I dedicate this book *War Cry* to my wife Mokhiniso who has been my total joy and inspiration over these last many decades of my life and all those others yet to come.
I love you, my Fireball.

WAR CRY

WILBUR SMITH
WITH DAVID CHURCHILL

HarperCollins*Publishers*

HarperCollins*Publishers*
1 London Bridge Street
London SE1 9GF

www.harpercollins.co.uk

This paperback edition 2017
1

First published in Great Britain by
HarperCollins*Publishers* 2017

A catalogue record for this book is
available from the British Library

ISBN: 978-0-00-753589-7

Set in Minion by Palimpsest Book Production Limited,
Falkirk, Stirlingshire

Printed and bound in Great Britain by
CPI Group (UK) Ltd, Croydon CR0 4YY

MIX
Paper from
responsible sources

FSC™ C007454

Two months had passed since war had been declared and the autumn sun that shone down from the clear blue skies over Bavaria was so glorious that it seemed to cry out for beer to be drunk and songs to be sung in hearty, joyful voices. But the Oktoberfest had been cancelled and the Double Phaeton limousine proceeding up the short drive of the villa in Grünwald, just outside Munich, bore tidings that were anything but joyous.

The car pulled to a halt. Its chauffeur opened the passenger door to allow a distinguished gentleman in his late sixties to disembark and a uniformed butler admitted him into the house. A moment later, Athala, Countess of Meerburg, looked up as the family lawyer Viktor Solomons was shown into the drawing room. His hair and beard might now be silver and his stride was less vigorous than it had once been, but the impeccable tailoring of his suit, the gleaming white of his perfectly starched collar and the flawless shine of his shoes reflected a mind that was still as precise, as sharp and as insightful as ever.

Solomons stopped in front of Athala's chair, gave a respectful little nod of the head and said, 'Good morning, Countess.'

His mood seemed subdued, but that was only to be expected, Athala reminded herself. Solomons's beloved son Isidore was away at the front. No parent could ever be light-hearted knowing that their child's very survival now lay at the mercy of the gods of war.

'Good morning, Viktor, what an unexpected pleasure to see you. Do please sit down.' Athala extended a dainty hand towards the chair opposite her. Then she turned her attention towards the butler who had shown the guest in and was now awaiting further instruction. 'Some coffee, please Braun, for Herr *Rechtsanwalt* Solomons. Would you like some cake, Viktor? A little strudel, perhaps?'

'No thank you, Countess.'

There was a sombre tone to Solomons's voice, Athala realized, and he seemed uncharacteristically reluctant to look her in the eye. *He has bad news*, she thought. *Is it the boys? Has something happened to one of them?*

She told herself to remain calm. It would not do to betray one's fears, especially not while a servant was still in the room. 'That will be all, Braun,' she said.

The butler departed. Athala felt a sudden desire to postpone the bad tidings for just a few seconds. 'Tell me, how is Isidore getting on? I hope he's safe and well.'

'Oh yes, very well thank you, Countess,' Viktor replied, with a distracted air, as though his mind was not fully engaged. But he took such pride in his beloved son that he could not resist adding, 'You know, Isidore's division is commanded by Crown Prince Wilhelm himself. Imagine that! We received a letter from him just last week to say that he has already seen his first action. Apparently, his major declared that he conducted himself admirably under fire.'

'I'm sure he did. Isidore is a fine young man. Now . . . what is it, Viktor, why are you here?'

Solomons hesitated a second to gather his thoughts and then sighed, 'I fear there is no other way of saying this, Countess. The War Office in Berlin informed me today that your husband, Graf Otto von Meerbach, is dead. General von Falkenhayn felt that it was better that you should hear the news from someone you knew, than simply receive a telegram message, or a visit from an unknown officer.'

Athala slumped back against her chair, eyes closed, unable to say a word.

'I know this must be very distressing,' Solomons went on, but distress was actually the last thing on her mind. Her overwhelming feeling was one of relief. Nothing had happened to her sons. And finally, after all these years, she was free. There was nothing that her husband could do to hurt her any more.

Athala controlled herself. She had been trained from her earliest girlhood to compose her fine, porcelain features into an image of calm, aristocratic elegance, no matter what the circumstances. It was now second nature to hide her true feelings behind that mask, just as the waters of a pond cover the constantly paddling feet that enable a swan to glide with such apparent ease across its glittering surface.

'How did he die?' she asked.

'In an air crash. I have been informed that His Excellency was engaged in a mission of the greatest importance to the German Empire. Its details are classified, but I am authorized to inform you that the crash occurred over British East Africa. The Count was flying aboard his magnificent new airship the *Assegai*. This was her maiden voyage.'

'Did the British shoot him down, then?'

'I do not know. Our ambassador in Bern was informed by his British counterpart merely that the Count had died. This

3

was a gesture of courtesy, in honour of your late husband's eminence. I gather, however, that the British do not have any Royal Flying Corps units in Africa, so we must assume that this was an accident of some kind. The gas used to elevate these "dirigibles" can, apparently, be very unstable.'

Athala looked Solomons straight in the eye and very calmly said, 'Was she on board the *Assegai* at the time?'

The lawyer did not need to be told who 'she' was. Nor, for that matter, would anyone remotely acquainted with German high society. Count von Meerbach had long been a notorious philanderer, but in recent years he had become obsessed with one particular mistress, a ravishing beauty, with lustrous sable hair and violet-blue eyes called Eva von Wellberg. The Count had begged Athala to divorce him, so that he could make the Wellberg woman his wife, but she had refused. Her Catholic faith would not allow her to end her marriage. And so they had come to an arrangement. Countess Athala lived, with their two young sons, in her perfectly proportioned classical villa in the chic little town to the southwest of Munich where the smartest elements of Bavarian society could be found. Meanwhile, Count Otto had retained his family castle on the shores of the Bodensee. And there he kept his mistress, or as Athala thought of her, his whore, and saw his sons on the rare occasions he was able, or remotely willing to spare the time to attend to them.

'The *Assegai* was housed within the grounds of the Meerbach Motor Works,' Solomons said, referring to the gigantic industrial complex on which the family fortune was based. 'I am told by senior company officials who were present at the airship's departure that a woman was seen going aboard her. I was also informed by the War Office that the *Assegai* went down with all hands. No one survived.'

Athala allowed a slight, bitter smile to cross her face. 'I will not even pretend to be sorry that she is dead.'

4

'Nor can I pretend to criticize you for that. I am well aware how much you have suffered on her account.'

'Dear Viktor, you are always so kind, and so fair. You are . . .' She paused to correct herself, 'You were my husband's lawyer, yet you have never done anything to hurt me.'

'I am the family's lawyer, Countess,' Solomons gently corrected her. 'And as long as you were, and remain part of the von Meerbach family, then I will always consider you my client. Now, may I ask, are you ready to discuss any of the consequences of your husband's tragic demise?'

'Yes, yes I am,' said Athala and then, for reasons she could not quite explain, she suddenly felt the loss to which she had been numb up to that point. For all that she had suffered, she had always prayed that one day her husband might see the error of his ways and devote himself to his family. Now all hope of that had gone. She began to cry and started rummaging through the bag at her feet, trying to find a handkerchief.

'May I?' asked Solomons, reaching into his pocket.

She waved him away, shaking her head, not trusting herself to speak. Finally she found what she was looking for, pressed the handkerchief to her eyes, dabbed her nose, took a deep breath and said, 'Please forgive me.'

'My dear Countess, you have just lost your husband. Whatever difficulties you may have faced, he was still the man you married, the father of your children.'

She nodded and ruefully said, 'It seems that I do not have a heart of stone after all.'

'I, for one, never supposed that you did. Not for a single moment.'

She gave him a nod of thanks and then said, 'Please continue . . . I believe you were going to describe the consequences of . . .' She could not bring herself to use the word 'death' and so just said, 'Of what has occurred.'

'Quite so. There cannot be a funeral, sadly, for if the body

5

has been recovered, the British will by now have buried it.'

'My husband died serving his country overseas,' Athala said, straightening her back and resuming her air of poised composure. 'That is to be expected.'

'Indeed. But I think it would be entirely appropriate, indeed expected, to have a service of remembrance, perhaps at the Frauenkirche in Munich, or you may feel that either the family chapel at Schloss Meerbach, or even a service at the Motor Works, would be more appropriate.'

'The Frauenkirche,' said Athala, without a moment's hesitation. 'I don't think a factory is a suitable location at which to commemorate a Count of the German Empire and the chapel at the *schloss* is too small to accommodate the numbers of people who will wish to attend. Could someone from your firm liaise with the Archbishop's office, to secure a suitable date and assist with the administration of the event?'

'Of course, Countess, that would be no trouble. Might I suggest the Bayerischer Hof for the reception after the service? If you give the hotel manager your general requirements, the hotel staff will know exactly how best to provide exactly what you need.'

'I'm afraid I can't even begin to think about that just now.' Athala closed her eyes, trying to put the jumble of thoughts and emotions in her head in order and then asked, 'What will become of my sons and I?'

'Well, the extent and variety of the Count's possessions mean that his will is unusually complex. But the essential facts are that the family estate here in Bavaria, and a majority share in the Motor Works, all go to your eldest son, Konrad, along with the title of Graf von Meerbach. Your younger son, Gerhard, will have a smaller shareholding in the company. The various properties and the income they generate will be held in trust for each son until he is twenty-five. Prior to that point, they will each receive a generous allowance, plus the cost of their education, of course. Any additional expenditure will have to be approved by their trustees.'

'And who will they be?'

'In the first instance, you and I, Countess.'

'My God, fancy Otto allowing me such power.'

'He was a traditionalist. He felt that a mother should take charge of her children's upbringing. But you will note that I said "in the first instance". Once Konrad is twenty-five, and takes control of the family's affairs, he will also assume the role of trustee to his brother, who will then be eighteen years old.'

'So for seven years, Gerhard will have to go cap in hand to Konrad if he ever needs anything?'

'Yes.'

Athala frowned. 'It worries me that one brother should have so much power over the other.'

'His Excellency believed very strongly that a family, like a nation, required the strong leadership of a single man.'

'Didn't he just . . . I take it that I am provided for.'

'Oh yes, you need not worry on that score. You will retain your own family money, added to which you will keep all the property, jewellery, artworks and so on that you received during your marriage, and receive a very generous annual allowance for the rest of your life. You will also have a place on the board.'

'I don't care about the damn board,' Athala said. 'It's my boys that I worry about. Where are we meant to live?'

'It is entirely up to you, whether you wish to reside here in Grünwald, or at Schloss Meerbach, or both. His Excellency has set aside monies that are to be spent on the maintenance of the castle and its estate, and on employing all the staff required to maintain the standards he himself demanded. You will be the mistress of Schloss Meerbach once again, if you choose to be so.'

'Until Konrad's twenty-fifth birthday . . .'

'Yes, he will be the master then.'

* * *

When Solomons had gone, Athala went upstairs to the playroom where Gerhard was playing. She looked on him as a gift from God, an unexpected blessing whose birth had brought a rare moment of joy to a marriage long past rescuing. Gerhard had been conceived on the very last night that Athala and Otto had slept together. It had been a short, perfunctory coupling and he had been away with Fräulein von Wellberg on the night Gerhard was born. But that only made her baby all the more precious to Athala.

She wondered how she was going to explain to him that his father was dead. How did one tell a three-year-old that sort of thing? For now, she didn't have the heart to interrupt Gerhard while he played with the wooden building bricks that were his favourite toy.

Athala always found her son fascinating to observe as he arranged the brightly coloured bricks. He had an instinctive grasp of symmetry. If he placed one brick of a certain colour or shape on one side of his latest castle, or house, or farm (Gerhard always knew exactly what he was building), then another, identical one had to go on the opposite side.

She leaned over and kissed his head. 'My little architect,' she murmured, and Gerhard beamed with pleasure, for that was his favourite of all her pet names for him.

I will tell him, Athala told herself, *but not yet.*

She gave the news to both her boys after Konrad had come home from school. He was only ten, but already regarded himself as the man of the house. As such, he made a point of not showing any sign of weakness when told that the father he took after so strongly was dead. Instead he wanted to know all the details of what had happened. Had his father been fighting the English? How many of them had he killed before they got him? When Athala had been unable to give him the answers he required, Konrad flew into a rage and said she was stupid.

'Father was quite right not to love you,' he sneered. 'You were never good enough for him.'

On another day, Athala might have smacked him for that, but today she let it go. Then Konrad's fury abated as fast as it had risen and he asked, 'If Father is dead, does that mean that I am the Count now?'

'Yes,' said Athala. 'You are Graf von Meerbach.'

Konrad gave a whoop of joy. 'I'm the Count! I'm the Count!' he chanted, marching around the playroom, like a stocky little red-headed guardsman. 'I can do whatever I want and nobody can stop me!'

He came to a halt by Gerhard's building, which had risen, brick by brick, until it was almost as tall as its maker.

'Hey Gerdi, look at me!'

Gerhard looked up at his big brother, smiling innocently.

Konrad kicked Gerhard's wonderful construction, scattering its bricks across the playroom floor. Then he kicked it again, and again until it was completely obliterated, and nothing remained but the colourful rubble carpeting the room.

Gerhard's little face crumpled in despair and he ran sobbing to his mother.

As she wrapped her arms around her baby, she looked at the boy count now standing proudly over the destruction he had wreaked and she realized with bitter despair that she had been freed from her husband, only to be enslaved anew by her even more terrible son.

The skinny little girl wore a pair of jodhpurs that flapped around her thighs, for she lacked the flesh with which to fill them. Her short, black bobbed hair, which was normally unconstrained by bands or clips of any kind, had been pinned into a little bun, to be worn beneath her riding hat. Her freckled face was tanned a golden brown and her eyes were the clear, pure blue of the African skies that had looked down upon every day of her life.

All around her the grassy hills, garlanded with sparkling streams, stretched away to the horizon as if the Highlands of Scotland had been transported to the Garden of Eden: a magical land of limitless fertility, incomprehensible scale and thrilling, untamed wildness. Here leopards lounged in the branches of trees that were also home to chattering monkeys and snakes, like the shimmering, iridescent green mamba, or the shy but fatally poisonous boomslang. The head-high grass hid lions sharp in fang and claw and, even deadlier still, the buffalo, whose horns could cut deep into a man's guts as easily as a sewing needle through fine linen.

The girl barely gave a thought to these hazards, for she knew no other world than this and besides, she had much more important things on her mind. She was stroking the velvet muzzle of her pony, a Somali-bred chestnut mare from which she had been inseparable ever since she had received it as her seventh-birthday present, eight months ago. The horse was called Kipipiri, which was both the Swahili word for 'butterfly' and the name of the mountain that stood tall on the eastern horizon, shimmering in the heat haze like a mirage.

'Look, Kippy,' the girl said, in a low, soothing murmur. 'Look at all the nasty boys and their horrid stallions. Let's show them what we can do!'

She stepped around to the side of the pony and, waving away the offer of a leg-up from her groom, put one foot into the nearest stirrup, pushed off it and sprang up into the saddle as nimbly as a jockey on Derby Day. Then she leaned forward along Kipipiri's neck, stroking her mane, and whispered in her ear, 'Fly, my darling, fly!'

Possessed by an exhilarating swirl of emotions in which pride, anticipation and giddy excitement clashed against nervousness, apprehension and a desperate longing not to make a fool of herself, the girl told herself to calm down. She had long since learned that her beloved Kippy could sense her emotions and be affected by them and the very last thing she needed was a nervous, skittish, over-excited mount. So she took a long deep breath, just as her mother had taught her, before letting the air out slowly and smoothly until she felt the tension ease from her shoulders. Then she sat up straight and kicked the pony into a walk, stirring up the dust from the peppery red earth as they moved towards the starting gate of the show-jumping ring that had been set up on one of the fields of the Wanjohi Valley Polo Club for its 1926 gymkhana.

The girl's eyes were fixed on the fences scattered at apparently random points around the ring. And a single thought filled her mind: *I am going to win!*

A loudspeaker had been slung from one of the wooden rafters that held up the corrugated iron awning over the clubhouse veranda. The harsh, tinny sound of a man's amplified voice burst from it, saying, 'Now the final competitor in the twelve-and-under show jumping, Miss Saffron Courtney on Kipi-pipi-piri . . .' Silence fell for a second and then the voice continued, 'Awfully sorry, few too many pips there, I fear.'

'And a few too many pink gins, eh, Chalky!' a voice called out from among the spectators lounging on the wooden benches that were serving as spectator seating for the annual gymkhana the polo club laid on for its members' children.

'Too true, dear boy, too true,' the announcer confessed, and then continued, 'So far there's only been one clear round, by Percy Toynton on Hotspur, which means that Saffron's the only rider standing between him and victory. She's much the youngest competitor in this event, so let's give her a jolly big round of applause to send her on her way.'

A ripple of limp clapping could be heard from the fifty or so white settlers who had come to watch their children compete

11

in the gymkhana, or who were simply grasping any opportunity to leave their farms and businesses and socialise with one another. They were drowsy with the warmth of the early afternoon sun and the thin air, for the polo fields lay at an altitude of almost eight thousand feet, which seemed to exaggerate the effect of their heroic consumption of alcohol. A few particularly jaded, decadent souls were further numbed by opium, while those who were exhibiting overt signs of energy or agitation had quite likely sniffed some of the cocaine that had recently become as familiar to the more daring elements in Kenyan society as a cocktail before dinner.

Saffron's mother Eva Courtney, however, was entirely clear-headed. Seven months pregnant, having had two miscarriages since her daughter's birth, she had been forbidden anything stronger than the occasional glass of Guinness to build up her strength. She looked towards the jumps that had been set up on one of the polo fields, whispered, 'Good luck, my sweet,' under her breath, and squeezed her husband's hand.

'I just hope she doesn't have a fall,' she said, her deep violet eyes heavy with maternal anxiety. 'She's only a little girl and look at the size of some of those jumps.'

Leon Courtney smiled at his wife. 'Don't you worry, darling,' he reassured her. 'Saffron is your daughter. Which means she's as brave as a lioness, as pretty as a pink flamingo . . . and as tough as an old bull rhino. She will come through unscathed, you mark my words.'

Eva Courtney smiled at Leon and let go of his hand so that he could get to his feet and walk down towards the polo field. *That's my Badger,* she thought. *He can't bear to sit and watch his girl from a distance. He has to get close to the action.*

Eva had given Leon the nickname Badger one morning a dozen years earlier, soon after they had met. They had ridden out as dawn broke over the Rift Valley and Eva had spotted a funny-looking creature about the size of a squat, sturdy, short-legged dog. It had black fur on its belly and lower body and white and pale grey on top, and was snuffling round in the grass like an old man searching for his reading glasses.

'What is it?' she had asked, to which Leon replied, 'It's a honey badger.' He told her that this unlikely beast was one of the most ferocious, fearless creatures in Africa. 'Even the lion gives him a wide berth,' Leon had said. 'Interfere with him at your peril.'

He could be talking about himself, Eva had thought. Leon had only been in his mid-twenties then, scraping a living as a safari guide. Now he was just a year shy of forty, the look of boyish eagerness that had once lit his eyes was replaced by the calmer assurance of a mature man in his prime, confident in his prowess as a hunter and fighting man. There was a deep groove between Leon's brows and lines around his eyes and mouth. With the frustration felt by women through the ages, to whom lines were an unwelcome sign that their youth and beauty were fading, Eva had to admit that on her man they suggested experience and authority and only made him all the more attractive. His body was a shade thicker through the trunk and his waist was not as slender as it had once been, but – another unfairness! – that only made him seem all the stronger and more powerful.

Eva looked around at the other men of the expatriate community gathered in this particular corner of Kenya. Her eyes came to rest on Josslyn Hay, the 25-year-old heir to the Earl of Erroll, the hereditary Lord High Constable of Scotland. He was a tall, strongly built young man and he wore a kilt, as he often did in honour of his heritage, with a red-ochre Somali shawl slung over one shoulder. He was a handsome enough sight, with his swept-back, matinee-idol blond hair. His cool blue eyes looked at the world, and its female inhabitants in particular, with the lazy, heavy-lidded impudence of a predator eyeing its next meal. Hay had seduced half the white women in British East Africa, but Eva was too familiar with his type

13

and too satisfied with her own alpha male to be remotely interested in adding to his conquests. Besides, he was far too young and inexperienced to interest her. As for the rest of the men there, they were a motley crew of aristocrats fleeing the new world of post-war Britain; remittance men putting on airs while praying for the next cheque from home; and adventurers enticed to Africa by the promise of a life they could never hope to match at home.

Leon Courtney, though, was different. His family had lived in Africa for two hundred and fifty years. He spoke Swahili as easily as English, conversed with the local Masai people in their own tongue and had excellent Arabic – an essential tool for a man whose father had founded a trading business that had been born of a single Nile steamer but now stretched from the gold mines of the Transvaal to the cotton fields of Egypt and the oil wells of Mesopotamia. Leon didn't play games. He didn't have to. He was man enough exactly as he was.

Yes, Badger, I am lucky, Eva thought. *Luckiest of all to love and be loved by you.*

S affron steadied herself at the start of her course. *I've simply got to beat Percy!* she told herself.

It was Percy Toynton's thirteenth birthday in a week's time so he only just qualified for the event. Not only was he almost twice as old as Saffron, both he and his horse were far larger and stronger than she and Kipipiri. Percy was not a nice boy, in Saffron's view. He was boastful and liked to make himself look clever at other children's expense. Still, he had got round the course without making a mistake. So she absolutely had to match that and then beat him in the jump-off that would follow.

'Don't get ahead of yourself,' Daddy had told her over breakfast that morning. 'This is a very important lesson in life. If you have a big, difficult job to do, don't fret about how hard it is. Break it down into smaller, easier jobs. Then steadily do them one by one and you'll find that in the end you've done the thing that seemed so hard. Do you understand?'

Saffron had screwed up her face and twisted her lips from side to side, thinking about what Daddy had said. 'I think so,' she'd replied, without much conviction.

'Well, take a clear round at show jumping. That's very difficult, isn't it?'

'Yes,' Saffron nodded.

'But if you look at a jump, I bet you always think you can get over it.'

'Always!' Saffron agreed.

'Very well then, don't think about how difficult it is to get a clear round. Think about one easy jump, then another, then another . . . and when you reach the end, if you jump over all the jumps, why, you'll have a clear round and it won't have seemed difficult at all.'

'Oh, I understand!' she'd said, enthusiastically.

Now Saffron glanced at the ragged line of her fellow competitors and their parents that ran down one side of the ring, and saw her father. He caught her eye and gave her a jaunty wave, accompanied by one of the broad smiles that always made her feel happy, for they were filled with optimism and confidence. She smiled back and then turned her attention to the first obstacle: a simple pair of crossed white rails forming a shallow X-shape lower in the middle than at the sides. *That's easy!* she thought and felt suddenly stronger and more confident. She urged Kipipiri forward and the little mare broke into a trot and then a canter and they passed through the starting gate and headed towards the jumps.

Leon Courtney had made sure not to convey a single iota of the tension he was feeling as Saffron began her round. His heart was bursting with pride. She could have entered the

15

eight-and-under category, but the very idea of going over the baby jumps, the highest of which barely reached Leon's knee, had appalled her. She had therefore insisted on going up an age group, and to most people that in itself was remarkable. The idea that she might actually win it was fanciful in the extreme. But Leon knew his daughter. She would not see it that way. She would want victory or nothing at all.

'Come on, Saffy,' he whispered, not wanting to shout for fear of spooking her pony.

She cantered up to the first fence; steadied Kipipiri then darted forward and sailed right across the centre of the jump, with masses of room to spare. Saffron smiled to herself. She and Kippy were both strong-willed, stubborn characters. As her mother used to say, 'You two girls are both as bad as each other!'

On days when Saffron and her pony were at odds with one another, the results were invariably disastrous, but when they were united and pulling in the same direction, it felt as though they could take on the world. The energy with which Kippy had jumped, her perfect balance on take-off and landing, the rhythm of her strides, and the alert, eager way her ears were pricked gave Saffron hope that this could be one of the good days.

Now, however, the challenge became much harder. The next fence was a double: two railed fences with a single stride between them. 'Good girl!' said Saffron as Kippy scraped over the first element of the pair, took her single stride perfectly then jumped the double rail too.

Now all the nerves had gone. Saffron was at one with the animal beneath her, controlling all the power that lay coiled up in the muscles bunched beneath Kippy's rich, dark, glossy coat.

She slowed the pony, turned her ninety degrees to the right and set out along the line of three fences that now presented themselves to her. The first was a plain white gate and she made easy work of it. Saffron had long legs for her age, even if they were as thin as a stork's, but she kept her stirrups short, all the better to rise out of the saddle as she jumped and drive her pony up and over the obstacle. Next came another single rail, although it was placed over bundles of flame-tree branches, still bedecked in their blazing red and yellow flowers: again it proved no match for Saffron and Kipipiri.

I say, Courtney, that girl of yours is as light as a feather in the saddle,' said one of the other spectators, a retired cavalry major called Brett, who also served as the local magistrate, as she tackled an oxer, comprised of two railed fences side-by-side. 'Lovely touch on the reins, too. Good show.'

'Thank you, Major,' Leon said, as Saffron brought Kipipiri round again to tackle the next couple of fences strung diagonally across the ring: a wall and the water jump. 'Mind you, I can't claim any credit. Saffron's absolutely her mother's daughter when it comes to riding. You wouldn't believe the hours that Eva's spent with her in the schooling ring, both as stubborn as each other, fighting like two cats in a bag, but by God it pays off.' Leon smiled affectionately at the thought of the two most precious people in his life then said, 'Excuse me a moment,' as he switched his full attention back to the ring.

For some reason, his daughter's pony had a terrible habit of 'dipping a toe in the water', as Leon liked to put it. She would leap over the highest, widest, scariest fences, but it was the devil's own job to persuade her that the water was an obstacle to be avoided, rather than a pool to be dived into.

As Saffron steadied herself before the challenge in front of her, Leon took a deep breath, trying to calm his racing pulse.

I don't know how Saffy feels jumping this course, he thought. *But I'm absolutely shattered watching it.*

One fence at a time, one fence at a time,' Saffron repeated to herself as she fixed her eyes on the wall. 'Here we go, girl!' she said and urged Kippy on across the parched turf.

17

The wall was high. They got over it without knocking any of the painted wooden tea-chests from which it had been improvised, but the pony stumbled on landing and it took all Saffron's skill to keep her upright, maintain their forward momentum and have her balanced and moving strongly again by the time they approached the water jump.

Saffron was absolutely determined she wouldn't make a mess of the water this time. She galloped at full pelt towards it, misjudged her pacing, had to take off miles away from the jump, but was going so fast that Kipipiri flew like a speeding dart over the rail, and the shallow pool of muddy brown water beyond. It was all Saffron could do to slow her down and turn her again – hard left this time – before they charged out of the ring.

Saffron was out of breath, but inwardly exultant. *No faults! Almost there!*

In front of her stood a low fence made of three striped poles on top of each other. The polo club's gymkhana committee had decided to make this a particularly gentle challenge to the riders, for just beyond it stood the last and hardest jump: a vicious triple combination of a plain rail fence, another hay-bale and rail, and finally an oxer, each with just a single stride between them. Some competitors had scraped the first element of the triple, hit the second and simply crashed into the third, completely unable to manage another jump. None apart from Percy had managed to get through without at least one fence down.

Saffron had to clear it. She summoned every shred of energy she still had in her and rode along the side of the ring nearest to the spectators, her mind replaying the pattern of steps she would need to enter the triple combination at the perfect point, going at just the right speed. She barely even thought of the poles as Kipipiri jumped over them.

As the pony's hind hooves passed over the jump, Saffron thought she heard a bump behind her. She glanced back and saw that the top pole had been rattled but it seemed to still be in place, so she thought no more of it. She barely even saw the people flashing by beside her, nor did she hear the faint gasp they emitted as she approached the first element. She met it perfectly, jumped the rail, kept Kippy balanced through her next stride, made it across the second rail, kicked on and then pulled so hard on the reins that she more or less picked up her pony and hauled her over the oxer.

I did it! I did it! Saffron thought exultantly as she galloped towards the finishing line. She crossed it and slowed Kipipiri to a trot as they exited the ring. She saw her father running towards her, dodging in and out of the applauding spectators and gave him a great big wave. But he didn't wave back.

Saffron frowned. *Why isn't he smiling?*

And then she heard the loudspeaker and felt as though she had been kicked in the tummy by a horse's hoof as the announcer called out, 'Oh, I say! What awfully bad luck for plucky Saffron Courtney, hitting the last-but-one fence when she was so close to a clear round. My goodness, that pole took an age to fall off! So that means the winner's rosette goes to Percy Toynton. Well played, young man!'

Saffron hardly knew what was happening as her groom took hold of Kipipiri's bridle. All she could think was, *How could I knock down that silly, stupid, simple little pole?* Her eyes had suddenly filled with tears and she could barely see her father Leon as he lifted her out of the saddle and hugged her to his chest, holding her tight before gently putting her down on the ground.

She leaned against him, wrapping her arms around his legs as he stroked her hair. 'I'm better than Percy, I know I am,' Saffron sobbed. And then she looked up, her face as furious as it was miserable and wailed. 'I lost, Daddy, I lost! I can't believe it . . . I lost!'

Leon had long since learned that there was no point trying to reason with Saffron at times like this. Her temper was

19

as fierce as an African storm, but cleared as quickly and then the sun came out in her just as it did over the savannah, and it shone just as brightly too.

She pulled herself away from him, tore her hat off her head and kicked it across the ground.

Leon heard a disapproving, 'Harrumph!' behind him and turned to see Major Brett frowning at the display of juvenile female anger. 'You should read that little madam some Kipling, Courtney.'

'Because she's behaving like a monkey from *The Jungle Book*?' Leon asked.

The major did not spot the presence of humour, or perhaps did not feel this was the time and place for frivolity. 'Good God, man, of course not! I'm referring to that poem. You know, triumph and disaster, impostors, treat them both the same and so forth.'

'Ah, but my daughter is a Courtney, and we've never been able to live up to such lofty ideals. Either we triumph, or it is a disaster.'

'Well that's not a very British way of seeing things, I must say.'

Leon smiled. 'In many ways we're not very British. Besides, that poem you were quoting, "If"—'

'Absolutely, that's the one.'

'As I recall, Kipling wrote it for his son, who died in the war, poor lad.'

'Believe he did, yes, rotten show.'

'And the point of the whole thing is summed up in the final line which is, if memory serves, "And – which is more – you'll be a man, my son."'

'Quite so, damned good advice, too.'

'Yes, to a boy it is. But Saffron is my daughter. She's a little girl. And not even Rudyard Kipling is going to turn her into a man.'

* * *

20

'Darling Leon, how good of you to come,' said Lady Idina Hay.

'My pleasure,' Leon replied. A select few members of the gymkhana crowd had been invited back to the Hays' house, Slains, which was named after Josslyn Hay's ancestral home, to have dinner and stay the night afterwards. Leon had thought twice before accepting the invitation. Idina, a short, slight woman with huge, captivating eyes, who matched her husband in his appetite and seductive power, had swiftly become as much of a source of scandal to Kenyan society as she had been in London. Now on her third marriage, with armies of lovers besides, she was apt to greet guests while lying naked in a green onyx bath; to entertain while wearing nothing but a flimsy cotton wrap, tied at the bust in the native style, with nothing underneath; and to hand guests a bowl filled with keys to the Slains' bedrooms, invite them to take one, inform them which room it opened and suggest that they slept with whomever they found within it.

'Apparently it's impossible for the servants,' Eva had said, when she passed on the gossip on to Leon. 'They pick up all the dirty laundry off the floor, get it all cleaned and pressed but then have absolutely no idea whom to return it to.'

Tonight, however, Idina was on her best behaviour and was dressed as if for the smartest salons of Paris in an impossibly short, translucent but just about decent dress of fluttering, champagne-coloured silk chiffon. Leon felt sure Eva would be able to identify it in an instant as being the work of some celebrated designer of whom he had never heard.

'So sorry to hear that Eva wasn't up to it,' Idina said, as if reading his mind.

'Well, she gets jolly tired, lugging the baby around inside her,' he replied. 'She swears it must be a boy, says it's twice the size Saffy was at the same stage. So she's gone back to Lusima with Saffy and the pony.'

'She's not driving, I hope!'

'She wanted to, you know. Absolutely determined to get behind the wheel. But I put my foot down and said absolutely not. So Loikot, my estate manager, is taking her back in the Rolls. He'll be back for me tomorrow.'

Idina laughed. 'You're the only man in Kenya who would even think of driving on the appalling, unmade roads in such a wildly extravagant car!'

'On the contrary, it's an extremely tough, practical machine. It was built as an armoured car, spent the war charging around Arabia and Mesopotamia. When peace came the army had far more than they needed, so I bought one. I smartened it up a bit, but underneath it's still a military vehicle,' Leon grinned at Idina. 'If the balloon ever goes up again, I can weld on some armour plating, stick a gun turret over the passenger seats and drive straight off to war.'

'Perhaps I should get one,' Idina mused. 'I have my Hispano–Suiza, of course and she's a wonderful thing.'

'I'll say. At least as grand as my Roller, and that silver stork on the bonnet rivals the Spirit of Ecstasy for style.'

'True, but she'd still rather be toddling around Mayfair than bumping about on the dirt tracks of Africa . . . Now I must get on and make sure dinner is being prepared properly,' Idina concluded. 'Just because one is a long way from home, that's no excuse for lowering one's standards.'

Apart from swapping the room keys, thought Leon, heading off to get dressed for dinner. *Unless they do that in Mayfair, too.*

The guests had gathered for drinks before dinner and split along gender lines, with the men, all dressed in white tie and tails, engaged in one set of conversations and the ladies, like a flock of brilliantly plumaged hummingbirds, all gathered in another. Leon Courtney was cradling a whisky in his hand as he talked with a small group that included his host, Josslyn Hay. The two men stood out from the rest, both because they were taller than the others, but also because they were so obviously the dominant males in that particular pack: a pair of magnets for watching female eyes.

'I rather think I'm going to make a play for Leon Courtney,' said the Honourable Amelia Cory-Porter, a well-dressed, brightly painted young divorcée with fashionably short, bobbed hair who had decided to lie low in Kenya until the fuss over her marriage, which had been ended by her adultery, died down. 'He is quite utterly scrumptious, don't you think?'

'Darling, you'll be wasting your time,' Idina Hay informed her. 'Leon Courtney's the only man in the whole of Kenya who refuses to sleep with anyone other than his wife. He barely even eyes one up. It's quite disconcerting, actually. Makes me wonder if I'm losing my touch.'

Amelia looked startled, as if confronted by an entirely new and unexpected aspect of human behaviour. 'Refuses sex? Really? That hardly seems natural, especially when his wife is in no condition to oblige him. You don't suppose he's secretly a queer, do you?'

'Heavens, no! I have it on good authority that in his younger days, he was quite the ladies' man. But the moment he clapped eyes on Eva, he fell head over heels in love and he's been besotted ever since.'

'I suppose one can't blame him,' said Amelia, though her air of disapproval was plain. 'I saw her at the gymkhana and she's perfectly lovely. What is it they say in romantic novels – eyes like limpid pools? She has those, all right. But even so, she's enormously pregnant. No one expects a chap to live like a monk these days just because his wife's blown up like a barrage balloon.'

'Well perhaps Leon Courtney's just an old-fashioned gentleman.'

'Oh, don't be silly. You know as well as I do that there's never been any such thing. But anyway, darling, do tell all about Eva. It's very strange. I thought I could detect a Northumbrian lilt in her voice – Daddy used to go shooting up there and we'd all go up with him, so I know the accent from the staff and gamekeepers and so forth. But I've heard that she's actually a German, is that so?'

'Well,' said Idina as the two women moved fractionally closer together, like conspirators sharing a deadly secret, 'the real British East Africa hands, like Florence Delamere, who've been here for years and years, can still remember the first time Eva pitched up in Nairobi, about a year or so before the war. Some ghastly German industrialist arrived in town on the most lavish safari anyone had ever seen, accompanied by a magnificent open motor car in which to go hunting, numerous lorries to cart all his baggage and two huge aeroplanes, made by his own company.'

'Good lord, what an extraordinary show,' Amelia said, clearly impressed by such a display of power and wealth.

'Absolutely,' Idina agreed. 'Of course, the whole town turned out to see the flying machines, but by the end of the day there was just as much talk about the ravishing creature who was parading around on the industrialist's arm, making no bones whatever about being his mistress and calling herself Eva von something-or-other.'

'And that was the same Eva I saw today?'

'Indeed she was. And guess who was the white hunter acting as the Germans' guide?'

'Goodness, was it Leon Courtney?'

'The very same. Anyway, Eva and the industrialist – apparently he was the absolute picture of the bullying, bullet-headed Hun – went back to Germany, and that seemed to be that. But then, really very soon after the start of the war, she was mysteriously back in Kenya, having parachuted down to earth from a giant Zeppelin.'

24

'Oh, don't! That's just too extraordinary!' Amelia laughed.

'Well, that's the story and I've heard it from enough people who were here at the time to believe it. Apparently, the Zeppelin crash-landed deep in the heart of Masailand. And it was shot down by . . . ?' Idina paused, teasingly.

'No! Don't tell me! Not Leon again?'

'Absolutely . . . and out of the wreckage, looking as pretty as a picture and as fresh as a daisy, steps the lovely Eva and falls, swooning into his arms!'

'Lucky girl. I'd happily swoon into his arms right now, if he'd have me.'

'Well, he won't, so you'll just have to find another man to swoon at!'

'Are you sure?' Amelia asked, wrinkling her porcelain brow with a little frown. 'It really is too bad to give up without a fight. After all, Leon's rich as well as divinely handsome. Lusima must be one of the biggest estates in the country.'

'He paid cash for the land, you know,' Idina said. 'Half a million pounds for a hundred and twenty thousand acres, didn't have to borrow a penny. I know that for an absolute fact because I heard it from the chap who conducted the sale.'

'Half a million? Cash?' Amelia gasped.

'Absolutely. I once plucked up the courage to ask Leon where his money came from it, but he was very coy. First he described it as "war reparations" and then he said it was payment for various patents that had belonged to Eva's father.'

'Perhaps he's a gangster and it's all the proceeds of his evil crimes!' said Amelia, excitedly. 'I rather like the idea of being – what's the phrase? – a gangster's moll.'

'I'm sure you do, duckie, but whatever else he might be, Leon Courtney's not a criminal. My guess is that it's something to do with the war.' Idina's eyes suddenly sparkled with mischief. 'I tell you what, darling, I shall set you a challenge. I'm going to change the placement I'd planned for the dinner table tonight and put you next to Leon. If you can find out where he got his gold by the time we retire to leave the men to their brandy and cigars I shall be very impressed indeed.'

'Done!' said the Hon. Amelia. 'And I'll seduce him, too, just you watch me, wife or no wife.'

Idina arched an eyebrow and concluded their little chat: 'Now, now, darling, let's not be greedy.'

Thanks to the combined efforts of Idina Hay and her formidable housekeeper Marie, the kitchen staff at Slains had been trained to produce French cuisine that would not have shamed the dinner table of a château on the Loire. The wine, notoriously difficult to keep in good condition in the tropics, was of equally high standard. Leon had long ago learned to pace himself when drinking at altitude, but the woman sitting next to him, who introduced herself as Amelia Cory-Porter, seemed determined to force as much Premier Cru claret as possible down his throat. She was attractive enough, in an obvious, uninteresting way, and covered in far too much make-up for his taste. She was also very clearly determined to get something from him, but Leon was not yet sure quite what that might be.

At first he'd thought she was flirting, for everything he knew about women told him that if he made a pass at her she would very happily oblige. But as the starter of *confit* duck breasts served with a salad of vegetables from Slains' own gardens gave way to superb *entrecôte* steaks served in a pepper sauce, he realized that Amelia was not after his body – or not at this precise moment anyway – but was instead angling for information. It was, of course, good manners to show interest in one's dining companions and any woman with half a brain knew how to make a man feel as though he was the wisest, most fascinating and witty fellow she had ever met. But Amelia was not flattering, so much as cross-examining him, working her way through his life and becoming more intense in her

26

questioning as she went on. His war service seemed to be of particular interest to her. Leon had done his best to fob her off by saying he never talked about the war, adding that in his experience any man who did was a bounder who was almost certainly lying. 'Unless, of course, he's a poet,' he'd added, hoping she might, like many an idealistic young woman, be distracted by thoughts of Wilfred Owen, Siegfried Sassoon and the other bards of war.

Amelia, however, wasn't distracted for a second. She was like a terrier with the scent of a particularly juicy rabbit in its nostrils. 'I heard the most extraordinary story about how you'd shot down a giant Zeppelin, single-handed. Do tell, that sounds so brave, is it actually true?'

'That sounds pretty improbable to me,' Leon said. 'Damned hard thing to shoot down, a Zeppelin, just ask any pilot. Now, I've talked far too much. You must tell me everything that's happening in London, what's new and interesting and so forth. Eva will be thrilled if I can pass on any news of home.'

Leon had been telling the truth, up to a point. It really was extremely hard to down a Zeppelin with machine-gun fire, which was one reason why he had never done any such thing. And Eva would indeed be keen to hear about the latest clothes, plays, novels and music that were captivating London society.

Amelia, however, was having none of it. 'Oh, who cares about silly dresses and even sillier books? I want to hear about that Zeppelin.'

Leon sighed. This was not a subject he had any intention of discussing, but how could he evade this woman's steely clutches without being unforgivably rude? He was just pondering his next move when he heard a man's voice, clearly somewhat the worse for wine, braying across the table.

'I say Courtney, is it true you have a Masai blood brother?'

The voice belonged to a newcomer to Kenya, who called himself Quentin de Lancey and affected the mannerisms of the upper class, though his appearance was far from noble. He was overweight and prone to become both red-faced and very sweaty in the heat, which caused his thin, reddish-brown hair to lie in damp strings across his pale, flabby skin.

'Something of that sort,' Leon replied, noncommittally.

When he was a nineteen-year-old Second Lieutenant in the Third Battalion of the King's African Rifles his platoon sergeant had been a Masai called Manyoro. Leon had saved Manyoro's life in battle, and when Leon had then been court-martialled on trumped-up charges of cowardice and desertion it had been Manyoro's evidence that had saved his neck. There was no man on earth whose friendship he valued more highly.

'And a coon name? Bongo-something, was what I'd heard.' A few people smiled at that, one of the women tittered. 'Bongo from Bongo-bongo-land, what?' de Lancey added, looking delighted by his own rapier wit.

'The name I received was M'Bogo,' said Leon, and a wiser, or more sober man than de Lancey might have heard the note of suppressed anger in his voice.

'I say, what kind of name is that?' de Lancey persisted.

'It is the name of the great buffalo bull. It represents strength and fighting spirit. I count myself honoured to have been given it.'

Again, it took a fool not to heed the warning contained in the phrase 'strength and fighting spirit', and again de Lancey was deaf to it. 'Oh, come-come, Courtney,' he said, as if he were the voice of reason and Leon the common fool. 'It's all very well getting on with these people, I suppose, but let's not pretend that they are anything but a lesser race. A chap I know was up-country a few months ago, looking for a good spot to start farming. He hung a paraffin lamp by his tent when he stopped for the night. The next thing he knew there were half-a-dozen nig-nogs coming up out of the bush, absolutely stark bollock naked apart from those red cloak things they wear.'

'It's called a *shuka*,' said Leon.

Beside him, Amelia Cory-Porter's eyes had widened and she was breathing just a little more heavily as she sensed that the man beside her was readying himself to impose his authority, possibly by force.

'Yes, well, whatever it's called, the poor chap was absolutely terrified, real brown-trouser time,' de Lancey said. 'Turned out the niggers just wanted to sit by his tent, cocks swinging gently in the breeze, gawping at the light – my chum didn't know where to look! They'd never seen anything like it, thought it was a star trapped in a bottle.'

Leon realized that he had clenched his napkin in his right fist and recognized the signs of an imminent explosion. *Control yourself*, he thought. *Count to ten. No point making an exhibition of yourself over one blithering idiot.*

He consciously relaxed his body, much to Amelia's disappointment as she felt her own gathering anticipation subside.

'It's true that the first sight of a white man and his possessions comes as a surprise,' Leon said, as dully as possible, hoping to close the subject and move on.

'Of course it does,' said de Lancey, who was equally keen to prolong the thrilling sensation of being the centre of everyone's attention. 'These people haven't developed anything that remotely passes for a civilization.'

Leon gave an impatient sigh. *Damn! I'm just going to have to put this buffoon in his place.*

'The Masai have no skyscrapers, or aeroplanes, or telephones in their world, that is true. But they know things that we cannot begin to understand.'

'Go on then, what sort of things?'

'Even a Masai child can track a stray animal for days across open country,' Leon said. 'They'll spot the faint outline of an elephant's footprint on a patch of rock-hard earth where you or I would see nothing but dirt and stones, and identify the

29

precise animal to which the print belongs. If the Masai soldiers I once had the privilege to command came across the trail of an invading war-party from another tribe they would at once know the number of men in the party, the length of time since they had passed and the destination to which they were heading. And if you doubt the capacity of the African brain, de Lancey, answer me this: how many languages do you speak?'

'I've always found the King's English perfectly adequate, thank you, Courtney.'

'Then you are two behind a great many Africans, who speak three languages as a matter of course: their tribal tongue; the lingua franca spoken by everyone in the nation of which their tribe is part; and the language of their colonial masters. So the particular Masai who calls me M'Bogo grew up speaking Masai. As a young man he joined the King's African Rifles where the ranks spoke Kiswahili, which he swiftly mastered. In recent years he has become fluent in English. These men are not niggers or coons, as you like to call them. They are a proud, noble, warrior race who have grazed their cattle on these lands since time immemorial, and in their own environment they are every bit our match and more.'

'Well said,' said a small man, with a bald pate and a scattering of silver hair, peering across the table through a pair of steel-framed spectacles.

'Well, I still say that there is a reason why we are their masters and they our servants,' de Lancey insisted. 'They're just a bunch of bone-idle savages and we are their superiors in both mind and body.'

Having dismissed the option of beating de Lancey to a pulp, Leon had been wondering how he could teach him the lesson he so richly deserved, and now a stroke of inspiration came to him. 'Would you like to put that proposition to the test?' he asked.

'Ooh . . .' purred Amelia. 'This is going to be fun!'

'How so?' de Lancey asked, and for the first time a note of caution entered his voice as it occurred to him he might just have blundered into a trap.

Leon thought for a moment, working out a way to draw de Lancey in, while still ensuring his ultimate humiliation. 'I will bet that one Masai from my Lusima estate can outrun any three white men you put up against him.'

'In a race, do you mean?'

'In a manner of speaking. What I have in mind is this . . .' Leon leaned forward onto the table so that everyone could see and hear him clearly. He wanted this to be public. 'One week from today, we will all meet up again at the polo field. String a rope around all four sides of one of the fields. The competitors will run around the field, outside that rope. D'you follow?'

'Yes, I believe so,' said de Lancey. 'They all run round the field and if a white man wins the race I win the wager, and if your darkie wins, you do?'

Leon smiled. 'Actually, that would be too easy for the Masai. They would be insulted by the very idea and say that one of their young boys, or even a woman, could win.'

'Listen here, old man, you sound like you hate your own race.'

'I wouldn't say that. I just think that you're either a good man or you're not and skin colour's got nothing whatever to do with it. The most appalling bully and bounder I ever met was a white man.' Leon paused for a moment and looked around the table at the disapproving faces. Then he added, 'Mind you, he was a German.'

The frowns turned to smiles and laughs at that and someone called out, 'I say, what happened to this horrible Hun?'

'His chest got in the way of a bullet from a .470 Nitro Express hunting rifle.'

'Was that what passed for your war service?' asked de Lancey acidly. 'Better than nothing I suppose.'

The man in the steel-rimmed glasses cleared his throat. There was a philosophical, almost sad look in his eyes and a wry cast to his mouth, as if he were all too aware of the imperfections of man and the shortness of his life. Yet at once the table fell silent. This was the Right Honourable Hugh Cholmondeley, Third Baron Delamere and the unquestioned leader of Kenya's white population. He had been among the first British settlers in British East Africa, owned two huge estates and was famed for the fortune he had spent trying to establish cattle, sheep and grain farming on his farmland, while preserving the wildlife in the vast areas of country that he left untouched. There was a cane resting on the back of his chair, for he walked with a limp, the result of being mauled by a lion. Yet there was real strength behind those faraway eyes.

'Gentlemen, gentlemen, let's not have any unpleasantness,' Delamere said. 'I can testify to the fact that Courtney here served alongside me throughout the war, chasing that infuriating German rascal von Lettow back and forth across East Africa. It may also interest you to know that Mrs Courtney assisted us as an aircraft navigator and pilot and was, at my particular request, awarded the Military Medal for her courage under fire. The Courtneys did their bit, you have my word on it.'

Leon gave a little nod of gratitude. 'Thank you, sir.'

'Think nothing of it, dear boy. Now, pray finish telling us about your wager. As you know, I rather share your opinion of the Masai.'

That, too, was something known to all the British in Kenya. Delamere even built his homes with the same mud and thatch that the Masai used for their huts. 'Of course,' he continued, 'I maintain that our European civilization as a whole is more advanced than the native African. Still, the individual Masai is a fine man and I might even put a guinea or two into the pot, once I know what I'm betting on. Courtney?'

'Very well then,' Leon began. The argument about the war

had been entirely forgotten and there was a palpable air of growing excitement as he spoke. 'I propose that the three white men run in a relay against the solitary Masai. One of them will start alongside him, the starter will fire his pistol and they will both set off around the field. The white man keeps running until he either gives up, or the Masai laps him.'

'Is that really likely to happen, Courtney?' Josslyn Hay asked. 'A polo field must be twice the size of a football pitch. It's a long way round.'

'Possibly not,' Leon replied. 'I just don't want anyone to get away with walking. This has to be a race that is run.'

'Fair point. But I take it your rules apply the other way around, as well. That is to say, you lose the wager if the Masai stops first or is lapped.'

'Of course.'

'I see, so then what?'

'Then the second man takes the first one's place, under the same conditions, then the third. My wager is very simple. I will bet you five thousand pounds de Lancey, that when the last of the three white men either stops or is lapped, the Masai will still be running.'

The blood drained from de Lancey's face as all eyes were fixed on him. 'I say Courtney, five thousand's a bit steep,' he objected. 'Rather beyond my means, what?'

'All right,' said Leon. He took a thoughtful sip of his claret, trying to suppress a huge grin as inspiration struck him. 'I suppose you don't want me taking the shirt off your back, eh?'

'I'd rather you didn't, old boy.'

'But that's exactly what I'd like to take. Here's my wager. If I lose I won't give you five thousand pounds. I'll give you ten.'

There was a gasp around the table. Idina Hay smiled to herself. Ten thousand pounds, given to her by her mother, had bought her car, Slains and the dresses she took such pride in receiving direct from the couturier Molyneux.

'And if you lose, de Lancey,' Leon went on, 'you will indeed give me the shirt off your back, and every other stitch of clothing that you are wearing, and you won't get them back until you've completed a lap of the polo field.'

'What . . . run around the field? In my birthday suit?' de Lancey gasped, as the other diners each formed their own mental picture of him naked and on the run. Laughter began to spread around the table.

'As naked as God made you.'

'He's got you there, de Lancey,' said Joss Hay, grinning from ear to ear. 'Ten thousand pounds against a trot round a field, you can't say no to that . . . What was that splendid phrase you came up with? Oh yes, with your cock swinging gently in the breeze. I'll bet every white woman in Kenya will be there, just to see the view.'

De Lancey could see that his only hope now was to brazen it out. 'Let me get this straight: you are betting me ten thousand pounds against a run round a field that one African native can beat three British gentlemen?'

'Absolutely.'

'I see . . . oh, one last thing.' De Lancey paused for a second and then asked, 'Will your chap run naked too? Isn't that what the natives do?'

'I should imagine so,' Leon replied. 'Is that a problem?'

'Worried that the Masai might make you look small, de Lancey?' one man asked to more peals of laughter.

'No, of course not. Just thinking of the ladies. Don't want them getting upset.'

As a number of the female diners glanced at one another with rolled eyes and little shakes of the head, Leon made an offer. 'I'll tell you what, I will provide a pair of shorts for my chap to wear, how's that?'

De Lancey looked around the table, knowing that his name in the Colony depended on what he said next. Like a man jumping into an ice-cold pool he steeled himself, breathed deeply and took the plunge: 'Then in that case Courtney, you've got a bet,' he said as a cheer went up, more drinks were called for, and the night's festivities began in earnest.

Leon Courtney emerged from the Great War with a fortune even bigger than Amelia or Idina had imagined. Having once been close to destitution he found himself with the means to buy one of the finest estates in East Africa. He named it Lusima, in honour of Manyoro's mother, whose skills as a healer, counsellor and mystical seer he had come to cherish deeply. Leon planned to follow the example of Lord Delamere who kept much of his land untouched, for use as a nature reserve, and gave over the rest to agriculture. When it came to setting up a safari business that would attract rich customers from Europe and the Americas, Leon was in his element, but the farming was a different matter. He could not help noticing how many British settlers lost everything they had trying to marry European agricultural techniques with African land, weather and pestilence. He therefore decided to work with the grain of Kenyan life, rather than against it. So he made an agreement with Manyoro, by which he and his extended family could have the freedom of the entire Lusima estate, provided that they also herded and cared for Leon's cattle alongside their own. Since the Masai measured a man's worth not in money, but by the number of his cows and of his children, Leon paid his people in their preferred currency. For every ten calves born to Leon's cows, the Masai kept one for themselves.

This arrangement had a few teething problems. The Masai believed that every cow on earth belonged to them and, as a consequence, felt perfectly entitled to rustle from non-Masai. They also lived off their animals' blood and milk and so kept their cattle alive for as long as possible, rather than sending them to the slaughterhouse. The concept of keeping another man's cattle until such time as they were taken away to be sold and killed struck even Manyoro, accustomed as he was to British customs due to his time in the army, as bizarre.

On the other hand, the offer of huge areas of grazing and a guaranteed increase in his and his people's herds was too good to turn down. As the years had gone by, he had prospered mightily, particularly once he had seen how much money his cattle could fetch and how useful money could be in a world now run by white men. The arrangement had worked perfectly for Leon, too, since his herds did not suffer anything like the same rates of disease as those of his fellow farmers. His Masai herdsmen knew which ground was corrupted by plants that produced poisonous feed or insects that carried disease and so they kept to areas of safe, sweet grass. They guarded their animals and Leon's against lions and other predators and they lived well on the blood and milk that they took from the animals they were herding, a practice to which Leon turned a blind eye once he realized that it did the cattle no harm whatsoever.

In time Manyoro had handed over the day-to-day running of the estate and its buildings to his kinsman Loikot, whom Leon had watched grow from an impish boy to a young man worthy of his trust and respect. Manyoro now lived in the village where his mother had raised him. It stood atop Lonsonyo Mountain, a mighty tower of rock that rose from the plains by the eastern escarpment of the Great Rift Valley, at one corner of the Lusima estate. Two days after the dinner at Slains, Leon drove out to the mountain. He left the Rolls at its foot, guarded by two of his men (their job was to deter curious animals, rather than larcenous humans, for no man who valued his life would touch M'Bogo's property and thereby risk Manyoro's wrath). Then he set off up the footpath that zigzagged back and forth across the steep slope, recalling, as he always did whenever he visited, the first time he had made the journey.

He had been half-starved and parched with thirst, his feet bloody and blistered, the skin flayed from his heels, the wounds so severe and the pain so great that he had managed no more than a couple of hundred feet up the climb before he had collapsed and been carried the rest of the way on a *mushila*, or litter, borne on four men's shoulders.

That had been twenty years ago, yet the memories of that time and his first encounter with Lusima were as vivid as if mere days, not decades had elapsed. He remembered too the times he had spent with Eva in this, their secret shelter from the outside world, the love they had made and the times they had swum in Sheba's Pool, a crystalline sanctuary nestled beneath a waterfall that fell from the mountain summit. He smiled as he recalled the sight of her, dashing down the path towards him, heedless of the precipitous drop that fell away beside her, then throwing herself into his arms. He felt himself harden and it was not the climb that made his heart beat faster and his breathing deepen as he thought of her naked body, so lithe and graceful in the water, her legs locked around his waist and her soft warm lips pressed to his.

Oh, Eva, my darling, my love, you were so beautiful then, so delicate, so fragile and yet so fierce and so strong. And then he smiled to himself as he thought, *And I'd still rather make love to you than any other woman on earth.*

They had both grown older since then, but the mountain itself remained as it had always been. On the lower slopes the path was shaded by the groves of umbrella acacias, whose branches flared upwards and outwards from the trunk, like the spokes of an umbrella, before bursting into a broad, but virtually flat canopy of leaves at their top. But as he climbed higher the air cooled and grew moist, almost like mist, and the plants around him became more lush. Tree orchids bloomed in vivid hues of pink and violet in the branches of tall trees where eagles and hawks made their eyries. Leon watched the birds wheeling in the vastness of the cloudless sky scanning the bush far below them for any signs of prey.

When he reached the top he was greeted by a gaggle of small children, grinning with delight and squealing, 'M'Bogo! M'Bogo!' A young woman, whom Leon knew to be one of Manyoro's new wives, looked at him with unabashed appreciation, for it was the custom among the Masai for a man to share his wives with valued guests, but only if the wife liked the look of the guest in question. She had the final and decisive say in the matter.

When Leon had first known Manyoro he had but one wife, for that was all the army would allow. She had produced three fine sons and two daughters. The Masai were, however, polygamous by tradition and it was an unspoken part of his bargain that Leon allowed them to live as they wished on his land. Having prospered mightily, Manyoro now had four wives to his name and a dozen or more new children, all of whom lived under the command and supervision of his first, senior bride. This had always been a prosperous community, whose inhabitants had been well-fed and housed in finely built huts. When Leon first arrived there, the women were bedecked in splendid ornaments of ivory and trade beads and the cattle were fat and sleek. All that was still true, but now Leon noticed a couple of paraffin lamps and, placed outside the largest and most splendid of all the huts, the incongruous sight of a set of rattan patio chairs arranged around a glass-topped table.

Manyoro was sitting in one of the chairs drinking a bottle of Bass pale ale. He must, Leon realized, be more than fifty now and had put on a good deal of weight over the years, as the visible proof of his power and prosperity. Yet there was no sense of softness about Manyoro and when he stood to greet Leon, the Masai was still the taller of the pair.

'I see you, Manyoro, my brother,' Leon said, speaking in Masai.

38

Manyoro's face broke into a huge grin. 'And I see you, M'Bogo, and my heart sings with joy.'

Manyoro lifted a bottle of beer from a metal wastepaper basket filled with ice-cold spring-water and offered it to Leon. He was delighted to accept, for the walk had given him a powerful thirst.

'You are the only Masai I know who always has a crate of pale ale ready to hand,' said Leon as he took the cold, wet bottle.

'More than one crate, I assure you,' Manyoro replied. 'It is a habit I learned in the army. They served this beer in the sergeants' mess.' He smacked his lips with relish. 'This is the best thing you British ever brought to Africa. Cheers!'

'Cheers!'

The two men raised their bottles in mutual salute, and then savoured their drinks in silence for a moment. After a while they began to speak in English about their wives and children, Leon feeling almost embarrassed at having just one of each in this company, though Manyoro was keen to hear news of the son that he felt sure Eva was bearing, and of Saffron's near-victory in the show jumping.

'Ah, she has her father's spirit, that one,' Manyoro said, approvingly, when he heard how Saffron had responded to being beaten. 'I have never understood how your people talk of being a "good loser". How can losing be good? Why would a man take pride in accepting defeat? Miss Saffron is right to feel anger and shame. That way she will not make the mistake of losing a second time. Ah, but you must be proud of her, brother. She will be as beautiful as her mother, when she is grown.'

'Not quite as beautiful as a Masai maiden, though, eh?' said Leon, knowing Manyoro's unshakable faith in the superiority of his tribe's females to all others.

'No, that would be impossible,' Manyoro agreed. 'But a great beauty among her own people, and with that fighting spirit in her heart . . . Believe me, M'Bogo, it will take a strong man to win her heart.'

Next they moved on to the latest developments on the Lusima estate. Though he seldom ventured down from his mountaintop, and the estate covered the best part of two hundred square miles, Manyoro still knew everything that happened on it and there was never any need for Leon to discipline any of the herders. In the extremely rare event that one of them did anything wrong, Manyoro would already have dealt with the matter himself before Leon even heard about it.

'So, *Bwana*, what brings you here today?' Manyoro asked, calling Leon 'Master' not out of servility, but respect.

'I come to you with a request, one that I hope you will find of interest,' Leon said. 'I dined at *Bwana* Hay's house two nights ago, and talked to a man by the name of de Lancey. He was disparaging of the Masai. He said they were lesser men, inferior to his own white tribe.'

'Then this man is no more than a baboon, and a very stupid baboon at that. He should count himself lucky that I did not hear him say those words.'

'Indeed he should,' Leon agreed. 'I, however, know the truth. So I assured him that my Masai brothers were proud warriors who have ruled this land since time began and I suggested a way in which I could prove their strength.'

Manyoro grinned. 'Will there be a fight? It has been too long since my assegai tasted blood. It keeps moaning to me, "Give me blood, for I am thirsty!"'

Leon fought back laughter as he adopted a pose of outrage at such rebellious sentiments. 'Sergeant Manyoro! Have you forgotten the oath you swore to defend my people? Have you become a rebellious Nandi, slithering like a snake upon the dirt?'

Manyoro's broad shoulders broke into a regretful shrug. 'You are right, M'Bogo, I have given my word and I will stand by it.

But please, never compare me to a Nandi, not even in jest. They are the lowest people on all the earth.'

'I apologize,' said Leon, reflecting that it had been a Nandi arrow, stuck in Manyoro's leg, that had first brought him here to Lusima. 'But let me assure you that neither you nor any of your people will be called upon to fight anyone. The *morani* will keep their blades sheathed. All I need is a man who can run.'

Leon began to explain what he had in mind. But Manyoro's reaction was not what he expected. Far from being amused by the challenge, still less inspired by it, he seemed offended.

'M'Bogo, forgive me, but I am insulted to the depth of my soul. Why did you only pit three whites against one Masai? It is too easy. Ten would be more of a contest, possibly twenty.'

'Now you insult my people, Manyoro. We are not all weak or lacking in endurance. I carried you on my back for thirty miles to this very mountain, when you were too badly wounded to walk.'

Manyoro nodded. 'That is true. But you are not like the others. You have the strength of the buffalo himself. That is why my people consider you our equal.'

'I am proud to bear that honour,' Leon replied. 'That is why I have set this challenge, so that the Masai should receive the respect that they are due.'

'For one day maybe,' said Manyoro, and suddenly Leon heard the voice of a proud man whose people were reduced to second-class status in their own land. 'But that is better than no days at all. Who will de Lancey find to run against my man?'

'No one that you need fear, but some whom you should respect,' Leon replied. 'De Lancey is putting the word out. He'll round up some pretty tough customers, don't you worry about that. We're not all bone-idle idiots from Happy Valley, you know.'

Manyoro thought for a moment then asked, 'You say you will lose ten thousand pounds if De Lancey's man wins?'

'Yes.'

'So if my man wins he will save you that amount. He will have done all the work. Should he not receive some reward for his efforts?'

Leon inwardly winced. Brother or no brother, Manyoro was always determined to wring the most out of any negotiation. 'Good point,' he conceded. 'What do you suggest?'

'A man who performs a great feat should have a wife to mark his triumph.'

'Sadly, I can't provide one of those.'

'Then give him the cattle with which he will attract a bride and make her father think, "This is a man who deserves to have my daughter beside him."'

'Very well, I will give him a bull and three cows . . .' Leon could tell from Manyoro's face that the offer, which he had thought generous to a fault, had somehow fallen short of the mark. And then it occurred to him and he wondered how he could ever have been so stupid as he said, 'And a bull and five cows to you too, though heaven knows your herds are already so mighty that you will not notice a few more.'

Manyoro smiled with delight, both at the offer and the fact that Leon had understood that it should be made. 'Ah, M'Bogo, a Masai always notices a new cow. You, of all men, should know that!'

'So, can I count on you to bring one of your best men to the polo fields?'

'You can count on me to bring a man. And you can count on him to win your bet. But whether he will be my best man, that I cannot say. My best might feel that this challenge is too easy. But fear not, M'Bogo, your money is safe . . . and so are my five cows and my bull besides. Now, come with me. You know there is someone else here who would rage like thunder if you should leave without seeing her.'

'You know that I would never dream of doing that.'

'Then come . . .'

Like an empress on her throne, Lusima Mama was sitting on a chair cut into the stump of what must once have been a towering tree. She rose as she saw Leon, her face wreathed in a loving, maternal smile, for since Leon had saved her son Manyoro's life he had become a son to her too.

Leon had no knowledge of Lusima's exact age, but she could not be less than seventy and was probably a good many years older than that. Twenty years ago she had seemed entirely impervious to the passing of time, but not even her wizardry could keep it at bay forever. Her hair was white now, her bare breasts a little saggier and less full than they had once been and her tattooed belly was just a fraction softer, the skin like crepe paper. But she held herself as tall and straight as ever, her walk still possessed a feline grace, and though there were lines around her dark eyes, their gaze could still look right through Leon, into the very depths of his soul.

A sense of great peace and security came over him, as it always did when he met Lusima. Being with her felt like stepping into a sanctuary, a place where he was always safe and cared for and he returned her smile with a warm and open heart. He held out his arms to hug her.

And then he saw something flicker in Lusima's eye and she halted in her approach towards him. Everything about her posture and expression tightened, as if she were suddenly aware of danger: as if the devil had crossed her path and something evil was prowling through the trees, waiting to attack.

'What is it?' asked Leon, alarmed by the change that had come over Lusima and conscious that it had happened while her eyes were focused on him.

'It . . . it is nothing, child.' Lusima forced a wan smile. 'Here, come and let me hold you.'

Leon held back. 'Something happened. You saw something. I know you did.' He paused, summoning up his courage as if

43

he were still a boy, rather than a grown man at the height of his powers. 'You have never been false with me, Lusima Mama. Never. But I fear you are being false with me now.'

Lusima dropped her hands to her side, her shoulders sagged and when she looked at him again the years seemed suddenly written upon her face. 'Oh my child,' she said softly, gently shaking her head. 'You will be sorely tested. You will know pain such as you have never endured before. There will be times when you will not believe that you can survive it, times when you will pray for the release of death. But you must believe me . . .' She reached out, took Leon's hands and looked at him with feverish, imploring eyes, 'You will find peace and happiness and joy one day.'

'But I have those things already!' Leon cried. 'Are you telling me that they will be taken from me? How? Tell me, for God's sake . . . what is going to happen?'

'I cannot tell you. It is not in my power. My visions come to me in riddles and half-formed images. I see a storm coming for you. I see a dagger in your heart. But you will survive, I promise you that.'

'But Eva . . . and Saffron . . . and the baby. What about them?'

'Truly, I do not know. I see blood. I feel a great emptiness in you. I wish I did not. I wish I could have lied to you. But I cannot deceive you M'Bogo, and I cannot deny it. I see blood.'

Leon spent the next few days with his stomach in knots and a permanent sense of suppressed anxiety dragging on his mind like a dog on a lead as he tried his best not to dwell on Lusima's intimations of disaster. He did not doubt that she was absolutely serious nor that there was truth in her words, for she had been right too often in the past for him to doubt her powers now. Yet experience had also taught him that there was nothing he could do to alter what fate had in store. So there was no point fretting over matters that he could not control.

Even so, when Eva reported feeling dizzy he insisted on driving her to see Doc Thompson.

Before the war, Dr Hector Thompson (to give him his proper title) and his wife had provided the expatriate community's medical care virtually single-handed. Since then, however, a European Hospital had been set up to care for the white community and the Thompsons had moved into semi-retirement, running a small general practice up-country. The Doc, a genial, reassuring Scotsman with a full head of white hair and a neatly clipped beard to match, took Eva's blood pressure and murmured, 'Hmm, one-thirty-five over eighty-five, a little on the high side. Tell me, my dear, have you had any other symptoms apart from dizziness? Headaches, for example, or blurred vision?'

'No,' Eva replied.

'Not felt sick or vomited?'

'Not since the morning sickness passed, but that was a couple of months ago.'

The doctor thought for a moment. 'You have had trouble in the past carrying a baby to term and we don't want to lose this one. On the other hand, we live at a much higher altitude than our British bodies were designed for and in a tropical climate, so there are all sorts of reasons why you might feel off-colour. I advise plenty of rest and no great exertions of any kind. I'll also give you some aspirin. Take two if you feel either a headache or nausea and if symptoms persist for more than an hour or two, get in touch. Don't worry about calling me out in the middle of the night. That's what I'm here for.'

The wager with de Lancey that Leon had thought so important now seemed entirely irrelevant. 'I'm going to call him to say that the whole thing's off,' he told Eva when they got home from their visit to Doc Thompson. 'If he makes me forfeit the money, so be it. What matters is staying here with you and making sure you're all right.'

'But I am all right,' she insisted. 'I felt a little dizzy, that's all, and you heard what Doctor Thompson said, it was probably just a spot of altitude sickness. I want you to win your wager. And I want to be there to see you win.'

'Absolutely not!' Leon insisted. 'You're not supposed to have any great exertions, those were the doc's own words.'

She laughed, 'Being a passenger on the drive down to the polo club is hardly an exertion, and nor is sitting in a comfortable chair in the shade when I get there. In any case, where do you think the Thompsons will be on the great day? Watching the race, just the same as everyone else for miles around. So if I do happen to feel a bit poorly, that will be the best place to be. Won't it?'

Leon could not dispute his wife's logic. And so, on the seventh morning after the dinner at Slains, he, Eva and Saffron, who was bouncing up and down with excitement at the thought of the event, set off before dawn and drove through the cool morning mist to the Wanjohi Valley Polo Club. Loikot came behind them, driving one of the estate's trucks, filled with everything the family would need to get them through the day and as many of the domestic and estate staff who could cram into the cabin and cargo area, or simply cling on to the outside of the vehicle.

The whole country seemed on the move. Farms and businesses stood deserted by their managers and workers alike. Shops and restaurants had put 'Closed' signs in their windows. Many of the chefs and shopkeepers, however, had simply shifted their operations to the polo club where an impromptu market had mushroomed, with stalls selling parasols, folding chairs and bottles of pop, alongside pits where fires were being stoked as whole sheep and great sides of beef were rotating on spits, while chops and sausages sizzled on griddles.

It was not just the colonists who had come to witness the

spectacle. Once word had reached the native Kenyan population that one of their number was taking on their white masters, tribal antagonisms had been set aside, for the time being at least, and half the country seemed to be on the move – men and women of the Masai, Kikuyu, Luhya and Meru peoples – coming by foot, ox-cart, bus, or any other means they could find to join the carnival.

The settlers were all arrayed along one side of the polo field around which the race would be held, in front of the clubhouse, with native Kenyans massed opposite them on the far side. The actual field itself had been kept empty, so that the competitors could be seen at all times, to prevent any possibility of cheating. The team principals would remain in the centre of the field, with those of the white runners who were still awaiting their turn to compete. Major Brett was serving as umpire while a dozen African police constables, arrayed around the course and supervised by a single white sergeant, would have the dual tasks of reporting any breaches of fair play, and also keeping the crowd in order.

'I'll be frank, Courtney, I'm not entirely happy about this whole palaver that your damned wager has sparked,' Major Brett told Leon soon after he, Eva and Saffron had arrived at the club.

'I had no idea there would be quite such a turnout,' Leon replied.

'Well, that's as may be. I'm a fair man, have to be in my position, so I accept that you could not reasonably have anticipated this level of public interest in a private wager between two gentlemen at dinner.'

'Precisely.'

'Nevertheless, I foresee the potential for considerable unrest when the native is defeated. John Masai's an excitable chap when his spirits are inflamed, particularly if he's got his hands on alcohol. I banned sales to the native population, of course, but I don't doubt they'll find a way to have a drink or two. And if they think that we have in any way conspired to make their chap lose, well, I just hope you don't have anything serious on your conscience when the day is out, that's all I can say.'

For a second, Leon suddenly wondered whether the blood Lusima had been talking about might be that of the spectators. He was shocked to realize that he felt relieved at that possibility. It seemed almost like a reprieve for his family.

Major Brett interpreted Leon's silence as a refusal to accept any responsibility.

'For God's sake, man, you can't possibly believe that three Englishmen can't beat a single native, can you?'

The question dragged Leon's mind back to the here and now. 'I would hardly have staked ten thousand pounds, Major, if I didn't think the Masai would win.'

Brett shook his head disapprovingly. 'Don't have much time for de Lancey. He strikes me as a bit of a bounder, not pukka at all. But he's got a point when he says you love the black man more than your own race. Wouldn't put it quite that strongly myself. But he's got a point.'

The major took out his pipe and started stuffing it with tobacco, tamped it down, put a match to the bowl and started puffing away, encouraging the tobacco to burn. Leon was looking around, trying to spot Manyoro, but it was his competitors who appeared first.

'Speak of the devil,' said Brett, looking past Leon. 'De Lancey's arrived. Got his team with him too, by the look of it.'

Leon turned and, sure enough, there was de Lancey, already red-faced and sweaty though the sun had barely begun to burn away the cloud that tended to hang over the valley in the early part of the day. Behind him were three men arrayed in various combinations of tennis shoes, boots, shorts, vests, shirts, scarves and cricket jumpers. A couple had actual running spikes hanging from laces tied around their necks. One wore a jumper with dark blue stripes around the V-neck and the waist and the letters 'OUAC' surmounted by a laurel crown on the chest. The other had an almost identical jumper, save that the stripes were a pale sky-blue and the letters on his chest read 'CUAC'. Leon was familiar with the traditional rivalry between Dark Blues and Light Blues: these two were Oxford and Cambridge men, and that being the case, the letters 'UAC' would surely stand for 'University Athletics Club'.

You never know, they might just be long jumpers or javelin throwers, he thought, cheering himself up as de Lancey stuck out a moist palm and gave Leon one of the softest handshakes he'd ever experienced. 'Morning, Courtney, hope you've brought the lolly,' de Lancey said. 'I've recruited as good a team as you'll find south of Suez. Would you care to be introduced?'

'By all means,' said Leon.

'Right-ho! Well, first I'd like you to meet Jonty Sopwith, though everyone calls him "Camel", you know, after the fighter plane.'

Leon nodded. 'Yes, even we Africans are aware of the Sopwith Camel. Good to meet you, Sopwith.'

He exchanged handshakes, a much firmer one this time. Sopwith was pale-skinned, ginger-haired and blue-eyed. He was tall and rangy, with long legs and a barrel chest, suggesting that he had a good stride, with the heart and lungs to power it. He looked as though he was in his early to mid twenties, just young enough to have missed the war, but in the prime years for an athlete. 'You're an Oxford man, I see.'

'Yes, sir. Ran in the Varsity team all three years I was there.'

'What was your event?'

'I'm a pretty decent half-miler, turned out a few times at the three-A's, got to the final twice, actually.'

So you're good enough to reach an Amateur Athletics Association final, competing to be British champion. No wonder de Lancey looks so cocky, Leon thought.

'And this is Dr Hugo Birchinall,' said de Lancey proudly as the man in the Light Blue jumper held out his hand. 'Birchinall works at the European Hospital – his specialty was the sprint back at Cambridge.'

'Good morning, doctor,' Leon said, sizing Birchinall up. As befitted a specialist in the longest of the sprints, Birchinall was slightly shorter than Sopwith, but more powerfully built, heavier in the hips and the shoulders. He had short dark hair, and a swarthy complexion so that he seemed an altogether more brooding, almost menacing figure than his more boyish teammate.

A smirk crossed de Lancey's face, as if to suggest that while he had begun his introductions with two renowned athletes, he had left the very best till last. 'Now for the final member of our team. I confess, he is not an Englishman, but he is white, and very proudly so, which was, I think you will agree, the essential element in our wager. So, Courtney, may I present a gentleman who has recently arrived in Kenya in search of opportunities as a farmer, Mister – or should I say *Mijnheer* – Hennie van Doorn. He's like you, old boy, a bit of a native African.'

Van Doorn did not shake Leon's hand. 'You any relative of that bastard Sean Courtney?' he said, in his guttural Afrikaaner accent.

'Distant cousin, why?'

'Because I lost most of my family in the war against the British, that's why.'

Leon knew he meant the Boer War, rather than the more recent conflict.

'My father died fighting men like General Courtney,' van Doorn went on. 'My mother and my baby brother perished in the Bloemfontein concentration camp. Now I do not have any family left. Not even distant cousins.'

'I'm truly sorry that your family suffered so badly,' Leon said.

'But I was born in Egypt. My father made his money trading up and down the Nile, and when he went to war, it was against the Mahdi at Khartoum. We had no part in what happened in South Africa.'

'You have a big estate here, *jah?*'

'Yes.'

'We had *'n klein plaas*, a small farm. It was on the Highveld, sixteen hundred metres up, not much lower than it is here, eh. Every day I would walk to school, six kilometres there, six kilometres back. Every day. But most of the time I did not walk, because if I walked I had to start before the sun was up and I did not like walking across the veldt in the dark, with all the wild animals out there, just waiting to have little Hennie for their breakfast. So I stayed in bed until the sun came up. But now I have a problem, for if I am late for school my teacher shall beat me and when I get home my father shall beat me even harder. So therefore I must run to school. Every day. Six kilometres there and six kilometres back. At sixteen hundred metres' altitude. So maybe this *kaffir* of yours can beat these *rooinek* Englishmen. But trust me, Courtney, he cannot beat me.'

Leon could not deny that de Lancey had rustled up a strong trio to win him his ten thousand pounds. But where were Manyoro and the man he was bringing to be de Lancey's opponent?

Leon looked around, scanning the crowd for the two tall, imperious Masai he expected to see striding towards him. Then he heard a voice shouting across the polo field, 'M'Bogo!' Leon turned and spotted Manyoro, emerging from the natives' side of the ground. As was his custom when venturing into the white man's world he had pinned the regimental badge of the King's African Rifles to his red ochre *shuka*. The badge was polished as brightly as if Company Sergeant Manyoro were stepping out onto the parade ground and beneath it were arrayed his many medals for bravery, campaigns against the enemy and long service. The message was very clear: *I have served the British Empire with honour and distinction and I deserve respect.*

Leon was about to call out his own greeting, but then he paused, dumbstruck. For Manyoro was not accompanied by a proud *morani* warrior who had earned his right to be considered as a true Masai man by killing a lion with nothing but his assegai to defend him. Instead there was a diminutive figure who could barely be twenty, if that. He was far shorter than any normal Masai, the shiny top of his shaven head barely reaching Manyoro's shoulder. And while the Masai tended to be both taller and much more slender than typical Europeans, this profoundly unimpressive specimen was not so much slender as scrawny, a fact made all the more apparent by the absurdly over-sized pair of British army shorts, presumably loaned to him by Manyoro, that were tied around his waist with string and hung down to halfway down his twig-like calves. This unlikely garment billowed around him as he walked so that he looked like a small child who'd dressed up in a pair of granny's old bloomers.

'I see you, Manyoro,' Leon replied, and did not bother to hide the irritation in his voice as he said, in English, 'You promised me a good man.'

Manyoro looked back at him and flatly said, 'No, I did not promise, brother. You demanded. And I told you that my best men would think this challenge beneath them. And so I have given you a runner and *Bwana* de Lancey can decide if he wants to race against him or not.'

'He's hardly going to say no to that, is he?' said Leon, pointedly.

'Shall I take him away, then? You can forfeit the wager if you wish.'

Leon forced himself to take his time and calmed down before he or Manyoro talked each other into a corner from which they could not extricate themselves.

'Very well, then, you had better introduce us.'

Manyoro switched to Masai as he said, 'M'Bogo, this is Simel. He is the son of one of my sisters. Simel, pay your respects to my brother M'Bogo. When you run for him, you run for me too, and for all our people. Do not let us down.'

'I see you, Simel,' Leon said.

'I see you, M'Bogo, and I promise you I will run like a wind over the grass that blows all day without ceasing.'

Aye, you might at that, thought Leon. For when he looked more closely he saw the lad had a flat, well-muscled stomach hidden behind the absurdly bunched-up waistband of his shorts. And he certainly seemed healthy. He stood as straight-backed as a guardsman and his eyes were bright with life and youthful optimism. *Ah well, nothing for it now. Better introduce him to the opposition.*

Leon walked Simel over to the part of the polo field where de Lancey had set up his camp. A large tent had been erected, within which stood a couple of camp beds on which his runners could rest before their exertions, or recover after them. There were deckchairs for de Lancey and his cronies – a thoroughly rum crowd of chancers and remittance men, so far as Leon could see – and the women they had brought with them. A steady stream of porters had brought crates of champagne and Tusker, Kenya's first brand of locally brewed beer. A campfire stood ready to provide sustenance to his opponent's entire party. A large iron kettle was coming to the boil and the smell of sausages sizzling on the grill, the whole set-up under the control of a couple of *totos*, suggested a late but hearty breakfast was being prepared.

A female face that Leon half-recognized caught his eye. It took him a second to place, but then he realized it belonged to Amelia Cory-Porter, his dinner companion a week earlier. He waved politely at her and she very pointedly did not wave back. Leon grinned to himself: *Hell hath no fury, eh? Fair enough, I showed her no interest, so now she's pitching her tent in de Lancey's camp. At least she'll be well fed.*

'Here's my man,' said Leon once he had found de Lancey. He could practically see the cogs working in the other man's mind as he tried to decide whether this was some kind of set-up. Simel was grinning at de Lancey in an amiable, unthreatening fashion. He was so diminutive that his three competitors, who were now emerging from various corners of the camp to discover what they were up against, looked like champion middleweight boxers up against an untrained flyweight.

De Lancey gave Simel one last once-over, saw no threat and said, 'Very well, then. You're on.'

Jonty Sopwith had been running long enough to know that good athletes came in all shapes and sizes. This little Masai had the look of a distance runner about him. He'd said as much to Hugo Birchinall who'd agreed. 'Looks like a classic Nilotic ectomorph to me. That means thin, Camel,' he added, knowing that Sopwith had studied Land Economy and was unlikely to be familiar with physiological terminology. 'Their light body-mass sheds heat more quickly than a more burly chap like me. Also helps them run long distances because they don't overheat, the way we do, like a car engine boiling over.'

'Then we'd better get this done as quickly as possible,' Sopwith said. 'I'm going to take it out hard. Then he has to decide whether to match me or not. If he doesn't he'll fall way behind. If he does go with me, I reckon I can run the strength out of him, same way I did to Bobby Snelling in the '21 Varsity match, do you remember?'

'I certainly do. Dear old Snellers hung on to your coat tails right up to the final bend, then you kicked again and he

54

practically collapsed on the spot. Poor chap just didn't have another ounce of energy left in him.'

'Exactly. Now, I reckon I'm good for a pretty sharp mile, at the very least. So I'm going to give it absolutely everything and hand over to you when I feel myself start to weaken.'

'And then I'll come on and pick him off. Good work, Camel. That's a damned sound plan.'

'So let's do the job ourselves, eh? Can't let it be said that two good Varsity men needed help from the *hoi polloi.*'

'No, we certainly can't.'

The tall, fair-skinned figure of Jonty Sopwith stood on the starting line beside the diminutive Simel. The two men shook hands and Sopwith said, 'Good luck, old man,' because it was the done thing to treat one's opponents with good manners and respect even if you then intended to grind them into the red African earth.

The starter fired his pistol and the two men set off to the sound of great roars of encouragement from the native Kenyans along one side of the polo field and the settlers on the other. As promised, Jonty Sopwith began at a punishing pace. In his introduction to Leon Courtney, he had understated his achievements, for he had a very good chance of making the British team for the Paris Olympics, two years earlier, until a badly twisted knee rendered him unable to compete. Sopwith therefore had every reason to believe that he could beat Simel, and get the job done pretty quickly too.

For a few seconds, Simel tried to keep up with the man whose hair was the colour of flame-tree flowers. But then he remembered the words that Manyoro had told him, just as they were walking to the start. 'Do not try to race any of them. Just run. And keep running. Think to yourself, "I am running back to Lonsonyo Mountain to see Lusima Mama and so I must run all day." But do not let the white men make you run any more quickly or slowly than you want to go. You must be a wildebeest, not a cheetah. Just run.'

Now Simel understood the point of Manyoro's words. This man who had introduced himself so politely was trying to tempt him into running fast, like a cheetah. But a cheetah could not run for long at top speed. If it did not catch its prey within a few seconds it stopped, gathered its strength and then tried again, some while later. The wildebeest, on the other hand, kept moving, running all day with its brothers and sisters, from one horizon to the other.

Now I will be the wildebeest, Simel thought, and he slowed from the near-sprint in which he had started and settled into an apparently effortless, loping stride, his feet springing as lightly as an antelope's hooves from one step to the next and his hands held up high by his chest.

Within a matter of seconds a gap of five yards had opened up between the two runners. It grew wider, to ten, then twenty yards. The cheering in the white stands rose in volume. In de Lancey's camp the hangers-on were all slapping him on the back, while the women shrieked encouragement to Jonty Sopwith.

This man's even better than he said he was, Leon thought to himself. Sopwith's stride was much longer and more powerful than Simel's, like a stallion on the gallops.

Hugo Birchinall was already warming up. *They're going for the quick kill: the middle-distance man breaks him then the sprinter runs him down. Good tactics. They might just work.*

Leon looked at Manyoro. He was watching Simel intently, giving away no trace of emotion.

'You see what he's doing?' said Leon, looking towards Sopwith, who had opened up a gap of the best part of fifty yards.

'Of course.'

56

'And will it work?'

Manyoro looked at the two runners out on the course then glanced across to Birchinall. 'He certainly thinks so. He is singing his victory song before the lion has been killed.'

'That's never a wise thing to do.'

'No, M'Bogo, it is not.'

Jonty Sopwith came round the final bend of the polo field and headed towards the finishing line at the end of the first lap, with the main mass of the settlers clustered in front of the clubhouse just ahead of him to his right. He glanced back over his shoulder and saw the distant figure of Simel, barely passing the corner, half the length of the polo field behind him, falling further back with every stride.

'Right, Sonny Jim, let's see how you like this,' Sopwith muttered. And then he kicked again, an athlete of Olympian quality revelling in his God-given ability.

Simel felt a shot of alarm when he saw this opponent speed up again. He did not seem to be tiring like a cheetah. On the contrary, he was gaining in strength. He heard a deep sigh, almost a groan, coming from his people on their side of the field which was quickly swallowed up by the shouts and cheers of all the white *bwanas* and their women.

Fighting the urge to try and keep pace, Simel told himself that all was not yet lost. He still felt as fresh as he had when the race had begun, and although the gap between him and the man in front was widening, still it was not even half the full distance around the field. As he ran past the whites a few of them shouted insults at him. The words meant nothing to him, for he did not speak English. But he did not have to. The looks on their faces, the waving of their fists and the way the men shouted and the women screamed at him bore an unmistakable stamp of hostility, even hatred.

Then a thought struck Simel. *These people fear me. They are scared that I might be as good as them, or even better.*

Though he showed no expression in his face, in his heart Simel smiled. For he knew that the white men were right to be afraid. All his life he had been ashamed of being so small, but now he had a chance to prove that he could do as much for his people as any man among them.

I am a Masai. Now I must show these people what that means.

In the clubhouse Saffron was jumping up and down with excitement and attracting pursed-lipped looks of disapproval from the women all around her as her high, piping voice shouted out encouragement to the Masai runner. She had a problem, however. It was very hard to see the race. There were too many grown-ups in the way.

Saffy had been told to stay with her mother and was positioned beside the chair in which Eva was sitting as calmly as she could so as to expend the minimum possible energy. As determined as she was not to let Leon treat her like an invalid or be made to stay at home, Eva could hardly disobey a doctor's orders, even if her natural inclination was to leap to her feet and shout just as excitedly as her daughter for the little man who had been given the role of acting as her husband's champion.

As the runners disappeared off towards the far end of the field, Saffron turned to Eva and begged her, 'Please Mummy, may I go and stand by Daddy in the middle of the field?'

'I'm not sure that's a good idea, my darling,' said Eva, reaching out to take Saffron's hand. 'I don't want you getting lost or trampled in the crowd. And I'm not sure Daddy really wants to have to worry about you when he's trying to concentrate on the race.'

'Oh, I can get through all those people!' Saffron insisted, looking dismissively at the human barrier created by the

58

grown-ups all around her. 'And I promise I'll be as good as gold with Daddy. I won't be naughty at all.' She fixed her huge blue eyes on her mother, almost daring her not to be charmed and repeated, 'Please Mummy . . . please!'

Eva smiled. *I pity any poor man who tries to resist those eyes*, she thought, suddenly seeing an image of exactly how Saffron would look when she was grown into womanhood. *I certainly can't.*

'Do you absolutely promise me that you'll go carefully?' she asked.

'Yes, Mummy,' Saffron nodded with a look of the utmost sincerity.

'And do you promise to be good and not to cause Daddy any trouble?'

'Yes, Mummy.'

'Very well then, you can go.'

'Thank you, thank you!' Saffron squealed, smothering her mother in kisses. 'You are the kindest, nicest, sweetest mummy in the whole wide world!'

'Oh, and one last thing . . .'

Saffron paused in mid-stride and turned back to Eva: 'Yes?'

'Tell Daddy not to worry about me. He needs to concentrate on his race. So tell him I've got a very comfortable chair and plenty of staff to look after me if I need anything. I will be quite all right. Can you remember all that?'

'Daddy's not to worry because you've got a comfy chair and everything's all right.'

'Very good. Now, be gone with you!'

Eva watched as her little girl disappeared into the crowd, fearlessly darting between the adults around her. Then she gave a sharp little sigh, closed her eyes and dropped her head for a moment as a sudden sharp stab of pain struck her, like a dart thrown at her forehead, hitting right above her eyes.

It's just a little headache, she told herself as it was followed by a slight sensation of nausea. *A migraine, probably. Nothing to worry about.*

She thought for a second about sending one of the club's staff to take a message to Leon and then immediately rejected the idea. *No, I mustn't bother him. He has other, much more important things on his mind.*

Saffron sneaked under the rope and dashed across the track and onto the polo field before anyone could stop her. She paused for a second and looked around. It was only a week since she and Kippy had been jumping on this very same field, but it seemed like years ago. Everything looked so different now. There was a crowd of people clustered round a large tent, and she scanned them all in case she could see her father. Then she saw him a way off to one side, talking to Manyoro, and she realized she'd been looking at the enemy camp and scampered off in the right direction.

'I see you, little princess,' said Manyoro as he spotted Saffron running towards him. She stopped in her tracks, two or three paces away from him and, with the utmost seriousness replied, in Masai, 'I see you, Uncle Manyoro.'

The tall, stately African's face broke into a broad, affectionate smile, for he considered this little white girl just as much of a niece as any of his Masai brothers' and sisters' offspring.

'Hello, Daddy,' Saffron said, turning to her father.

'Saffy!' Leon exclaimed. He picked her up and swung her into the air, laughing as she squealed with excitement. He hugged her to his body, planting a kiss on the top of her head and then put her down on the ground.

'So, what brings you here, eh?' he asked.

'Mummy said I could,' said Saffron, wanting to establish that she had permission. 'I couldn't see the race from the clubhouse because of all the people in the way. But I promised Mummy I'll be very, very good and won't cause any trouble at all.'

'Hmm . . . I doubt that somehow. So, tell me, how is Mummy feeling?'

Saffron dutifully repeated Eva's message, virtually word for word.

'Good,' said Leon, putting his daughter down. 'I'm very pleased that Mummy is so well set. And very well done to you for remembering everything.'

Saffron beamed with pleasure at her father's praise. 'What's your runner called, Daddy?' she asked, once her feet were back on terra firma.

'Simel.'

'He's very small.'

Leon gave a rueful chuckle. 'Yes, that's what I thought, too, when I first saw him. But I think he's putting up a pretty good show.'

Saffron looked at the two runners who were now separated by slightly more than the length of the back straight. Sopwith had completed his second lap while she had been negotiating with her mother and making her way to where her father was standing, and was now halfway around the third. He no longer appeared to be running ahead of Simel so much as chasing him from behind.

'Is that man going to catch up with Simel?' Saffron asked.

'I hope not, my darling. But if he doesn't then Mr Birchinall – he's the chap over there doing stretches and looking terribly keen – is going to take over.'

'Oh,' said Saffron, thoughtfully. 'That doesn't sound very fair.'

'Well, those are the rules I created.'

'Well I think those rules are beastly to Simel. I'm going to go and cheer him up.'

Saffron raced off to the far corner of the field and waited for Simel to run past. When he was a few paces away from her she cried out, 'Come on Simel! Come on Simel!' and then dashed along beside him. Saffron could only keep up with him for a handful of strides, but the sight and sound of her encouraging their man brought heart to his supporters and they raised their voices again to urge him on.

Manyoro, however, had his eyes elsewhere. 'Look at *Bwana* Sopwith, brother. His stride has shortened and his pace has slowed.'

'By God you're right,' Leon agreed. He had brought a pair of field glasses with him and he trained them now on Sopwith, who would shortly cross the line for the third time. 'He's gasping for breath. It's the altitude, probably, he's just not used to it.'

'But Simel keeps running,' said Manyoro. 'Soon the gap will start to open up again.'

Birchinall had now taken up his position on the track at the end of the clubhouse straight, urging his teammate on. Sopwith made one final effort, summoning every last ounce of strength as he ran to where Birchinall was standing with his hand held out behind him, as if waiting for a baton. Sopwith reached out, slapped the hand and then fell to his hands and knees on the grass, his head slumped down and his chest heaving.

Now it was Birchinall's turn and he was a very different kind of athlete. He ran like a true sprinter, arms pumping, back straight, knees up high and suddenly the gap between him and Simel up ahead seemed to be narrowing again, and even more quickly this time. The spectators on the colonists' side of the field roared for their man. They flooded forwards towards the rope that marked the track and the few police constables detailed to cover that side of the course – for no one had even considered the possibility that the white crowd might give way to disorder – found themselves trying to hold back a tide of shouting, fist-pumping farmers and businessmen.

Within the length of the back straight, right in front of Simel's own supporters, Birchinall had taken another fifty yards out of the gap. By the time he had run across the width of the polo field and turned the corner into the clubhouse straight, Simel was only just passing the finishing line.

The little Masai was starting to worry, darting nervous glances over his shoulder, but still he did not increase his pace.

'For God's sake, run harder, man!' Leon shouted, though he knew that Simel could not possibly hear him over the noise of the crowds.

Manyoro shook his head. 'No, he must hold his nerve. That is his only hope.'

'Tell that to de Lancey. He thinks he's in the money.'

Sure enough, the opposition camp was already celebrating. A crate of champagne had been dragged from within the tent and the *totos* were busy opening bottles and pouring glasses. The victory toasts were just about to be poured.

Simel rounded the turn at the end of the clubhouse straight, his eyes wide with the fear of defeat, but sticking to the instructions Manyoro had given him, for he was even more scared of disobeying his chief than of losing the race.

Birchinall was coming up hard, still gaining, still maintaining his pace though he was far beyond the limits of his usual racing distance. His face bore an expression of savage fury, the look of a man who is fighting past the point of exhaustion, ignoring the screaming pain of his muscles, the bursting of his heart and the desperate craving of his lungs for air.

He was going to win if it killed him. He knew it. The crowd knew it. Simel knew it.

The distance between them closed. Twenty yards . . . fifteen . . . ten . . .

Simel could hear the Englishman's feet pounding towards him and the rasping of his breath, like a wild animal at his heels.

He could not help himself. He broke into a sprint.

Birchinall increased his pace still further, pushing himself far beyond his normal limits, further than he'd gone in any race he'd ever run in his life.

Still he kept coming.

Simel closed his eyes, barely even conscious that he was still running, steeling himself for the moment when Birchinall would overtake him.

And then he heard a sudden scream of pain. He opened his eyes, glanced around again, and there was Hugo Birchinall on the ground, writhing in agony, clutching the back of his right thigh, desperately rubbing at the hamstring that had given way under the intolerable stress of the race and snapped.

Simel slowed to little more than a walk. He looked back again, not knowing what to do. Another human being was injured and in pain. Surely it was right to care for him. Should he go back, or keep running?

Confused by what had happened and breathless from the additional exertion required to keep himself that fateful hair's breadth ahead of Birchinall, Simel was unaware of the shouts and gestures of both Leon and Manyoro who were now running towards the corner of the polo field where the injury had occurred, hotly pursued by Saffron and behind her both de Lancey and Jonty Sopwith. The Masai was barely moving now and de Lancey was yelling, 'Umpire! Umpire! He's stopped!' But his voice was entirely lost in the pandemonium that had broken out among both sets of supporters.

Then Birchinall displayed the depths of his courage and fighting spirit. Grimacing in agony at the effort, he hauled himself to his feet and set off after Simel once again, hobbling and hopping on his one good leg. The sight of such a mighty runner reduced to this desperate parody of his former self was enough to reduce many of the women gathered under the clubhouse veranda to tears, and not a few of the men around them dabbed discreetly at their eyes or suddenly found the need to blow their noses.

Simel, however, had an entirely different reaction. He knew that a wounded animal could be the most dangerous of all, so when he saw Birchinall coming towards him again, no matter how slowly or awkwardly, his sympathy vanished. He had a chance now to open his lead up again, and he was not going to waste it.

He did not even see Birchinall finally accepting that he was beaten and his place being taken by van Doorn. In the time it took the South African to reach the point on the track where Birchinall had finally collapsed, Simel was able to open up the gap by a couple of hundred metres.

Barely ten minutes had passed and he was two-thirds of the way to proving that even the smallest Masai was more than a match for any white man.

In her chair on the clubhouse veranda, Eva slipped into a light sleep that gave her a brief respite from the worsening headaches and nausea she had been experiencing. But her dreams were troubled, incoherent and suffused with a sense of threat so menacing that they woke her.

Now her head felt like it was splitting in two. *Mustn't trouble Leon*, she thought to herself, feeling slightly dizzy, as if she'd had too much to drink, though she'd not touched anything stronger than a cup of tea with lemon all day. *A couple of aspirin should make me feel better.*

Eva smiled weakly at a passing waitress. 'Do you think you could possibly get me a glass of soda water, please?'

'Of course, Madam,' the waitress replied.

'Thank you so much,' Eva replied, and slumped, exhausted, back into her chair.

Hennie van Doorn possessed the bitter, unyielding tough-ness of a man born to pioneering Afrikaaner stock. For generations his family had struggled to take, hold and cultivate their land on the high veldt. They fought the land itself, the elements around them and the other peoples who coveted that territory for themselves, be they Zulus who considered it theirs to begin with, or British fired by an insatiable greed for more land and a greater Empire. They prayed to a God who was as hard and unforgiving as they were themselves, a God who taught them to hold grudges, seek retribution and left the turning of other cheeks to weaker, more gullible folk than them.

Simel could feel the menace emanating from this very different breed of white man, as it did from a growling lion or an angry snake. This was not a man whose limbs would betray him as Birchinall's had done. Everything about him told the world that Hennie van Doorn was going to win. No other outcome was possible. Every time Simel looked back, van Doorn was just a little bit closer to him.

The sun was rising now and the growing heat was making more and more people seek out shade wherever they could, be that within the clubhouse, in the shade of a tree or beneath an umbrella or parasol. But still the runners kept going. For Leon, the very fact that van Doorn was drawing out the kill over such a long period made it all the more horribly fascinating. It was like watching a spider taking hours to weave its web, knowing that the insects that were its prey would inevitably be caught and die when the task was complete. And Simel was finally starting to weaken.

Leon and Manyoro were now playing a much more active part in the race. Every time Simel passed their position, they marched to the side of the track, shadowed by Saffron trotting along beside them, and while the little girl cheered her hero on and Leon clapped and called out his encouragement, Manyoro provided instructions in Masai, urging Simel on and advising him how best to conserve his strength. At first, Leon understood everything that Manyoro said, for he had himself been fluent in Masai for more than twenty years. But then a time came when Manyoro's words sounded foreign to him. He had slipped into some kind of slang or dialect that even Leon could not follow.

'What were you saying to him, just then?' Leon asked.

The big man shrugged his shoulders. 'It was nothing, M'Bogo.'

Leon was about to pursue the matter, but suddenly he noticed that Simel's metronomic stride had started to shorten. With his hunter's instinct for a weakening prey, van Doorn was looking stronger and picking up pace. The gap between them was narrowing much more quickly.

Leon sighed and looked up to the heavens, as if seeking some kind of divine intervention. Something caught his eye. Far in the distance, beyond the furthest hills, a great mass of storm clouds had appeared over the western horizon and was now marching across the sky towards the polo fields. Leon could see lightning flashes many miles away.

Rain stops play, thought Leon. *That might be our only hope.*

Simel's head was rolling from side to side and his stride had lost its spring. He could feel van Doorn getting closer. His looks back down the track were becoming ever more frequent and wide-eyed. The South African was actually grinning at him now, relishing his impending triumph, picking up his pace all the time.

They were running across the field, about to turn into the back straight. Van Doorn was no more than thirty paces behind him and gaining all the time. Simel saw Manyoro, *Bwana* Courtney and his little daughter waiting by the side of the track up ahead. He had almost reached the three of them, and the gap between him and van Doorn had halved once again when he saw his chief give a fractional nod of the head. That was the signal they had agreed over the previous circuits and Simel understood precisely what it meant.

Like a man waking from a prolonged slumber, Simel came alive again. His body lost its heavy, lifeless torpor, his head lifted and his stride lengthened. Within a dozen strides he was moving at something close to his full speed. The Kenyans massed along the back straight burst back into life as they saw that Simel's apparent exhaustion had been a ruse to draw his opponent on. They hooted with delight at the Masai's cleverness and the white man's foolishness and for every one of them shouting for Simel, there was another loudly mocking van Doorn.

The Afrikaaner paid them no attention whatever. His entire being was focused on the business of running. His smile was replaced by a grimace as he forced himself to match Simel. But matching him wasn't good enough. He had to go faster. Van Doorn had come too close to snatching an outright victory to be content with anything less now.

Simel had never known such pain. His whole body was on fire, every muscle burning, every breath a desperate, rasping inhalation, sucking air into lungs that still felt starved and a heart whose beating was like an army of drummers, pounding their sticks against his ribs.

He had been running for so, so long. And provided that he kept his pace steady, measured, moderate, he could have kept going for even longer still. But this was different. This was running like the cheetah. And the cheetah did not run for long.

Simel started to slow, and this time he was not pretending.

Eva's headache had become unbearable. She tried to call for a waitress to get her some more water, but when she tried to speak, she could not hear herself speak over the shouting, cheering, stamping crowd. There was a roaring sound in her ears, like surf crashing on the shore, and she was blinded by a flashing, flickering sensation as if someone was shining a light right in her eye.

She gave a cry of, 'Help!' but the sound that emerged from her mouth was a feeble, incoherent moan.

A moment later a waitress passed by her chair, and the scream of horror she gave was enough to cut through the hubbub around her. A dozen or so of the people crammed onto the veranda turned and looked in horror at the sight of a woman jerking helplessly, unconsciously, like a marionette in the hands of a mad puppeteer while a dark crimson stain spread across the front of her skirt.

'Doctor!' a man's voice shouted. 'For God's sake someone get a doctor!'

Van Doorn was at the very limits of his physical resources. But he saw the little man tying up and understood that if he could only keep going, just for a very short while, he could yet have his victory.

But could he keep going? He was suffering badly from the sun and heat and lack of water. His mouth was parched and a crust of desiccated white foam had formed at the corners of his lips. He felt light-headed, his vision was starting to blur around the edges and there was a rushing sound in his ears as if he were on the verge of fainting.

No! van Doorn told himself. *I will not give in. Only the weak let pain or discomfort affect them. I will beat this* verdoem kaffer *yet!*

He drove himself into one last effort and forced his shattered body to keep going, denying its pleas to slow down.

The gap was closing once again.

Well, it was a good try,' Leon said.

'Simel's not beaten yet, Daddy!' Saffron insisted, defiant to the last.

'I'm afraid your father is right,' Manyoro said, in a voice heavy with disappointment. 'Simel fought with the heart and courage of a lion. He saw off two hunters, but he could not defeat the third. There is no disgrace in that.'

'I don't care what you say,' Saffron insisted, folding her arms in front of her chest and glaring up at the two men, 'I think he'll win.'

Leon gave a rueful sigh. He was about to lose ten thousand pounds in public, and to a man like de Lancey . . . *Let that be a lesson to you. Don't make any more stupid bets at dinner tables.*

The African faces opposite him that had been so gleeful a few moments ago were now downcast. Silence had fallen as they waited for the end.

And then, from somewhere in the crowd, a single voice sang out:

We are the young lions!

A few other men joined in, somewhat tentatively:

When we roar the earth shivers!

And then more voices, more strongly:

Our spears are our fangs!

And more again:

Our spears are our claws!

An exultant smile spread across both Leon and Manyoro's faces. This was the Lion Song, passed down to all Masai boys as part of the teaching that would lead them towards manhood. Their fathers and brothers sang it, as they would one day too, when they went out to attack lesser tribes and plunder their cattle and women, or confront the mighty lion with nothing but an assegai in their hands. This song both celebrated strength and provided it. And Leon joined in with all the other Masai voices, coming together in the rich, sonorous, exultant harmonies that were one of the glories of Africa, from the velvety resonance of the basses to the highest, piping falsettos.

Fear us, O ye beasts, they sang.

Fear us, O ye strangers!

Across the field, Simel heard the voices of his people calling to him and now he was panting out the next lines along with them:

Turn your eyes away from our faces, you women!
You dare not look upon the beauty of our faces!

Simel was barely aware of the power surging back through him, as if carried through the air by the song itself, for his running now seemed effortless, his body almost weightless as though his spirit had left it somehow and was looking down from on high.

The Masai saw the effect of their singing on Simel, and their volume became still greater as they let him know that they and he were one:

We are the brothers of the lion pride!
We are the young lions!
We are the Masai!

Simel ran down the home straight, past the crowds of his people's white masters, barely registering their presence. The music had filled him, refreshed him and driven him on.

He was unaware of all the people rushing towards him and when the first arms caught hold of him and broke the music's enchantment he struggled and lashed out, shouting, 'No! No! I must not stop.'

Then Simel heard Manyoro's voice and felt the strength of his embrace as he said, 'Be still, little warrior. Be still. The battle is over. The victory is won. Look . . . turn your head and look.'

Simel did as he was told and stared back down the track. He saw a body lying on the turf, and men rushing towards it as they had towards him. He realized that the body belonged to van Doorn and for a terrible moment thought that he might be dead.

'Have I killed him?' Simel panted, though he was gasping for air so desperately that he barely had breath enough to talk.

'No,' Manyoro reassured him. 'Watch. He rises.'

Simel screwed up his eyes and, sure enough, arms were reaching down, grasping the fallen runner and slowly lifting him back to his feet.

'Good,' Simel gasped. 'I am glad.'

'You won,' Manyoro said. 'You ran like a true Masai, a true *morani*.'

Simel smiled. And then, only then, he passed out from sheer exhaustion.

Saffron was still filled with the excitement of the final minutes of the race and the elation of Simel's win. But the sight of him fainting in Manyoro's arms plunged her into an abyss of fear and concern for him until he came to, blinked a few times and looked around as if unsure where he was. And then all those bad feelings vanished and she was jumping up and down and cheering at the very top of her voice as Simel was hoisted onto Manyoro's shoulders as even the white spectators joined in the riotous applause for what was so clearly such a mighty effort and a splendid triumph.

'Make that ten cows!' Leon called to Manyoro. 'Simel deserves it. And, yes, ten for you too!'

The native crowd had burst past the police who had all been far too busy cheering the victory themselves to stop them and were now flooding across the polo field towards the clubhouse, dancing and jumping for joy as they went.

Amidst the pandemonium it suddenly struck Saffron that Mummy ought to be there, enjoying it all with her and Daddy.

I wonder if I should go and get her, she thought.

And then she saw Doctor Thompson pushing his way through the crowd. Of all the people all around her, whether black or white, his was the only face not alight with the sheer thrill of what they had all just witnessed. He looked sombre, and she could see him becoming cross as he had to force his way through all the people blocking his way.

The doctor was looking from side to side, clearly searching for someone. Then he spotted Saffron. He'd often treated her for colds and upset tummies and general bumps and bruises so he recognized her at once and came towards her.

'Hello, Saffron,' he said, not giving her his usual smile. And before she could even say hello back, he asked, 'Where's your father?'

'He's over there, by Manyoro,' she said, pointing towards them. 'Is something the matter?'

The doctor didn't reply and suddenly Saffron had a terrible, frightening feeling that she knew what the matter was. She reached up and tugged on the doctor's sleeve. 'Is Mummy all right?'

He looked down at her, his face grave, opened his mouth, but then closed it again, as if he did not know what to say. He turned his head, looked towards her father and pushed his way through the mass of people lining up to offer their congratulations.

Saffron watched the doctor talking to Daddy. She saw the happiness drain from her father's face, to be replaced by a look as sad and serious as the doctor's. Then her father turned to Manyoro, and said something. Both men looked towards her and then they started moving: her father with Doctor Thompson, heading back up to the clubhouse, Manyoro towards her.

Saffron knew what that meant. Daddy was going to see Mummy, who must be really ill, or he and the doctor wouldn't be looking so worried. Manyoro was supposed to be looking after her.

Saffron loved Manyoro. But she loved her mother more and she had to see her, no matter how ill she was. She just had to.

She thought for a second. *Black people aren't allowed in the clubhouse. Not unless they're staff. So if I can get there before Manyoro he can't come in after me.*

She looked towards Manyoro. For a second their eyes met. Then Saffron turned and dashed away, nipping between the much bigger grown-ups all around her while Manyoro had to go slowly and steadily, asking permission of all the settlers to let him through. Saffron knew that she was being cruel, forcing a man as proud and dignified as Manyoro to lower himself to men and women who weren't half as fine as him, simply because of the colour of his skin. But she had no choice. She had to see her mother.

Saffron kept moving, constantly expecting to feel the weight of Manyoro's hand on her shoulder until she reached the short flight of steps leading up to the clubhouse veranda. She dashed up the steps, knowing that once she'd reached the top she was safe and only then looked around to see where Manyoro was.

The Masai wasn't hard to spot. He was a good head taller than any of the settlers around him and he was looking at her with an expression of disappointment and something else Saffron had never seen in him before. She frowned, wondering what it was and then she realized that Manyoro was in pain. He clenched his fist and bumped it against his chest, over his heart.

The pain he's feeling is for me, Saffron thought as she turned and made her way to the spot where Mummy had been sitting. Her chair was empty, but her handbag was still there, on the table beside the chair, and the book she had brought with her to read, *The Green Hat*.

Saffron remembered the first time she'd seen it, a few days earlier. 'Who wants to read a book about a hat?' she'd asked.

Mummy had laughed and said, 'It's not just about a hat. It's more about the woman who wears it. She's called Iris Storm and she's very daring and rather wicked.'

'Is she the baddie, then?'

'No, she's more like a tragic heroine – someone beautiful and rather wonderful, but doomed.'

'Oh . . .' Saffron had not been entirely sure what Mummy had meant by that, but then she'd perked up when Mummy leaned over, with a cheeky smile on her face and a wicked glint in her eye, and whispered, 'Would you like to hear a secret about this book?'

'Ooh, yes please!' cried Saffron, who loved secrets and could

74

tell from Mummy's expression that this was going to be a really good one.

'Well, Iris Storm is a pretend character, but she's based on a real person.'

'Is that the secret?' asked Saffron, disappointedly.

'It's part of the secret,' Eva said. 'The other part is that the real woman is someone you know.'

Now that was interesting. Saffron's eyes widened. 'Who?' she gasped.

'I can't tell you, because it's a secret . . . but . . .' Mummy let the word hang tantalizingly in the air, 'In the book, Iris Storm drives a great big yellow Hispano–Suiza car with a silver stork on the bonnet. What do you think about that?'

Saffron frowned in concentration. And then it struck her. She had seen a great big yellow car with a stork. 'I know, I know!' she squealed excitedly. 'It's . . .'

'Ssshhh . . .' Mummy had put a finger to her lips. 'Don't say a word. It's a secret.'

Moments like that, when she and Mummy were sharing things and it felt as though they lived in their own little world – although Daddy and Kippy were allowed into it too, of course – were one of the things Saffron loved about her mother. So now she smiled to herself as she picked up the book and put it into Mummy's bag, taking care not to let the bookmark fall out, so that Mummy didn't lose her place.

'Hey you . . . Missy!' someone called out. 'What do you think you're doing with that bag?'

Saffron turned and saw a cross-looking man she didn't recognise.

'It's my mummy's bag,' she said. 'I'm going to take it to her.' Then she stopped and, suddenly feeling very frightened, said, 'I don't know where she is.'

The man's face fell. He looked around as if looking for an escape route.

75

'My mummy is Eva Courtney,' Saffron said. 'Do you know where she's gone?'

'Ah . . . I . . . that's to say . . . must dash,' the man said and disappeared into the crowd.

Saffron was surrounded by people yet utterly alone. More alone than she'd ever been in her life. She wished she'd let Manyoro look after her. She always felt completely safe when she was with him.

A waitress came up to her and got down on her haunches in front of her. 'I will take you to your mother,' she said, and held out her hand.

Saffron took it. The feel of the waitress's smooth warm skin calmed and comforted her a little. She walked with her into the main body of the clubhouse, still clutching her mother's handbag tight to her body with her spare hand. There was a bar inside where children weren't supposed to go, filled with men talking about the race, settling up their own side bets and loudly calling for more beer. No one paid Saffron any attention as the waitress led her across the bar and opened a door with a wooden sign on it that said 'Committee Room'.

'You go in there, Miss,' said the waitress, softly, opening the door and gently ushering Saffron into the room.

Saffron crept in, knowing she was not supposed to be there and not wanting to disturb anyone.

She saw three people grouped around the table that stood in the middle of the room. A woman was standing at the far end with her back towards her. Saffron recognized her as Mrs Thompson, the doctor's wife. Daddy was next to her, also with his back towards the door. Between them Saffron could just see the snowy-white top of Doctor Thompson's head on the other side of the table. He seemed to be looking down at something in front of him. There was someone next to him and as she crabbed her neck to see better Saffron realized that it was the runner, Dr Birchinall, still in his shorts and a white cricket jumper, but with a white bandage wrapped around his injured thigh.

Only then did Saffron see her mother's legs and shoeless feet on the table, lying between her father and Birchinall.

Mummy's feet were jerking up and down, as if she were shaking or kicking them, but the way they were moving was really strange, not like anything anyone would normally do.

Saffron crept around the side of the room, until she was almost opposite the end of the table. She hadn't looked up at all, not wanting to catch anyone's eye. But finally she turned and looked down the table.

Mummy was lying on her back with her arms to her side. The Thompsons were up by her head with their arms pressing down on her shoulders. Daddy had his arms on Mummy's legs. And the reason they were all pushing down was that she was throwing herself from side to side, her body shaking and her limbs twitching.

Saffron didn't understand what was happening or why her mother was moving the way she was, or why her eyes were open but she didn't seem to be seeing anything. The beautiful face that had always looked at her with such love in its eyes was twisted into something ugly and unrecognizable. Mummy's dress had ridden up and there was a wet, dark stain between her legs and on the surface of the table. And then she groaned and it was a ghastly sound that was nothing like her mother's normal voice but more the howl of a wounded animal and Saffron could not control herself a second longer. She screamed out, 'Mummy!' dropped the bag and dashed towards the table.

'Who let that girl in here?' Doctor Thompson shouted. 'Get her out at once!'

Saffron saw her father let go of Mummy's thrashing legs. He stepped towards her with such an angry desperate look on his face that she burst out crying and this time when he picked her up there was no happiness, not even any affection, just his angry face and his hands holding her so tightly that it hurt.

'Mummy!' Saffron screamed again and then a third time, 'Mummy! I've got to see Mummy!'

But it was no use. Her father was carrying her out of the room and across the bar and no matter how hard she punched or kicked him or how loudly she shouted, 'Let me go! Let me go!' he would not loosen his grip on her.

He pushed his way through the crowd on the veranda, and walked down the steps to where Manyoro was waiting.

Then, and only then, did Leon Courtney drop his daughter to the ground, though he still held her arms so that she could not get away. He glared at Manyoro with fury in his eyes and there was not the slightest trace of brotherly affection in his voice as he snarled, 'I thought I told you to look after her.'

Manyoro said nothing. He just took Saffron's hand, a little more gently than her father had done, but still holding her just as tightly. Leon Courtney waited for a moment to see that his daughter was finally secured. Then he turned on his heels and ran back up the clubhouse steps.

As Saffron watched him go she felt abandoned, desolate and completely unable to understand what was happening. Her whole world that had seemed so secure and so happy just a few minutes earlier was falling apart around her. Her mother was desperately ill. Her father hated her. Nothing was as it should be and none of it made any sense.

Just then she felt the first drops of rain fall on her and spatter across the red earth all around her. There was a sudden explosive crack of thunder and only a couple of seconds later a dazzling flash of lightning. The wind whipped at her dress and within an instant her tears were washed from her face by torrential rain, and the sound of her crying was drowned by the roaring of the storm.

'How is she?' Leon shouted for the hundredth time, trying to make himself heard over the straining of the engine and the pounding of the rain, and received much the same answer from the back of the car as he had on every previous occasion. He was leaning back in the driver's seat, his head half-turned to the back of the Rolls-Royce.

'She's very weak, Mr Courtney. But she's still here.' Dr Hugo Birchinall was behind him, sitting on the back seat with Eva cradled in his arms. 'She's a fighter, sir, you should be very proud of her. But Mr Courtney, may I give you a word of advice . . . as a doctor?'

'Go ahead.'

'Your wife is very ill indeed. There's no guarantee she'll make it. But she certainly won't make it if we crash. So please, focus all your attention on your driving. It'll help take your mind off things.'

Leon said nothing, but he turned his eyes back to the road ahead. Birchinall was right. It was an act of sheer desperation even to try to make the drive to Nairobi in this kind of weather. The distance wasn't an issue. The Rolls's six-cylinder, eighty-horsepower engine would make short work of the seventy-five miles between Gilgil and the Kenyan capital if the journey ran along flat, straight roads. But the truth was very different.

Like most of western Kenya, Gilgil lay within the confines of the Great Rift Valley, the stupendous tear in the earth's surface that ran in a great arc southwards for almost four thousand miles, from the Red Sea coast of Ethiopia through the heart of East Africa to the Indian Ocean in Mozambique.

Nairobi, however, lay outside the Rift and the only way to reach it by car was a dirt road, surfaced with gravel that ran up the towering escarpment, as much as three thousand feet of virtually sheer rock at its highest points, that formed one side of the valley. The road clung to the side of this gargantuan natural wall, snaking and twisting, seeking every possible scrap of purchase as it rose and rose towards the summit.

There were no barriers of any kind at its side, nor even any markings to indicate where the road ended and the plummeting drop into the void began. Occasional trees clung to the scraps of rocky soil by the side of the road and a few enterprising, or possibly just foolhardy tradesmen had set up shacks, selling food and drinks on the very few patches of flat land, just a few yards wide, that lay between the road and the edge of the cliff.

On a clear, sunny day with a dry road beneath the wheels, the view from the road, looking out across the apparently limitless expanse of the Great Rift Valley, was a sight so heart-stopping in its magnificence that it justified the nervousness that even the most cool-headed driver or passenger felt when braving the escarpment road. And the fearful could console themselves that this petrifying stretch of their journey was less than ten miles in length. But when rain fell as hard as this it might as well have been ten thousand miles, for no sensible person even attempted to negotiate what swiftly became an impossibly treacherous cross between a muddy track and a rushing stream. The water didn't just fall onto the road from the sky. It cascaded in torrents from the heights up above. So it was by no means uncommon for sections of the road's surface to be washed away in really bad storms and any hostess who invited guests for a weekend anywhere within the valley did so on the mutual understanding that, if the weather turned bad, they might be there for a week.

But Eva Courtney could not wait a week, or even a day. Her only hope was to get to a hospital and the nearest one of any size at all was in Nairobi.

'I'll try to get a message through to let them know you're coming,' Doc Thompson had said. 'Birchinall, you look after

Mrs Courtney along the way. Courtney, you'd better pray that fancy car of yours is as powerful as you always tell us it is. And may God be with you, for you'll need all the luck He can give.'

It was barely midday by the time they had set off. Eva's first fit had passed, though others could be expected. Her face had lost its normal golden tan and was a ghostly, greyish white. Yet she seemed to be at peace, as if she were just sleeping as she was taken on a stretcher to the car and then laid on her side along the back seat. Leon had relented a little and let Saffron see her mother and whisper, 'I love you,' in her ear, but he had resisted his daughter's increasingly frantic pleas to be allowed to come with them to the hospital and she had been taken away, kicking and screaming, to be driven back to Lusima in the truck with Manyoro, Loikot and the staff.

The first section of the drive was relatively straightforward as the road ran southeast along the valley floor. The rain was far too much for the Rolls's windscreen wipers to cope with, but Leon knew the route so well that he only needed a few visual clues, no matter how blurred by water, to tell him where he was, and there was almost no other traffic on the road to worry about. He was even able, in a desperate attempt to talk about something, anything other than Eva's plight, to tell Birchinall, 'This storm has come at just the right time for your Mr de Lancey.'

'How do you mean?'

'Well, I doubt he's stripped down to his birthday suit and run round the polo field in this weather. Even if he did there'd be no one still left to watch him.'

'I'm glad your chap won,' Birchinall said. 'Pluckiest thing I ever saw, taking on the three of us like that. It would have been rotten if van Doorn had come on and beaten him at the last. Can't say I liked the cut of that Boer's jib, truth be told. Charmless bunch, aren't they?'

'True enough. But they'd probably say that charm's a luxury

they can't afford. And to do the man justice, he's not like ninety-nine per cent of the other white men and women who were at the race today. He's not a settler, or a colonist. He's a proper African.'

'So are you, from what I hear . . . If you don't mind me saying so.'

'Absolutely not, I take it as a compliment, which was how this ridiculous bet ever happened in the first place. Christ, I wish I'd never set de Lancey that wager. We'd have spent the day at home, no excitement. Eva would have been right as rain. I'll never forgive myself if anything happens to her. Never!'

'Don't say that, Mr Courtney. Your wife has eclampsia. It could have struck her at any time, in any surroundings. As it was, it happened at a place that was a lot closer to Nairobi than your estate is, with two doctors immediately at hand. If anything, your wager has improved her chances, not lessened them.'

The road was starting to rise upwards now, passing through groves of spiky-leaved sisal and candelabra euphorbia, whose succulent stems branched out and up from a central tree trunk like a myriad green candles. As they went higher, more and more of the valley and the hills that rose from it were displayed before them.

'Astonishing, isn't it?' Birchinall said. 'Looks like something from the dawn of time. Just the power of it all.'

Leon knew just what the doctor meant, for the sun had entirely disappeared and the only illumination came from lightning bolts that could be seen flashing across the sky, striking one mountain ridge after another with their searing blasts of pure white light – the mountains just a darker shade of black against the deep purples and charcoal greys of the sky. It truly seemed as though the bolts were being hurled down from the heavens by unseen gods, as though the vast power they contained held the spark of life itself, as well as the destructive force of death.

82

And then the road swung upwards again, curled this way and that and suddenly they were on the side of the escarpment, on a road that seemed barely wider than the car itself and, just at the point when the surface became most treacherous, so it was almost completely exposed to the full force of the wind and rain. Leon had ordered the most powerful headlights possible for his car, but the beams barely penetrated the watery, murky gloom. He could see a small patch of road surface directly in front of the bonnet, but beyond that there was nothing but darkness, and it was quite impossible to tell whether the blackness was simply that of the track itself, just waiting for the light to strike it, or the empty space beyond the precipice, waiting to hurl them to their destruction.

Leon longed to put his foot down on the accelerator, for every extra minute spent on the journey lessened Eva's chances of surviving it. From time to time he would hear her groan or whimper and it struck him that these moments came not when she emitted sound, but when the chaos outside the car had temporarily abated enough for him to catch the audible evidence of her suffering. But as they crawled up and up, the road became steadily more treacherous.

The gushing water was dislodging rocks that hammered against the wheels and the underside of the chassis, and digging out potholes where just hours before the surface had been relatively smooth. Where the gravel had been washed away the earth below was dissolving into a muddy slurry as slippery as ice. More than once Leon felt the car sliding across the road, towards the side of the track, and he had to wrestle with the wheel to control the skid and keep them moving forwards.

Is this it? he asked himself. *Is this the disaster that Lusima Mama foretold? But how can it be? She said I would live. She made it sound like a curse. If Eva and I could go together that would almost be a blessing.*

And then he caught himself. *No! Whatever happens, I have*

to live. There must be one of us, at the very least, to look after poor Saffy. But, oh God, please let there be two. Please, I beg you, let my darling Eva survive.

Do you believe in God?' Saffron asked Manyoro, as they drove back to Lusima through the same storm, but on much friendlier roads.

'Of course. I believe in the Father, the Son and the Holy Ghost,' replied Manyoro, whose formal education had all been provided by missionaries.

'I've already prayed to them. I prayed and prayed to make Mummy better. Do you have another God, a Masai one I can pray to as well?'

'Yes, we have a God we call Ngai. He created all the cattle in the world and gave them all to the Masai. When we drink the blood and milk of our cattle, it is as if we are drinking the blood of Ngai, too.'

'Christians believe they drink Jesus's blood, don't they?'

'Yes, and that is why I believe in your God. I think he is really Ngai!'

Manyoro burst out laughing at the cunning of his theology. Then he told Saffron, 'Ngai has a wife called Olapa. She is the goddess of the moon. You can pray to them if you like.'

'Thank you.'

'Also we believe that every person on earth has a guardian spirit who has been sent to watch over us and keep us safe. So when you pray, ask that your mother's guardian spirit is kept strong and wide-awake so that it can protect her now.'

So Saffron prayed to God and Jesus and Ngai and Olapa. She prayed for Mummy and for her guardian spirit. She promised God that she would be good all the time, and never do anything naughty ever again, if only Mummy could get better.

Then she told Manyoro all about her prayers and when she

had finished listing them all she asked, 'Do you think that will make any difference?'

The nurse standing by the main entrance of the European Hospital in Nairobi screwed up her eyes against the glare of the headlights coming towards her. 'Look out for a big car that has a lady with wings at the front of its bonnet,' Dr Hartson had told her. But she could not see the front of the car because the lights were so blinding. Then the car turned as it followed the drive round and now she could see it from the side and there, sure enough, was the flying lady. The nurse turned on her feet and burst through the double swing-doors into the hospital. 'They are here, doctor!' she called out as she ran down the corridor. 'They are here!'

Leon saw the nurse disappear into the building as he pulled up under the awning that covered the driveway in front of the entrance. He had not spoken for the final few miles of the journey, for fear of hearing words that would be unbearable. But now, as the engine spluttered and died, he could restrain himself no longer.

'Is she still breathing?' he asked.

'Just,' Birchinall replied. 'But her pulse is very faint.'

'Thank God,' Leon muttered, grateful that he had delivered Eva to the hospital alive.

'I'm afraid you're going to have to help lift her out,' Birchinall said. 'My leg has pretty well seized up.'

'Of course.'

Leon got out of the Rolls just as the hospital doors crashed open and an orderly appeared, pushing a wheeled stretcher. Behind him came the nurse and a man in a doctor's white coat whom Leon recognized as Frank Hartson, the hospital's sole consultant surgeon. They had met once or twice at social occasions, and so far as Leon could tell, Hartson seemed like a perfectly decent, intelligent fellow, if not the liveliest mind one

85

was ever likely to encounter. Now this man would have Eva's life in his hands.

Leon ran round to the rear door of the car and opened it wide as the stretcher came to a halt just a few feet away. Then he put one foot into the well in front of the passenger seat, leaned in and placed his arms under Eva's shoulders, between her body and Birchinall's.

'I have the legs, *Bwana*,' the orderly said.

'Lift on three,' Leon told him. 'One . . . two . . . three!'

The two men lifted Eva's limp, unresponsive body up off the seat and Leon watched in horror as her head rolled helplessly against his arm. Her eyes were closed. There was crusted spittle at the corners of her mouth. When he looked down at her skirt it was wet and pungent with blood and urine.

'Oh my poor darling,' Leon murmured.

He placed her on the stretcher and watched as the orderly strapped her down. Then he took her hand and looked down at the face that had captivated him so utterly for so long. 'Good luck. God speed. I love you so very, very much,' Leon said and for a second he thought he saw, or perhaps it was just his longing that made him imagine a flicker of her eyelids and the tiniest fraction of a smile.

'I'm sorry, Mr Courtney, but we really have to get your wife ready for surgery,' Hartson said.

'I understand.' Leon forced himself to let go of Eva's fingers.

'Dr Birchinall is in the car,' Hartson told the nurse. 'He needs crutches. Please get some for him and then come straight to the operating theatre.' He turned to the orderly. 'Tell Matron I need to operate as soon as possible. So please prepare Mrs Courtney for surgery immediately. Got that?'

'Yes, doctor.'

'Off you go then.'

As the orderly pushed the stretcher away towards the heart of the building, Hartson turned to Courtney. 'I'm sorry we have to meet in such grim circumstances. Look, I don't know how much Thompson has said to you about your wife's condition . . .'

'Nothing beyond what he said when she first went to see him. We didn't really stop and chat today, what with the convulsions.'

'Quite so. Well, here's the situation. As Birchinall may have told you, we're pretty certain your wife is suffering from eclampsia, which is what we call a hypertensive disorder. In layman's terms, she's got very high blood pressure and excess protein in her blood and urine. The seizures she's suffered are characteristic of the condition. But I have to warn you that eclampsia can also lead to kidney failure, cardiac arrest, pneumonia and brain haemorrhage. I'm afraid to say that these can, on occasion, prove fatal.'

'Why in God's name didn't Thompson do something about it days ago, if she was so ill?' Leon asked, failing to keep the anger out of his voice.

'With the resources available to him he couldn't have predicted what would happen. The initial symptoms of dizziness, headaches, mild nausea could apply to all manner of conditions, many of them relatively trivial. And your wife is a pregnant woman living at altitude. She could feel sick or have a sore head and there'd be nothing whatever to worry about. The advice he gave was entirely appropriate. It's just rotten luck that there was in fact something serious going on.'

'So what can you do now?'

'Ideally I would give your wife something to lower her blood pressure, but I fear we may be past that now. With your permission I will try an emergency delivery by caesarean section. I have to tell you that there is a high chance that we will lose the baby and a somewhat smaller but still significant chance that your wife will not survive the operation, also. It rather depends on the degree of organ damage she has already suffered.'

Leon tried to cut through the emotions that were crowding out his rational mind and make some sense of what Hartson had just said: that calm, unflappable English voice delivering such devastating, heartbreaking news. Leon wanted something he could fight, an enemy he could defeat, for what in God's name was the point of his existence as a man if not to protect his woman and his child? But there was nothing to be done, for the war was all within her, out of his reach.

'Do I have your consent?' Dr Hartson repeated.

Leon nodded. 'Do whatever you think is best, doctor. And if it comes to a choice . . .' Leon stopped, choking on his words as he fought back desperate tears, 'for God's sake, please . . . save Eva.'

'I'll do my very best, I promise you,' Hartson said. He half-turned, about to walk away, then stopped and looked back at Leon. 'There's a waiting room just down the corridor. Take a seat in there, why don't you? I'll have someone bring you some tea, good and sweet to keep your blood sugar up, eh?'

Hartson had taken half-a-dozen steps down the corridor, when Leon said, 'Doctor?'

Hartson stopped: 'Yes?'

'Good luck.'

Hartson said nothing, just looked for a couple more seconds at Leon, then went away towards the operating theatre.

Leon watched him go, gave a heavy sigh, then went in search of the waiting room.

An hour passed in the waiting room. There were four battered old armchairs and Leon sat in each one of them as he tried to find somewhere he could be still without needing to get up and pace around the room, just to work off the tension that had his guts as tight as drumskins. A low wooden table sat in the middle of the room, surrounded by the chairs. A few dog-eared old issues of *Punch* were scattered across its surface, next to a dirty Bakelite ashtray. Leon picked up the magazines in turn, flicked through their pages, gazed blankly at the cartoons, hardly even seeing the drawings, still less appreciating their jokes. The tea arrived after the best part of half an hour's wait and he gulped it down in a couple of minutes. The sugar perked him up, as Doctor Hartson had predicted, but the additional energy only made his restlessness worse.

As Leon was leaving the clubhouse, back at the polo club, Doc Thompson had pressed a packet of Player's Navy Cut cigarettes into his hand, saying, 'These may come in handy.'

'I don't smoke,' Leon had replied but in the chaos Thompson hadn't heard, so Leon had shoved the cigarettes into his trouser pocket and forgotten all about them. Now he took out the crushed and crumpled pack. Thompson had stuck a book of matches into the pack. The words 'Henderson's General Store, Gilgil, Kenya' were printed on the flap of card that covered the matches.

As a boy, Leon had grown up with the smell of the cheroots that his father Ryder Courtney kept clamped between his teeth as he navigated his river boats up and down the Nile or haggled with the men from whom he bought and sold. When the clash of wills between father and son became too intense for them to remain in the same house, Leon had left the family home in Cairo to seek his fortune in the new colony of British East Africa, as Kenya had then been known. The smell of cigar smoke had always been associated in his mind with his father, and everything he was trying to escape, and the only time he had ever smoked had been during the war when, like virtually every other soldier in the British army, he did it to pass the time and ease the tension in the long hours of tedium and apprehension that preceded the start of any battle. The day he left the army, he threw away his smokes, but now he realized that Doc Thompson had not so much given him the packet of Player's as prescribed it for precisely this helpless period of waiting for news that might very well be bad.

Leon lit up his first cigarette, felt the familiar sensation of the smoke filling his lungs and then the long, slow, relaxing exhalation as it poured back out again. There were eight more in the packet and Leon smoked them all over the next two hours. By that point the air in the waiting room was thick with smoke, his clothes stank and his mouth tasted as filthy as the ashtray that was now half-filled with his fag-ends.

Leon suddenly felt a desperate need for fresh, clean air. He walked out of the waiting room, along the corridor and through the two swing-doors into the world beyond. The area in front of the European Hospital and the road on which it stood was laid out in a pleasant garden, bounded on three sides by the drive, and on the fourth by the wall that ran along the road on which the hospital was located. Benches had been placed for patients and their visitors to sit on. The storm had passed, night had fallen and the air was as cool and refreshing as water from a mountain stream. Leon wiped the rainwater off one of the benches with his hand then sat down on it, stretched his legs out in front of him and leaned back, gazing up at the majestic, infinite beauty of the stars in the southern sky. There was no traffic on the road outside and the only sound to be heard was the noise of the insects chattering away in the bushes and trees. Leon closed his eyes and for a moment a sensation of deep peace and relaxation spread through him, easing the tension from his muscles.

Then he heard the clatter of the doors.

Leon opened his eyes, sat up straight on the bench and looked towards the hospital entrance. In the harsh white glare of the light that illuminated the spaces beneath the awning, Leon saw Dr Hartson walking towards him. His shoulders were slumped, his tread was heavy and there was an air about him that Leon had seen in soldiers who had just taken a beating and lost comrades in the process.

And then he knew the message that Dr Hartson was bearing

with him on that slow, exhausted trudge across the lawn and it was as if all the constellations had suddenly vanished from the sky and blackness fell upon Leon Courtney. For he had lost the sun and moon and stars that had illuminated his existence.

Hartson had reached him now. He must have known that he had no need to tell Leon what had happened. So he just said, 'I am so very sorry, old man. We did everything we could, but . . .'

Hartson may have finished his sentence, but if he did Leon Courtney never heard him. For now the dam inside him broke and all he could hear was the sound of his own sobbing.

In her room at Lusima, Saffron lay awake for what seemed like hours before she dropped into a fitful sleep, plagued by dreams that were filled with anger, danger and a terrible sense that something was missing, no matter how hard she tried to find it. Then she woke suddenly. There was someone in her room, she knew there was. She sat up straight, eyes wide, staring from side to side, straining her ears for any sound, but although that sense of another presence very close to her remained, there was no sign at all of anyone she could see or hear.

She turned on her bedside light.

The room was empty. The door was closed.

And then, as suddenly as it had appeared, the presence vanished and, in a moment of absolute clarity, Saffron understood.

'Mummy!' she cried out. 'Mummy! Come back!'

But Mummy was gone and she wasn't ever coming back. Saffron knew that now, and with that knowledge all the comfort and security her mother had brought with her disappeared from Saffron's life and an entirely new chapter of her existence began.

At the age of thirteen, Leon sent Saffron to Rodean, a girls' boarding school in Parktown. 'It's time you got a proper education,' he'd told her. 'When I'm gone, you'll be in charge of the estate, and all my Courtney business interests. You need to know about more than cookery, needlework and flower arranging.'

'But why do I have to go all the way to South Africa?' Saffron protested. 'I'm sure there are good schools in Kenya too.'

'Indeed there are. But I've asked around and it seems that none of them offers the kind of education for girls that you will get at Roedean. It's the sister establishment of a very famous girls' school in England. Literally so, apparently: three sisters started the place in England and then a fourth one came out to South Africa and started the place in Jo'burg with a chum. That was thirty years ago and apparently it's gone from strength to strength since, a really top-notch place. And Saffy . . .' Leon's voice had softened as he started to speak from the heart, rather than the head, 'it's no life for you here, rattling around the estate with just me and the staff for company.'

'But I like rattling around the estate! It's my home. And all the people on it are my family,' Saffron pleaded.

'I know, my darling, and there's not one of them that doesn't love you as their own. But you need to be around girls your age, and you need women you can look up to and learn from. There are things I just can't teach you. Things only women know. And . . . well . . . you know . . .'

Yes, of course Saffron knew. In the end, so many conversations with her father came back to the great hole in their lives where her mother should have been. He had never found another woman to replace her. There had been plenty of women who liked the idea of being Mrs Leon Courtney and mistress of one of the largest, best run and most breathtakingly beautiful estates in East Africa. Several of them had found their way to Lusima and done their best to impress Saffron's father by sucking up to her.

'If one more silly woman tells me that she's sure we shall be the most terrific chums, I am going to scream,' Saffy had told Kippy, during one of their daily heart-to-hearts (though in truth the pony was only really interested in the apple that she knew her mistress was hiding behind her back). But each of the women disappeared within a matter of days, weeks, or in one case a full three months, and Saffron had long since given up paying any attention to any of them.

That did not, however, mean she loved her father any less, or was bored with her home. Lusima was a magical kingdom in which she was the Crown Princess and there was nowhere else in the world she wanted to be. So she had fought with every logical argument she could muster and every emotional trick she could play, but it had done her no good. Her father had made up his mind, and when Leon Courtney did that, no force on God's earth could budge him from his decision.

Going to Roedean meant that Saffron would have to leave home for the first time. Leon knew that the experience was bound to be hard for her, so he was keen to make it as exciting as possible, to distract her from any thought of home-sickness for as long as possible. To that end, he did not take her on a steamship to Durban, the nearest port to Johannesburg, but instead booked tickets on the final legs of the brand new Imperial Airways service from England to South Africa. And he did not take her to Johannesburg. Instead, shortly after Christmas 1932, he and Saffron flew all the way to Cape Town.

'I thought it was time you met the South African branch of the family,' Leon told her, 'starting with your cousin Centaine.'

'That's an odd name,' Saffron replied.

'It's French, and it means a hundred. So "*Une centaine d'années*" means "a century".'

'Well that's even odder. Who calls a girl "Century"?'

'Someone whose daughter is born in the first hour of the first day of the first month of the first year of a century might, if they

93

were French. Centaine's maiden name was de Thiry and she met my cousin Michael in France when he was stationed there with the Royal Flying Corps during the war. Michael was a fighter pilot.'

'Did they fall in love?'

'Yes.'

'How romantic!' Saffron's imagination instantly conjured up an image of a dashing pilot and a beautiful French girl swooning at one another, though she still knew too little about love to have much of an idea what would happen after that.

'I've decided that Centaine is a lovely name,' she said, with characteristic decisiveness. But then something struck her. 'You said Michael was a fighter pilot, and you haven't said we're meeting him in South Africa. So . . .'

'He died, yes. The damn Germans shot him down.'

'So how did she end up in South Africa?'

'Well, Michael and Centaine got married,' Leon began. In truth, he had always had his doubts as to whether the knot had ever been tied, but the family had accepted Centaine as one of their own and any doubts had been discreetly swept under the carpet. 'When he died Centaine was pregnant with his baby, and she had no family left in France so it was decided to send her down to South Africa because she and the child, when it came, would be safer there.'

'Wasn't there any war in South Africa, then?'

'Nothing to write home about. South West Africa had been a German colony, so plenty of people there were on the Kaiser's side. So were some of the Boers, because they hated the British. The Germans actually planned to help the Boers rise up and conquer South Africa but . . . well, that never happened.'

Mostly because your mother and I stopped it happening, Leon thought, but did not say. Instead he went on, 'Anyway, there was far, far less fighting of any kind in South Africa than there was in France, so it should have been much safer for Centaine to be here, except for one thing . . .'

'Ooh, what?' asked Saffron, who was becoming more curious about Centaine by the minute.

'The ship Cousin Centaine was on was torpedoed by a German submarine. Somehow she survived and was washed ashore on the coast of South West Africa.'

'What a lucky escape!'

'Yes, but her troubles weren't over, because, as you should know if you've been paying attention in geography lessons, the coast there is part of the Namib Desert, which is one of the oldest and driest deserts on earth. That's why they call it the Skeleton Coast. There's no water there, no food, nothing. Not for a white man, anyway.'

'So why didn't she die?'

'She was rescued by a San tribesman and his wife. The San have an extraordinary ability to survive in the desert and they kept Centaine alive until her baby son was born. Anyway, while she was travelling with them, she found a diamond, just lying on the ground.'

'A diamond!' Saffron exclaimed. 'Who'd left it there in the middle of a desert?'

'No one left it there,' Leon laughed. 'It was an uncut diamond. It was there naturally. So Centaine claimed the land and all its mineral rights and it turned out that there were a lot more diamonds where that first one had come from. So she became the owner of a diamond mine.'

Saffron's eyes were as wide as huge sapphire saucers. 'Goodness! Cousin Centaine must be the richest woman in the world!' she exclaimed.

'Well, she has been very rich, that's true. But these are hard times for everyone and there's not much of a market for diamonds these days, or anything else, come to that. I think she's been lucky to keep hold of the mine at all, to be honest, but now I gather she's putting her home outside Cape Town on the market. All its contents too, apparently: pictures, furniture, family silver, the lot. That's one of the reasons I wanted to see her. Thought I might be able to help.'

Saffron thought that this was a rather sad subject, so she decided to change it. 'Can you tell me about Centaine's son? What's his name? How old is he?'

'He's called Shasa and I suppose he must be fifteen by now. I think you were born about eighteen months apart.'

'What's he like?' she asked, really meaning to say, 'Is he handsome?' but not daring to be that obvious.

'I honestly don't know,' her father replied. 'I've met Centaine a couple of times, but not her lad. But I'm sure you two will have plenty to talk about.'

When they landed at Winfield Aerodrome, just to the east of Cape Town, the first thing Leon and Saffron saw was an enormous yellow Daimler parked on the field, barely twenty yards from where the Atalanta had come to a halt.

'Look at that car!' Saffron said to her father, pointing in the Daimler's direction. 'It's even bigger and yellower than Lady Idina's Hispano–Suiza!'

Before Leon could reply the driver's door swung open. A car like this was usually driven by a uniformed chauffeur, but what emerged instead was a woman so striking that Saffron stopped dead in her tracks and simply gazed at her in wonder.

'Is . . . is that Cousin Centaine?' she gasped.

'It is indeed,' Leon replied.

With just one look, Saffron was lost in admiration for Centaine. She was as beautiful as a queen in one of Saffron's old books of illustrated fairy tales, as slender as a wand, with impeccably bobbed black hair and eyes so mesmerizingly dark that they seemed almost black too. But it wasn't just her beauty that made Centaine regal. It was the way she carried herself and the fierce determination in the line of her jaw.

Saffron had spent almost half her life without a female role model, but now, looking at Centaine, she was gripped by an emotion that she did not quite recognize at first, though she knew somehow that she had felt it before. And then she realized that this was just like seeing her equally beautiful, stylish mother when she was a very little girl: that same sense of awe in the presence of feminine beauty and grace and the same longing that maybe, just maybe, she might look a little like that herself one day.

Leon strode over to say hello and as he approached, Centaine smiled and suddenly revealed the other side to her personality: charming, flirtatious, deliciously female in the presence of a man.

What a couple they'd make, Saffron thought, looking at her tall, strong, handsome father beside this ravishing woman. Taken aback by this entirely unexpected idea she chided herself. *Don't be so silly!*

Then another figure emerged from the car. And suddenly Saffron had something much more important to think about.

Shasa Courtney had not been keen on being dragged out to the aerodrome to meet his cousin from Kenya. She was being sent to Roedean, for a start, and everyone knew that Roedean girls were plain, spotty swots who all wore glasses and did nothing but read books. They weren't interested in boys. They just wanted to go off to university and get jobs that were meant for men. Plus, this Saffron girl was only thirteen, whereas he was only a few months from his sixteenth birthday and was just about to go back to his school, Bishops, as Head Boy. Clearly she could not possibly be of any interest to him.

Then he saw a girl get off the plane. And that had to be Saffron because there was only one other female emerging from the Atalanta and she was a silver-haired granny on the arm of an equally elderly man. But on the other hand, that girl – the one with the shiny, dark chocolate coloured hair blowing against the breeze, wearing a skirt that the wind was pushing against her long legs so that he could see the shape of her slender thighs and her flat tummy and the wicked, tantalizing, infinitely mysterious bit in the middle – that girl, who had now spotted him, he could tell, and was looking at him, staring at him in fact, so that he felt as though she could see right through him . . . *that* girl couldn't be Saffron Courtney. Could it?

'Centaine! How splendid to see you again,' Leon said.

'And you Leon,' she replied, kissing his cheeks with the elegant affection of a born and bred Frenchwoman.

He stepped back and gave her an appraising up-and-down. 'You look . . .' he was about to give her appearance a conventionally flattering compliment when the warmth of her smile and the way it lit up her eyes made him change his mind. 'D'you know, you look extraordinarily happy. Good news?'

'Yes!' she said.

'May I ask what it involves?'

'Later.' She took his arm and turned back towards her car. 'Your daughter is quite ravishing, Leon. It will not be long before she is driving men wild. Perhaps you should forget school and send her off to a convent!'

'Steady on, old girl,' Leon replied. Like any doting father, he had always taken it for granted that his daughter was the prettiest little girl in the world. But the thought of her as a sexual creature, even as a hypothetical, far-distant possibility, had never occurred to him. But now he followed Centaine's eyes and watched as Saffron and Shasa approached one another.

'By God, you really can see the family resemblance,' he said.

'Mmm . . .' Centaine murmured in agreement, for it was true that the two youngsters were so similar as to look more like siblings than cousins. Shasa's eyes were an even darker blue than Saffron's, perhaps, but they both shared the same dark hair and slim, limber build. He was only just growing out of an almost girlish beauty, but was not yet a man. She still possessed the last vestiges of her tomboy days, though faint traces of approaching womanhood were beginning to appear in the slight broadening and rounding of her hips and the first traces of her breasts.

'Look at them, sizing one another up,' Centaine said.

'Like young lions.'

'I wonder how long it will take them to realize that they share a sadness: Shasa without a father, Saffron without a mother. Both of them so rich in one way, and so deprived in another.' She snapped herself out of her reverie. 'Come! You must be exhausted after your journey. I must drive you back to Weltevreden.'

'Have you had to let the chauffeur go? So many people one knows have done that,' Leon asked, hoping that his tone was sufficiently sympathetic that the remark did not seem tactless.

Centaine laughed. 'Heavens no! I don't believe in having chauffeurs. I refuse to be controlled by any man. Even if he's just driving my car!'

Saffron and Shasa spent the journey from the aerodrome to his mother's estate talking about his school and speculating about hers. Each was forced to conclude that their prejudices were, perhaps, unfounded. As Centaine had anticipated, they soon established that they had each lost a parent. Neither of them wanted to talk about the experience, but a mutual understanding had been established: they had both been through a similar ordeal and it gave them a bond that did not need to be expressed.

Saffron was charmed by Weltevreden. Like Lusima it was set among hills, but this country was not so newly claimed from Mother Nature. Europeans had lived in the countryside around Cape Town for centuries and they had somehow softened the edges of the landscape; the earth seemed richer, the Kikuyu grass greener. Weltevreden even had its own vineyard, and pretty whitewashed cottages were dotted about the place.

'Oh look, Daddy, a polo field!' Saffron exclaimed.

'Yah,' said Shasa, coolly, 'we run a team here, the Weltevreden Invitation. We won the junior league here a couple of weeks ago, actually. I scored the winning goal.'

'I love polo!' sighed Saffron.

'A lot of girls do,' Shasa said. 'I think it's a bit like the olden days. You know, medieval maidens watching all the knights jousting and stuff.'

''No, I don't mean *watching* polo. I suppose that's all right. But it's not half as much fun as *playing* polo.'

'But you can't play polo!' Shasa protested. 'You're . . . well, you're a girl!'

Neither of the two youngsters saw Leon roll his eyes as he contemplated the terrible mistake the lad had just made, or noticed Centaine's smile as she found her unswerving loyalty to her son being trumped by her support for a fellow female.

'I do so!' Saffron protested. 'And I'll prove it, too!'

Before the argument could go any further, Centaine was calling out, 'We're there.'

White-jacketed male staff and housemaids in smart black uniforms were waiting to greet them as they stepped out of the Daimler.

'Welcome to Weltevreden,' Centaine said.

Saffron looked around in wonder at a full-sized reproduction of a French château that made her home at Lusima look like a tumbledown farmhouse. She was led into a cool, quiet hallway lined with paintings.

'I love your pictures, Cousin Centaine,' she said.

'Thank you, my dear. If you like, I can show you around some of the other ones in the house, as well. I think you would like them.'

'Thank you, I would.'

'Mater's got a landscape by a chap called Alfred Sisley that was painted on the estate where she was born, and a Van Gogh picture of a wheat field,' Shasa boasted.

Centaine flashed him a frown of disapproval and then turned to her guests, 'Now I'm sure you'd like to freshen up and change before . . .'

'Actually,' Saffron interrupted her, earning a cross look from her father in turn, 'I would like to play polo with Shasa. If he doesn't mind playing with a girl.'

'Oh, all right,' he grouched.

'Well you can't play in that dress,' Centaine pointed out. 'You can borrow some of my riding breeches and a pair of my boots. I can't promise that they'll fit but it's better than nothing.' She signalled to one of the maids. 'Could you please show Miss Courtney where my riding gear is kept?'

'Yes, Ma'am. Come this way please, Miss.'

'I'll get changed too and meet you back here in a few minutes, then,' said Shasa, and dashed up the stairs to his room.

'Saffy's mad keen to be up and doing. But I must say I would appreciate the chance of a bath, a shave, a fresh change of clothes and, if you have it, a nice glass of whisky,' Leon said, when he and Centaine were alone.

'Of course,' Centaine said. She glanced at an antique grandfather clock whose gentle ticking could be heard now that their children had disappeared. 'It's quarter to six now, so by the time you've freshened up the sun will be – what is it you English say? – over the yardarm.'

'That's the one.'

'Then it will certainly be time for a drink.'

Leon Courtney sank into the welcome embrace of a leather armchair that could have come straight from a gentleman's club in Pall Mall, gratefully took the heavy crystal glass of single malt Scotch that the footman had presented to him on a silver tray and looked at Centaine. She had changed into a crystal-beaded evening dress and was cradling a freshly shaken martini.

'So,' he said, 'tell me about that smile. It's hardly left your face since we arrived here, and I don't believe it's entirely due to the pleasure of our company.'

'Not entirely, no,' Centaine agreed, 'though it is very nice indeed to see you here.'

'I'll be honest: I was expecting to find you on your uppers. The word on the family grapevine was you'd called in the chaps from Sotheby's and everything was up for grabs. But I never in my life saw anyone less on their uppers than you have looked today.'

'The stories were true,' Centaine said. She took a sip from her cocktail glass and placed it on a table beside her. 'I was in real trouble. Who isn't these days?'

'Who indeed . . .'

'But I had a stroke of good fortune on the stock market. I happened to be holding a great many shares in mining companies when the government took South Africa off the gold standard.'

'Ah, I see,' said Leon thoughtfully. 'Clever you.'

For years, many of the world's major currencies had been pegged to the gold standard, meaning that their worth had in theory been backed by gold. This had kept the price of currencies artificially high, so they were hugely overvalued when the Crash of 1929 was followed by economic depression across the western world. As countries came off the gold standard, their currencies were able to drop in value, making their exports much cheaper to foreign buyers and thus boosting their economies. South Africa had been one of the very last countries to remain tied to gold, sending the exchange rate of the South African pound far above that of British sterling and thus making

South African gold, diamonds and wool so expensive that no one bought them any more. The decision to come off the gold standard and let the South African pound find its true value had been made only a matter of days earlier. The immediate effect had been to transform the country's trading position. Shares in mining companies suddenly rocketed. Anyone who had bought at the bottom of the market stood to make an enormous profit.

'I won't ask how you pulled off your coup,' Leon went on, though every commercial instinct he had told him she must have had inside information about the government's decision. 'I shall simply congratulate you on becoming a true Courtney. We've always found ways to make a killing. The first Courtneys got rich by looting Spanish treasure ships in the service of our King.'

'Looting other people's treasure – that's the basis for the whole British Empire,' Centaine said, with a wry smile.

'That . . . and defeating the French.'

'Touché!' she laughed.

Just then the doors to the drawing room in which they were sitting were flung open and two hot, flushed adolescents, with dust-covered clothes and hair matted by sweat, burst into the room.

'So, how did it go?'

'I showed him!' Saffron cried triumphantly. 'I made him back off.'

'Only because I let you,' Shasa retorted.

'Calm down, Shasa, and tell me what happened,' Centaine commanded.

'Well, Mater, we went down to the stables and I told her that I had two ponies, and one of them was Plum Pudding, who's really steady and experienced, and the other one was Tiger Shark, who's quicker and stronger, but wild and really hard to control. And I said she could choose which one she wanted to ride, and I thought she was bound to pick Plum Pudding . . .'

'But I chose Tiger Shark!' said Saffron.

'Of course you did,' said Leon, who had seen that one coming the moment he heard Shasa's descriptions of the two beasts.

'And we played for a bit, just knocking up and it was fun and Shasa was quite good . . .'

'I'm better than "quite good"!' Shasa protested, indignantly but also accurately.

'And then the ball was in the middle of the field and we both went for it,' Saffron said.

'We went "down the throat"; Shasa said. 'Just like I did with Max Theunissen in the final, do you remember, Mater?'

Centaine's face suddenly whitened. 'Going down the throat' was the polo expression for a full frontal charge between two players, riding directly at one another, head-on, and Shasa had pulled off the very same trick to win his polo tournament. It had been one of the most terrifying moments of Centaine's life, seeing a berserker madness seize her son as he'd hurled Tiger Shark at the Theunissen boy and his pony. If the two horses had collided at full gallop they would certainly have had to be put down and both their riders could have been seriously injured or even killed. At the very last instant, Theunissen's nerve had cracked, he had pulled away and Shasa had smashed the ball past him and into the goal.

The idea that he had even considered pulling off the same trick on a guest, and, what's more, a guest who was a relative, a girl and younger than him, appalled her.

'You did what?' Centaine gasped. The question was rhetorical. Before her son could answer she got to her feet, looked Shasa in the eye and rasped, 'How dare you? How *dare* you? That is unforgivably bad-mannered, stupid, irresponsible, and dangerous behaviour. You're lucky both of you aren't on your way to hospital. Go to your room right now. Right now!'

Shasa looked mortified. He bit his bottom lip, trying to hold back his tears. Then Saffron piped up, 'Excuse me, Cousin Centaine, but it wasn't Shasa's fault. I was the one who charged at him. And he got out of the way . . . And I know you weren't being a scaredy-cat, Shasa, even though I said you were. You just didn't want to hurt me.'

Silence fell upon the room. Leon hesitated for a moment, not wanting to take charge in someone else's house, and with their child, but he realized he was the only person in the room not yet involved in the argument.

'Right,' he said, 'let's sort this out, shall we? Saffron, you did very well to own up. But you shouldn't have charged Shasa. You put both of you in danger and you and I both know that you only did it because you were being pig-headed about doing anything a boy could do and wanted to show Shasa up. Now you've got him into trouble and I think it's a pretty poor show. You owe him an apology.'

Saffron screwed up her face, realized that she was in the wrong and said, 'I'm sorry, Shasa. I didn't mean to get you in trouble.'

'That's all right.'

'As for you, Shasa,' Leon went on, 'let this be a lesson. It's both rude and extremely unwise to be ungentlemanly to a lady, particularly a Courtney lady, because believe me, my boy, they fight back. Honestly, if there is any young man on earth who ought to know what women are capable of, it's you. Just think of your mother, for heaven's sake, and all she's achieved. Do you doubt her abilities, just because she's a woman?'

'No, sir.'

'And are you sorry for doubting Saffron?'

'Yes, sir.'

'Good. That's settled then, and no harm done. Now, Saffron, you've had a very long day. I think you should go and have that bath and perhaps, if you ask Cousin Centaine nicely, she'll have some supper brought to your room. A bit of food and an early night is what you need, my girl.'

'An excellent idea,' said Centaine. 'And I think you should do the same thing, Shasa. Bath, supper and bed . . . and then we can all have a fresh start in the morning.'

Shasa and Saffron walked upstairs together. When they got to the landing they paused before they went off to their rooms.

'I wouldn't have backed down, you know, when I went down the throat,' Saffron said. 'Even if you hadn't got out of the way.'

'I know,' said Shasa. 'And I wouldn't have got out of the way, either, if it had been anyone else coming towards me.'

'I know,' she said.

With that they each satisfied their pride and went off to their baths with their honour and dignity intact, knowing that now they would be friends for life.

Saffron was sad to leave the haven of Weltevreden. As a motherless only child, she had loved having a relative her age to play with, and an older female role model to look up to. But after the blissful bucolic luxury of Centaine's Cape Town estate, the size and noise and bustle of Johannesburg were an overwhelming assault to her. The city was five times as big as Nairobi, with more than a quarter of a million inhabitants, and they all seemed to move with a speed and urgency she had never experienced before, as if every single one of them had something urgent they simply had to achieve, right this very second.

'That's the Johannesburg Stock Exchange,' Leon told her as they passed an ornate building, fronted by great marble columns, that covered an entire city block on Hollard Street. 'The companies that control half the world's gold and diamonds are traded there.'

'It looks like a palace,' Saffron said.

'Well it is, in a way. It's the palace of Mammon, the demon of money.'

106

Over lunch, Leon gave Saffron a quick explanation of how company shares and stock exchanges worked and was surprised by the speed with which she picked up the ideas he was presenting to her. So far, he felt, the day had gone well. He'd been perfectly happy purchasing Saffron's tuck box, on which her name was even now being painted in elegant black capital letters. And having led countless groups of travellers and hunters across the wilds of British East Africa during his pre-War days as a safari guide he was completely at home debating the best possible trunks to buy to carry all Saffron's increasingly vast amounts of baggage.

After leaving the restaurant where they had lunched, they arrived at the school outfitters. Suddenly talk turned to dresses, blouses, pinafores and other items of youthful female attire and Leon's expertise gave way to bafflement. When the shop's manageress, who'd had no need even to glance at the list to know what it contained, got on to the subject of gym knickers a look passed across her father's face that Saffron had never in all her life seen before.

Oh my goodness, he's blushing! she thought to herself, desperately trying to keep a straight face. *He's so embarrassed he doesn't even know where to look.*

'Perhaps it would be best if Father took a seat and let Miss Courtney and I proceed by ourselves,' the manageress said. 'I take it, sir, that I have your permission to select the items that Miss will need for her time at Roedean?'

'Yes, yes, absolutely, whatever she needs, excellent plan,' Leon had blustered. Saffron couldn't swear to it, but she was almost certain the manageress, who had seemed rather fearsome when they had first been introduced, actually winked at her as they walked away to deal with those mysterious aspects of female existence that were best kept hidden from the uncomprehending eyes of men.

Saffron had felt as though she was being initiated into some mysterious but exciting new world as the manageress, whose name was now revealed to be Miss Halfpenny, took an appraising look at her chest, said, 'Someone should have bought you a brassiere by now, young lady.' She sighed, 'But that's a mother's job . . .'

'I don't have a mother,' Saffron said. 'She died when I was seven.'

'I'm very sorry, but I'm afraid I feared as much. When a girl walks in with her father . . .' She left the sentence unfinished, but then gave a brisk sigh and said, 'Never mind, best just get on with it, hadn't we? Lots of children don't have a mother, or a father, or even both, what with the war and the Spanish Flu and who knows what. But they find a way to manage and I'm sure you will too. Just let me help you and I'm sure we'll sort you out with everything you need.'

Saffron had been hearing this kind of stiff-upper-lip encouragement for years, but she sensed a genuine kindness in Miss Halfpenny's voice. As she rummaged in glass-fronted drawers for bras and knickers and stockings, occasionally holding up an item in front of Saffron's coltish, long-limbed frame, checking it for size and either discarding it on one pile or placing it on another, much larger heap of things to be tried on, Miss Halfpenny chatted away about what Saffron could expect at Roedean, and what the teachers and girls were like.

'Your father couldn't have picked a better place. Roedean girls, in my experience, are bright, independent, thoroughly modern young ladies. Plenty of them go on to university, too. And they are all trained to be able to earn their own living.'

'Daddy said I needed to know about more than cookery and needlework and flower arranging.'

Miss Halfpenny gave an approving nod. 'Well said, that man. And I'm sure he's thinking about your mother and what she would have wanted for you and he's trying his very best to make her happy.'

'I hadn't thought of that,' said Saffron. But from the moment Miss Halfpenny said those words, her attitude to her new school changed. She resolved that she would do everything to make her mother happy, too, with the result that having turned up at Roedean in mid-January for the first day of the new academic year she plunged into school life with all the energy she possessed. Her naturally athletic physique and fiercely competitive nature made her a demon on the hockey pitch and netball court and her rapidly growing height saw her cast for many a male role in the school's dramatic productions. It took her a term or two to learn how to adapt to boarding school life, which requires pupils to be able to get along with people with whom they share not only classrooms but also dormitories, bathrooms and every meal of the day. Saffron soon made friends, however, for her classmates knew that while her temper could be stormy she was neither malicious, nor deceitful: she said precisely what she thought, for better or for worse, and once decided on a course of action stuck to it, come hell or high water. If her ancestors were looking down from on high they must have smiled, for no Courtney had ever done anything else.

Soon after his return from South Africa, Leon had to go into Nairobi to carry out various administrative chores related to the Lusima estate. He took a room at the Muthaiga Country Club, a private, membership-only institution that was the social hub of the expatriate community in Kenya. For all its social cachet, the Muthaiga was not a particularly impressive piece of architecture, being little more than a greatly expanded bungalow, with pink pebbledash walls, painted metal window frames (for wooden frames soon rotted away in the sub-tropical climate) and a few classical columns by the entrance to provide a sense of colonial prestige. Inside, one walked over floors of highly polished wooden parquet, past walls painted in shades of cream and green. It looked, as Hugh Delamere had once remarked to Leon, 'Like a cross between my old prep school and a suburban nursing home.'

Arriving back at the club one evening, after a long day of meetings with lawyers and accountants, Leon sank into one of the chintz-covered armchairs that dotted the members' lounge. A uniformed waiter immediately appeared and took his order for a gin and tonic. The drink appeared beside him only moments later and Leon signed for it on a coloured paper chit: nothing as grubby as money was ever seen to change hands within the club's portals. Leon took a sip of the ice-cold drink, put the glass back on the side table and leaned back in his chair, eyes closed as he let the cares of the day slip away.

Then he heard a familiar voice: 'Evening, Courtney, mind if I join you?'

'By all means, Joss,' Leon replied.

Over the past few years a lot had changed in Josslyn Hay's life. For one thing, he was now the twenty-second Earl of Erroll, having inherited the title on his father's death, along with the honorary post of Lord High Constable of Scotland. He had not, however, inherited any money, for his father had not been a wealthy man, and the lack of cash had led to the breakdown of his marriage to Lady Idina. His second wife, Molly, was, like Idina, a wealthy divorcée and, once again, Joss saw no reason whatsoever why his marriage vows should apply to him. He still looked as he always had done: his hair swept back and blond, his head slightly turned, so that his half-closed blue eyes looked slightly sideways at anyone he was talking to. And one look was still enough to land the great majority of women who happened to catch his fancy.

So far as Leon was concerned, Joss Erroll, as he now liked to be known, was an unprincipled rogue, no matter how elevated his title might be, and if he ever so much as glanced at Saffron he'd horsewhip him all the way to the Mombasa docks and throw him onto the first outbound steamer he could find. But until that time, Leon was perfectly happy to enjoy Joss's company. It was certainly more agreeable than that of a great many other expats he could think of.

'Have you heard about this business at the Oxford Union?' Joss asked, once he had been served a drink of his own.

'What business is that?' Leon replied.

'A bloody rum one, I can tell you.' Joss took a cigarette from a slim silver case, tapped it against the table, lit it and sat back, savouring the first inhalation. 'They had a debate with the motion, "This House will under no circumstances fight for its King and Country."'

'Bloody Hellfire! I trust the motion was soundly defeated.'

''Fraid not, old boy, it was carried by almost three hundred votes to one hundred and fifty. A two-to-one majority.'

Leon looked aghast. 'Are you seriously telling me that the flower of young English manhood, the fellows who are supposed to be the brightest and best of their generation, have declared that they will never fight for their country?'

'Apparently so,' Joss replied. 'The Huns, or the commies, or even the damn French can pitch up on our shores, march across the country, rape our womenfolk and pitchfork our babies, and the brightest brains in the kingdom will simply say, "By all means, feel free."'

'I don't believe it,' said Leon. 'Of course the last war was bloody. And I know people say it was the war to end all wars. But this lily-livered pacifism is nothing but cowardice and treachery. There are times when the nation simply has to be defended and a man has to answer the call.'

'Couldn't agree with you more, Courtney. But then again, you and I are simple, straightforward chaps. We're not like these intellectual Oxbridge types.'

'Well, I grant you,' said Leon, 'there is no one on earth as dangerous as a really clever fool. But even so, how in God's name were the audience at the Union persuaded to support the motion?'

Joss took a long lazy drag on his cigarette as a sly smile played across his lips. 'Oh, you'll love this . . . the chap proposing the motion, Digby I believe was his name, said that we should all follow the example of Soviet Russia, which was the only country fighting for the cause of peace . . . a rather interesting paradox, that, I thought: fighting for peace.'

'Perhaps that's what the Reds were doing when they seized power in a bloody revolution and murdered the Tsar and his family,' Leon observed.

'Ah, yes, that must have been it. How foolish we were not to spot their peaceful intentions. Anyway, when Master Digby had said his piece he was supported by a philosopher called Joad – can't say I've ever heard of him but apparently he's considered quite the coming man in philosophical circles – and he suggested that if Britain should ever be invaded there was no point fighting our enemies with weapons. We had to engage in a campaign of non-violent protest, like Mister Gandhi goes in for, in India.'

'Good grief,' gasped Leon. 'Can you imagine it if these people get their way? Enemy planes will start bombing London and their tanks will roll down Whitehall, and all we'll have to defend us will be Joad and a bunch of conscientious objectors from Oxford University sitting in the middle of the road, chanting for peace?'

'Well, look on the bright side, Courtney. Most people don't go to Oxford University.'

'Well, I suppose that's a reassuring thought. Care for another drink?'

The following evening, Leon wrote one of his regular letters to Saffron. He gave her a vivid account of the debate, as discussed by him and Erroll, and let her know in no uncertain terms of his extreme disapproval of its outcome and of the

Oxford students who had voted for it. 'I warn you now, my girl, if you should ever be courted by an Oxford man I will refuse to allow him into my house. I'm sure you will read these words and think, "Oh, the old boy's just having his little joke," and you may be right. But I am shocked to think that a supposedly great university should have become a nest of Reds, traitors and pacifists and I would disapprove most strongly of you having anything whatever to do with it.'

Saffron received the letter a week later in South Africa. She had never given much thought to any universities, let alone Oxford, but the idea of students being so provocative and so tremendously annoying to their elders pricked her curiosity. So she asked her form teacher, 'Please, Miss, can girls go to Oxford University?'

'Indeed they can, Saffron,' her teacher replied. 'None of our pupils has ever gone to Oxford, or not yet, at any rate. But our sister school in England regularly puts girls up for both the Oxford and Cambridge entrance examinations, with considerable success.'

'So if I went to the other Roedean, I might be able to get into Oxford?'

The teacher laughed. 'Well, I suppose so, Saffron. But you would have to work rather harder than you do presently. There are very few places for young women at England's great universities, so competition to get in is very fierce indeed.'

To some teenage girls, those words might have been enough to put them off the very idea of university education. But Saffron was different. The thought of going halfway across the world to engage in a winner-takes-all contest filled her with excitement and enthusiasm.

'Have I been any help to you, my dear?' the teacher asked.

'Oh yes, Miss,' beamed Saffron. 'You have been a very great help indeed!'

113

Of all the discoveries Saffron had made since arriving at her new school, the most surprising was that she enjoyed her lessons much more than she'd expected. She was hardly an intellectual, for whom thought was preferable to action, but she had a quick mind, grasped ideas easily and, because she enjoyed the feeling of getting things right, worked to make that happen as often as possible. Sadly, however, there were so many other things going on in her life that work was not always possible, or not in Saffron's view at any rate, with the result that her school reports were filled with teachers' pleas that if only Saffron could possibly give her studies her full concentration and effort, great things would surely follow. Now, however, she had a purpose, a goal at which to aim. And once she had her mind set on something, she pursued it with a determination a terrier would have envied.

In mid-January 1934, Saffron flew back down to Johannesburg with her father for the start of the new school year. She assured him that she was perfectly capable of handling the journey alone, for she had already flown unaccompanied from South Africa to Kenya and back again for her mid-year holidays, but he insisted. 'What kind of a father would I be if I didn't take my daughter all the way to school, at least once a year,' he said. 'Besides, who's going to pay for all your shopping if I'm not there to do it?'

That was a point to which Saffron had no counter, for another expedition to the emporia of Johannesburg was required to replace everything that she had either broken, worn out or grown out of during her first year. When they went to the outfitters, Leon doffed his hat to Miss Halfpenny, gave her a winning smile as he said how charmed he was to see her again and obediently did as he was told when Miss Halfpenny said, 'Father may leave us now. We ladies will manage quite nicely by ourselves.'

Leon felt an unexpected pang of disappointment at his

dismissal. But there was something else, too, a bittersweet realization provoked by two little words: 'We ladies.' That was what Miss Halfpenny had said, and she was right. Saffron was becoming a young lady. She wasn't just his little girl any more. And as much as Leon was proud at the woman he could see his daughter becoming, it saddened him, too, to say goodbye to his little girl.

Five thousand miles from Johannesburg, at the Meerbach Motor Works, a sprawling citadel of industry that covered several square kilometres in the southeast corner of Bavaria, Oswald Paust, the Head of Personnel, was coming towards the end of his annual report to the company's trustees. 'After many months of hard work, the task of ridding the company of all Jewish employees, as well as other undesirable races, workers with any form of mental or physical deformity, no matter how minor, and sexual or political deviants is very nearly complete,' he proudly asserted. 'I can now confirm that Jews, who used to form some 4.2 per cent of the workforce, have entirely disappeared from all our factories, workshops, design studios, maintenance depots and offices . . .'

His next words were drowned out as the trustees banged the palms of their hands against the boardroom table around which they were gathered as a sign of approval.

'As I was saying . . .' Paust went on. 'There are six remaining cases of so called "*Mischlinge*", which is to say mongrels who have one Jewish parent, or one or more grandparents. I am presently in discussions with representatives from the SS Race and Settlement Main Office to determine whether the fact that none of them shows any signs of Jewish appearance, or practises any Jewish religious or domestic customs, entitles them to any special consideration. I am deeply indebted to *Herr Sturmbannführer* von Meerbach for his assistance in this regard.'

More palms were slapped against the great oak tabletop and

the massive, brooding figure at the end of the table nodded his head in acknowledgement of the tribute.

'The work has not, of course, been without difficulties,' Paust said, in the tone of a man who has taken on a great burden, but borne it willingly. 'It was relatively easy to weed out the communists, since we already knew who the troublemakers and strike leaders were. These people have never kept their affiliations quiet. Establishing the deviancy of suspected homosexuals, however, required considerable investigation, which proved expensive. Nevertheless, a little over one per cent of our workers were found to be practising homosexuals and lost their jobs as a consequence. It must be noted, unfortunately, that the loss to our workforce from these two groups was disproportionately skewed towards higher skill occupations, so that our legal, accounting, marketing, design and research departments have been quite severely affected and may take some months to recover from the loss of experienced and, if I may say so, talented personnel. Of course it is no surprise that the Jew, with his greedy, disputatious nature, should gravitate towards legal and financial work, while the effeminacy of homosexuals may give them a certain aesthetic flair in the design of advertising posters, for example, or even aircraft fuselages. But I feel sure that the trustees will accept that any short-term loss of company income will be more than outweighed by the benefits of knowing that our workers are all decent, healthy Aryan folk.'

This time the banging was markedly less hearty. As keen as the trustees were to ensure that they maintained the highest standards of racial, sexual and political purity, they were even more interested in maintaining the highest possible profit. *SS-Sturmbannführer* Konrad von Meerbach had dropped his aristocratic title in favour of his Nazi rank, but he remained chairman of the company that bore his name. Clearly irritated by the want of enthusiasm for Paust's conclusions, he made a point of slamming his great lion's paw of a hand, its back covered with a furry mat of ginger hair, so hard that all the pens and coffee cups sitting in front of the company trustees rattled with the impact.

'Thank you, Paust,' said von Meerbach, rising to his feet. He was still young, in his very early thirties, but his physical stature – for he had the massively muscled shoulders, thick chest, tree-trunk neck and glowering brow of a heavyweight boxer – and inborn air of dominance gave him the authority of a much older man. 'I am deeply appreciative of your efforts and I am sure that all my fellow trustees would wish to join me in applauding your achievements.' He gave half-a-dozen hearty claps, prompting six of the eight other attendees at this meeting of the Meerbach Family Trust to take the hint and join in with equal heartiness.

The only two whose applause seemed perfunctory at best were a thin, nervous-looking woman in her mid-sixties, whose fingers were otherwise occupied holding a long, black cigarette holder, and a young man sitting next to her. He was not clad in a formal business suit and stiff collar, as the other men present all were, but preferred a jacket cut from heathery grey-green tweed, a flannel shirt and a knitted tie over a pair of grey worsted trousers. He looked like an academic or some form of intellectual – neither of which was a remotely complimentary description in Germany any more – and the impression of nonconformity was reinforced by the sweep of dark blond hair that insisted on flopping down over his right eyebrow no matter how often he swept it back up to the side of his head. He could, however, afford to treat Konrad von Meerbach more casually than the others did for he was his younger brother, Gerhard, and the woman sitting next to him was their mother, the dowager Countess Athala.

'You may go now,' said Konrad, and Paust scuttled from the room. Konrad remained standing. He looked from one side of

117

the long, rectangular table to the other, scanning the faces pointing back at him.

'I am shocked, gentlemen, truly shocked,' he said, 'at the idea that anyone here . . . any . . . single . . . one,' he repeated, jabbing a finger onto the table with each word, 'could possibly consider it more important to grab a few more Reichsmarks than to carry out the work to which the Führer has sacrificed his entire life, namely the purification of the Aryan race. Anyone would think that you were Jews, the way you place money first, above all else, when we all know that our first duty is to our Führer. I would give away these factories here, all the estates around them, even the *schloss* that bears my family name, all the great works of art and furniture within it, everything I own, in fact, before I parted with this . . .'

Konrad pointed to the Nazi badge on his jacket lapel: the black swastika on a white background surrounded by a red ring and outside that a gold wreath, running right around the badge. 'The Führer himself pinned this golden badge, awarded for special services to the Party, on my chest, because he remembered me from the early days, this rich kid, not even twenty, who joined the march through Munich, November the ninth, 1923 . . .'

'Oh God, here we go again . . .' Gerhard sighed to himself

' . . . who stood shoulder to shoulder with the others who were proud to call themselves National Socialists, who did not break ranks when the police fired on us. Oh yes, the Führer remembers those who stood by him then and who remain true to him now. That is why I combine my role as the head of this great company with the even greater honour of serving as personal assistant to *SS-Gruppenführer* Heydrich, and why I am privileged to enjoy the confidence of the most senior members of our Party and government. And this is where I come full circle, gentlemen – and Mother – for it is precisely because I put the Party first, and everyone knows it, that I am now able to tell you that the Meerbach Motor Works is about to enjoy the greatest prosperity we have ever known.'

He put his hands on his hips and looked around triumphantly as the room once more echoed to the sound of flesh and bone upon wood.

'Over the next four to five years the Reich will embark upon a period of military expansion that will make its enemies quake in fear. German factories will build aircraft by the thousands and tanks by the tens of thousands. The days when our nation was forced to bow its head by the Allied Powers will be gone for good, just as the Jews whose betrayal undermined our country and led to its defeat will be gone. And all these fighter aeroplanes and bombers and transports – warplanes unlike any the world has ever seen before – will need engines. All these new tanks, with designs far, far superior to any other tanks on the face of this planet – for who can match Germany for engineering genius? – will require engines to power them, too. And who will supply these engines? Who else but a company cleansed of Jews and commies and perverts, a company whose loyalty to the Party is unquestioned, a company, in short, like the Meerbach Motor Works!'

Konrad bowed his head in modest appreciation of the applause his words had provoked, sat back down again and then, when order had been restored, said, 'And so, let us proceed with the private element of the meeting. Herr Lange, perhaps you would give us your report on the state of the Meerbach Family Trust's funds at the present time.'

A short, bespectacled man consulted the papers in front of him and proceeded to give a long and extremely detailed account of capital, income and expenditure, delivered in a flat, nasal monotone. His droning intonation, however, could not disguise one salient, inescapable fact. The Meerbach family was extraordinarily wealthy: not merely rich, but blessed with a fortune on a par with the Rothschilds, the Rockefellers and the Fords.

The Meerbach estate stretched for more than thirty kilometres from one end to the other along the shores of the Bodensee. The bank deposits in Frankfurt, Zürich, London and New York matched the reserves of many a nation.

When the recital of facts and figures was complete, various other items on the meeting's agenda were dealt with, before Konrad said, 'Very well, I think we can now break for a very well-earned lunch. Unless there is any other business anyone wishes to raise?'

His tone very strongly suggested that there ought not to be and there was much shaking of heads from the men in suits. But then Gerhard von Meerbach raised his hand. 'Actually,' he said, 'I do have a request to make.'

'Oh really, what is that?' Konrad snapped back, with no suggestion whatever of brotherly love.

'I'd like some more money.'

When Oliver Twist asked for a second helping of gruel he did not provoke a more horrified response than the collective gasp that went up around the table.

'More money?' Konrad sneered. 'You have a perfectly good allowance. You must be far better off than all your layabout student friends. Besides, I thought you commies weren't interested in money or material possessions.'

'For the thousandth time, Konnie, I am not, nor have I ever been a communist. Besides, I can't see why you hate them so much. You belong to the National Socialist Party. The communists worship Russia, or as they insist on calling it, the Union of Soviet Socialist Republics. You're a socialist, they're socialists. Excuse me if I can't spot the difference.'

The words were intended to provoke and the only reason Konrad didn't charge round to where his brother was sitting, haul him bodily from his chair and give him the thrashing he deserved was that he knew he was being baited. Breathing hard as he fought to control his temper he said, 'How much do you want? And why do you want it?'

'I'd like five thousand Reichsmarks, please. I want to buy a Mercedes.'

'So you want to spend our money on a competitor's car?'

'Think of it as a form of industrial espionage. I want to see what the competition is up to.'

'But you can buy a perfectly good car for far less than five thousand.'

'I don't want a perfectly good car. I want the best. And I want it because I'm a von Meerbach and, unlike you, Konnie, I actually know and care about technology. You may be a good Party man, but can you strip down a car's engine, clean and service its parts and then put it back together again? I can. And the car I want, the Type 29 Mercedes 500K, may look like a runabout for playboys and their girlfriends, but it has a five-litre, supercharged engine that can produce one hundred and twenty kilowatts of power and reach top speeds of more than one hundred and sixty kilometres per hour. It also has a suspension system that is undoubtedly the most advanced in the world. Finally, it is unquestionably, indisputably German. The Führer himself is driven around in various models of Mercedes-Benz. How can you object if I want the same car as him?'

Konrad von Meerbach looked at his younger brother with steely blue eyes. *You may be able to take engines apart, baby brother,* he thought. *But you have never been in the basement of the Gestapo headquarters at number eight, Prinz-Albrecht-Strasse, just down the road from Heydrich's office, where I work when I am in Berlin, and seen a man being taken apart, seen his mind and soul . . . what was it you said? Ah yes, stripped down and cleaned and put back together again. But I have. I've heard them scream in pain and beg for mercy. I've seen them betray themselves, their friends, their families, anything and everything just to make the pain go away. And don't think that you, with all your arrogance, your privileges and your smartarse student attitudes, would be any different.*

'Fine,' he said. 'Have your money. But don't blame me when you crash your stupid car.'

The meeting broke up. Konrad was first to leave the boardroom, with the others trailing in his wake. As they were about to follow everyone else through the door to the hall outside, Athala von Meerbach put a bony hand on her younger son's arm. Once upon a time she had been a great beauty, with ash-blonde hair, high cheekbones and delicate features that made other women feel that their own appearance, no matter how attractive, was somehow clumsy and unrefined in comparison. But an unhappy marriage and half a lifetime of loneliness and disillusion had ravaged Athala, leaving her cheeks gaunt and her skin lined and blue veins clearly visible through her wrinkled, semi-translucent skin. Now she looked up at Gerhard and said, 'Wait a second.'

He stopped in his tracks. 'Yes, Mother?'

She looked at him with the eyes of a woman who has heard too many male lies, excuses and bogus arguments not to be able to spot another. 'Tell me, darling boy,' she said, 'why do you really want that money?'

Once he had delivered Saffron to school, Leon did not fly back to Nairobi, but headed down to Durban and boarded the first passenger vessel he could find that was bound north. While he was in Johannesburg he had received a telegram from his brother David, who was now the managing director of Courtney Trading, the firm their father had founded. The message simply read.

CT SITUATION DESPERATE. FAMILY'S FUTURE IN JEOPARDY. PLEASE COME TO CAIRO SOONEST.

Your part of the family's future may be in jeopardy, Davey-boy, but not mine,' Leon muttered when he first received the telegram.

122

'I've only got ten per cent of the company, and one hundred per cent of my own loot, thank you very much.'

He had been about to draft a reply in that ungenerous vein, but stopped himself just in time: *Don't be such a bloody idiot. No need to make the same mistake twice.*

More than twenty-five years had passed since the day Leon had left home and he hadn't returned to Cairo since. His stubborn refusal to go back and make peace with his father had been one of the few subjects on which he and Eva had disagreed. Having lost her father when she was still a girl, she could not bear to see the man she loved deliberately cut himself off from his.

'You're just being stubborn,' she used to say. 'All you have to do is go to Cairo, shake his hand and make your peace.'

'Why should I go there?' Leon would reply. 'He's as rich as Croesus. He could come down to Kenya any time he wanted.'

'Because you were the one who left. And because he's just as stubborn as you are and one of you has to be man enough to end this stupid feud.'

'I'll do it when this damn war is over,' Leon would say. But then the war had ended and he changed his excuse for not doing anything to, 'How can I leave you when you're pregnant with our child?' Then Saffron had arrived and no matter how many times Eva had said, 'I'll come with you. I'm perfectly well and a baby is very portable,' or, 'Very well, then, I will stay here with Saffron and we shall be perfectly able to take care of ourselves until you return,' it still was not enough to make Leon take the first step north to Cairo.

Then his father had died and was buried by the time the news of his passing reached Leon. The opportunity to make his peace with his old man had gone forever and Leon bitterly regretted his failure to do anything while he still had the chance. Eva had been right. It had simply been a matter of stubbornness and foolish pride and now that he was a father too he realized how much Ryder must have missed him and how deeply his mother must have been hurt by their falling out.

The ship that was taking Leon back up to Mombasa was en route to Suez so he simply extended his ticket and cabled his brother in Cairo:

ON MY WAY. INFORM OF DEVELOPMENTS C/O P&O SHIP BRABANTIA.

The journey north, around the Horn of Africa and then up the Red Sea to the Suez Canal, took three weeks, and virtually every day saw Leon in the ship's radio room, either dictating a cable to Cairo or receiving one in reply. The situation was very clear, and all too typical of the times they were in. In the ten years after the end of the war, Courtney Trading had built on the legacy left by its founder. With Leon, the oldest of Ryder Courtney's sons, absent from the family, and Francis, the second son, so badly wounded in action that he was unable to work full time, responsibility for managing the company had fallen upon David, the third son, named after his maternal grandfather David Benbrook, who had died defending his family at the siege of Khartoum. With the global economy booming and mass production making cars affordable to millions of new customers, and the aircraft industry expanding at breakneck pace, David had concluded that, of all the family's interests, their investments in Persian oilfields had the best long-term prospects. Accordingly he had borrowed heavily to finance expansion of both their drilling and prospecting operations, and the tanker fleet that carried the oil to refineries in Great Britain and Europe. The strategy would have paid off handsomely had not the Wall Street Crash of 1929 sent the global economy plummeting into a terrible depression. With the supply of oil increasing, for all the world's petroleum

124

companies had been expanding, and the demand suddenly falling, the bottom dropped out of the market and the price of oil fell through the floor.

Backed by Francis and also Dorian, the youngest of the four Courtney brothers, David had held his nerve. He had not cancelled his contracts with shipbuilders. Instead he had renegotiated new, lower prices, knowing that yards were willing to cut their profit margins to the bone rather than lose work completely. He even bought out some of his partners in the Persian fields whose pockets were not as deep as his for a fraction of the true value of their holdings. Eventually, he reasoned, the world would go back to work again, demand for oil would pick up and the price would rebound.

But the world wasn't returning to work. The depression continued to get worse and worse. Now Ryder Trading was not the hunter but the prey. The debts accumulated by the expansion programme could no longer be financed and the company was facing the very fate it had imposed on others: selling everything at a rock-bottom price, and giving every penny from the sale to its bankers. The only hope was for someone to come to the rescue. And in the eyes of his younger brothers, that someone had to be Leon.

Gerhard von Meerbach walked along the street that led towards the marshalling yards, his jacket collar raised to ward off the chilly winter wind and his cap rammed over his eyes. The noise of the people and the occasional cars and trucks all around him was drowned by the sound of the locomotives and rolling stock being shunted into place to serve the tens of thousands of people who would be leaving Munich Central Station, three kilometres down the tracks, within the next few hours. This was Laim, a tough, uncompromising, working-class neighbourhood, where the pristine streets in the smarter parts of the city gave way to cracked pavements strewn with discarded newspapers, rotting vegetables and dog mess. It was crammed with men and women: some quietly going about their business; others leaning on doorways and lamp-posts, cigarettes in their mouths, watching the world go by; others again pointing fingers, shouting and swearing in coarse accents that made Gerhard feel nervous about opening his own mouth and revealing his educated, aristocratic intonation.

He had dressed for the occasion in his oldest, scruffiest suit, one he'd been wearing to lectures, building sites, parties and countless late nights in smoky bars and cabarets throughout his student years. Its black fabric had been rubbed to a greenish sheen with age and over-use, there were patches on the elbows and close examination would reveal crude darning where a former girlfriend had mended one of the trouser pockets that had almost been ripped off in a particularly wild bout of student horseplay. He was wearing his oldest shirt without the stiff collar that would normally be attached to it, and had borrowed one of the oily flat-caps, worn by the mechanic when he was servicing the family's fleet of cars.

He passed a tailor's shop on whose window someone had painted a crude Star of David in whitewash, with the word '*Jude*' scrawled next to it. Underneath it was a poster that screamed, 'Don't buy from Jews!' The shop was closed and the door padlocked. The dummies in the window were covered in dust and one had fallen over. The Jews, it seemed, had been driven out.

From a *bierkeller* came the smell of stale drink and the sound of raucous voices joining in the old drinking song 'Lang Lang Ist's Her' to the accompaniment of an accordion. A man outside the *bierkeller* looked furtively to one side and then another and then shoved a crudely printed pamphlet into Gerhard's hand. 'You look like a friend,' he said, then scuttled back into the shadows.

Gerhard glanced at the pamphlet, which was entitled, 'ISK

– Journal of the International Socialist Combat League' and carried the headline, 'International Socialism on the Autobahn!' Below that was a picture showing men working on a brand new stretch of high-speed motorway between Frankfurt and Darmstadt, the first of its kind in the world and Adolf Hitler's pride and joy. The story beneath it described the workers' discontent with their poor pay and intolerable living conditions. But they were striking back, the writer said. They were staging protests, slowing the pace of construction, even daubing slogans on the new bridges across the road.

Gerhard stopped dead in his tracks. Could any of this possibly be true? The cinema newsreels had been full of stories about the new autobahn and none of them had mentioned discontent among the workforce, who were always pictured with broad smiles on their faces as they toiled for the good of the Fatherland. Nor had anyone said a word in public about any painted slogans. *Well, they wouldn't, would they?* Gerhard thought, crumpling up the pamphlet and shoving it into the nearest rubbish bin. Then he, too, looked around, just as the ISK activist had done, just as everyone did in Munich, the city that had spawned the Gestapo, where the eyes and ears of the secret police were assumed to be ever vigilant, everywhere. Gerhard had taken a tram to Laimer Platz, watching all the other passengers as they got on and off and then checking to see that no one had followed him when he alighted. On the walk down Fürstenrieder Strasse he'd paused every so often to look in shop windows and see what was happening behind him, just as he had seen actors do in films. But there had been no sign of anyone on his tail, so he'd pressed on towards his destination.

And now here he was, walking up the short flight of cracked stone steps to the entrance of an apartment building. The brickwork around the door was stained where water had flooded down the wall from overflowing guttering above and the mortar between the bricks was crumbling away and in desperate need of repointing. The front door was not locked. Gerhard pushed it open and walked into a hallway lined with bicycles propped up against both walls. A small board showed the numbers of the flats that opened off the staircase rising up in front of Meerbach. He saw a name scrawled by the final number, 12(b): Solomons.

Oh, Izzy, has it come to this? Gerhard thought, remembering the days when his mother used to take him to visit the Solomons at their splendid house on Königinstrasse – Queen Street – just opposite the English Garden. The Solomons had been family lawyers to the von Meerbachs for generations and were so perfectly assimilated into upper-class German life that, as Gerhard's mother used to say, 'One would hardly know that they were Jews at all.'

A display cabinet in the dining room proudly bore the decorations Isidore Solomons, the family's golden boy, had won in the war. He had fought as proudly and valiantly for Germany as any man in the Kaiser's army and, as he miraculously survived while so many others died around him, he had risen from a humble *Leutnant* to *Oberst*, or colonel, in the process. Solomons had served in the 15th Bavarian Infantry Division, part of the Fifth Army under Crown Prince Wilhelm of Germany, the Kaiser's heir. The Prince's handwritten letter of commendation, praising Solomons for his gallantry, had taken pride of place in the cabinet, next to his *Pour le Mérite* medal, the legendary Blue Max. It was the highest honour that any German military man could receive and had been awarded to him in recognition of his extraordinary courage under fire at Verdun, and his selfless willingness to risk his own life to protect those of the men who served under him.

Solomons did not like to talk about his wartime experiences. But Gerhard could remember sitting on the great marble staircase at Schloss Meerbach one New Year's Eve, watching the guests arrive for the night's celebrations. Gentlemen had been invited to wear their decorations. Isidore Solomons had walked in, looking tall, saturnine and impeccably dressed with the blue cross on his chest, hanging from a black and white ribbon, surrounded by a cluster of golden oak leaves, with the words '*Pour le Mérite*' inscribed upon its face. Men had taken one look at it and greeted him with the kind of deference they might have shown to royalty, while women seemed like moths drawn to his flame as other richer, more powerful, even more famous men – for the guest list included a number of celebrated actors, writers, painters and musicians – walked by entirely unnoticed.

And now the Solomons were reduced to this, walking up and down the stairs that Gerhard was now climbing, where the paint was peeling off damp-ridden walls and the pervasive odour of stewed cabbage and stale sweat mingled with the stench of human filth from the toilets – one to every two floors, Gerhard noticed as he recalled the gleaming marble bathrooms of the old Solomons house.

Finally he reached the top floor. He walked along a cramped corridor, barely wider than his shoulders, then knocked on the door marked '12(b)'.

'Come in, my dear fellow,' said Isidore nonchalantly, as if nothing had changed, ushering Gerhard into a cramped sitting room, filled with incongruously grand furniture that Gerhard recognized from the house on Königinstrasse. Solomons was as impeccably dressed, shaved and groomed as if he were still one of the smartest lawyers in Munich. He waved a hand at a room that looked immaculately maintained, save for the bed-linen neatly folded up at the end of a sofa on which one member of the family must have slept.

'You look well,' Gerhard said. 'As if you're just about to go to the office.'

Solomons shrugged. 'One tries to maintain one's stand-ards. And actually I do keep my hand in – unofficially. In this neighbourhood there are always people in need of legal advice. Most of them can't afford to pay, but it keeps me occupied and . . . well, let's just say that some of my clients are in a position to make sure that no one bothers us here. That is worth a lot these days.'

'Is Claudia around?' Gerhard asked. 'I suppose the children must be at school.'

'Actually the children are being educated at home these days. It was made clear to us that their presence was no longer welcome at their school. Ah well, I would have found it hard to pay the fees anyway . . . So, to answer your question, Claudia is not in at the moment. I sent her off to the park with the children and my mother. I thought it best that we spoke alone. I hope you agree?'

'Absolutely . . . of course,' Gerhard replied, trying to maintain the pretence that they were chatting casually, just as in days gone by. But it was impossible. 'Izzy . . . Mr Solomons . . . I'm so, so sorry. It shames me to see you like this.'

'Nonsense, dear boy, think nothing of it. We have a bedroom, a kitchen, a shared bathroom and toilet on the next floor down. Hardly the same as Königinstrasse, of course, but it's positively palatial compared to my quarters at Verdun. And there are far fewer rats.'

Gerhard laughed. Solomons was more than twenty years his senior, old enough to be his father. He had inherited the position of family lawyer from his late father at the end of the war. Having grown up without a father of his own, for he had only been three when his was killed in action at the very start of the war, Gerhard had needed an older man to turn to for advice, or just a pair of ears willing to listen to his troubles, and Isidore Solomons – quick-witted, urbane, steeped in legal knowledge, utterly loyal to the von Meerbach family and blessed with an innate wisdom worthy of his name – was the natural choice.

'Konrad should never have dismissed you. He should have fought harder to persuade his friends in the Party to grant you an exemption from the anti-Jew laws. You were awarded the Max, for heaven's sake.'

Solomons gave a shrug and a wry, sad smile. 'It turns out the *Pour le Mérite* isn't what it used to be. I don't blame Konrad. The fact is, I couldn't do my job properly any more and it wasn't going to get any better, either. Mark my words, Gerhard. What has happened so far is only the beginning.'

'Then he should have given you a proper settlement. After all these years, these generations, it's the very least my family could do for yours.'

'Well, that's true. But Konrad has his own career to think about. I hear he is working directly for Heydrich now, as some kind of adjutant, no?'

'That's right. He's Heydrich's personal secretary. They're working in Berlin now that Heydrich's got the whole Gestapo and Security Police under him. Konrad travels with him everywhere. He's even been up to the Führer's chalet at Berchtesgarten.'

'Tea on the terrace with Adolf and Eva, how *gemütlich*!'

'Not so charming really, I suspect. Anyway, you can rest assured there's at least one of us who understands the concept of a debt of honour. I managed to get five thousand Reichsmarks from my trust fund. The trustees think I'm buying a Mercedes. Let's just hope they don't ever expect to see it.'

'Thank you, Herr von Meerbach,' said Solomons, suddenly sounding much more formal as Gerhard removed an envelope from his inside jacket pocket and handed it over. 'You are too generous. Most people could not earn that in a year. It will help us more than you can know.'

'Most people aren't von Meerbachs or Solomons.' Gerhard paused. 'I won't ask what you're going to do with it. I don't want to know. But whatever you do, and wherever you may go, I will always wish you well. And . . .' Gerhard sighed. 'This isn't just about all that family stuff, though I did mean what I said. It's personal, too. As long as I live, I will never forget your kindness to me, or all the times you took the trouble to listen to me and help me. Never.'

Solomons put a fatherly hand on Gerhard's shoulder. 'You are a good man, but these are not times for good men. So remember, you must be as hard, and determined and, if necessary, as ruthless as the bad men who are on the rise, all across Europe. You have to fight their fire with fire, or they will triumph and all will be lost. Tell me, are you familiar with the work of William Butler Yeats?'

Gerhard shook his head.

'He is an Irish poet, very good I think. He has a poem called "The Second Coming". He writes in English of course, but I have his works in a German translation.' Solomons walked across to a rickety wooden bookcase and took out a small volume that proudly bore the marks and creases of a much read and much loved book.

'Yeats wrote this in 1919, when the blood had not yet dried from the last war, but he was already, like a prophet, seeing the next one approaching,' Solomons said, leafing through until he had found the right page. 'Ach so, I have it! Listen to these few lines, Gerhard, for they tell us much:

Things fall apart; the centre cannot hold;
Mere anarchy is loosed upon the world,
The blood-dimmed tide is loosed, and everywhere
The ceremony of innocence is drowned;
The best lack all conviction, while the worst
Are full of passionate intensity.

You are one of the best, Gerhard. One of the very best. And so you must have as much conviction and as much passionate intensity in the good things that you do as the worst in all the evil acts that they commit. And stay alive. For God's sake,

Gerhard, do as I did at Verdun and above all, whatever else may happen . . . stay alive.'

The four Courtney brothers met for lunch on the terrace of Shepheard's Hotel in Cairo, where Leon was staying, having taken the train there from the port of Suez. The weather was pleasantly warm, which meant blissfully cool by Cairo standards. Leon had booked the table and arrived early, sipping a pre-prandial gin and tonic as he watched the world go by: Europeans in suits and hats; Arabs in their flowing robes; street traders calling out for customers as they walked down the street bearing large baskets laden with almonds and apricots; street urchins begging for strangers' spare *piastres*; horse-drawn carriages fighting for the right of way against donkeys and carts and drivers furiously tooting their horns. The women's clothes had changed while Leon had been away, there were many more cars and bicycles, and the smell of exhaust fumes now mingled with the eternal aroma of dust, dung, woodsmoke and spice that had hung in the air here since time immemorial, but the essential nature of the city remained the same.

But what of his brothers? Would he even recognise them after all this time?

A white-jacketed waiter appeared at his table and said, 'Your guests have arrived, *effendi.*'

Leon looked past him to see the three men walking towards him. He spotted David at once. He had been a tall, skinny stick of a lad when Leon had last seen him and he looked exactly the same even though he was now approaching forty. Even his sandy hair, the fairest in the family, was as tousled and apparently unbrushed now that he was a serious businessman as it had been when he was a schoolboy. Dorian, too, was immediately recognisable. Dark and elfin in the slightness of his body and the quickness of his movement, he had inherited their mother's artistic talents. By the time he was ten or eleven he could draw brilliantly wicked cartoons of his big brothers, or turn his hand to watercolour landscapes that could have been mistaken for the work of adults. Judging by his crumpled, sand-coloured linen suit, with the trousers held up by a tie rather than a belt and a dark blue shirt open at the neck to reveal a cotton neckerchief, he was still the artist of the family.

That left Francis, the closest of the three brothers to Leon in age: too close, perhaps, because Leon had always felt that Francis looked on him with rivalry rather than love. But the best part of thirty years had passed since those days, and those years had included a war in which Francis had suffered more than any of them, and been changed more than any of them, too.

But had he changed for the better, or the worse? That, thought Leon as he watched Francis walk towards him, limping slightly and carrying a stick to help support him, was the key to the plan he had in mind: the key, indeed, to the survival of Courtney Trading itself.

Davy's a reasonable chap. If he sees that I'm being fair, he'll accept it. Dorian will tag along with him. But what about you, Frankie-boy? Which way are you going to jump?

Captain Francis Courtney had been serving in the Mediterranean Expeditionary Force that had landed at Cape Helles in western Turkey in April 1915. On the northern side of the Cape lay the waters of the Aegean. To the south were the Dardanelles, the straits through which all sea traffic between the Mediterranean and the Black Sea had to pass. The Dardanelles lay in the hands of the Ottoman Empire, which had sided with Germany in the war. If they could be secured by the Allies, however, that would enable direct communications between British forces in North Africa and the Middle East and their Russian allies on the far shores of the Black Sea. The original aim of the Dardanelles Campaign, as it was initially termed, was to use French and Royal Navy battleships to force a passage through the straits by sea. In the eyes of Winston Churchill (or 'that damn fool Winston' as Leon Courtney termed him from that moment on), the operation should have been straightforward. The Ottoman Empire was decadent, inefficient and weakened by internal revolt. The Royal Navy was the greatest maritime force the world had ever seen.

Unfortunately, however, a combination of minefields in the water and Turkish gun batteries on the shore devastated the British and French fleets and forced a humiliating retreat. It was then decided that the Turkish guns had to be attacked from the land and so the second phase of the campaign began. It was a campaign involving British, French, Indian, Australian and New Zealand troops and it was the Australasian forces and the casualties they suffered that epitomized the combination of heroic fighting by the troops and total strategic failure by their commanders. For this was Gallipoli, and even by the standards of the Great War, a conflict not short of blood-soaked catastrophe, this was a disaster of spectacular dimensions. Contrary to public perception, the British troops, who formed the great majority of the Allied army, comprised around two-thirds of all the killed and wounded. And one of them was Francis Courtney.

To his father's disappointment, when Francis had first been called up, his poor performance in basic training led to him being adjudged as 'not officer material' and sent to the ranks. By the time of the Gallipoli campaign he was a lance corporal working for the regimental quartermaster, for whom he was a clerk, checking supplies in and out. While Ryder Courtney may have regarded this as a sorry state of affairs, Francis was delighted. The honour of starting one's military service as a second lieutenant was far outweighed in his eyes by the appalling casualty rates among young subalterns. Let them lead charges against trenches defended by machine guns: he was much happier in the quartermaster's stores, filling out chits and keeping orderly accounts. But then, towards the very end of the Gallipoli fiasco a man called Garden, a captain in the Special Brigade of the Royal Engineers, arrived at the front, hot foot from Egypt. He brought with him three thousand cylinders of chlorine gas, for some desperate desk-wallah, two thousand miles away at the War Office in London, had suggested that gas might be the way of dislodging the Turks from their positions and turning disaster into triumph. This, however, was not only an immoral idea but an impractical one. The sea breezes that swirled around Cape Helles were far too changeable and just as likely to blow a cloud of gas straight back onto the British lines as to send it across to the Turks. To make matters worse, the Turkish positions were on higher ground than the Allied ones and chlorine, being much heavier than air, tends to sink downhill, rather than floating up.

So the plan was abandoned and the gas canisters put into storage until such time as they and Captain Garden could be sent back to Alexandria. By complete chance a stray Turkish shell exploded near the dump where the gas canisters had been piled and a piece of shrapnel from the shell pierced one of the cylinders. Francis Courtney had been inspecting the dump at the time, to check that the records showed the correct quantities of munitions in storage. He had in fact been walking past the chlorine cylinders when the shell landed. The explosion threw him, shocked but unhurt, to the ground just as a heavy stream of chlorine was emitted from the ruptured canister.

A burning pain ripped through his eyes and throat, a giant fist seemed to clamp itself around his chest and his lungs seized up, so he felt as if he were suffocating. He somehow managed to stagger to his feet and stumble away from the gas, an action that saved his life. Even so he was seized by spasms of coughing and retching. His eyes were blinded by the tears produced by his desperate body as it sought to remove the irritation. His mouth, meanwhile, went to the opposite extreme: he was parched with thirst and his tongue felt thick and furry. Francis collapsed to the ground where he was found by a stretcher party, lying on his side with his head aching and his mouth open in a desperate attempt to let the fluid in his lungs flow back out of his body. His face was a pale greenish yellow, and over the next few hours other parts of his body put on a macabre display of vivid colour as the gas and the oxygen deprivation that it caused took their toll: the jaundiced pallor of his face slowly gave way to a vivid, violet red complexion, while his fingernails went from a healthy pink to a deathly blue. He was exhausted and yet restless, struggling for breath, seized by the anxiety, bordering on panic, that comes with an inability to breathe. Everything hurt, his whole body was erupting in protest: coughs, vomit and diarrhoea, one after another in an endless, random succession.

Finally Francis slept. He awoke feeling much better. But a few hours later a second wave of physical torment broke over him as his shattered body, its defences broken, gave way to an acute bronchial fever. The coughing returned and the white handkerchiefs he held to his face were soon coated with green, blood-streaked mucus. As his temperature rose beyond one hundred and four degrees Fahrenheit, his pulse became faint yet rapid. For a few hours he became delirious and the doctors at the military hospital felt certain that he would be another addition to the ever-growing list of fatal casualties. But then, when all seemed lost, the fever broke. Francis had survived.

'It was being a Courtney that saved him,' Leon's mother had written in her letter telling him what had happened. 'Frank was just too stubborn to die and your pa refused to take no for an answer. He went all the way to the War Office to get permission to ship Frank back to Alexandria and then made damn sure that he had the best doctors and nurses in the Levant to look after him. With God's will, we hope he will pull through.'

It was a slow business, even so. Francis spent almost four years recuperating: first in hospital, then at a sanatorium and finally at home. In the end, he had emerged much weaker and with an acute sensitivity to bright light: hence the stick and dark glasses. But compared to many of the blind, the crippled and the mutilated veterans who had become such a horribly familiar sight on post-war streets, Francis Courtney had got off lightly.

'I'm so glad to see you looking so well, Frank,' Leon said, in a tone that left no doubt that he meant what he said.

Francis reacted as if insulted. He gave a dismissive little grunt and his mouth was twisted into a bitter grimace as he said, 'So, you wouldn't come back when your brother was lying wounded for months on end. And you still wouldn't come when your father was dying. But the moment your money's at risk you come running. Excuse me if I'm not impressed.' His voice had a wheezy edge to it and when he'd said his piece he gave a rasping, hacking cough that seemed to Leon to be as much a sign of his brother's anger as any purely physical gesture.

'Steady on, Frank,' said David. 'No need to rake over old ground, eh?'

Leon ignored the provocation. 'Well, it's good to see you, anyway,' he said and held out a hand.

Francis pointedly ignored it.

'Thank you so much for coming all this way, Leon,' said David, playing the peacemaker. 'I very much hope we can sort something out for all our benefit.'

His handshake was firm and confident, the grip of a man who was used to taking responsibility and standing by his word.

Dorian stood back for a second, eyeing Leon as if he were sizing him up for a portrait. Then he said, 'Hmm . . . somewhat battered by old age, but still essentially the same big brother.'

Then he grinned and, to Leon's surprise, gave him an affectionate hug. 'Good to see you, old man.'

'You too,' said Leon. Then he waved a hand towards his table and said: 'Why don't you sit down and order some drinks? They make a damn good G'n'T, as this empty glass can testify.'

'That sounds like a splendid idea,' said David.

Dorian thought for a second. 'I think I'll have a vodka martini, if that's all right, big brother.'

'By all means. How about you, Frank?'

'Johnnie Walker, neat, no ice, and make it a double.'

The drinks were obtained, food was ordered, served and consumed. All the while, the four men's conversation was just the normal talk of brothers who have long been parted from one of their number. Leon asked after their mother and sister and caught up on the details of their various families. David was married with two children: a boy of ten and a girl of seven. Francis had been married but his wife Marjorie had long since left him and he had not found anyone new. Dorian, meanwhile, was entirely unencumbered by any marital ties, clearly preferring to play the field with a constant stream of women.

'I don't believe he's ever painted a woman's portrait without taking her to bed,' David remarked.

'Oh, that's not fair,' Dorian insisted. 'A chap asked me to paint his mother a few years ago. He told me that he wanted something to remember her by when she was gone. She was a splendid old bird, seventy-five if she was a day, but still in remarkably good physical fettle, and bright as a button with it.'

'Tell me you didn't . . .' said Leon, laughing.

'Of course not!' Dorian exclaimed, as if outraged by the very suggestion. 'That's precisely the point I was trying to make. I do have my limits.' He paused for a moment and then added, 'Though I have to admit the thought did cross my mind . . .'

'I really don't think that Dorian's total absence of sexual

continence is either an interesting or fruitful topic of conversation,' said Francis irritably. 'Can we just get on with our business? That's why we're here, isn't it? And, let's be honest, Leon, you wouldn't have come all this way to discuss it unless you thought you could profit from our misfortunes. So why don't you tell us exactly how, precisely, you intend to do it?'

Leon looked at his brother. He understood now that Francis carried his deepest scars on his soul, rather than his body. That was where the real damage lay and it was all the more dangerous as a result.

He took his time, refusing to let Francis goad him into haste or ill temper. Instead, he summoned the waiter and ordered coffee for them all, then said, 'Very well, why don't I start by summarizing the situation as I see it. And then we can discuss what to do about it. I have my ideas, but I'm sure you will all have ones of your own, too.'

'That sounds fair enough,' said David. 'Fire away.'

'Right then . . . The first thing I want to say is that I think you acted entirely reasonably, Davy. It's absolutely clear to me that the demand for oil-based fuels is only going to grow – even ships are as likely to be powered by diesel as coal these days – and there was no reason why you should have predicted this endless damn depression when absolutely nobody else did. So, I see no need for recriminations.

'On the other hand, there's no getting away from the fact that Courtney Trading is in dire straits. It's not just the oil. All Dad's investments in the South African mining industry are suffering. Gold and diamonds are the last things anyone's buying these days. Even Egyptian cotton's going through a slump. And of course shipping has come to a virtual standstill because no one can afford to trade. So there's nothing taking up the slack. And the company's total debts stand at a little over six million pounds by my rough calculation . . .'

'Six million, two hundred and thirty-nine thousand, four hundred and seventy-two pounds, seventeen shillings and tenpence was the precise figure when our chief accountant last worked it out,' said David.

'Well, the seventeen and ten shouldn't be any problem,' said Dorian, blithely.

'And it's borrowed at an average of around eight per cent per annum interest,' said Leon.

'About that, yes,' David agreed.

'Which means that in round figures Courtney Trading needs to find half a million pounds a year to meet the interest, let alone repay any of the principal, and that's impossible when none of its businesses are making any money.'

'Thank you so much, Leon, for telling us what we already know,' said Francis.

'Indulge me, Frank, there's a good chap. You see, I think that the very scale of the company's debts is what will give us leverage with the bankers. Any creditor with half a brain will know that if we have to sell up, we'll get a pittance and they'll be lucky to get a tenth of their money back. It's far better for them if we stay in business.'

'Frank does have a point, Leon,' said David. 'We have managed to work this out for ourselves and I've been hammering the message home to the banks for months. In fact, that's the only reason they haven't foreclosed on us already. But they're getting to the point where they're ready to write off the loss.'

'Quite so . . . But if they knew that the interest would be covered for a period of, say, four years – absolutely guaranteed – they would be much calmer, wouldn't they? And if they knew that their capital investment was safer, then they might be amenable to renegotiating the terms of the loan. After all, interest rates now are far lower than they were when you made these deals. The Americans are down to about two per cent.

I don't see why we couldn't get our creditors to accept a four per cent return, if they knew they were going to get paid.'

'But they're not going to get paid, are they?' Francis protested. His voice rose in volume as he raged, 'It doesn't matter if the interest is eight per cent, four per cent or the square root of bugger-all, we can't bloody well pay it.'

'I really don't think it's a good idea to let the whole of Cairo know that,' said Leon. 'And in any case it's not true. You may not be able to pay it. But I can.'

'How?' asked Francis, bitterly. 'Magic beans?'

'No, gold sovereigns. One million pounds' worth of them.'

'And you have that, do you, one million pounds in gold? Are we really expected to believe that? What did you do, dig up a treasure trove of pirate gold?'

Leon shrugged, 'This is not the time to go into details, but that's as good a way of describing it as any other.'

David frowned. 'This gold of yours, Leon, assuming that you have it . . . It is legal, isn't it? I mean you didn't come by it criminally, or anything?'

'I didn't rob a bank if that's what you're worried about. It was the spoils of war, if you really want to know, taken from our nation's enemies. Which, as our dear, departed father would surely have said, if he were here now, was how we Courtneys made our family fortune in the first place.'

'"The fine Courtney tradition of barely legalised piracy" . . . wasn't that his phrase?' asked Dorian with a grin. 'You must admit, Davy, the old man was – in the nicest, most charming possible way, of course – an absolute rogue and a scoundrel. He'd be thrilled to hear that his oldest son had taken after him so splendidly. A million pounds in gold, eh? Dad would have been proud of you, Leon . . . and a little jealous too, I dare say.'

'Suppose you give us this money,' said Francis. 'What do you want in return?'

'Good question, Frank,' said Leon. 'I've been trying to work that out for myself. The first place, I've been wondering whether to do anything at all. I don't mean to sound callous, but the plain truth is that if Courtney Trading goes bust it really won't trouble me – financially, at least. On the other hand, it will cause you chaps very considerable inconvenience. What's more it will destroy Dad's legacy, which means more to me than I dare say you imagine. But what troubles me most of all is that our mother and sisters will be left without a means of support, and I'm not prepared to accept that under any circumstances. So the company has to be saved.

'Now, Dad left you three twenty-five per cent of the company each because you'd stayed in Cairo and could be expected to run the show. My share was cut to ten per cent because I'd walked out . . . and before you say anything, Frank, I have never had any complaint about that. And Mater, Penny and Becca each got five, which should have been ample to keep them decently supported for life.

'I could, of course, simply give them each enough to make up for the loss of their Courtney Trading shares. That would be much cheaper for me in the short term, but there's no possibility of profit in the long term and I am absolutely convinced that the company has a very fine future if it can survive the present crisis. So here is what I will propose. I will give Courtney Trading one million pounds. And in return I will receive an additional forty-one per cent of the company, taking my share up to fifty-one per cent. I have to be the majority shareholder, after all, to make sure my investment is protected.'

'But that's daylight robbery!' Francis exploded. He looked around at the others. 'What did I say? He's just a bloody thief.' Then he turned his acid gaze on Leon. 'You bastard! You know perfectly well that it's worth far, far more than that.'

'Not at the moment it isn't,' David wryly observed.

'Precisely,' said Leon, doing his best to remain calm. 'And this way you will still retain a stake, and keep it for long enough to see it grow in value so that you will actually be much better off in the meantime. Look, Frank, I'm staking virtually all of my liquid assets on this company. If this goes wrong, I could end up on Queer Street too. So I want a damn good premium or I'm walking away and keeping my money safe and sound in the bank vault where it now resides.'

'How do you propose we give you this forty-one per cent?' Dorian asked.

'Essentially, you transfer a proportion of your shares to me. It's up to you to decide who gives me what. But I think Davy should have the second biggest holding after me, because he's the poor sod who'll have to make the whole project work. I don't want the womenfolk to lose out too badly, and by the way, I'll cover their living expenses for the next four years because one of my conditions is that no one, myself included, gets a dividend from the company in that time. Of course, you three can claim wages for the work you do. Again, Davy gets the lion's share.'

Leon looked around the table. David had taken a notebook from his jacket and was writing calculations as he worked through the financial implications of Leon's proposal. Dorian was leaning back in his chair, casually smoking a cigar and making eyes at a very pretty woman at the next table, whose husband had his back to him and was therefore none the wiser. Francis angrily stubbed out a cigarette and beckoned a waiter over to him. 'Get me a whisky,' he said. 'And make it a damn strong one.'

'I agree with Leon that the ladies should only have to hand over a minimal amount,' said David, looking at the numbers jotted on the notepaper in front of him. 'I suggest a contribution of two per cent, shared evenly between them. That leaves us chaps to find thirty-nine per cent, which divides very neatly by three into thirteen each. Jolly kind of you to offer me more, Leon, but we should do this equally or not at all. I take it, incidentally, that we aren't seeing any of the actual money.'

'No, it all goes into the company's accounts,' Leon said. 'If we can halve the rate of interest, a million pounds should tide the company over for four years, and if things still haven't got any better by then, well, it really won't make any difference if Courtney Trading goes under because the whole world will be bust.'

'Excuse me for my limited appreciation of financial matters,' said Dorian, 'but if I understand you correctly, your basic proposal to us is that half a sixpence is better than none.'

'Correct.'

'But if things do get better, then you will have an awful lot more sixpences than the rest of us. I take the point that you're the one who's risking his money. But we are giving up our birthright, handing over our mess of pottage, or whatever that chap in the Bible did. It seems to me that if things go well, and your money is completely safe, and suddenly worth an awful lot more than one million pounds, we should have some of our pottage back. If you see what I mean.'

Leon smiled, 'Ma always used to say that you weren't as green as you're cabbage-looking, Dorian, and I can see that she was right. Very well, here's what I suggest. If, at some later date, Courtney Trading is back on its feet and, as you say, its value is greatly increased, then you can buy back half of the shares you gave me, for their face value, plus four per cent interest for every year I've held them.'

'By God, is there no end to your greed?' Francis sneered. 'Charging your own brothers interest? Are you sure you're not a Jew, Leon? Shylock himself would be proud of you.'

'Is there no end to your bitterness, Frank?' replied Leon, in a tone less of anger than regret. 'In the situation Dorian is envisaging, the shares will be worth far, far more than they were – twice, perhaps even ten times as much. So if I am charging four per cent interest, you can happily pay it and still be hugely in profit. All I am doing is making sure that I am not actually losing money, bearing in mind that it could just sit in a bank earning interest anyway.'

'What do you think, Davy?' asked Dorian.

'I think it's a very fair offer. Leon still stands to make a very considerable profit if things go well, which is fair enough in the circumstances. But he's giving us a chance to share in that profit. And since we have no chance of profit whatsoever at the moment, that strikes me as a very fair deal.'

'So do you accept my terms, David?' Leon asked.

'Yes. We'll have to get lawyers to draw up the papers, but in principle you can count me in.'

'Dorian?'

'Oh, I'm just the layabout artist of the family. If it's good enough for Davy it's good enough for me.'

'How about you, Frank? I want unanimous agreement on this. I can't have us split from the very beginning. There's no chance of the plan working if we aren't all committed to it.'

'I don't trust you,' said Francis. 'You'll find a way to trick us, I'm sure of it.'

'That's what the lawyers are for,' said David. 'To make sure no one tricks anyone and all the contracts are completely above board.'

'But why would I want to trick anyone?' Leon asked. 'I have no reason to do that. I'm doing this for all the reasons I've already stated: to preserve Dad's legacy, to help Mother and the girls and, yes, because I think there's a genuine business opportunity here – for all of us. Look, if you don't trust me, I will get up from the table right now, walk away and you won't ever have to hear another word about any of my wicked schemes.'

'Leon's right, Frank,' said David. 'He doesn't need Courtney Trading, but we do need a million pounds.'

'So we should accept his terms because he's got us over a barrel, is that what you're saying?'

'No, we should accept his terms because we won't get better

ones anywhere else and because we owe it to our parents and our sisters not to let our personal feelings get in the way of doing the right thing.'

There was still a little whisky left in the bottom of Francis Courtney's glass. He downed it, slammed the glass back down on the table and glared at Leon. 'Very well then, I can see I have no alternative but to accept your terms. I'll sign whatever papers the lawyers put in front of me. I'll put on a brave face in public. I'm used to that. But don't think I like it, dear brother of mine. Because I don't. Not one little bit.'

A short while later, as the four Courtney brothers all went their separate ways, Dorian stayed behind for a moment to have one last word with Leon.

'Are you going to see Mother while you're here?' he asked.

'Absolutely. I was planning to have dinner with her tonight, as a matter of fact. Just thought it was best to get this business out of the way first.'

'Yes, that makes sense. Look, I'm sorry about Frank. He can be awfully unreasonable these days.'

Leon shrugged. 'Well, he's had to endure a hell of a lot, what with his wounds, losing his family. It's enough to make anyone testy.'

'Hmm . . . You're right, of course, but it's not quite that simple. It wasn't actually getting wounded that made Frank this way. It was when he got better.'

'How do you mean?'

'In a sort of way, I think he quite enjoyed being the family invalid. He was the centre of attention. I mean, Dad was absolutely obsessed by doing everything possible to make Frank better . . . as he would have been for any of us, of course, including you, Leon. So Frank was endlessly being fussed over and made to feel special. The whole business of going to see him was tremendously dramatic. The windows would be shaded

147

and Frank would be lying in bed, coughing feebly. Only Marjorie was allowed to approach him.'

'It must have been terribly hard for her. I don't suppose one can blame her for not coping.'

'Quite so,' Dorian agreed. 'But oddly enough, that wasn't the part she couldn't cope with. I mean, Marjorie's a smashing girl and she was an absolute brick when Frank was in hospital. The problems started when he came back home.'

'Why so?'

'Well, there was no reason for Frank not to lead a perfectly normal life, and I don't think he liked it. Suddenly, people weren't paying him nearly as much attention. Everyone said, "Jolly good to see you, old man," and then just got on with things as usual. Frank couldn't seem to cope. I think the gas affected him in the head more than the body. He changed, psychologically. I mean, he wasn't such a bad chap, really, in the old days. But now there was this air of gloom and self-pity all around him. And then, of course, Dad became ill . . .' Dorian stopped, looked at Leon and sorrowfully said, 'You really should have come home.'

'I know . . . Believe me, I know. I don't think there's anything I regret more.'

'Ah well, no point fretting about it now. Anyway . . . as I was saying . . . Dad became ill and of course everyone's attention turned to him and his needs.'

'And Frank felt let down by that? Surely not.'

'I'm rather afraid he did. He certainly became more and more bitter, that's for sure. And that's what drove Marjorie away. She just couldn't stand the person he became. And if you ask me, that's what has stopped him finding a new wife, too.'

Leon gave a rueful sigh. 'It's so sad, and so counter-productive. It sounds like Frank has got himself trapped in a really vicious circle. The more bitter he is, the less people warm to him, and that only makes him more bitter.'

'And more dangerous,' said Dorian. 'I know he's gone along

with your plan for the time being. He knows he doesn't have a choice. But I don't think he wants it to succeed. I think he wants you to be proved wrong, even if it means him losing everything.'

'Oh, come on. He surely wouldn't go that far. Once the money starts rolling in, he'll come around.'

'No, he won't. That's the whole point. If the money comes in, that means you were right, and it also means that you're getting more than the rest of us. No, I couldn't care less, because all I need is paint, canvas and a place to lay my head. And Davy won't mind because he's a pretty decent sort, really, and he understands that this is the only way that the company can survive. But Frank is different. He would rather we all failed than that you succeeded.'

'I see.'

'I hope you do, big bro. So take my advice, even if I am the baby of the family. Keep your eyes wide open. And watch your back.'

L eon dined with his mother, and it was good to begin the process of rebuilding a relationship that for more than a quarter of a century had consisted of nothing more than occasional letters from her and even less frequent replies from him. She had cried. He had felt a whole host of emotions that he couldn't quite make sense of. This was the kind of time when he missed Eva more than ever: she would have helped him untangle the knots in his head and his heart. But for now the unresolved feelings made him restless. There was no point going to bed, he knew he wouldn't sleep. So when she returned to Shepheard's Hotel Leon headed for the bar, grabbed a stool and ordered a brandy.

'Kind of a pity to drink alone, don't you think?'

The voice was female, American. It took Leon a second to realize she was speaking to him. He turned on his stool and saw the woman the voice belonged to. She'd gone for the Jean Harlow look – platinum hair, Cupid's bow lips, big come-hither eyes and a black cocktail dress that left her creamy shoulders completely bare and her splendid breasts only marginally less so. The Blonde Bombshell look wasn't exactly subtle. But no man with red blood in his veins could deny that it was effective.

'Are you gonna say something, maybe invite me to sit down, or do I gotta stand here all night while you look at me like a starving man in a butcher's shop?'

Leon smiled. 'I apologize. You took me by surprise. My mind was, ah . . . elsewhere.'

'Well bring it back here then and ask me what I want to drink. Hell, I'll save you the trouble. Hey, Joe!' She waved the barman over. 'You know what I want, right?'

'Certainly, Mrs Kravitz. An Old Fashioned, made with Bourbon and not Scotch, easy on the water with an extra cherry on top.'

'Attaboy.'

'Good evening, Mrs Kravitz,' Leon said. 'My name is Courtney . . . Leon Courtney.'

'Good evening to you, Mr Courtney. My name is Mildred, but I'd rather you called me Millie.'

'How about Mr Kravitz, what does he call you?'

'Oh, I don't know. "Sweetheart" if he's feeling friendly. "You dumb bitch" if he ain't.'

'Will he be joining us for drinks?'

'God, I should hope not! Far as I know he's off in the desert somewhere, looking at pyramids and ancient mummies. Though he could be in a whorehouse right here in Cairo, for all I know.'

'Is he an archaeologist?'

'Hymie Kravitz, an archaeologist? Ha! That's a good one. He's no kind of -ologist, trust me. Not unless you can get an -ology in ass-licking. No, my Hymie's a studio executive

150

at Metro-Goldwyn-Mayer. His boss, Mr Thalberg, he's Head of Production, has an idea to make a motion picture set in Ancient Egypt. You know, King Tut, Cleopatra, all that jazz. Maybe get Cecil B. DeMille to direct it. And he's thinking, maybe they should make it right here in Egypt. Y'know, so it feels real. Anyways, he sent Hymie over here to take a look. And, I mean, it was obvious within ten minutes you could never make a Hollywood picture in this dump. But Hymie can't just say that. He's got to give it his best shot, so he's off scouting locations and talking to folks that know about dead Egyptians.'

'And he left you here in the hotel? Foolish man. Must be very boring for you.'

'Tell me about it, Leon. I thought it would be romantic. Y'know, me and Hymie cruising down the Nile, riding camels, posing by the pyramids and whatnot. Instead, all I do is sit around this damn hotel. Hell, I can sit on my ass at home in Bel Air. What's the future in that? But, say, what about you . . . and Mrs Courtney?'

'Well, I'm here on business. And I'm widowed. My wife died a few years ago.'

'Oh gee, I'm sorry. Damn, I can be dumb sometimes.'

'Don't worry about it. You meant no harm.'

'Maybe I should have that on my tombstone: *Here lies Millie Kravitz. She meant no harm.*'

'Either that or: *She was a good girl, really.*'

Millie looked at Leon over the top of her Old Fashioned. 'Well aren't you the sly dog, Leon Courtney?'

He knew for certain then that they were going to end up in bed. They each had another drink and then went up to his room. 'I guess your business pays well,' Millie said when she saw its size and luxury.

She stepped out of her teetering heels and barely came up to his shoulder, but he wasn't complaining. As petite as she was, every inch of Millie Kravitz was built to please. Her figure was a true hourglass, with a full, round, peachy backside that just begged to be caressed, grabbed or spanked, depending on the mood of the occasion, and a waist so slender she looked like she could be snapped in two if a man tried hard enough. When she slipped out of her dress, letting it slide down her body and land in folds at her feet, Leon saw that her breasts owed nothing to corsetry or the cut of her dress: they really were just as full and soft and inviting as advertised.

As he looked at her, Leon grinned, even as he felt himself swelling. 'I see you're blonde all over.'

She looked down at her platinum pudenda. 'Yeah, the peroxide stung like a bitch, but the rug gotta match the drapes, right?'

Leon didn't say anything. He just grabbed her, pulled her to him and laid her down on the bed; she looked up at him as he mounted her. There were times when he could take it nice and slow, teasing and petting and gradually bringing a woman to that point of arousal and hunger at which the act of penetration had become an overwhelming need for them both. But this was not one of those nights. He just took her because that's what he wanted and he knew that she did too. This was not romance. It was sheer animal instinct and it was hard and fast and he knew from her screams and the clawing of her scarlet nails down his back and the desperation with which she arched her spine to let him further and further into her that she wanted it that way too. As her moaning and writhing and desperation reached its climax he felt the muscles far inside her fluttering around him and knew that she had come. He let himself go then, thinking of nothing but his own pleasure as he drove even faster, even harder, even deeper, the tension growing more unbearable until that final, explosive release came and he collapsed onto the bed beside her.

They both lay there, sweaty and exhausted, staring up at the ceiling.

'God, I sure needed that,' Millie gasped.

'Me too.'

She snuggled up to him with her head on his shoulder, her legs wrapped around his thigh and her fingers playing idly with the hair on his chest. Then her fingers fell still and her breathing changed and a moment later Leon realized that she was crying.

'What's the matter?' he asked.

'Oh I don't know,' she sniffed. 'It's just, that was great and I'm not kidding, I really needed it so bad. But I guess I need something else, you know? Something more.'

'Yah, I know.'

'And I ain't gonna get it from you, am I? Which is a real pity, cause you're a handsome bastard, and you're a lot more loaded than Hymie . . . in more ways than one.'

'Thank you for the compliment.'

'Believe me, honey, I'm thanking you. Anyway, I should stop going on. Who needs a broad getting weepy on them in the sack? But . . . you know what I mean, right?'

'Yes, Millie, I know exactly what you mean,' Leon said.

They fell asleep in each other's arms. When Leon awoke, the sun was streaming into his room through a gap in the curtains and he was alone in the bed. There was a piece of hotel notepaper on the pillow. Leon rubbed the sleep from his eyes and picked it up. The note read,

Nice knowing you, Mr C. Love M xxx

He looked for her in the hotel dining room when he went down for breakfast and in the bar before lunch, but there was no sign for her. As he got into the taxi that would take him to the station and the train to Suez, Leon knew that he would never see Millie Kravitz again. But he also knew that she was right. He needed something more.

In the late 1850s, having made his fortune from manufacturing steam engines, Gerhard von Meerbach's great-grandfather was invited to join a royal hunting party at Hohenschwangau Castle, the recently built country home of King Maximilian II of Bavaria. The castle stood atop a rocky crag on the site of a medieval fortress and was built in keeping with that style. It was ringed by high, crenelated walls, around whose battlements guests could stroll and look down upon the frigid, crystalline waters of the Alpsee, the lake that washed against the foot of the crag, or gaze up at soaring peaks, marching away in serried ranks as far as the eye could see. Within the walls stood a mighty, foursquare keep, that looked ready to withstand any invading army. The medieval theme continued within the keep, where chambers were decorated with murals showing kings and queens going about their fairy tale lives and the heavy wooden furniture was carved in a Gothic style. Yet the sense of antiquity was deceptive, for the castle had been built with every modern comfort and luxury that the mid-nineteenth century had to offer.

Old Man von Meerbach was so taken with the king's castle that he immediately decided to build one just like it, except that his was bigger and named after himself. Thus Schloss Meerbach had risen from an equally picturesque site on the shores of the Bodensee near Friedrichshafen, west of Munich. The *schloss* had been the most magnificent residence in the kingdom of Bavaria until Maximilian's successor, 'Mad' King Ludwig II, embarked upon a programme of castle building so wildly extravagant and excessive that not even his richest subjects could possibly compete.

Gerhard von Meerbach was born at Schloss Meerbach. He knew every single square centimetre of the huge building, from the subterranean depths of the lowest cellars, which had been designed to look like medieval dungeons and in which four generations of von Meerbach fathers had threatened to lock their misbehaving sons, right up to the servants' quarters crammed in under the roofs. And the older he had grown, the more Gerhard concluded that he really hated the place.

There was something oppressive about the monumental, overbearing scale of Schloss Meerbach. The main reception rooms were panelled in wood stained almost black by years of smoke from candles, gaslights and cigars, from which hung larger than life-sized portraits of von Meerbachs, past and present. The men had a very particular look about them. Much like the castle that bore their name they were undeniably powerful and imposing, but their strength seemed deigned to intimidate and bully those weaker than themselves, rather than protect them.

Gerhard's father, Count Otto, had chosen to be painted in his flying gear, standing in front of a biplane powered by one of the rotary engines that had propelled the Meerbach Motor Works and the family's fortunes to even greater heights than before. He was standing with his legs apart, his hands on hips and his eyes boring into anyone who looked at the picture, as if daring them to defy him. Gerhard had only been three when his father died and had few memories of their time together, but he felt that he must have been very frightened of him, for he could not look at that hard, obdurate face beneath the bristle of short-cropped ginger hair without feeling a tremor of anxiety. That, not the pain of losing a father's love, was what he had been left with.

Gerhard himself was of a very different physical type, inherited from his mother's side of the family. Though by no means weak-looking, he was much slimmer in build: lithe rather than thickset and with more conventionally handsome, regular facial features. His eyes were a soft marble grey but had the unusual property

155

(which Gerhard had discovered from the way that the women he seduced gazed at them) of appearing to change colour depending on the light around them, so that they carried a hint of blue, or even hazel, depending on the circumstances. His tastes, too, were far removed from the Gothic grandeur of Schloss Meerbach. He was a child of his times, training to be an architect in the modernist style, in which walls were white if they existed at all, light flooded in through the biggest possible windows, and form was reduced to pure, clean, geometric simplicity.

Still, even Gerhard had to admit that there were times when the sheer grandeur of the castle could make it a splendid back-drop for the family to entertain their guests. Tonight for example was the moment at which Konrad von Meerbach had shown himself to be a man whose influence straddled the old Germany and the new. He was entitled, as the eldest son of an aristocratic family, to call himself *Graf* or Count von Meerbach, yet chose not to, declaring such a badge of inherited privilege unbefitting to his National Socialist principles. Tonight he had hosted a grand dinner at which the guests were taken from the finest old aristocratic families of Bavaria, the wealthiest indus-trialists of the region and their new Nazi masters, who were now busily constructing the foundations of the Thousand Year Reich. The guest of honour was *SS-Gruppenführer* Reinhard Heydrich himself, the newly appointed commander of both the Gestapo, the national secret police and the SD, or *Sicherheitsdienst*, the Nazi Party's own intelligence agency.

Heydrich's arrival at the party reminded Gerhard of the effect Izzy Solomons's Blue Max had created a dozen years earlier. In this case the magnetism was provided not by a decoration for valour, but by the black dress-uniform Heydrich was wearing, or more specifically, its jacket. This was short, cut like a tailcoat from which the tails had been removed so that it stopped at the waist. The only colour came from the slash of lipstick red on Heydrich's left arm, where he wore a swastika armband.

156

There were silver braid epaulettes on his shoulders, denoting his rank, which was also indicated by a collar patch on which were embroidered the three silver oak leaves of a *Gruppenführer*. On the right side of his chest a silver death's head grinned at the world around it in horribly macabre good humour.

Gerhard was very far from being a Nazi supporter, but with his trained eye he could not deny the evil genius with which everything about the Party's visual image, from the vast scale of the Nuremberg Rallies, with the Cathedral of Light formed by the searchlight beams rising like giant columns into the night sky above the Zeppelin Field, to the piercing gaze of that little silver death's head, was designed to underline the idea of absolute, inevitable dominion over the world. And Heydrich, the prodigy of the Nazi Party, could carry it off with an *élan* that was entirely missing from most of the Nazi leaders.

Gerhard had always thought of Hitler, Himmler, Goebbels and their ilk as laughably far removed from the master race of which they spoke so avidly. Heydrich, however, was different. He was a tall, slim, elegant man, as glamorous as a film star, with blond hair brushed back from his temples, narrowed, quizzical eyes, a long, fine-boned but slightly hooked nose and surprisingly full, sensuous lips. He came from an artistic family – his father was a modestly successful opera singer and composer – and he possessed almost film-star-like charisma. To his discomfort, it struck Gerhard that had he met Heydrich in other circumstances he might have found him very likeable. In conversation, he did not rant, or pound the table, or berate any of the other men and women around it. He laughed, he gave way graciously to let others have their say, and he was courteous to a fault to the women on either side of him. It was only when one listened closely to what this handsome devil with his honeyed voice was saying that one began to get a glimpse of the cold, calculating malice that lurked, like a viper in a flowerbed, behind that delightful façade.

When dinner was over, Gerhard had planned to slip away to his room. Though he had been brought up to be able to make polite conversation to anyone at any time, he had very little in common with anyone else in attendance that evening and wanted to write a letter to a girlfriend in Berlin, describing his impressions of the night while they were still fresh in his mind. But as he was discreetly making his way to the door of the large drawing room to which the guests had all retired, he felt a tap on his shoulder.

It was his older brother Konrad, proudly wearing his *SS-Sturmbannführer*'s uniform: a rank equivalent to an army major. 'Come with me, please,' he said, with chilly politeness, as if talking to a suspect apprehended on the street, rather than a member of his own family.

'Thanks, but I'm just going up to bed,' Gerhard replied, affecting not to hear the menace in Konrad's voice.

'You misunderstand me. That was not an invitation. That was an order. Come with me. Now.'

Members of the von Meerbach family did not make scenes in front of their guests. So Gerhard went with Konrad, smiling at a couple of other guests who caught his eye as they walked out of the drawing room and across the marble-flagged great hall of the castle to an oak door, studded with black nails on the far side. This was the door to Konrad's study, but to Gerhard's surprise he knocked and waited for a call of 'Enter!' from within.

Gerhard followed his brother into the study. Directly opposite the door, sitting behind the desk that had for more than a hundred years belonged to the head of the Meerbach family, was a now familiar, golden-haired figure. He stood and held out a hand.

'Ah, Herr von Meerbach, thank you for joining us. I don't believe that we have been properly introduced. My name is Reinhard Heydrich. Won't you please sit down?'

Gerhard shook the proffered hand and took one of two

158

wooden chairs arranged opposite the desk. His brother sat in the other.

Doing his best to maintain his composure in the face of a summons to the most powerful secret policeman in Germany, Gerhard asked, 'May I ask to what I owe the pleasure of meeting you, *Herr Gruppenführer*?'

Heydrich smiled as if this were just a casual social encounter. 'Oh, we can come to that in a moment,' he said. 'But first, tell me a little about yourself. You are twenty-three years old, is that correct?'

'Yes.' Gerhard noticed that a pale grey cardboard file, containing a number of sheets of typed paper, was open on the desk in front of Heydrich. *My God, is that my file?* he thought. *Is that what Germany is coming to?*

'And you are studying architecture in Berlin, no?'

'That's right. I am a student in the College of Architecture at the Berlin University for the Arts.'

'And before that you spent three years at the Bauhaus School, formerly known as the Great Ducal Saxon Art School, in Dessau.'

'Yes.'

'May I ask what attracted you to the Bauhaus?'

'Certainly. I was a great admirer of its first director, Walter Gropius, and of the modernist principles that he advanced. By the time I arrived, however, his place had been taken by Ludwig Mies van der Rohe. He was in my view an even greater architect. Aside from that, some of the greatest artistic minds of our time have been teachers at the Bauhaus. For anyone of my generation who is interested in the arts it was a natural choice to make.'

'By "greatest minds" I take it you refer to men such as Paul Klee, Wassily Kandinsky and László Moholy-Nagy?'

'That's right.'

'I take it you are aware that we now consider their work to be degenerate trash?'

159

'I am aware of that. Of course, that particular critical analysis had not yet been made at the time I applied for admission to the Bauhaus.'

Heydrich's eyes bored into Gerhard, as if deciding whether the latter's words had been unacceptably mocking, then he wrote a brief note on the file.

'This modernist trash has strong Semitic influences, I am sure you would agree,' Heydrich remarked, putting down his pen.

Gerhard stood his ground. 'With respect, *Herr Gruppenführer*, it is correct to say that Moholy-Nagy is of Jewish descent, but the other men you have mentioned were not. Indeed, there were men on the faculty who held opinions on the Jews that you might find sympathetic. Certainly there were very few, if any Jewish students at the Bauhaus during my time there.'

Heydrich frowned, looking uncertain for once. Gerhard did his best not to smile. *You didn't know that, did you? Now what are you going to say?*

Heydrich cleared his throat, glanced at the file. 'You were still enrolled at the Bauhaus when it moved to Berlin . . .'

'That is correct.'

'Where it was closed on political grounds.'

'Strictly speaking, Mies closed the school voluntarily, having received permission to continue.'

'Don't try to be clever with me, Herr von Meerbach. The Gestapo closed the school. Maria Ludwig Michael Mies, alias Mies van der Rohe, known to close associates as Mies: born 27 March 1886 in Aachen, Prussia . . .' Heydrich paused for a beat to let Gerhard appreciate the depth of his knowledge and what that implied ' . . . appealed to my predecessor in Berlin and was given a reprieve. He then understood that it was not in fact wise for him to continue. He is currently unable to find work in this country. People do not want this "modernist" architecture you value so highly, Herr von Meerbach. You should bear that in mind. But, to return to our discussion: Gestapo agents in Berlin were rightly concerned that the Bauhaus was a nest of communist subversion that actively promoted anti-German ideas and therefore could not be tolerated by the Reich. Tell me, are you a communist?'

Gerhard could not help himself. He burst out laughing. 'Not you too! As I told your colleague, my brother, I am not a communist. Look at me, *Herr Gruppenführer*. Here I am, in my family's castle dressed for dinner in my white tie and tails. Do I seem like a communist to you?'

'This is not a laughing matter, and I strongly advise you not to treat it as such. Answer my question. Are you a communist?'

'No, I am not, nor have I ever been a communist, nor voted for the Communist Party. Yes, there were plenty of students at the Bauhaus who had communist sympathies, as there were at every other university in the land. But I was not one of them, nor were they allowed to form an organization within the Bauhaus. And if you must know, I will tell you what I actually believe, which is that a modern form of architecture, based on the latest principles of engineering, science and manufacturing, is in keeping both with my own family's industrial heritage and with the thoroughly German principles of craft and quality as represented by the German Association of Craftsmen, of which I am a member. I want to tear down the slums of our industrial cities and produce clean, airy, healthy homes for ordinary, hard-working German families to live in. What the hell is communist about that?'

As the impassioned question hung in the air, Heydrich leaned back in his chair and his cold, sceptical eyes examined Gerhard like a butterfly collector looking at a specimen pinned to a board. 'Do you have any idea how privileged and how arrogant you sound?' he asked in a calm, untroubled voice that was far more unnerving than any furious shouting would have been. 'The very fact that you, a mere student, feel free to address me of all people in this way, in front of your brother, without considering the very grave risk you are running, or the embarrassment and shame you are bringing upon your family . . . Trust me, Herr von Meerbach, no ordinary German would be so foolish as to speak as you have done.'

'I apologize if I have caused offence, *Herr Gruppenführer*,' Gerhard said, respectfully, but still looking Heydrich in the eye. 'That was not my intention. I was merely seeking to establish the truth, which is that I am not a communist.'

'You are, however, a Jew-lover.'

The words hit Gerhard like a blow from a Brownshirt's truncheon. 'I'm . . . I'm sorry . . . ?' he stammered. 'What do you mean?'

'Exactly what I say. Some five weeks ago, on the morning of 7 March – my birthday, as it happens – you drove to the outskirts of Munich from where you caught a tram to Laimer Platz. From there you walked down Fürstenrieder Strasse, making a series of hopelessly amateur attempts to check whether you were being followed. You were, of course, even if you clearly did not know it. You paused to accept an item of forbidden communist literature . . .'

'I did not accept it!' Gerhard protested. 'The man shoved it into my hand.'

'And you looked at it with considerable interest for one who says that he does not have communist sympathies before throwing it away. You then proceeded to your destination, the apartment where your family's former lawyer – the Jew Solomons – now lives. Do you deny that this is the case?'

'You know that I can't deny it. That is what happened. And excuse me if I am being arrogant again, but may I ask, is it a crime to speak to someone who gave loyal service both to my family, and to our country, just because he is a Jew?'

'No,' Heydrich admitted. He pondered a moment and then added, 'Thank you. You have made me realize that we must tighten the laws regarding all forms of association between Aryans and Jews. But even now, a case could be made against you for providing the financial means to allow a Jew to leave Germany without permission.'

'What do you mean?'

'Oh, come now. You gave Solomons five thousand marks. It was your preposterous attempt to persuade your trustees that you needed money to buy a smart car – as if a student, even one from your family, would drive around in a Mercedes grand tourer – that alerted your brother to what you were up to. He very properly informed me and a watch was placed on you.'

Gerhard turned, aghast, to look at Konrad. 'You betrayed me? Your own brother? How could you?'

'Because he is a patriot and a good Nazi,' Heydrich said before Konrad could answer. 'And perhaps because he is a good brother and hopes to save you before it is too late.'

'Save me from what? How can it possibly be a crime to talk to a man who was awarded the Blue Max for his courage at Verdun? Isidore Solomons was a colonel, personally commended by Crown Prince Wilhelm himself. To me, he is the very best kind of German.'

'He's a filthy Yid, a greedy, treacherous, conspiring rat, like all the rest of his race,' sneered Konrad.

'How can you say that?' Gerhard asked, his voice rising in appalled incomprehension. 'He was our friend. We went to his family's house. We stood there, you and I, while he told us about the history of the *Pour le Mérite*, our eyes popping out of our heads when he took it out of the case and showed it to us. You thought he was a hero. You did! How can you deny it?'

'I was a child. Now that I am an adult, I have learned the truth about the Jews. They are nothing but sub-human scum. All of them.'

Heydrich held up a hand in admonition. 'No, *Sturmbannführer*, your brother has a point. We must be aware of the existence of what one might call "the good Jew". People may know such a person – their doctor, for example, or a kindly woman who mends their clothes, or even, as in this case, a war-hero. They will think to themselves, "Well, Herr Levy or Frau Goldschmidt isn't such a bad sort. They can't be as bad as these Nazis say." It is for us to educate them so that they understand that these good apples are the exceptions and that all the rest are rotten. And since it is not possible to sort out the minuscule number of good from the vast numbers of bad, then they must all be dealt with in the same way. But to get back to this particular Jew, Isidore Solomons and his family. Do you happen to know where they are now, Herr von Meerbach?'

'I assume that they are still living at the same apartment on Fürstenrieder Strasse.'

Heydrich sighed. 'Really? You think Solomons and his spawn are still sitting there in that disgusting slum block – the very kind that you wish to tear down and replace with shiny modernist houses – when he has five thousand Reichsmarks sitting in his wallet, along with all the gold and diamonds you can bet he has hidden away? No. Try again.'

'He did not look to me like a man who had diamonds hidden away anywhere. As you say, why would he be living like that if he had?'

'Because, Herr von Meerbach, Solomons is a Jew. And Jews have learned that their greed and usury and vile treachery inevitably bring down the justifiable anger of the decent people amongst whom they live. So they always – but always – have the means to run away, like the rats they are. And diamonds – so small, so light, but so very valuable – are the perfect form of portable wealth. So, tell me, please: where is Solomons now?'

'I don't know. I promise you, *Herr Gruppenführer*, on my life I do not know.'

Gerhard's heart was beating hard now, his body flooding with adrenalin as it responded to the threat Heydrich posed and the fear he induced. He felt the sweat starting to prickle under his arms. 'I'm telling the truth. I swear it!' he added, unable to keep the note of desperation from his voice.

'What do you think, *Sturmbannführer*? Is the suspect telling the truth?'

'I think he's a filthy liar,' said Konrad as the word 'suspect' echoed around Gerhard's brain.

Gerhard looked at his older brother and saw the hate etched into his twisted features. The two of them had never got on particularly well. They were very different characters. But he had never had the faintest idea that such bitter hostility had been burning away inside Konrad's heart.

'I am not lying,' he repeated, trying not to scream the words in frustration. 'I do not know where the Solomons family has gone, or even if they have gone anywhere at all. I gave him some money because I believed he deserved some kind of settlement from our family after all he had done for us. I gave him as much as I could manage, though it was far less than he deserved. I did not ask him what he planned to do with it and he did not tell me.'

Heydrich said nothing. He let Gerhard sit there and watched as he wiped a hand across his brow to rid himself of the beads of sweat collecting there. Finally he said, 'Actually I believe you. Solomons is too good a lawyer to tell you anything that might incriminate you or, more importantly from his perspective, himself. I am satisfied that you do not know where the Jew has gone. Luckily, however, I do. He and his family crossed the border into Switzerland – without proper papers, naturally – some three weeks ago and are now resident in Zürich, where he has found employment in a the legal firm of Grünspan and Aaronsohn – fellow Jews, of course. I assume he had already arranged the position there before he left, indeed before he took your money. Hmm . . . I wonder if he will pay it back?'

'I would not ask him to.'

'Just as well, since that would be against his religion.'

Konrad snickered sycophantically at his boss's wit as Heydrich went on, 'The Swiss authorities have asked us whether we wish them to deport the Solomons and we have decided, on balance, that this will not be necessary. Your protestations about Solomons's military record might well be echoed in the press, particularly the foreign correspondents. A man who fights nobly for his country is a hero in any language, even if he was once an enemy. If anything were to happen to Solomons, it would be a distraction for us to have to explain that away. So he is better off in Switzerland where he will keep a low profile, I am sure, for he knows that we could reach out and deal with him at any time, should he even think of causing trouble.

'You, however, have caused trouble, and you are right here. Let me be frank, Herr von Meerbach, the Reich rewards loyal citizens, but punishes dissenters and deviants mercilessly. Two years ago, my commander *Reichsführer-SS* Heinrich Himmler opened a camp near the town of Dachau, just outside Munich. Do you know the place?'

'I know the town of Dachau. I was not aware of any camp there.'

'No? Well, let me tell you about it. This camp is intended for political and social undesirables: communists, criminals, sexual deviants, intellectuals . . . Jew-lovers. People, in short, who have no place in a healthy Aryan society. The regime there is hard. Inmates are completely isolated from the outside world: no visits, no letters in or out, no newspapers or radio broadcasts, nothing that in any way connects inmates to the society they have themselves rejected. There is forced labour, every day. There are no weekends or holidays in Dachau. The rations provide the absolute bare minimum required for survival, so there are no fat inmates at Dachau, either. Discipline is absolute and punishments brutal. A man who commits the most minor infraction has his wrists bound behind his back and then

166

attached to a hook, three metres above the ground. He then hangs there, in agony, as his arms are slowly torn from their sockets. For more serious offences, execution is carried out instantly, without either trial or any form of appeal.'

Heydrich paused. 'You look pale, Herr von Meerbach. Could you be so good as to get your brother a glass of water, please, *Herr Sturmbannführer*? I believe he needs it.'

It took Konrad a little under three minutes to leave the study, go to the drawing room, find one of the crystal jugs filled with iced water, pour a glass and return to Heydrich and Gerhard. In that time Heydrich did not speak. He sat quite motionless and simply looked at Gerhard with reptilian coldness, letting the description of Dachau sink into his mind and fire his imagination with vivid images of unspeakable suffering.

Konrad placed the glass in front of his brother and Gerhard downed it in one.

'Better?' Heydrich asked. 'Now, listen very carefully to me Gerhard von Meerbach, for your life and your family's repu- tation depend upon it. I could have you arrested this instant and sent directly to Dachau. You will be sleeping there tonight and you will never set foot outside its fence, if I say so. Do you understand?'

'Yes.' It was just a single syllable, but Gerhard found he could barely force it out of his mouth, so tightly was his throat constricted.

'However, you share one quality, apart from treachery with Isidore Solomons, which is to say, you are a potential embar- rassment. The Meerbach Motor Works is a vital part of our industrial armoury. Furthermore, your brother's commitment to Nazi ideals is a very clear sign to other members of the social and commercial elite that their class is as much a part of the new order in Germany as anyone else, and that as much loyalty is expected from them as it is from those whom they regard as their inferiors. It is very tempting indeed to punish you, and do so publicly, in such a way as to make it clear to all classes of the population that no one is above the law of the Reich and no one can escape its justice and its retribution. As you can imagine, that would be a message greatly welcomed by the lower orders in society. But it is an unfortunate fact of life that the Reich needs the great industrial families as much as they need us, and while it may be necessary to secure their co-operation by fear, it is preferable to have them as allies, and even – as in your brother's case – enthusiastic supporters. Again, there is part of me that relishes the idea of making an example of the two of you as a sort of Cain and Abel of the Reich: the good, noble brother versus the wicked betrayer of his family's honour. Even now . . .'

Heydrich sighed, '*Ach*, what a story Goebbels would make of that! But you are lucky. Your fate hung in the balance as I arrived here. But then I met your mother. Such a charming lady, so proud of both her sons, but widowed so young. "This woman has already lost a husband," I said to myself. "Can I now deprive her of a son?" So, in the end, I decided upon a different solution to the problem. Would you like to know what that is?'

'Yes . . . yes please,' Gerhard was shocked to realize that he was almost begging.

'Very well, then, this is it. You, Gerhard von Meerbach, will become a model citizen of the Reich. You may continue your architectural studies, but not at the Berlin University of the Arts. Instead I will apprentice you to Albert Speer, First Architect of the Reich. You will learn about the true, Nazi principles of archi-tecture, as laid down by the Führer himself, as you work on buildings designed to glorify the Reich. In your spare time, you will busy yourself with an activity that is perfectly suited to your family's proud history of providing engines for our nation's warplanes.'

'You want me to work in our factory?' Gerhard asked.

Heydrich laughed. 'Well, if you insist . . . But no, I had something else in mind. As you doubtless know, Article 198 of the Treaty of Versailles prohibits Germany from having an air force. This is an absurd limitation on our right to self-defence and one of many good reasons why the Führer has totally repudiated the Treaty in its entirety. As a result we are now training pilots as reservists for the Luftwaffe, so that when the time comes to show the world the true strength of the Third Reich there will be enough men to provide us with absolute command of the air.

'You will therefore become one of these reservists. You will spend weekends, and a prolonged period every summer training to be a pilot. You will wear your Luftwaffe uniform with pride. At no time, whether at work, or in training, or when you are with your family and friends, will you deviate by so much as a millimetre from the approved Party line. You will give the Nazi salute, declaim, "Heil Hitler!" and mean it. Should the topic of the Jews arise in conversation, you will let no man outdo you in your condemnation of their race and its evil, scheming ways. Should the discussion turn to the arts, you will denounce the decadence of abstract daubs that look like nothing more than something a monkey could produce by flinging paint at a canvas.'

'You want my soul,' Gerhard said.

'Yes,' Heydrich replied. 'I want your soul, and should you be filled by some misguided spirit of principle or nobility and decide that you would rather sacrifice yourself than give in to me, let me add this. If you are denounced as a political dissenter and Jew-lover, I will not stop there. All your friends, your fellow students, the women you have loved – everyone who has ever had anything to do with you will find their lives examined in every detail by the Gestapo. They will be arrested and questioned. Their property will be searched. And if my men find anything, no matter how trivial, that suggests that they are undesirable, they will join you at Dachau. So you will not just be condemning yourself. You will condemn them too. So, do you accept my conditions?'

'What choice do I have?'

'None. I want your solemn agreement to commit yourself wholeheartedly to the Nazi cause, given to me and witnessed by your brother. Now.'

Gerhard swallowed hard. He longed to spit in Heydrich's face, to tell him where he could shove his demands and to hell with the consequences. He didn't care what Dachau was like. Better to suffer there and be true to oneself, than to live a lie in comfort. But he could not betray his friends. He could not condemn them to the camps.

'I will,' Gerhard said, and it felt like handing his soul to the devil himself.

'Thank you,' said Heydrich. 'That wasn't so hard, now, was it?'

He stood up straight, as did Konrad, then looked hard at Gerhard.

Gerhard stood too.

Heydrich flung out his right arm in front of him and shouted, 'Heil Hitler!'

'Heil Hitler!' echoed Konrad.

Silence fell for a second. Then a third arm rose into the air and was held out in the Nazi salute.

'Heil Hitler!' cried Gerhard von Meerbach.

In May 1934, Francis Courtney set off for England, taking a ship from Alexandria to Piraeus, the port of Athens, and then travelling across the Continent by train to London. His older brother, he knew, increasingly chose to travel by air, but he made it very plain to the other members of the family that he disapproved of such extravagance. 'It's all very well for Leon to throw money around. He stole our shares from us, he can

170

afford it. But I am quite content to travel in a more modest style, as befits an English gentleman.'

'I wasn't aware that any of us were either English or gentlemanly,' Dorian had replied. 'But if that's how you want to get to Blighty, Frank, who am I to tell you otherwise?'

Frank's principal reason for making the journey was to see his surgeon, Dr Harold Gillies. He had been suffering minor problems with his skin graft: a small patch appeared to have died off, leaving a sore, small suppurating area that had to be covered at all times by a dressing. But that was not the only reason Frank wanted to be in London. There was another man he wanted to see: Oswald Mosley, leader of the British Union of Fascists, or the Blackshirts as they liked to call themselves.

His was a name that was increasingly heard among the men who discussed politics at the Cairo Sporting Club, where Frank liked to play the occasional round of golf, demanding a special handicap as he did so, to allow for his war wounds. 'Of course the man's an absolute bounder,' one of Frank's cronies, a liquor importer called Desmond 'Piggy' Peters, declared one morning as they were walking to the first tee. 'I'm reliably assured that he married the Curzon girl, Cynthia I believe she's called, for her money and is now having it off on the side with her sister and her stepmother.'

'Bloody hell,' said the third member of the game, a cotton trader by the name of Hatton. 'You have to admire the nerve of the man.'

'And the stamina,' said Frank.

When the men's laughter had abated, Piggy Peters continued, 'But Mosley's no fool. Been a Member of Parliament for the Tories and the Socialists and would have made a better Prime Minister than any man in either party, so I'm told. But he couldn't be doing with the old way, d'you see? Times are too serious, more radical measures required, that's his assessment of the situation, and who's to argue with that, eh?'

'No one with any brains,' Frank agreed. 'It's patently obvious the whole bloody world's going to the dogs. Capitalism's on its uppers. The Reds just want to control the whole world. And the bloody Jews don't care who wins because they control the banks and the commies, both.'

'The Hebrew only thinks about two things, himself and his money, not necessarily in that order,' Hatton observed, to harrumphs of approval.

'It's not just that. Look around the colonies, the darkies are as bad as the Jews. That Gandhi fellow in India wanting independence, ungrateful little man, after all we've done for that country.'

'Well, that's Mosley's point, as I understand it,' Piggy said. 'He thinks it's time we put ourselves first, looked after number one, as it were. He says there's a third way that's not capitalism and not communism, but fascism. And when you look at what that Hitler chappie's doing in Germany, you can't argue, I don't think.'

'God knows he's a ridiculous-looking man and what was he in the war, just a corporal, wasn't it?'

'So was Napoleon and he didn't do so badly,' Hatton pointed out.

'But he's putting Germany back on its feet,' Frank went on. 'Damned impressive, I call it. He's given the people back their self-respect.'

'Exactly! And that's what Oswald Mosley is going to do for the British, you mark my words,' said Piggy Peters.

'I'm going home in a few weeks' time, have this damn skin graft attended to. I think I might just make it my business to find out a bit about this Mosley fellow.'

'I think I may be able to help you there, Frank. Couple of chaps I do business with in London are quite prominent supporters of the Blackshirt movement, absolutely hugger-mugger with Mosley himself. Let me know when you're going and I'll wangle you an introduction to the great man.'

* * *

Gillies repaired the skin graft and Frank spent two weeks in a sanatorium by the sea at Eastbourne while the operation healed. On the morning of 7 June, feeling better than he had done in months, he took the train to London, checked into a respectable but modest hotel, and then set off for the Olympia exhibition hall on the Hammersmith Road in West London, where Mosley was holding a rally of his supporters.

Twelve thousand fascist sympathizers were due to attend the event. But ranged against them were thousands of protesters who had come to attend a demonstration organized by the London District Committee of the Communist Party. A press release had been sent out to all London's newspapers, the newsreel-makers and the British Broadcasting Corporation declaring that 'the workers in the capital city will resist with all means the fascist menace'.

That very morning the *Daily Worker*, a Communist mouthpiece, had warned the Blackshirts that 'the workers' counter-action will cause them to tremble'.

For their part the Blackshirts made it perfectly clear that they had no intention of cancelling the event or backing down in any way. Left and right were going to war, and neither much minded who got in the way.

Frank emerged from Olympia station, just yards from the hall, to find that the short journey to the main entrance had become a gauntlet as anyone who wanted to watch Mosley speak had to run as fast they could past an angry mob of protesters waving anti-Mosley placards and red banners bearing the yellow hammer and sickle of the Soviet Union. They were met by hard-faced fascists, dressed in black from head to toe, and only too ready to trade a punch to the head or a kick to the guts for every word of abuse shouted at them by a protester. Between the two forces a thin blue line of policemen, a few of them mounted on horseback, tried to maintain a safe passage for civilians caught in the furore.

The deafening noise, the press of bodies and the overwhelming impression of chaos that could at any moment tip into outright anarchy only served to fire Frank with more enthusiasm for Mosley's cause. Any man who could provoke such hatred from people Frank despised must be doing something right. And the way the mob was behaving merely underlined the desperate need for order and discipline to be imposed upon the people for their own good by a strong man, and damn democracy and the people's rights. Those were old ideas, failed ideas. The times required something new.

As he walked at a steady pace, refusing to be driven into a run by the mob, his temper rising with every pace he took, Frank suddenly felt something wet strike the left side of his face. He put a hand up to his cheek, examined what it found, saw a warm, bubbly blob of saliva and realized he'd been spat on.

Outraged at the insult, Frank turned to his left and saw a young woman just a few feet away. She was scruffily dressed, standing with a group of men, all with their shirts undone at the neck, not a hat between them. And they were all laughing at him. The girl looked right at him and mimicked the act of spitting in his direction. Then she laughed again.

It was more than he could stand. He took a couple of swift paces towards the group, propelling himself forward with his walking stick, its steel tip striking sparks as it hit the paving stones. 'Don't fall over, Dad!' one of the men shouted at him. Frank's face was contorted in a furious snarl as he raised his stick and lashed out at his tormentors. He hit the girl flush in the face. She screamed and bent double, blood seeping between her fingers as she pressed her hands to her head. Her companions dashed towards Frank. He flailed at them with his stick but they kept coming and one landed a punch on Frank's shoulder that knocked him back. Still they kept coming, as possessed with blind anger as he had been, bent on exacting revenge. Suddenly, Frank felt desperately afraid. He had provoked these hooligans and now they wanted their revenge. He lashed out again, but someone caught his stick in mid-swing and ripped it from his grasp. Desperately he cowered like a boxer caught on the ropes, hunching his shoulders, holding his hands up by his head to try and protect himself. He was waiting for the first punch to land when he felt a rough hand grabbing his shoulder and pulling him back out of the way. Frank fell backward onto the pavement. He propped himself up on his elbows to see a knot of Blackshirts piling into the demonstrators, laying into them with practised, brutal efficiency. Frank scrabbled for his hat, which was lying on the ground beside him and put it back on. Then he rose rather shakily to his feet. The Blackshirts had put the opponents to flight. One of them emerged from the mêlée holding Frank's stick. 'Does this belong to you, sir?' he asked. His accent was lower-class, but efficient and respectful, Frank thought, like a sergeant speaking to an officer.

'Yes, yes it is, thank you.'

'Rotten, isn't it, the way them commie scum assault decent gentlemen like yourself? Don't you worry, sir, we don't stand for it.'

'Well said, young man,' said Frank and he touched the brim of his hat in salute as he went on his way. Inside the hall there was more fighting, for some demonstrators had managed to get hold of tickets and infiltrate the event itself. The start time was delayed for thirty minutes, then forty-five and almost an hour had passed by the time the house light suddenly dimmed. A great roar went up as mighty spotlights cut through air made heavy by the countless cigarettes smoked by the audience as they had waited for this moment. The bright white beams picked out the blazing red banners of the British Union of

Fascists, each bearing the party symbol of a white lightning bolt inside a blue circle. The banners were being carried two abreast by twenty Blackshirts marching down the aisle that ran down the centre of the auditorium, past thousands of supporters all holding out their arms in the fascist salute. At the head of the party marched another Blackshirt, the commander of their unit.

A chant went up, thousands of voices shouting, 'M-O-S-L-E-Y! Mosley, Mosley, Mosley!' And then the beams swept past the banners and found the man marching behind them, the man who had filled the hall and the streets outside: Oswald Mosley himself.

Everything about his appearance was designed to create an impression of strength and virility. Mosley was thirty-seven, the absolute prime of a man's life, tall and straight-backed. He wore black trousers held by a broad black leather belt. A close-fitting black polo-neck jumper covered his strapping chest and he held his head high, more like a gladiator entering the arena than a politician about to make a speech. His hair and moustaches were as black as his clothes. This was Britain's Hitler.

Frank found himself caught up in the hysteria, saluting, applauding, chanting as Mosley reached the front of the crowd and mounted the steps to the platform from which he would speak. Only now did Frank notice that Mosley had a slight limp, but somehow that discovery did nothing to detract from his conviction that this was the strongman the country and the Empire so desperately needed.

The standard bearers took up their positions on either side of the platform, all standing to attention.

'Colour-party, present arms!' shouted the Blackshirt commander, as if they were Guards at the Trooping of the Colour.

At once, the men lowered their flagpoles to the diagonal,

pointing out at the crowd. A few voices of dissent could be heard, scattered around the huge arena. Mosley and his Blackshirts ignored them.

'Colour-party, stand easy!' the commander cried, and as one the men stood legs slightly apart. Mosley remained silent, motionless, waiting for his people to calm themselves.

The hubbub ebbed away and the thousands who had been on their feet took their places in their seats. Then Mosley began. 'Thousands of our fellow countrymen and women have come to hear our case and thousands have joined the fascist ranks,' he said, in a voice that was unmistakably upper-class, without being absurdly highfalutin'. He had the rich, sonorous tone and perfect diction of a great Shakespearian actor, so that the words he said were imbued with significance and gravitas. And the very sound of his voice gave him an air of authority, one that immediately impressed itself upon a crowd raised since birth to respect their betters and obey their leaders.

'This movement is something new in the political life of this country, something that goes further and deeper than any other movement this land has ever known,' Mosley went on, and Frank Courtney, sitting halfway back on the floor of the Olympia hall, felt special because he was part of that movement, a cog in the machine that was going to transform the Empire.

Then the spell was broken as a couple of protesters leaped to their feet and shook their fists at the stage as they shouted at Mosley.

He gave an easy, confident, reassuring smile as black-shirted stewards found the hecklers and dragged them from their seats. 'Take no notice of these small interruptions,' Mosley said. 'They don't worry me and they needn't worry you.'

The crowd roared in approval, feeling that they had been as defiant as their leader. Nothing would stop him stating his case, or prevent them hearing it.

'This meeting is symbolic of the advance of the Blackshirt

cause in the first twenty months of its existence,' Mosley continued. 'In that time, fascism in Great Britain has advanced more rapidly than in any other country in the world. Not because our people had to adopt fascism. Not under the lash of economic necessity, as in other lands, but because they desire a new creed and a new order in our land.'

The speech continued for an hour as Mosley spoke, entirely without notes, yet without stumbling or repeating himself or at any moment losing the power and flow of his argument. Frank was overwhelmed. He felt as though he had been waiting his whole life to hear the words that had just been laid before him. They made sense of so much. They addressed his bitter sense of grievance and injustice and promised a world in which he could be one of the winners, one of the new masters. Piggy Peters had been as good as his word and spoken to his friends in the Mosley camp, who had ensured that Frank's name was added to the list of guests at a small reception, held backstage after the event was over. His sense of privilege was raised even higher as he saw the envious glances being cast in his direction as the Blackshirts guarding the way to the reception parted to let him through.

Frank found Piggy's contact and introduced himself. 'Mr Courtney, how splendid of you to come all the way from Egypt, just for us, what? Look, Oswald will be dashed keen to meet you. He's very keen on spreading the word out to the colonies and anyone who can lend a hand is greatly appreciated.'

A few minutes later, Frank found himself in the presence of the great man himself. Mosley was as impressive close up as he had been when performing to his thousands of followers. His grand oratory gave way to overwhelming charm. He focused all his attention on Frank, noticed his stick, inquired how he had come by his injury and said, 'Good man. You served our country with honour, and I salute you. I have a bit of a dicky leg myself, as you may have notice. I picked it up in '16 when I was with the Royal Flying Corps. I wish I could say I came by my wounds in honourable combat, but the truth is I pranged my plane while I was trying to impress my mother and sister with my prowess as a pilot. Damn foolish, don't you agree?'

Before Frank could answer Mosley went on, 'Now, I hear you're quite the coming man in Cairo. Let me assure you that I would appreciate any help you could give the cause out there. We have to bring the Empire with us if we are to succeed. Excuse me one moment . . .'

Mosley turned away for a second and waved towards the most beautiful woman Frank had ever seen in his life. She was as slender and graceful as Botticelli's Venus, brought to life in modern dress. Her hair was a dark honey blonde and her clear, pale blue eyes were framed by eyebrows shaped like perfectly drawn arches. Her nose was straight, fine and very slightly tilted upwards, her scarlet lips were disdainfully sensual and her chin, fractionally too strong to be conventionally pretty, merely added to the sense that she was in every possible way a thoroughly superior being.

'Darling, do come and meet Mr Courtney,' Mosley said. 'He's going to do wonderful things for us in Egypt. Mr Courtney, may I introduce Mrs Diana Guinness.'

'I'm so pleased to meet you,' said this vision of female loveliness. 'Anyone who fights for our cause will always be a friend of mine.'

'I do assure you, Mrs Guinness, that you can absolutely count on me,' said Frank.

She clasped his hand, looked deep into his eyes and said, 'Thank you so much, Mr Courtney.'

A moment later, Mosley and his mistress had disappeared without a backward glance. Their work was done. Frank Courtney was utterly won over to the cause of British fascism.

On a fine afternoon in high summer Gerhard von Meerbach clambered into the tiny open cockpit of the Grunau Baby glider that sat on the runway of the private airfield that formed part of the Meerbach Motor Works complex. He bent his head, making sure not to hit it on the raised wing that swept in a single pure and uninterrupted sweep of fabric and plywood over the top of the feather-light craft. This was the Ford Model T of gliders, a design barely more complicated than the sort of kit a schoolboy might build with balsa wood and paper, but it had opened up the skies to tens of thousands of Germans. And, in so doing, it had enabled a nation banned from possessing an air force by the Treaty of Versailles to train its next generation of pilots.

Gerhard strapped himself in, pulled his leather helmet over his head and did up the chinstrap. He checked his controls to make sure that the glider's flaps were all working. Then he waved his arm to indicate his readiness.

A member of the ground crew raised a white flag, and more than one thousand metres up the runway another flag was lifted to indicate that the signal had been received. The second flagman was standing by a hefty Mercedes L6500 truck on which a massive motorized winch – powered, naturally, by a Meerbach engine – had been mounted. The engine had been thrumming for the past couple of minutes as it was brought to full power. Now a lever was thrown, gears engaged and the drum of the winch started rotating, slowly at first and then gathering speed.

A cable of light, high-tensile steel wire ran from the winch to the nose of the glider. For a few seconds the winch did nothing but take up the slack. Then Gerhard felt the tug as the line tightened and then the forward motion and the breeze in his face as the Grunau Baby began rolling down the runway. The breeze turned to a gale as the glider reached its take-off speed of eighty kilometres per hour and then, just as a sail fills at the touch of the breeze, so the wing responded to the rush of air across its surface and Gerhard felt the first glorious moment of release as the glider left the grasp of the earth below and, defying gravity, rose up into the sky.

When the altimeter showed a height of five hundred metres, Gerhard released the clip that held the cable, which plummeted back down to earth. Now, at last he was truly free.

The glorious armies of alpine peaks, the lush green meadows and the dazzling sparkle of the waters of the Bodensee were magnificent enough when seen from the windows of the Schloss Meerbach. They provided endlessly changing backdrops of colour, light and form to walks, cross-country ski trips or hunting expeditions on the estate. But nothing compared to their loveliness or majesty when seen from the air. And gliding, Gerhard had discovered, was the purest of all forms of flight. An engine gave off deafening noise, constant vibration and choking exhaust fumes. But a glider was as silent as a soaring eagle, as it rode the invisible currents of hot air that picked it up and carried across the sky.

Gerhard's face was wreathed in an exultant smile. *Thank you, Konrad! Thank you,* Gruppenführer *Heydrich! You have no idea of the gift you made to me when you ordered me to fly!*

Here, in this most joyous solitude, he was liberated from the cares of the world down below. Over the past three months his life had been transformed. He had been forced to drop many of his old acquaintances; for fear that he might lead the Gestapo towards them. Other friends, including his very closest, had dropped him of their own accord, appalled by his apparent capitulation to the bigotry and wickedness of Nazi ideology. To them, the sudden appearance of a Party badge on Gerhard's shoulder and his appointment to the staff of Albert Speer's design office was evidence that he had chosen to betray his conscience, political ideals and architectural creativity. 'Once a spoiled rich kid, always a spoiled rich kid,' one of Gerhard's oldest, closest companions had sneered. 'In the end, you couldn't resist it, could you? They put it all on a plate for you:

privilege, advancement, a seat at the top table. And you couldn't say no.'

It tore Gerhard apart that he could not tell anyone the truth. He hated himself every time he nodded approvingly or even spoke up in support when a guest at the family dinner table made an anti-Semitic remark. He barely said a word at work without first running his comments through in his mind to check that they were in accordance with approved Nazi thinking. Konrad had asked him one day, 'Berlin is a city of four million people. How many Gestapo men do you think it requires to keep every one of them in order?'

'I don't know,' Gerhard had replied. 'Ten thousand? Twenty thousand?'

'No, you are completely wrong. There are barely five hundred Gestapo officers in all Berlin. But then again, there are also four million. That is the genius of the system. Everyone watches everyone else. Everyone is a policeman. You have no idea how much information is brought to our attention every day. So many people reporting so many neighbours, workmates, friends, even family members. It is all we can do just to file all the accusations.'

Konrad had looked at Gerhard then and the smug, bullying look in his eyes was as clear as any spoken threat: we are watching you, we have eyes and ears everywhere, you are never safe. It could be that pretty girl who works as the office secretary, or that friendly fellow who invites you out for a drink, or the landlady of your flat. It could be absolutely anyone. You are never safe from us. Never!

But up here, high in the Bavarian sky, there was no one to spy on Gerhard, no one to report him for independent thoughts or rash bursts of improper speech. Up here he could recover some sense of his true self. And as his eyes ranged over the wondrous scenery and towards the Swiss shoreline on the far side of the Bodensee – how tempting it was, sometimes, just to turn the nose of the glider towards that safe haven and leave his cares behind! – so his mind returned as it often did to the postcard he had received just ten days after his encounter with Heydrich. It was a typical tourist card that showed a view of the steam engine that carried passengers up what was said to be the steepest railway line in the world to the top of a mountain called the Rothorn. And the message was equally innocent:

Hey Gerd, you should come to Switzerland. The girls here look even better than the mountains! Looking forward to seeing you again. If you need anything from here – cheese? chocolate? fancy watches? – just let me know.
Your pal, Maxi.

Gerhard had known at once that Maxi was Isidore Solomons, the proud holder of the Blue Max. *Thank God the card arrived after I met that SS bastard*, he thought now. *I could never have lied to Heydrich that I didn't know where Izzy was. He would have seen through me at once.*

'If you need anything . . .' that was the key line, Izzy's sign that he had a debt of honour to Gerhard. One day, it might be called upon. Until that day, however, Gerhard would not mention anything to anyone. And when the glider came back down to earth and real life began again, he would not allow himself even to think about Isidore Solomons.

By the time her third year at Roedean began, Saffron had that wonderful feeling of being completely at home in her school and wholly at ease with everything involved in getting there and back. Leon, too, was far more relaxed, not least because his daughter's evident enjoyment of her education brought him tremendous pleasure, even if it was even harder for him that he could not share it all with Eva. 'Off to see the splendid Miss Halfpenny,' he said, straightening his tie before they left for the outfitters. 'Pity she'll kick me out within ten seconds of our arrival. Damned handsome woman, that one.'

'Daddy, really!' Saffron exclaimed in mock outrage. 'You can't talk about Miss Halfpenny like that. She's not one of your lady friends. I mean, she's much too old, for a start.'

Leon laughed as he opened the car door for Saffron to get in. 'My dear girl, I would estimate that Miss Halfpenny is only around thirty. And in case you haven't noticed, I will celebrate – or possibly mourn – my forty-seventh birthday this year. A woman of thirty may seem ancient to you, but to me she's a mere slip of a girl.'

As they drove into central Johannesburg, Saffron turned her father's words over in her head. She had never really stopped to think about Miss Halfpenny's looks, not least because the way the manageress dressed was intended to make her seem eminently respectable rather than attractive. But now that she considered the question, Saffy decided that she could see what her father meant. Miss Halfpenny had lovely auburn hair, even if she did wear it in a prim little bun. And though her features were not pretty-pretty – her nose was too long, her cheekbones too pronounced – they were elegant, symmetrical and fine-boned. She had nice hazel eyes, too, and, though her job did not encourage levity, Saffron had seen Miss Halfpenny smile enough times to see how it lit up her face.

Having considered all these questions in the abstract, Saffron was keen to see the object of her deliberations again to observe her more closely in the flesh. But when she and Leon arrived at the shop they discovered that Miss Halfpenny was no longer employed there. 'Her mother took poorly and she had to go back to England to look after her,' the new manageress said. 'But I would be pleased to cater to your requirements. Come this way . . .'

'Well, I'll leave you to it,' said Leon, looking much less cheerful than he had as they arrived at the shop. Saffron had hardly been any more cheerful as she followed the unfamiliar face off towards the clothes racks and drawers.

It had not been an auspicious start to the new school year, but things had improved since then and now here Saffron was, just three weeks away from Christmas, coming in to land at Nairobi. She had taken her School Certificate exams in English language and literature, mathematics, science, history, geography, art, French, Latin and (to Saffron's tremendous indignation at the very idea of being examined in the skills that her father had so strongly dismissed) domestic science. She was reasonably sure that she had passed them all, with Credit or even Distinction grades in most of them. Between gritted teeth, if sufficiently tortured, she might even have admitted that she quite enjoyed her cookery lessons and was actually rather proud of the pineapple upside-down cake she had produced in her exam.

But those days were behind her now. She was sixteen years old, legally entitled to leave school and, so far as she was concerned, practically a grown woman. Her father would be waiting for her on the aerodrome's flat grass field. Kippy, who was by now far too old to ride, but still tended with loving care by the stable-boys, was waiting for her at Lusima. And there was a surprise waiting for her. A happy smile spread across Saffron's face.

Home! she exulted. *I'm almost home!*

'Would you care to give me your coffee cup, please, Miss Courtney?' the Imperial Airways steward asked the poised young lady of sixteen whom he was serving, almost shouting to make himself heard over the roar of the four rotary engines that powered the Armstrong Whitworth Atalanta airliner. 'We'll be landing in Nairobi soon.'

Saffron smiled up at the steward in his smart white uniform. His peaked cap made him look like a naval officer who had, quite by chance, found himself acting the role of a cabin boy on this Imperial Airways flight.

'Of course, Symons, here you are,' she called back, handing him the bone china cup and saucer. 'I thought it was particularly good today.'

Symons smiled. 'I made it nice and strong for you, just the way you like it, Miss. Almost home, eh?'

'Yes.' After three years of air travel, Saffron was well used to the volume required to converse in the air. 'My father cabled me just before we left Jo'burg. He said he had a surprise for me when I got home. I'm a little worried because he didn't say if it was a nice surprise or a nasty one. I do hope it's nice.'

'I'm sure it will be. I'll bet he's bought you something extra special for Christmas. The way your father talks about you when he flies with us, I know he'd only ever want nice things for you. Proud as punch he is, though better not tell him I said so!'

'I won't, but thank you very much for saying so, anyway, Symons. That was very sweet.'

The steward beamed affectionately and walked back between the cabin's seven pairs of passenger seats towards his galley in the rear of the plane. He and his colleagues, who were permanently stationed in Africa by Imperial Airways, along with the company's own pilots, navigators, mechanics and ground staff, had all come to know Saffron very well over the past three years as she flew back and forth between Nairobi and Roedean, on the northern edge of Johannesburg.

The Imperial Airways Atalanta came to a halt on the landing strip at Nairobi Aerodrome. When she'd emerged from the plane and had her passport stamped, Saffron looked around the tiny terminal that served both departing and arriving passengers before spotting her father and dashing towards him with a jubilant cry of, 'Daddy!' But as she disentangled herself from their hug – that wonderful moment, so long anticipated, when she could relish the feeling of absolute safety that came from having his arms around her and the man-smell of him as she put her head to his chest – she saw a woman, waiting patiently for father and daughter to finish their greeting, clearly waiting to say hello.

She was wearing a loose linen robe that hung to her knees. It was white, but decorated with delicate, brightly coloured embroidered flowers around the neckline and on the hems of the three-quarter-length sleeves. Beneath it she wore pyjama-like trousers, also white, which gathered at the ankle. Her shoes were simple, open sandals. Her short, grey hair was held in place by a silk scarf around her head, she was wearing dark glasses, and she carried an open straw bag, which hung from her shoulder on a leather strap. The grey hair suggested that she must be quite old, but her figure was slim and lithe and there was something about both the way she dressed – which was quite unlike anything Saffron had ever seen before – and the way she carried herself that seemed irrepressibly youthful.

Who is she? Saffron wondered. And then an appalling possibility struck her: *Is this Daddy's surprise? Does he want me to meet his new wife?*

The woman caught her eye, smiled and said, 'Hello, my dear. My name is Saffron Courtney.'

Saffron's head spun: *What did she just say?*

'Saffron . . . meet Saffron,' Leon said, seeing her confusion. 'This is your grandmother, darling. My mother. We named you after her.'

Oh, thank goodness for that! Saffron was hugely relieved, but also dumbfounded. She had never in her life met a grandparent before, and the woman in front of her now wasn't at all the sort of cuddly old creature she'd always imagined as a granny.

'I am so, so pleased to meet you at last,' her grandmother said. 'Come here and give me a hug.'

Saffron did as she was told and found herself enveloped in

a scent that seemed impossibly spicy and mysterious, as if it had been stolen from the innermost chambers of a sultan's harem. With every second that passed, Saffron found herself becoming more captivated by her newfound relative.

'I think your clothes are just wonderful,' she said. 'It's midsummer, but you look as cool as a cucumber.'

Her grandmother smiled. 'Thank you, my dear, how sweet of you to say so. The truth is, I've lived in North Africa all my life and I long ago realized that it was absolutely potty to go around dressed in clothes designed for cold, wet days in England when one was right next door to the Sahara Desert. I know people are always saying that white women can't survive the sun . . . Do people still have that lunatic habit of putting their daughters into hats lined with heavy red felt?'

'Oh yes, lots of girls have to wear those,' Saffron said. 'But I never have.'

'Well, that's because you come from a family that actually knows how to live out here. Personally, I took my cue from what I observed on my travels through Mesopotamia, Ethiopia, Egypt, Morocco . . . all over the place, actually . . . and adapted the local clothes to my tastes and needs. I'm a painter, you see. So I have to have clothes that are comfortable to work in. No corsets. No stockings. Can't be doing with that nonsense, unless I'm forced to dress up.'

'I agree,' said Saffron. 'It's so lovely to get out of school uniforms and starched dresses and spend my holidays in my riding breeches or just some shorts.'

'That's my girl! Now, before we go any further, we need to decide upon names. I know that some grandmothers are happy with "Granny" and "Nanny" or even "Nan" – though not in polite society, I might add. I, however, like to be known as Grandma. So can we agree on that?'

'Absolutely, Grandma,' Saffron said, loving this unexpected chance to say the word.

'Good. And you, my boy, may call me Mother, or if we are feeling particularly friendly, Ma.'

'Yes, Mother,' said Leon, wearily, not noticing the wink his mother had aimed in Saffron's direction.

'Very well then,' Grandma declared. 'You may now take us all to lunch.'

I thought we'd eat at the Stanley,' Leon said as he drove them away from the airport, towards Delamere Road, where the New Stanley Hotel stood. 'The Muthaiga's really not a suitable place for mothers and daughters. It's become even rowdier than usual lately. Chaps swinging from the lights, pretending to be monkeys, getting drunk in public and taking all their clothes off.'

'Oh but I love all that!' Saffron exclaimed. The night she always spent at the Muthaiga before catching the plane to Johannesburg was one of the highlights of the whole journey to school.

'Well, I'm sure your grandmamma would not.'

'Oh Leon, really!' Grandma objected. 'I'm hardly a doddering old maid. I was a married woman by the time I was fifteen, and I'd already lived through the Siege of Khartoum by then, practically seen my poor dear father killed before my eyes and had a few adventures with your own father that really aren't suitable for young ears.'

'Grandma!' Saffron gasped, instantly forgetting about the Muthaiga. 'How could you be married at fifteen? That's not even legal!'

'It is in Abyssinia, which is where your grandfather and I had our wedding. And I may say, it was quite an occasion. The Emperor and Empress themselves attended the service.'

Saffron's eyes opened wide in astonished admiration. 'An Emperor . . . and an Empress?' she gasped.

'Oh yes, my dear, Empress Miriam and I were the best of

189

friends. Like you, she was kind enough to take an interest in the way I dressed. She used to come to me for advice, actually, although in her eyes I was rather an old maid. She'd been married at thirteen, you see.'

'Goodness.'

'How old are you, Saffron?'

'Sixteen, Grandma.'

'A fine age. I was sixteen when your father was born.'

'Oh,' said Saffron, who now understood why her grand-mother looked so unusually youthful.

'Well, anyway,' Leon continued, struggling to lead the conversation back to safer ground, 'Mayence and Fred Tate, who've run the hotel for as long as anyone can remember – good chap, Fred, bumped into him a lot in the war – have just done the place up and I must say they've done an excellent job, and—'

'Were you shocked when Grandpa asked you to marry him?' Saffron asked, ignoring her father.

'Well, it wasn't really a case of him asking me,' Grandma replied. 'You see, what happened was—'

'I really don't think Saffron wants to hear this story,' Leon interrupted.

'Oh yes I do!'

Saffron snuggled deeper into the leather passenger seat, making herself comfortable, feeling very much as she had done as a little girl, safe beneath her blankets as her mother read her a bedtime story as Grandma continued, 'My sister Amber and I were supposed to go to live with your great-uncle Penrod's family, the Ballantynes, at their estate in Scotland, to be brought up as good British girls with a governess. We were due to sail from Djibouti on a ship called the *Singapore*. But I was desperately in love with Ryder Courtney . . .'

'How old was he, Grandma?'

'A little more than twice my age, but I didn't care. I knew he was the love of my life, knew it in the depths of my heart, and I wasn't going to let him go. So I ran away, and the ship had to leave without me. Ryder found me eventually – after I'd sent him off on a false trail down the road to Abyssinia, rather cleverly I thought . . .'

Grandma flashed a cheeky little smile at Saffron, who suddenly saw a glimpse of the impish, rebellious, but adorable girl she must have been. 'The poor man tried to be cross with me but I could see that his heart wasn't in it because I knew that he loved me just as much as I loved him, he just hadn't realized it himself. So I told him that we were to be married and that it was quite all right because I had already spoken to the Empress. She thoroughly approved of the plan and had agreed to sponsor our union, so really there was absolutely no good reason not to get married and he, bless him . . .' Now the smile on Grandma's face was wistful and Saffron thought she could see the beginning of a tear in her eye as Grandma said, 'That darling man said that it was not the worst notion he had ever heard of, and then he kissed me, and I was the happiest girl in the world.'

'Oh, Grandma . . .' Saffron sighed. 'That is such a beautiful story.'

'Don't you worry, my dear, that is only one tiny part of a much, much longer tale and I dare say I will tell you a bit more before I leave.'

'Please, please do, that would be marvellous!'

'Well, here we are,' Leon said with relief, pulling up outside the hotel.

It was a white-painted three-storey building. The entrance was flanked by two towers topped by little cupolas that made them look like a matching pair of pepper grinders. The façade was pierced by high arches that rose up to the first floor to reveal bedrooms set back behind balconies decorated with baskets of brightly coloured flowers. They were to lunch outside, but just before the maître d' escorted them to their table,

Leon said, 'Excuse us one moment,' and then told his mother and daughter, 'Come with me.'

He led them across to an old acacia tree, and when they came closer they saw that the trunk was ringed by a series of cork noticeboards, all of them covered with letters, telegrams, or just pieces of folded paper with names scrawled upon them. 'This is the New Stanley Hotel thorn tree, Nairobi's unofficial post office. If you want to get in touch with someone in Kenya, and you don't know exactly where they are, just stick a message here and sooner or later it will be found.'

'I'd like to stick a message that says, "I'm hungry. Where's lunch?"' Granny said.

'I'm starving too,' Saffron agreed.

They ate well, as one always did in Kenya, for the land was so fertile and the climate so balmy that virtually all fruits and vegetables grew year-round and the huge tracts of grazing produced delicious pork, lamb and beef. Grandma quizzed Saffron about her sporting triumphs, discovering that in the past year she had been the captain of the school hockey and netball teams as well as winning the individual tennis trophy.

'She also rides as well as any horseman I've ever seen. She can hit a gamebird on the wing like Dead-Eye Dick's little sister. And not only can she drive a car, she also knows how to change a tyre, top up the oil or water . . .'

'And I know how to turn one of my stockings into a fan-belt!' Saffron added.

'I wouldn't let her set off around the estate unless she could manage a few basic running repairs,' Leon explained. 'Can't have her being helpless if she has a breakdown while she's miles from home.'

'I see . . .' said Grandma thoughtfully. 'Tell me, Saffron, have your lessons been going well, too?'

'I think so, Grandma. I'm just waiting for my exam results. I think they shouldn't be too bad.'

'What she means is she's hoping for Distinctions all round,' beamed Leon.

'Good . . . good . . .' Grandma said, though she sounded surprisingly unimpressed, for a woman who had just been informed that her granddaughter was both a sporting and academic paragon. 'Tell me dear girl, since you are so formidably well educated, what do the following three people have in common: Elsa Schiaparelli, Main Rousseau Bocher and Madeleine Vionnet?'

Saffron was flummoxed. She glanced towards her father but he simply shrugged as if to say, 'I haven't got a clue.'

'Umm . . .' she desperately wracked her brain, remembered that Grandma was a painter and took a guess. 'Are they all artists?'

'In a manner of speaking, I suppose you could say they are. But what sort of artists?'

'Uh . . . Uh . . .' Saffron's voice rose in something close to panic. 'Sculptors? Painters?' Desperately she tried to think: *What other kinds of artists are there?*

'They are all couturiers,' Grandma said, and then, realizing from the continued look of bafflement on Saffron's face that she did not know what a couturier was, added, 'They create very beautiful, expensive, perfectly made-to-measure dresses and evening gowns for rich and fashionable women.'

'Oh,' said Saffron, feeling utterly crestfallen.

'And you, my darling child, would look utterly ravishing in any of their creations, which is why they would fight to have you as their customer. Do you have any idea at all how perfectly lovely-looking you are, Saffron? . . . No, one look at your face tells me that you don't.' She turned towards her son. 'Leon, your daughter is a marvel. You have provided for her as well as any father could. You have given her a splendid education. Your love for her is as delightfully obvious as hers for you. The one thing you have not done, because you could not possibly do it, is to show her how to be a woman.'

'If Eva hadn't died . . .' Leon began, and then fell silent.

Grandma reached out her hand and placed it on her son's arm. 'I know, darling, I know . . . You suffered a terrible loss and you have been nothing short of heroic, raising a daughter and, by the way, keeping your mother and sisters very well provided for too. Courtney Trading seems to be flourishing.'

Leon grinned with relief. 'Yes, things have been picking up lately. The world's still a long way from being properly back on its feet. But I think we're actually ahead of the pack. All the bankers have been paid off ahead of schedule, so we're debt-free. It's Davy you should be thanking, though, Ma. He did all the hard work. I just signed the cheques.'

'Well, he couldn't have done it if you hadn't come to our rescue. That was a very fine thing you did, Leon, even if not everyone recognizes the fact. Now, I'm going to take Saffy off to do some shopping.'

'What for?' asked Saffron, wondering whether her grandmother was suddenly going to make expensive hand-made dresses appear by magic in the modest little shops of Nairobi.

'Christmas presents!' announced Grandma decisively. 'Have you bought your father one yet?'

'Actually . . . no.'

'I suspected as much. Now, Leon, you stay here and have a nice cup of coffee, chat to your chums in the Long Bar – I'm quite sure you know half the men there – and generally pass the time until we ladies return. Saffron?'

'Yes, Grandma?'

'Follow me!'

Saffron was thrilled by the sudden arrival in her life of this extraordinary woman. First she had met Cousin Centaine, now Grandma Saffron. Bit by bit a proper family, with all sorts of relations, was starting to assemble itself around her. Together they went off and browsed the shops in the new Stanley Arcade, set into one outside wall of the hotel. In one of the shops, which sold menswear, Saffron went off in one direction, to look at a rack of ties that might provide a possible candidate for a present, while Grandma busied herself elsewhere. Saffron was just running a couple of rather beautiful, brightly patterned silk ties through her hands, wondering whether she could ever persuade her father to wear one, when she heard a harsh, female voice say, 'You must be the Courtney girl. My, haven't you grown up?'

Saffron turned around to see a woman whose type was all too familiar in Kenya. She had obviously once been quite pretty and from her haughty attitude, extravagantly coiffed, bright blonde hair and thick make-up she believed that her looks were still intact. But that fatal combination of too much sun and far too many drinks over rather more years than she would care to admit had left her skin as leathery as her crocodile-skin handbag. There were deep wrinkles around her eyes and her top lip was grooved with the lines that come from being so often pursed around a cigarette.

'I'm sorry,' said Saffron. 'I don't think we've been introduced.'

'I dare say you're right,' the woman said. 'My name is Amelia Cory-Porter. I used to know your father, briefly. He made quite a pass at me, as a matter of fact.'

I don't believe that, Saffron thought, and then something in the bitterness of the older woman's voice told her, *but I bet you made a pass at him, didn't you? And I bet he blanked you, too.*

'Really?' she replied. 'How interesting.'

Amelia Cory-Porter looked at Saffron with something she had rarely if ever before encountered in her life: undiluted malice. 'By God, you're as arrogant and full of yourself as he was, too. Look at you, pretty as a picture, rolling in money. Who'd ever guess that your mother was a tart?'

The words hit Saffron like a punch to the gut. It was as if all the air had been knocked from her body. She could hardly breathe. Somehow she managed to gasp, 'No she wasn't.'

'Oh, I'm afraid she very much was, my dear. She made her living spreading her legs for some fat German until she decided she fancied a bit of younger meat and set her sights on your father. Poor chap didn't know what hit him, from what I heard.'

'No, no she wasn't like that,' Saffron sobbed. 'She wasn't like that!'

Through her tears, Saffron saw her grandma coming towards her and heard her asking, 'What on earth is going on here?'

'She . . . she . . . she said Mummy was a tart,' Saffron sobbed.

'I think I'll be going now,' said Amelia Cory-Porter.

'Stay right there!' Grandma commanded in a voice that would have made presidents and generals halt their stride. 'What on earth do you think you are doing, reducing a sweet young girl to tears with such vile filth?'

'You call it filth, I say it's nothing but the truth. Her mother was a German's whore. She was a tart . . . and a traitor too.'

Grandma took another step closer to Amelia. 'I dare say you'd know a thing or two about sleeping with men for money, yourself, though by the look of you you're probably finding it rather harder to work up any interest these days.'

'I'm not going to stay here and listen to rubbish like that.'

'You are going to stay here until I tell you to go. Now, listen here, you common little minx, if you spread another word of this vile slander to anyone, anyone at all, our family will come after you with every legal means at our disposal, and we will ruin you, utterly and completely. Do I make myself clear?'

'I really don't think there's any need to make threats . . .'

'I will ask you again: have I clearly conveyed the consequences of any further vile slanders?'

Amelia Cory-Porter seemed to be deflating before her eyes, like a balloon filled with poison gas that had just been pricked by a sharp pin. 'Yes,' she muttered.

'Good. Now, consider this . . . my son, Leon Courtney, is at this moment less than two hundred yards away. He is an exceptionally decent, honourable gentleman, but when he hears what you have said to his daughter he may not be able to stop himself giving you the thrashing you so soundly deserve.'

'Well, I think I should be going then,' Amelia said, though she did not actually move.

'Yes, I think you should. And I'd go a long way away, too, if I were you. Now, be gone with you. And pray to God I never set eyes on you again.'

'Thank you, Grandma,' Saffron said, watching Amelia Cory-Porter scuttle out of the shop. 'But all those horrible things she said . . . I have to know if they're true.'

Leon waited until they had all returned safely to Lusima and had a light supper before he took his mother and daughter into his study, the most private and intimate corner of the house. His mahogany desk stood by the bay window, facing inwards into the room. One wall was entirely covered in bookcases, an open fireplace dominated another. Above the mantelpiece hung a portrait of Eva, painted a year after Saffron's birth. The artist was a White Russian called Vassileyev who had fled the Revolution, washed up on the shores of Kenya and made a modest living from the commissions he obtained from the expatriate community and tourists. Vassileyev did not pretend to be anything more than a jobbing painter, yet in this one work he had excelled himself, for he had perfectly caught Eva's beauty, and also the joy in her heart. Here was a young woman, blissfully married, with a baby she adored, living in paradise and preserved in all her perfection forever.

Leon made sure that Saffron and his mother were comfortably settled and provided with drinks: a good, stiff whisky for Grandma and a small gin with a lot of tonic and lemon for Saffron. He poured himself a brandy and placed himself by the fire. For some reason he didn't feel that this was a tale he could

197

recount sitting down. He wanted to be able to move and work off a little of the tension that telling it would generate. He sipped his brandy slowly as he looked up at Eva's portrait. Even now, almost a decade after her passing, his love for her had not dimmed. 'Please forgive me, my darling,' he whispered to the picture. Then he turned to face his audience.

'I had always hoped, perhaps naively, that I would never have to tell you what you now want to know,' Leon began. He spoke slowly, choosing his words carefully and bestowing upon them a certain formality. 'This was in part because some of what I have to say concerns matters that are officially classified. I am about to break the law by speaking about them to you, and you both will break the law if you discuss them with anyone else. And I really do mean anyone else at all, ever. So first, I must ask you both to promise, on your words of honour, never to repeat a word of what you hear tonight. Do you promise me that, Saffron?'

'Yes, Father,' she replied, with equal seriousness.

'And you, Mother?'

'Yes, of course dear, I quite understand.'

'Very well, then . . . There was a second reason why I hoped that this moment would never come, Saffron, and that is because I know how much it would upset your mother. She was the love of my life. She was as brave as she was beautiful. She brought me more happiness than I ever dreamed possible. She gave me you, my darling, the finest daughter any man could wish for, and she loved you with all her heart, as she loved me too.'

'I know, Daddy,' said Saffron, and her eyes filled with welling tears.

'She was also a true patriot. You already know that she served the British Empire during the war and was decorated for her valour . . .'

'Yes.'

198

'But what you don't know is that she served the Empire before the war too.'

'May one ask how?' Grandma inquired.

Leon nodded, 'Yes, on this one night you may.' He took another drink from his brandy and then said, 'Eva was a spy, an agent for the Secret Service Bureau, in its foreign espionage department, or the Secret Intelligence Service as they call it nowadays. So now I hope you understand why this is all top secret.'

'Good heavens,' Grandma said as Saffron asked, 'What kind of a spy?'

'I'm coming to that, but first you need to know a little about Eva's background. She was born in Northumberland. Her father, Peter, was English but her mother was German – you must remember, Saffron, that in those days the links between England and Germany were very strong, and our two countries were not enemies. Her parents were not rich, but they loved each other and they loved her, so she grew up in a happy home. But then, when she was twelve, her parents both contracted a disease called polio myelitis. Eva's mother died . . .' Leon looked at Saffron. 'Yes, I know, to think that Mummy would herself die young is almost unbearable. Her father survived the disease but it left him crippled. His legs withered away and he was confined to a wheelchair.'

Leon paused to finish off his brandy. He placed the empty glass on the mantelpiece above the fireplace, looked up at Eva's portrait for moral support and went on. 'Your mother, like you, Saffy, was a bright girl and had the chance to go to Edinburgh University, but she turned the offer down because she wanted to stay at home and care for her father.'

Leon paused and gave a wistful smile.

'What is it, Daddy?' Saffron asked.

'Oh, nothing, I just remembered Mummy saying that she called her father "Curly" because he didn't have a hair on his head. Anyway, Curly was a brilliant engineer and inventor, and he came up with brilliant ideas for high-powered internal combustion engines. He patented his designs, but he didn't have the money to develop them and bring them into production. But a German industrialist did have the money. He offered Curly a partnership and waved a contract under his nose. Curly, being a boffin, didn't know the first thing about contracts and he couldn't afford a lawyer, so he put his name to the contract and, to cut a long story short, signed away all his rights to his life's work and his patents. The German went away and made his already massive fortune even larger, while poor Curly died in poverty.'

No need to tell her how he died, Leon thought to himself. *Blowing his brains out with a shotgun, Eva having to clean the bloodstains off the wall.*

'Your mother was sixteen – your age – at the time, and she was left all alone in the world, penniless, with no one to look after her,' he said.

'Oh, but that's awful!' cried Saffron. 'Why didn't the German take care of her? He'd made so much money out of Curly's inventions. He could afford it.'

'He could indeed, but he had the hardest, meanest, cruellest heart of any man I ever met.'

'You met him? How?'

'Wait, my darling. All in good time . . . Now, young Eva had to find some way to support herself, so she went to work as a factory girl in a nearby mill. But then, one day, a woman called Mrs Ryan arrived at her doorstep, saying that she had known Eva's mother, had heard of the tragic events of the past few years and wanted to help. Eva went to live in Mrs Ryan's house in London. Mrs Ryan was a firm believer in the greatness of the British Empire. She used to talk endlessly about what a blessing the Empire was to the world and what a privilege it was to serve it, if one was ever called upon to do so. And Eva agreed, because she was suddenly enjoying all the benefits of living in the Empire's capital city. She had her own room, all nicely furnished; smart clothes; a tutor to teach her etiquette; a riding master and her own horse – a filly called Hyperion. All in all she soon became a very proper young gentlewoman. She also had German lessons. That was the one thing Mrs Ryan absolutely insisted upon – daily German lessons.

'What your mother did not know, however, was that she was being trained. You see, there are many ways in which a spy network can obtain secret information. It can infiltrate enemy organizations with its own agents, operating undercover. It can bribe, persuade or blackmail enemy personnel to betray their own cause. It can beat or torture enemy captives. Or it can take advantage of the male sex's irrepressible desire to impress, seduce and conquer the female of the species, particularly if she is very, very beautiful.

'Eva, of course, was incomparably lovely. She was also very bright – she could have gone to university, remember. And finally, she was burning with the desire to avenge her father and right the wrong that had been done to him. All this made her extremely useful to the Secret Intelligence Service. For by now, the political winds had shifted. The Germans were making no secret of their desire to challenge the British and take over the mantle of the world's greatest power. Germany's armed forces were expanding at a tremendous rate, as was its armaments industry, part of which was owned by the very man who had stolen Curly Barry's designs. So Eva Barry was given a new identity. She became a haughty German aristocrat called Eva von Wellberg. She was introduced to the man who had ruined her father and . . .' Leon paused, steeled himself, took a deep breath and said, 'and she became his mistress.'

Saffron could not help herself. 'So she *was* a tart!' she sobbed. 'That horrible woman was right.'

Grandma took her in her arms. 'No, darling, she wasn't . . .

201

that's not what your father is saying at all. Sometimes, we women have to make very hard choices. We do what we must to survive, as my own sisters did when they were prisoners of the Mahdi, after the fall of Khartoum. Or we do what our country requires of us. We can't fight with our fists or guns in the way men do, so . . .'

'So we become prostitutes?'

'That's quite enough!' Leon snapped. 'I will not have you talking about your mother like that. She did something she knew was rotten because it had to be done. Look at me . . . look at me, girl!'

Saffron raised her head from her grandmother's embrace and turned her eyes back to her father.

'I have killed more men in the service of my country than I care to think about,' Leon said. 'Killed them with these hands. I've left them crying for their mothers, bleeding their lives away into the dirt. So if your mother is a prostitute, then I am a murderer, and a mass murderer at that. But I know that I did what I did in a just cause, serving my King, standing up for freedom and decency, just as my darling Eva did too. And how some cheap little tramp like Amelia Cory-Porter has the brass nerve to throw vicious accusations at your mother, who had more goodness and decency in her little finger than that woman has in her whole raddled body, is completely beyond me.'

For a moment no one said anything. Saffron looked at her father, trying to make sense of everything she'd heard. There had been so much to take in. And she'd never heard anything like the way he had spoken just then, with so much raw passion. Her breathing calmed and her tears stopped flowing. 'Here . . .' Leon said, taking the silk handkerchief out of his lapel pocket and handing it to her. She used it to wipe her eyes and nose and handed it back. She sniffed, gave him a brave smile and said, 'At least now I know what to buy you for Christmas.'

'A man can never have too many handkerchiefs,' Leon agreed.

'Might I ask how the story of Eva and the mysterious German ended?' Grandma asked.

'The two of them came on safari to East Africa, just a few months before the war. I was their guide. Eva and I fell in love. When the safari ended, she had to go back to Germany and we both feared that was the end for us. But then the war broke out, and the Germans conceived a plan to join up with the old Boer rebels in South Africa and rise up against British rule. The rebels needed arms and money to pay troops. Eva's German industrialist had just the means of getting the cargo to them much more quickly than any conventional means of transport – a mighty airship, even bigger than a Zeppelin, called the *Assegai*. He insisted on commanding the expedition and on taking his mistress with him, unaware that she was spying for the enemy and had alerted us of the plan. I intercepted the *Assegai*. I didn't have the means to shoot her down so I dropped fishing nets down onto her engines, tangled up the propellers and crippled her that way.'

'But Mummy was on board!' Saffron exclaimed.

'She wasn't supposed to be. I saw her just as I was making my attack.'

'And you went ahead, anyway?'

'Yes, of course. I had no choice. It was my duty. We both understood that.'

'But Mummy survived . . . how?'

'Thanks to the one decent thing that damn German ever did. He stuck a parachute harness on her and threw her off the airship.'

'Did he die on his airship?'

Leon thought for a moment. *Should I tell her? Why make things even worse? But how can I let Eva be the only one who bears any blame?*

'No,' he said. 'He had a parachute too. It got caught in some trees, just before he landed. Mummy found him hanging there, wriggling as helplessly as a fish on a line, but she didn't have the heart to kill him in cold blood. Some of his men came up and captured her. He was about to give her a very nasty, painful death when I came upon the scene.'

'Did you . . .' Saffron could not finish the sentence.

'Yes, girl, I did. I shot that bastard through the chest and have never suffered a single second of remorse since. He deserved it. And as he roasts away in Hades he should count himself lucky that I got to him before Manyoro did, or his death would have been a lot longer, drawn-out and infinitely more painful.'

'Ah, Leon, how like your father you are . . .' Grandma sighed. 'He would have loved that story, and understood it perfectly, too: both your role and Eva's. But tell me, how much money was this airship carrying?'

'Approximately five million German marks, in gold coins.'

'How much would that be in pounds sterling?'

'A little less than two million.'

'And was it ever recovered?'

'Yes.'

'Who by?'

Leon said nothing.

'Ahh . . .' said his mother, putting one and one together and coming up with two million.

'Oh . . .' said Saffron, suddenly understanding why she lived on such a magnificent estate. Then her brows furrowed as a thought struck her and she said, 'Daddy?'

'Yes?'

'You never told us what the German man was called.'

Leon paused, thought for a moment and then said, 'I don't suppose there's any reason now not to tell you, not after you've heard everything else . . . Very well, then, his name was von Meerbach. Count Otto von Meerbach, to be precise.'

*　*　*

Three days before Christmas, as they were all sitting around the breakfast table, one of the house staff came in bearing a telegram for Leon, sent to him by the headmistress of Roedean. It read:

PLEASED REPORT SAFFRON EXAM RESULTS. FOUR CREDITS, SIX DISTINCTIONS (INC DOMSCI FUNNIEST). SPLENDID.

'Well done, you brilliant girl, well done!' he exulted, reaching out his hand to squeeze hers. 'I couldn't be more proud of you.' He leaned back in his chair and took another, puzzled look at the piece of paper in his hand. 'There's only one thing I don't quite understand. What on earth is "domsci"? And what's so funny about it?'

Now it was Saffron's turn to be baffled. 'I don't have any idea, Daddy. May I have a look?'

Leon handed the telegram over to his daughter and watched her face go from frowning concentration to wide-eyed horror as she gasped, 'Oh no!' followed in immediate succession by helpless fits of the giggles.

'I'm sorry,' he said, 'but would someone please tell me what on earth is going on?'

'Oh, Daddy, don't look so worried!' Saffron laughed. 'D-O-M-S-C-I is short for "domestic science". Miss Lawrence knows I hated it. So it's funny that I ended up doing quite well.'

'You did a lot better than "quite well". I'd have given my eye teeth to get a Distinction in anything at all.'

'You could have got any result you wanted in any subject you chose, dear boy, if only you had also chosen to do some work,' Grandma pointed out. 'There was never anything wrong with your brain, merely your desire to actually use it.'

'I was an idle young beggar, wasn't I?' Leon admitted. 'So, now that you've got these wonderful exam results, what are you going to do with them? Back to Roedean for Sixth Form, I suppose?'

'Hmm . . . yes . . . in a way . . .' Saffron said, mysteriously.

'What do you mean, "in a way"?' Leon asked.

'Well, I do want to go to Roedean for Sixth Form . . . but I want to go to Roedean in England.' Saffron saw her father was about to say something, but kept talking, determined not to let him get a word in until she'd made her case, particularly since her opening gambit had been carefully calculated to make it almost impossible for her father to deny her. 'The thing is,' she said, 'I've been thinking a lot about what I want to do, and I was so sad when you told me about Mummy, who never went to university, even though she was clever enough. It was awful that she never had the chance to show what she could do as a student. So I think it's really important that I should make the best of my ability and my opportunities.'

'I agree,' said Leon, though there was a hesitation in his voice that betrayed his strong sense that his clever little girl was laying a very large trap, into which she expected him to fall.

'So I've been talking to some of the mistresses at Roedean and they've been telling me about their sister school in England. Apparently it's tremendously strong academically, even more than the one in Jo'burg, and it sends tons of girls off to university, including Oxford and Cambridge.'

'You are not going to Oxford!' Leon snapped, suddenly seeing precisely why she'd been leading him on. 'It's a nest of cowards, traitors and Reds. I absolutely forbid it!'

Saffron groaned inwardly. She hadn't forgotten her father's letter on the subject, but she had hoped that for once in his life he might have moderated his opinion just a little. 'For goodness sakes, Daddy, all the people who voted in that silly debate must have left Oxford by now. All I care about is that it's one of the greatest universities in the world.'

'Well go to one of the other greatest universities then.'

'I can't. Oxford is the only one that has the course I want to do.'

'What's that, then: waving the white flag?'

'Oh for heaven's sake, Leon, don't be so ridiculous,' said Grandma. 'What on earth has put these silly ideas into your head?'

'There's nothing silly about them at all, Mother. You must know perfectly well that the Oxford Union voted that its members would never, under any circumstance, fight for their King and country. I'm sorry, but that's simply unacceptable. Too many fine young men died fighting to keep us free, including some damn good friends of mine. It's just an insult to their sacrifice for the next generation to turn into a bunch of bloody conshies.'

'Is it?' Grandma asked. 'I should have thought that a conscientious objection to war was the only decent, moral response to its horror. You forget, my dear, I grew up with war. I saw it destroy my childhood home. It took my father and, indirectly, my oldest sister. When I became a mother it turned my second son from a kind, loving, delightful boy into a bitter and twisted man. I'm sure that if, God forbid, there should ever come a time when the British Empire needs defending from another barbarian horde, the young men of England will do their part, just as they always have done. But for now, let them stand up for peace. There's not a woman on earth who wouldn't applaud them for it.'

Saffron's head had been turning from her father to her grandmother and now back to her father again, like a spectator at a tennis match watching the ball hit from one end to the other. Leon took a deep breath, composed himself and then said, 'Look, Ma, I know how utterly vile war is. It was bad enough charging round East Africa after von Lettow. God only knows how much worse it was for the poor chaps in the trenches. And yes, it's terrible to see what's become of Frank. But it's just not right for young men now to turn their backs and say,

"That's not for me." It makes us veterans wonder what any of it was for.'

'It was for the freedom to have debates and speak out on both sides and vote on the result, my darling,' said Grandma, with a much gentler, more comforting tone to her voice. 'You fought so that those young men could say their piece. And you also fought so that your daughter could make her own way in the world. So, Saffron, tell us why you want to go to Oxford, and why your father should doubtless have to pay a handsome sum for you to be able to do so.'

Greatly relieved that peace seemed to have broken out again, Saffron said, 'Well, Daddy has his estate and all his business interests and eventually he'll need someone else to run them, and he doesn't have a son, so . . . well, I just thought I should to be prepared, in case I ever have to do it. And Oxford has a course called P.P.E., which stands for Philosophy, Politics and Economics, which I think would be terribly interesting, and also really useful.'

'Given the fact that your father's business interests now stretch all the way from the gold and diamond mines of South Africa to the oilfields of Mesopotamia, an understanding of economics will indeed be essential,' Grandma said. 'And since his assets in Abyssinia, obtained by his father from the Emperor himself when we were very first married, are now threatened by that ghastly little man Signor Mussolini, I should say that you may well be in need of a grasp of politics too. A study of philosophy should make you a more logical and even more moral thinker. Well done, Saffron. That's a first-rate idea.'

'Thank you, Grandma. But Daddy . . . do you really own all those things?'

'I have shares in a family firm that has those interests, yes.'

'I had no idea that there was, well . . . so much. I just thought it was the estate and . . . actually I'm not sure what else I thought there was.'

'That was exactly what I'd hoped you would think, Saffy. I didn't want you growing up a spoiled little rich girl, who only thinks about money and how to spend it. That's not what life should be about.'

'I don't think money matters at all, Daddy, really I don't.'

'Well, it matters when you don't have any, believe me. But I know what you mean, my darling, and I'm very pleased you feel that way. Now, Ma, you evidently approve of Saffron's plan to go to Oxford – although I imagine it's extremely hard to get in, so we can't take it for granted. What do you think about her going to school in England first?'

Grandma smiled, 'Well, I'm a fine one to talk, since I spurned the chance to go there myself. Mind you, I was desperately in love, and my man was in Africa, so that was rather different. You aren't secretly planning to marry a much older lover, are you, Saffy?'

'No Grandma, I am absolutely not!' Saffron laughed.

'Just as well. It was a miracle my marriage worked as well as it did. But to answer your question, Leon, I think it's a splendid idea. Whether or not money is a good thing, Saffron is going to inherit an awful lot of it, and the social position that comes with that. She needs to learn how to act like a British gentlewoman, rather than an African tomboy.'

'I say, Ma, that's rather harsh!' Leon objected. 'She's a perfectly lovely girl.'

'Of course she is. But at this precise moment, she would be as out of place and ill-equipped in a smart Mayfair cocktail party as a London debutante would be if you picked her up and dropped her in the middle of the African bush.'

'I would much rather be in the bush . . .' Saffron sighed.

'I'm sure you would and I have no doubt you could cope without the slightest trouble. But you need to learn about the supposedly civilized world, too, because it's every bit as much of a jungle. The predators – male and female alike – have just as sharp claws as any lion or cheetah, and just as hungry appetites.'

'That sounds awful. I'm not sure I want to go now.'

'Yes, you do. Life in a city like London, or Paris, or even Cairo can be wonderfully stimulating, exciting, thrilling . . . Oh, my dear, what I would give to be as young and as pretty as you. You will have the whole world at your feet and it will be the most marvellous feeling in the world. You just have to know the rules of the game. And you'll never learn them living out here in the back of beyond.'

'I just want to get away from horrible old women like Amelia Cory-Porter. I hate the way it is here, everyone knowing everyone else, sticking their noses into each other's business, spreading beastly lies about other people.'

'I'm afraid you'll find women like her wherever you go,' Grandma said. 'And men who are utter rotters and scoundrels too. But it's different in a great city. You have more room to be yourself. No one can watch you as closely as they can in a smaller community.'

'Then I do want to go . . . Please, Daddy, do you think you might say I can?'

'Well,' said Leon, thoughtfully, and Saffron beamed in delight because she knew from that moment that he wasn't going to say, 'No.'

'If I recall correctly, the British school year begins in September,' Leon continued. 'So that means you wouldn't be able to start for nine months. The question is, what should you do until then?'

'Why do I have to wait until September to go back to school?' Saffron asked. 'I'll be seventeen by then and nineteen by the time I leave. That's too old to be at school. I'd rather start right away.'

'But you will have missed a term, so you'll be behind the other girls,' Leon pointed out.

'Then I'll just have to work harder and catch up. I'd rather that than be the old maid of the class.'

'You are no one's idea of an old maid, my dear,' Grandma pointed out. 'But I do take your point.' She thought for a moment. 'You must go with her, Leon. And when you get to England, stay there for a few months. Speaking as one of your shareholders, albeit a very minor one, I believe it's time Courtney Trading had a London office. Perhaps you could set it up while Saffron spends her first two terms at school, and then you could both go travelling around Europe in the summer.'

'That would be wonderful!' Saffron enthused.

'Very well, then, that's settled.'

'Hold on a minute,' Leon interjected. 'We don't know whether Saffron can go to school in England. They may not have a place for her. Even if they do, everything has to be organized in a couple of weeks. She can't just turn up and say, "Let me in!"'

'My darling boy,' said Grandma, 'this is the modern age. There are telegrams and telephones with which to communicate and aeroplanes to take you halfway around the world in a matter of days. Use your initiative, Leon. Get in touch with the headmistress in Jo'burg, ask her to pull strings, make a discreet donation as a parting gift to the school if that helps oil the wheels. You have always been able to achieve whatever you wanted, when you put your mind to it. So . . .'

'I'll put my mind to it,' Leon said.

Leon made calls, sent telegrams, pulled strings and booked tickets. By the second of January 1936, with school due to start on the sixth, he and Saffron were both in London. But after a couple of days in London, Saffron was wondering whether she'd made the right decision to come to England. The weather was cold and damp and grey. The pavements were covered with a slurry of semi-molten slush and grime. They could see Green

211

Park from their hotel window, but as she looked at the mono-chrome tones of the dead grass, the bare trees and the footpaths, Saffron moaned, 'It looks more like Grey Park to me.'

The sun never seemed to shine in the daytime and thick, choking fogs, heavy with the smell of car fumes and coal fires, descended at night, making it impossible to see more than a few feet into the murk. The filthy air seemed to have seeped into the buildings, so that all the great monuments to which her father dutifully took her, from Buckingham Palace to Westminster Abbey and St Paul's Cathedral, all the great department stores, all the government offices on Whitehall were stained in shades from pigeon grey to a blackness so deep and dirty that they seemed to be hewn from coal, rather than constructed in brick or stone. The greyness was reflected in the dullness of the clothes people wore, the pallor of their complexions and the tasteless food they ate. Even the last few Christmas decorations still hanging in shop windows or draped across the streets seemed to have been leached of all their festive colours. And however much Saffron had been overwhelmed at first by the size of Johannesburg, London was on a different scale altogether.

Coming into the centre of the city from Croydon Aerodrome they drove for mile after mile past identical streets of terraced houses and one town centre after another: each clustered around an Underground station; each with its own municipal hall, library, baths, shops, pubs and restaurants; each with streets more crowded than any Saffron had ever seen, and each just one of a myriad separate suburbs of the great, sprawling city.

Leon did his best to show his daughter the very finest that the centre of the Empire had to offer. He booked a suite of rooms at the Ritz, which was gloriously indulgent, with a bedroom for each of them, huge beds with mattresses thick and comfortable enough for the fussiest princess and a bathroom that shone with the reflections from the polished marble walls and floor and the gleaming chrome of the baths and taps. He took her to the London Palladium, to see the Crazy Gang, and even though she did not have the first idea who all the performers were, nor why the audience lapped up their catch-phrases with such delight and obvious familiarity, still she found herself caught up in the atmosphere and was soon laughing and clapping along with everyone else. Leon also discovered the joys of the Lyon's Corner House tearooms that seemed to be present on half the streets of central London. 'They know how to make a proper cup of tea here,' he said approvingly. 'Good and strong, in a simple cup, reminds me of the army.' But even so, though both Saffron and Leon did their best to keep their spirits up, they both had the same thought repeating itself in their minds: *I wish I were back in Kenya.*

But they had both come too far to change their minds now, even if that were something that ever came easily to either of them. So they had to make the best of it. Once again Leon found himself heading off with Saffron on another expedition to buy yet more school uniforms and equipment and, having asked the Ritz concierge where one went for such things in London, was directed to Daniel Neal, the leading light in school outfitting, whose flagship store was in Portman Square, just north of Oxford Street.

'Goodness, it's huge!' Saffron said as they emerged from the taxi and found themselves confronted by three plate-glass windows, each as wide as a typical London townhouse and all decorated with mannequins of impeccably dressed schoolchildren. The shop filled the ground and first floor along half the length of a massive modern mansion block that took up most of one side of the square.

'Well, I think we can assume it will have everything you need,' said Leon, who was keen to buy the maximum number of necessary items in the minimum number of shops and the smallest possible time. 'Come on, let's find out.'

They walked in and then stopped dead as they looked around and tried to work out where on earth they could find everything they required. Across the floor they could see a woman in a smart black dress. Her back was turned to them, but she was clearly giving instructions to one of the shop assistants.

'That's the ticket, someone in authority,' said Leon and started making his way towards her. By now the woman had sent her underling on her way but, clearly being the kind of perfectionist who noticed the smallest fault and felt bound to correct it, was bending over a table, making fractional adjustments to a display of jumpers.

'Excuse me, Miss,' said Leon. 'My daughter and I need assistance.'

The woman straightened and turned to face them. A puzzled expression crossed her face, the look of someone who has just seen something or someone in an entirely unfamiliar context yet knows that they are familiar, but can't quite work out how.

A similar bafflement, now turning to mutual embarrassment as both grown-ups found themselves in the same predicament, had seized Leon and for a moment he and the woman both just stared at one another, neither knowing quite what to say.

And then Saffron realized exactly who the woman was.

Miss Halfpenny! It's me, Saffron Courtney . . . from Jo'burg. I went to Roedean.'

The manageress's face was at once lit up by a warm, engaging smile. 'Of course! I knew I remembered you . . . and your father, too.'

'Leon Courtney,' he said, holding out a hand. 'I don't believe we've ever been properly introduced.'

'Harriet Halfpenny . . .' She frowned. 'Hmm . . . I'm not sure whether I should be quite so familiar with customers, but it really is an unexpected delight to see you both again. May I ask what brings you here?'

'The same as brought us to the last shop we saw you in: school uniforms for Saffron.'

'May I ask which school in particular?'

'The same one, Roedean,' said Saffron. 'Except this one's in England.'

'Very well then, you will need a blue blazer, blue skirts, white shirts and a tie striped according to your house colours.'

'I don't know what house I'm going to be in. It's all been awfully sudden,' said Saffron.

'Never mind, I'm sure you can get the right one at the school itself. You'll also be requiring shoes, stockings, gym kits, of course, as well as nighties. We only have a limited range of those, I'm afraid, I suggest Selfridges or John Lewis if you want a wider selection, and likewise for dressing gowns and undies.'

'Oh Lord . . .' groaned Leon.

Miss Halfpenny looked at Leon, then turned her eyes towards Saffron, who gave a little shrug that said, 'No, it's still just the two of us.'

'Would you like me to take care of everything, Mr Courtney?' Miss Halfpenny asked. 'As I recall, Saffron and I used to manage pretty well by ourselves.'

Leon was about to agree, but then changed his mind. 'Actually, I think I'll come with you. When I think of all the dangers I've faced like a man, it seems a bit feeble to run away from a bit of shopping.'

'Well said, sir!' Miss Halfpenny said, with a little clap of her hands. Leon looked delighted by the compliment and Saffron, observing the way the pair of them were grinning at one another, suddenly realized that her school uniform was suddenly a very long way from being the most important thing about their shopping expedition.

She thought about the care her father had taken to dress smartly and look well groomed on the days when they had visited the school shop in Johannesburg, and of his disappointment when he was told that Miss Halfpenny had been forced to return to England. She thought of all the women who had told her that they would be her friend: *But Miss Halfpenny already is my friend. I really like her because I know how nice she is.*

As they went round the shop Saffron did everything she could to include her father in her conversations with Miss Halfpenny and was delighted when he said things that made her laugh or say, 'Quite right, Mr Courtney.' It struck Saffron that she was seeing a completely new side to her father. He was relaxed with Miss Halfpenny, more ready to laugh at himself and even flirtatious in a way that was really quite sweet because he was so obviously unaware he was doing it. *She makes him happy,* Saffron thought. And then, *But what would people say if Leon Courtney married a shopgirl?* And then, *Who cares what anyone else thinks? She's the right person for him, that's all that matters. In any case she's not a shopgirl, she's a manageress. And Daddy hates snobs, anyway, so that's that.*

By the time Miss Halfpenny was ringing up all Saffron's new clothes at the till, while assorted underlings packed them away in carrier bags, Saffron had decided that it was her job to keep the two grown-ups as close to one another as possible for as long as it took for them both to realize what was best for them. She was just pondering how to do this when Miss Halfpenny said, 'There are an awful lot of bags. If you don't want to be troubled with them I can have them sent round to wherever you're staying.'

'Thank you,' said Leon. 'We're at the . . .'

'Oh, don't you worry, Daddy, I'm sure we can manage,' Saffron interrupted, feeling absolutely certain that if Miss Halfpenny knew they were staying at the Ritz, she would immediately feel that they were far above her station and abandon any thought of romance.

'Oh, well, if you don't mind lugging a couple of bags yourself, darling.'

'Not at all,' said Saffron and then, feeling that strong and purposeful action was required, said, 'Would you like to have tea with us, when you finish work, Miss Halfpenny? It would be so nice for us to talk to someone else who knows Africa. And Daddy has developed an absolute passion for Lyon's Corner Houses.'

'I quite agree, they're admirable institutions,' said Miss Halfpenny. 'But I don't get off until five, and I'm sure you have better things to do this afternoon than take tea with me.'

Leon didn't say anything. Saffron, who was standing next to him, with the counter between them and Miss Halfpenny, gave him a hefty kick on the ankles, just as if she were booting a horse into action.

'Nonsense!' he said, nobly resisting the temptation to kick his daughter right back. 'I can't think of anything more pleasant.'

Miss Halfpenny pondered the invitation. 'Is Piccadilly Circus at all convenient for you?' she asked.

'Absolutely. It's just down the road from our hotel.'

'Very well, then,' said Miss Halfpenny, becoming her usual, businesslike self again. 'Do you know the Trocadero on Piccadilly Circus? It has a magnificent entrance, with great big columns and a pediment above it, just like a Greek temple. It's quite the tourist attraction. And it's even run by Lyon's, just like the Corner Houses, so the tea should be to your taste.'

'In that case, Saffron and I will meet you at five thirty, just inside the magnificent entrance. How does that sound?'

'Like the most tremendous fun,' said Harriet Halfpenny.

Welcome to the Troc,' said Miss Halfpenny when she met Leon and Saffron.

'You look nice,' Leon said.

'Thank you.'

'I love your hair, Miss Halfpenny,' Saffron said. 'It looks so nice down.'

She had noticed at once that Miss Halfpenny had unpinned

her hair, which now fell in auburn waves around her oval face. She had put mascara and liner around her hazel eyes, too, and rouged her lips and cheeks. Saffron was delighted. *You want to look nice for him. And you really do!*

'Ah, so that's what it is. I knew something was different,' Leon said. 'Well, it's jolly nice, anyway. Now, there seem to be a stack of different rooms to go to in here. What do you suggest?'

'That depends,' said Miss Halfpenny, 'do you like music and dancing, Saffron?'

'Oh yes, but I'm useless at dancing. I've never really learned how to do it at all.'

'Then it's time you learned. Follow me.'

The interior of the Trocadero resembled a grand opera house, rather than a tearoom. A grand, red-carpeted staircase decorated with murals depicting the legend of King Arthur and his knights of the round table rose through the heart of the building, wrapping around a bronze statue of a classical goddess, who held up a light designed to look like a flaming torch. Palm fronds sprouted from pots and urns at the foot of the stairs and along the first-floor landing. There was a splendid bar with a sign by the entrance that said, 'Gentlemen Only'.

'That really makes me want to go in it,' Saffron whispered to Miss Halfpenny as they walked by.

'I shouldn't think we're missing very much,' she replied.

Saffron heard a jazz band, playing somewhere in the building. The music grew louder as they drew near and then they entered a great salon. Small round dining tables, crowded with people, were packed close together on the floor, with the only open space reserved for the shiny wooden dance floor. Saffron looked up and saw the band, seated on the balcony that ran right around the room, with more tables, from which diners could look down on the scene below.

'Let's go up there!' she said, pointing to the balcony.

'Excuse me,' said Leon and went in search of the maître d'.

'So . . . this is the Empire Hall,' said Miss Halfpenny to Saffron. 'What do you think?'

'It's amazing! I'm so glad you suggested it.'

'Ah! I think we may be in business. Your father is calling us.'

Sure enough, Leon was waving at them from across the floor. He was standing next to a plump, moustachioed man in a black uniform.

'*Ah, cosi belle signorine!*' the maître d' exclaimed. 'Signor, you did not tell me that your wife and daughter were so beautiful.'

'Well . . .' Leon began, and then stopped himself and instead said, 'They are rather lovely, aren't they?'

Well done, Daddy! Saffron thought as she followed the maître d' up the stairs.

'One little moment,' he said as they reached the balcony. He flicked his fingers, summoning two waiters as if by magic. Then he issued instructions in a flurry of words and gesticulations and, by another act of conjuring, space appeared where there had been none and was instantly filled by a table, right by the balustrade, covered in a crisp white cloth, polished cutlery and gleaming glasses.

'Would the *signore* care for anything to drink?' the maître d' asked when they had all been seated.

Leon consulted his watch. 'Hmm . . . very nearly six o'clock. It's really too late for tea, don't you think? A bottle of champagne will do very nicely.'

An ice-bucket appeared on a stand beside the table, followed soon after by a wine waiter who deftly popped the cork, poured champagne for all three of them – Saffron was thrilled that her father did not stop the waiter as he filled her glass – and then placed the bottle into the bucket.

'Cheers!' said Leon, raising his glass. 'Here's to Africa . . . and London . . . and to you, Miss Halfpenny. Where would we be without you?'

'Somewhere not nearly as nice,' said Saffron, raising her glass.

The conversation did not flag for a second as they enjoyed their drinks. Then Miss Halfpenny said, 'I think it's time I taught you a few dance-steps, Saffron.'

'What? In front of all these people?'

'Go on,' said Leon. 'I dare you.'

'Promise you won't laugh if I'm hopeless?'

'I promise. I shall stay up here, watching you both from afar.'

The two women went down to the dance floor, where half-a-dozen couples were dancing to the waltz that the band was playing.

'I'll be the man,' said Miss Halfpenny. 'So, start by putting your right hand in my left hand . . . good. Next, put your left hand on my right shoulder . . . excellent. Now just watch my feet and try to follow them with yours, as if you were looking in a mirror. Off we go!'

They set off across the floor and within a few steps Saffron's feet were hopelessly tangled up and Miss Halfpenny's toes were smarting from having been trodden on.

'I'll never get the hang of this!' Saffron protested.

'Yes, you will. Now try again.'

By the sixth try, Saffron had mastered the basic step. By the end of the second song she was moving almost gracefully. When the song ended, she looked up at the balcony and saw her father clapping. He gave her a little nod, to signal his approval. Then, as the music started again, she saw him get up from the table and make his way along the balcony towards the stairs. Miss Halfpenny had seen him too. They stepped to the side of the dance floor and waited for Leon to join them.

He arrived a few moments later. 'Well done, Saffron, you picked that up very quickly. I'm impressed. Now it's time your clumsy old father had a go. May I have the pleasure of the next dance, Miss Halfpenny?'

'Yes,' she said. 'You may.'

He took her in his arms and Saffron saw that her father was

not in the slightest bit clumsy, nor did he resemble an old man. As they stepped onto the dance floor and joined the other couples, Leon held Miss Halfpenny with an air of confident command and she, Saffron noticed, responded by relaxing her shoulders and molding her body to his, just fractionally, but enough. She tilted her head so that she was looking up at him and their eyes met and Saffron caught it, at once, the spark between them, the instant connection.

Saffron skipped upstairs, her feet hardly touching the steps beneath them, so happy that it was almost as if she were the one falling in love. After all these years, her father had finally found someone. Saffron raised her eyes, as if to the sky. She wondered if her mother was looking down on them. Saffron knew that if she were, she would be happy too.

The school had reserved two coaches on the Brighton train and the platform at Victoria station was filled with schoolgirls, and their parents saying goodbye. Like the others, Saffron was already dressed in her uniform, for school rules applied from the moment the girls stepped on board the train. Leon tipped the station porter, who had taken Saffron's luggage on board, then turned to her and said, 'Good luck, old girl. I hope you have a splendid first term. Just keep your nose down, work hard, be your usual charming self and I'm sure you'll find that you'll have fitted right in before even you know it.'

'Don't worry, I will,' Saffron replied. 'And Daddy . . .'

'Yes?'

'I really, really like Miss Halfpenny.'

'We seem to be in agreement, then, because I rather like her, too.'

'I know. And I don't mind at all.'

'Oh don't you now?' Leon grinned. 'How very gracious of you! Now, come here and give your father a hug.'

Saffron snuggled into her father's embrace, got up on tiptoe to give him a kiss on the cheek and then said her final goodbye. A moment later, she was on the train and instantly turned her mind to school and the term ahead, with barely a thought for the father she was leaving behind.

Her first problem was where to sit. Every compartment she looked into seemed to be filled with girls, all abuzz with conversation, picking up their friendships after the weeks apart over Christmas. Finally she came to one in which there was just a single girl. She was blonde and Saffron noticed that while all the other girls seemed to have found ways of making their well-worn uniforms just a little bit more relaxed, some even verging on the scruffy, this girl's was as smart as a new pin. Saffron had been feeling a little self-conscious in her own immaculate uniform and had been well aware of the inquisitive eyes being turned in her direction and the huddled whispers as girls speculated on who the new girl might be. But perhaps she was not alone, after all. She opened the compartment door and stepped inside.

'Do you mind if I sit here?' she said, indicating the seat opposite the one on which the blonde girl was perched.

'Not at all, please go ahead,' the girl replied. She sounded a little nervous and her accent was foreign, though Saffron could not place it.

'Hello,' she said. 'I'm Saffron Courtney.'

'Good afternoon, Saffron. My name is Francesca von Schöndorf.'

'Oh, are you German?'

Francesca's face fell. 'Yes,' she sighed, as if she knew that this would not be welcome information.

'Are you a new girl too?' Saffron asked.

'No, already for one term I have been at Roedean.'

'I'm only just starting. I used to be at the other Roedean, in South Africa.'

'There is a Roedean in Africa?' Francesca sounded amazed at

222

the very idea. 'I did not know that. So you are South African, *ja*?'

'No, I come from Kenya. So what's school like?'

'Difficult, I must say,' Francesca admitted. 'The teachers are very good, yes, and the situation is remarkable, right by the sea on high, how you say . . . *klippen*?'

'Cliffs?'

'Yes, of course, cliffs. So the sea is very beautiful, although often it looks grey because the sky also is grey . . .'

Saffron laughed. 'I know! Everything in England is grey!'

For the first time Francesca relaxed enough to smile. 'I think so, too!'

'How about the other girls?'

Francesca's smile turned to a grimace. 'Not so good . . . I mean, many of the girls are very nice. But there are some who do not like me.'

'Really? Why not?'

'Because I am German. Maybe they have fathers who died in the war, or they think all Germans are monsters, but in any case they let me know that I am not welcome.'

'I think that's beastly! It sounds to me as if they're just bullies. They're looking for any excuse they can find to be horrible to other girls, so they pick on you for being German.'

'Yes, this is maybe true. Of course, I cannot tell my parents what happens. They would not believe it because they have lots of friends and family in England. My father used to know the Kaiser and of course the grandmother of the Kaiser was Queen Victoria of England. My grandmother was English, too, actually.'

'What a coincidence! My grandmother was German.'

'Really? You are not teasing me?'

'Not at all. She was my mother's mother. I never met her because she died when my mother was just a girl.'

'Oh that is so sad. But your mother can tell you about her, no?'

Saffron shrugged. 'No, my mother died when I was seven.'

'Oh, I am so sorry.'

'That's all right. You weren't to know. But tell me all about your family. Fancy your father knowing the Kaiser. Is he terribly grand?'

As it turned out, he was. The von Schöndorfs were an old Bavarian family, although for all her talk of palaces and castles, Francesca gave the impression that her people were not as rich or as mighty as they once were and were increasingly forced to sell family portraits, heirlooms or properties just to make ends meet. For her part, Francesca was thrilled by Saffron's descriptions of Lusima and amazed when Saffron described encounters with rhinos, elephants and even lions as everyday occurrences.

The two girls talked all the way to Brighton, and then on the coach that took them to the school. They stood together in line as the girls all snaked past the teaching staff who were, as school custom dictated, lined up to shake the hand of every girl in the school, and then Francesca, who told Saffron that her family all called her Chessi, showed her around. Both girls now knew that they had at least one person they could always sit next to and at the start of any school term that made all the difference.

Leon walked back across Green Park to the Ritz, glad of the chance to stretch his legs. He felt as though he had a lot of nervous energy to work off. *By God, I feel like a bloody schoolboy*, he thought to himself. *Get a grip of yourself, man!*

Earlier in the day, while Saffron was busy packing, he had sent a messenger round to the Daniel Neal store, with a note addressed to Miss Halfpenny, inviting her to meet him for dinner at the Ritz. The messenger had been instructed to wait for her reply, and duly brought it back to the hotel.

'Thank you for a delightful, but rather sudden invitation,' Miss Halfpenny had written in a neat, feminine hand. 'I need to think about it. But I will send you a proper answer as soon as I can.'

None had arrived before Leon had taken Saffron to her train. The business of getting his daughter off to school had occupied his mind until she was actually on the train, but the moment their farewells were complete, Leon's attention, like Saffron's, had shifted elsewhere: in his case, right back to Miss Halfpenny. He stepped through the gate from the park onto Piccadilly, turned right and had to restrain himself from running the final few yards along the street, underneath the hotel arches, through the front entrance in and up to the reception desk.

'Is there a message for Mr Courtney?' he asked, when he reached his destination, doing his very best to seem offhand.

The young man behind the desk had to concentrate hard, as if dragging the very deepest recesses of his memory before he could finally answer, 'I believe that does ring a bell, sir, yes. Excuse me one moment.'

He went away to consult a rather older, more imposing functionary, further up the desk. The younger man returned, bearing a note, which he then looked at before saying, 'Miss Halfpenny called for you, sir. She says she would be delighted to accept your invitation and will meet you for dinner at eight.'

'Excellent news!' said Leon, and pressed a ten-shilling note into the young man's hand.

'That's very generous of you, sir, much obliged. And may I wish you a most enjoyable evening.'

Leon visited the hotel barber to have his hair neatly trimmed and his chin shaved as close as an expertly wielded razor could manage. He had already taken the precaution of having his dress shirt and dinner suit cleaned and pressed and was looking the picture of manly elegance as he went downstairs at half-past seven. The same staff member was still behind the desk and was only too happy to oblige when asked if he could direct Miss Halfpenny to the Palm Court when she arrived.

Leon went on ahead and procured a table nestled in the most discreet corner he could find, which was no easy task in a white, pink and gold-painted salon, with a glass ceiling and mirrored walls whose entire purpose was for guests to see and be seen. Then he ordered a whisky on the rocks and waited for his guest to arrive.

Harriet Halfpenny stepped out of the cab, gave a shilling to the footman who had opened the door and stood for a moment on the pavement as she composed herself. She forced herself to hold her head up and walk into the Ritz as if she owned the place. Her first destination was the cloakroom, where she deposited her overcoat, which suddenly seemed embarrassingly cheap and tatty, though it was a perfectly warm, serviceable garment. Next she went to the ladies' room and inspected her reflection. Her delay in replying to Leon Courtney's invitation had owed nothing to any reluctance to see him. She had simply been unable to contemplate walking into the Ritz in the dress she wore to work. In her lunch hour she had dashed out to Selfridges and spent a sum of money that was way beyond her means, one that would have her living on bread and water for the next month, in fact, on a long evening dress in green silk. Harriet did not think of herself as having the body of a great seductress, but she was reasonably tall and long-limbed and had, thanks to her many years of membership of her local netball club, kept her figure reasonably trim. Her breasts were neat, and actually rather fuller than might have been expected from her naturally slender, narrow-hipped build. And now she came to look at herself, the dress did seem to fit very well, and whatever assets she had were being displayed to her best advantage. *Right you are, girl*, she told her reflection in the mirror. *Over the top you go.*

She went to the reception desk, could not help smiling when the young man behind it said, 'Mr Courtney is going to be *very*

226

pleased to see you, Miss,' and made for the Palm Court. She had to make an effort to keep her jaw from dropping as she walked in, for the room was sumptuous. The palms after which it was named were dotted around the edge of the room, but her eye was struck by a huge floral centerpiece at its heart, which was festooned with huge, pink roses whose blooms seemed to defy the winter outside.

Harriet searched for Leon Courtney. And then, there he was, in the far corner, rising to his feet to greet her. *By God, you're a good-looking man*, she thought. With his height, his broad shoulders and his immaculately tailored dinner jacket, Leon cut an imposing figure. But it was his face that she loved. That deeply tanned skin made all the Englishmen around him look pallid and whey-faced. It set off the white of his strong, square teeth, just as the lines around his eyes framed his clear, dark eyes. Oh, those eyes! There was strength, and intelligence, and warmth, and the hint of possible anger in them, but also there was sadness.

This was a man whose wife had died and never been replaced, though goodness knows enough women must have tried. So why did she, a spinster who worked in a shop, think that she stood a chance when all those others had failed? It was an absurd proposition, or at least it should have been. But Harriet had seen the way he looked at her when he thought her attention was elsewhere. She knew how pleased Saffron had been to see her and how much her approval would mean to her father. It had been Saffron who had made the running on her father's behalf, acting the matchmaker. But none of that really counted for anything now. All that mattered was the feeling that had filled her when Leon had first held her on the dance floor at the Troc, the look in his eyes when he gazed at her, and the unmistakable evidence of his arousal when she pressed her body against his.

He had seen her now and a broad grin was crossing his face,

in an expression of undiluted, boyish glee. *He's thrilled to see me!* she thought and then they were saying hello and not quite sure whether to shake hands, or kiss, or what to do at all.

'Remind me, what did I say you looked like, the other evening at the Troc?' Leon asked.

'You said I looked nice.'

'Did I now?' He looked at her again and now his eyes conveyed an entirely new message that Harriet had never seen in them before. Now they were hungry, predatory, penetrating so deep into her she had to grasp the top of the chair by her side for fear that her knees would give way completely if she did not.

'Well, you don't look "nice" now, my darling. You look absolutely ravishing.'

Harriet's pulse was racing as his eyes continued to bore into her. She felt the molten heat between her legs as a little devil inside her head was saying, *Just throw me over the table and take me now!* But then Leon smiled, the spell was broken and he said, 'I ordered champagne cocktails for us both. Just like last time . . . only a little more exciting.'

Harriet sat down, composed herself again as she sipped her drink and then, doing her very best to sound like a sophisticated woman making polite conversation, asked, 'Are you staying here, while you're in London?'

'Saffron and I took a suite. It's a bit fancy for me, to be honest. I'm just a scruffy old African at heart.'

'You don't look very scruffy.'

He shrugged. 'That's the army for you, teaches you to scrub up smart when required. Honestly, I'd be just as happy sleeping under the stars, next to a nice campfire. But this isn't really the weather for it, or the place, so here I am. It was nice for Saffron, anyway.'

'She's a wonderful girl.'

'Yes, she is . . .' Leon paused and looked at Harriet again, not quite as hungrily, perhaps, but still his eyes were dark and serious as he said, 'She thinks the world of you, too, you know. It's, ah . . . it's the first time she's felt that about anyone. Since her mother died, I mean.'

Harriet knew full well that Leon was speaking about himself, as well as Saffron. 'Look, Mr Courtney . . .'

'Please, for heaven's sake, call me Leon.'

'Very well, Leon . . .'

'Should I still call you Miss Halfpenny?' he asked, with a teasing look in his eye, before she could go any further.

'No,' she giggled. 'Call me Harriet.'

'All right, then, Harriet it is. Now, what were you about to say before I so rudely interrupted you?'

'Just this: you are obviously a very successful man. You fly from Africa to England at a moment's notice and book a suite at the Ritz. Your suit is beautifully tailored . . .'

'By a splendid Indian gentleman in Nairobi who charges me almost nothing . . .'

'Well, wherever you get it, the point is that you are you, and I am just a 35-year-old spinster who works in a shop. And I can't quite see how I can hope to be worthy of you.'

'Well, if you are a 35-year-old spinster then I am a 48-year-old widower, so that makes us even,' he replied. 'And as for working in a shop, let me tell you the way I see it. I respect anyone who gets up in the morning, stands on their own two feet and puts in a hard day's work for a fair day's pay. I admire you for doing your job, and doing it damn well, I might add, far more than some la-di-da society woman who lives off her daddy, or her husband, or her trust fund and never does a hand's turn in her life.

'Look, Harriet, let me put my cards on the table. I know . . . Hell, I've probably known from that first day in Johannesburg . . . that you are not only the most attractive woman I've met in God knows how long, but you're also the best woman, too. You're strong, and independent, but also kind and funny and warm. I saw the way you took Saffron off, that very first time, and looked after her and made her feel at ease. I thought of all the other women I've known, because I've not been a monk, believe me. Not one of them ever got on as well with Saffy, no matter how hard they tried, as you did from the moment you met her. That told me a helluva lot about the kind of woman you were.'

'Thank you,' murmured Harriet, who suddenly found that she wanted to cry.

'You don't have to thank me. I should thank *you*. The third time Saffy and I went back to Jo'burg, I told myself I'd buck up and ask you out for a drink, or dinner or something. Then the woman there told me you'd gone back to England and I was kicking myself. I couldn't believe I'd been so stupid and let you get away. But now you're here, and you're giving me another chance. And believe me, Harriet, I intend to take it.'

He paused. 'That's all I have to say,' he added and gave her a sweet, self-deprecating smile.

'Don't worry. That's all you need to say.'

'Good. Now, shall we order some food? I don't know about you, but I am absolutely famished.'

Harriet did not sleep with Leon Courtney that night, though she was sorely tempted. Denying herself as much as him, she restricted their intimacy to a brief kiss as they were saying goodbye, while the hotel footman summoned a taxi. After their second dinner she let him see her home and had the very great pleasure of kissing him at length, and feeling his hands exploring almost – but not quite – every inch of her body in the back of the cab as it drove to her very modest little terraced house in the deeply unfashionable backstreets of Fulham. She had inherited the place from her mother, who had died a year after her return to England. It shamed Harriet to find herself feeling grateful for her mother's passing: it meant she was free to do as she pleased.

On their next date they went to the pictures, just like a pair of courting youngsters. The film they chose was *The 39 Steps*. All Harriet's friends said it was tremendously good, but she emerged from the cinema none the wiser for most of the film had been spent smooching with Leon in the next seat, rather than watching Robert Donat's adventures on the screen.

They continued in this fashion for another fortnight, both deliriously happy but increasingly frustrated. Leon was generous, kind, amusing and never once made her feel that she owed him anything in return for the dinners he bought her, and then the dresses to wear to the dinners, and then a pair of earrings and a pearl necklace to go with the dresses. 'Without you, I would be alone, and bored and completely lacking in any idea of where to go,' he said. 'And with you, I'm the happiest man in London.'

Harriet found herself wanting to tell Leon if something funny happened to her, or she saw a newspaper story that she knew would interest him, or even if she had been forced to endure an exceptionally rude customer and just needed to get it off her chest. She was fascinated by the life Leon had led in Africa, and when he talked about his estate at Lusima, she longed to see it, not just because she knew it would be quite unlike anything she had ever experienced in her life – wilder, more beautiful, filled with extraordinary animals and people – but because it was his place, and he loved it so, and she wanted to be part of that love.

Then one day, he said, 'Do you fancy a weekend in the country? I've been invited to meet all my English cousins. They have a place down in Devon. It's called High Weald, been in the family since the seventeenth century. I've never been there myself, but I'm told it's very lovely.' He paused and stroked his chin in mock contemplation. 'Hmm . . . hope they've improved the plumbing and heating since they moved in. Maybe installed the odd lavatory or two, that sort of thing.'

Harriet giggled. 'I thought you were the hardy outdoorsman who liked to sleep out under the stars. Why would you care about plumbing and heating?'

'I must be getting soft since I met you.'

'Soft in the head, certainly.'

'Anyway, would you like to come along?'

'Are you sure? I don't want to feel like I'm spoiling a family occasion.'

'Nonsense, you won't spoil anything. I've told them all about you and they can't wait to meet you. We can leave after you finish work on Friday afternoon and I promise I'll have you back in London, safe and sound in time for Monday morning. Please . . . I really would like it very much. And before you ask, yes, of course you will have your own room. We aren't married and the English members of the Courtney clan are sticklers for etiquette. Though I dare say our rooms won't be too far apart . . .'

Harriet had never been to a country house party, but she'd read enough novels to know that while the social rules might be scrupulously observed on the surface, blind eyes were turned to anything that happened once the lights were out. Leon's invitation was a declaration of intent.

'Yes,' she said, 'that sounds wonderful. I'd love to come.'

High Weald was nestled between rolling hills that looked out towards the sea. Its lawns ran down to a low cliff, where a path descended to a sandy cove. On a cold, still day in late January, with the sky as cloudless as midsummer, mirrored in the flat-calm sea, it was a perfect place for two lovers to walk to hand-in-hand, for the man to lead his woman safely down the steep, stony path and for the two of them to stand, arm in arm, and look out across the waters.

They held each other differently now, in the way that two lovers do after their bodies have joined as one, with that perfect, effortless match of one form to another that told them both that they were made to be together. Harriet pulled Leon still closer to her and sighed contentedly. Then her sigh became a yawn.

'Bored of me already?'

'Just tired,' she said, her voice muffled by the way her head was half-buried in his overcoat. 'You've completely exhausted me, you wicked man.'

'Well the fresh sea air should wake you up. Come on . . .' He pulled her off him. 'Take a few deep breaths, that's the spirit!' Harriet did her best to oblige but then he said, 'Right, now for some bracing exercise. Ten star jumps . . . One! Two!'

'No, shan't!' she said, defiantly yawning again.

'Oh all right, you win . . . lazy-bones,' Leon said. He wrapped his arms around her again. 'You must admit though, it was a very nice way to get exhausted.'

'Mmm . . .' she nodded and he bent down to kiss the top of her head.

'I love you so much, Hattie, my darling.'

She looked up at him. 'I love you, too. With all my heart. And I love the way you kiss me, and I love the way you touch me, and stroke me and . . .' She reached out and stroked his crotch, gently rubbing her hand up and down the front of his trousers until she could feel him and then she said, 'And I love that most of all. I love when you're inside me. I love the way you taste and I love your smell.'

Leon grunted like a lazy, contented lion.

'Do you want to know a secret?' she asked him. He nodded and she said, 'Remember that first dinner we had together, just the two of us, at the Ritz?'

'How could I forget?'

'When we first said hello, the way you looked at me, the things it did to me . . . you could have had me there and then.'

'I'm going to have you now,' Leon said. He led her back up the beach to where the sand was dry. Then he took off his coat, placed on the ground and she lay down upon it.

233

'Christ!' he muttered, placing himself on top of her. 'It's bloody cold. I might get frostbite on my cock.'

She gave a low purring laugh. 'Silly man. Why don't you put it somewhere hot?'

He reached down and she opened her legs and lifted her bottom off the ground so that he could tug her skirt up around her hips and pull her knickers down her legs. She kicked them off and his hand felt for the soft, hot, wet, yielding core of her. Then it was her turn to feel for his fly buttons and the slit in his underpants and then she had him in his hands and he sprang free from the clothes that had confined him and she guided him into her, groaning with pleasure as she took him again.

Now he didn't give a damn about the cold. He couldn't care less that they were right out in the open and if any other members of the house party walked down to the cliff's edge they would certainly be spotted. All Leon cared about was his love and desire for his woman. He wanted her to feel it and know it in ways that went far beyond words. He wanted her to take pleasure in him and from him and his whole being was focused on her, all his senses alert to every sound, every movement she made. He kissed her and she responded and the boundaries between them blurred, like two water-colours on a piece of paper, joining as one to create something entirely new. She was his woman now and they would never be divided.

'Marry me,' he said. 'Please, I beg you. Marry me.'

'Oh God,' she moaned. 'Yes,' and then, her voice rising with every repetition, 'Yes, yes, yes, yes, yes!'

The other members of the house party were delighted that the weekend had been graced by such a happy event. Champagne was brought up from the cellar, corks popped and toasts drunk to the happy couple. When Leon and Harriet had arrived at High Weald on Friday evening, they did so as strangers to his English cousins. But they were such an obviously delightful and well-matched couple and their happiness was so infectious that by the time they came to say their farewells on Sunday afternoon, both sides felt like family.

'Thank you so much for having us,' Leon said to his host, Sir William Courtney, while the staff loaded his and Harriet's luggage into the car that would take them to catch the London train.

'My dear chap, it's been an absolute pleasure. It's not every day an engagement is announced beneath one's roof. It'll be the talk of Devon before the week is out, you mark my words. And well done, old man, Harriet's a splendid girl. You've found yourself an absolute cracker there.'

Harriet meanwhile was kissing goodbye to Lady Courtney. 'You must both promise to come to stay again before you go back to Kenya,' her hostess said, with a squeeze of Harriet's hand to emphasize that this was a genuine invitation, not a mere pleasantry.

'We'd love that,' Harriet replied, thinking how strange and also how wonderful it was to have become one half of a 'we' after so many years of just being 'I'.

'And do bring Saffron down with you. I'm greatly looking forward to meeting her.'

They were all smiles as they waved goodbye and the happy glow lasted all the way to Exeter station. But once they were settled in their first-class compartment and the train began the journey as dusk fell on the Devonshire countryside, Harriet became quieter, more melancholy.

At first Leon assumed that she was simply exhausted. Neither of them had slept more than a few hours over the entire weekend and their nights had been anything but restful. But as the time went by he realized that something was clearly bothering Harriet. This was the first time he had ever seen her unhappy and it troubled him deeply.

'What is it, my darling?'

She sighed, 'I don't know . . .'

Leon knew enough about women not to believe that for a moment. But he also knew that there was no point forcing the issue. 'Well, if there is something on your mind, you can tell me. I love you very much, Harriet Halfpenny, and nothing you say could ever change that.'

'I fear that this might,' she said, looking up at him with such sadness in her eyes that he had to reach out and take her in his arms.

'Darling Harriet,' he said, kissing her hair and gently stroking her, trying with every means at his disposal to make her feel safe, and loved, and protected. She was crying now and, once again, Leon was grateful for the handkerchief he always wore in his breast pocket.

He waited until the crying had passed, then pulled back a little so he could look her in the eyes and very quietly said, 'Please tell me. I just want to help.'

'I'm just so worried that you'll be disappointed in me.'

'Never!'

'It's just I would have told you before you asked me to marry you but you . . .' Harriet managed a faint smile, 'You took me by surprise.'

'I took myself by surprise, come to that! But it was a jolly nice surprise, don't you think?'

'Oh yes . . . the nicest. But there's something I have to tell you, and if it makes you want to change your mind, then I won't blame you or hold it against you.'

A note of anxiety entered Leon's voice. 'What could possibly make me do that? For goodness sakes, darling, please tell me. You've really got me worried.'

'Well, it's very simple,' Harriet said, gathering herself. 'When I was very young, during the war, I had a sweetheart. We were going to get married, but he was killed in the Hundred Days

Offensive, just a month before the Armistice. But he'd come home on leave in the spring and, well, I was pregnant . . . and I lost the baby . . . and, and . . . oh Leon, I can't have any more. I won't be able to give you a child!'

The resolve that had enabled her to tell her story cracked and Harriet fell back onto Leon's chest, sobbing.

'Oh, Harriet, you silly, wonderful, beautiful girl, I don't mind about that. I don't mind at all.'

She looked up, hardly believing that could be true. 'Really?'

'Really . . . In fact, I had been wondering how I was going to tell you that I didn't want us to have children. I thought you would be terribly disappointed. It's partly because I'm getting on a bit and I don't want to be a doddery old man who's old enough to be his children's grandpa. But the real truth is, I have already lost someone I loved very, very much because she was carrying my child, and I simply could not bear to lose you the same way. Even now, after all these years, there's a little voice in my head that tells me I killed Eva.'

'But you didn't. You mustn't think that,' said Harriet, reaching out to Leon, their roles reversed as she offered comfort to him.

'I know it's foolish, but I can't help it. And if you were pregnant . . . well, I'm not sure how I would cope, to be honest. So you don't have to worry in the very slightest. I am blessed with a wonderful daughter and that's good enough for me. All I want from you, my darling, is you. You are perfect in my eyes, and I want you till the day I die.'

'I think you're just as silly as me,' Harriet said, snuggling up against her man.

'Then we're the perfect couple, aren't we?' he replied.

Saffron was granted a weekend exeat from school to attend her father's wedding. Leon married Harriet at Chelsea Town Hall and Saffron was both the bridesmaid and the only guest, for this was a very private occasion. Afterwards they lunched at the Troc, where Mr and Mrs Courtney had their first dance as a married couple. The same maître d' who had looked after them before was on duty. He recognized the gentleman with his two '*belle signorine*' at once and his smile only broadened when Harriet held up her left hand, with its gold wedding band and the diamond and sapphire engagement ring Leon had bought her at Garrard & Co, the Mayfair jewellery house that had catered to British royal families for the past two hundred years. She was beaming with delight as she said, 'And this time, I really am his wife!'

They were all going on from the Troc to Victoria: Saffron to take the train back to school, while Leon and Harriet boarded the Simplon Orient Express service to Venice, but first Saffron and Harriet retired to the ladies' room for a private, woman-to-woman chat.

'I just wanted to say, thank you,' Harriet said as they were both standing by the mirror, attending to their faces. 'I'm sure that lots of girls in your position would hate the idea of their father finding someone new, and they'd be absolutely poisonous. I can't tell you how much it means to me that you have been so nice and so welcoming.'

'Oh, I would have been poisonous . . . really poisonous if I'd wanted to be,' Saffron said, making them both laugh. 'But not to you, because I knew that you weren't like all the others. You didn't want anything from him. You didn't try to suck up to me.' Saffron took Harriet's hand in hers. 'I think you're lovely, Harriet . . . Oh, is it all right if I call you Harriet?'

'Of course! It is my name and you certainly can't call me Miss Halfpenny any longer.'

'Well, I might sometimes, just to tease.'

'Don't you dare!'

'Anyway, I love how happy Daddy has been since he met you, and I love it that of all the people in the world who could have been my stepmother, you're the one who is. And I really,

really hope you have an absolutely super-smashing time on your honeymoon. There's only one thing I'm sad about . . .'

A look of alarm crossed Harriet's face. 'Really? What's the matter?' she asked.

'I don't know, I just wish I could be there when you see Lusima for the first time. It's so magical.'

'I wish you could be there too. But we won't be going out until Easter. I have to finish working my notice . . .'

'Do you really have to do that? Can't you just leave?'

'I could, yes. But then I would be letting my employer down and making more work for my colleagues and I would hate to think that I was the kind of woman who would do such a thing. Besides, the girl who's replacing me needs to be taught how everything's done.'

'You know, you're a bit of a bossy-boots . . . in the nicest possible way,' Saffron laughed.

'I dare say I am,' Harriet admitted. 'But in any case, your father needs to get the new office up and running and we think we might get a little house so that we all have somewhere to stay when we're in town. Perhaps you can help me decorate it. We can choose curtains and carpets and whatnot.'

'I'd love that!'

'Good, then that's settled. We'll do all that before we leave, and it then won't be long before you come out for the summer holidays. I will still be terribly new to Kenya, so you can show me all around Lusima, and take me to all your favourite places.'

'I will, I promise,' Saffron said. 'Now. We'd better get back to our table. Daddy will be wondering where you are. Come on, Mrs Courtney, your husband awaits you.'

'Mrs Courtney . . .' murmured Harriet, still trying to get used to her new name. 'Fancy that.'

As an architect, Albert Speer stood for everything that the modernists who had taught Gerhard von Meerbach at the Bauhaus most despised. His work did not look forward, but back. His desire was not to build modern homes and workplaces, but to create monstrous copies of ancient Greek and Roman buildings, on a monumental scale that dwarfed even the mightiest Classical temple or amphitheatre. And he did this not to improve the lives of ordinary people, but to glorify his master Adolf Hitler.

Yet however much Gerhard hated to admit it, even to himself, there was something profoundly exciting in finding oneself so close to the centre of power in Germany. The Führer saw himself as a frustrated artist and architect, so took a close personal interest in all the plans that Speer drew up, for they envisaged nothing less than a total rebuilding, even a re-imagining of Berlin. It did not matter what existing streets or buildings stood in the way, Speer and his team, among whom Gerhard now found himself, were free to design on the basis that anything that stood in their way would simply be obliterated, if Hitler liked what they proposed to put up instead.

The scale on which Speer was planning gave Gerhard entry into the magnitude of Hitler's ambitions, for what they were creating was not the capital of a country, or even an expanded Reich, but of a global empire. Elsewhere in Berlin another architect, Werner March, was supervising the construction of a Olympic Stadium seating one hundred thousand spectators. It frustrated Speer that March was working in concrete, steel, bricks and mortar, while he was still restricted to pencil, ink and paper, but he got his own back by proposing structures that would make March's apparently splendid stadium look like an insignificant pimple.

There would be a grand, triumphal boulevard called the Avenue of Splendours slicing through the heart of the city. Its commencement would be marked by a triumphal arch, many times larger than the Arc de Triomphe or the Brandenburg Gate, and it would lead to a Great Square covering three hundred and fifty thousand square metres of open space. Along one side would rise the Führer's own palace, built on a scale that would dwarf Versailles. Directly opposite the Arch, on the far side of the Great Square, would stand the People's Hall, whose domed design was inspired by Hitler's own sketches. The dome of the hall was intended to be two hundred metres high and two hundred and fifty metres wide: so huge, in fact, that one of the tasks assigned to Gerhard was to conceive of ways to prevent clouds forming inside the dome and raining on the people within it.

Craftsmen had been working for months to create a room-sized model of the entire scheme showing a huge section of the new city with all its streets and major buildings.

One day in late February 1936, Speer told his staff that the Führer himself would be paying a personal visit to their studios to examine the model and go over the plans.

'The Führer is under great strain at the moment,' Speer explained. 'There are matters which I am not at liberty to discuss that may very soon transform the position of the Reich, and make the German people a power within Europe once again. The Führer bears the entire weight of responsibility for our glorious future upon his shoulders. He needs, and deserves the chance to relax, to take his mind off his responsibilities, if only for a few brief moments. It is our great privilege to be able to provide him with that opportunity. I therefore call on all of you to do everything in your power to make our glorious leader's visit an enjoyable one.'

The announcement threw the entire office into something close to a frenzy. The female staff dashed to the ladies' rooms to make themselves look beautiful for their master. The men put on jackets, straightened ties, combed their hair and tried to adopt the proper attitude. 'But what should that be?' they asked one another. Did Hitler want to see confident, purposeful men who could be entrusted with the creation of his capital?

Or should they be deferential, modest and silent until spoken to?

And then, suddenly, he was there, that instantly recognisable face, already known to all the world, but dressed in a tweed suit, rather than the usual brown uniform jacket: the great architect now, rather than the great leader.

Gerhard was as transfixed as everyone else. *If Jesus Christ himself had appeared here we could not be more in awe of him*, he thought, suddenly realizing that he was no different to anyone else, no more capable of remaining independent or sceptical in the presence of the Führer.

They had been told to keep working while the visit was in progress: 'The Führer wants to see activity and progress,' Speer had said. So Gerhard dragged his eyes away from Hitler and back to his drawing board. He was drawing a ventilation duct for the dome of the People's Hall when he heard a coughing noise, clearly designed to attract his attention, just over his left shoulder.

Gerhard looked round and there, less than two metres away, was Adolf Hitler, with Albert Speer beside him. Gerhard jumped from the high stool on which he had been perched and, as an immediate reflex action, saluted the Führer with a cry of 'Heil Hitler!'

Hitler responded with a salute that was little more than a flick of the wrist and then Speer said, 'This is one of our most promising young staff, Gerhard von Meerbach.'

'Of the engine-making family?' Hitler inquired, looking at Gerhard.

'Yes, my Führer. My brother Konrad is the present Count von Meerbach.'

'Von Meerbach is not only a promising architect, he is also a volunteer pilot in the Luftwaffe.'

Hitler nodded approvingly. 'You see, Speer, this is National Socialism at its best. Here we have a young man from an aristocratic family, yet he does not waste his time in a world of privilege. He helps to build the Reich and also to defend the Reich.' Then he stepped forward and gave Gerhard an avuncular pat on the arm. 'Well done, young man,' he said, and his blue eyes looked right at Gerhard, who found himself transfixed. Hitler possessed a form of charm that was something close to mesmerism. To be in the Führer's presence, eye to eye, was to be utterly persuaded of his greatness so that one wanted nothing more in life but to do whatever one could to serve his cause.

'*Ach so*, I see you are working on the Great Hall. So, tell me von Meerbach, what do you think of my scheme for the building?'

And Gerhard found himself saying, as if no other words were possible, 'I think it is magnificent, my Führer.'

Saffron and her new friend Chessi von Schöndorf had made a deal in the very first days of their friendship. Chessi would help Saffron to learn to speak German and in return would be taught enough Swahili so that, as she put it, 'I can to my parents the most great shock give! They send me to England to speak English better, but now I shall pretend that I am at Roedean only speaking African. They will not know what has happened.'

This was, Saffron agreed, an excellent scheme. In the event, however, she only learned two words. '*Hujambo*', which meant 'Hello' or 'How are you?' and '*Sijambo*', which was the conventional reply, meaning, 'Fine.' When Saffy and Chessi were overheard using '*Hujambo?*' '*Sijambo!*' as their greeting to one another, their in-joke became an instant craze throughout the entire school as four hundred and fifty English schoolgirls and a very few foreign students put on their idea of African voices and pretended to be Zulu or Masai princesses.

The craze was over in a matter of weeks, but by that time its two originators had entered the ranks of the most popular girls in their year, a position that only became stronger for Saffy when her skill on the sports field, allied to her good looks, made her the target of a hundred adoring 'pashes' – as the younger girls' crushes on the older ones were known – from the junior end of the school. Popularity had always found Saffy without her having to look for it. For Chessi, on the other hand, this sudden acceptance by girls who had previously been cold to her was a thrilling new experience. She immediately set her Swahili studies aside and plunged into her exciting new social life. Saffron, meanwhile, stuck to her guns, gradually improving her German until she and Chessi could chat to one another, even if she regularly had to reach for English words and phrases when the German ones were still unknown to her.

After weeks when it seemed as though the Easter term would go on for ever, it suddenly seemed to be over in no time at all. She spent the first half of the four-week holiday in London with Leon and Harriet. They had bought a flat in Chesham Court, an apartment block newly converted from a Victorian mansion on Chesham Place in the heart of Belgravia, just a few minutes' walk from Sloane Square in one direction and Knightsbridge in the other: right in the heart of one of the smartest and most attractive parts of town.

'You can stay here when you need to spend a night or two in town,' Leon told Saffron. 'We've hired a part-time house-keeper, Mrs Perkins. Give her a couple of days' notice before you arrive and she'll have the whole place freshened up. I dare say she'll even cook you a meal or two if you ask her nicely.'

As promised, Harriet let Saffron help her with the decoration of the flat and the two of them spent a week scouring depart-ment stores like Peter Jones and Harrods, and a mass of antiques shops, upholsterers, carpet-sellers, fabric merchants, furniture shops and purveyors of sheets, carpets, curtains and knick-knacks of all sort. They also shopped for clothes, for Harriet needed outfits suitable for her new life in the tropics, from safari clothing to wear on the estate to the evening dresses required for the annual horse-racing week in Nairobi for which female guests at the Muthaiga Club (and no one stayed anywhere else for race week) were expected to appear in a new gown every night. Saffron, meanwhile, had already received her first invitations to her new friends' birthday parties and country-house weekends and so required everything from party frocks to hunting tweeds.

Leon made a show of immense distress at the bills the two women in his life were running up, but they all knew it was just a sham. He was by nature a generous man and it pleased him that he had the means to indulge a wife and daughter who gave him so much happiness in return. Since Saffron would have to look after herself for long stretches of the year, when she was in England and Leon was in Africa, he opened an account for her at Coutts bank, complete with chequebook, to be funded by an allowance of thirty pounds a month – a sum which left Saffron wide-eyed with amazement and gratitude. He also said that she might take advantage of the account he had set up at Harrods, on two conditions: first that she should only buy things because she truly needed them, rather than wanted them, and second that she informed him, in writing, of any purchase over five pounds, so that he could make sure than the first condition was being met. 'I am treating you like an adult, rather than a child, and giving you access to grown-up sums of money. Now it's up to you to be grown-up in how you use them.'

This seemed entirely reasonable to Saffron, who appreciated the trust and responsibility Leon was bestowing on her and, as a result, was determined not to betray his faith in her.

'Bear this in mind,' he said. 'I wouldn't want any daughter of mine to seem like a poor relation. But I wouldn't want her looking like a spoiled brat either. So find the middle way, and stick to it.'

* * *

Saffron, Harriet and Leon spent the second weekend of the Easter holiday at High Weald, where Sir William and Lady Violet assured Saffy that she was always welcome to come and stay for half-terms, or holidays, for it simply wasn't possible or practical to go all the way to Kenya more than once or twice a year. The Courtneys' own children, Philippa and Michael, were six and four years older respectively than Saffron. Mike was halfway through his officer training course at the Royal Military College, Sandhurst, and Philly was already married to a City stockbroker, with her first baby on the way and a half-timbered mock-Tudor house in the Surrey suburbs to look after. 'I'm afraid we're just a pair of old sticks,' Lady Violet, who was only in her mid-forties and still retained much of the delicate, English-rose prettiness of her youth, told Saffy. 'But a lot of the other families round about us have children your age and there's always masses going on – riding, sailing, tennis parties and all that sort of thing – so we'll make sure you don't have to sit around being bored by us for too much of the time.'

The Courtneys kept a stable with half-a-dozen horses in it. Saffron was very taken by one, a powerful stallion, whose rich brown coat was as glossy as a well-polished mahogany dining table.

'Ah, that's Tanqueray, Mike's hunter,' Lady Courtney told her. 'Mike calls him Tank because he's such a great big brute of a beast. He's over seventeen hands, you know.'

'Would Mike mind awfully if I took Tanqueray out?' Saffron asked. Before they'd all gone out to the stables she had put on her jodhpurs and was carrying her riding cap, just to be ready in case she had the chance for a ride.

'Are you sure that's a good idea, my dear? He really is a man's horse. Mike is six foot tall and played rugby for the county when he was at school and even he says it takes all his strength to keep Tank under control sometimes.'

'I'm five feet nine and a quarter,' Saffron said. 'Everyone at school calls me Saffy Stringbean because I'm so tall. So I can ride a big horse.'

There was a paddock just beyond the stable yard, where half-a-dozen elderly fences, their paint now flaking and wood slowly rotting, had been arranged many years earlier, when the Courtney children were in their gymkhana-going years. Saffron pointed in that direction. 'Perhaps I could take him out there just for a little trot, to see if it was too much for me,' she suggested. 'He wouldn't able to run away with me because it's all fenced in.'

'Hmm . . .' Violet pondered. 'What do you think, Leon? Is Saffy up to it?'

'There's only one way to find out,' he replied. 'But listen to me, Saffron: take it nice and easy, do you hear?'

'Yes, Daddy.'

'Just a gentle trot, and if that goes well enough a nice easy canter. But no more than that!'

'No, Daddy.'

'Well, if you're sure, Leon,' Violet conceded, making it quite plain that she regarded this as a highly unwise exercise. She told the stable-boy to saddle Tanqueray and soon the sound of horse's hooves on cobblestones echoed around the yard. Saffy went up to Tanqueray, who looked at her with something close to disdain. Evidently he was as sceptical as Lady Violet that this long, slender slip of a female human could stand a chance of controlling him. Saffron stood by Tanqueray's massive, sculpted head, stroked his hard, muscular cheeks, talking to him all the while, getting him used to the sound of her voice. When the trip to the stables had been mooted over lunch, she had taken the precaution of discreetly sneaking a half-eaten apple out of the dining room. She now removed this from her pocket, still hidden within her hand, checked to see that Leon and Violet were engaged in their own conversation and not, at this precise moment, paying any attention to her and slipped it under Tanqueray's nose. He took the hint at once and snaffled the apple in the blink of an eye. Saffy gave Tanqueray's cheek a final pat and asked the stable-boy for a leg-up.

'You sure, Miss? Hell of a beast, this'un, pardon me saying so.'

'Quite sure, thank you.'

She placed one foot in the lad's cupped hands and sprang up into the saddle. A second later, before Tanqueray had any opportunity to object, she was walking him across the yard towards the five-bar gate that led into the paddock. The stable-boy ran ahead and opened it to let the horse and rider through. Leon and Violet followed them and stood by the rails that surrounded the paddock to see what would happen next.

'I do hope she will be all right,' said Violet, apprehensively.

Leon put a foot on the lower rail and leaned forward onto the fence. 'I'm more concerned for the horse. He has no idea what's about to hit him.'

Saffron trotted, just as she had promised . . . but only for a matter of seconds. She managed a nice, relaxed canter, for as short a span of time again. Then she leaned forward and said, 'Right, my lad, let's see what you're made of,' and kicked Tanqueray into a gallop, riding full pelt across the paddock towards the first fence.

Saffron whooped with delight. Now, for the first time since she had landed in England, three months earlier, she felt absolutely in control. For the next five minutes she drove Tanqueray back and forth across the paddock, approaching the fences from every conceivable angle, in every possible sequence, getting a feel for the horse beneath her, learning his individual mannerisms and quirks, feeling for the perfect, natural rhythm between her and him, like a yachtsman finding the perfect balance between his boat and the wind.

For animals, as for people, authority is best exercised as something so inevitable, so assured that neither side ever questions it. Men and women will happily follow a leader who gives them a sense of absolute confidence and control over his destiny and theirs. And horses will obey the hand of a rider who conveys that same air of command. Saffron had never considered how or why she could make a horse do what she wanted. She just knew that she could, knew it without the faintest shadow of a doubt and, like the perfect self-fulfilling prophecy, the horses she rode knew it too.

'My goodness,' said Lady Violet Courtney as Tanqueray thundered past her with Saffron crouched over him in her characteristic jockey style. 'That girl rides like the wind.'

'I know,' grinned Leon. 'Just wait till you see her shoot.'

A fortnight after Hitler's visit to Speer's studio, German troops marched into the Rhineland. Since the end of the war this great swathe of German territory on either side of the Rhine had by order of the Treaty of Versailles been a neutral, de-militarized zone into which no German forces were allowed. Until the start of the 1930s it had been occupied by French and British troops. Now Hitler had defied the Allied powers and demonstrated that he could get away with it, for there had been no response to his unilateral action. The Rhineland was truly German once again and there was nothing anyone could do about it.

Irrespective of his politics, Gerhard was a patriot and he too was caught up in the jubilation that had filled the overwhelming mass of the German people in the wake of Hitler's triumph. Three-quarters of his life had been led in the shadow of defeat and the shame that came with it. Foreigners had drawn up treaties that denied Germany the means to defend itself and imposed reparations that beggared a once-prosperous people. Gerhard had never suffered materially, as so many of his fellow countrymen and women had done, but he felt the humiliation of his country's debasement just as acutely. So he felt the renewal of national pride as well, and shared the pleasure of it too.

With the march into the Rhineland still fresh in the nation's mind, Hitler called a national referendum. It took the place of a conventional election and asked for a single yes or no response to what were in fact two questions: do you approve of the re-occupation of the Rhineland and of the election of the following candidates (all of whom were members of the Nazi Party, bar a few token and entirely spurious 'independents') to the Reich parliament? Of forty-five million voters, more than forty-four million voters responded, 'Yes.'

Gerhard was one of them. Then, on the morning after the result of the referendum came in, he had the chance to take a brand new fighter plane up for a training flight. It had been developed by the brilliant engineer Willy Messerschmitt at his company Bayerische Flugzeugwerke – another Bavarian company with which the Meerbach Motor Works had long had close links, which was the reason Gerhard received an invitation to try the new aircraft. It had been given the designation Bf 109 and it represented, he instantly realized, little short of a revolution in fighter design.

It looked sleek, yet also tough and purposeful, with wide, up-tilted wings that were squared off at the tips and a glass canopy that kept the pilot protected from the elements but provided perfect all-round vision. There were a few drawbacks with the 109. The cockpit was cramped for a man of Gerhard's height and, once landed, the aircraft sat with its tail on the ground and its nose tilted upwards, making it hard for the pilot to see where he was going when taxiing on the runway. It also took a bit of getting used to a single-winged craft that was bigger and heavier than the flimsy, but nimble biplanes with open cockpits that the veteran Luftwaffe pilots were accustomed to.

'They're like a bunch of old women, complaining that everything's going to hell and nothing is as good as the old days,' Messerschmitt had told Gerhard. 'But you are young. You never knew the old days. I think you will like it.'

Messerschmitt was right. From the moment the 109 was airborne it was a revelation to Gerhard: so fast, agile and strong that no matter how roughly Gerhard threw it about the sky it responded without complaint.

His only disappointment was that this prototype model was fitted with a British engine, a Rolls-Royce Kestrel; 'God in heaven, Willy, why didn't you ask us?' Gerhard asked. 'We could have made an engine worthy of such a magnificent design.'

Towards the end of his flight, as he was heading back to the airfield, with the adrenalin-driven excitement of the aerobatics he had been performing giving way to the deep contentment that he always felt in the air, Gerhard found himself looking back on everything that had happened to him and to his country over the past month.

The Rhineland was only the very first step on a much longer path, so far as Hitler was concerned. That much was obvious from the plans for the rebuilt Berlin. It was also very clear to Gerhard, from his own responses to Hitler's personal presence and to the whole nation's joy at his success, that the Führer had the power to make Germany do whatever he wanted. And if Willy Messerschmitt's Bf 109 was anything to go by, and there were tank designers and naval architects producing similar weapons for use on land and sea, the German armed forces would have the tools with which to carry out any tasks the Führer set them. On the surface that seemed like a glorious prospect but then there was that other vision of Nazism: the one Gerhard had received on that night in his father's study, when Heydrich had sat behind the old man's desk and painted a picture of a very different Germany, one in which the government had absolute power, individuals were helpless and Jews, or communists, or homosexuals – anyone, in fact, who did not fit the Nazi vision of an acceptable German – could be persecuted, punished and killed without the slightest right to any defence. That would be the empire that Hitler would rule from his palace in the new Berlin.

Leon had now set up the London branch of Courtney Trading and got it running to his satisfaction. Now it was time to take his bride to Kenya. As always, Leon was going by air.

'I've never been up in an aeroplane in my life, I've always travelled by boat,' Harriet admitted to Saffron as they stood in the main bedroom of the Chesham Court flat, surrounded by open trunks, suitcases and strewn clothes. 'Now I'm going all the way to Africa.'

'Don't you worry. It can be noisy, and smelly, and bumpy sometimes and some people get air-sick though I never do,' Saffron said, and then, seeing the look of alarm on Harriet's face, quickly added, 'But I'm sure you won't be bothered by any of that at all. And just wait till you fly over the Alps, and past the pyramids, and along the Great Rift Valley. Even if you are feeling a little poorly, you'll soon forget about it when you look out of the window and watch the world going by.'

Saffron, too, was on her travels a few days later, making her way by rail to Nuremberg, where Chessi von Schöndorf and her parents would meet her. At about the time that Gerhard von Meerbach had been taking the Messerschmitt through its paces, Saffy had been changing trains at Cologne and walked across a concourse packed with German soldiers in uniform. A week earlier, the Führer himself had paraded through the streets of the city at the head of a massive column of grey-uniformed troops and the station was still bedecked with the scarlet Nazi banners that had been hung to celebrate the great day and there were posters everywhere declaring the achievements of National Socialism.

Nuremberg was even more Nazified for this was the site of the great annual rallies that Saffron had read about and seen in newsreels even when she was in Africa. But there was Chessi on the platform, waiting to greet her with a great shriek of delight, a flurry of hugs and giggles and high-pitched, over-excited cries of '*Hujambo?*' '*Sijambo!*' The von Schöndorfs could not have been more welcoming and charming and it was all Saffron could do to persuade them, as politely as possible, that they really did not have to speak English to her and that she was actually very keen to practise her German. They drove to Regensburg, which was the nearest town to their family's ancestral home, and took her down narrow streets past high medieval houses with steepled roofs, and an old cathedral with two ornate spires, and through an arch in a building like a castle gatehouse onto a centuries-old bridge across the River Danube. 'It's just like a fairy tale!' Saffron sighed. 'I've never seen a more beautiful town in my life!'

For the next ten days she lived as a member of the von Schöndorf family and what struck Saffron was how similar their life was in so many ways to that of the Courtneys in Devon. The food was a bit different, of course. She came down to breakfast on the first day to find slices of cheese and cooked meats, black bread and coffee, when the Courtneys never began the day without a good bowl of porridge, followed by any combination they fancied of kippers, devilled kidneys, eggs, bacon, sausages, tomatoes, mushrooms and, of course, a proper cup of tea, with plenty of toast and marmalade to follow, if required. But those gastronomic details aside, the country life of long walks, cross-country rides, long conversations on rainy afternoons and songs around the piano in the evening was really no different. And though Chessi's father was, perhaps, a little more formal and regimented than Saffron's, there was no difference at all in the obvious love he felt for his daughter and her three younger brothers.

One night, Baron von Schöndorf announced that there was a film being shown at the local village hall that night. After supper the entire household, staff and family alike piled into an assortment of cars and drove down to the village. It was clear when they walked into the hall that absolutely every man, woman and child present knew the von Schöndorfs, who were greeted like something close to royalty and shown to a row of seats that had been specially reserved for them. The film turned out to be Charlie Chaplin's *City Lights*. It was a silent film and, there being no language barrier, could be enjoyed by anyone, anywhere, equally. Here was an English comedian, who lived in America, reducing two hundred German country folk to helpless laughter at Chaplin's foolery, and tears at the plight of the blind flower-girl that the little tramp with his bowler hat and cane befriended.

As Saffron and her new German friends drove back up to the Schöndorfs' house, Saffron thought about the common humanity that was so evident in the fact that her responses to the film had been no different to any of the Germans in that hall. They wanted nothing more than to live in peace and get on with their lives, which was all anyone in England, or Kenya for that matter, wanted too. Surely their leaders would realize that. Surely they wouldn't lead the world into war again.

For thousands of years people had lived in the place that Egyptians called al-Qahira. The pharaohs, Macedonians and Romans had come and gone. Coptic Christians, Jews and conquering Arabs had all created their own communities. But for Francis Courtney, Cairo was, and had always been a British city. He grew up in a large house close to his relatives the Ballantynes in the Garden City, where quiet, winding streets, planted with shady trees, were lined with the villas and mansions of the colonial elite. Life in those houses was essentially British and when the Courtney brothers had been taken to the Gezira Sporting Club, which stood on an island in the middle of the Nile, surrounded by another European suburb, Zamalek, they played tennis, cricket, golf and polo, as English gentlemen did wherever they went in the world.

Now, though, Francis was getting to know another Cairo. This was a much more crowded, dirty, but also more vibrant world, heady with spices, the aroma of thick, dark Turkish coffee and the smoke from countless shisha pipes. This was where, in great secrecy and taking endless precautions to ensure that he was not followed, Francis Courtney, director of Courtney Trading, stalwart of the British community in Cairo, had on three separate occasions come to a small room behind a modest restaurant on a shadowy sidestreet to meet Hassan al-Banna, founder of the Muslim Brotherhood.

Al-Banna was a decade younger than Francis, but, like Oswald Mosley, he was fired by a vision. And that vision touched something in Francis, just as Mosley's had done. For in the two years since that moment of revelation at the British Union of Fascists meeting at Earls Court, Francis had come to the realization that he not only wanted to see the creation of a new, better, purer Britain, he wanted the destruction of what had gone before. His motivation did not arise out of idealism, but from hatred and resentment. These emotions had their roots in his feelings about his brothers, Leon in particular. But they had grown from there to encompass everything he had always taken for granted but now found himself despising: all the cocktail parties filled with women who would not sleep with him; the sports he could no longer play; the friends whose numbers seemed to shrink with every passing year; the family business that was now thriving again and – despite his smaller shareholding – making him richer than he had ever been in his life. Yet that very growth in Courtney Trading's profits and the expansion of its businesses only made Francis even more embittered for it was making Leon richer still.

Francis wanted to tear the whole stinking edifice of British rule in Egypt to the ground. And, while he was at it, he wanted to bury the country's Jews in the ruins. Hassan al-Banna shared both these ambitions. He was, like so many revolutionaries, the child of a relatively prosperous, privileged family, and had been working as a schoolteacher in Ismalia, close to the Suez Canal, when he founded the Muslim Brotherhood. Ever since, he had denounced the rule of Islamic lands by colonial, infidel overlords and called upon his co-religionists to prepare themselves for a great *jihad* that would see them take back control of their own destinies.

It had been his old chum Piggy Peters who first alerted Francis to al-Banna's dreams of a great uprising. 'Mark my words, Courtney,' he said over his third pink gin, one long, hot afternoon, 'the wogs are getting restless. Chum of mine who works on the Canal tells me that there's some new gang called the Muslim Brotherhood, campaigning among the workers, getting them all het up about the evil infidels, telling Johnny Arab he should be leading a life of purity and devotion, reading the Koran all day long, God knows what other nonsense. Anyway, the upshot of it all is, rebellion is brewing in the ranks. Still a way off anything actually happening. But it's on the way.'

'Bloody hell, Piggy, that's a damned unhappy prospect,' Francis had said, but privately he was intrigued. He made further inquiries, discovered that al-Banna had relocated to Cairo and wrote to him, signing himself 'An Admirer' and offering financial assistance to the Brotherhood.

Hassan al-Banna had been wary in the extreme, fearful that he was being led into a trap. But when one five-hundred-pound donation was followed by another and no police came smashing through his door, he sent an intermediary to a rendezvous with his mysterious donor and that meeting was followed by face-to-face encounters with Courtney himself.

'Your assistance has helped me greatly,' al-Banna told him.

'The Brotherhood's message of liberation and religious observance is spreading. We have friends throughout the *ummah*, both here in Egypt and elsewhere. We are talking to them, planning with them, preparing for *jihad* together. Look to the north, my friend. Observe the gestures of the Black Hand. You will see what your money is buying.'

Francis had already learned that the '*ummah*' was the greater Islamic community around the world, irrespective of national boundaries. At Easter 1936, when the Arabs in Palestine, stirred up by a militant Islamic group that called itself the Black Hand, took the first steps towards outright rebellion against British rule and thereby launched a general strike, he understood what al-Banna had been talking about.

But that had not been the only message the leader of the Muslim Brotherhood had brought him. 'You are not the only inhabitant of *Dar-al-Harab*, the infidel empire that we call the House of War, who shares a common cause with us,' al-Banna had said. 'Others agree with us that our greatest of all enemies, even above the British, can be found in Zion. They have come to me offering assistance, just as you did, and I have taken the liberty of directing them to you, believing that you may be their friend as you are mine. They will make contact soon.'

Not long afterwards, Francis Courtney was invited in his role as a director of Courtney Trading to attend a form reception at the German Embassy, held to mark the visit of a German trade delegation to Egypt. It comprised officials from the Reich Ministry of Trade and Commerce, accompanied by a number of prominent businessmen, almost all of whom, Francis noticed, had a Nazi Party badge pinned to the left lapel of their dinner jackets.

One of the ministry men, who introduced himself as Manfred Erhardt, made it his business to introduce Francis to a number of the most influential businesspeople and to make it plain to them that Courtney Trading was a highly successful, influential and potentially useful company of which Francis was a very senior director and shareholder. 'Herr Courtney can supply us with oil for our factories, cotton for our mills and diamonds for our mistresses,' the official had said to his fellow delegates, and the laughter that followed had set the mood for some very positive and potentially profitable conversations.

'Thank you,' Francis said afterwards. 'That was damn kind of you. We could have spent years trying to break into the German market and not achieved as much as this one evening has done.'

'My dear fellow, think nothing of it,' Erhardt replied. 'I gather that we have mutual friends and mutual interests that – how shall I put it – extend beyond the world of commerce, no?'

'Ah, yes, I believe we do. I assume you have been following recent events in Palestine?'

'Of course, with great interest. Now, I must not detain you any longer. But I feel sure that tonight is the start of a partnership between Courtney Trading and the Third Reich that will prove beneficial to both parties. And I hope, also, that you and I will be able to have further discussions, about subjects of mutual interest in the weeks and months to come.'

'You're staying here in Cairo, then?'

'For a while, I think, yes.' He smiled affably. 'How would an Englishman say it? Ah yes . . . You haven't seen the last of me, old boy.'

Mr Brown was very clearly a man of considerable eminence, for he spoke very casually and without any sense of showing off about his encounters with Prime Ministers, from Gladstone – Mr Brown had been a very young man at the time of the great man's fourth and final administration – through to the present occupant of No.10 Downing Street, Stanley Baldwin. His opinions were judicious, measured, but not without a certain cutting edge. 'Mr Baldwin has already served two Kings of England in his first year in office, and it would not at all surprise me if, within a very short while, he is serving a third,' he remarked over dinner at one of the finest ducal dining tables in England, one June evening in 1936. He had saved his remark until the ladies had left the table for, as he liked to say, 'It is foolish, and even unfair to expect confidentiality as well as beauty from the fairer sex.' (In truth, Mr Brown's career had relied very considerably on the ability of women to extract secrets from hopelessly indiscreet men. But then, little about him was entirely as it seemed.)

'Dash it all, man, you can't say a thing like that,' the duke had exclaimed, calling over a footman to refresh his glass of port. 'His Majesty's a young man, still in the prime of his life. No reason at all to suppose he won't live for a good long while yet. Outlast us all, I dare say.'

'With respect, your grace, I was not suggesting that the King would die, merely that he would no longer be our monarch.'

Six months later, Edward VIII had indeed abdicated, giving up his throne for the love of a serial adulterer whose lovers, if Mr Brown's information was correct, included the German Ambassador in London, Joachim von Ribbentrop. At another dinner, just before Christmas, the duke who had been Brown's host told his guests, 'I'll tell you the queerest thing. A chap called Brown, sitting right here, at this table, as good as said that Edward was going to give up the throne, months before the balloon went up. I pooh-poohed him, said he was talking rot. Well, it just goes to show how wrong one can be, eh? Funny old cove, Brown. I'm damned if anyone knows exactly what he does, but he seems to have all the inside gen.'

'D'you know,' one of the other guests remarked, 'I'm not even sure that I've ever heard anyone address him by his Christian name. Don't have an earthly what it is, as a matter of fact. Isn't that strange?'

'Mr Brown's very charming,' the attractive marchioness

whom the duke had insisted should be sat next to him said. 'Of course, he must be seventy if he's a day, but he still has a rather naughty little twinkle in his eye, which is quite sweet.'

'Well, I'm almost seventy. I hope I can still twinkle sweetly!' said the duke.

'I wouldn't say you twinkle sweetly. I think you do it rather naughtily.'

The duke was delighted with that. Once the laughter died down, the conversation turned back to the crisis in the House of Windsor. 'How can one have a King who can't string two words together without gobbling like a Christmas turkey, that's what I want to know?' the duke had asked. It was only later, when the women were in the drawing room, waiting for the men to finish their conversation, that one of them mentioned Mr Brown again and said, 'The thing I like about him is that he listens to what one has to say. One spends so much time having to pretend to be fascinated by the most frightful bores droning on about themselves, but he is actually interested in one's life and one's opinions. And so one finds oneself saying all sorts of things that would never normally pop out of one's mouth. I have a feeling that he was quite a ladies' man in his day.'

Mr Brown was indeed a great listener. He knew that he was expected to sing for his supper and so made sure to have a few carefully selected titbits of Westminster or Whitehall gossip to pass on to his hosts, be they the owners of grand houses on Park Lane, or the Masters of Oxford and Cambridge colleges who regularly invited him to dine at their high tables. But he had long since learned that he didn't have to talk very much at all, provided that what he said was sufficiently interesting to make an impression. For the rest of the time he paid attention to what everyone else was saying. And as he went about his business in the eighteen months after the abdication, Mr Brown kept hearing snatches of conversation about a remarkable girl who had arrived in England from darkest Africa and caused quite a stir in the closed little world of upper-class England in which everyone knew one another, had gone to the same schools, served in the same regiments or come out at the same debutante balls. All the most important families were inter-related and women in particular could explain in great detail the ties of blood and marriage that linked them to this great landowner, or that political titan. So when someone new arrived on the scene, blessed with gifts that marked them out from the herd, they very soon made a name for themselves.

So it was with Saffron Courtney. 'I was down in Devon the other day, spent a weekend with Gilbert and Gladys Acland, down at Huntsham,' a retired general told Mr Brown over sherry at the Army and Navy Club, or 'the Rag' as its members called it in Pall Mall.

'How is Acland?' Mr Brown had asked.

'Same as always. Splendid fellow, decent as the day is long. His proudest boast is that in all the years he has been the Member for Tiverton he has never seen fit to open his mouth in the Chamber. "You won't find a single trace of me in Hansard," that's what he says. Typical Acland!'

'He is known as a good Committee man, though. He does a great deal of work behind the scenes.'

'He was a damn good soldier, too. Served in South Africa and in the war, colonel of his regiment, won an MC. Of course he's also Master of the Tiverton Foxhounds and the weekend I was there, he was hosting a meet at Huntsham. The Aclands had some other chums over for the weekend, the Courtneys, do you know them? Sir William and Lady Violet, live at a place called High Weald, charming couple.'

'I believe we've met,' said Mr Brown, whose ears had pricked at the mention of the name 'Courtney'.

'Well they'd brought a young cousin of theirs over, name of Saffron Courtney. Roedean girl, parents live in Kenya, staying with them for half-term, or some such. Well, I'm getting on a bit, same as you Brown, but I don't mind saying, if I were a young subaltern again, full of the joys of spring, I'd have made a play for young Miss Courtney. By God, she was a pretty young filly. Tall, mark you, looked me in the eye, but deep blue eyes, rosebud lips. What I'd give to be young again, eh?'

'Did you happen to catch who her people were?' Brown asked, thinking, *Can this possibly be Eva's little girl?*

'Funnily enough, Violet did mention something, let me think . . . Yes, that's right. Her father's a chap called Leon Courtney. Used to be a white hunter, I think. You know the sort, made a living taking rich tourists out on safari. He's as rich as Croesus himself now, apparently. No one's entirely sure how. He lost his first wife, the girl's mother, but remarried recently. Young Saffron's rather in favour of her new stepmother, as I recall.'

Yes, it is! After all these years, Mr Brown thought as he casually asked, 'Did you join the hunt?'

'I certainly thought about it. Won't deny it was damned tempting, but I'm afraid my days of riding to hounds are over. Wish I had gone, though, because once everyone got back, all that anyone could talk about was the Courtney girl's performance.'

'How so?'

'Well, the general gist of it was that they'd never seen anything like her. Her mount was a bloody great hunter that the Courtneys keep for their son, seventeen hands if it was an inch, absolutely not a lady's horse. Plenty of chaps, experienced horsemen, old cavalry types – some of 'em were speculating about how long it would be before the girl came a cropper, and serve her right, getting on a horse like that. Well, the hunt trotted off to some copse where the local peasantry claimed to have seen foxes. They all waited around, the way one does. Hunting is like war in that respect: endless waiting interspersed with sudden bouts of extreme activity. But anyway, the hounds eventually took the scent, gave tongue and it was tally-ho and off they all went, what?'

'Absolutely.'

'Now, I don't know if you're familiar with hunting in that part of the West Country . . .'

'Not especially.'

'Quite unlike anywhere else. You see, the fields tend not to be separated by walls or hedges, but by banks. About head high, I suppose, very steep, with just enough width on the top for a horse to gather its feet before it jumps down the other side. Of course, riders who aren't used to this sort of thing tend to need a bit of time to master the technique, get used to it all.'

'I can well imagine.'

'But not our Miss Courtney. She had that brute of a stallion up and over the tallest, steepest banks without even blinking. Acland said it was like watching Fulke Walwyn take Reynoldstown over the jumps at Aintree. The girl was a complete natural, apparently. Wonderful seat, brave as a lion, but unfortunately had not the first idea about proper behaviour. Not surprising, I suppose, if she's grown up in the wilds of Africa. At one point, I'm told, she dashed past the whippers-in and was riding alongside the Huntsman, which is as far from the done thing as one can possibly get. Acland had to have a word with Bill Courtney afterwards, ask him to read his young cousin the rules, as it were. But he couldn't bring himself to be angry with her. No one could. She was just such a splendid horsewoman, d'you see?'

'I knew her mother,' Mr Brown said, unable to keep an uncharacteristic note of sentiment from his voice and immediately regretting his indiscretion.

'Was she a beauty too?' the general asked.

Mr Brown decided he might as well continue to play the game. 'She was, without a doubt, the single most beautiful woman on whom I have ever clapped eyes.'

'I see . . . know her well, did you?'

Mr Brown gave an enigmatic, but suggestive shrug.

'You sly old dog!' said the general and then repeated, 'Ah what I'd give to be young.'

Saffron arrived back in Kenya for the summer holidays to find Lusima in a state of frenzied activity. A team of Indian builders and decorators – for in Kenya, the settlers always hired Indians to build and maintain their homes, just as they chose Somalis to serve in them – had set up an office and dormitory in one of the outbuildings, while Harriet supervised the total transformation of the interior of the house. Saffron's initial reaction was shock: Harriet had written to her to say that she was doing 'a little bit of redecoration', but Saffy had no idea that this was what she had in mind.

'Nor did I,' confessed Harriet when Saffron asked. 'But as soon as I started making one room look nice, well . . . come with me. I'll show you what I mean.'

She led Saffron into the drawing room, whose most striking feature were two sets of French windows what opened onto a terrace beyond which one could see the garden and a spectacular view of the Aberdare mountain range, rising up in the distance. Saffron's first impression was how much brighter the room seemed and then she began to spot all the changes that had made it that way: the fresh white paint around the windows, the cornicing around the top of the room and the ceiling itself: a new, pale rose coloured carpet; fresh wallpaper and large vases filled with lovely roses from the garden. She also noticed something else: Harriet hadn't changed the pictures on the wall or the framed photographs on the piano, some of which showed the family when Eva was still alive. She had put her stamp on the room, but acknowledged everything that had gone before her.

'It looks really nice,' Saffron told her.

Harriet heaved a sigh of relief. 'I'm so glad you like it. I've been so worried in case you didn't. Now, let's go into the dining room.'

Saffron walked into the room where she had eaten so many meals, always sitting in her chair, always looking across the table to the antique mahogany sideboard in which the china and silver were kept. The furniture had all been removed, for the Indians were due to start work on the room within the next few days. But that only served to highlight how dowdy and faded the floor-to-ceiling curtains over the windows were, how worn the carpet, how cracked and dirty the paint on the skirting boards.

Saffron saw at once why the process of redecorating, once started, was bound to consume the whole house. But she had to bite her lip, for the sight of a room she had loved for so long looking quite so dowdy and sad made her want to cry. 'Oh . . .' she said, for once in her life quite lost for words.

'I know,' said Leon, walking into the room behind her. 'Makes you realize how I just let the place go to seed.'

'No you didn't, Daddy. You just didn't . . .' Saffron cast around for the right word.

'I didn't pay attention,' Leon interrupted her. 'I suppose I was just being a typical man, concentrating on business and the estate and all the things that interested me and not actually paying any attention to the house, or anything in it.'

'I've had to change all the bed-linen,' Harriet said. 'The sheets were so worn I could practically see right through them and the towels . . . well, the least said about them the better.'

'Not really my sort of thing, buying linens,' Leon admitted. 'And I'll tell you something else, Saffy, the grub's a lot better round here these days, too.'

'Dinner last night was delicious, now you come to mention it. I had a chat with *Mpishi* and his *totos*,' Harriet said, as Saffron and Leon exchanged amused glances at how fast she had picked up the Swahili words for a cook and kitchen-boys. 'In my experience staff actually like to be kept on their toes. It shows

265

them someone cares. If they cook well, I make a point of complimenting them and if they don't they soon hear about that too. I think we all understand one another.'

'I think they're all completely petrified of you, my darling,' Leon said. 'But devoted to you, too, which is as it should be. Now, the reason I was looking for you two was that I suddenly realized that the rest of the estate might have been quietly wasting away for the past ten years, just like the house has done. And since my study is about to get the Harriet Courtney treatment, it seemed like a good time to go on a proper tour of inspection. So I'll be heading off at crack of dawn tomorrow, Manyoro's coming with me, just the two of us, on foot, sleeping under the stars. It will be like old times.'

'I wish he was that enthusiastic about spending time with me,' Harriet remarked, with mock disappointment, though the smile on her face suggested that she knew very well how much Leon loved her company.

'Did you say that you're redecorating the study?' Saffron asked, with a note of anxiety in her voice. 'What are you doing about . . .' she paused and glanced apologetically at Harriet before concluding, 'about Mummy's picture?'

'That's a very good question,' Leon replied. 'Harriet and I talked about it at length. I don't think it would be right for any man to start a new life with his second wife if the first one is still hanging around the house like Marley's ghost.'

'But Mummy's not . . .'

'Wait! Hold your horses, Saffy, and let me finish . . . I love that picture as much as you do. Which is why, at Harriet's suggestion, I have asked Vassileyev to copy Mummy's head as a much smaller portrait, which we will hang somewhere, though I haven't decided exactly where just yet. Meanwhile the original portrait will be properly packed for storage so that you can have it when you are old enough to have a place of your own.'

'And we're going to get a new picture done . . . of us,' Harriet said, stepping across to Leon and taking his arm. The two of them looked at Saffron and she realized from the way they were looking at her that they were hoping for her approval.

This role reversal was something she had never experienced before, but their happiness and their hope that she would be included in it was so obviously sincere that she was completely won over.

'I think that's a lovely idea,' she said. 'But when it's done, you shouldn't hide it away in the study. You should put it in the dining room where everyone can see it.'

'Well, that's a thought,' said Leon. 'Now, if you ladies will excuse me, I have to sort out my kit for the great trek around the estate.'

'It makes such a difference, you being here,' Saffron said to Harriet when they were alone again. 'It's like the secret garden coming to life again.'

'Oh, I loved *The Secret Garden* when I was a girl!' said Harriet.

'Me too, though I always cried and cried when Colin's father came back to the house, no matter how many times I read it. I think I was really imagining Mummy coming back to me.'

'I never knew my father. He left my mother before I was even born. I still wonder if he's out there somewhere, just waiting to see me again . . .'

Saffron rushed across and gave Harriet a hug. Harriet squeezed her back, but then, after a few seconds, stepped back and said, 'So, shall we go and have a look at your room? I didn't dare touch a single thing without your permission, and you have my promise that if anything is done, it will be exactly as you like it.'

The following morning, Saffron was awake before dawn. She pulled on a pair of shorts and a jumper and went downstairs to the kitchen where she made herself a cup of tea and then took it outside. The air was still chilly as the very first faint light of the new day drew a pale golden line along the eastern horizon as Saffy sat down on the steps that led from the kitchen into the back yard, with her knees drawn up to her chest and her mug clutched in both hands to keep them warm.

Slowly that side of the house began to stir into life as the first *totos* emerged from their sleeping quarters to start work baking the fresh rolls for breakfast.

They grinned to see Saffron, who greeted each man by name, for she had known them all her life. Speaking in Swahili, scattered with the occasional Arabic phrase, she asked after their families, some of whom were thousands of miles away in Somalia, taking the trouble to listen to their answers and respond with as much interest as she would to one of her friends.

Finally the reason for her early rising appeared.

'Uncle Manyoro!' she cried and dashed towards him just as if she were still a little girl.

They exchanged greetings and then he looked at her with a serious, almost frowning expression on his face and said, 'You have changed, my little princess. You have become a woman.' Then his face was illuminated by a huge smile as he said, 'Now I shall call you my queen.'

A *toto* appeared, without needing to be called, and respectfully handed Manyoro a cup of the strong, black, heavily sweetened coffee without which he could not properly begin his day.

'So, Saffron, what has made you wait for me here, outside on this step, in the cold morning air, when you could be warm in your bed inside?'

'I needed to know something.'

'And what would that be?'

'What do you think of Harriet? Do you like her? Do you think that everyone on the estate will like her?'

268

'Hmm . . .' he replied, sipping his coffee. 'I can hear from your voice that you like her very much and that you want me to say yes.'

'Don't you want to say yes?' Saffron asked, suddenly alarmed.

Manyoro took some more coffee then said, 'You know that I loved your mother very much. She was my brother's woman and so she was like a sister to me.'

'Yes, I know.'

'When she was gone, the light went out of my brother's life. He walked and talked and appeared to be a man, but he was really just an empty shell. The loss of your mother had taken away his heart.'

'I know . . .'

'So for all those years, I felt his sadness and it made me sad too. I had my wives and my children and they made me happy. I wanted my brother to be happy too. Now he has a new Mrs Courtney . . .' he paused and Saffron could scarcely bear the tension until Manyoro said, 'And now the light has returned to my brother's eyes. Now his heart beats again. Everyone can feel it. Their chief has a woman. She has made him a man again. And that makes them happy. That makes me, very, very happy.'

'Oh, Manyoro, I'm so glad!' said Saffron wrapping her arms around one of his strong biceps. 'I feel just the same way. It's like the house. I didn't realize how shabby it had become until I saw how Harriet was making it all new. And I didn't really know how sad Daddy had been until I saw how happy he was with her.'

'She is a strong woman, too . . . I like that. A man like M'Bogo needs a mate who can match his strength with hers.' He chuckled. '*Mpishi* told me a story about his new mistress. He said she is very strict. Everything has to be done in exactly the right way, just as she commands it.'

'I know,' giggled Saffron. 'I've seen her giving orders.'

269

'So he asked himself, "What will happen if I do not do exactly as the mistress says? Will she notice it?"'

'Oh dear . . .'

'So one day, when he cooked dinner, he made the meal perfectly, everything as it should have been . . . except for the potatoes. He had been told to make boiled potatoes, but instead he fried them. He fried them as well as he could. But still they were not boiled.'

'So what happened?'

'The meal was served. Every scrap of food was eaten. Afterwards, Mrs Courtney came into the kitchen. She praised *Mpishi* and the *totos* for the meal. She said the food was delicious and that the boys had served it very well. She turned to leave and then, just as she got to the door, she turned around and said to *Mpishi*, "But if you ever cook the potatoes the wrong way again, I will have to have words with *Bwana* Courtney and ask him to have you dismissed."'

'Oh no!' Not even Saffron had thought Harriet would be so severe. 'How terrible for *Mpishi*!'

'Not at all, he was extremely delighted. He said to me, "I have been invisible since the first *memsahib* died. Now they see me again and all is well." And he is right, all is well.'

Manyoro got to his feet and said, 'Now I must leave you. Your father will be wondering where I am. And I must not keep him waiting. It would make Mrs Courtney very angry, and she might have me dismissed!'

And with that, guffawing mightily at his own joke, Manyoro went into the house, leaving Saffron glowing with happiness on the step behind him.

Gerhard and Konrad von Meerbach did not make a habit of spending time together, not if they could avoid it. But on a perfect summer's evening, with the air warm and still, Konrad happened to find himself at a reception held on a terrace by the bank of the River Spree to celebrate the successful completion of all the preparations necessary to ensure the complete success of the Olympic Games that would be held in the city in barely two weeks' time. Konrad was delighted to have received an invitation, since this was very much an occasion for the rulers of the Reich, who had issued all the orders, than the bureaucrats, artisans and labourers who had done all the work. He was wearing his SS dress uniform, which was all the more impressive since a recent promotion had put a silver oak leaf on his collar tab, and feeling all the more smug for all the admiring glances he was receiving from the women that he passed by.

There was, Konrad well knew, an infallible correlation between the wealth and power of the men at any given occasion and the beauty of the women. On this occasion, the men were the most powerful in all the Reich and the female guests were correspondingly lovely. The balmy weather had inspired many of them to wear light silk dresses that exposed their arms, their shoulders, their décolletages and, in some cases, draped so low around their naked backs, barely covering the tops of their buttocks, that they could not possibly be wearing any undergarments. It was on nights like this that Konrad was grateful for his wife Trudi's acceptance of his decision that she should remain in Bavaria to raise their two-year-old son and newly arrived baby daughter. Trudi was a pretty, docile, but insipid blonde whose most appealing feature was that she was a great-niece of Gustav von Bohlen und Halbach, or Gustav Krupp as he now liked to be known, having married the heiress to the great Krupps steelmaking and armaments company. It was good for Konrad's personal status and the Meerbach Motor Works business to be in with the most powerful industrial dynasty in Germany. And it was good for his sex-life if his wife was several hundred kilometres away in a delightful house in the grounds of Schloss Meerbach while he was chasing women in Berlin.

He was just deciding which of the women to target first when his eye was caught by the sight of a familiar figure in an elegant, but rather too casually cut suit, smiling charmingly at three little beauties who seemed enthralled by his company.

No, it can't be . . . God in heaven, it is. Damn him!

Konrad forced himself to grit his teeth and paste a sickly smile across his face: it was a worthwhile sacrifice if it got him any closer to the women. 'Gerd, what a pleasant surprise to see you here. Come now, brother, introduce me to your delightful friends.'

'Of course,' smiled Gerhard, while the young women simpered at the big, tough-looking SS officer who had just arrived on the scene. 'Konnie, let me introduce you to Gerda, Sabi and Jana. Ladies, this is my big brother, *SS-Standartenführer* Konrad Graf von Meerbach.'

Konrad clicked his heels and nodded his head to the ladies. 'I am honoured to meet you.'

Gerhard smiled, for all the world like an affectionate younger brother who was delighted to be able to show off his impressive older sibling. 'You picked a perfect time to pop by, Konnie. I was just about to tell the girls about my recent meeting with the Führer himself.'

'Your what?' Konrad replied, completely unable to keep the shock or incredulity out of his voice. The smart-arsed little pup had to be up to some kind of tomfoolery. It was inconceivable that he was telling the truth. 'Is this some kind of a joke? I have to tell you Gerhard, it is in very bad taste if it is.'

'Fear not, old man, this is nothing other than the absolute honest truth. It was my genuine honour and privilege to meet the Führer when he paid a visit to the Speer architectural practice, where I work. He even patted me on the arm and said I was an example of National Socialism at its best.'

Konrad felt the sense of self-satisfaction that had been buoying him up so pleasurably just a few moments before evaporate into the Berlin night, leaving him bitterly deflated.

For years he had boasted of his closeness to the most powerful figures in the Nazi hierarchy, and he was telling nothing but the truth. He worked every day with Heydrich, spoke frequently to Himmler and had been introduced to Bormann and Goebbels. He had often even been in the same room as Hitler. But never, not once had he actually exchanged words with the Führer.

'How did this encounter take place?' Konrad said, doing his very best not to let too much of the poison in his heart seep into his words. It would not do him any good with the women if he were seen to envy his younger brother.

'Well, I have the honour of working on the plans for the future transformation of Berlin into a capital worthy of the Reich. This is a project very dear to the Führer's heart, and so . . .'

Gerhard told the story of his meeting with Hitler. It was painfully obvious to Konrad that he was telling the truth, not least because of the relish with which he described the Führer congratulating him for both building the Reich and defending it.

'How can you be an architect and a Luftwaffe pilot?' one of the girls – Konrad thought she might have been the one called Jana – asked.

Because I damn well ordered him to be! thought Konrad.

'Oh, I'm just a reservist, a part-time fighter pilot,' Gerhard said, with a self-deprecating smile that had the three girls practically melting into a puddle in front of him.

'Do you like flying?' Sabi piped up, casting big brown doe eyes in Gerhard's direction.

'I absolutely love it,' he said. 'There is absolutely nowhere in the world where I feel more at peace, more absolutely in control of my destiny, and more surrounded by the glory of this wonderful planet than when I am up in the sky, as free as a bird. It's the most wonderful feeling you can imagine.'

As the girls sighed adoringly, Konrad contemplated the bitter irony of the situation. He had sent Gerhard off to do a job he should have hated, and join a branch of the armed forces to which his free-spirited character should have been entirely unsuited. And the little bastard had ended up becoming the Führer's personal pet – Gerhard had returned to the story of his meeting and was recounting every word of his conversation about the Great Hall.

'It's really just boring stuff, lots of talk about vents and air-circulation,' Gerhard said.

'How can it be boring, telling us what the Führer said?' asked Sabi.

'Is it true that when you meet him, it's not like meeting anyone else on earth?' Trudi wondered.

'Yes,' said Gerhard, 'that is absolutely true. It is a quite extraordinary experience.'

Konrad didn't think that anything could top the surprises that had already been flung at him, but Gerhard's awestruck praise of Hitler beat them all.

'So you, my sceptical, rebellious brother now accept that the Führer is the greatest man of our times?'

'I accept that he has a power that is truly unique,' Gerhard replied. 'When he looked right at me, standing as close to me as I am to you all now, it was like nothing I have ever known before, and for that moment there was nothing he could have said that I would not have believed and no order he could have given that I would not have obeyed. And I am absolutely certain that any one of you would have felt exactly the same thing if you had been in my place.'

Silence fell over the little group. No one knew quite how to follow that. Konrad cleared his throat. 'Well, I must be going. People to meet, things to do – this is a working event for me, I'm afraid. Good to see you, Gerd. My congratulations on your remarkable encounter with the Führer. That is a rare privilege. Ladies . . .'

He bowed again and walked away. There had been no point at all in staying. He simply couldn't compete with Gerhard.

Konrad paused by the balustrade at the edge of the terrace and looked out across the river, taking in the scene. He lit a cigarette and smoked it thoughtfully, and as he did so his spirits, so recently deflated, began to rise again. This evening might have appeared to be a triumph for Gerhard. But surely, on reflection, he, Konrad, was the true victor. For he had taken a rebel who had to be forced, virtually on pain of death, to toe the Nazi line and set him on the path to becoming a true believer. Gerhard's conversion to Hitler's cause, that afternoon in Speer's office, had been a modern-day equivalent to St Paul's conversion to Christianity, when he saw God on the road to Damascus.

You belong to us now, little brother, Konrad thought as he threw the end of his cigarette into the murky waters of the Spree. *You belong to Adolf Hitler!*

Gerhard asked Sabi if she wanted to leave with him, then Jana asked if she could come too. So he slipped a ten Reichsmark note into one of the wine waiter's hand and was given a bottle of the excellent French champagne that the waiters had been serving in return. They went back to Gerhard's apartment where they quickly polished off the champagne and then a bottle of schnapps that Gerhard had in his drinks cabinet. Then he discovered that there was most of a bottle of an excellent Riesling in his refrigerator, so he took that into his bedroom and the girls followed him in one on each arm, giggling as they kicked off their high heels and slipped out of their dresses. Then Gerhard had both of the girls and then lay against the quilted headboard of his king-sized bed, watching while they played at kissing and petting one another until he was fully restored and able to join in again, too.

When every permutation had been worked through and they were all exhausted Jana and Sabi fell asleep, one on either side of him. Gerhard, however, was still wide-awake, still restless despite his physical fatigue. He slipped out of the bed and watched as they rearranged themselves in their sleep until they were curled up in a tangle of soft curves, gold and chestnut hair, and warm, sweet skin like two pretty, pampered little kittens in a basket. He went out onto the balcony of his apartment and, in an unconscious echo of his brother's actions, smoked a cigarette as he looked out at the sleeping city.

Gerhard had been corrupted, he knew that. Not completely perhaps, but even if he had not sold his soul – not beyond redemption – he had at least allowed it to be used for causes in which he did not believe. In return he had received a new form of status to go with that which he had inherited, for the Führer's personal approval had marked him out as a coming man and, like a singer becoming a star overnight after a single brilliant performance, he was now regarded everywhere as a coming man in the Party and the Reich. He was not exactly famous, but, as the women in his bed demonstrated, he received the perks of one who was.

He consoled himself with two thoughts. The first was that his flying still remained pure and unsullied as an expression of his true self. And the other was that he had been more careful than anyone realized when he described Hitler's effect upon him. He had seen how furious Konrad had been when he discovered that his despised brother had been blessed by the Führer in a way he had never been. But he had also seen the first signs of the smugness returning to Konrad's features when he heard what must have sounded, to his ears, like the praise of a besotted, adoring devotee. For it would never have occurred to Konrad that Gerhard did not glory in Hitler's powers of mesmerism, just as he would have done, that in fact Gerhard was terrified by the way that he had been seduced and what that told him about the way that the whole country had fallen under Hitler's spell.

But can I escape that spell? Gerhard asked himself. *Do I have the willpower and the courage to resist it?*

And the reason he was still so wide-awake and quite unable to sleep was his fear that the answer was: *No.*

Saffron went back to Roedean in September and settled down to the final year-and-a-bit of school. When the autumn term ended, two weeks before Christmas, she found that she was almost sorry to be flying out to Kenya for the holiday: not because she did not want to see her father and Harriet, but because it meant missing so many of the balls and house parties to which her school friends and family members had invited her. She arrived back at Lusima, where all the renovation work had finally been completed, to discover that Harriet had created a miniature gallery of family pictures that ran up the stairs from the front hall to the bedrooms. She had contacted Grandma Courtney in Cairo who had sent her a small pencil portrait of Leon as a boy, and some ancient photographs of him with his parents and brothers. Centaine had contributed a photograph that she had taken of Saffron and Shasa during the visit to Cape Town four years earlier, and another shot of Shasa in his polo gear, about to compete for South Africa in the Berlin Olympics. Harriet's own childhood was represented too, along with a photograph of all the shopgirls, herself included, at the school outfitters where she had first met Leon and Saffron. And there, discreetly placed among them, was the head of Eva that Vassileyev had copied from his own portrait of her. He had somehow added a slightly wistful air to her expression that gave a sense of her absence, as if she were gently regretting that she could not be there among them all in person. By including Eva as part of a wider family, Harriet had found a way to honour her importance to Leon and Saffron without in any way being overshadowed by the past.

Saffron was touched by the thoughtfulness of the gesture and the trouble Harriet must have taken to assemble all the various pictures. But there was no hiding who was mistress of the Lusima estate now. Harriet presided over a great Christmas tea-party for all the estate workers and their families, with little presents for all the children. There was a dinner to celebrate Saffron's arrival from England, attended by local families she had known all her life. When the ladies retired from the table, Saffron was struck by the degree to which the other women in the local expatriate community, even those who came from much smarter backgrounds, had not only accepted Harriet as her own, but even deferred to her a little. Of course, Harriet happened to be the wife of one of the richest men in the entire country, but that would not, of itself, have prevented catty remarks designed to put her in her place: gentle, and even not-so-gentle reminders that she had been a shop manageress not so very long ago. There was an assurance, however, about the way she carried herself, and a strong suggestion of barely hidden steel that silenced any doubters, even before they had opened their mouths. If anything, by transforming the appearance of Lusima, and raising the standards of the household so dramatically, from the delicious food, to the impeccable service, to the basket of perfectly ironed hand-towels in the spotless downstairs lavatory (where amusing cartoons hung on the walls and a small vase of scented flowers was placed on the deep-set windowsill), she had made people see Leon in a different light. He had been looked on as a former white hunter: handsome, even charming when he wanted to be, but still a little rough around the edges, who happened to have come into a large amount of money in mysterious circumstances. Now he was fast acquiring a new identity as a gentleman landowner and pillar of the community.

It struck Saffron, as she lay in bed after the dinner party running over the evening's events in her head, that she was changing too, just as her father was. Thanks to the flat in Chesham Place she had been able to spend weekend exeats, a half-term and a few days waiting for her flight up in London. She was getting to know the city a little better now and leading a life that was very different to her tomboy existence in Kenya. She saw girlfriends for lunch or tea in fashionable restaurants and cafés. They furthered her education in the pleasures of shopping, even when one didn't really buy very much but just scouted all the nicest shops, looking at the other customers as much as the goods on the shelves or the dresses on the rails, getting a sense of what was or was not stylish; what did or did not suit. She bought magazines like *Vogue*, *Tatler* and *The Queen* and found herself becoming equally familiar with the names of the smartest London and Paris fashion designers, and of the beautiful women – actresses and aristocrats – who wore the dresses that the designers made and went to the parties where one simply had to be perfectly dressed if one was to be taken even remotely seriously. And with every party she herself went to, Saffron realized that even if she didn't know Lady This, or the Hon Mrs That, she did know her younger sister or her niece.

Having spent another fortnight with the von Schöndorfs in Bavaria at Easter, Saffron took her Higher School Certificate exams in June 1937 and her Oxford entrance papers in December that year, for Oxford and Cambridge both insisted on selecting their students by their own specific examinations. She spent the Christmas holidays in England this time, enjoying ten days of parties in London, before taking the train down to Devon to spend Christmas with her Courtney relations, then taking the train up from Exeter to London, then catching the sleeper up to Edinburgh for a Scottish Hogmanay with her Ballantyne cousins. Two months later she discovered that she had been given a place at Lady Margaret Hall to study Politics, Philosophy and Economics, exactly as she had planned.

Saffron spent the early months of 1938 in London. It was obvious to her that Germany was the rising power in Europe, and Britain's relations with the Reich, whether peaceful or otherwise, would be the dominant theme of the next few years. So she decided to improve on the conversational German she had picked up from Chessi and her family and signed up for three lessons a week with a tutor, based in South Kensington. Her aunt Penny Miller, the older of Leon's two sisters, had been widowed very young in the war and never remarried. Like Dorian, Penny had inherited Grandma Courtney's artistic gifts. She had recently moved from Cairo to London and was renting a studio-cum-flat in Tite Street, off the King's Road in Chelsea.

It was a colourful, bohemian quarter and Penny's friends were all painters, poets, musicians and actors, none with two pennies to rub together, and all of them filled with a variety of passions, be they creative, political or sexual. Here was another new world for Saffron to explore and she soon learned that she had to dress down for evening at Aunt Penny's just as she had to dress up for cocktails at the homes of her debutante friends. But she loved the free and easy world of late-night dinners in cheap Greek restaurants and endless conversations on the meaning of life and love over bottles of rough red wine just as much as the smartest ball in Eaton Place or Park Lane, where knots of passers-by would gather on the pavements to watch the girls arrive in their gowns and family jewels, before dancing the night away to Ambrose and his orchestra. And every Friday afternoon, without fail, found Saffron at one of London's mainline rail termini, en route to that weekend's house party, where some combination of hunting, shooting, dancing and dining awaited. For no one, not even the most radical of Aunt Penny's friends, spent a single weekend in London if they could possibly avoid it.

As winter turned to spring and the first cricket matches of May heralded the onset of another English summer, Leon and Harriet arrived back in England. Leon attended to business at the office on Ludgate Hill while Harriet helped prepare Saffron for the Season. This was the summer-long round of events, both private and public – for the Wimbledon tennis, Henley regatta and the cricket match between the schoolboys for Eton and Harrow (all of them future husband material for the debutantes) were all a part of it – that formed the 'coming out' of upper-class girls as they left the shelter of their family homes and were thrown on the marriage market.

Saffron had not the slightest intention of finding a husband: she had Oxford to attend and, though she had not yet mentioned this to her father, a business career of her own to start first. Still she played along with the game, going to the annual Queen Charlotte's Ball where the girls all curtseyed before a giant cake, and then curtsying again, this time for the King himself when she was introduced at Court by her Cousin Violet. In order for a girl to be allowed this honour, she had to be accompanied by a sponsor who had herself been introduced in the past and Violet was only too happy to do it.

In July, Saffron, Penny and Harriet persuaded Leon to accompany them to the London exhibition of German Expressionists, internationally renowned artists including Kokoschka and Kandinsky who had all, to a man, been banished by the Nazis. Just that month, Hitler had raged against them as 'lamentable unfortunates who plainly suffer from defective sight. They can live and work where they choose, but not in Germany.'

'I'm hardly an admirer of Mr Hitler, but I think he may have a point,' muttered Leon, as he looked at the paintings, most of which, in his view, came under the category of 'a six-year-old could have done better' or, in some extreme cases, 'a monkey'. But then he stopped in front of a painting by an artist called Magnus Zeller, which the card beside it revealed was called 'Der Hitlerstaat (The Hitler State)'. It showed a ruined landscape across which an army of slaves, whipped by men in black SS uniforms, were dragging a giant cart on which was mounted the monumental statue of a seated ruler who looked like an

Ancient Egyptian pharaoh. The entire picture was painted in a bleak palette of grey and browns, and the only splashes of bright colour came from the Nazi banners that fluttered around the great king's feet.

Leon stopped dead in front of the picture and stared at it intently, not saying a word. Finally, he turned to Saffron and asked, 'You've been there, tell me: is this how it will all end?'

Saffron thought of all the banners she had seen on her visits to Germany. She cast her mind's eye over all the propaganda posters. There were more of them every year and their tone was becoming progressively more hostile: not celebrating the Nazi government's achievements but berating its enemies, particularly the Jews. There were more anti-Jewish slogans painted on walls and shop windows – or perhaps there just seemed to be more because she could understand them so much better now. But then she thought of the von Schöndorfs and their friendship and generosity towards her, feelings that had been echoed by the overwhelming number of people she had met in Germany. And yet, she had seen those black uniforms, too.

'I don't know,' she said, finally. 'But I fear that it might.'

Two days later Saffron was at home in Chesham Place when her father came back from the office. 'I've been talking to Hartley Grainger. I told him not to renew any of our German contracts when they come to the end of their terms. No need to do anything dramatic just yet, so we won't cancel any that are still active. Just won't look for new deals, that's all. Your uncle Frank won't be happy. The German trade is his baby. But I think you're right, Saffy. I think we're in for rough weather and it's time to start battening down the hatches.'

For the past two years Mr Brown had found himself encountering mentions of Saffron Courtney wherever he went. In Oxford she was regarded as Zuleika Dobson, Max Beerbohm's fictional *femme fatale*, whose beauty drives university men mad with passion, brought to life. In Scotland, staying with her Ballantyne cousins over the New Year, she had caused as much astonishment with her marksmanship on a pheasant shoot as her skill and daring on a horse had done in Devon. A fellow guest at the house party told him, 'The ghillie turned to Ballantyne and said, "Yon wee lassie's putting every gun in Scotland tae shame."'

'Of course, the Courtney girl's absolutely ravishing.' Lady Diana Cooper, one of the great beauties of a slightly earlier age, and still ravishing in her early forties, had mentioned Saffron to him one evening at a cocktail party in Berkeley Square. 'What I rather admire is the way she handles her money. It's perfectly obvious that she has an awful lot of it. I can assure you that any woman looking at her would know at once that all her dresses are hand-made, and not by some little old lady-who-does, either. I was talking to Hardy Amies just the other day and he was in raptures, talking about what a delight it was to dress her. Eddie Molyneux adores her too, he'd use her as a mannequin if he could. Of course she has that slightly boyish figure, which all the queers love, and dresses hang so much more elegantly if one's not too curvy. But the admirable aspect is her understatement.'

'How do you mean?'

'Well, she's very young and, not to put too fine a point on it, colonial. She hasn't grown up in smart homes, surrounded by well-dressed women, who know how to be *comme il faut*. In a way, that's part of her charm. She has a slight air of wildness. One gets the impression she could go off hunting lions without turning a hair. So one might expect her to be a little vulgar, overdone.'

'Just a little too flashy?'

'Exactly. Dear Mr Brown, you are so nice to talk to. You always understand just what one means.'

'I do my best, Lady Cooper. But how does this absence of vulgarity manifest itself?'

'Well, by its absence!' she laughed. 'I mean, whenever one sees Saffron Courtney one always thinks, that's a very well-dressed girl. Her shoes are always just right for her dress and for the occasion. Her handbags are delightful. Her jewellery is very nice but discreet. Actually, that's the word for it: discreet. Either someone has told her, or she's worked out for herself, that with looks like hers and that dazzling personality, she doesn't need her clothes to be anything but a very chic, elegant backdrop.'

'I hesitate to make an observation about women, particularly with regard to their relations with other women . . .'

'Very wise. It's not a subject upon which men are likely to have anything remotely useful to say.'

'But let me suggest something, just as a hypothesis . . .'

Lady Diana smiled. 'Very well then, Mr Brown, just this once, since you are really quite perceptive, for a man.'

'I think Miss Courtney's intelligence is evident in the freedom with which you, and other ladies to whom I have spoken, compliment her. I can imagine a girl like her, arriving in England, blessed with wealth, looks, a remarkable sportswoman . . . Well, such a creature might cause considerable ill feeling among some members of her sex. Not you, of course, Lady Cooper, you have no need whatever to fear competition . . .'

'You said that just in time.'

'But other women, particularly of Miss Courtney's own generation, and perhaps a few years older than her, might resent the competition she presented to them and feel inspired to spread malicious gossip, or criticize her behaviour. You know the sort of thing.'

'I'm afraid to say that I do. I dare say I provoked a bit of it when I was Saffron Courtney's age.'

'And yet, while she seems to have made a tremendous impression upon society in the past year or two, I have not heard a single bad word about her, aside, perhaps, from the disappointment of the mothers whose sons have failed to win her heart.'

'Yes,' mused Lady Diana, thoughtfully, 'one hasn't heard the slightest suggestion of a love-affair, which is unusual, with a girl that attractive.'

'She is very young, you know, only just nineteen.'

'True, but even so . . .'

'Perhaps she simply can't find a man who's good enough for her. In my experience, women – and I apologize again for my impertinence – do like to be able to admire and even look up to the men they love.'

'Well, we certainly like to look up to them in the purely literal sense. I can't bear a man to be shorter than me, and that must limit her choices, being such a tall girl.'

'I don't believe she will give her heart, or anything else, to any man who isn't as remarkable as she is. And that, I fear, may be hard to find.'

'Why, Mr Brown, I had no idea you were so sentimental. I do believe you have a little *tendresse* for Saffron Courtney.'

'An old man's affection, perhaps. Though I should add that it's purely a matter of speculation. I haven't actually met the girl.'

'Well, we really must do something about that!'

Yes, thought Mr Brown, *I really must.*

Saffron's parents, for she regarded Harriet as a true mother figure now, stayed on until September when they accompanied her as she went up to Oxford to begin her new life as an undergraduate. It was a perfect early autumn day with which to start the Michaelmas Term. There was still a hint of warmth in the sun that shone from a cloudless sky and the City of Dreaming Spires was looking at its best. Ancient buildings that had seen countless generations of students come and go looked down on all the young freshmen, their faces filled with excitement and ambition, but also the nervousness and uncertainty of newcomers to whom everything is unfamiliar, as they made their way across their college quads, looking for the staircases on which their new rooms would be found.

'I so envy you,' Harriet said. 'To have the chance to come to a place like this, and study with some of the world's finest minds . . . It's the most wonderful opportunity that anyone could have.'

'I'm proud of you,' Leon told Saffron, as he and Harriet were taking their leave. 'You said you were going to come here. You worked damn hard, and you jolly well did it. Well done. Now you have to make the best of it because I'll tell you this: if you leave Oxford and you haven't done yourself or the university justice you will regret it for the rest of your life.'

Her father was right, Saffron knew it. But still, there were times in her first few weeks when she really did wonder if an Oxford education was all that it was cracked up to be, for women at any rate. The female dons who ran Lady Margaret hall seemed to be obsessed with the dangers posed to their students by the uncontrollable urges of their male peers. The hours during which young men were allowed into the college were strictly limited to the afternoon and early evening and it was even considered unsuitable for young ladies to be seen walking with men unless they were both pushing their bicycles.

Saffron considered herself to be an intelligent girl but she simply could not see the logic of that instruction. 'It's so that you can always have your bicycle between yourself and him,' one nervous-looking girl explained over their first dinner in college. 'That way it's a barrier between you and him.'

'Hmm, I see . . .' said Saffron who had walked down countless streets and over all manner of landscapes with a great many male friends, some of whom were obviously smitten with her, without feeling the need to protect herself with a wheeled vehicle of any kind. And then, because the other girl looked so earnest, and so fearful of the opposite sex, Saffron couldn't resist adding, 'I find that once men have seen me shoot, they don't give me any trouble at all.'

'Oh,' squeaked the other girl, nervously, and sat there, unable to eat for a good couple of minutes as she tried to come to terms with the entirely unfamiliar species of female sitting next to her. Another girl piped up, 'My big sister's at Somerville. She has a spiffing trick she uses if she's in a taxi and a chap tries to get too fresh with her. She looks out for a chestnut seller and asks the cabbie to stop. Then she says to the chap, "Would you mind terribly getting me some hot chestnuts?" Of course, he can hardly say no. So he buys the chestnuts and then they drive on and the next time he leans over and tries to kiss her, she just pops a burning hot chestnut in his mouth. And then what can he do?!'

Saffy was fascinated by the idea of men as strange, hostile creatures to be fought off at all costs. She enjoyed male company and traditionally male pursuits and had always felt able to match any man as she had once matched small boys. Of course, she also loved looking pretty and dancing with a handsome beau in his white tie and tails. As tall and relatively strong as she was, there was nothing like being in the arms of a man she liked who was taller and much stronger still. She had kissed numerous men and been pursued by many more. But still she had not given herself completely to any of them.

It was not that she was a prude, or had a mystical regard for her own virginity, or was saving herself for her husband. It certainly wasn't because she lacked an appetite for sex, that much she knew for sure. It was simply that she knew that she could not be truly happy unless she could find a man who was her match, and more. She never wanted to have to hold back, for fear that her husband could not cope with her intelligence, or her independence, or her money, or any of the other blessings she possessed that could be burdens too. It was, she often thought, a great unfairness that all the things that made it harder for her to find a man would make it much easier to find a girl, if she were a man. A male student who was the handsome, wealthy heir to a Kenyan estate would have girls queuing all down the High Street and would happily work his way through those that took his fancy.

For her, though, it was different. She was like the dominant lioness in the pack, who would mate only with the alpha male. He was waiting for her somewhere, Saffron just knew it. But until she found him, she would just have to be patient, even if there were times when every inch of her body and every deep, primal instinct cried out, 'I want a man!'

M y darling, you need a wife,' Athala von Meerbach said to her son Gerhard one afternoon as they walked along a path through the woods at the Schloss Meerbach.

He groaned in frustration and annoyance. 'Not you too, Mother! Konrad is forever telling me that it is my duty as a good German and Party member to find a nice, Aryan wife and start producing the soldiers and mothers of the future. I always tell him that I haven't yet found the right Aryan . . . and it's true. I haven't.'

'I'm not surprised if you insist on having affairs with girls like that little blonde thing, the baker's daughter?'

'Her name was Jana, mother.' To Gerhard's surprise, his fling with two young women had turned into an affair, of a sort, with one of them. He had never truly loved Jana, but she had been good company, out of bed as well as in it, and they had spent a pleasant enough year together. She had always known that she had no long-term future with Gerhard and, in the end, had left him to marry a nice young detective in the Berlin Criminal Police. Gerhard had hardly been broken-hearted, exactly, but he had missed her and his big bed had suddenly seemed emptier without her.

'Her father was a perfectly respectable tradesman,' he went on. 'You seem to forget that we live in a socialist country now. The idea that one class is superior to any other is no longer acceptable.'

'Politicians come and politicians go, but a great family goes on forever.'

'The Reich will last a thousand years. The Führer said so. Our family had better get used to it.'

Athala looked at her son. She did not say anything. No one ever said anything that might be interpreted as criticism of the Führer or his government. The risk of being overheard and reported was too great, even for a dowager countess in the grounds of her own family's castle. But her look let Gerhard know that she wasn't standing for that sort of nonsense from him.

'Look, Ma,' he said, softening his voice, 'the truth is that I just don't feel it would be right for me to marry anyone at the moment. I have my work to do for Herr Speer, and most of my spare time is taken up with my duties as a Luftwaffe reservist. How could I give a wife the time that she needs? How could she ever get to know the real me?'

That was as close as Gerhard dared come to stating the truth, which was that he was living a lie. Any woman who entered into marriage believing that the man she loved was really the one she saw in front of her – with his Party badge, his work planning the Führer's new Berlin and his devoted service to the country's armed forces – would be marrying that lie. That was simply not fair to her. He would not ask any woman to be his wife on the basis of a great deceit.

Athala stopped, took his hand and looked up into his eyes. 'I understand, my darling. But you are a good man, a kind man, a generous man. That is the real you and any woman would be glad to have a husband with those qualities. God rest your father's soul, but he had none of those things.'

'Perhaps. But he had power, and energy and complete

self-confidence. A man can go a very long way if he doesn't spend too much time worrying about anyone else's feelings.'

'Maybe . . . but you are not such a man, and I am glad of it. Now, listen, I have arranged a dinner on Saturday night, nothing special, just a dozen guests. I have asked the von Schöndorfs to come. They have a very pretty daughter, Francesca. Come to think of it, I'm sure you've met her . . .'

Gerhard laughed, 'My God, Mother, I remember Chessi, she's just a little girl! You can't go marrying me off to a baby.'

'She was a little girl. But she isn't any more, just as you are no longer a shy little schoolboy or a teenager covered in pimples. She is nineteen, I believe, and quite sophisticated for her age. The von Schöndorfs sent her to be educated in England. She knew some very smart people there. You might be surprised.'

Gerhard sighed. 'Very well, then. Sit Chessi next to me at supper. I promise to be nice to her, but I absolutely do not promise to go down on one knee and marry her.'

'Well, just meet her. You never know, you might find that you like her more than you expect.'

Do I have to go to dinner at the Meerbachs?' wailed Chessi von Schöndorf. 'Konrad is a brute and his poor wife just sits there looking pregnant and downtrodden.'

She was sitting in her bed with a breakfast tray on her lap. Her mother was perched on the end of the bed, occasionally reaching over to steal one of the grapes that lay in a little bowl on the tray.

'There is another son . . .' the Countess von Schöndorf replied, letting the words hang in the air for a second before she added, 'and he doesn't have any kind of wife at all.'

'If he's anything like his brother, he will only want to talk about two things: how Meerbach engines are better than any other engines on earth and how the Führer is better than any other leader on earth.'

'Shh!' her mother hissed. 'When will you learn you are not

in England now. You cannot say the first thing that comes into your head!'

'All right, I'm sorry . . . but we're in my room. There's no one listening here.'

'How do you know? Now, for your information, you have actually met Gerhard, when you were a little girl.'

'I don't remember him.'

'No matter, the point is, he is not at all boring. He works as an architect and in his spare time he is a fighter pilot in the Luftwaffe.'

The look on Chessi's face told her mother that her attitude might be changing. She decided to press home her advantage while she could, 'So he is creative and also dashing and brave.'

'Is he handsome?'

'Ahh,' said the Countess, 'that you will have to decide for yourself.'

Chessi thought for a moment, 'I suppose I could wear the Norman Hartnell dress – you know, the one that Saffy bought me.'

'It still bothers me, that she spent so much. You should not have let her. It's not fair.'

'But she wanted to, Mutti! She said it was her way of repaying me for all the times she has stayed with us. And it is a very lovely dress . . .'

'Yes, it is, and you do look adorable wearing it. No man could possibly resist you.'

'Of course not!' Chessi smiled. 'But if he is a Meerbach, even a Meerbach who is a pilot and an architect and a great scientist, and heaven knows what else, then I will certainly be able to resist him.'

That Saturday evening, Athala von Meerbach waved her younger son over to her and said, 'Gerhard, do meet the Count and Countess von Schöndorf.'

'It's my great pleasure,' he said. 'How good of you to come. I have very happy memories of visiting your home when I was a boy.'

'And this is their daughter, Francesca . . .'

Gerhard cast his eyes upon the girl who was being served up to him as marriage-bait and could not believe what he saw. The little brat with her hair in pigtails and freckles across her nose had turned into a ravishing blonde goddess who was to Jana what Botticelli's Venus was to a cartoon strip. He had always thought that the Schöndorfs were as poor as church mice, but her dress was fit for a Hollywood movie star: a shoulderless satin evening gown in palest pink that cupped her full breasts – Gerhard had to make a conscious effort not to stare at them – corseted her tiny waist and then tumbled in a waterfall of glossy fabric to the floor.

Mein Gott! Gerhard thought to himself. Then he gathered his senses, took Francesca's and kissed it as he said, 'It is an absolute pleasure to meet you, *Komtesse.* You know, when my mother told me that you were coming here tonight, I said, "But she's only a little girl!"'

The von Schöndorfs laughed politely and Gerhard continued. 'But my mother said, "You silly boy! Francesca is a grown-up now, and she is very pretty."'

Francesca appeared a little embarrassed at that, though her parents looked at her with indulgent pride.

'Mother, you were entirely mistaken,' said Gerhard, and for a moment, exactly as he had intended, the harshness of his tone alarmed the others. He waited a second, and then, before anyone could protest, he added, 'Francesca is not just pretty. She is absolutely ravishing.'

Francesca gripped her mother's arm tight. The gesture might have appeared to be one of embarrassment: a girl taken aback by a man's compliment. In actual fact, it was simply a matter of necessity. Francesca was afraid that if she did not hold on to something, immediately, her legs might simply give way.

She had watched Gerhard as his mother gestured to him across the drawing room where the guests had gathered for pre-dinner drinks. He had been talking to a woman who looked a good few years older than him. He was dressed in white tie and tails, but the way he stood, one hand in his trouser pocket, his weight shifted onto his right hip with his left leg slightly out to one side, made his formal evening wear seem as relaxed as if he had just strolled down to dinner in a comfortable old jacket and a pair of slacks. He had smiled at his mother and politely bid the woman goodbye and as he strolled across the room, greeting a couple of the other guests on the way, the woman he had been talking to had followed him with her eyes, as if unable to tear them away from him.

I don't blame you! Chessi thought. Gerhard von Meerbach was the best-looking man she had ever met and when he walked up to her and her parents she realized that the attraction lay in the combination of very different qualities within him. He carried himself with the cool confidence of the daring aviator, with that tall, lean figure and the dark blond hair that fell over one eyebrow, so that it was all she could do not to reach up and push it back. But his eyes and his mouth, when one was close enough to study them – and oh, how she studied them! – had a look of sensitivity and perceptiveness about them that belied the devil-may-care first impression. This was a man who saw, and felt. And he was also, it suddenly struck Chessi, a man who was wounded. There was pain in him. She could not say precisely how she knew that, but she was sure of it. And suddenly there was nothing in all the world she wanted more than the chance to make that pain go away.

In the distance she heard a gong sound. 'Ah,' said Gerhard, 'time to go in to dinner. Francesca, will you do me the great honour of walking in with me?'

He held out his arm and she took it. They walked into the dining room past many an admiring eye, for they made such a splendid couple. And behind them their two mothers looked at one another and exchanged a private smile, as if to say, 'Mission accomplished!'

Mr Brown had very few, if any close friends: he did not allow himself the luxury of the shared revelations of one's true self upon which real friendship is based. But the great many people who counted him among his acquaintances would have been surprised to discover that this quiet gentleman, so understated in his manner, so disinclined to make flamboyant gestures or grand entrances, so utterly un-theatrical in every way, did in fact consider himself a sort of impresario. He was, after all, in the business of spotting, unearthing, grooming and then exploiting talent. He scoured the country for brilliant young people: the cleverest, toughest, best-looking or even those who were like him, exceptionally good at fading into the background. He took note of the way that other people regarded them, researched their characters and opinions and then auditioned them, just as a Broadway or Hollywood producer might to see whether they would be right for the parts he had in mind for them.

The difference, however, between Mr Brown and those other professional talent-spotters was that his subjects were unaware of his interest until a very late stage in the process, and, should they eventually choose to be recruited, gave their performances in absolute secrecy. Eva Barry, a clever, exceptionally beautiful girl from a humble home in Northumbria had been one of Mr Brown's finds and had served both him, and her country with exceptional dedication, self-sacrifice and courage. Now, a quarter of a century after she had gone to work for him, Mr Brown was on a train to Oxford to see whether Eva's daughter might prove equally useful.

He knew perfectly well that Saffron Courtney would be very unlikely to sacrifice her virtue for her country in the way that her mother had done. Eva had been dirt-poor, desperate and sufficiently motivated by the desire for revenge that she was prepared to prostitute herself to Count Otto von Meerbach, the man who had destroyed her father, if it helped destroy von Meerbach in his turn. From all that Mr Brown had gathered about Saffron, her situation was infinitely different. She was blessed by wealth as well as brilliance. Her mother's death had been a tragic twist of fate, for which no individual could be held to blame. Her father was alive and well and his relationship with Saffron was in many ways the keystone of her young life.

That did not, however, mean that she might not be useful one day, and that day might well come in months rather than years. Once again, Hitler had dared the rest of Europe to stop him as he announced his determination to send his troops into Czechoslovakia. Once again, he had got away with his effrontery. Neville Chamberlain, who had taken Balfour's place as Prime Minister a year earlier, had gone with the French premier Édouard Daladier to meet Hitler and his crony, the Italian dictator Mussolini, in Munich. Chamberlain and Daladier had given away the freedom of the Czechs in the hope of preserving what Chamberlain had described as, 'Peace with honour. Peace in our time.'

Chamberlain's political rival Winston Churchill had retorted, 'You were given the choice between war and dishonour. You chose dishonour and you will have war.' But the people were just grateful for any shred of hope that war might be averted. As one newsreel, showing footage of Chamberlain's car travelling down roads lined with cheering, waving citizens of the German Reich, had intoned, 'Let no man say that too high a price has been paid for the peace of the world until he has searched his soul and found himself willing to risk war and the lives of those nearest and dearest to him, and until he has attempted to add up the total price that might have had to be paid in death and destruction.'

There's no 'might' about it, Mr Brown had thought, watching the newsreel himself, for he enjoyed an occasional visit to his local picture-house. *There will be war. The only issue is when.*

With that in mind, and being also aware of the eternal truth that all wars are started by the old but fought by the young, Mr Brown was on the lookout for the fresh blood his service would require once hostilities began. And from everything he'd heard, Saffron Courtney might be just what he was looking for.

As a crowd of undergrads spilled out of the Oxford University Department of Economics, a small group stopped by the line of bicycles propped up against the wall outside. A young man called out to one of the very few women emerging from the lecture on the subject of 'Marshall and Pigou's Neoclassical Paradigm': 'What ho, Courtney! Will I be seeing you at the library this afternoon?'

Saffron stopped and smiled at her friend Quentin Edery. Although he might be putting on the voice and mannerisms of a real-life Bertie Wooster, Edery was in fact a fiercely intelligent grammar schoolboy from a modest home in the West Midlands town of Dudley. He had won a scholarship to New College and made no secret of his ambition one day to be the Chancellor of the Exchequer in a Labour government.

'I'm sorry but I can't,' Saffron replied. 'Manners wants to talk to me about my essay. He suggested we discuss it over tea and crumpets.'

'Hmm . . . that sounds fishy. You'd better watch out. When a man offers a girl a hot, buttered crumpet, it's a sure prelude to a pass.'

Saffron laughed. 'I hardly think Manners is going to make a pass at me. I don't think I'm his type at all.'

'Fair point. He's not a ladies' man, it must be said. In which case I think he's going to make a last desperate bid to shake you out of your absurd, outdated belief in the future of capitalism and put you on the socialist road to righteousness.'

'I think that's closer to the mark. My essay took issue with Keynes and suggested that economic growth would be stimulated more effectively if governments made it easier for private companies to find credit, rather than wasting resources on inefficient public expenditure.'

'My God, Courtney, there are times when I realize that behind that lovely façade there lurks the mind of a robber baron, whose only desire is to grind the noses of the poor even further into the dirt.'

'And you, darling Quentin, just want to be a Soviet Commissar, telling the people what's good for them. But since I have actually seen how jobs can be saved and wages increased if fundamentally sound companies can be saved from going under during an economic collapse, by the simple expedient of providing access to credit, allowing them to keep trading until they can flourish again under their own steam, I think the poor would be better off under my system.'

'Good luck persuading Manners of that. He worships the ground on which John Maynard Keynes treads. Anyway, must be off . . .'

Saffron watched her friend pedal off down the road and thought about how strange it was that one could like someone so much and disagree with them so fundamentally. Quentin Edery wanted to create an entirely new society, one in which people like her would no longer enjoy the privileges of wealth and possession and ordinary men and women, like the people he grew up with, would have their fair share of the prosperity they worked to create. In principle, Saffron could hardly argue with that proposition: she could hardly say that she believed in unfair shares. But she was African at heart, used to a world of predators and prey, in which life was an eternal contest for survival and the strongest always came out on top. So as much as she liked the idea of everyone living in peace, sharing everything equally, she simply couldn't believe it could ever work in practice. Her ideals, therefore, were aimed at working with the grain of human nature, accepting man as the competitive, but also fallible animal that he was, and making the best of what was sometimes bound to be a bad business.

She was rehearsing this argument in her mind, wondering how she could persuade Dr Jeremy Manners, the brilliant don who was supervising her Economics course, as she walked from New College Lane into the college itself, past the porter's lodge and into the Front Quad. Dusk was settling on the city and the lights in the college chapel were on, illuminating the medieval stained glass windows like a series of brightly coloured lanterns as Saffron followed the path around the oval lawn in the centre of the quad until she came to an arch at the far end. She passed under it and entered into Garden Quad, so called because it was open on one side and looked onto the gardens that were one of the glories of Oxford. Had this been a summer's afternoon, she might have looked down from the windows of Dr Manners onto the great expanse of lawn (on which, unlike the one in the Front Quad, students like Saffron were allowed to walk), the tree-topped mound that stood at one corner of the garden and the ancient city walls that enclosed the entire space, with magnificent herbaceous borders at their base that provided a blaze of colour when their shrubs and flowers were all in bloom.

This, however, was not the season for flowers. This was the time of chilly, wet afternoons and the single thing that drove Saffron most quickly down the path and up the stairs to the second-floor rooms was the thought of a hot fire, a steaming cup of tea and, yes, a freshly toasted crumpet.

She knocked on the heavy oak door and heard her tutor's voice call, 'Come!'

She walked into a large room, lined with bookshelves and strewn, on every possible surface, with more books, both open and closed, assorted journals and academic papers, sheets of foolscap covered in students' handwriting or Manners's own typing, and framed pictures of Manners himself, with friends, his academic peers and the occasional politician who had sought his advice on economic policy.

Manners himself was a tall, quite bulky man in his early forties, with an unruly shock of ginger hair, fading to grey at his temples. He was wearing a pair of baggy tweed trousers and an Aran sweater, beneath which a shirt and tie were just visible.

'Ah, Saffron, how good of you to join us,' Manners said, and it was only then that Saffron noticed that there was another man in the room, sitting so quietly in one of the armchairs Manners had arranged around the fire that he barely seemed present at all. He was small and slightly built, dressed in a perfectly tailored charcoal grey suit, a stiff collared white shirt and a plain, dark blue tie, and was, to judge by his silver hair and the lines on his face, well into old age. Yet she now realized that he was looking at her with eyes that were still very much alive and somewhat unsettling in the cool, unapologetic frankness with which they were examining her.

Now the man rose to his feet, waving away Manners's offer to assist him as he emerged from the armchair's deep embrace.

'Saffron, this is Mr Brown. He's an old chum of mine and, I might add, a veritable *éminence grise* of Whitehall. He knows absolutely everyone who matters in government and has done for, what, fifty years, would you say, Brown?'

Mr Brown gave the merest trace of a half-smile and a barely perceptible shrug, 'Oh, I don't know, Manners, but I've been around the place for quite a while, I suppose.'

He looked at Saffron. 'I'm delighted to meet you, my dear,' he said, shaking her hand.

'Sit down, Saffron, please,' Manners said. 'Can I get you a cup of tea? Crumpet?'

Saffron said yes to both and then Mr Brown said, 'I'm afraid I owe you an apology, Miss Courtney. Manners has invited you here under false pretences. So let me reassure you that there is nothing wrong with your essay.'

'I thought it was well argued, interesting use of first-hand evidence – one seldom teaches a student who can support their thesis with a first-hand account of the means by which their own family firm was saved from bankruptcy – and really rather impressive,' said Manners. 'Of course, I disagreed with every single word, from the opening capital letter to the last full stop. But still, beta double-plus, good work.'

'So why am I here?' Saffron asked, looking from one man to the other.

'Mr Brown particularly asked to meet you,' said Manners.

'Would it be rude to ask why?'

Mr Brown gave another hint of a smile. 'Of course not, Miss Courtney. The truth is that His Majesty's Government always has need of the brightest and best of the country's young people. One of my tasks, therefore, is to keep an eye out for those who show particular promise and, though you may not be aware of this, you are much talked about by your elders.'

'Really?' said Saffron, somewhat taken aback.

'Oh yes. I have heard tales of everything from your skill on the hunting field to your good taste in clothes. Now, here's Manners complimenting your academic ability. I may say, incidentally, that I cast an eye over your essay. I hope you don't mind. I agree with Manners that it was a nicely written piece, and I also agree with you that the market, not the state, is the driving motor of a successful economy.'

'How can a Whitehall man say a thing like that?' Manners asked.

'Precisely because he knows what the other Whitehall men

are like, and wouldn't trust most of them to run the proverbial whelk-stall.'

Saffron did her best to suppress a giggle at the look of horror on Manners's face and said, 'Thank you, Mr Brown.'

'Not at all, my dear. Oh . . . there's one other thing I forgot to mention. Old age is catching up with me, I fear.'

'What was that?'

'Simply that I had another reason for wanting to meet you in particular. You see, I used to know your mother, a long time ago. Knew her rather well, in fact, when she first came to town.'

G*ood girl!* thought Mr Brown. *You knew exactly what I was talking about, and it caught you completely off-guard, but you recovered in a flash.*

He looked at Manners and realized that he had not noticed anything out of the ordinary, beyond the obvious surprise of an unexpected connection between two people who had never before met one another.

'Good Lord, Brown, you never told me that!' said Manners. 'I wouldn't have bothered with all the cloak-and-dagger stuff if I'd known you were an old family friend.'

'I wouldn't go quite that far,' said Mr Brown. 'But, yes, I knew Eva Barry, as she was called before she married Saffron's father. And a remarkable young woman she was too. She won the Military Medal, you know, Manners, for her bravery in the East African campaign. The War Office had their doubts, being the stuffed shirts they were, but Delamere absolutely insisted on it, said she'd had as much guts as any of the men under her command. Of course, that was a few years after I knew her.'

Mr Brown was addressing his words to Manners, but his attention was all focused on Saffron. He wanted to see how she would react, now that he had made it absolutely plain that he had known Eva in her spying days. And Saffron clearly knew all about those days because she wasn't asking any of the obvious questions that any girl, particularly one who had lost her mother so young, would normally pose to someone who had known her in days gone by.

When we've trained you properly, you'll know not to make those kinds of mistakes, Mr Brown thought. But that was just a trifling detail. This girl was every inch her mother's daughter. Not only was she just as beautiful, perhaps even more so if such a thing were possible, but she also had the same steely core that Eva had possessed. Mr Brown could see it in the dark blue eyes that were looking at him now with such cold, implacable fury, though her mouth was smiling sweetly. Saffron knew the whole story, that was obvious, and she had naturally, and correctly, jumped to the conclusion that Mr Brown had been responsible for what her mother had been obliged to do.

Brown let Manners chat on for a while, asking who wanted their tea-cup refilled or another crumpet on their plate – 'More butter? Strawberry jam?' – and then asked Saffron, 'Would I be right in thinking you have visited Germany more than once over the course of the past few years?'

'That's right. My closest friend at school was a German girl, Francesca von Schöndorf.'

'What did you make of the place?'

Saffron paused for a second and then said, 'Well I felt the same way about Germany as Dr Manners did about my essay. I thought the country was beautiful, it's culture – you know, the architecture, the music, the literature and so on – was magnificent and all the people I ever talked to were charming. But I disagreed with every single word of Nazism from the first capital letter to the last full stop.'

Manners burst out laughing and clapped his hands. 'Now that deserves an alpha!'

'What makes you say that?' asked Brown.

'Because it's hateful . . . I mean literally filled with hate. The way the Jews are degraded is appalling. And there's a bullying feeling to it: all those huge red banners with swastikas on them, and beastly men swaggering around in fancy uniforms like little tin gods. Every time I went there it got worse.'

'Do you think the Germans want a war?'

'No, I'm absolutely certain that the average German is terrified of another war. It's not till you get there that you realize how many more men they lost than we did in the Great War. But it's not a matter of what they want, is it? It's a matter of what Hitler gives them.'

'Ah yes, der Führer . . . tell me, what did your hosts think of him? I imagine, with a name like "von Schöndorf", they were what we might call upper crust.'

'Yes, they were. As for what they thought about Hitler . . .' Saffron cast her mind back and tried to come up with a fair description of how Chessi's parents viewed their leader. 'I suppose they feel the way upper-crust people in this country would do if the royal family disappeared and some ghastly little corporal with a funny moustache suddenly set himself up as the country's supreme ruler in their place. They'd be appalled. They'd find it unbelievable. And they'd do their very best to carry on as if he simply didn't exist.'

'Plenty of members of the English upper crust are rather sympathetic – too sympathetic, in fact – to Herr Hitler,' Brown observed.

'Yes, but only as ruler of Germany. They wouldn't much like it if he was lording it over them.'

Mr Brown was struck by the self-confidence and directness with which Saffron expressed her opinions. He'd expect that of a bright young Oxford man, though not, perhaps, one who was still a fresher. But even the brightest bluestocking, who privately held very forceful opinions, was apt to feel constrained by the rules of ladylike behaviour. It wasn't that the Courtney girl was in any way shrill or hectoring. He had asked her straight questions. She had given him straight answers. It was more

303

that it clearly did not occur to her to behave in any other way.

Your mother never had that, he thought. *She was just as beautiful as you, just as brave, just as bright. But she didn't have that inner self-belief, not at first, anyway. That, my dear, is your great privilege.*

He looked at his watch. 'My goodness, is that the time? I really must be going. Manners, thank you so much for your hospitality, which is as generous as ever.'

'It was my pleasure, sir.'

'And Miss Courtney, I greatly enjoyed our conversation. I think you are a young woman to be watched and I would very much appreciate the chance to talk with you again. For example, should you happen to make another trip to Germany, I should be very interested to hear your observations.'

'That's very flattering,' said Saffron, with a suitably appreciative smile. 'I should be delighted to provide them, though I'm sure you already know far more about the place than I ever will.'

'Ah, but there's nothing like a fresh pair of eyes . . . Well then, I'll be off. Don't worry Manners, I'll find my own way out.'

And with that, Mr Brown walked out onto the wooden staircase, and as he made his way back down to ground level he thought to himself, *We will have a use for you, Miss Courtney. Oh yes, you will certainly come in handy one day.*

Just before the end of term, as she was packing up for Christmas, Saffron received a letter from Chessi von Schöndorf. It was written in her usual chatty style, full of news about her family, and questions about Saffy's life as a student at Oxford. Chessi's big news was that she had been invited to join a group of friends who were going to St Moritz for a fortnight, just after Christmas. 'Of course the skiing will be wonderful, though I know that is of no interest to you!!' she had written, making Saffron smile, for it was one of the running jokes in their life that in the three years she had visited Chessi and her family, all of whom were put on skis almost as soon as they could walk, Saffy had never really developed any great skill on snow. It baffled them both, for there had never before been a sport that Saffron had not taken to like a natural, but for some reason – they agreed that it must be something to do with her African upbringing – she was, though brave enough to tackle any slope, no more than a competent skier. Chessi had been thrilled to discover that here at last was something at which she outshone her otherwise brilliant friend and Saffron made a deliberate decision to set aside her usual, ferociously competitive nature because it seemed only fair to let Chessi get her share of the limelight for once. But the subject of skiing was soon forgotten because then there came some really interesting news:

'Now, Saffy my darling friend I must tell you the most wonderful news of all – I AM IN LOVE!!!! He is called Gerhard and he comes from a very good family (a very rich family, too, as Mutti keeps telling me!). He is an architect by profession, but also in his spare time he is in the Luftwaffe and he flies fighter planes. So he is an artist AND he is a brave warrior AND he is tall, and handsome, like a film star, but he has lovely eyes, that are so kind and gentle. Oh Saffy, when he looks at me with those eyes I am in heaven!! So, he will be joining us in St Moritz, towards the end of our stay and I think that he may propose marriage to me and if he does I will say Yes because I love him so and I want to be with him forever!!'

Saffron could just hear Chessi's voice, filled with giddy happiness, as if she were in the room beside her, and the two of them were giggling with excitement and going into every tiny detail of what he had said and done, and what it all meant. It was such a contrast to the earnestness of her Oxford life, which seemed filled with fascinating but deeply serious debates about important subjects with dons and fellow students, all determined to set the world to right. She wrote back to Chessi, congratulating her on her good fortune, assuring her that she absolutely insisted on being a bridesmaid at her wedding and adding, 'I'm off to Scotland for Christmas and New Year with the Ballantynes, which is lovely, but it does mean having to fend off my cousin Rory. Do you remember, I told you about him at Easter? He's an estate manager rather than a brave warrior, but he's quite good-looking I suppose. The thing is, he's perfectly sweet and I do like him, but only in a friendly, family sort of way. I just hope he doesn't start getting fresh after he's drunk too much on Christmas Day. If he makes a pass at me I shall have to slap him in the face and then where will we be?!'

Rory had done his best. He had gone to the trouble of drawing out a family tree on the back of an old roll of wallpaper. On the afternoon of New Year's Day he unfurled his masterpiece on a table in the library and showed Saffron that the two of them were only cousins by marriage, because her great-aunt had married his great-uncle, so there was no blood link and therefore no impediment to their getting married. 'Not that I'm proposing, or anything,' Rory had added.

'That's just as well,' she replied, 'because if you were, I would have to say no, and I'd much rather not do that because then we couldn't be such good friends. I think you're a smashing chum, and I love you very much as part of my family, even if we don't have any blood in common. But I'm not in love with you. It's nothing you've done or not done. I just don't feel that way about you, that's all.'

'I suppose there's some brainy chap at Oxford you're sweet on, the lucky blighter.'

'Don't be silly, of course there isn't! There isn't anyone at all.'

'Then maybe I still have a chance.'

Saffron didn't reply to that. She simply said, 'Come on, let's get back to the drawing room. Tea will have been served by now. Everyone will be wondering where we've got to.'

To Saffron's surprise there was a telegram waiting for her on a silver salver. Her first thought was that something awful had happened to her father or Harriet but when she opened it she saw that it had been sent from the Badrutt's Palace Hotel in St Moritz.

HAVING WUNDERBAR TIME STOP HE WILL ARRIVE IN TWO DAYS STOP SO EXCITED STOP WISH YOU WERE HERE LOVE CHESSI

I've been to St Moritz, you know,' said Rory, when Saffron told him about the message. 'Splendid place. I'm proud to say I went down the Cresta Run, which was without doubt the most terrifying thing I've done in my life but hellish good fun. You know that cricket jumper I wear, the one with the burgundy stripes around the collar – that's my St Moritz Toboggan Club jumper. It proves I've been down the run and jolly proud of it I am too!'

A mischievous smile crossed Saffron's face and her eyes twinkled with the light of an idea forming in her mind. 'Just out of curiosity, how would one get from here to St Moritz?'

'Ah, well, I can tell you exactly because of course I've done it. One simply takes the midday Flying Scotsman from Edinburgh to King's Cross, getting in at about half-past seven. Then nip across London on the Tube to Victoria and hop on the overnight boat train to Paris. That gets you into the Gare du Nord at nine in the morning . . . I say, I'm not boring you am I, with this recitation?'

'Not at all. Please continue.'

'Well then you have to get across Paris, on the Metro this time, of course, to the Gare de Lyon, catch the first train to

307

Zürich, which is another five hours or so. From there you go to a place called Chur, change again, for the final time thank goodness, and that takes you all the way to St Moritz, arriving just in time for a nice drink before dinner.'

'Well that sounds splendid,' said Saffron. 'Do you think your ma and pa would mind awfully if we set off for Switzerland tomorrow?'

'I'm sorry . . . what did you say?'

'I said I think we should go to St Moritz. It will be a lovely surprise for Chessi and you can show me the Cresta Run. I think I'd like to try it too.'

'But . . . but you can't!'

'Why on earth not?'

'Because you're a girl. Female riders were banned about ten years ago. They're absolutely not allowed.'

'All the better,' said Saffron. 'Now I absolutely insist on going down it.'

A call to the Edinburgh office of the Thomas Cook travel agency, first thing the following morning, revealed that they could book trains and even hotel rooms in St Moritz, but it would take a day at the very least to arrange. A little over twenty-four hours later Saffron strode through the door of Thomas Cook with Rory in her wake, paid for and collected two return rail tickets to St Moritz and was informed that they had been unable to find two rooms at the Palace Hotel but had procured a pair at the Suvretta House. 'I am assured that you will find it more than satisfactory, Miss,' the lady serving her said, with a pursed-lipped look of a respectable Edinburgh woman who senses something of which she should disapprove, even if she has not yet decided precisely what that might be.

Saffron sent a telegram to Chessi:

ON MY WAY SEE YOU SOONEST LOVE SAFFYXX.

She and Rory lunched on the train to London; dined, slept and breakfasted en route to Paris; grabbed a *croque monsieur* and a cup of coffee each at the station café in Gare de Lyon and got off the train at St Moritz to find a member of the hotel staff waiting to meet them.

Saffron ate a hearty supper, went up to bed immediately afterwards and slept like a log till half-past eight. She ordered breakfast to be brought to her room and was sitting up in bed, sipping a large cup of hot chocolate and looking out at the wonderful view down the valley towards the frozen lake, when there was a knock on the door.

'Who is it?' Saffron called out.

'Just me,' came Rory's muffled voice. 'Can I come in?'

'Yes!' replied Saffron, pulling her robe a little tighter over her chest to cover up the faintest hint of cleavage.

'Goodness, aren't you up yet?' Rory said when he saw her still luxuriating in bed. 'I thought you'd want to be dashing off to see your chum.'

'It's too late for that. I know what Chessi's like when she gets anywhere near a ski-slope. She'll have been heading for the slopes and absolutely raring to go by eight at the latest. So I'll see her this evening instead, and what I thought was that it would be really fun if I had a story to tell her all about how I went down the Cresta Run.'

'You're not still set on that, are you? I was rather hoping you might have gone off the idea.'

'Why on earth would I do that? I raided your wardrobe and your pa's for men's clothes. I don't have any other reason to wear them.'

'But honestly, Saffy, you could hurt yourself.'

'I could just as easily hurt myself skiing, plenty of people do, but you wouldn't try to stop me doing that.'

'I know, but no one would blame me if you hurt yourself. But the only way you can go down the Cresta is if I help you do it.'

'Oh I wouldn't worry about that,' Saffron said. 'No one would ever blame you for not being able to persuade me to be sensible. No one can. Just ask my poor father.'

'Very well then. This is your funeral and you can't blame me if you break your silly neck. And that being the case I suggest we meet at ten o'clock in the hall. And then I will take you to meet Herr Zuber.'

'Ooh, that sounds mysterious, who's he?'

'The man without whom neither you nor anyone else is allowed anywhere near the Cresta Run, no matter how much of a man you might be.'

Saffron had eaten, showered and allowed herself the indulgence of some particularly pretty underwear. *Just because I have to look like a man on the outside, I'm jolly well going to still feel female on the inside.* She pinned her hair up into a bun and shoved a man's woolly hat down over her head. She was as tall as most men, so that wasn't a problem, and a thick woollen jumper worn beneath a blouson windcheater bulked up her shoulders and hid her pretty but not particularly large breasts. Her face, though, was far from manly, which was normally a very good thing, but not today. She wrapped a scarf around her neck and up over her mouth and covered her big blue eyes and long thick lashes with a pair of dark glasses.

Having done her best to look like a man, she now got to work on acting, moving and sounding like one too. For years, Saffron's height had condemned her to play the man's roles in school plays: she had made a fine Romeo, but she would far rather have been Juliet. But now, quite unexpectedly, that experience was coming in useful. She stood in front of the mirror, stuck her hands in her trouser pockets and slouched. *Men are so lucky to be able to do that!* she thought. *We have to keep our backs straight and our heads up and cross our legs when we sit down. We hardly ever just relax, the way they do. And that reminds me – knees apart when I sit down!*

She practised her man-walk up and down the room a couple of times, not moving from the hips as women did, but leading with her shoulders. Next item on the agenda was her voice. She had decided to limit the chances of being caught out by keeping her speech to a bare minimum. She lowered her voice as much as she could and tried out a couple of manly grunts, indicating yes, or no, and then a few brief phrases: 'Right-ho', 'Absolutely', 'Got it' and 'Can't wait'.

I know plenty of men who never say anything more for them-selves than that, she thought, and told herself on no account to giggle, squeal or describe anything as either 'sweet' or 'ador-able'. She was reasonably sure that she'd be screaming like a banshee once she set off down the run itself, but once she was sliding down the ice at fifty miles an hour, there was absolutely nothing that anyone could do about it until she reached the bottom.

She gave herself one last look in the mirror, gave a manly shrug of her shoulders and set off to find Rory and the myste-rious Herr Zuber.

Gerhard had also arrived in St Moritz the previous after-noon, although he had driven the two-hundred-odd kilometres from Schloss Meerbach. Having once pretended that he wanted money to buy a Mercedes, he had acquired a newer model a couple of years ago, a gloriously sleek, bright red two-seater 540K cabriolet, with whitewall tyres and pale beige, almost honey-coloured leather seats, and never once regretted the decision: the thrill of driving it at the unlimited speeds allowed on the new autobahns was almost a match for being at the controls of a 109. Gerhard had chosen not to stay at the Palace due to a sense that he ought not to see Chessi before he proposed to her: it seemed more romantic that way, somehow. He had stopped off at home for a night on the way down from Berlin because it broke his journey very conveniently and he wanted to tell his mother that he was about to propose to Francesca von Schöndorf.

Athala was, as he had expected her to be, delighted by the news. 'Oh I'm so happy for you both!' she exclaimed, wrapping her arms around her son. 'From the first time I saw the two of you together I thought that you looked so perfect together. She really is such a beautiful creature, and so charming. She will make you a wonderful wife, and you, my boy, must be as good a husband to her.'

'Of course, Mother. Why else would I marry her?'

Gerhard had meant it, too. He really did want to be a good husband. His father and older brother might have regarded their marriage vows as an irrelevance that had no effect whatever on their sexual liaisons with other women. But he would be different. He would treat his wife with the respect she deserved. And surely that would not be difficult. Chessi was just as lovely and as sweet-natured as his mother had said and they really did make a fine pair together: everybody said so.

If only he loved her just a little bit more. Oh, he liked her well enough and he never had the slightest trouble in finding her attractive, though he wished she had not been quite such a good Catholic girl or insisted quite so fiercely on remaining a virgin until her wedding night. He was sure that if they had made love then he would no longer be quite so beset by . . . not doubt exactly, more a feeling that he was not quite as swept up in the overwhelming passion that he had always imagined true love would bring.

He had been working very hard, of course, and spending a

312

great deal of his spare time with the Luftwaffe, so there had been very little of his time, or mind to spare for thinking about love. And Chessi, bless her, was so filled with excitement and anticipation, so enraptured the very idea of becoming his wife that she seemed to have enough love to spare for them both. Still, there was a very small, quiet but insistent voice in the back of his mind wondering whether he felt quite as strongly, or as certainly about the whole idea as she did.

Well, it was too late to worry about that now. He was about to offer his hand in marriage to Chessi and what man would not envy the thought of waking up next to her for the rest of his life? Gerhard had made a point of keeping her away from Konrad, not because he had the slightest fear that he would steal Chessi away from him – he might very well try, but she would certainly not respond – but because something about his mere presence would feel like a sort of bile or poison, making everything just that little bit meaner, less joyful than it should be. Once they were married, at the wedding reception, then Konrad could meet Chessi, but not before.

So, tonight he would propose to Chessi and all would be well. Yes, that would surely make all the difference. In the meantime, he intended to spend the day reacquainting himself with another old flame, a mean old bitch he had conquered three years earlier but wanted to master again. By God, she could treat a man badly. But damn her, she was worth the pain!

Herr Zuber was an avuncular, grey-haired man, whose family had lived in St Moritz for as far back as anyone could remember, and who ran a shop in the middle of town that not only supplied normal skiing equipment but also the particular accoutrements required by riders on the Cresta Run. From the top down the complete outfit began with a helmet with flaps that covered one's ears and buckled under the chin. There were pads to protect one's elbows and gloves that resembled a cross between winter mittens and a knight in armour's gauntlets, with a metal plate over the top of the wearer's hands and knuckles to protect them from hard, rough-edged ice. Another pair of pads protected the knees and the whole ensemble was completed with boots tipped with steel toecaps from which protruded two wicked, jagged-edged steel tips.

'They'd come in jolly handy on the dance floor sometimes, what?' joked Rory, to which Saffron responded by nodding and grunting, 'Huh!'

She thought her male impersonation had gone rather well, but as she was leaving Herr Zuber said, 'May I wish you good luck, Fräulein. I have always admired women who have real courage.'

She stopped dead by the doorway and was about to bluster it out but then thought it was wiser to find out now what she'd done wrong. That might stop her being caught out again later.

'How did you know?' she asked.

'So many ways . . . You had to take off your . . . I do not know the word . . .' He pointed at his eyes, 'Sonnenbrille.'

'Dark glasses,' said Saffron.

'Ach so . . . And your eyes, ah, no man could have any so beautiful.'

'Thank you . . . I'll make sure I keep my dark glasses on all the time.'

'Also your hands. You should always your gloves keep on because you have very, ah . . . slender fingers, sehr hübsch.'

'What does that mean?' Rory asked.

'Herr Zuber very sweetly said that my fingers were pretty. Vielen dank.'

'Bitte, you are welcome, Fräulein. But finally I could not help but notice that you were wearing a scent, I do not know its name, but no man would smell this way. Not unless he was, you know, how shall I say? Not a true man?'

'Oh goodness, my Shalimar! I must have put it on this morning after my shower, without even thinking.'

'I have a little *toilette* at the back of the shop. There is a basin there. If you shall wash your face the scent will go. Then keep your glasses and your gloves on and maybe you will be able to go down the run. You can tell me all about it when you bring this equipment back. Until then, *viel Glück* . . . good luck!'

Saffron washed around her neck, and behind her ears. Then she put her dark glasses and gloves back on: it was time to get back into character. As she and Rory walked out of the store she was vaguely aware of the presence of a tall man coming the other way, but then the door shut behind her and Rory was sniffing the air and saying, 'Can't smell a thing. Excellent. Tally-ho!'

They walked together up the path that ran alongside the Cresta Run. Rory still felt that he had one card left to play in his bid to prevent his cousin from killing herself.

'We won't be going all the way to the very top,' he said. 'There's a special start for novices halfway up. Everyone uses it for their first few runs. It's actually a rule, now I come to think of it.'

'So is prohibiting female riders and I'm not obeying that one, either,' she retorted. 'Now, you'd better let me know what I can expect to find on my way down.'

'All right then,' Rory sighed. 'The run is about three-quarters of a mile long and it drops rather more than five hundred feet. The average gradient is one-in-eight which is jolly steep, I can tell you, and the steepest bits are much worse. Look, Saffy, I really don't think it's a good idea to . . .'

'That's enough! I've made up my mind. The best thing you can do now is just to help me. Tell me what I need to do to make it down in one piece.'

'Dig your toes in. You should be good at that. Just stick the

315

ends of your boots into the ice and go slowly at first, till you get the hang of it. Don't be embarrassed, or think you look stupid. You'll look a lot more stupid going too fast and then having a crash than getting down to the bottom in one piece at a nice steady pace.'

'Would you tell another man that?'

'Yes, actually, I would. And I'd also tell him that the Cresta is full of tricks and surprises. Some of the bends are deliberately made to spit riders out and send them flying off the track, unless they maintain complete control of the sled. Which brings me to the matter of Shuttlecock . . .'

'What's that?'

'The deadliest turn on the course, Cousin Saffron, assuming you get that far. Which you probably won't if you are mad enough to set off from the very top . . .'

Saffron gave Rory a look that a gorgon would have been proud of.

'Very well, then,' he conceded, 'you start out from the very top, go past Stable Junction and over Church Leap, so called because of the rather picturesque parish church that stands beside the top of the track . . . then round a few more corners, past the beginners' start and onto the Junction Straight. Now, unless you're very careful you may find yourself picking up rather more speed on the straight than you – or any novice, including a man! – can handle. You zoom up and around the right-hander at Rise, crash down on the other side, whizz under Nani's Bridge, take a turn called Battledore and then you're at Shuttlecock, which is the perfect example of the type of corner I was talking about.'

'The type that spits you out?'

'Exactly. That's what it's there for, to dispose of riders who are going too fast. It's like a kind of safety-valve, so that they can't come to even more trouble further down. There's even a Shuttlecock Club for people who come off there. They have a club tie and everything.'

316

'Perhaps I can have a Shuttlecock Club garter-belt made for me.'

'I wouldn't say that sort of thing while you're in any other chap's hearing.'

'By the way,' Saffron asked, 'what happens if you come off on the wrong side of the track and go flying straight off the mountain?'

Rory shook his head sorrowfully. 'Nothing to be done, I'm afraid. There's a special little cemetery, down by the lake, just for people who died on the Cresta Run. Hell of a way to go, what?'

'Yes . . . yes . . . hell of a way,' Saffron muttered and this time Rory could see she was genuinely shaken.

'Don't worry,' he said. 'I was only teasing. There's no cemetery. There are nets at the side of the track, wherever it's near a bad drop, so they catch anyone who crashes. Look,' he pointed up the hill, 'there's one up there, on that curve, d'you see?'

'You brute!' Saffron exclaimed. 'I have a good mind to punch you with my metal gloves. That will teach you not to be so cruel!'

They walked on and Saffron occasionally caught sight of prone figures flashing by in a dark blur, the metal runners of their skeleton sleds rattling furiously against the ice.

'This is the novices' start,' Rory said as they passed a group of beginners standing by the side of the track, taking instruction from an old hand.

'Goodbye, novices!' said Saffron, walking up the hill.

Finally, they came to the start of the Cresta Run. It wasn't much to look at. A small wooden hut stored the sleds and provided shelter for the timekeeper who recorded all the runs. There was a small iron stove inside to keep him warm and ease the chill for the riders on really cold days. This, however, was perfect alpine weather, with clear blue skies, dazzling sunshine and thick snow on the ground. A group of riders, all in their helmets, gloves, pads and boots, were sitting on a wooden bench facing the top of the run, which was blocked by a plank hinged to a post by the side of the track. A man in a St Moritz Toboggan Club sweater was standing by the plank, acting as the starter.

No rider could go down the track until the one before had got off it, either because he had made it to the end, or because he was lying in the snow, somewhere to the side. At that point, a signal was sent up to the hut, the starter raised the plank and the next rider set off.

One of the men sitting on the bench seemed to be looking at Rory and Saffron with particular interest as they walked towards him. Saffron felt her skin flush, thinking he must be looking at her, seeing something wrong, but then a grin broke out across the man's face and in an American accent he said, 'I got it! You're Ballantyne, right? You were here in '37.'

'That's right. And you must be . . .'

'Holland Moritz.'

'Of course, Moritz . . . Didn't you like to tell the ladies that ol' Saint Moritz himself had been an ancestor of yours?'

'I might have used that line once or twice,' he admitted and Saffron had to make a conscious effort not to look too obviously at his perfect white teeth, his suntanned skin and the twinkle in his black-brown eyes.

'Say, who's your friend?' Moritz asked.

'Oh, this is my cousin, S . . .' he paused for a second, 'Stephen Courtney.'

'Good to meet you Steve,' said Moritz, giving Saffron a hearty handshake.

'You too,' she replied doing her best not to wince as the bones in her hand seemed to be crushed by the Moritz's grip.

Just behind him, Saffron could see a man pick up his sled and walk to the start. The plank was lifted. The rider took two or three quick steps then dived forward, holding his sled in front of him and landing on his stomach, his head right up at the front just inches from the ice as he raced off down the track and around the first bend.

'So, you as fast on the run as your cousin?' Moritz asked her.

'Actually, Stephen's a novice. This is his first day on the course.'

'Is that so? And you're going from the top?'

Saffron nodded, 'Uh-huh.'

Moritz whistled in admiration. 'Well you've got balls of steel, I'll say that for you.'

'Oh yes, Stephen's got balls all right,' said Rory.

Saffron nodded and gave another grunt.

'You don't want to talk, I get it. Don't blame you, first time on the run and all. Just get down it and everything will be grand. You'll feel as high as a kite and you'll want to come straight back up here and do it all over again. Uh-oh, time for me to go . . .'

A few seconds later Moritz was running towards the start, going much faster than the previous rider, hurling himself onto the ice and going like a human bullet down the mountain.

'Don't be fooled for one second by that wide-eyed, all-American charm,' Rory said. 'Holland Moritz is as tough a rider as ever went down the run and he wins practically every event he enters. Damn nice chap though and an absolutely first-rate rider.'

'It's my turn next,' said Saffron.

'Now, be honest, are you absolutely sure you want to do it?'

Saffron looked at the track. Suddenly it didn't look like a gradient of one-in-six, it looked like a vertical tunnel of ice that would hold her in its icy claws for three-quarters of a mile, beating and battering her, terrifying her for every single second until, if she survived at all, she arrived in a heap at the far end.

She was scared witless.

'Yes,' she said, 'I'm sure.'

'Very well then, don't even try to emulate Mr Moritz and his flying leap at the start. Walk steadily up to the edge, put the sled down, lower yourself onto it and only at the very end give a gentle push with your standing foot. So long as you are moving, no matter how slowly at the start, the track will do the rest.'

'Mr Courtney, the run is all yours,' said the starter.

Saffron picked up one of the sleds and was startled by how light and insubstantial it felt in her hands. The body of the sled was little bigger than a metal tea-tray with a padded top and a pair of steel runners attached to the bottom. This flimsy device was all she had to carry her down the Cresta Run.

'Mr Courtney . . . ?' the starter asked.

'Just coming,' Saffron grunted.

Then she took two steps forward, past the raised plank, bent forward with her arms out in front of her, so that the sled was only a foot or so off the ice, took a final deep breath, lunged forwards, felt the sled hit the ice, flung herself down on top of it and then, as the sled tipped over the edge, felt the ice beneath its runners and in an instant she was away.

The speed: that was what hit her, overwhelmed her, robbed her of any control over her destiny and filled her with a combination of raw fear and absolute excitement unlike any she had ever experienced. Saffron had ridden horses flat out, pushing them as hard as they could go, and jumping them over obstacles that seemed impossibly high. She had driven trucks at speed across the African savannah, heedless of the potholes or termite mounds that could wreck them at any moment, and taken cars out for spins around the narrow lanes of Devon, where every turn was blind and the fear of collision constant. On holiday with the von Schöndorfs she had insisted on throwing herself however gracelessly down the steepest ski-runs the Bavarian Alps could provide.

some kind of bolt from above and he suddenly realized that this was the feeling, that immediate connection, deep in the heart, between one soul and another.

And he had experienced it with a man.

Gerhard's pulse had been racing just standing looking into those eyes, which had not left his but seemed caught by the same magnetism as his own. But now his heart beat still faster in panic as he thought, *No, it can't be! I'm not a homo! I've had so many women. I can't be . . . can I?*

Finally the man seemed to emerge from his dazed state. He put his hand to his face and then, in a voice that sounded almost as alarmed as Gerhard felt, said, 'Dark glasses . . . fell off . . . you seen them?'

Gerhard looked around. The glasses were lying on the snow just a couple of paces away. He picked them up and handed them to their owner who said, 'Thank you,' in a soft, low voice and smiled shyly at him: shyly and so prettily that Gerhard would have sworn that . . . *No, how can that be? Only men can ride the Cresta Run. It's a rule. And the English are like us Germans. They obey their rules.*

'Well, ah, better find my cousin. He'll be worried. You know, about me falling off,' the mysterious rider said. He turned to walk back up the hill.

'I'll come with you,' said Gerhard, who suddenly saw a golden opportunity to get to the bottom of the mystery. 'It would be sensible to have someone with you after such a shock.'

'Second thoughts, I'll wait for him at the bottom.'

'Very well . . . by the way, what's your name?'

'Courtney,' said the rider, over his shoulder as he walked away. Gerhard watched him go and then, just as he was about to turn back up the hill, the mysterious Mr Courtney gave a little wiggle, just a quick, utterly feminine swish of the hips, and Gerhard burst out laughing. *Thank God for that!* he thought and continued on his way.

A couple of minutes later he met a wild-eyed Englishman coming the other way in a state of great alarm. 'Have you seen my cousin?' he said. 'Chap by the name of Courtney. I think he's crashed, but I don't know where.'

'*Ach so* . . . yes I saw Courtney. The crash was at Shuttlecock. But please, do not concern yourself. Courtney is alive and well . . .' Gerhard grinned, 'And she is waiting for you at the bottom of the run.'

Saffron could not help it. She knew it was madness to give the game away, but she had to let him know that she was a girl. She had felt it, just as he had, that sudden overwhelming certainty that she had just met her man, the one she had been waiting for, and it had come as even more of a shock than the crash. She had heard about love at first sight, of course, in songs and films and silly romantic novels. But she had never really believed that it happened in real life. But it had, and of all the rotten luck, she had been pretending to be a man and she had seen the alarm in his eyes as he thought about what that meant, and even if she never saw him ever again, she had to let him know that it was all right to love her. But how were they ever going to meet again?

She was lost in thought, pondering the best way to find one tall, handsome man – no, he was more than handsome: he was a beautiful man – amidst the crowds of tourists at the height of the season in St Moritz when Rory came racing up behind her.

'There you are! I was so worried. You were going at such a lick, I knew you were going to have a prang. Thank heavens you're still in one piece.'

'I'm perfectly all right,' Saffron assured him. 'I landed in a great big heap of snow and was rescued by a rather charming German gentleman.'

'I think I met him on the way down. Looking rather pleased

with himself, I thought. He'd worked out you weren't a man.'

'Oh dear,' said Saffron, doing her best to sound concerned although her heart was turning cartwheels of delight. 'Do you think he'll give the game away to anyone else?'

'Probably. You can't trust a German, that's what I think.'

'Oh, don't be ridiculous, Rory. Do you know any Germans?'

'Well no, not personally . . .'

'Well I do and they are delightful. I shall introduce you to my dear friend Chessi von Schöndorf this evening and I promise you that you will think she is perfectly delightful. You never know, she may even have a nice German girlfriend who'll change your mind about her nation.'

'I don't want a nice German girl. I want—'

'Ssshh . . .' Saffron put a finger to his lips. 'I'll have none of that talk around here. I am going to go to the Palace to leave a message for Chessi, asking where we are all to meet this evening. Then we shall lunch and I don't know about you, but I am going to spend the afternoon making up for the horrors of having to be a beastly man by indulging all my most frivolous female instincts. I shall have a nice, hot, steamy Turkish bath, followed by a massage. Then I will have my hair done and my nails. I might even go shopping for a new dress.'

'That seems like an awful lot of trouble to go to just to see another girl.'

'In the first place, it's not trouble, it's the most perfect fun. In the second, another girl will appreciate the trouble I've taken more than any man ever would. And in the third . . .' Saffron caught herself just in time. Her third reason was that she was completely certain that she would see him again and she wanted to look her absolute best, because . . . 'Oh,' she said.

Rory was looking at her in the manner of a man who was completely baffled by whatever was going on in the head of the woman next to him.

'Oh, what?' he asked.

'Sorry?' Saffron said, plainly distracted and not really paying attention.

'Well you were just about to tell me the third reason why all this rigmarole you were planning wasn't really a lot of trouble when you stopped, and then you went "Oh", and I just wondered what that was about.'

'Oh . . . nothing. Forget I said a word. You're completely right. I'm a foolish female and I'm sure that whatever you do this afternoon will be a lot more sensible.'

Now she sounded put out and Rory could not for the life of him work out what he had done to deserve it.

But of course, Rory hadn't done a thing. He was, indeed, the very last thing on Saffron's mind. She was fully occupied trying to come to terms with a train of thought that had connected a whole series of fragmentary ideas, memories and perceptions floating around in her subconscious and come to a ghastly conclusion.

For the awful feeling had suddenly struck Saffron that she knew who that beautiful German man, the one she was destined to make her own, had been. He was the man that Chessi was expecting to marry. And if he hadn't proposed to her already, then he would do so very soon, quite possibly tonight. *I'm supposed to be her best friend*, she thought. *How can I possibly come between her and the man she loves?*

Saffron thought a little more. *Hold your horses, girl! You don't know that he actually is her man. And you didn't come between them. You literally landed at his feet AND it was a complete accident AND what happened – whatever it was – was completely unintentional. You didn't plan to look into his eyes and fall head over heels for him. It just happened.*

She considered all that she had learned from a single term of Philosophy and concluded: *So that means that you bear no moral responsibility for what may or at not have occurred.*

Ah, but what about what might happen in the future? the angel on her shoulder asked.

Saffron considered the question and came up with her response. *It's not my decision. It's this man's, whoever he is. If he prefers me, then he shouldn't be with Chessi anyway and she would never have been happy with him. And if he chooses her then I will be extremely cross, but I will have a clear conscience and know that she is perfect for him and I have helped him prove that.*

Which led her to her final verdict: *He's a big boy. He can make up his own mind which one of us he wants.*

That said, she was going to give him every reason to want her. Because, after all, she still didn't know if he really was Chessi's man . . . did she?

Chessi and the others had all gone up to the galleried first floor of Chesa Veglia, where four of the little tables with their red, white and blue checked tablecloths had been pressed together to accommodate their party. Gerhard, however, had decided to stay downstairs a little longer and have another drink. 'Do you need a little extra courage, old man?' one of the others had said. 'I wonder what could possibly make you feel like that?' Everyone had laughed and Chessi had blushed happily because they all knew that this was the night when Gerhard von Meerbach would propose to her and she would of course say 'Yes', because even if she weren't as madly in love as Chessi obviously was, what girl in her right mind would ever turn away a young man as handsome, charming, rich and in every way blessed as him?

So Gerhard stayed downstairs, drank a beer, smoked a cigarette and looked around at all the other wealthy men and their beautiful, pampered women enjoying their evening at the restaurant that the Badrutt family had created inside an old farmhouse. It had opened only three winters earlier but the skill of the conversion had been the way that everything had been designed to create the feeling that people had been eating and drinking here for decades, centuries even. No attempt had been made to disguise the basic structure of the building. In that respect, Gerhard mused, as he cast a professional architect's eye over the place, even his old modernist tutors at the Bauhaus would have approved. The massive wooden posts that held up the floors of pine planks, dark with age (or simply stained to look that way), were left as they were, undisguised and unadorned. Ceilings were simply the underside of the floor-boards of the room above them. Stone walls were either whitewashed or covered with wooden panels decorated with pots of flowers painted onto their surface in a very basic almost childlike style. It created an effect of hearty, rustic simplicity for people who lived very sophisticated, urban lives: *It's a modern version of Marie Antoinette's farmhouse at the palace of Versailles.*

Gerhard's beer glass was empty. He had no reason to stay down here. There was only so much time he could spend looking at the room around him, trying to postpone a proposal which he now knew for certain could never lead to a happy marriage. But he stayed in the hope that she might walk into the room, the woman who had dressed like a man, with her blue eyes he would happily gaze into for all eternity and that cheeky little flick of her rump that had lit a fire of raw lust that he knew would never go out.

It was ridiculous. Why should she come here? There were plenty of other places in St Moritz to eat, and if she was with the Cresta crowd they would all be at their unofficial clubhouse, the bar of the Kulm Hotel. By now, he imagined, the truth behind her escapade would have got out and all the Englishmen would long ago have forgiven her for breaking the rules and be competing for her attention. But she would never look at any of them the way she had looked at him, Gerhard was sure of it.

Ach, don't be so pathetically sentimental! he told himself.

It was a fleeting moment. It has nothing to do with reality. So grow up, stop believing in daydreams and go and propose to the beautiful girl upstairs, who will make such a wonderful wife.

Gerhard paid the barman. He picked his packet of cigarettes up off the counter and got down from his stool. He turned to face the room and was about to walk to the stairs.

And then, as if she had just materialized in the Chesa Veglia, more like a ghost than a living, flesh-and-blood woman, there she was, looking like the heroine of a Russian novel in a black fur coat and hat. Her skin looked very pale and her scarlet-painted lips and blue eyes were bursts of colour against that black and white background. Her cousin was talking to the restaurant manager who was pointing upstairs. Meanwhile, she was darting her eyes from side to side, scanning the room, and Gerhard realized at once that she was looking for him. *I must not call out to her or wave. That would only give the game away. We have to find each other's eyes. It has to be a matter of chance, or destiny.*

So he did no more than look in her direction, trying not to make it too obvious, and as he did, he saw her sense his gaze, like an animal catching a predator's scent on the wind. But she did not try to escape, as a hunted animal might. She turned her head and looked back at him. And in that instant, Gerhard knew that his fate was sealed.

If I've understood the restaurant chappie correctly, your friend and her chums are all upstairs and the stairs are just over there so we should be able to find them in a jiffy,' said Rory, looking suitably pleased that his efforts had proved successful.

Saffron did not appear to have heard him, which was hardly surprising given the hubbub being generated by all the people thronging the restaurant. Rory decided to try again, but more loudly, slowly and clearly this time, as if speaking to someone who was hard of hearing, tremendously stupid, foreign, or all three. 'I say, Saffron dearest . . . your . . . chums . . . are . . . upstairs.'

'What? Oh yes, Chessi . . . Well, can you be a darling and go up there by yourself?'

'Why on earth would I want to do that? I don't know a soul up there. She's your friend.'

'Oh, Chessi's very easy to spot. Blonde, very pretty and she has a rather splendid bosom. That seems to be the first thing chaps notice about her.'

'But what about you? Don't you want to see her? I mean, you've come all this way for the express reason that you want to see your closest girlfriend and now you don't seem to have the slightest interest at all. I'm sorry, Saffy, but what on earth is going on?'

She gave him her most dazzling, ingratiating smile. 'Nothing's going on, darling. It's just that by the most extraordinary co-incidence I've spotted the mysterious knight in shining armour who rescued me after my crash this morning. And it really would be jolly rude not to go over and say thank you to him. I'm sure you don't want to hang around twiddling your thumbs while I do that. So why don't you toddle along and introduce yourself, and you can tell Chessi that I'll be along to join you, just as soon as I've said my words of thanks.'

'Well, I can just as easily wait down here for you to do that.'

'Please don't, there's a dear,' said Saffron, with a very heavy hint that Rory heard loud and clear: for whatever reason she didn't want anyone getting in the way when she went to say hello to this man.

'Oh all right,' he said. 'I know when I'm not wanted.'

'Oh, thank you, darling Rory,' she said. Then she gave him a peck on the cheek and was off across the room like a hound after a fox.

I should have gone down to Shuttlecock before her run, thought Rory bitterly. *I knew she was going to come off. The girl's never done anything slowly or steadily in her life.*

He sighed with resignation and went off to find the Schöndorf girl and her friends. It wasn't difficult. They were all clustered around a long line of tables and a seriously pretty blonde girl – *By George, she really does have some really cracking boobies!* – was at the head with empty seats to either side of her, clearly intended for her husband-to-be and her best friend.

'Ah . . .' said Rory to himself, suddenly wondering whether those two seats were ever to be filled. Oh well, no time to worry about that now. He went over to the girl and said, 'Hello, my name's Rory Ballantyne. I'm Saffron Courtney's cousin. She asked me to say that she'll be up in a second.'

The girl frowned. 'Really? What has detained her?' she asked, in English.

'Oh nothing of any importance really, she just had to say thank you to a chap, a German, actually . . . Frightfully funny story, actually. You see . . .'

Then Rory told the story of Saffron's attempt to defy the rules that banned women and go down the Cresta Run. And though he said so himself, he really thought he told the story jolly well, with lots of amusing little jokes and observations. But he had the horrible feeling that the longer his story went on, the flatter it fell, and at the end, instead of the laughter he might reasonably have expected at the tale of a girl landing head-first in the snow, and all the questions and requests to tell this bit or that bit of the story again that would normally follow such a splendid yarn, there was nothing but silence.

Chessi said something in German, addressed to the table as a whole, and made as if to get up from the table. Then one of the other Germans, a man, spoke to her in the universal tone of a man letting a woman know that she was being very foolish but it did not matter because he would solve her problem. He got up and walked off towards the stairs.

Rory watched the man go down the stairs and a couple of minutes later he saw him come back up again, alone. He walked to the end of the table where Chessi was sitting, glared at Rory as if to suggest that this was all somehow his fault, then got down on his haunches and, with one hand placed consolingly on Chessi's shoulder, spoke to her with quiet, unsmiling earnestness. She listened to what he had to say, thanked him politely, though Rory could see that she was fighting back the tears. Then she stood up. Numerous voices were raised from around the table, but she ignored them and stalked off towards the stairs.

Rory was now getting a very strong feeling that his presence at the table was not welcome. Clearly he was being blamed for Saffron's absence, as if he had been part of her deception. He would have loved to have had the chance to explain that he was just as much in the dark as anyone else, but this was clearly not the time or place for that conversation. So he got up, gave a polite little bow to the table and took his leave.

When he got to the bottom of the stairs, Rory met Chessi coming the other way. 'She is not here,' Chessi said, her sweet, doll-like face now radiating barely controlled fury. 'She has left and taken the man who is to be my husband with her. Tell her from me that she has one day in which to explain herself, apologize and then leave St Moritz, so that I and my man may get on with our lives. And if she does not agree to those conditions, then our friendship is at an end.'

'Golly, yes, I'll pass that on. Absolutely,' said Rory Ballantyne. 'Look,' he said desperately, feeling almost as hurt as the woman in front of him at Saffron's apparently appalling behaviour, 'I don't know if it's any consolation, but this sort of thing is in her blood. Her mother was just the same. She ran off with some German chap, von-something, can't remember exactly . . . anyway, he went off to Africa and that's how she met Saffron's pater, my ma's cousin, because he was their white hunter . . .'

The anger on Francesca von Schöndorf's face had faded like mist in the sun. Now something close to a smile was playing around her face. 'Tell me,' she said. 'I hope I am not being too personal, but I sense that maybe Saffron has hurt you, too.'

Rory frowned. 'Well, yah, she has, rather. I mean, I'm dashed fond of her and so forth, but yes, she rather let me down, actually.'

'Then we have something in common. I have to go back to my friends now and try not to be too upset when my girlfriends tell me how sad I am when all the time I know that they will be thrilled because they were jealous of me getting Gerhard von Meerbach and now that I have lost him they will be thinking, "Maybe I have a chance." But tomorrow, maybe, you and I should talk and you can tell me all about Saffron's past, because she has always kept it very secret from me.'

'Well, she only told me a few bits and bobs, but there was a lot of family gossip, you know, things people had picked up on the grapevine. I say, did I hear you correctly? Is your fiancé chap called von Meerbach?'

'Yes . . . why?'

'Well, it rather complicates things actually. I mean, I wonder if it would really be a good idea to talk. Not really the act of a gentleman, what? Spilling the beans about a lady?'

'My dear, Rory, do you think that Saffron's actions are those of a lady?' Chessi asked, making his eyes pop as she wiggled her body in such a way as to present her spectacular breasts very close to him, directly in his line of sight.

Rory felt his pulse quicken, his trousers bulge and his brain scramble, all at the same time. 'Well no . . . no, I suppose not.'

'Then we should certainly talk. Why don't we meet for coffee? Eleven o'clock, in the foyer of the Palace Hotel. Would that suit you?'

'Um . . . well, I don't see why not.'

'Splendid! I really cannot tell you how much I am looking forward to our conversation.'

* * *

333

When Saffron reached him they did not even say hello. He simply told her, 'We must go. Now!'

She did not ask him why. She already knew the answer, but she did not want to hear it said. She did not even want him to give her his name. That way she could maintain the pretence of ignorance.

When they got outside he asked, 'Where are you staying?'

'The Suvretta House.'

He grinned. 'Me too. Here, I have my car. We can drive back.'

'Ooh,' Saffron purred, when she saw the sleek lines of the Mercedes.

'You like cars?' he said, opening the doors for her.

'I like going fast.'

'Once again . . . me too.' He turned his head to smile at her and his face was so handsome that when he looked away to drive the car she felt as though she had been given a wonderful present at Christmas, only to have it snatched away again.

It took less than five minutes to drive through the snowy streets to the hotel, but it was enough for a feeling to build inside Saffron: a combination of desire, frantic impatience – she had an almost desperate need to feel his arms around her and press her body close to his – and apprehension. It was like standing at the top of the Cresta Run. She knew what was going to happen and there was not the slightest possibility of turning back.

She tried to distract herself by watching him drive. He drove fast, but without any sense that he was showing off, for his every movement was calm, precise, always in total control. He was not even close to the limit of his abilities and that sense of his confidence and assurance was both comforting, for it made her feel entirely safe, but also profoundly attractive. *He will know exactly what he is doing, even when I don't*, she thought, and longed all the more for that moment to come.

Just as they were arriving at the hotel, he said, 'I am in Room

424. I will take the stairs. You take the elevator. That way, no one need suspect anything.'

He pulled up outside the entrance and a uniformed doorman opened Saffron's door. She got out and waited while he tipped the man and handed over his car keys, trying to seem no more than polite, as she would wait for any male friend. Then they walked into the hotel, not even holding hands.

'Goodnight,' he said when they reached the lifts.

'Thank you for a lovely dinner,' she replied and got in without even giving him a peck on the cheek. 'Fourth floor, please,' she said to the operator.

Saffron tried to stay calm and control her breathing, hoping that the young lad with his funny pillbox cap could not tell that her pulse was racing and that the molten heat between her legs was almost more than she could bear.

'Thank you,' she said, with a polite, ladylike smile when the lift came to a halt, the operator pulled the metal grating wide and the doors slid open.

She walked slowly and steadily, just in case anyone should be watching, until she got to his room. The door was very slightly ajar. She pushed it open and there he was. He kicked the door closed as he took her in his arms and kissed her, hard, not hesitating for a single second.

Saffron gave a muffled moan as their mouths locked together. His lips and his tongue were strong and assertive, as though they were taking possession of her, and she yielded to him, giving herself without restraint, exploring his body and his face with her hands, taking in the man-smell of him, pressing herself against him and thrilling to the sure sign of his arousal. She had been kissed before, but it had not excited her. She had felt a man's erection before, but just felt amusement, embarrassment or repulsion. She had ridden all her life and did not need to be told about the delicious, tingly, melty feeling of having an animal between her thighs or rubbing her crotch against the saddle.

But this was totally different. This was raw, animal passion and she knew that she had provoked that feeling in him too, and that sense of achievement, of power over him only aroused her all the more.

They had barely got more than a couple of steps into the room, but neither of them could even wait to get to the bed. He shoved her up against the wall and, still kissing her, pulled her hat from her head and threw it to the floor. She gave a shake of a head to release her hair and he ran his fingers through it and then clenched his fist, grabbing a handful. She moved her head and that pulled at her hair and made it hurt a little so she tried to shake free, but she didn't want to succeed and he didn't let her. He held her harder, trapping her and she shuddered as a shock of pure pleasure shivered through her. Now his other hand lifted her skirt with practised dexterity. She lifted her bottom forward away from the wall to make it easier for him and the higher the fabric rose and the more exposed and utterly vulnerable she felt, the more excited she became.

She was wearing a pair of French camiknickers in pale peach silk, trimmed with lace, and now his hand was running over the soft, slippery fabric, over the hot wetness between her legs and she pushed herself against his hands, making her hunger obvious, glorying in her shamelessness, Now his fingers were inside the elasticated waistband of her knickers, easing them down over her bottom, running over her skin as they went, and tugging them over her hips and now she didn't need any help from his hand because she could let them fall down her legs to the floor and step out of them, and while she was doing that, and the kissing was still not stopping and her head was still caught in his grasp, he was undoing the front of his trousers and she could feel him against her and his fingers sliding up and down and into her. She felt as though she were being lifted up and up and up, like a boat riding to the top of a wave, but never getting there because the wave kept growing and growing. Except the wave was inside her, that feeling of pleasure building and building, that longing for release. And suddenly he had let go of her hair and his hand had left her crotch, but she could still feel him there. Now his hands were going behind her back and around her bottom and he suddenly lifted her up, so that she had to wrap her arms around his neck to cling on and he was lifting her, like the wave lifting her and then bringing her down and he was in her and the heat of him, the size of him, filling her up from within was like no feeling she had ever known.

She gave a little cry, 'Oh!' of surprise and just the tiniest moment of discomfort and he paused for a second and she groaned, imploringly, 'Don't stop!'

He thrust even deeper inside her, and then again and again and she couldn't think any more, but was just a mass of sensations, inside her, outside, touch, smell, taste, sound and of course the sight of his own ecstasy on his face. She was utterly helpless and her only desire was for him to consume her, take her, break down the barrier between her body and his until they were just fused together in one being. Now he groaned, a deep, guttural, animal expression of pleasure and the intensity and desperation of his movements increased still further. She knew that he was feeling it too, this unbearable intensity of excitement, and she suddenly realized that she was moaning and screaming and she just didn't care because her entire existence was focused on the joy of this mutual possession, the two of them, and then she reached the top of the wave and the wave crashed down and it was like an explosion, an earthquake, an eruption and she felt him come inside her and knew that he had felt it too. 'Oh God . . . oh God . . .' she gasped.

He held her for a moment, his chest heaving as he caught his breath and she felt little spasms of pleasure hitting her like aftershocks, and when he withdrew she pleaded, 'Don't go,' for the loss of him, the absence of him inside her was almost unbearable.

He tucked himself back into his trousers, then gently pushed a strand of hair away from her face, smiled and said, 'Here, let me help you with your coat.'

She laughed at the absurdity of it: all that had happened, her life had been changed utterly, forever and she'd not even taken off her coat. He took it and placed it over a chair, then he returned to her and said, 'Now let me help you undress.'

He undid her dress at the back and when she stepped out of it he took it and laid it over the coat with that same sense of confident, easy precision with which he'd driven his car. By the time he'd got back she had taken off her bra and was about to remove her suspender belt and stockings when he said, 'Wait.'

He stepped back and looked at her and although his eyes were entirely frank in the way they ran up and down her body, taking in every detail, Saffron realized that she did not feel in the slightest bit embarrassed, still less ashamed to be examined so freely or to display herself so openly.

He took her in his arms again and said, 'Thank you. I wanted to fix you in my mind, every last bit of you, so that in years to come, no matter where I am or how much time goes by, I will always have the memory of you, at this moment. The memory of the most beautiful woman in the world.'

Then she slipped out of her stockings, casting glances up at him as he removed his own clothes, and her gaze was as greedy as his as it took in the straighter, harder lines of his body, the breadth of his shoulders and the narrowness of his waist and hips, the way the muscles moved in his torso, his arms and legs and even, with affectionate gratitude, the soft, wrinkled remnant of what had been so hard and smooth. She had never looked at the details of a man's body before, not at any rate from the perspective of a woman who has just experienced that magical fit between the male and female forms. She had never seen a man's forearms and known how the strength of them felt, or seen his buttocks and felt an overwhelming desire to sink her red-painted nails into them as she pulled him ever closer, ever deeper into her.

'I will remember you too,' she said as they got into bed. 'Always and anywhere, forever.'

He nodded, lying on his side, his face almost touching hers, looking at her with an expression of profound gravity, understanding that they were bound together now and that any public vows they might make would only be the formalizing of a bond that had long since become unbreakable. Then he smiled and said, 'Do you realize that after all this, we still have not been introduced?'

She giggled, 'Nor we have.'

'Very well,' he said, pushing himself up into a sitting position and holding out his right hand. 'It is my very great pleasure to meet you, Fräulein. My name is Gerhard von Meerbach.'

If he had slapped her in the face, she could not have looked more shocked or more appalled. 'I'm . . . I'm Saffron Courtney,' she managed to say, her voice barely rising above a whisper. Then she asked, 'Did you say, "von Meerbach", like the company that makes engines?'

'Yes, that is my family.'

'So you're related to Count von Meerbach?'

'Yes. The present Count is my older brother Konrad. My father was Count before him. Why do you ask? And, please . . . why do you look so unhappy, my darling Saffron? *Liebchen*, what is the matter?'

'Because of all the men in the world to fall in love with, you are the very last I should have chosen. Chessi von Schöndorf is . . . I suppose now that should be "was" . . . my best friend.'

Gerhard reached out an arm to touch her shoulder, feeling far more nervous and uncertain trying to reassure her now than when he was stripping her and taking her, ravishing her

339

just a short while earlier. 'You cannot blame yourself for that,' he said. 'You did not even know my name.'

'I knew, though . . . I just knew . . .'

He nodded sympathetically. 'I understand. I suppose I knew too. But neither of us set out to hurt Francesca. What happened was a matter of fate. If anyone is to blame it was me. I had a choice. I could have ignored what happened this morning and gone ahead with my proposal. If we had met at dinner, I could have been polite, but no more than that. But in truth that was impossible. I had to have you. And if that was the case, how could I be untrue to Chessi even as I was asking her to be my wife? So, as I say, I had a choice to make and I chose you.'

Saffron smiled, but it was a sad, ironic smile that struck fear into Gerhard's heart. 'So that's another thing we have in common: our logic. I told myself it was up to you to choose and if all we had to worry about was that choice, then I could live with that. If the price of having you was losing Chessi, I would pay it. It would make me sad, but I wouldn't think twice. But that isn't our problem, is it?'

Gerhard frowned in bafflement. 'I don't know . . . I don't understand. What are you trying to tell me?'

'So the name "Courtney" means nothing to you?'

'No, should it?'

'How about Eva von Wellberg?'

'No . . . who is she?'

'She was my mother. She was also your father's mistress. She married my father, Leon Courtney . . . after . . . after . . .'

'After what?'

'After he killed Count Otto von Meerbach by shooting him through the chest with a hunting rifle at point-blank range.'

Saffron had maintained her composure up to that point, but that broke it and she burst into desperate sobs and he could only catch occasional words and phrases as she tried to speak through the tears. 'How can we? . . . Oh God, of all the people

. . . so cruel, so unfair . . . How can we possibly love each other now . . . ?'

Gerhard held her and calmed her, and the very fact that he did that, rather than throwing her out of his bed, seemed to ease her distress a little.

'I was only very small when my father died, so I hardly knew him,' he told her. 'But I know how much he hurt my mother, and I know what kind of a man my brother is, and everyone says how much he takes after our father, so . . . It's strange, but this does not seem to upset me as much as it does you. I'm not sure why that is. It seems wrong somehow, and yet that is how I feel . . . Hold on a moment . . .'

Gerhard reached for the phone by the bed and asked the operator to be put through to room service. He ordered a cold supper for two to be brought up to Room 424: a selection of cold meats and chicken, smoked salmon, bread and butter, a little cheese, some grapes and, because this no longer seemed an occasion for champagne, a bottle of Riesling: 'An Auslese,' Gerhard said, specifying the bold, honeyed wine made from the ripest and thus the richest tasting grapes. 'The best you have, please. And also a bottle of cognac and some Perrier. We will need an ice-bucket for the wine, of course.'

Then he turned back to Saffron and said, 'We have much to talk about and a lot more love to make. We will need to keep our strength up. Now, you have a long and complicated story to tell me, that is obvious. So start from the beginning, tell me everything, and when you have finished, then we will decide what to do next.'

And so she told it all, from her grandfather's ruin to the Zeppelin crash on a mountainside in Kenya and its consequences, while Gerhard listened intently, only interrupting occasionally to make sure that he had understood her correctly. She was less than halfway through her tale, with her mother on the way to Germany to seduce the man who had ruined

341

her father, when supper arrived. Gerhard was struck by Saffron's self-possession at being found in bed by the waiter. She had wrapped a cotton bathrobe around her to preserve her decency and talked to the waiter in confident, almost fluent German about all the various items on the trolley, specifying which ones she wanted on her plate with that combination of ease, good manners but unspoken assumption of command that marked someone used from birth to dealing with staff. *This girl can barely be twenty, maybe less, but if she became the mistress of a great house tomorrow, she would be able to run it and everyone would accept her as their mistress.*

The waiter opened the wine and poured out the first two glasses then disappeared, cheered by a suitably generous tip. They each took their glasses and tapped them together. 'To you,' Gerhard said. 'Now, eat, and then tell me more of your story.'

He grinned at the relish with which Saffron demolished the substantial plate of food that the waiter had prepared for her. Clearly this was not the kind of girl who spent hours talking about her diet and lived off nothing but lettuce leaves and water.

She saw him looking at her as she set about a chicken leg like a lioness consuming her dead prey and grinned: 'I had no idea how much of an appetite one can work up by making love.' She put the leg down, stripped bare of its meat and took another drink of wine. 'Or a thirst.'

'Now you must tell me the rest of your story, like Scheherazade and the Sultan, and I will feed you grapes from time to time, just to encourage you.'

And so she kept talking and every so often he would pop a grape between her lips, or simply kiss them himself, and somehow the telling of this tale of treachery, theft, infidelity, betrayal and killing seemed to bring them together, rather than driving them apart. Finally Saffron said, 'My father hid the five

342

million marks at the bottom of a pool, halfway up the mountain where the Zeppelin landed. After the war he and my mother went back there . . .' she smiled, 'and I went there, too, in a way, because my mother was already pregnant with me. They recovered the gold and my father used some of it to buy our estate in Kenya . . . Oh, I'd love to take you there one day. It's so beautiful, rolling hills with wonderful views of mountains in the distance . . .'

'That sounds like our estate in Bavaria,' he said.

'Does your estate have lions, and cheetahs, and rhinos, and hippos, and zebras, and giraffes, and . . .'

He laughed. 'Is this an estate or a zoo?'

'It's Africa,' she said, quite seriously. 'And if you want to know me truly, never forget this. I may be a subject of His Majesty the King, and I may study at Oxford and have cousins all over England and Scotland. But I am not really English at all. I am African.'

A mischievous grin crossed Gerhard's face. 'There was something I was going to say. Something very important about us, and our love, and our future . . . But the way you said that, "I am African," was so . . . what is that new word you English have? . . . Ah yes, so sexy that I am afraid, my darling, that I am obliged to seduce you all over again.'

'Are you sure that's a good idea?'

'Yes . . .' he said, taking the robe off her, without the slightest resistance on her part, and laying her down on the bed. 'I want to explore you, like Dr Livingstone and Mr Stanley exploring Africa . . .' He gave her a little kiss on the lips, but then his head moved down her body, following his right hand as it ran down her breastbone and then around each of her breasts in turn. They were not large, but they were pretty and in proportion to the sleekness of the rest of her; the long, flowing lines of a body that was naturally athletic, gifted with speed and strength but still entirely feminine.

Her nipples were a delicate shade of coral pink and they were standing up for him as proudly as little guardsmen on parade. 'Here for example,' he whispered, taking her left nipple between his finger and thumb, squeezing it slowly, gently, just to the point where she gave a little gasp and arched her back, and then he ran the palm of one hand over that same nipple touching it as faintly, delicately as he possibly could while his other hand squeezed her right nipple so that she was engulfed by two totally different feelings at one and the same time. Then, still working her right breast with his hand, he lowered his head over her left breast and started playing with it with his lips and tongue and teeth: sometimes kissing her skin, sometimes flicking the nipple with his tongue, then very gently biting it, taking infinite care to apply just the right amount of pressure. Her hands were running through his hair and then stroking his back and then, as he brought his head over to her other breast, she moaned and shuddered with pleasure, her fingernails tore at his skin and her buttocks began to writhe as the need for him took hold.

'Now, I must look for the source . . .' he murmured and slid his body down the bed so that his lips and tongue slipped lower and lower until she was crying out, 'Oh God . . . oh God . . . please!' He drove into her with all his force, as if he could somehow put his entire body and soul within her, consuming her, feeling like a conqueror, but knowing that she had overwhelmed him absolutely, too.

Afterwards, they lay there together until he summoned up the energy to pour some more of the sweet, rich wine and they shared a glass. 'Here,' he said, 'try some of this with it.' He passed her a piece of Emmentaler and the combination of the two flavours, the honey wine and the strong salty cheese, was magical.

'My God, that's almost as good as the you-know-what-ing,' Saffron said, and now there was nothing in her smile but the

344

absolute happiness, with a slight degree of smugness, of someone who has just enjoyed a bout of wonderful loving. 'Now, tell me your important thing, the one that you were about to explain before we were so delightfully interrupted.'

'Ah yes ... It is really very simple ... Terrible things happened between our families in the past. Great wrongs were done, on both sides. So now we must decide: do we live in the past and concentrate on old hatred, or do we live in the present and concentrate on our love? If we live in the past, the hatred gets worse, nothing is solved and we are both unhappy. If we live in the present we will be adding happiness to our own lives and, in some tiny little way, to the world. So, I say we should love.'

'And I say, I love you, Gerhard von Meerbach.' She wrapped her arms around his neck again and kissed him. Then she said, 'I love a man called von Meerbach. Good heavens ... what an utterly extraordinary idea!'

They talked and made love all night long. Saffron told Gerhard about her life in Africa: how her mother had died and her father had brought her up alone for almost a decade until he had finally found happiness with Harriet. She described Manyoro: how he and her father considered themselves to be brothers; all the years that he had always been there whenever she needed him; and her own delight when Manyoro had told her that she was no longer his little princess and, 'Now I shall call you my queen.' When Gerhard heard the heartfelt respect and affection she felt for this black African, he knew that Saffron would have nothing but contempt for the hatred of other races that lay at the heart of Nazism and that their love would have no chance of lasting unless he was completely open about the life he had led for the past five years.

So he told her about his meeting with Heydrich and how

345

the second most powerful man in the SS had united with his brother to force him into a pact with the devil of Nazism. He confessed to all the benefits that he had gained from being seen to be a good Nazi and to the joy he had found as a pilot, alone in the air. 'Now I know why people talk about being as free as a bird,' he said, 'because up there is where I find true freedom.'

He recounted his meeting with Hitler and realized that even this English girl, who considered herself an African and despised racial prejudice, was still fascinated by the idea of his personal encounter with a man whose fame was now universal, among those whom he appalled as well as those who adored him. The one part of his story that he did not tell in full was its beginning: his gift to Isidore Solomons. He did not want to sound as though he was making excuses, or portraying himself as better than he was. But Saffron saw at once that something was missing. 'How was Heydrich able to make you join the Nazi Party?' she asked. 'Surely, even in Germany, you can't force an innocent man who has done nothing wrong to give up everything he stands for and stand up for something he doesn't believe.'

'I would not be so sure about that,' Gerhard replied. 'I imagine that if you come from a land that is truly free, where you can say and think whatever you like without fear, and criticize the government, or have political arguments with your friends over dinner or in a bar, then it is impossible to imagine what losing that freedom is like. In Germany you cannot argue, because you cannot trust the person who argues against you. Even your oldest friend, or your brother, or your child might report your opinions to the secret police. My brother and Heydrich could have labelled me a communist and thrown me in a camp, just for studying architecture at a school that was later banned, even though I have never voted for a communist candidate, or supported communist ideals in my life.'

'But there must be trials, surely? You must be able to defend yourself.'

'Five years ago, maybe . . . just. Now the judges belong to the Party too and justice is defined by the Party's ideals.'

'My God . . . I had no idea. That's awful.'

'Yes, it is, but I can only say so because we are not in Germany and you are not a German. Look . . .' he paused, sighed and then said, 'There is someone you should meet, someone here in Switzerland. He is, you could say, my own Manyoro. When you talk to him everything will make more sense.'

Saffron left Gerhard's room just as the first rays of the sun were prising their way through the gaps between the mountains. She collapsed into her own bed and slept like a log until ten. Three messages had been left for her at the concierge's desk and then slipped beneath her door. Each had been placed inside a hotel envelope, so that she had no idea who had written them, although it wasn't hard to guess. So she took pot luck and opened up one of the envelopes at random. It contained a furious, heartbroken, devastating indictment of her behaviour from Chessi von Schöndorf that left Saffron in tears, for she knew how much her friend had adored Gerhard and how utterly crushed and humiliated she must feel at losing him. No matter what finely reasoned, impeccably logical justifications Saffron could dream up to justify what she had done, still the fact remained that someone who had trusted her absolutely had been absolutely let down.

The second note, from Rory, was no less irate.

I might, perhaps, begin to understand, if not forgive your actions if you had prostituted yourself for an Englishman, but to throw away your honour on a damned Hun is unspeakably low. Of course, as the whole family knows, your mother did the same thing. Clearly you take after her. I shall remain in St Moritz for a few days, enjoying the company of the decent, honest chaps from the Tobogganing

> *Club. I will then make my own way home and I expect you
> to do the same. I dare say you are worried now that I will
> besmirch your reputation once I return to England by telling
> people the truth about what you have done. You may rest
> assured that my lips will be sealed. I have no desire to lower
> myself into the same gutter as you. I pride myself on being
> a gentleman. You, however, are no lady.*

Saffron felt as though she had been physically attacked. She
lay on her bed, defeated, and distraught. In one fell swoop,
one moment of reckless passion, she had lost her two closest
friends in the world. Chessi had been the first person to show
her any kindness on that train to Roedean. Over three Easter
holidays she and her family had welcomed her into their home
and treated her like one of the family. How could she have
repaid such generosity with such selfishness? And poor Rory
. . . Saffron knew that his letter must have been motivated as
much by his envy of Gerhard and his own frustrated, rejected
love for her as by his disapproval of her immorality. *He
wouldn't have thought it was so immoral if he'd been in the bed
with me last night.* But that didn't make his outrage any less
justified or less sincere. She had behaved like a tramp, a slut,
a harlot. She had given herself to a man, and done it gladly,
wantonly, heedless of the consequences of her actions. And
now, for the very first time, the most obvious consequence of
all occurred to her: *My God, what if I'm pregnant?*

Saffron was starving hungry, but she could not eat. She was
exhausted, but unable to sit still. She had to escape, but she
had nowhere to go for once she stepped outside the four walls
of her room she would be in enemy territory.

Her only hope was the third note. It must surely have been
sent by Gerhard, but her fingers were shaking so much she
could barely open the envelope, for if he had rejected her too
she would be left with nothing.

My darling,

I have written to Francesca, explaining that I cannot marry her and taking full responsibility for my actions. In the circumstances it is best that I should leave St Moritz. I am going to Zürich. I would like it very much if you could join me there, so that I can introduce you to my own 'Manyoro'. He will explain everything. I am thinking of you and my heart is breaking for you because I know how much pain you will be in today. Just know that I love you with all my heart. This is a very difficult day, but you are a good, kind, beautiful person. Do not forget that. I love you with all my heart – G

PS: I will wait for you between 15.00–18.00 at Zürich station. If you miss me there, I will be staying at the Baur au Lac.

Finally, Saffron had a shred of hope. And she also had a plan to follow, something to do, a train to catch. With that renewed sense of purpose came a slight lifting of her spirits. She was a long way from being happy, but the crushing, hopeless despair was beginning to lift from her soul. She ordered breakfast and ate it, all while composing two short notes to Chessi and Rory. Though she made it plain that it had never been her intention to cause pain, she did not attempt to justify what she had done, or make excuses, or pretend that they had no right to be hurt. She simply apologized, in the most straightforward, sincere terms she could find, without even begging their forgiveness for she knew she had no right to ask for that. It was for them to give, in their own time, if they ever so desired. And in the meantime the best thing she could do – the only thing that would justify everything else – was to put her heart and soul into loving Gerhard von Meerbach.

It was only later that a thought struck her. She had promised, well, not promised exactly, but certainly agreed to tell Mr Brown

349

about her impressions of Germany and its people. Did that mean she had to tell him about Gerhard? She hadn't actually been to Germany again, after all, even if – and here Saffy could not resist a giggle – she did know an awful lot more about at least one of its people.

No, this was her private life. It was none of his business. And with that matter settled, she got on with the rest of her day.

Gerhard was waiting on the platform at Zürich when the train from Chur arrived. Saffron had been nervous as the end of her journey drew closer. What if she saw him in the cold light of day, away from the excitement and glamour of St Moritz, and suddenly realized that she had made the wrong choice? What if she should have ditched him and gone back to Chessi and Rory on her bended knees begging them to take her back? It was not an appealing prospect: begging did not come naturally to Saffron Courtney. Then she smiled to herself as she thought: *Except when I'm begging him to take me, wicked girl that I am!*

That thought sent little tremors through her body, for she had discovered that she could almost recreate the sensation of having Gerhard inside her, simply by thinking about how that had felt. And that delectable reminder of the wonderful night she had spent with her man reassured her that all would be well.

And so it was. Gerhard looked as edible as ever in a long, olive green loden coat, with a scarf draped around his neck with a casual elegance that made her wonder why none of the male students who thronged Oxford in their college scarves ever looked half as dashing. She ran into his arms and from the moment he was holding her again there was nothing else in the world but them, and she would have given up anyone and everyone in order to keep him. 'I was wondering if you could possibly be as lovely as I had remembered,' he said, echoing her own thoughts. 'And here you are, even more beautiful today than you were yesterday. Kiss me.'

She looked around and gave a nervous little laugh. 'But there are so many people! They'll all see us.'

'Let them. Every man will envy me.'

And every woman will wish she were in my place, thought Saffron, willingly surrendering to his lips and his tongue and wishing they could just stay there, in that wonderful embrace, forever.

All too soon, he pulled away. 'I have booked a room for you at the Baur au Lac . . . If we were in Paris or Nice, we might be able to share a room. But the Swiss are even more orderly than us Germans. They would certainly not approve.'

'You never know, I might refuse to share a room with you. I'm a respectable young lady, you know . . .' And then, before he could say anything, she added, 'Well, I used to be, anyway.'

'One day, if I am very lucky, perhaps I will be able to make you respectable again.'

'May I finish university first?' she said. 'You needn't worry. There's not a man in all Oxford that could tempt me away from you.'

'Ah . . . wouldn't it be nice to be able to make plans? But this world we are in . . . I fear that none of us can plan for anything . . .'

'Don't say that,' she said, squeezing his arm with hers to cling to him as tightly as she could. 'It frightens me.'

'You? . . . Frightened? That is one thing I would never expect from you.'

'I'm frightened of losing you. I've always done my best to beat the boys at everything.' She looked up at him with an impish smile. 'That's why I went down the Cresta Run . . . But I'm still a girl. You know . . . underneath.'

'Oh, I know . . . *mein Gott*, how I know! Now, come, my car is waiting to take us back to the Baur. You can drop off your cases and then we have an appointment.'

'With your mysterious Manyoro?'

'Exactly!'

A short while later, in the car, on the way between the hotel and the meeting Gerhard had arranged, he said, 'You know, I have been thinking a lot about something that happened last night . . .'

'Mmm . . . me too!' Saffron purred.

Gerhard laughed. 'Not that! Well, not just that, should I say.'

'What else, then?'

'The way I reacted when you said that your father had killed my father. I should have been shocked, no? I should have been angry, outraged. It should have been the end of any love or even friendship between us. But instead I felt nothing. That is not normal, surely. So ever since I have been asking myself why that was. I thought maybe it was because I was so young when he died and therefore I do not have memories of him, nothing that would make me miss him and all the things we did together. But no, that cannot be right, because that is exactly what should make me angry: your father robbed me of the memories a son should have of his father; all the times they went hunting or skiing together; all the games they played when the boy was little, even the fights they had when the boy was fifteen or sixteen, rebelling against his old man.'

'I know exactly how that feels. That's how it is for me, too, not having my mother. We never did all the things that a mother and her daughter should do. I never learnt from her how to be a woman.'

'Yes, but your mother was good and kind. I am sure she loved you and always wanted the best for you. But I would never have had those good memories, even if my father had lived. I know that he was a bully. It was bad enough growing up with my brother Konrad. All the time, whenever he could, he tried to push me down, sometimes with words, sometimes with his fists.'

'He sounds horrible.'

'He thinks that being in the SS – arresting people, torturing them, ruining their lives – is the best job in the world. And for him it is. That is the kind of man he is and the kind of boy he was. But we were only boys, not men, and even though he always used to say that he was the head of the family, he could not control me, or stop me being the person I wanted to be.'

'Not then, at any rate . . .'

'No, not then . . . and maybe not now . . . or at least not in the future, I don't know. But my point is, if my father had been alive, he could have controlled me. He and Konrad would have thought the same way. Konrad used to tear up the drawings I made when I was small. He said that only girls played with pencils and paints.'

'But that's stupid! Think of all the men who were great artists!'

'Konrad doesn't think. Or not like that, at any rate. But even though he made my life hell, my mother encouraged me and supported me when I said I wanted to be an architect and he could not stop her. But I'm sure my father would have overruled her, and prevented me from studying architecture. I could not have been myself if he had been alive. And so what I have concluded is that by killing my father, your father saved me.'

'I see what you mean,' Saffron said. 'But it's sad that you should think that. Even worse that you might very well be right.'

'Mmmm . . .' murmured Gerhard. His eyes were on the road. They were in an area of narrow cobbled streets with tall, old buildings on either side, many of them with cafés or restaurants on the ground floor. Now Gerhard seemed to find what he was looking for, turned sharp right and went down an even more cramped sidestreet that opened onto a little square. 'I think we've arrived,' he said.

Gerhard parked the car, they got out and he led the way to a café–patisserie called Konditorei Kagan. A handwritten sign in the window beside the entrance said, 'Koscheres Essen serviert hier.'

'Kosher food served here,' Saffron translated, murmuring to herself.

But Gerhard heard her and said, 'One used to see signs like that in Germany, you know. All over Berlin there were Jewish bakeries, butchers, delicatessens. But now . . .'

He led the way in. Saffron saw a serving counter to the left of the door, close to the window with tables and chairs beyond it, many occupied with people enjoying coffee and cakes to warm up the cold winter afternoon. A middle-aged man, presumably the proprietor, Kagan himself, was standing behind the counter serving his customers. It was obvious to Saffron, from the way he had a word for everyone as he fetched them their food, or made their coffees, or handed back their change, that these were all regulars. And she could see from the looks being cast in their direction that she and Gerhard were very obviously strangers and that his loden coat, such an obviously German piece of clothing, marked him out all the more clearly.

He approached the counter and spoke to the man behind it. 'Herr Kagan?' he asked.

'Yes . . . who is asking?' The suspicion in his voice was palpable.

'My name is von Meerbach. Max said I should ask for him here.'

At once, Kagan's attitude was transformed. He leaned forward and clasped Gerhard's hand. 'I am honoured to meet you, Herr von Meerbach. You are a *mensch*.'

Saffron was puzzled. '*Mensch*' was simply the German word for 'human being'.

'I hope so,' said Gerhard, sounding equally bemused.

'*Oi vey iz mir!*' exclaimed Kagan. 'Did my old friend never teach you anything? In Yiddish a *mensch* is not just a man, but a man of honour, a good man, someone to admire. You did a fine thing, Herr von Meerbach. You are a *mensch.*'

Saffron realized that although Kagan's words had made her smile she was suddenly very close to tears, so moved by hearing Gerhard described in such fine terms.

'And you, Fräulein,' Kagan said, turning his attention to her. 'Ei-yei-yei, such a *shainer maidel!*'

'I hardly dare ask what that means,' Saffron said, hoping that her German grammar and accent weren't too terrible.

'It means that you are a beautiful girl, my dear . . . but not a German girl, I think.'

'No, I'm English.'

Gerhard looked at her with a little smile, as if to say, 'I thought you said you were African?'

And she gave a little shrug of her shoulders that meant, 'It's easier just to say "English".'

'A handsome German man and a lovely English rose, so obviously in love,' Kagan said. 'Maybe there is some hope for this sad world, eh?'

'I hope so,' agreed Gerhard.

'But I am keeping you and Max will be wondering what has happened. Go through to the back and take the door on the right-hand side. Then up the stairs. You will find Max when you get to the top.'

They walked between the tables and Saffron was conscious that they were being appraised in a very different way now. The women in particular were openly curious, wondering what these Gentiles had done to earn such a warm reaction from Kagan, whom they knew to be no friend of the new Nazi Germany.

The unashamed inspection made Saffron smile, so that the moment they were through the door Gerhard asked, 'What was so funny?'

355

'Just that they reminded me of Masai women. They stare at people, men in particular, in just that same way, you know, really having a good look, completely unbothered by all the conventions that say it's rude to stare.'

'Ah, my lovely African girl . . . Come on, let's find our man.'

They climbed the stairs and came to a landing that served as the hall of the apartment where Kagan and his family lived above their shop. But when one of the doors that led off the landing opened, the figure that walked out was not Frau Kagan or any of her children, but a distinguished-looking man who appeared to Saffron to be about the same age as her father. He wore a pinstripe suit, with a waistcoat and stiff collared shirt and tie, and when he saw Gerhard his face broke into a look of absolute delight as he opened his arms and said, 'My dear boy . . .'

'Izzy!' Gerhard replied and they hugged and slapped one another's backs.

So he does have a father in his life, after all, Saffron thought.

Gerhard disentangled himself and said, 'Izzy, I would like you to meet Miss Saffron Courtney. She is the woman I will love for the rest of my life.'

'And who could blame you?'

'Saffron, this is Isidore Solomons, who was for many years my family's lawyer, as his father and grandfather were before him. He is also a true hero.'

'*Ach*, please . . .' Isidore rolled his eyes at Saffron and, switching to English, said, 'It is my very great pleasure to meet you, Miss Courtney. I am sorry that I could not invite you to my home. I should love you to see it, Gerhard, our circumstances are much improved since you last saw me. But it might not be wise. Even here, in Switzerland, I can feel eyes upon me. But please, come through into the Kagans' sitting room, which they have kindly placed at our disposal. Herr Kagan has made a big pot of coffee and you must try the cakes, Miss Courtney. If there is one thing a Jew cares about it is his food, and I doubt there is a finer baker in Zürich than Yavi Kagan. In fact, I know there is not.'

'It sounds as though you and he are close, Herr Solomons,' Saffron said.

'Yes, I suppose we are. It has become my habit every morning to stop here on my way to work for a cup of coffee and a couple of Mandelbrot. Look, Kagan has put some out for us this afternoon.' He pointed at a small pile of hard biscuits shaped like little slices of bread. 'They are flavoured with orange, lemon and vanilla and covered in slices of freshly toasted almonds. Dip them in your coffee, Miss Courtney, you will not regret it.'

Saffron did as she was told and then took a bite, 'Mmm . . . delicious!' To Isidore's evident approval, she polished off the biscuit in her usual brisk style and then asked, 'When we came in, Gerhard asked for Max. I can see now why you might not want to use your real name. But is there any reason why you chose Max instead?'

'It's nothing really . . .' Isidore said.

'Nonsense!' Gerhard protested. 'The truth is, I chose the name because Izzy won the Blue Max in the war. That is the highest award for gallantry that Germany has to offer. It is like the Victoria Cross for the British.'

'Oh . . . goodness,' said Saffron, feeling a little overawed.

'I am sure you are not the slightest bit interested in old men telling war stories,' Isidore said.

'On the contrary, Herr Solomons . . .'

'Please, call me Izzy.'

'May I call you Max? After all, that is how I first knew you.'

'You may call me anything you like. And I believe you were about to make what we lawyers would think of as a counter-argument.'

357

'Yes, I was. You see, I was brought up among Masai warriors in Kenya . . .'

'She's an African, Izzy, can't you tell?' Gerhard said, earning himself a playful slap on his leg for his cheek.

'So I was taught that there was no higher praise for a man than to call him a great warrior. I salute you for it.'

'Thank you my dear, I shall treasure that compliment,' Izzy said. 'And now, I dare say you are wondering why Gerhard has brought you here. So I will tell you . . .'

And so it was that Saffron discovered what Gerhard had done, why a Jewish café proprietor in Zürich should call him a *mensch*, and what had made two Nazis so determined to force him to abandon his principles. When the story was over, she got up, walked around to Izzy's chair, said, 'Thank you, Max. Thank you from the bottom of my heart,' and gave him a little kiss on the cheek.

Then she walked back to where Gerhard was sitting. 'Stand up,' she said. 'I want to hug my man.' So she hugged him and told him how proud she was of him and then she giggled and hissed, 'Not now, you wicked man!' as she felt the effect that her words were having.

Saffron sat down and for the next while was happy to sit and listen as the men caught up with everything that had happened since they had last met. She loved to see the affection between the two of them and was fascinated by all she heard, wanting to know absolutely every single thing she could possibly learn about this man who had walked away with her heart.

Then Gerhard asked, 'Izzy, is it wrong that I love flying so much and that I take pride in being part of the Luftwaffe and having an aircraft as fine and fast and deadly as a 109?'

'Was it wrong for von Richthofen to be proud of being our greatest ace or to love flying his little red Fokker?'

'Well no, but that was different.'

'Why?'

'You, of all people know why, Izzy.'

'I know two things, Gerhard. I know that I was proud to serve my country, our country. And I know that I hate Hitler and everything he stands for. But as much as Hitler would like to pretend that his Nazi Party and our country are one and the same thing – which is one of the many reasons I despise him, incidentally – he is wrong. Germany will still survive when he and his evil henchmen are gone, and all that I ask of God is that I should be allowed to live to see that day and have my country returned to me. So I say, no, you are not wrong to be proud. But I have a question for you, my boy . . .'

'Go ahead, ask it.'

'When you were very young, and had all the arrogance and invincibility of the young, you took a crazy risk to help me.'

'And I don't regret it, not for an instant.'

'I do not doubt that, but here is my question. You are five years older now. You are making a reputation as an architect . . .' Isidore held up his hand to stop Gerhard from interrupting. 'I know, it is not in the style of design you would have sought, but still it is there. Also you have a position within your squadron and the Luftwaffe, one in which you take pride. And now, you have met the woman who will be your companion through life, I have no doubt at all about that, if only the fates will allow. So my question to you is this. If you knew another German family, who happened to be Jewish, would you give them, too, five thousand marks to help them escape? For we surely know now, if we did not in '34, that there is no future for them in the Nazi Reich. Would you give them the money, and with it the gift of life?'

Saffron could see that the question had taken Gerhard completely unawares. He wanted to say, 'Of course!' She could see him trying to frame the words. But she could also see that his honesty forbade him from saying them. In the end, he shook his head sadly and said, 'I don't know . . . I really don't know . . . but I very much fear I would not.'

Isidore nodded sympathetically. 'I understand, and I do not think any the worse of you. You have done your good deed. If every man in Germany were even half, even a tenth as generous as you, my people would not be in the mortal danger that confronts us today. So all I ask of you Gerhard, is that you carry in your heart the memory of the reckless, but fine young man that you were. Treasure it like a candle that must be kept burning. Do not let the light go out. One day you may have need of it.'

Saffron watched as Isidore's eyes went from her to Gerhard and back again and they seemed to her to be filled with a sorrow so profound that she could hardly bear to look at him: the sorrow of an entire people, an echo of persecution and suffering that stretched back into the mists of time.

'Do you remember that poem I read you, the one that said the centre could not hold: "The blood-dimmed tide is loosed and everywhere the ceremony of innocence is drowned"?'

'Yeats,' Saffron said, quietly.

'Indeed . . . My children, that time is upon us. I can feel it coming. That evil barbarian will not be satisfied until he has engulfed the whole world in war and death. I fear for us all, and I fear for you, the young whom the old will sacrifice, just as they sacrificed my generation. I want to see you together, living in peace, with your children running around, playing happily between you. I want to be there, with my silver hair and my walking stick, smiling to see life being created and love being shared.

'And so I say to you both now, as I once said to you, Gerhard: whatever happens, for God's sake stay alive.'

It was pure chance that Mr Brown discovered that Saffron had been in St Moritz, and when he did the information did not come from an intelligence officer or secret agent, but simply from a snippet of gossip, overheard at a wedding reception. He had been threading his way through the mass of people thronging the reception rooms of a country house in Wiltshire when he caught a young, female voice saying, 'Did you hear what Saffy Courtney got up to in St Moritz this year? It was too, too wicked.'

Mr Brown stopped and adjusted his posture to be able to see one of the bridesmaids talking to a girlfriend.

'Oh do tell!' said the girlfriend, leaning in expectantly.

'Well, first she insisted on going down the Cresta Run, which is strictly chaps-only.'

'Golly, how daring!'

'I think it's rather show-offy, myself. And she came flying off, which rather serves her right.'

The bridesmaid's friend gave an appreciative giggle at the thought of the famously, and, to her mind, rather annoyingly beautiful Saffron Courtney making a fool of herself.

'But that wasn't the really wicked thing she did . . .'

'Oh, my dear, what did she do?'

'She ran off with a German! Stole him from his fiancée, right under her nose, and spent the night with him. And she'd never even clapped eyes on him before!'

'No! How awful!' the friend gasped, wondering why she never had adventures like that.

'I know! Poor Rory Ballantyne, who'd taken her to St Moritz and smuggled her onto the Cresta, much against his own better judgement, was absolutely furious, apparently. They've been on absolute non-speakers ever since.'

'Dear Rory . . . he's so sweet.'

'A bit dull, though . . . but terribly sweet.'

A week or so later, Mr Brown made sure that he just happened to be in Oxford during the last week of Hilary term (why they did not call it the Spring, Lent or Easter term, like everyone else, Mr Brown – who was a Cambridge man – could not imagine) and invited Saffron Courtney to a spot of lunch at the Randolph Hotel.

'I thought it would be nice to catch up,' he said. 'Did you go anywhere jolly for Christmas?'

'I was up in Scotland with my cousins, the Ballantynes,' Saffron said. She paused fractionally and Mr Brown could tell that she was trying to decide how much he did or did not know. 'Then I went skiing in St Moritz. It was a complete spur-of-the-moment sort of thing.'

'Did you have a nice time?'

'I did actually, yes.' Saffron leaned over to him and stage-whispered, 'You mustn't tell anyone, but I did something that is totally *verboten*. I had a bash at the Cresta Run.'

'Ah yes, I gather women are not allowed.'

'No, I had to dress up as a man. I'm not sure I was very convincing.'

Mr Brown smiled amiably. Then, like a poker player making his opening bet, he asked, 'Did you learn anything interesting while you were there?'

She looked him right in the eye, didn't miss a beat, and like an opponent seeing the bet and raising it said, 'Yes, actually, I did. I met a rather interesting man.'

'Really? Did he say anything that might interest me?'

'Yes . . . He was a Jew . . .'

Saffron left the sentence hanging just long enough to make Mr Brown wonder if she had slept with a German Jew, and then continued by telling him the story of a lawyer who had been a hero in the Great War but been forced to flee the country he had served so valiantly. She told the story very well, so that it was as moving as it was genuinely informative. And while she was rather vague about exactly how and where she had met this gentleman, whose name she said she had sworn not to reveal, it was plain that her tale was true. But she said not one word that even hinted at a lover, let alone a German one.

Mr Brown left the meal in high spirits. He had rarely seen

362

information withheld so effortlessly, and such a good cover story put in its place. The girl was an absolute natural.

Saffron and Gerhard met one more time, that Easter, when she found an excuse to visit Paris. The plans that Speer had drawn up for the new Berlin, guided by his Führer's fantasies, were very strongly based on the drawings of an eighteenth-century architect called Étienne-Louis Boullée. His works were collected at the Bibliothèque National in the French capital and, having assured Speer that a direct study of the old master's work would greatly assist his own endeavours, and promised that he would meet all the expenses himself, Gerhard was given permission to pay the Boullée archive a personal visit. He booked a quiet room at the Ritz, spent many delightful hours in bed with Saffron, had their photograph taken in front of the Eiffel Tower – both smiling at the camera and locked in a passionate embrace – and even, having kissed Saffron goodbye at the Gare du Nord, managed one exhausted day in the Bibliothèque before returning to Berlin.

While they were in Paris, Gerhard and Saffron talked for longer than either of them would have wanted about the war they both felt certain was coming. They agreed that they had each of them an obligation to do their bit for their country. They also agreed that they would never say a word about any detail of their service to the other. If they did, and were intercepted, that would lead to suspicions of espionage or treachery. Furthermore, if either of them knew what the other was doing, and had any idea of the danger they were in, it would be impossible to bear. And finally, their love depended on being able to forget their nations' political and military differences and see one another as individuals. All they really needed to know was that they were still alive and still in love.

Gerhard had worked out a way by which they could communicate. In order to protect her and the other people involved, the only information he gave her was Isidore Solomons' office address in Zürich. All he wanted from her in return was an address in England to which Izzy could safely write. She provided her Aunt Penny's house in Tite Street.

'You don't mind, do you?' Saffron asked, a few nights later when she and Penny were having dinner in a little Italian restaurant in the backstreets of Chelsea, between the King's Road and the river.

'That depends on your answer to three questions,' Penny replied.

'Well then you'd better ask me them.'

'Very well. First: do you know that you love him?'

'Oh, absolutely, from the bottom of my heart,' Saffron replied and Penny knew at once that she was telling the truth.

'Second: are you sure that he loves you?'

'Absolutely, without a doubt.'

'And thirdly: is he a good man?'

'Oh yes, he truly is,' Saffron assured Penny and then told her the story of Isidore Solomons, and described the way they had been received at Herr Kagan's café in Zürich. By the end of the story, both women were in tears and Aunt Penny's cooperation and absolute discretion were assured.

When she went back to Oxford for the summer term, Saffron volunteered for the local branch of the Mechanised Transport Corps, a voluntary organization founded in the '14–'18 war to provide trained female driver–mechanics to the armed services, so that men could be freed for duties on the front line. Leon and Harriet came over to London for the month of June, as they had done before, and as they ate their strawberries and cream at Wimbledon and took in the Summer Show at the Royal Academy, they were all three painfully aware of the sense that twenty years of peace were drawing to a close.

'When war does break out, I'm going to leave Oxford,' Saffron told Leon. 'I want to do my bit.'

'But there's no need to do that right away. You won't be called up. Finish your studies and then if, God forbid, the bloody war still isn't over you can decide how best to serve your country.'

'But what's the point of staying at Oxford when it's half empty and all the boys one knows have gone to war? It would be miserable. I can do my bit, even if it is only driving a car or a lorry or something and then go back there afterwards. Oxford will still be Oxford, no matter what happens in the war.'

Leon could see there was no budging her and for all that he wanted to keep his baby girl safe, he admired her courage and determination. So rather than fight her, he decided to redirect her, for the thing he feared above all was for Saffron to be stuck in London when the bombs started falling. For if there was one thing all the military experts seemed to agree on it was that modern bombers could inflict death and destruction on a scale never before seen in time of war.

Saffron had not been home to Kenya for a year and went back to Africa with Leon and Harriet. On the way they stopped off in Cairo, staying with Grandma at the old Courtney family home in the Garden City. For a couple of days after their arrival in the city, Saffron could not help but notice that her father seemed to be unusually busy and secretive. But finally, he came clean.

'I dare say you've been wondering what I've been up to,' he said to Saffron as they were having a drink before dinner.

'I have rather, yes,' she replied.

'As have I,' Harriet interjected. She looked at Saffron, 'He's not said a word to me either.'

'Well, I'm in the fortunate position of having a bit of influence in this city. Courtney Trading will be a major asset to the war effort, if and when the show begins, what with our oil, ships and whatnot. So I've been able to pull a few strings. It turns out that the army has just appointed a new General Officer Commanding the British and Empire troops in Egypt. He's Major General Henry Maitland Wilson, who's known to one and all as Jumbo, for reasons that will become apparent when you meet him. Anyway, he's just arrived in Cairo, barely knows a soul and is in need of a driver. I said I'd be happy to show him the ropes, introduce him to everyone, get him set up at the Sporting Club and so forth. And in return, all I asked was the chance to provide him with a trained MTC girl to chauffeur him around: my own dear daughter in fact. So, how does that sound?'

'Interesting . . .' said Saffron, in the sceptical tone of someone waiting to hear what the catch is.

'Oh, it's more than interesting, darling,' said Harriet. 'Any girl would jump at the chance to drive a general.'

'Of course, he wants to meet you,' Leon added, 'Make sure you're presentable, know how to drive, aren't some silly little thing who won't be able to deal with him. I assured him he need have no concerns. So we're meeting him for lunch at the club on Saturday. If all goes well I thought I'd invite him duck-shooting in the Delta. I'm sure he'll be all the happier once he's seen you shoot.'

'Well, it does sound like a tremendous opportunity. But what if there isn't a war?'

'Then you go back to university. But I'll be honest with you, Saffy, I think there will be. I think Hitler wants to get his paws on Poland. He has to move before the weather turns bad, and when he does I can't see how we can let him occupy another country without the slightest protest.'

Leon had only one demand to make of Saffron, and Jumbo Wilson, which he raised over lunch at the Gezira Sporting Club.

'I think it's important for Saffron to have some means of self-defence. I've taken the liberty of procuring a little Beretta 418 pistol. It's an ideal lady's gun: small, very light and fits very neatly into a handbag.'

'I do assure you, Mr Courtney, I have no intention of taking your daughter into battle, or danger of any kind, if I can possibly avoid it,' said the general, who was just as tall and stout as his name suggested.

'I'm absolutely sure you don't, General. But I have fought a war in Africa and it's not like Europe. The front lines aren't drawn nice and neatly on the map. You never know when or where you might suddenly run into trouble.'

'Do you have any idea how to shoot a gun, Miss Courtney?' the major general asked.

'I have a fair bit of experience, yes sir.'

'Tell you what, General,' said Leon, 'why don't you come duck-hunting with us in the Delta? We'll put a party together, make a day of it.'

Jumbo came shooting. Saffron picked him up from his quarters and drove him out to the lake where the shoot would take place. Her driving was perfectly competent and her shooting was exceptional, at least the match of any man there.

'I would be happy to make you my driver and consent to you being armed, though I would be grateful if you kept quiet about our agreement. You are both civilian and female and on both grounds should not be carrying a gun about your person.'

'Not a word,' said Saffron, 'I assure you.'

The following morning she reported for work. Leon and Harriet returned to Kenya delighted by the thought that Saffron was unquestionably doing her bit for her country, but in a way that minimized the actual danger to herself, should hostilities begin.

Less than a month later, Hitler invaded Poland. The Second World War had begun.

The Christmas season of 1939 was a joyous time in Germany. Poland had been conquered with the loss of fewer than twenty thousand men killed or wounded. After the horrors of trench warfare on the Western Front in the First War, when so many men had been slaughtered with so little to show for their passing, the *blitzkrieg* of the new conflict offered a painless military victory to go along with all the conquests Hitler had already made without a gun being fired. The Reich now straddled the heart of Europe, from the French border in the west to the Russian in the east, and there were many who hoped that the Führer would be satisfied with what he had achieved. Germany's pride and status had been triumphantly restored. Why not now take time to enjoy this new position as one of the great global powers?

The ballrooms and dining halls of Bavaria's aristocratic palaces and castles were filled with happy revellers in that holiday season. Gerhard von Meerbach was still based in Poland and could not get home leave for Christmas or the New Year. But for Konrad, who divided his time between Heydrich's headquarters in Berlin and the Meerbach Motor Works, it was no trouble at all to attend a number of the most prominent social events, though his freedom to do as he pleased was constrained by the presence of his wife Trudi. This was, of course, frustrating, but it was important to be seen with his wife in public. It reinforced his image as a good family man, which was important within the Party.

At one such occasion, shortly before Christmas, he happened to have been separated temporarily from Trudi, who had gone to gossip with a little cluster of her female friends. The hostess of the party took his arm and led him a few paces towards another guest who found herself without company, a blonde, whom Konrad reckoned was at least a decade younger than himself. She was a pretty little thing all right, with a more than satisfactory pair of breasts displayed by her ballgown like a pair of peaches in a bowl. She looked at him with distinct interest: that black uniform working its usual magic. *By God, I wonder if I've time to have her before that dumb bitch Trudi notices I'm missing?* Konrad asked himself.

'Chessi, may I introduce Count von Meerbach?'

The woman seemed to tense up, as if the name were not welcome, and then hostess suddenly remembered why, realized she had made a terrible *faux pas* but had no option but to continue: 'Count von Meerbach, this is Countess Francesca von Schöndorf.'

Konrad had noticed the blonde's unease, too, for if there was one thing that his increasing experience in the business of interrogation had taught him it was the ability to spot signs of tension or discomfort in the person opposite. *So this is the girl Gerhard discarded*, he thought. *He must have been out of his mind!*

Konrad clicked his heels, bowed and said, 'I am enchanted to meet you, Countess. And I hope you will allow me, as the head of the von Meerbach family, to offer you my most sincere apologies for the appalling and unforgiveable conduct of my brother towards you. And may I say that he was not only an unmannered oaf, but also a blind fool to have treated a woman as beautiful as you as stupidly as he did.'

Chessi was not about to let a second member of the same family flatter her into losing her wits, but Count von Meerbach's words deserved a polite response and so she said, 'Thank you, that is very kind.'

'Well I can see that you two have a lot to talk about,' said their hostess, who was clearly desperate to extract herself as quickly as possible. 'Ah! There are Fritz and Amélie Thyssen. Please excuse me while I say hello.'

Chessi saw the tightening of von Meerbach's mouth at the mention of Thyssen's name. The industrialist, a strong supporter of the Nazi Party in the early days, had fallen out with the Führer over the government's hostility towards the Catholic Church and the obsession with making rearmament the focus of Germany's industrial efforts. As an SS officer and the head of a company whose engines helped power the German war effort, von Meerbach was bound to disapprove.

As she waited for him to turn his attention back to her and make the next move in the conversation, she examined the man in front of her. *So this is the infamous Konrad! If only you knew the things your brother said about you!* He was not at all as handsome or elegant as Gerd and had none of the sensitivity or finesse of his younger brother. But though he had crude features and a peasant's body – stocky, thick-limbed, like a carthorse rather than an Arab stallion – there was an unmistakable aura of power around Konrad von Meerbach that Gerd did not possess. Here was a man who would take what he wanted and crush anyone who got in his way. She had no doubt that he was a bully and a bastard. But that could be made to work to her advantage. Because if Konrad's feelings towards Gerhard were as negative as Gerhard's towards him, well then, that animosity could yet be used effectively.

'I dare say you know that my brother and I don't get on,' Konrad began, when his attention switched back to Chessi. 'I know he parades around, playing the part of the fighter-ace, but that is just a façade, as carefully designed as one of those buildings he likes to draw. I know the real man underneath.'

Chessi had an ace to play in this game with von Meerbach and at a party like this, where conversations could be interrupted at any moment, she could not afford to delay it. 'Tell me, did Gerhard tell you why, or rather, for whom he broke his word to me?'

Von Meerbach smiled. 'Believe me, I am the last person on earth to whom he would confide any matters of the heart.'

'Then I will tell you. Some friends of mine and I were on holiday in St Moritz in January. Gerhard made a special effort to get there to join us for a few days. He was going to make his formal proposal to me, I absolutely know it. But it happened that an old school friend of mine, who knew where I was staying, had taken it into her head to come and join me. I don't know if you are aware of this, Count von Meerbach, but I spent two years of my education in England. That was where I met my friend. So she came all the way from Scotland, where she had spent Christmas, to Switzerland, just to see me, her dearest friend. You understand, of course, that we met in '36, when there was still a friendship between our two nations.'

'Of course, Countess,' Konrad agreed. 'The Führer endeavoured up until the final moments before the British declaration of war to find a way to live in peace with Britain and its Empire.'

'Quite so . . . The point is, this young Englishwoman came to St Moritz to see me. But before we had a chance to meet one another she fell at the feet, quite literally, of your brother Gerhard and decided, at once, that she wanted him for herself.'

'Was she aware of the connection between you and him?'

'She knew that I was in love, but she swore to me that she had no idea that he was my man. Foolishly, perhaps, I believed her. Had she respected our friendship, withdrawn her claws and given him back to me, I might have been able to forgive her, and Gerhard. But she would not let him go, and he seemed only too happy to be taken.'

'So my brother's lover was an Englishwoman?'

'Yes . . . but why do you say "was"? How do you know that he is not still in love with the same Englishwoman?'

Chessi had a friend who was forever going to expensive clinics in her futile attempts to lose weight. Her problem was very simple. She was greedy and ate too much. And while she could just about withstand a week's compulsory starvation, she no sooner stepped out through the clinic's gates than she went back to her old ways. The look that came across Konrad von Meerbach's face when he realized that he was being presented with a means to destroy his brother was very like Chessi's friend's expression when, immediately after her latest cure, she

371

was confronted with a large plate of *späztle* noodles, thickly covered in cheese.

'Do you know the Englishwoman's name?' he asked, practically salivating.

'Yes,' said Chessi. The hostess was heading back in their direction, so there was no time to lose. 'Her name is Saffron Courtney. She grew up in Kenya where her father has a great estate. Her mother was called Eva. She was the mistress of a very rich and powerful German industrialist before the First War. This industrialist actually died in Africa, at the start of the war. Saffron's father killed him.'

Konrad's face had gone pale. His jaw was clenched as tight as a bull mastiff's. The edges of his lips were white with suppressed rage and his voice was thick and hoarse as he asked, 'How do you know this? If you are lying to me, or trying to tease me . . . If you are getting back at my family with slurs and slanders . . .'

Chessi suddenly felt very afraid. She could not understand why her story had made Konrad react so strongly. 'I promise you, Count, that I am telling you the truth,' she insisted, with a plaintive desperation. 'I was told the whole story by one of Saffron's cousins. He was in love with her himself. We both felt betrayed. He was only too happy to tell me everything.'

Konrad looked at her, jutting his massive head forward, making no attempt to be in the slightest bit polite as he searched her face for any telltale signs of deceit. He nodded. 'Yes, I believe you. There is no way you could know these things unless you had learned them in the way you described. Are there more details that you could tell me?'

'Yes.'

'But you do not know the name of the German industrialist?'

'No, I . . .' and then it all became obvious. 'Oh . . .' she said, thinking, *Why didn't I see it sooner? The von Meerbach boys grew up without a father. Of course, it had to be him!*

372

'We will talk soon,' Konrad said. 'We have much to discuss. And I believe our conversation can be to both our mutual advantage.'

Rory Ballantyne imagined that storming a pillbox was a rather exciting activity. But somehow the officer standing before him in the classroom of 161 Officer Cadet Training Unit, or the Royal Military College, Sandhurst, as it had been known before the war, was making it as boring as Latin grammar. So it came as a huge relief to him when the class was interrupted by a lance corporal coming in and approaching the instructor.

'Excuse me, sir,' the corporal said, 'but the adjutant has asked me to fetch Cadet Ballantyne. There's a gentleman here to see him.'

'Can't it wait till the end of the class?' the instructor asked.

'I'm sorry, sir, but I'm to bring Cadet Ballantyne at once. The adjutant was most particular.'

The instructor gave an irritated, put-upon sigh and said, 'Very well then, Ballantyne, off you go.'

Rory rose from his desk, looked at a couple of the men in the same row as him and gave a wide-eyed shrug, as if to say, 'I haven't got a clue what this is about,' and followed the corporal over to the adjutant's office, where he was introduced to a small, elderly gentleman with thinning, snow-white hair, whose name was Mr Brown.

'Why don't we go for a walk?' Mr Brown said. 'A stroll to Upper Lake, perhaps. How about that?'

'Absolutely, sir,' Rory replied. 'I think I know the way.'

'So do I, dear boy . . . so do I.'

And so they went out into the chilly winter air. Mr Brown walked slowly, well wrapped up against the cold in a heavy overcoat, scarf and hat, with his hands in leather gloves while Rory walked beside him in his khaki battledress, wishing he could go a bit faster, just to warm up a bit. Finally, when they were on a path well away from the college buildings, where no one could possibly overhear them, Mr Brown said, 'Before we begin, I need to tell you, in the strongest possible terms, that everything we say must remain absolutely confidential. You are to tell no one at all about the content or purpose of our meeting. Do I make myself clear?'

'Yes sir, absolutely,' Rory replied.

'When you return to your fellow cadets, tell them that I am an old family friend, who is an official in the War Office. I was visiting the college and asked after you.'

'I understand, sir. I'm just not quite sure, what actually is the purpose of our meeting?'

'I'm here to ask you about your cousin, Saffron Courtney.'

Rory felt a sudden stab of alarm. 'Is she all right? I say, she's not in trouble, is she?'

Mr Brown chuckled amiably. 'Oh no, no . . . nothing like that. No, this is more a matter of assessment. Miss Courtney's name has come up for a possible job and we wish to make sure of her suitability, that's all.'

'It sounds rather cloak-and-dagger. There were always rumours in the family that Saffy's mater was a spy before the last war.'

'That sounds rather improbable to me. One shouldn't pay too much attention to family rumours. Facts, Ballantyne, that's what I'm after. So . . . I gather that you and Miss Courtney are very close.'

'Not as close as we used to be, I'm afraid, sir.'

'Oh really, how so?'

And so Rory found himself telling the story of the trip to St Moritz. And while he honestly didn't want to say anything that would discredit Saffron, for she was still part of the family after all, there was something almost hypnotic about the gentle way that Mr Brown asked one question after another. He seemed to be able to draw out information without one really noticing how much one was giving away. Then Rory found himself describing how Saffron had insisted on going down the Cresta Run and gone off afterwards with a German called von Meerbach.

Mr Brown's ears had pricked up at that particular name for some reason and he insisted on hearing all the gory details, despite Rory worrying that it really wasn't very gentlemanly of him to be saying all these things about a lady, particularly his own cousin.

'But dash it all,' he concluded, 'it really wasn't on. I mean, the war hadn't started, obviously, but we were all worried it might be on the way, and if we did fight the Germans would be our enemies again. And there she was going off with a bloody Hun!'

'You sound as though you were quite upset by the whole thing.'

'I suppose I was rather cross about it, yes. Wrote Saffy quite a stiff letter, telling her what I thought. Haven't seen her since, if you must know.'

'Did you think she might have had Nazi sympathies?'

'Saffy . . . a Nazi?' Rory was incredulous. 'God no! I didn't think much of her behaviour, still don't, but Saffy's no Hitler-lover. It's just not in her nature. All that marching and goose-stepping – not her kind of thing at all!'

'So why did she fall for a German, do you suppose?'

'Why does any woman fall for a man? He was bloody rich and not bad-looking, I suppose, if you like foreigners. The real question is, why did she not give a damn about him being German?'

'Quite right, Cadet Ballantyne, that is indeed the question. And what would you give as your answer?'

'Oh, that's easy. Saffy didn't give a damn because she just doesn't give a damn. She's not like other girls . . . that's what's so special about her. She just does whatever she wants and to hell with the consequences. Women aren't supposed to go down the Cresta Run, but that didn't stop Saffy. English girls aren't supposed to love Germans, but . . . Well, I don't know if she loves him, but you get my drift.'

'I do indeed.'

They were standing beside the lake and Rory was looking out across the water. The more he'd talked about Saffron, the less he'd wanted to catch Mr Brown's eye.

'You care for her very much, don't you, Cadet Ballantyne?'

Now Rory turned his head. He nodded.

'Are you worried that you may have said too much?'

'Yah, I am, rather.'

'Don't be. Everything you have said is safe with me. And I agree with you. I, too, think that Saffron Courtney is a very remarkable young woman.'

'I'd hate to think I'd said anything that would cause her any harm.'

'Rest assured, Ballantyne. I don't for a single second think that your cousin is in any way disloyal to this country. As I said, I'm just collecting information by way of an assessment.'

'If you're assessing her, I suppose you know she's a terrific shot and rides like the wind.'

'So I've heard.'

'It's funny, here I am with all the other cadets, training to be an officer. But if Saffy was a man, she'd be a better soldier than any of us.'

'What makes you think she won't still be a better soldier, even as a woman?'

Mr Brown left the question hanging in the air for a moment and then said, 'I think it's time we were getting back, don't you?'

* * *

The man who had been known to Francis Courtney as Manfred Erhardt was a senior agent of the Abwehr, the German military intelligence service. He was certain that Francis Courtney could be developed as an extremely useful asset, but felt that his value would be all the higher if he had greater influence within his family firm. But it was clear from everything Courtney said that his way was blocked by his brothers, Leon and David. Erhardt considered Leon Courtney less of an immediate issue, since he lived in Kenya and was not involved in the day-to-day running of Courtney Trading. It was David Courtney, the chief executive, who presented the greater impediment to Francis's advance. On the other hand, he was also much more vulnerable than Leon.

Erhardt accordingly sent word to Francis asking for any plans his brother might be making to leave Cairo within the next month or two. Francis made up a story about planning a family party and wanting to know when David would be out of town, so as not to leave him out, and though his brother's secretary was extremely doubtful about the likelihood of the famously antisocial Francis suddenly becoming a party host, she could hardly say no to a Courtney. The information was provided and passed on to Erhardt.

Four weeks later David Courtney paid one of his regular visits to Alexandria, to spend some days at the family's shipping operation based there. While he was there he had a convivial dinner with his brother Dorian and, since it was a lovely night and Alexandria had an atmosphere quite unlike Cairo's – much more relaxed, Mediterranean and open to the idea of romance – David decided to stroll back to his hotel on foot, rather than taking a taxi. Knowing the city well, he took a short-cut that at one point led him down a sidestreet so narrow that it was hardly more than an alley.

He didn't hear or see the man who slipped out of a shadowy doorway, stepped up behind him, grabbed the bottom of his face from behind, so that his jaw was lifted up and back and then slit open his throat from one ear to the other.

David's wallet, watch and even his hand-made shoes were all stolen. The city's police chief expressed his profound regret to the Courtney family. Clearly this appalling crime was the work of brigands, but despite the most arduous and exhaustive searches, the culprits had not been tracked down.

So far as Erhardt was concerned the operation had worked perfectly. But then came an unexpected drawback. Having flown up to Cairo for his brother's funeral, Leon Courtney decided to move to the city full time for the foreseeable future, to take over the running of Courtney Trading for himself. He placed Loikot in charge of the cattle at Lusima, left Manyoro to continue as the unofficial leader and law enforcer of the local Masai community and appointed an ambitious young South African, Piet van der Meuwe, to look after the burgeoning agricultural side of the estate, growing everything from green beans to coffee beans. He already had the best lawyers and accountants in Nairobi and so, with his land in safe hands, he and Harriet established themselves in Cairo and Courtney Trading got used to life under its new boss.

On reflection, Erhardt was not too disappointed with the way things had worked out. Francis Courtney was even more convinced that the fates and his family were united against him. And there was, in Manfred Erhardt's considerable experience, nothing quite like bitterness, resentment and a sense of having been betrayed to make a man a traitor himself.

Konrad von Meerbach now had three great tasks in his life: to assist Heydrich, to lead the family firm, and to come up with a strong enough case against Gerhard to have him sent without trial to a concentration camp. A series of conversations with Francesca von Schöndorf had provided him with a veritable treasure trove of incriminating gossip, and enough leads to assist him in turning that gossip into genuinely incriminating evidence. He and Francesca celebrated their private alliance with a dinner in Berlin and she willingly accompanied him back to his apartment afterwards. But although her body was even more inviting when naked than it had been when clothed, there was still something unsatisfactory for both of them about the occasion. Gerhard's shadow seemed to hang over the bed, and the more they told themselves that this was their way of getting back at him, the more power it seemed to give him – that he could still matter that much to both of them – and the more hollow their triumph became.

That did not, however, mean that Konrad was going to go easy on his brother. With the infinite patience of a poisonous spider, he set about creating a web in which to snare his prey. He wanted proof that Gerhard and this Courtney woman were still in touch with one another. For with every day that passed, the difficulty of bringing a charge of treachery against his brother grew.

In April 1940, units from the 77th Fighter Wing, including Gerhard's squadron, were tasked with supporting the invasion of Norway. He shot down two Royal Air Force fighters during the campaign. And even if they had been antiquated Gloucester Gladiator biplanes, they still counted towards his tally of kills. One more, and he would be an ace.

That fifth kill was a Wellington bomber, shot down over France during the invasion of France. Two more victims, a Hurricane and Spitfire – and they were anything but antiquated – followed in the hectic weeks that saw the British driven back to the sea and forced to make a humiliating retreat from the beaches of Dunkirk, leaving all their equipment behind them. By then, *Reichsmarschall* Herman Göring, the commander-in-chief of the Luftwaffe himself, had pinned an Iron Cross on Gerhard's chest. With that, and the famous pat on the arm from the Führer himself, Gerhard was acquiring a status that, however undeserved, would make him very hard to bring down.

So Konrad thought: *If I loved a woman who belonged with the enemy, how would I stay in touch with her?* Any man who was away at the war wanted to write to his sweetheart and to receive letters from her. But Gerhard and the Courtney woman – Konrad could not bring himself to think of her as Saffron, for it made her sound too human, as though she might almost be likeable – could not write to one another directly, for there was no communication between the Reich and the British Empire. Nor could she write to him, even indirectly, in English, or he to her in German. After all, there were censors in both countries, intercepting mail coming in and going out and any communication written in an enemy language would immediately set off alarms.

So there had to be an intermediary, who could render communications safe in both directions. One could only reach such an intermediary, and he or she would only be able to pass messages on, if they lived in a neutral country. And this person would have to be capable of writing in both English and German. Furthermore they would have to have a reason why they would go to such trouble, and run a certain degree of risk, in order to help two lovebirds.

Konrad had been lying in bed with a long-limbed, and remarkably flexible member of the chorus line at one of the Berlin vaudeville theatres, relaxing after an energetic bout of lovemaking, when he realized precisely who the intermediary must be. The girl had taken the smile that had crossed his face as a sign that he was happy to be with her, but her satisfaction had been short-lived because he immediately kicked her out into the night. He wanted solitude, peace and quiet in which to think, not the inane prattling of a dim-witted dancing girl.

Within a week, Konrad had set up the surveillance and mail interception operation that, by August, had come across the first communication from the intermediary to London, though the letter was not sent directly to Saffron but to a relative, Penelope Courtney, who lived in London. At roughly the same time a letter came in from London, though it was almost certainly the reply to a much earlier communication. Letters from Switzerland to Britain, if they got through at all, went on a very long-winded, circuitous route via neutral countries like Portugal or Sweden, so these two lovers would be communicating very occasionally and very slowly. But if they were in love that would be enough to keep the fires burning in their hearts.

There was just one problem. No matter how hard the German agents assigned to the case tried, they could not establish the next link in the chain: from the intermediary to Gerhard. Somehow the letters were being smuggled in and out of the Reich in such a way that the chain was not visible. So then Konrad considered the other end of that chain. Someone in Germany must act as the final link to Gerhard, just as this Penelope Courtney woman did to Gerhard's bitch.

Another man, whose character was formed very differently to Konrad's and who did not live in a system like Nazism might have hesitated before coming to the conclusion that he did. And they would then have felt a great deal less willing than him to institute a second programme of mail interception to prove that their hunch had been correct. But Konrad was not such a man. He had his hunch, he acted upon it and he was proved correct. He then discovered that the first individual he had uncovered, the one who operated from neutral ground, was involved in a multi-faith organization. Its aim was to assist and resettle families, in particular children, who had suffered as a result of various Nazi policies, and one of its other leading members was a Catholic priest. And with that discovery, the last link in the chain fell into place.

* * *

Konrad's web had been spun. Gerhard was trapped, though he did not know it. But then an unexpected problem arose.

'I really don't think it would be wise to have your brother arrested,' Heydrich said, one evening in late August, after Konrad had presented him with his findings. 'He is a decorated fighter-ace currently engaged in combat operations. If we were to seize him, the fuss would go all the way to the top. Then we would have *Reichsmarschall* Göring fighting with *Reichsführer* Himmler over a man whose crime is that he fucked the wrong woman. Sooner or later, they would both wonder why the hell they were bothering, and then they would both turn their fire on me. At that point, believe me, I would step aside and let the full weight of their joint fury fall on you.

'I am sorry, Konrad, but this little family feud of yours is really not worth the trouble it will cause. We have a war to win: a war against the international Jewish conspiracy. We will only achieve total victory when we have wiped the entire race from the face of the earth. Concentrate on that task, if you please, not your brother's sex-life.'

'Yes, sir,' Konrad said, but inside he was thinking, *That is what you say now. But if I can find just one word, in one letter, that gives away the slightest shred of sensitive military information, then I will change your mind, and Himmler's and Göring's too.*

Just then the air-raid sirens began to wail. Heydrich remained as glacially calm as ever behind his desk. Konrad felt equally unperturbed. It must be some kind of practice drill. Göring himself had assured the German people that no British bomber would ever be able to reach the Ruhr, on the western edge of the Reich, closest to England. Berlin was five hundred kilometres to the east of the Ruhr, and thus that much further away from the British Isles. There was no need to be alarmed.

Then the phone rang on Heydrich's desk. Konrad could not hear what the man on the other end of the line was saying, but his tone was certainly very agitated. Heydrich listened quietly, with no more than the occasional, 'Are you sure?' and 'I see.' Finally he said, 'Very well, I will inform my staff accordingly.' Then he put down the phone and looked at Konrad. 'It appears I misjudged the situation – this is not a mere drill. Approximately fifty RAF bombers are on a course that will take them directly to Berlin. They are expected to be over the city within the next ten minutes. It seems that we are under attack.'

There was heavy cloud over the city that night. The British bombers could not find their way to the heart of the city. Two people were slightly injured when a bomb fell close to the wooden summer house in the garden of their home in Rosenthal, a suburb to the north of the city. The rest of the bombs fell harmlessly on farmland, hitting crops and livestock, rather than buildings and people. A joke ran round the city: 'The British can't defeat us in battle. So now they are trying to starve us out.'

But the Führer was not amused. Göring was deeply embarrassed. Revenge would have to be taken against Britain's cities and London in particular and every single Luftwaffe pilot would be required to assist in the campaign. If ever there had been any hope in persuading anyone to have a fighter-ace removed from the front line, that time was past.

So now Konrad had to find another way to destroy his brother.

Steady, now, boys. Eyes open, total concentration. Tommy will be saying hello soon . . .' The voice of his squadron captain, Dieter Rolf, crackled in Gerhard von Meerbach's earpiece. Five thousand metres below them the river Thames ran like a ribbon of silver, gleaming in the afternoon sun, right into the heart of London. Gerhard did his best, as always, to try not to think about Saffron. Just before the war began she had written to him saying that her father wanted her to go home. He presumed that she meant back to Africa. But perhaps he was wrong. Or perhaps she had not been able to get there and was now stuck in Britain for the duration of the war. Gerhard still assumed that England would eventually fall just as Poland, France, the Low Countries, Denmark and Norway had done. There were times when he would lie in his bed and imagine him, a conqueror, finding Saffron again and . . . what then?

She would be a traitor in the eyes of her people if she consorted with one of their occupiers.

Gerhard could not bear the thought that he would never hold her in his arms again, never lie with her and make love. He thought of the scent of her hair; the sound of her laughter, and the moans when they made love; the light that flickered deep in the sapphire pools of her eyes; the way she arched her back when he entered her; the feel of her breasts when his hands were cupped around them; the line of her hips, the swell of her buttocks and the swoop into her slender waist; the hot, wet grip of her pussy around him and . . .

Enough, man! Keep your mind on your job!

Between the Messerschmitts and the river were fifty Dornier 17 bombers flying in perfect formation at low altitude, their pilots ignoring the distraction of the anti-aircraft batteries whose shells were already exploding like black pom-poms in the air around them and heading inexorably towards their target.

It wasn't hard to spot. Up ahead the smoke was rising from the London Docks. The route up the Thames had become so familiar that Gerhard's 109 could practically have flown there without his assistance, but he questioned the change of strategy. The original policy of attacking RAF Fighter Command's airfields had been working perfectly. The RAF was losing so many planes, in the air and on the ground, that he could not believe they could possibly replace them. Even more importantly their experienced pilots were being killed and replaced by beginners who had scarcely learned to fly a trainer aircraft, let alone survive in aerial combat against hardened veterans. True the Royal Air Force was now using Spitfires and Hurricanes that were a match for the German 109s, but even so, the boys in the Luftwaffe fighter wings had felt confident of victory.

But then that damn bomb fell on Berlin: one bomb in a damned summer house. And suddenly everything changed. Sure, it was good for the German people to see newsreel footage of London on fire. But it was also good for the Royal Air Force. They had been given time to regroup, to fill in the bomb craters in their runways, repair their aircraft and give their pilots more training and more rest. Even within the past two or three weeks it had become possible to tell the difference. The English were fighting fit again, and they had brought in some friends to help them, a squadron of Polish flyers, all veterans of the invasion, and all willing to do anything to get their own back on the hated Germans.

So now Gerhard settled into the rhythm that any fighter pilot who wished to stay alive had to maintain: his eyes constantly flicking across the sky, searching for the enemy aircraft he knew must be on their way. But where were they coming from? The fighter squadrons on both sides were playing a game of hide-and-seek, using the scattered clouds for shelter, but also knowing that, as long as they could not be seen, neither could they see: in the end they had to come out into the sun. And it was as Gerhard's flight of four planes, with him in the leading position, emerged from the clouds that another voice clamoured in his earphones. 'Enemy at six o'clock, low! Hurricanes! Looks like a single squadron coming in from the city, heading straight for the bombers.'

'I see them!' Gerhard responded, for the Hurricanes showed clearly as black silhouettes against the dazzling river. The 109s peeled away, one flight after another in a perfect sequence born of endless repetition, and soon it was Gerhard's turn as he banked right and then dived at full speed, reaching almost six hundred kilometres an hour as he rocketed towards the Hurricanes below. The roar of air against his cockpit was almost enough to drown out the engine as the numbers on the altimeter rotated as quickly as the fruit on a slot machine, unable to keep up with the velocity of his descent.

Gerhard felt the dizzy sensation as his heart struggled against immense gravitational forces to pump blood up to his brain. It was all too easy to black out in a full dive and just keep plummeting all the way down to the ground and certain death. But if he pulled up too soon, that would simply expose the belly of his aircraft to the enemies' guns. He just had to keep going, down and down, aiming for a Hurricane that he had picked out as his prey, hoping that they wouldn't see him until it was too late, throttling back towards the end to ease the speed, so as not to overshoot the target.

He was almost there, so close he could see the head of the Hurricane's pilot inside his cockpit. He flattened the dive then wrapped his fingers around the firing grip, and flicked down the trigger that operated his two machine guns. On top of the grip there was a button that fired the canon. *Now!* Gerhard squeezed the trigger with his index finger and pressed on the button with his thumb, feeling the airframe shudder as the guns all fired.

And at that precise moment the alarm must have been sounded for the Hurricanes suddenly scattered like a flock of starlings menaced by predatory hawks, some climbing, others diving, yet more twisting and corkscrewing to the side. The pilot Gerhard had aimed at heaved on his joystick and hauled his plane into a steep climb . . . Right into Gerhard's path.

He banked hard right and for a fraction of a second that seemed to drag on for an age he could do nothing but pray as the 109 twisted onto its side, the wings almost vertical as they skimmed past the Hurricane.

Gerhard was fighting for control of his aircraft now and at that moment of vulnerability he became the prey for suddenly his left wing was peppered with bullet holes, right up by the fuselage, just centimetres away from his leg. He looked around to see where the fire was coming from, looked in his mirror, couldn't see anything and then he heard his wingman, Berti Schrumpp, shouting, 'He's behind you, Meerbach, right behind you!'

Gerhard reacted just as his earlier target had done, he pulled back on the joystick and as the nose of his plane came up he felt another burst of bullets hit the fuselage from behind, just behind his cockpit. *Two close misses! He won't miss a third time.* Gerhard climbed, almost vertically, in the reverse of his earlier dive. Now the gravity that had impelled him down so fast was pushing against his climb, slowing the plane so that it was on the verge of stalling. One second before that could happen, Gerhard applied the rudder to full yaw, turning it around so that it rolled off the top of its climb and came right back down the way it had come, picking up speed again and, in theory, bringing it right back onto the pursuing enemy plane.

Except that the Hurricane wasn't there any longer. In the pell-mell chaos of the mass dogfight it had itself been engaged by a 109 and been forced to take evasive action. All across the sky, as the bombers continued on their droning, unvarying path to their target, the fighters were turning, diving, firing, missing.

But some were hitting. A sudden explosion of dazzling orange and gold erupted from the engine of one of the Dorniers, which fell away to one side, trailing a plume of smoke. 'For God's sake, get out!' Gerhard shouted, as if anyone could possibly hear. He looked for a further second or two for any sign of parachutes, but that was all the time he could spare, for there was danger all around him, and also targets, too.

There was a cry of triumph over the squadron radio as

someone hit a Hurricane and then, as if some celestial referee had blown a full-time whistle, the dogfight was over. There was only a certain amount of time and fuel that they could afford to expend if they were to make it back to France in one piece. There was a plaintive cry of complaint, 'Now that bastard will be able to get away. I'd have finished him off if I'd had a few more seconds.'

'And his friend might have finished off you.' That was Rolf talking. 'The bomber boys got through, that's what matters. Now let's bring them safely home.'

Heydrich was right. Konrad was kept so busy in the final months of 1940 that he had no time to plot his brother's downfall. In mid-November he was in Warsaw, acting as his master's eyes and ears as the final touches were put to the ghetto where the city's four hundred thousand Jews were imprisoned.

'As you can see, the walls are almost complete,' said Ludwig Fischer, the Governor of Warsaw, proudly as he and Konrad were driven along Okapowa, the street that formed one side of the ghetto. 'None of those filthy Yids will ever get out. Not until we decide to take them out.'

'Well they can't stay here forever, that's for sure,' Konrad agreed, as the car turned left onto Jerusalem Avenue. 'But at least you are only wasting a small portion of the city on them. I counted only twenty city blocks from one end of the wall back there to the other.'

'That's right. I am proud to say that we have managed to fit one-third of the city's population into one fortieth of its total area.'

'Very impressive. How did you do that?'

'It is simply a matter of the efficient utilization of space,' Fischer explained. 'There are approximately twenty-seven thousand apartments within the ghetto, so that gives us fifteen Jews per apartment, which works out at six or seven of them for each room of each apartment. So yes, they must all lie very close together at night, but they will not mind this, I assure you.'

'Why not?'

'Because we do not intend to waste heating fuel on Jews in wintertime. So if they all lie together like sardines in a tin, then they will keep each other warm, even if they have no coal for their fires!'

Konrad laughed heartily at this splendid witticism. 'I shall be sure to tell *Obergruppenführer* Heydrich you said that, he will be greatly amused. But, to be serious, I imagine the numbers will in any case lessen through natural attrition.'

'Of course. The combination of forced labour, minimal rations and cold will swiftly weed out the weaker members of the population. But I hear that you are already working on other ways to do that.'

'Ah, have you had a visit from the Kaiser's Coffee Company van?'

Fischer's face lit up like a child being promised a trip to the circus. 'No, but I am very keen to see it.'

'You should. It is operated by a *kommando* led by a fellow called Lange. The van is airtight and it is equipped with a canister of carbon monoxide gas, which, as you may know, is odourless but deadly poisonous. We have been testing it on imbeciles, inmates of mental asylums and so forth as part of the euthanasia program. It's very important to rid the population of these defective individuals who are using up resources that could be put to better use elsewhere.'

'"Useless eaters," as they say.'

'Exactly.'

The question of 'useless eaters' became an even greater part of Konrad's life in the New Year as Heydrich was placed in charge of the SS planning for the occupation of Russia. An invasion was planned for the spring and the SS would have a vital role, following in the army's footsteps and dealing with the necessary task of cleansing the entire population of Jews and Bolsheviks and that required an immense amount of organization.

'One cannot just walk into Russia and say, "Let's kill all the commies and the Israelites,"' Heydrich would say. 'It requires planning. Where will we find these people. How will we kill them? What will we do with the bodies? How will we persuade our men to slaughter defenceless women and children? This is vital work. It has to be given an immense amount of thought.'

Konrad was happy to oblige. It was fascinating, thrilling work. To be in at the start of an empire's creation was a privilege granted to few men. So Konrad was in a good mood as he took his regular morning shower, shortly after waking at five thirty as he always did these days. As he soaped his body he sang a French song that seemed to be everywhere in Berlin that spring. It was called 'J'Attendrai', or 'I will wait', and its subject was the pledge that every woman made to her man as he went off to war, that she would wait day and night, waiting forever until he came back.

Then you're screwed if he doesn't come back, aren't you, my little darling, Konrad thought and laughed at the image of the woman growing old while her man lay rotting on some far-flung battlefield. And then he laughed even harder for he had just had another one of his bright ideas. And this one was an absolute beauty.

In Zürich, Isidore walked into the Konditorei Kagan as usual, but instead of Yavi Kagan greeting him in the usual fashion, the proprietor beckoned him over, nervously. He leaned over the counter and whispered to Isidore. 'There is a man sitting at your table. I told him it was reserved, but he insisted. He said, "It is Herr Solomons that I have come to see." He's there now, a German. I think he is Gestapo or SS. I can smell those bastards.'

If Kagan said the man was SS, the chances were he was right. 'You can turn round now and walk out if you like,' he added.

Isidore shook his head. 'No, I've run enough. I'll not be made to run again.'

Before he had taken another five steps into the café, Isidore knew who was waiting to see him. 'Good morning, Count von Meerbach,' he said, taking his normal chair, directly opposite Konrad.

'Good morning to you, Solomons,' Konrad said. 'You look very well. You've put on a little weight since I last saw you. Good to know you're eating well. And it suits you, gives you a certain substance. Who wants a lawyer who can't afford a decent meal, eh? My compliments to your tailor. He cuts a fine suit. Must have cost you a pretty penny, eh? Have you paid my brother back his five thousand marks? If not, perhaps you could pay me. It was my money, after all.'

'As I understand it, the money came from the Meerbach trust,' Isidore said. 'I, of all people, know the terms of the trust, since I helped draft them, and the money that your brother chose to give me, rather than loan me – he was very insistent on that point – came to him as a beneficiary of the trust. There is, therefore, no sense at all in which that money was yours. So I have no obligation whatever to give it, or any portion of it to you.'

Konrad smiled, 'That's my clever little Jew-boy. Your kind have always got an argument for holding on to your money.'

'You forget yourself. This is not Germany. You have no power over me here.'

'Oh really, is that what you think?'

'No, it is what I know to be the law.'

'There are all kinds of law, Solomons. For example, there is also the law of the jungle in which the weak are crushed by the strong, so that inferior species are driven to extinction while the powerful thrive and spread across more and more territory.'

'Thank you for the lecture in natural selection. Now, tell me what you want, get it over and done with and then we can both go on with our day.'

'I want you to write two letters, one to my brother and the other to his English bitch lover.'

'I'm sorry, but I am unaware of anyone who answers that description, so how could I possibly write to them?'

'The same way you always do, Solomons. Ah, good, I can see from your face that we are making a little progress here. And here is your brother Yid with your Jew-bread and kosher coffee.'

Kagan bridled at that, but Isidore put a hand on his arm and said, 'Ignore him, Herr Kagan. He's not worth the trouble.'

'If you say so, Herr Solomons, but he should count himself lucky that you were here to restrain me.'

Isidore looked at Konrad: 'You were going to tell me the purpose of this meeting . . .'

'It's very simple. I know that you operate a kind of post office for my brother and his lover, who is English, meaning that both of them are consorting with the enemy, an offence for which my brother could be court-martialled and shot. That's the law, by the way, Solomons. I dare say she could be executed as a traitor too, if the English were ever given reason to believe that a young woman who acts as the driver for a general – I dare say you did not know that – was writing letters to an officer in the Luftwaffe.'

'What do you mean, "a kind of post office"?'

'I mean that you receive letters from England written by a Frau Penelope Miller, who is the aunt of Fräulein Saffron Courtney, Gerhard's lover. These letters appear to be from the older Courtney woman to you, but their content has in fact been composed by the niece and is intended for my brother's eyes. You then copy the key lines of the letter you have received onto a new document which you give by hand to Father Weiss, when you meet for the meetings of your inter-faith committee. He then sends it to his fellow priest Father Bauer who passes it on to my mother, who then incorporates what you have written into her letters to my brother. Then the whole process is repeated, in reverse, when my brother replies to Fräulein Courtney.' Konrad sighed. 'So many people risking their necks, just so two traitors can each betray their countries. Why would anyone do such a thing?'

'Because they understand that these are two good young people, in love with one another, and that love is a precious thing, and all the more so in a world filled with men like you, who spread hatred and death wherever you go.'

'I will spread death to Zürich, unless you do exactly as I say. I will have you killed and your wife and children smuggled back over the border to Germany, where they belong, so that they can be dealt with just like any other Jews. I will have my mother and her priest arrested for treason and my brother too. I will make sure that the English discover what Fräulein Courtney has been doing and have the evidence required to convict her. I will do all this, and gladly too, unless you do exactly what I say.'

Isidore looked at Konrad, frowning in puzzlement as he examined his face. 'What happened to you, Konnie?' he asked. 'I can remember when you were a little boy, letting you ride on my shoulders around the garden. I remember you playing in the sunshine with my younger brothers and sisters, with my cousins, all of you happy – some Christians, some Jews but all little German children. When did you become this . . . this monstrous perversion of a human being? I know you want me to fear you. I know that is what makes you feel strong. But I do not fear you. I pity you. You are doomed. Your soul is forsaken. May God have mercy for what you have become.'

For a moment, barely a second, Isidore thought he had

penetrated the thick walls Konrad von Meerbach had built around whatever fear or pain it was that now motivated him. But then the Nazi mask that Konrad now wore returned like a portcullis slamming down to block a castle gate. 'God does not exist,' he said. 'You Jews of all people should know that, for no true God would ever let his chosen people be abused the way that we have abused you. And believe me, what has happened so far is as nothing compared to what is to come. There will be horrors that you cannot even imagine. So now, remember what will happen if you dare to defy my demands.'

'Which are?'

'You will write two letters: one to my brother, the other to Fräulein Courtney, exactly as if you were passing on genuine messages from them.'

'What are these letters to say?'

Then Konrad told him, and Isidore understood what it must have been like for Dr Faustus, having to make his deals with the devil.

Victory! At last, after endless months of nothing but bad news, the British army, with considerable help from its Imperial allies, had an enemy on the run. And as driver to General Jumbo Wilson, Saffron felt like a spectator with the best seats in the stadium.

It had all begun with Mussolini's declaration of war against Britain and France on 10 June 1940, a decision he had postponed until the German army was practically at the gates of Paris and he was sure of coming in on the winning side. The Italians had an empire in Africa that included Ethiopia, Somalia and Libya, which shared a long land border with Egypt.

In September, the Italians launched an offensive into Egypt and advanced about fifty miles to the port of Sidi Barrani before a lack of supplies, modern equipment and enthusiasm brought them to a halt. The British regrouped and in early December launched a counter-offensive, codenamed Operation Compass. It was a stunning success. Within two days they had recaptured Sidi Barrani and taken forty thousand Italian prisoners for the loss of just six hundred men.

Jumbo Wilson was in jubilant mood and Saffron found her boss delightful company as she drove the khaki Humber saloon that contained the general and his closest aides around Cairo, or up the coast road towards Sidi Barrani and beyond as he paid visits to the forward command posts of the Indian, Australian and British divisions leading the charge back towards the Libyan border.

The Italian XXIII Corps under the command of Lieutenant General Annibale 'Electric Beard' Bergonzoli – so called because of his mighty, silver whiskers, topped by a flamboyant moustache – dug in at the town of Bardia. They turned the place into a veritable fortress ringed by an eighteen-mile-long anti-tank ditch that was peppered with strongpoints, armed with anti-tank guns and machine guns and positioned so that it was impossible for the enemy to attack anywhere without coming under fire from at least two different points. Almost one hundred and thirty tanks, ready to move at any moment to wherever the fighting was fiercest, underpinned Bardia's impregnability.

Mussolini placed great faith in his general. He wrote to Bergonzoli, praising him as an old and intrepid soldier and declaring, 'I am certain that "Electric Beard" and his brave soldiers will stand at whatever cost, faithful to the last.'

Bergonzoli assured *Il Duce* that he need have no doubt of the outcome of the battle: 'In Bardia we are and here we stay.'

The Allies had other ideas. The British 7th Armoured Division, who had given themselves the soon-to-be legendary nickname 'The Desert Rats', swung round behind Bardia to cut off any Italian retreat. On 3 January 1941, the Australian 6th Division went into the attack against the stronghold. By the time night fell, two days later, Bardia, and another forty thousand Italians were in Allied hands.

It was now, as the Australians pressed on towards the port of Tobruk, that Jumbo Wilson decided to pay a visit to the field headquarters of Major General Richard O'Connor, who had been given command of Operation Compass.

As Leon had predicted at lunch with Jumbo, Harriet and Saffron almost eighteen months earlier, warfare in Africa was very different to a European campaign. On the Western Front during the First War, the front lines that ran between a myriad French towns and villages had faced one another with immobile, near-impregnable certainty. In the emptiness of the Western Desert, where the local population consisted of little more than scorpions, vipers and thick clouds of flies, the battle moved at such a dizzying pace that there hardly was a front line at all. In this sea of sand the fighting took on some of the characteristics of naval warfare, where half the trick lay in just finding your enemy.

Or your friends, come to that.

How was your day?' Harriet asked after Saffron arrived home from work one day.

'Unexciting,' Saffy replied. 'Just a couple of errands in town and an awful lot of waiting in between.'

'Poor girl. Why don't I make you a nice cup of tea? That should raise your spirits. Oh, by the way, a boy came round from the company with a telegram for you.'

'A telegram? That's unexpected.'

'Good news I hope,' Harriet said, handing Saffron the message.

'Fingers crossed,' said Saffy, who was smiling as she opened the telegram.

Then the smile vanished, the blood drained from her face, the telegram slipped from her fingers and she stood white-faced and absolutely silent for several seconds before she broke down into convulsive sobs.

Harriet rushed to her side and took her arm. 'Come with me,' she said gently and guided Saffron to a chair, where she sat, bent over, still crying helplessly.

Harriet walked back to where the telegram lay abandoned on the floor. She wondered whether it was wrong to read it but then reasoned that if she knew what had happened she wouldn't have to make Saffron even more unhappy by asking.

GERRY SHOT DOWN MISSING PRESUMED DEAD STOP SO SO SORRY PENNY

Oh you poor, dear girl, thought Harriet. And then, *You kept him very quiet. I wonder why.*

'Would you like to talk about him?' she asked. 'You never know, it might help.'

Saffron shook her head. 'I can't. I can't ever say a word about him.'

'Oh, I'm sure that's not true.'

'It is!' Saffron insisted and turned her desperate eyes towards Harriet. 'You don't understand, Father would be devastated if he ever found out about him.'

'Surely not? He would be terribly sad for you, but he wouldn't be angry just because you were in love. You're perfectly old enough for that sort of thing.'

'It's who I was in love with – his family, where he came from. Please can we stop talking about this? I . . . I can't say another word. Really I can't.'

'I understand. If you change your mind, you can talk to me whenever you want. And if you don't change your mind, well, I understand that, too.'

'Thank you,' said Saffron.

She kissed Harriet and took herself to her bedroom. She

slept not a wink that night. She lay there for hours, obsessively running through every last moment she had spent with Gerhard. Remembering her first sight of him, the first smell of his body, the first time they had made love and she had taken possession of him, inside her, making him hers alone. She took out all the letters from her bag and read them again and again, though she already knew them all by heart. She realized that her stock of memories was pitifully small. They had spent so little time together. She had been robbed of so many years of love. How lucky Harriet was! She still had her man. They could hold one another, talk to one another, share their lives. They had a future. She did not.

Saffron brooded on the emptiness of the years ahead. Perhaps she could find a husband. He might even be a man for whom she might feel affection, companionship, the sort of love that arose from friendship and perhaps having children together. But they would not be Gerhard's children. She would never feel the immediate, instinctive, animal passion that told her that he was her man, above all others. And what was the point of a life without that?

It was dawn and in the distance, across the river, the calls to prayer were ringing out from the city's mosques when a thought suddenly struck her, very clearly, like a form of revelation. She realized that she was now blessed with a peculiar kind of freedom. If she had no future, then it did not matter what she did now, in the present, for any consequences of her actions were essentially irrelevant: she was lost anyway. So she could do precisely whatever she liked.

Which way do you want me to go, sir?' Saffron asked as the Humber came to a point, twenty miles inside the Libyan border, where the tank tracks that had served as a road for the past half-hour split in two directions. She could feel the tension in the car. In the desert they might just as easily bump into a hostile unit as a friendly one, so every turning became a gamble, with life and death as its stakes.

The constant stress was making the men around her edgy and short-tempered. But she actually preferred this sort of situation to a normal drive. The level of concentration was so high that she had no spare mental capacity left to waste thinking about Gerhard. And if she died, she didn't really care.

Just so long as I take a few of them with me.

'Left,' said the eager young staff officer, Captain Wright, who was sitting in the front passenger seat. 'I'm pretty sure it's left.'

'Pretty sure?' barked Jumbo Wilson from the rear of the car. 'That's not good enough. You should know the way as a matter of certainty.'

'Well, sir, the last message I received said that the field head-quarters had been established eight miles southwest of Bardia, in a wadi,' Wright replied and then added helpfully, 'That's a dried-up riverbed, sir.'

'I know what a wadi is, Wright. I've seen enough of them.'

'Quite so, sir. So, anyway, the map shows a wadi about two miles up ahead, to the left. Once we reach the wadi and follow it for another mile or so I'm confident we will reach O'Connor's HQ.'

'Let us hope your confidence is justified. Take the left-hand fork, Miss Courtney. Drive on.'

'Yes, sir,' Saffron said.

A couple of minutes later she heard Jumbo's voice again. 'For pity's sake man, could you please stop wriggling around like a man with ants in his pants. What on earth is the matter?'

'Bit of a gyppy tummy, sir,' came the strained voice of the other staff man in the car, Major Morgan. 'I'm rather in need of relief.'

Jumbo sighed. Sounding more like a parent talking to a fidgeting child than one senior officer addressing another, he said, 'Hang on till we reach this blasted wadi and see if you can find a spot to do your business there. Best to get it dealt with before we reach O'Connor, I suppose.'

Mamma mia! I thought you said you were a mechanic!'
Matteo Frescobaldi, a tough, bullet-headed sergeant from the Blackshirt Division, battle-hardened from service in the Spanish Civil War and the conquest of Ethiopia, was standing by the open bonnet of a battered army truck and he was not impressed by what he was seeing.

'I am, Sarge!' protested the oil-stained figure standing in front of him, wiping his black-stained hands on his filthy battle-dress uniform. 'But we're stuck in the middle of a godforsaken desert with no tools, no spares, at the bottom of a river that doesn't have any water.'

Frescobaldi grinned at the man's cheek and gave him a friendly pat on the face. 'Very funny,' he said. 'But there are eight of us, and only five, at most can fit in that . . .' He pointed towards the elegant lines of the Fiat 2800 staff car that he had appropriated, just as the supposedly impregnable fortress of Bardia was falling apart around his ears. 'You will be one of the three we leave behind unless you get that truck working.'

'You won't leave the truck. How else will you move the loot?'

They had sneaked out of the town on the night before it fell, taking the safe that contained the cash entrusted to General Bergonzoli to help fund his campaign. Or at least they thought that was what it contained. They had not been able to open it yet.

'You are quite right,' Frescobaldi growled. 'I will have to move the loot. In which case, you fix the truck or I leave five behind.' He glanced down at the Breda machine gun that was, as usual, cradled in his arms like a much-loved baby. 'Dead or alive, I don't care.'

Just then they heard the sound of an engine – a car rather than a tank – coming towards them. Frescobaldi raced to the top of the low ridge behind which he had concealed his men and their vehicles. He grinned at what he saw, then he went back down to their position.

'Forget about the truck,' he said. 'We have another way of getting out of here.'

Just up ahead, to one side of the stony, bone-dry bed of the wadi, stood a small clump of desiccated grey thorn bushes. Saffron slowed the car down and said, 'Might that be a good spot, sir? For Major Morgan, I mean.'

'Yes, that'll do. Stop her,' Jumbo replied.

She brought the car to a halt. Morgan hopped out and scuttled towards the thorn bushes.

'I hope he's all right, sir,' said Saffron. 'He'd better watch out for snakes, underneath the bush.'

Captain Wright was just suppressing a laugh when the shooting started. Suddenly the walls of the wadi were echoing to the percussive chatter of a light machine gun, the dusty earth around Major Morgan was bursting with the impact of bullets and the major was dashing back towards the Humber, followed by the gunfire. He was fifteen yards from the car when something seemed to pick him up and throw him forward. He lay on the ground, a red stain spreading through the back of his khaki shirt.

'Get him, Wright!' shouted Wilson. 'Courtney, get this car turned around.'

Wright leaped out and ran, bent double towards Morgan, drawing the fire towards himself. With the door still open, Saffron slammed her foot to the floor and the car leaped forward, then a couple of seconds later she wrenched on the handbrake, turned the wheel hard and the car slewed round, virtually on the spot, throwing a cloud of dust into the air that acted as a temporary smokescreen as she raced back the way she had come.

The Italians were still firing and there was a hammering on

the back of the car as a burst of rounds hit the boot.

Saffron stopped the car for just long enough to allow Wright to bundle Morgan into the back seat, screaming in pain, and then she was off again.

Behind them the firing ceased, but Morgan's cries of distress were louder than ever and the smell of diarrhoea filled the car as he voided his bowels. Saffron looked in the mirror. There was nothing behind her. She turned all her attention back to the wadi. It was littered with stones, rocks and even a few sizeable boulders, left by the receding waters of the river that had once run down it. On the way in she had taken it very slowly and carefully, all too aware of the perils of damaging the car out here in the middle of nowhere.

Now she was driving a little faster. Then she took another look in the mirror and sped up again.

'There's a car behind us!' she shouted.

Wright twisted the mirror so that he could see out of it. 'Looks like an Italian staff car. There's a chap leaning out of his window holding a gun. Duck sir, duck!'

The machine gun fired again, but the bullets passed harmlessly wide: the chances of hitting a fast moving car up ahead from the window of another vehicle when both were driving over uneven ground were meagre in the extreme.

That did not stop Wright pulling out his Enfield No.2 service revolver, winding down his window and firing off three rounds back at the Italians.

'Don't waste your ammunition, man!' Jumbo shouted.

They had passed over a relatively flat stretch of riverbed but now the ground was getting rougher again. Saffron found that she was not frightened by the gunfire, for her whole mind was taken up with the task of finding the best speed. Too slow and they would be caught by their pursuers. Too fast and they could hit a rock and become sitting ducks.

'What's happening behind us?' she asked.

'The chap with the gun is waving his arm around – typical Italian. Think he wants his driver to go faster.'

Saffron increased her speed a little, but not to the point where she felt out of control. Let the other man drive like an idiot. They would soon see who survived the longest.

'They're getting closer, sir!' Wright yelled. 'For God's sake, Courtney, can't you go faster?'

'Leave the girl alone,' Jumbo said. He twisted round in the passenger seat and then ducked as the machine gun spat fire again and the rear window shattered as it was hit by a round. Saffron felt a shower of glass particles against her back, but she was unhurt.

'Time for suppressing fire, I think,' said Jumbo and, with Morgan still holding his hands to the front of his shirt in a desperate attempt to staunch the flow of blood, the general turned until he had one knee on the passenger seat and was leaning on the back of the seat, facing backwards. He and Wright fired several times. A couple of rounds hit the chasing car, but to no obvious effect, though the man with the machine gun was forced to duck back inside the vehicle.

The Italians were gaining on the Humber with every second. As the range narrowed, Jumbo Wilson fired a shot that hit the pursuers' windscreen.

'Good shot, sir!' Wright shouted as the Italians veered to one side before the driver regained control and took up a new course, running parallel to the Humber but slightly to the left, on the passenger's side.

'I've got a better shot now,' said Wright, for the new course exposed the flank of the Italian car, and, by the same token, the side of the Humber too. He took careful aim at the man with the machine gun, heedless of the fire that was coming from it, and pulled the trigger.

It clicked.

The gun was empty.

'Damn!' Wright exclaimed. 'Do you have any spare ammunition, sir?' he asked.

'No,' Jumbo admitted. 'Didn't anticipate a need for it.'

'Me neither.'

The Italians had been blessed with a stroke of luck. The side of the wadi onto which they'd been forced was smoother. Now they were gaining fast. Their bonnet was level with the back of the Humber, with a gap of barely fifteen feet between the sides of the two cars. But now it seemed that the man with the machine gun had the same problem as the British soldiers. He had run out of bullets. Glancing across, Saffron could see him bend down, evidently scrabbling around on the floor of the car for now she could see the driver beyond him.

'Would you open the glove compartment please, sir?' she asked.

'I'm sorry?' Wright asked.

'Open the damn glove compartment!' Saffron snapped.

'Do as she says, Wright,' said Jumbo, beginning to grasp what she was up to.

'Now pull out my shoulder bag and open it.'

'A gun!' Wright exclaimed. 'What a stroke of luck!'

'Hand it to me please, sir.' Saffron glanced at the Italian car. The man still hadn't reloaded his machine gun but it could only be a matter of time.

'Do it!' Jumbo commanded.

Saffron took a last look through the windscreen. There was a short patch of relatively clear ground up ahead.

'Take the wheel, please, sir. Just keep it straight. Don't move it.'

Wright leaned over to hold the wheel. Saffron rested her right arm on his shoulder, aimed through the open passenger window of the Italian car and fired four rounds in quick succession.

'Thank you sir,' she said. 'I'll take the wheel again now.'

* * *

404

Frescobaldi knew he had another magazine. He had thrown a bunch of them into the car as they all leaped in to chase the British. But as he scrabbled around the footwell, with the car bouncing up and down like a whore's bedsprings, he couldn't find the damn thing.

When the four shots came they were so much quieter than the clatter of his Breda that he barely heard them above the noise of the engine, the wind and the crashing of the car against the rough ground. But then he saw his driver jerk back in his seat as two rounds hit his head.

The wheel slewed as the dead man lost his grip. The car swerved off course, ran at full speed for a further fifty metres, with every man inside it shouting out in panic, and smashed into the side of a massive boulder, twice the height of a man.

The car burst into flames. Frescobaldi pushed at the door beside him with all his strength but the frame was buckled and the door would not budge and as the fire took hold of him Frescobaldi wished he had one last round in his gun.

For then he would be able to use it on himself.

Major Morgan was dead by the time that they finally reached Major General O'Connor's headquarters. As his body was pulled from the car, O'Connor approached his visitor and said, 'Good heavens, Jumbo. You look like you got yourself into a bit of a scrape.'

'Yes,' Wilson agreed. He looked over towards the car. Saffron was sitting on the ground, exhausted, her hands wrapped round a much needed cup of strong, sweet tea. 'It was that chit of a girl over there who got us out of it, you know. She put four rounds into a man, cool as a cucumber, never seen anything like it. Tell me, Dick, do you suppose it is technically possible to mention a female civilian in despatches?'

'Not sure, to be honest. I dare say no one's even considered the possibility.'

405

'Seems only right, somehow. She'd probably be picking up a medal if she were a soldier and a man.'

There were men in both the British High Commission and the military headquarters in Cairo whose jobs involved the filing of discreet reports to units in London that did not officially exist. Mr Brown had asked these operatives to keep him posted on any interesting news about Saffron Courtney. Her exploits in the desert certainly qualified as that and Mr Brown devoured the reports of the incident with great interest. Saffron's ability to keep her head when others were panicking, and her willingness to shoot an enemy dead impressed but did not surprise him. She was, after all, known to be a good shot and any girl who willingly threw herself down the Cresta Run clearly had an appetite for danger.

Moreover, from the first time he met her, something about Saffron had given Mr Brown the impression that she might possess a character trait that was surprisingly rare in the population at large: the ability to kill another human being at close range, face to face. In times of peace, such an ability was not to be encouraged. But when the nation was at war it became an essential commodity.

That Saffron could kill when her own life was in danger had now been established.

But can you kill in cold blood?

That was what Mr Brown now wanted to know.

General Archibald Wavell, the British commander-in-chief in the Middle East, was in ultimate control of every British, Imperial and Allied soldier, sailor and airman in North Africa, the Eastern Mediterranean and the Middle East, including Palestine, Iraq and Iran. In February 1941 yet another country fell into his sphere of influence and he summoned Jumbo Wilson to his office in Cairo to discuss it.

Wavell was not a small man. He had a strong, square jaw and, though his hair was grey, his eyebrows and moustache were still dark. He had lost his left eye fighting at Ypres in the First War, but his right was still sharp enough. He was, in short, as imposing as his rank suggested, but still he was dwarfed by the height and bulk of Jumbo Wilson.

Wavell was Wilson's boss. On the other hand, Wilson was two years his senior in age. More significantly they were both very senior officers and so when they met in private they cast the formalities of rank aside and talked as old friends.

'I've got a job for you Jumbo,' Wavell began. 'Think there's a promotion in it, full general, if you play your cards right.'

'That certainly sounds interesting. What's the score?'

'As you know, the Greeks have done a terrific job against the Italians in Albania, given them a hell of a bloody nose. Now Mussolini's gone bleating to his big brother in Berlin, asking Hitler for help, and it seems he's about to oblige. The Greeks are convinced there'll be German invasion in the spring and have asked for our help.'

'I hope we've said that we're awfully sorry but we're rather busy at the moment. So no can do, but we wish you the very best of British luck.'

Wavell winced in discomfort at what he was about to say. 'Not exactly. A view has been taken that Greece is now our only ally left standing in Europe so we can't just stand by and watch them fall beneath the jackboot, too. So we're sending the First Armoured Brigade, the first New Zealand Division, the sixth and seventh Australian Divisions and the Polish Brigade to Greece, and I want you to be in charge of the whole show over there.'

Wilson said nothing.

'You don't seem overwhelmed with enthusiasm,' his commander-in-chief observed.

'Well, I'm very grateful for the job, Archie, of course I am. Appreciate you placing your trust in me and so forth.'

'You've earned it.'

'But, for pity's sake . . . Sending so many of our best units off to Greece, undermining our forces here, it's just madness. Surely those fools in Whitehall can see that.'

Wavell sighed. 'I'm afraid it's more the fool in Downing Street that's the problem. Winston's determined to open up a Balkan Front and he sees Greece as the place to do it. It's not just a matter of keeping Greece out of German hands. He's also got it into his head that we can use air bases in Greece to bomb the Romanian oilfields and cut off Germany's best source of fuel.'

'A Balkan Front?' Wilson repeated incredulously. 'God almighty, you think he'd have learned his lesson at Gallipoli. Someone has to talk some sense into him, or we'll have another disaster as bad as that one on our hands.'

'I don't disagree with you, but the Prime Minister must have what the Prime Minister wants.'

There are times when a man continues to plead his case, even when he knows that the effort is futile, simply because he cannot quite believe that anyone could be so foolish as to disregard it. Major General Wilson was now such a man. 'But it's obvious, surely, that we've got our hands full here in the desert, particularly now that the Germans have joined the party. We're not just facing a bunch of Italians any more. Rommel's a damn good general – he proved that with the 7th Panzers in France. What's more his troops are tough, battle-hardened and, above all, used to winning. But they're not invincible. Not if we hit him with everything we've got. He'll have the devil of a time keeping his army supplied, for one thing. Every gallon of fuel for his tanks, every drop of water, every bullet will have to be brought hundreds of miles along the coast road by truck. We can beat him, Archie, you know we can, but only if we have all the men and equipment we need for the job.'

Wavell knew that he was sending Wilson on a fool's mission. He also knew that, having sent him, his own chances of defeating Rommel would be greatly reduced. And both men knew that they were now likely to be held responsible for defeats in campaigns that could not have been won. But in the meantime, Wavell had his own orders to obey and that meant packing Wilson off to Greece.

'I agree with you, Jumbo, honestly I do,' Wavell said. 'We have a terrific chance here in the desert to send the Germans packing and show that we can actually go up against them in the field and win. But Winston has decided that Greece is the new priority. He's like a child in a toyshop . . . "I want that one!" "No, I want that one!" And he must have his way, whether we like it or not.'

'So what's the plan?'

'There'll be troop convoys leaving Alex for Piraeus every three days, starting from the first week in March. The Navy will provide escorts, of course. Meanwhile John D'Albiac is heading up the RAF side of things. Once his chaps are set up in southern Greece they'll be able to provide air cover, too, if needs be.'

Wilson frowned thoughtfully. 'That's less than a month from now. I'm going to need to be on the ground with my staff by the time the first men get off their troopships.'

'I agree.'

'Then I'd better get started.'

'Good man,' Wavell said. 'And Jumbo . . .'

'Yes?'

'Don't you worry. Whatever happens over there, I'll make damn sure it's not held against you.'

A number of Luftwaffe fighter wings were withdrawn from their bases on the Channel coast at the New Year of 1941 and sent to Poland to start intensive training. They were never told exactly what they were training for, but it was perfectly obvious from the huge build-up of forces just behind the easternmost border of the Reich, army as well as air force, that an invasion of Russia was on the way. But then, just when it seemed that they might at any moment receive the orders that would send them into action against the Ivans, they were suddenly sent in another direction.

'This is strictly between you and me, but I've heard we're off on a jaunt to the Balkans and Greece,' Dieter Rolf told Gerhard, one evening in the officers' mess. 'It appears our Italian friends have got themselves into trouble and we've got to pull them out of it.'

'Won't that hold up the, ah . . . the other big push?' Gerhard asked – for security's sake it was best not to say the word 'Russia'.

'It may well do. But that's not our problem, is it? We'll be flying over the Parthenon in a month or two.'

'Wonder if we'll be able to take some leave in the Greek islands? That would be nice.'

'I'll say . . . Oh, by the way, I've got a letter for you from home.'

Gerhard took it. He waited until after dinner, barely able to suppress a smile as he thought of the joy he would feel when he read Saffy's letter. Then he raced back to his bedroom, slammed the door behind him, ripped open the envelope and ten seconds later collapsed onto the bed.

He didn't know how long he spent sitting on the edge of his mattress, head in his hands, sobbing helplessly. At one point, he heard the door open, a couple of footsteps into the room and then Schrumpp saying, 'Sorry, old man, didn't mean to disturb you.' At some point in the night he fell asleep and had terrible dreams in which Saffron appeared, except that he could never see her face, or get any closer to her, no matter how hard he tried.

The following morning Gerhard walked into the mess. He couldn't face eating breakfast, but he very badly needed coffee to jolt his brain back to life. He didn't say anything and nor did anyone say anything to him. They were all used to the constant presence of death. For all the Luftwaffe's triumphs, the squadron had lost almost half its original complement of pilots over the past eighteen months of war, and many of those who had survived had lost brothers and friends who were serving in other areas of the Wehrmacht, or family members killed in air raids and accidents at home.

It was best not to dwell on these things. Best to let a man come to terms with his loss and then carry on as normal. There would be time enough for mourning when the war was over. So Gerhard said not a word. But his heart was broken and his soul scarred.

Saffron had been his love, his hope, his redemption. Without her, those things were gone. And without them, what was left of him at all?

W ilson was hard at work, planning, executing and supervising the movement of more than three full divisions of troops, with the prospect of more to come if the fighting became as serious as expected. Saffron found herself shuttling up to Alexandria and back as her boss and his senior staff officers met with their naval equivalents. In between those trips there was an endless round of visits to all the units that would be involved in Operation Lustre, as the expedition to Greece had been titled, more meetings with Wavell and more trips to Alexandria.

Wilson himself was due to fly from Cairo to Athens in the final days of February. Less than a week before his planned departure date, Saffron still didn't know if she would be accompanying him. Finally she plucked up the courage to ask.

'Been thinking about that myself,' Wilson said. 'No denying you might come in handy. I can always get a chap to drive me, but you know my ways, what to say, when not to say anything, all that kind of thing. Don't want to have to train someone

411

else. So my conclusion is yes, you will come. But I'm not letting you anywhere near the fighting.'

'But sir . . .'

'No "but sirs" about it, young lady. This is going to be hard, bloody fighting and the front line is no place for a woman, even if she can shoot straight. Once the balloon goes up, I'll be packing you off to Athens. You can make yourself useful there. And if things go badly and Jerry puts us on the back foot, I want you taking the first available aircraft or ship back to Alex.'

'Yes sir,' said Saffron, grudgingly.

'That's an order.'

'Yes, sir.'

There was a war on, an Empire to defend and the myth of British invincibility to uphold, so the English language newspapers always did their best to find the most positive possible interpretation of any bad news from the front. But even so, Leon could see that the Greek campaign was going badly and his fears were magnified a thousand-fold by the knowledge that Saffron was over there, doubtless perilously close to the fighting and in danger of capture, injury or even – though he made a conscious effort to avoid brooding on this possibility – death. Late one evening, barely a week after the first German forces had crossed the Greek border, Leon found himself summoned to General Wavell's Cairo headquarters. As one of the leading English businessmen in Egypt, with interests across Wavell's sphere of command, Leon had crossed paths with him once or twice at social events, but they had never had any professional dealings with one another. But here was one of the general's staff officers calling up at half-past ten to inform Leon that a car was on the way to pick him up, making it politely, but very firmly clear that this was an order, not an invitation, and adding, 'It would be a great help if you knew where all your ships were at the moment, so if you need to call anyone to find out, I advise you to do so right away.'

Leon didn't need to ask. He held regular morning and evening meetings to check on the whereabouts of Courtney Trading's fleet of six oil tankers and a dozen merchantmen of various sizes. Thus far, they had not lost a single vessel, unlike vessels on the North Atlantic run, whose every move was tracked by wolf packs of German U-boats. For the sake of the men who crewed his ships, quite apart from the state of his company bank balance, Leon intended to keep it that way if he possibly could.

Wavell sometimes preferred to wear civilian clothes when working late and so, on this chilly April night, Leon found the C-in-C sitting at his desk in a checked jacket and a white-spotted burgundy silk scarf, neatly tucked into a dark blue woollen jumper. The desk was covered in papers, but still there was evidence of a neat, ordered mind in the row of pens and pencils neatly lined up in easy reach to Wavell's right, and the blotter, ashtray and glass paperweights distributed as carefully as divisions on a battle-plan.

'Ah, Courtney, good of you to come at such short notice,' said Wavell, removing a pair of tortoiseshell reading glasses as he stood to greet his guest.

They shook hands and Wavell indicated that Leon should sit down on a leather-backed chair that had been placed opposite the desk.

'It's late and I'm sure you'd rather be at home in bed, so I'll get straight to the point. What I am about to discuss with you is a matter of grave importance and absolute secrecy. I trust I can count on you to respect that.'

'Absolutely.'

'Good man. Now, I dare say you've been following events in Greece.'

'Yes. Reading between the lines of the newspaper reports, one gets the impression that things are not going well.'

'That is putting it very mildly indeed, Courtney. Between you and me, the situation is disastrous. The Greeks had most of their army up in Albania, to the northwest, fighting the Italians, and the rest to the northeast, on the Bulgarian border. Field Marshal List sent the German 12th Army charging right between them, smashed the entire front to pieces in a matter of hours, typical *blitzkrieg* stuff. Now half of their forces have swung west to trap the Greeks on the Albanian front. The other half's swung southeast, cutting off the Greeks on the Bulgarian front, and raced to the sea at Thessalonica. We begged the Greeks to mount an orderly retreat from Albania before they were completely cut off, but they simply refused to give a single inch of it back to the Italians. So now they're being pounded by a couple of crack SS divisions and they'll have to surrender within days, possibly even hours.'

'What about our chaps?' Leon asked. 'I admit, I have a personal interest. My daughter Saffron is General Wilson's driver.'

'Hmm . . . can't be easy for you. My boy's a subaltern in the Black Watch. One worries, can't help it. I'm sure Jumbo will do his very best to get her out in one piece, but I must tell you, it's not looking good. We're falling back in as orderly a fashion as possible, but we're having to leave supply dumps – rations, petrol, even ammunition – and now Jerry's using our materiel to supply the troops attacking us.'

'Will we be able to get our chaps out of the country? It sounds like we're on the way to another Dunkirk.'

'Quite so. I fear the resemblance will extend to all the tanks and artillery pieces abandoned by the roadside as we run to the sea. You know, we hadn't even finished putting our chaps on the ground when the German offensive began. Some units have been getting off their ships and re-embarking before the tide has even turned because there's simply no point trying to get them to the front.'

'How long do we have?'

'A couple of weeks, at most. We might still be putting up some kind of a fight by the first week of May, but it could equally well be all over by then. That's why I need you to help me with the greatest possible urgency.'

'Of course, General, what can I do?'

Wavell took a cigarette from a silver box on his desk, which he then offered to Leon, who declined. He lit the cigarette and smoked it for a few seconds while he composed his thoughts.

'One of the less, ah, publicized issues raised by Herr Hitler's acts of conquest concerns the gold reserves of the nations he seizes. To be frank, neither we nor the governments of the countries concerned have had much luck keeping that gold out of Nazi hands. We don't want to make the same mistake with Greece. Our aim is to get it out of the country, across the Med, through the Suez Canal and down to South Africa before the Germans even know it's gone.'

'You'll have a hard time doing that if the Germans are moving as fast as you suggest.'

'Agreed. The chances of completing the entire journey before they reach Athens are very small. But if we could at least get it through the Canal, I would feel very confident of reaching Durban and from there taking it by train to Johannesburg.'

'And you want me to supply the ship that carries it.'

'Precisely.'

'Might I ask why you aren't entrusting the job to a naval vessel rather than a merchantman?'

'We are desperately stretched, Courtney, I'm sure I don't need to tell you that. I simply cannot spare a single destroyer, or even a frigate to undertake a mission that would take it thousands of miles away from the front. But just as importantly, I want to do this on the QT. The Germans do their damnedest to keep track of all our warships, just as we try to do of theirs. A single merchantman, on the other hand, is a much less visible proposition.'

'I see. And how large would this cargo be?'

Wavell took a last pull on his cigarette, stubbed it out and said, 'I am led to believe that the Greek reserves weigh somewhere in the region of one hundred and thirty tons. A ton of gold is currently worth around four hundred thousand pounds sterling, making the value of the reserves rather more than fifty million pounds.'

Leon gave a long soft whistle. 'That would buy Hitler a lot of new tanks.'

'About five thousand, and all their spares as well,' Wavell replied.

'I take it that if you can't spare a destroyer to carry the gold then you certainly won't spare one to escort the ship that does.'

'Even if I could, I wouldn't. It would rather give the game away, don't you think?'

'In that case I insist that my men have the ability to defend themselves. They'll need anti-aircraft guns in particular.'

'Again, I would argue that the less one does to draw attention the better. We haven't got time to mount any Bofors guns, let alone train your chaps to use them.'

'Let me be blunt, General. I am willing to send one of my ships to pick up that gold. I'll even give you the best I've got available. She's the *Star of Khartoum*, so called because my late father ran supplies into Khartoum when General Gordon was under siege there, back in '85. Seems apt that she should be doing this job now, and she's well-suited for it, too, because she's only a couple of years old, built to my specifications at the Swan Hunter yard on Tyneside and powered by a Parsons Marine Steam Turbine engine producing ten thousand ship horsepower. She can get from Athens to Alex doing twenty knots all the way, and that's allowing for all the ballast she's going to have to carry.'

'Why carry extra weight?' Wavell asked. 'Surely you want her to be as light as possible?'

'No, you don't, not if, as you say, the whole point is to be inconspicuous. If the *Star*'s only got a hundred-odd tons of gold in her holds she'll be riding awfully high in the water and any snoop hanging around the waterfront is going to ask himself why a ship flying the Red Duster is leaving Greece with nothing aboard when we have so much kit and so many people who need extracting.'

'Fair enough. When can you leave?'

'Just one moment. I have two conditions. The first is that I am not sending my men into harm's way without at least some means of defending themselves. Manning a Bofors may be beyond them, but there's no reason they can't fire a machine gun. The Navy mount Vickers point-fives in groups of four as short-range anti-aircraft defence. I'll have six of those mounts, if you please.'

'Well, I'll have to have a word with Admiral Cunningham and see—'

'The only words you have to have with Cunningham are, "That's. An. Order." I'm sure he'll take the point.'

'I'm sorry, Mr Courtney, but I really don't take kindly to being spoken to in this way.'

'And I don't like the idea of informing the families of good, brave men that their sons and husbands have died because they had no means of defending themselves against attack. There's fifty million in gold sitting in a vault in Athens. If you put the guns on the dock at Alex by 08.00 tomorrow, I'll have the *Star of Khartoum* on her way by midnight and into the dock at Piraeus forty-eight hours after that. I'm assuming the Germans won't have got there by then, of course.'

Wavell seemed to hesitate.

'Fifty million pounds,' Leon repeated. 'Worth the loan of a few Vickers guns, I'd say.'

'Very well, you will have your guns. Now, you said you had two conditions. What is the second?'

417

'It's not a condition, so much as a piece of information. I'm going to Greece on my ship.'

'There's really no need. Arrangements are already being made for the gold to be brought to the dockside and loaded.'

'Damn your gold, General. I'm going there for my daughter.'

Wavell looked at him. 'Mr Courtney, I must advise you, in the strongest possible terms, not to do that. You could be placing yourself and your daughter in very grave danger indeed.'

'I understand, General. But my daughter is already in danger and I would feel a very great deal happier if I could do my bit to get her out of it.'

'It is possible, you know, that you might be making her position worse, rather than better. I quite understand a father's desire to help his child, particularly a female one. But you should ask yourself why you are doing this. Is it really for her sake, or for yours?'

'Are you officially advising me not to go?'

'Yes, Mr Courtney, I am.'

'Well, I note that advice, but I must tell you that I reject it.'

Wavell shrugged, and for a moment Leon caught a sign of the profound mental exhaustion, the accumulated burden of so many life-and-death situations carried out in such stressful circumstances that accompanied his level of command.

'Very well then, I have done my bit to help you. Now you must go and do your bit to save your girl.'

I'm sorry, Leon, but you can't have the *Star*,' Francis Courtney protested. He looked at the other men around the table at the morning shipping review, looking for signs of support. 'She'll be fully laden with finest quality Egyptian cotton, bound for Bombay, there to be made into bed-linen fit for a Maharajah.'

'Good, then I won't have to worry about ballast. Anwar . . .' Leon looked at Courtney Trading's shipping manager. 'Please tell the chaps at the dock to clear the Number Two hold, just for'ard of the engine room. And assemble every maintenance man, welder and fitter we've got by the ship. Any minute now a convoy of trucks is going to turn up, laden with machine guns, courtesy of the Royal Navy, and we need to get them positioned. I'll be driving up to Alex as soon as this meeting is finished and will supervise the job when I get there.'

'Yes, Mr Leon.'

'Good man. I'll tell you where I want them mounted before I leave here, so they can get down to work right away.'

Francis wasn't giving up. 'This is outrageous! We can't go around arming our ships like a bunch of pirates.'

'Since that is precisely how our forefathers made their fortunes in the first place, I really can't see the problem. I have agreed with General Wavell to send the *Star* to Greece. I will discuss the matter further with you in private, but for now all I will say is that I am satisfied that we will be giving sufficient assistance to the war effort to justify the risk involved.'

'That is a practically new ship and you know as well as I do that if she is damaged or sunk, the compensation we will receive will not come anywhere near covering the cost of replacing her.'

'I am well aware of that, Frank.'

'Well then this is gross irresponsibility and I must protest as both a shareholder and director of the company.'

'I really don't think we should be having this argument in public, Frank. So let me just say this. If Hitler should win the war, then it really won't matter what our balance sheet looks like, will it?'

'I don't see why not. Herr Hitler has always made his respect for the British Empire plain. I am sure he would see no reason to wreck its economy or harm its commercial interests. Of course, he would want to bring our activities into line with his economic policies, as any leader does, but . . .'

'That's defeatist talk, Frank, and I won't have it. Gentlemen, our meeting is at an end. As the chairman and leading share-holder, I am ordering the *Star of Khartoum* to sail for Athens at the soonest opportunity. This meeting is at an end. Frank, I'd like a word with you. In private.'

Leon waited until the others had left the room, furious that he had given Frank the opportunity to speak as he had: reports of it would be all over the company by the end of the day, demoralizing the majority of workers who were loyal to the Allied cause and encouraging those few, and Leon knew there must be some, who secretly hoped for Nazi victory.

Finally the door closed behind the last man to leave and Leon turned on his brother. 'How dare you? How dare you come up with your ghastly pro-Nazi propaganda in front of other members of staff? Anyone listening to that might have thought you wanted the Germans to win this blasted war . . . Maybe you do . . . well . . . do you?'

'No, no, of course not . . . far from it,' Frank blustered. 'It's no secret that I'm disappointed that we have entered into what I believe to be an entirely unnecessary conflict. We allowed ourselves to become ensnared in Polish attempts to provoke Berlin and declared war at a time when there was no threat whatever to British or Imperial interests. It was a grave mistake in my view and is causing us to waste the Empire's human and material resources on war, when they would be far better served in peaceful trade and economic activity. And I cannot for the life of me see why anyone would think that opinion was unpatriotic.'

'You are, I suppose, entitled to your view on government policy. The freedom to express contrary views is one of the things we're fighting for. Not much of it in Germany, I fancy. But now that the war is here, and we have to win it, we all have a duty to do whatever we can to help the war effort, and that includes you.'

'How in God's name is sending one cargo vessel to Greece going to help the war effort?'

'I'm afraid I am not at liberty to tell you that. I gave my word to General Wavell that I would not discuss any of the details of the voyage or its mission.'

'You're sending our fastest ship to a country that is rapidly being overrun—'

'There's no reason to suppose that.'

'Oh, don't be ridiculous, Leon. I can read Arabic and believe me the Arab papers don't pussyfoot around bad news the way the English ones do. The Germans have us on the run, again. So Wavell wants you to get something or someone out of there before they march into Athens. I think I have a right to know what it is that you're putting in one of our ships.'

'Ask Wavell, why don't you? He can decide if he wants to tell you. Meanwhile I will be going to Greece with the *Star*, so you will be in charge while I'm gone.'

Francis's face suddenly brightened.

'Yes, I thought you'd like that,' Leon said. 'But it's purely a question of day-to-day management. No major decisions are to be made without my specific approval. And if I hear you have been expressing even the slightest lack of faith in our eventual victory, by God I'll horsewhip you out of the building.'

'I shall ignore that threat and the slander behind it. Neither does you any credit whatever, Leon.'

The phone at the head of the boardroom table by Leon's chair rang. He walked over and picked it up. It was Anwar: 'The guns have arrived at the dockside, Mr Leon. I am told there are six trucks carrying the guns and another two with ammunition and mounting equipment. If you could please tell me where the guns are to be placed, I will make sure the work begins at once. I am told the Navy has also supplied men to assist the fitting of the guns and also a dozen men to fire them. They insist that this is better than having untrained seamen who must, in any case, attend to their own duties.'

Leon could see the sense in that, and appreciated the generosity of the offer. Wavell must have made it clear to Cunningham that total cooperation was required. 'Very well,' he said, 'I want all the Navy men dressed in exactly the same clothes as our chaps.

421

Can't have them standing out. As for the positioning of the guns, it's very simple. One set should be mounted in the bows, and another in the stern. The remaining four go up on the top deck, above the bridge, one on each corner.'

'So that they form a square around the funnel?'

'Exactly.'

'It will be done as you instruct. And Mr Leon, I wish you a safe voyage.'

'Thank you, Anwar.'

'Will Miss Saffron be returning with you from Greece?'

'I sincerely hope so.'

'Then may God the all-powerful and all-merciful watch over her on her journey.'

Within the hour, Leon was on his way to Alexandria. At lunchtime, Francis informed his secretary that he would be out for an hour or so.

'Lunching at the club, are you, sir?' she asked.

'Something like that, haven't decided exactly where yet.'

'Very well.'

But the moment he left the Courtney Trading office, he did not head for any of the agreeable clubs and restaurants which the leading members of the British community in Cairo patronized. Instead he went to the Old City, into the backstreets where few white faces were seen, bound for the restaurant where he could leave a coded message for Hassan al-Banna. Its contents would be transmitted to Berlin by methods Francis was more than happy not to know. He assumed that the forward listening stations of the Afrika Korps could pick up a transmission from Cairo, sent at a particular time on a specific frequency, and then pass the message on to Berlin. But that was really not his problem.

* * *

eon was very nearly as good as his word. The *Star of Khartoum* cast off from the Alexandria docks at ten minutes past midnight. Once the captain, Jerry McAloon, a tough Ulsterman, pickled by sun, salt and alcohol, had seen the ship into open water and checked that a full blackout was being observed, he sat down with Leon and the Navy sub-lieutenant in charge of the gunners. His name was Jamie Randolph, his chin looked as though it had never had need of a razor and he seemed barely old enough to order a round of drinks in a pub, let alone command men in battle. But Leon remembered his own early days in the King's African Rifles and realized he had been no older when he took charge of his first platoon.

'Let me get one thing straight, Randolph,' McAloon growled. 'I don't like mixing merchant sailors with Navy men. Leads to trouble in my experience. But I'll have no fighting on this ship. Do I make myself clear?'

'Perfectly, sir,' Randolph replied, looking the skipper in the eye and not flinching in the slightest.

'I know I can control my men. What I want to know is, can you control yours?'

'I'd be a poor officer if I couldn't. If there is any disorder on board, it won't come from my men.'

McAloon looked at the youngster with the first glimmers of respect.

'Make sure that it doesn't,' he said.

As the *Star of Khartoum* was cutting through the waters of the eastern Mediterranean, bound for Piraeus, a young woman working in a building near the Buckinghamshire village of Bletchley, some fifty miles northwest of London – a building whose very existence was as closely kept a secret as Britain possessed – finished her translation of the decoded German signal to which she had been assigned. She took the

English version of the text to her supervisor. He read it and at once understood the significance of the signal's contents, for he had been briefed to expect something like it and to call a number in Whitehall if and when it came through.

The man on the other end of the line listened with interest to the contents of the signal before saying, 'That's excellent work. Well done.' He then turned to a colleague, a much older man, and said, 'They know.'

'Already? That's very fast.'

'Well, let me clarify that. To be precise they know enough to be able to work out the rest for themselves.'

'Do they have the name of the ship?'

'Yes.'

The older man sighed. 'Then I pity the poor souls aboard it.'

A year after he and his comrades had followed an invincible army through the Low Countries and northern France, Gerhard von Meerbach found himself doing exactly the same, though this time through Yugoslavia and Greece. It was incredible how little the British or their allies seemed to have learned, how unprepared they were for the decisiveness of the Wehrmacht's offences. Once again, enemy armies were outflanked, encircled and forced to surrender, or to run from the closing noose as fast as their legs and wheels could carry them.

In the air, the story was just the same. When the Luftwaffe had taken on the RAF in the skies over England, Gerhard had felt for the very first time that he was in a battle of equals. But here in Greece, the British flyers were hopelessly outnumbered and forced to operate from inadequate airfields without the central organization that had made them so effective in the summer of 1940. The campaign barely seemed to have begun before it was over and yet another vast expanse of sky belonged to the Stukas and the 109s.

The other pilots were jubilant at the ease of their victory, but Gerhard took no pleasure from it. They flew every day across clear blue skies, but without Saffron the sun had gone from his life and the world around him was dark.

'Cheer up, Meerbach,' said Schrumpp after they'd come back from yet another successful mission. 'You got another kill today. You should be strutting around like the cock of the walk, not moping about like a miserable old woman. What's got into you?'

Gerhard did his best to smile. '*Ach*, it's just too easy. I prefer to have more of a challenge.'

'Well I prefer to shoot down the enemy with as little trouble as possible.' Schrumpp grinned. 'But then again, I'm just a builder's son from Frankfurt. I dare say you Bavarian aristocrats have different standards, eh?'

'Precisely.' Gerhard raised his head, looked down his nose at Schrumpp and in his most lordly tones said, 'Now run along and get me some schnapps, there's a good man.'

'Oh yes, sir, absolutely sir!' Schrumpp said, bowing and scraping.

'Well go on then, get a move on!'

Gerhard managed to maintain the pretence of good humour as Schrumpp laughed and went off to the bar. But as soon as his friend had gone a few paces he slumped down into a battered armchair.

Ah, Schrumpp, what a decent, innocent, good man you are, he thought. *I don't want the enemy to be a challenge. I want them to be good enough to kill me.*

'Courtney! . . . Driver Courtney!'

Saffron opened her eyes to see a harassed-looking man in a crumpled linen suit, the top button of his shirt undone and his tie askew, trying to force his way through the crowds of people in the foyer of the British Embassy. Every Briton in

Greece was trying to leave the country and they all seemed to think that the route out led through the embassy, as if its harassed staff could somehow produce tickets for aircraft, when none were flying, or ships, when all civilian passenger ships had long since sailed away. They weren't the only ones hoping for a miracle. There were Jews, some of whom had already been forced to flee once from other conquered countries; artists, writers and intellectuals who knew they would be marked men under the Nazis; citizens of other Empire nations who looked to the mother country for help in their hour of need. All had congregated on the embassy. And there was no help that could be given to any of them at all.

That the Germans had been victorious did not take anyone by surprise. From the moment he had first sent his troops into the Rhineland, five years earlier, Hitler had never once faced an opponent he could not defeat. But even now the speed and inexorability of *blitzkrieg* warfare took people by surprise. Just eighteen days had passed since the first German soldier crossed the Greek border and now the war was almost over. Trucks filled with exhausted, filthy, demoralized Allied troops, many of them bloodied or bandaged, had been spotted heading for Porto Rafti, fifteen miles east of Athens itself, en route to the naval ships waiting to carry them back to Alexandria. They had to leave from there, people said, because the city's main port at Piraeus had been all but immobilized by German bombing.

How long would it be before the Germans marched through the streets of Athens? No more than a day, surely: two at the most. Saffron had been given orders to get out, and Wilson had repeated them when he paid Athens a flying visit to confer with the King of Greece and confess that his country was lost. She had been assured by some of the diplomats that her best way out was to leave with them, under cover of diplomatic immunity, after the Germans had arrived. 'Dress up in civvies and we'll say you're one of the secretaries,' a young diplomat had told her. 'Even the Nazis can't touch anyone who works for the embassy.'

Saffron had decided to count on that and not worry about even trying to find another way out, for there was none. And even if there were, she had no time to spare to find it. She had been working flat out, driving diplomats and other British worthies to and fro across the city, or just helping deal with the chaos at the embassy, making endless cups of tea for all the people crowded into the halls, corridors and even outside in the garden.

'Driver Courtney!' the man in the linen suit called again.

Saffron rubbed the fatigue from her eyes, got to her feet and called out, 'Yes, sir,' waving as she did so.

The man saw her and forced his way through the crowd towards her. 'There you are!' he said. 'Got another taxi ride for you. Off to the Bank of Greece again, usual two passengers. Dare say your old Humber can drive itself there by now!'

'I should think it can,' she agreed, for she had indeed been making regular visits to and from the spanking new Central Building on Panepistimiou Street over the past few days, always taking the same two men. One was a thin, balding, moustachioed fellow by the name of Watkins who said, in his fussy little voice, that he was a Bank of England official, though what he was doing in Athens was hard for Saffron to imagine. The other was a much tougher, smoother, more dangerous, and clearly (in his own eyes at least) more seductive figure called John Swift, who said he was a Second Secretary at the embassy.

'Watkins doesn't speak Greek,' Swift had explained, on their first drive down. 'It's all Greek to him, what?'

'Actually, I do have a little Ancient Greek,' Watkins protested, 'though that sadly doesn't seem to be much use in the present century.'

'So I'm here to be his liaison with his opposite numbers at

427

the Bank of Greece, make sure everyone has the right end of the stick.'

'I see,' said Saffron, whose own impression was that Swift carried himself a lot more like a military man than a diplomat. *He might be Watkins's translator,* she thought. *I bet he's also his bodyguard. But why on earth would a meek little man like that need a bodyguard? Who would ever want to hurt him?*

She had slung her ever-present bag with its vital contents of wallet, gun and letters from Gerhard over her shoulder, gone to get the Humber and was standing beside it on the pavement outside the embassy when her two passengers appeared. They seemed more than usually preoccupied and got into the back of the car without a word. She closed the passenger door behind them and drove off. As the Germans approached ever closer to the city, the Greeks seemed to have vanished from sight. Almost everyone had retreated into their own homes, waiting with their families for the moment when the first of their conquerors appeared on the streets of their capital city. Though there was plenty of petrol for military vehicles, for huge supplies of fuel, food and ammunition had accompanied the Allied expeditionary force, in anticipation of a lengthy campaign, the civilian garages had long since run dry, so the journey to the bank had become a very swift one, particularly at this time of the evening, for it was past seven and the sun was starting to go down.

This time, though, was different. She passed two trucks, then a third and a fourth all going the same way as her. Three were military, one Greek and two British. The fourth was civilian, with the name of the firm that owned it written in Greek script on its sides. But all four were big vehicles, capable of carrying heavy loads, and they were heading in the same direction as her, past the National Gardens, cutting the corner of Syntagma Square and then heading down Panepistimiou Street itself. Parked to the side of the road, by the National Library building, there was a British armoured car with a turret-mounted heavy machine gun and just beyond it two army trucks, surrounded by soldiers smoking, chatting and doing what Saffron had long since realized was what all soldiers do for most of the time: waiting for something to happen.

But by now the trucks that had been driving alongside her were slowing as military policemen were flagging them down and guiding them to the side of the road, each taking its turn in a line that began just outside the National Library, ran for a hundred yards or so up the road and came back down the other side towards the entrance to the bank itself. All along the way there were more police beside the parked trucks, sitting astride motorbikes.

Now Saffron herself was ordered to halt. She wound down her window as a policeman wearing a British uniform approached and asked to see her papers. She handed them over and added, 'I'm driving these two gentlemen to the bank. They are expected.'

Swift got out of the back of the car, approached the policeman and led him off to one side. Whatever he said must have worked because less than a minute later he returned to the car and said, 'It's all sorted, Miss Courtney. You can drive on.'

Sure enough the policeman was waving them through. Saffron followed the line of trucks, made a U-turn at the top of the road and came back down the other side, parking just ahead of another armoured car, which was itself positioned in front of the first truck in line.

'Wait for us here. This shouldn't take long,' Swift said as he and Watkins got out. It occurred to Saffron that Swift always did the talking for both of them, and that wasn't, she decided, because Watkins was naturally shy and retiring. It was because Swift was the man in charge.

Unless the weather was pouring wet Saffron had long since acquired the habit of waiting outside her car, rather than in.

On a hot day in Athens, the rays of the midday sun were actually less brutal in the open air than being roasted inside a motorized tin can. So she stepped onto the pavement and looked around.

The entrance of the bank resembled a modern take on an ancient Greek temple. It was all very clean, very simple: a white marble portico enclosed three high doorways, split by two classical columns. Normally the doors were closed, but this evening they were wide open and a stream of soldiers were coming out of two of the doors, pushing hand-trolleys laden with small wooden crates down the short flight of steps and then taking them along the pavement towards the trucks where other soldiers loaded them aboard. Then the empty trolleys were being taken back into the bank through the third door.

'Hey, Miss!' Saffron looked round to see the commander of the armoured car, a sergeant, whose body was now poking up out of the turret. Now he clambered out, jumped down to the ground and walked towards her.

'Planning on staying here long, love?' he asked.

'Just until the gentlemen I'm driving have finished their meeting, Sergeant. They told me it wouldn't be long.'

'Well you can't stay here, you're blocking the way and we're going to be on the move. Park up ahead, in that sidestreet. Right on the corner is fine, just so long as you're not causing an obstruction.'

'Well, I'm sure I'd hate to do that.'

The sergeant grinned. 'You can obstruct me any time, love!' he said and she laughed, because the impish cheek in his eyes was a nice change from the fear, fatigue and panic she had seen in so many faces for so many days.

She got back in the car and did as he had asked. A couple of minutes later, the sergeant disappeared back into his turret and the armoured car started up and slowly rolled down the street, past where Saffron was parked, followed by the leading trucks. About a dozen must have gone by before the line came to a halt. There were two trucks blocking the end of her street, but if she looked through the gap between them she could see the far end of the line, on the other side of the road, start to move.

The process was repeated half a dozen more times over the course of the following two and a half hours. The sun went down and in the blackout the only illumination came from the dimmed torches of military policemen, guiding the men with the trolleys to the trucks they were loading, like ushers showing cinema-goers to their seats. Finally she could see the process was complete. Just as the final trucks were rolling slowly past her, followed by the army vehicles bringing up the rear, there was a tap on her window. It was Swift.

'I'd be very grateful if you could get us to the front of the column, please, Miss Courtney. Don't be afraid to drive on the wrong side of the road. We'll be going to Piraeus, incidentally. We need to be the first to arrive.'

Saffron knew better than to ask why they were going to the port, or what was in the trucks. But the question was superfluous anyway. When a country that is about to be conquered empties the vaults of its central bank and sends them off to the nearest ship, it wasn't too hard to guess what those trucks might be carrying.

The chestnut trees along the Landwehr Canal were just coming into leaf opposite the headquarters of the Abwehr, a long, five-storey, grey granite building with a red tiled roof that Hitler's spies shared with the *Oberkommando der Wehrmacht*, or OKW, the supreme high command of all his armed forces. The room where coded transmissions from agents working in the field were decrypted was on the fourth floor and looked out at the chestnuts through windows decorated with curtains and flounced valances that seemed more in keeping with an apartment's parlour than an intelligence agency's nerve centre. But it was here that the transmission from Cairo, passing on the information that the British had sent a merchant vessel named the *Star of Khartoum* to Greece to collect a valuable, highly classified cargo, was eventually decrypted. It had not been assigned a high priority. The Abwehr's masters at the OKW needed hourly updates about the status of the Allied forces facing them on the battlefield in Greece. The suicide of the Greek Prime Minister Koryzis, brought on by his shame at his nation's collapse, had affected planning for the political administration of Germany's latest dominion. And even more important than either of those was the intelligence being gathered in preparation for the imminent invasion of Russia and the destruction of Soviet communism, the only cause that was even close to being as dear to the Führer as the annihilation of the Jews.

All that being the case, the *Star of Khartoum* was already docked in the bombed-out remnants of the port of Piraeus by the time that its potential significance was explained to Admiral Canaris, the head of the Abwehr, at a meeting with three of his senior subordinates. Canaris was a gentlemanly figure who seemed out of place among the cold-blooded careerists, Nazi ideologues and, as he was himself coming to realize, blood-thirsty psychopaths who populated the higher echelons of the Reich. But he had been a brilliant, daring junior naval officer in his youth and now he was a cunning, sophisticated spymaster in his middle age. One thing he was not, however, was impetuous.

'So, we know that this ship is sailing for Greece,' he said, having heard the contents of the signal from Cairo. 'We know that it is bringing a cargo of great value back to the British in Egypt. The question remains, however: what precisely is the cargo?' He held up a hand to forestall the words that might be about to be spoken by any of the other three men around the table. 'And let me be the first to say, before anyone else does, that it is very unlikely to be olive oil, retsina or Greek cheese.'

The others produced the degree of laughter required of a boss's witticism and one of them dryly inquired, 'Do they have anything else to offer?'

'Gold, of course,' said a second man, somewhat impatiently, for he was serious by nature and did not approve of tomfoolery at work. 'What else could it be? They are hoping to get the gold out of Greece before we can seize it and we must strain every sinew to stop them.'

'A very reasonable point, Hümmel,' said Canaris. 'I would say that there is at least a seventy-five per cent chance, maybe even a ninety per cent chance that you are right. But there is in my estimation one other cargo that the British might wish to take from Greece before we can take it back to Berlin: antiquities. They already have the Elgin Marbles. I am sure that they would be happier having the rest of the treasures of Ancient Athens under their own safe keeping than made available for inspection by the citizens of the Reich.'

'I suppose that might explain why they have only sent a cargo ship,' said Hümmel, conceding the point to a degree at any rate. 'I must confess I have been asking myself: if I wanted to transport six hundred million Reichsmarks in gold, would I really just send a single cargo ship? Surely I would load it aboard my mightiest battleship, with more smaller warships around it, and make it impossible for the gold to be lost.'

'Also reasonable,' Canaris agreed. 'But now I shall argue against myself. Consider the position of General Wavell and Admiral Cunningham. The expedition to Greece has turned out to be the disaster they must have feared, wasting men and equipment that would have been much better used in North Africa. What is their number one priority now: saving the gold? No. All their resources must be focused on a single task: getting as many of their men back to Egypt as they possibly can. And so where will they put

433

Cunningham's cruisers and destroyers? Surely alongside the troop-ships. The gold they must now move in a very different way, as inconspicuously as possible. So they choose one small cargo vessel, for we surely will not pay attention to that when there are so many other more important targets for us to look at.'

'Excuse me, sir,' said the fourth Abwehr officer at the table, 'but I do not quite understand what difference it makes what this British ship is carrying. Let us just sink the damn thing and let them worry about what they have lost.'

'It matters, Friedlander, because we Germans are proud of being the most cultured race on earth. We did not bomb Paris before we captured it, for to do so would be an insult to the very European civilization we exist to defend. If we sank a boat containing priceless treasures of antiquity, we would be handing the Allies a propaganda coup. "Look at these Nazi barbarians!" they would say. "See how they treat the masterpieces of classical art." Goebbels would not be happy at having to counter that. Nor would all the professors and museum keepers who have made Berlin the world centre of study into the antiquities.

'No, first we must beg General List please to speed up his advance to reach Piraeus before this ship leaves. If we capture the ship and cargo intact, that is the best outcome of all. At the same time we order our agents on the ground to observe the port as closely as possible. When this *Star of Khartoum* arrives, they must not let the ship out of their sight until they have established its cargo. Then if the army does not get there in time we act as follows. If the cargo is nothing more than old statues, we let it sail. Who knows, the way Rommel is going, maybe he will be on the quayside to greet the *Star of Khartoum* when it arrives in Alexandria. If the cargo is gold, we tell the Luftwaffe to sink the ship, at all costs. It would be bad enough for us not to have that gold. But for our enemies to have it would truly be a disaster.'

* * *

General Wavell had done Leon a great favour. At the bottom of one of his despatches to Jumbo Wilson he had appended a question. 'What are whereabouts of your driver, Miss Courtney?' Wilson had countless better things to think about but it did not do to ignore a superior officer's questions, even if he was also a friend, so he replied, 'Athens c/o UK Embassy'.

This information had been passed on to the *Star of Khartoum*, from which Leon had radioed the embassy shortly after arriving in Piraeus and been told that his daughter had gone to the Bank of Greece, acting as driver for a Bank of England official and his embassy liaison officer. Leon knew what was about to be delivered from the bank. The chances were that the bank man would want to see the cargo safely aboard ship, in which case Saffron would drive him.

Still he had a nervous wait until the army Humber appeared, the only sign of its approach being the slivers of light from its taped-up headlights, and Saffron got out, looking as smart as ever in her uniform, and politely opened the door for her passengers.

Leon waited until she was finished and then called out, 'Saffy!'

She started, looked around, peered through the near darkness and then a huge smile crossed her face as she cried, 'Daddy!' and ran towards him.

'What on earth are you doing here?' she asked.

'Well, this is my ship, and as my daughter was at its destination, I thought I'd come along for the ride. Now, get aboard, I've got you a cabin for yourself, so you should be very comfortable.'

'But I can't. I've got to take Mr Watkins and Mr Swift back to Athens.'

'No you don't. Wavell himself has given me his personal permission to bring you back to Alex.'

'Yes, but—'

'But nothing.' Leon looked around and saw a man whose

suit and tie did nothing to hide his toughness. This, it was perfectly obvious, was a man who knew how to look after himself. 'That Swift?' he asked.

'Yes.'

'Hold on a minute.'

Leon walked over. 'Mr Swift? My name is Courtney. This is my ship. And your driver is my daughter. I have General Wavell's permission to take her back to Alex. Do you have any objections?'

'Not at all. I can find the way back to Athens.'

'You and your colleague are welcome to come aboard if you need a passage back to Egypt.'

'Very kind, but no thanks. We've still got a few loose ends to tidy up and we'll both claim diplomatic immunity. The Germans won't touch us.'

'Good luck to you then,' said Leon. Then he shook Swift's hand and walked off.

Hell and damnation!' cursed Swift, as he settled into the driver's seat and started up the car. 'My orders were to get the Courtney girl out of Athens safe and sound.'

'Well that's not going to happen now,' said Watkins. 'But don't blame yourself, old boy. What could you have done? Old man Courtney wasn't going to take no for an answer and you could hardly tell him to find another ticket home without giving the whole game away.'

'I suppose you're right . . .'

'I know I am. In any case, you just have to look at the man to see he'd never even countenance deserting his own ship, and the girl's hardly going to leave her pater in the lurch, is she?'

'I know, but my orders were as clear as bloody crystal: Saffron Courtney gets out safe and sound. God knows why, but someone very high up is keeping an eye out for her.'

'I don't blame them. What man wouldn't?'

Swift gave a smile that was more of a grimace. 'No, it's not that. I think they have plans for her.'

'Well then they're going to have to find new plans. Look, the thing I always tell myself in circumstances like this is: think of the bigger picture. One can't go compromising an entire operation, just for the sake of a single individual, or even a hundred individuals.'

'I feel bad for her though. She was a damned good girl, that one.'

'Oh yes, she was a cracker. But think of the bigger picture.'

A German asset in Athens, whose cover was that of a left-wing Romanian journalist forced into exile in Greece, duly made his way to Piraeus. The one functioning wharf was ringed with armed guards. But the piles of rubble and the hollowed-out shells of warehouses and customs buildings that now littered the site provided plenty of cover and the blackout was a gift to anyone wishing to pass by undetected. So he had little trouble in getting to within fifty metres of the ship. What he saw was men handling shallow wooden boxes, no larger than the boxes of fruit one would find on a market stall. Whatever was in these boxes was a very great deal heavier than apples or peaches, however, for it was apparent in the way the men were carrying them off the trucks lined up along the quay and onto pallets that were then winched aboard the ship that this was hard, back-breaking work.

He made his way back to his attic apartment, pulled out a suitcase from underneath his bed and extracted his portable Enigma coding machine. Having translated his despatch into meaningless and, so far as he knew, unbreakable gibberish, he used the radio hidden in his wardrobe to send it.

This time the men in the decrypting room in the building on Tirpitzufer wasted no time in dealing with the message. The news that the British were trying to take the Greek gold reserves out of the country was passed immediately to both the OKW and the Führer's office at the Reich Chancellery. Prompted by Göring's personal insistence that the Luftwaffe would deal with the issue, his most senior planners responded that there was not time to organize a night-raid on Piraeus of a size large enough to provide any likelihood of hitting a single, relatively small target in a blacked-out area.

They did, however, propose that a close watch should be kept on the target vessel so that its precise departure time could be reported. Sunrise would be at 07.32. By that point a Junkers Ju 86 P-2 reconnaissance aircraft, capable of flying at altitudes higher than any Allied aircraft could reach, with a sixteen-hundred-kilometre range that would enable it to sweep a huge area of the Aegean, would be in the air, ready to find the gold-ship. There were, the planners believed, only two courses the *Star of Khartoum* could possibly plot en route to Alexandria. Both began by sailing south, but then one veered to the west of Crete, through the Antikythera Straits, and the other turned towards the Kaso Straits to the east. The target vessel, however, would only have been steaming for a few hours by the time the Ju 86 began its sweeps of the area, so the two possible courses would not yet have diverged greatly. One spotter plane would therefore be sufficient to find the ship and lead a formation of Stuka dive-bombers and their fighter escorts straight to it. This was just as well, since the Luftwaffe only had a single Ju 86 in the Balkan theatre of operations, but there was no need to tell the Führer that.

'The gold will not reach Alexandria, my Führer,' Göring assured Hitler. 'You have my word on that.'

'You gave me, and the German people your word that not a single bomb would ever fall on the Ruhr. You did not keep it that time, Herman. Why should I believe you now?'

'Because by this time tomorrow we will know that all the gold in Greece is sitting at the bottom of the sea.'

* * *

The agent who had sent the Abwehr news of the *Star of Khartoum*'s cargo was ordered back to the docks to report on its departure. It was three in the morning in Berlin when the message came in. The *Star* had left at shortly after two. The quarry was on the run. The hounds would soon be after it.

The men of Gerhard's squadron were roused from their beds before first light and informed of a vital mission: a precision attack on a small target at the very outermost limits of their range.

Squadron Captain Rolf briefed them on their task. 'The target is a British ship, carrying a strategically important cargo and, before you ask, no I don't know any more than that. But the orders have come from the very top, Göring himself has taken a personal interest, so it must be damned important.

'This ship will be almost five hundred kilometres to the southwest by the time we reach it. We'll be carrying droptanks with extra fuel, but even so, we'll have to be very careful. As for the Stukas, those lads will have to lean out of their cockpits and flap their arms because even with extra tanks they'll be flying on fumes by the time they're even halfway back. Our job, as always, is to escort our slow, fat friends, but once we get to the ship, we don't anticipate any RAF presence in the area, and they don't have any escort vessels there, so we can attack the ship ourselves. If we maintain a steady stream of strafing runs that will draw enemy fire, if there is any, away from the Stukas and let them drop their bombs right down the funnel.

'This strikes me as a tricky little assignment. On the face of it, the target is a sitting duck, all alone, bobbing up and down on the pond. But you never know, the duck may fight back, and it is, in any case, a very long way away and we have to be very conscious indeed of our fuel levels. So don't waste a drop doing anything you don't have to because I want all of you and your planes back here safe and sound in the evening when I read out the message of congratulations from Berlin.'

Gerhard felt oddly cheerful as he climbed into his 109 and went through his routine of pre-flight checks. This mission felt like a pleasant change, an interesting technical exercise with an important target at the end of it.

'You seem very cheerful this morning, sir,' one of the ground crew working on his plane observed.

'You're right, I am in a good mood,' Gerhard replied. 'It is a beautiful morning, not a cloud in the sky and I'm going to be up there soon myself.'

The Ju 86 tasked with finding the *Star of Khartoum* had flown over what remained of the Allied ground forces and aircraft in Greece at an altitude of thirteen thousand metres, one and a half times the elevation of Mount Everest, so far above the earth that no one had the slightest notion of its passing. Now, as Homer's rosy-fingered dawn spread its rays across the wine-dark waters of the Aegean, the pilot brought the aircraft down to a mere six thousand metres, at which point he and his two crew felt they could cover a wide area of sea in a single pass, but would still be able to see a solitary vessel on the water.

Their cabin was pressurised, making the Ju 86 infinitely more comfortable than most military aircraft, and a Thermos flask of coffee was chasing any lingering, early morning bleariness from their systems.

For three hours they swept back and forth across the Aegean like an airborne pendulum that lengthened its string with every swing. But although they encountered plenty of troopships fleeing across the water and even received a few desultory rounds of anti-aircraft fire from the destroyers escorting the defeated, retreating army, there was no sign at all of anything that matched the description they'd been given of the *Star of Khartoum*.

'It has to be here,' muttered the pilot. 'I'm going to go back the way we came, flying the same pattern but in the opposite direction. Maybe if we come at everything from a different angle, we'll spot something we missed before.'

'We didn't miss anything,' the navigator argued.

'We must have done. We're almost two hundred and fifty kilometres southeast of Piraeus. That ship has been in the water for no more than nine hours. It would have to be doing almost thirty kilometres an hour to have gone any further than this. It's a cargo steamer, for hell's sake, not a torpedo boat.'

'It's a steamer carrying a precious cargo and I bet the skipper and all his men are shit-scared. All alone on the water, no escort . . . I know what I'd do if I were them: run the boilers right up to the red zone and beyond and, if they burst, too bad. I tell you what else I'd do – stay away from all the other ships. They're going to attract attention. What do you bet the Italians have got submarines waiting for them? All the troopships we saw were heading to the west of Crete. I say we fly southeast and look for a ship going like a bat out of hell for the Kaso Straits.'

'I call that a waste of time,' the pilot insisted.

'Listen, we have nothing to lose. If we don't find that shitting boat we are going to get our arses kicked black and blue. We've got to fly back the way we came anyway, or we won't be able to get back to base, so if it is there, like you say, we'll spot it. But just in case it isn't, and while there's still plenty of fuel in the tanks, let's just try to see whether we can complete our mission successfully, eh Captain?'

'*Ja*, you're right, we have nothing to lose but our sore arses. Give me a bearing for the Kaso Straits.'

Ten minutes later, they had just begun to start having their doubts when a cry of 'I can see it! God in heaven, I see it!'

burst into their headsets from the third member of the crew, who was perched in the plane's glazed nose with a perfect view in all directions.

And sure enough, about three kilometres to the south, steaming flat out at very nearly forty kilometres an hour, there was the *Star of Khartoum*.

The sea was clearer than any Saffron had ever seen, the crystal water shading from a deep, purple-black to the purest blues and turquoises she could imagine. The islands, so sudden and sharp, emerging from the water like the tips of drowned church spires, were a mosaic of white houses and white mills and black olive trees against the dusty, khaki earth. She would have loved to explore them with Gerhard one day. But there was nothing to be gained in letting her mind dwell on that. She was on a ship that was fleeing for its life and she did not have her lover beside her, but a bunch of sailors manning the machine-gun emplacements, bragging to one another about all the things they planned to do when they got back to Alex – the drinks they would consume, the tarts they'd screw – occasionally saying, 'Sorry, Miss,' when their language became too explicit.

If only you knew . . . Saffron thought. She wondered how many of the boys around her, for they were none of them yet true men, had even kissed a woman properly, let alone made love to one. Yet she had given every inch of her body to Gerhard, and taken every bit of him in return and her hips squirmed a little at the wetness those thoughts induced.

'Gorgeous day, isn't it?' an upper-class voice said over Saffron's right shoulder. She turned, looked over the top of her dark glasses and saw Jamie Randolph coming towards her. *Speaking of virgins* . . .

'Yes, pity to waste it on a war.'

'Well, we seemed to have sneaked away without anyone knowing. With any luck we'll have a smooth passage back to

Alex. I know it sounds silly, but I'm almost sorry. I was rather hoping my chaps might get a spot of real action. It's all very well training for hours on end, but none of us have actually been under fire, as it were.'

'Then count yourselves lucky,' she said, and the tone of her voice made Randolph frown as he said, 'I say, do you mean that you have?'

'Yes. Only once . . . but it wasn't something I'd choose to repeat.'

'Well I should think not. Hardly the sort of thing a woman should have to endure. But as I was saying—'

'Wait a second,' Saffron interrupted him. She screwed up her eyes as she looked up to the sky behind the stern of the ship. 'We have company.'

'Where?' said Randolph.

'Off to the northwest, at high altitude. Follow the line of the wake, then go a bit to the right and look up. Do you see it?'

Randolph did as he was told, pulling the peak of his cap down over his eyes to shade them from the glare. 'Hang on . . . can't see anything . . .'

Saffron stood beside him and pointed up into the sky to guide him. By now the two lads on the nearest Vickers battery had caught on to what was happening and were peering at the heavens too.

'I see it, Miss!' one of them said. 'Look sir, just where the young lady was saying . . .'

'Got it,' said Randolph. 'Hang on . . . back in a jiffy . . .'

He disappeared off across the deck and down the ladder to the bridge. A minute later he was back bearing a pair of binoculars. He looked through them and his lips gave a little wince of frustration. 'It's an aircraft all right, but I have no idea what it is. Doesn't look like anything I've ever seen before, not even on those diagrams one has to memorize. You know, the silhouettes of enemy aircraft.'

'Can I have a look?' Saffron asked.

Randolph handed the binoculars over, conscious of the fact that this absurdly pretty girl, whom he'd approached in the hope of a bit of social conversation, maybe even mild flirtation, had turned out to have more battle experience than he or any of his men.

'I've seen that before,' Saffron said, and now she was the one with a puzzled, frustrated look on her face, 'but I can't for the life of me remember where or when. Not in the war, though, I'm almost sure it was before this all started.'

She looked again. 'Got it! I know this sounds silly, but I flew in a plane just like that once. I think it was a flight from Cologne to Munich . . . a girlfriend from school lived in that part of the world. I'm sure that's a German plane. But what on earth would an airliner be doing out here?'

'I think I can answer that,' said Randolph, thrilled to have something he knew that she didn't. 'After the last war, the Jerries weren't allowed to have bombers, Treaty of Versailles and all that. So they designed airliners that could be converted to be bombers. Typical underhand sort of trick those bloody Nazis go in for.'

'Do you want me to take a pop at it, sir? Let 'em know we've spotted 'em?' the gunner asked.

'No, we'd only be wasting ammunition and I fear we're going to need every round we've got. Excuse me, Miss Courtney . . .' he cleared his throat. 'Listen here, men. Jerry knows where we are. If he sent a plane all this way to find us, then it's because he thinks we've got something worth chasing on board.'

'I should think 'e bloody does, sir, seeing as 'ow we've got the contents of the Bank of bleedin' Greece down there in the 'old.'

'Well, I can't say quite what we've got, but I dare say you're right, Bowyer. The point is, they'll be coming after us. More aircraft, I imagine. If they're flying all the way from Greece,

444

they'll be at the very outside limits of their range, so they won't hang around for long. We've got to make sure that while they're here, they don't get a decent shot at us. That means keeping clear heads and firing concerted bursts at specific targets, not just blazing away and hoping for the best. Now, check your guns, make sure they're all working. Tin hats on. Let's put on a damn good show, shall we? See if we can't impress Miss Courtney.'

'Tell you what, sir, she don't 'alf impress us!'

'Perhaps you would like to accompany me to the bridge, Miss Courtney,' Randolph said, 'and leave these ruffians to do their worst? I'd better let the captain know we're expecting company. And then, if you don't mind, I will leave you. Need to pass the word to the chaps in the bow and the stern. Good to know that our presence here isn't being wasted, eh? That's the main thing. We've got something to do.'

There was no point in changing course or trying to hide the ship somewhere among the islands. As long as the Germans had that plane, with its huge, triangular wings like black sails in the sky, circling high overhead, watching their every move, there was no possibility of escape. And so Captain McAloon took the complete opposite course of action. He had the radio operator send out their course, speed and position, along with the message that they were anticipating an imminent attack from the air. That way, with any luck, if the ship went down, any survivors might stand a chance of being picked up.

Saffron had been given a helmet and a lifejacket. She pinned up her hair and put the tin hat on top. There was still no sign of any more enemy aircraft in the sky so while she still had time she went to the ship's kitchen and asked the cook for some greaseproof paper, which she wrapped around her package of letters and photographs and over the barrel of her gun.

Then she smeared a thick layer of lard over both wrappings to make them more waterproof. The cook also gave her a ball of twine which she wound like a cocoon around her bag. Then she slung the bag across her body and put the lifejacket on top. If she was going to die, there wasn't a lot she could do about it. But if she was going in the water, then she wasn't going to lose her most precious possessions.

Her preparations complete, she went back up to the bridge. Her father was there, talking to the captain, making plans for what they would do with the Courtney Trading fleet when they could finally get back to being a normal peaceful business again. 'I wouldn't listen to a word my father says, Captain,' Saffron said, going up to them and allowing herself the brief indulgence of wrapping her arm around her father's tall, solid, comforting form. 'He knows perfectly well that when this ghastly war is over, I will be taking control of everything.'

'I wouldn't be so sure of that, young lady,' said her father, pretending to be cross. Then he squeezed her tight and kissed the top of her head, just as he had done when she was a little girl and she had exactly the same feeling that she had done then: that as long as her daddy was beside her, like a wall protecting her from any harm the world might throw at them, nothing could possibly go wrong.

Then Jamie Randolph walked down the ladder to the side of the bridge, came in and said, 'They're on their way: Stukas, with an escort of Messerschmitt fighters. I estimate they'll be here in a couple of minutes. Better sound the alarm.'

McAloon sounded two long blasts on the ship's horn and all over the vessel men snapped into action. Down in the engine room, the turbines were revved still higher and further beyond their limits to squeeze the last little bit of speed from them, for the faster they were moving the harder, surely, they would be to hit.

Men who had been assigned to fire parties took their positions, as did those who had the carpentry or welding skills to be able to make emergency repairs. Leon had taken the precaution of recruiting the firm's best medical officer for the trip and he was ready in the sick bay with a couple of orderlies. A silence fell over the ship as men retreated into their own thoughts, their own fears, their own love for all the people they had left behind and might never see again.

And then, like a breaking storm, the first Stukas hurled themselves at the ship and the battle began.

Saffron had heard the scream of diving Stukas on cinema newsreels enough times. It was the sound of the *blitzkrieg*, the sound of the Nazis crushing everyone in their path. But nothing had prepared her for the sheer volume and almost physical aggression of that banshee shriek, rising in pitch and volume, the sound echoing around the bridge as the first three planes dived down towards their prey, rising to a shrieking, hysterical climax just before the Stukas released their bombs, one after another, no more than a few seconds apart, flattened out their dives and rose again into the sky.

For the first few minutes, this was a battle she heard, more than saw. The frantic chatter of the Vickers guns, desperately trying to fend their attackers off; then the roar of the German fighter planes and the hammer of their cannons as they made their runs, trying to silence the guns on the *Star of Khartoum* so that the Stukas could finish off their prey at their leisure; the roar of Captain McAloon's voice as he shouted out the commands that sent the helm spinning this way and that as he tried to make the ship jink and swerve in a bid to make the dive-bombers miss.

And it worked. The first three bombs all missed, sending up huge geysers of seawater that crashed down like waves onto the *Star*'s decks but did no serious harm. But still some damage

447

was being done. The fire crews had been sent to put out a blaze ignited by one of the Messerschmitts' incendiary rounds in the after deck house by the stern of the vessel. The rear battery had been mounted on the deck house roof. The blaze had to be extinguished before they were forced to abandon the guns.

Then Randolph reappeared in the cabin. His face was white with shock and pain and his left arm hung, bloodied, limp and useless at his side.

'Three of my lads are down. One of the gun batteries is out of action. The guns work, just don't have anyone to man them. Can you spare me anyone, Captain?'

McAloon didn't even acknowledge that he had heard Randolph. It was very likely that he hadn't. The cacophony of battle was deafening and the captain was at the very limit of his powers, just trying to keep his ship moving forward.

But Saffron heard. 'We'll do it,' she shouted back. She looked at Leon. 'Come on, let's go!'

He paused for a moment, as if about to tell her to stay under cover, but then he nodded and followed her out.

'The guns fire in two pairs, one gunner for each!' Randolph shouted as he led them up the ladder, finding it hard to keep his balance with only one hand to hold the rails. 'Don't worry about ammo, they're self-loading. There are two hand-wheels. One makes the gun mounting rotate. The other controls the elevation of the guns. You'll get the hang of it.'

Coming up behind Randolph, Saffron put her dark glasses back on, feeling that the gesture was oddly frivolous but knowing that she would be able to see much more clearly if she was not screwing up her eyes against the glare of the midday sun off the glittering sea. They reached the top deck. Two hours ago, when Saffron had been sunning herself and watching the view, it had seemed like a lovely, airy place to be. Now she felt utterly exposed, with nothing to protect her from the bullets and bombs as she dashed across the deck, following Randolph

448

to the silenced gun battery. There was a dead man lying on the deck at the base of the guns and another semi-upright, his feet on the ground but his torso draped across one of the drum-shaped magazines that contained the ammunition. Saffron recognized the sailor who had said that she impressed him. Half his skull was missing and brain matter was dribbling down the remains of his face and onto the top of the magazine.

Randolph did his best to make himself heard as a Messerschmitt roared across the bows, aiming for the guns there. 'You'll have to move them!'

Her father took the one who was standing, heaving him out of the way. Saffron grabbed the lying man under both armpits and dragged him backwards so that she had room to get past him and stand behind the guns.

The 109 that had strafed the bows came back for a second run. Somehow the men behind the guns down there had survived the first run and they were still firing as the pilot swooped down and came in at them again, so low over the water that he was firing directly at the gunners, and they at him, like duellists with banks of machine guns, rather than single pistols to fight with. And then one of the gunners was hit, his body jerked by a series of impacts in lightning-fast succession that drove him backwards, with the back of his lifejacket disintegrating in a bloody mess as the bullets went straight through him. He took one step back, then a second and finally a third before he fell, his legs bent under him, his arms flung out to either side, his dead eyes looking up at the German fighter as its racing shadow passed across his corpse.

'Try your wheel!' shouted Leon.

Saffron reached down to the wheel. It was about a foot wide, mounted horizontally atop a steel rod, with a vertical handle for her to grip. She rotated the handle clockwise and saw the barrels of the guns point up: anti-clockwise and they came back down.

'My turn!' Leon said and he got the feel for the identical control that made the guns rotate. They each had a gunsight, fixed parallel to the guns, with an eyepiece and a round sight, criss-crossed with aiming wires about two feet beyond it.

'Ready to give it a go?' Leon asked.

Saffron nodded.

'Right. The bow is twelve o'clock. To the left is nine, to the right is three, to the stern is six. OK?'

'Yes!'

Overhead the Stukas were circling, waiting for the fighters to finish their job. Another of the 109s began his run, determined to finish off the bow battery, coming in from the opposite direction to the previous plane.

And the guns in the bow were pointing the wrong way. Saffron and Leon saw it at the same time, the sole surviving gunner dashing round to his dead comrade's position, frantically turning the abandoned wheel so that he could bring the guns round to bear on the incoming plane.

But he wasn't moving fast enough.

'Three o'clock, low!' Leon yelled.

He put all his strength into turning his wheel as fast as possible but the guns seemed to move with agonizing slowness. Saffron was working her wheel anti-clockwise, bringing the guns down until the end of the sight was pointing barely twenty feet above the bow deck.

The 109 raced towards the *Star of Khartoum*, closer and closer.

'Wait!' shouted Leon.

The plane was speeding over the waves, its guns firing.

'Wait!'

The man by the Vickers flung himself to the deck as the bullets ricocheted off the steel deck and the bow rails.

The plane was so close Saffron could actually see the leather helmet and goggles of the pilot in his cockpit.

'Fire!'

The hammering of the four guns battered Saffron's eardrums, but then, in the blink of an eye, the plane was past them, keeping low for a couple of seconds and rising up into the sky as it climbed and banked and prepared to come back in again.

'Keep that elevation. Don't think we were far off him. I'll bring us round for the next go,' Leon said as the guns tracked back across the bows.

While they had been occupied at the front of the boat, another plane had been attacking the stern. Suddenly, behind them they heard an explosion. Saffron turned and saw that the entire stern section of the ship was ablaze. She could not see the after deck house at all for all the smoke. But then she spotted a figure emerge from the inferno, apparently walking in the air. She realized he must be on the deck house roof, which meant that he was one of the gunners. And he was ablaze, a walking torch, his arms waving, beating at his body in a futile attempt to keep the fire at bay. He stumbled and fell to his feet and then the flames engulfed him as they gathered him into their white-hot embrace.

'Saffron! Saffron!'

She heard her father's voice as if from a great distance and turned to see the 109 coming in for another run. The bow gunner was curled up on the deck, his arms wrapped around his head, his nerve broken by the repeated assaults.

Saffron forgot about him. She looked through her sights, imagining she was out on a shoot and that the Messerschmitt was really a pheasant or a duck and that she shouldn't find this metal bird any harder to kill than the real one.

Leon had been thinking much the same thing. Having turned his guns towards the attacking aircraft, he now planned to bring them back again, moving ahead of the 109's course, knowing that its speed would bring it into his sights and that the motion of the guns would throw the hail of half-inch rounds in a wider arc, like the pellets from a shotgun, increasing their chances that some at least would hit.

The plane came in.

Once again they waited.

And then, when she judged the moment right, without waiting for an order, Saffron fired.

Gerhard was impressed. The first three Stukas had gone in expecting an easy kill, but the British had made this harder than any of them had expected. The *Star of Khartoum* was surprisingly fast and agile, moving through the water more like a warship than a normal cargo vessel and she had sharp teeth with those machine-gun nests. So the 109s had gone to work, knowing they had to act fast to neutralize the guns, for every few seconds spent over the target cost the Stukas another kilometre of range.

Schrumpp had gone in first to take out the guns in the bow and almost finished the job. Now it was Gerhard's privilege to apply the coup de grace. His first run peppered the area around the guns and sent the one remaining man there diving from his post. Now he intended to put a few of the shells from the 20mm cannon mounted in the nose into the guns themselves, disabling them and possibly even setting off their own ammunition.

He pulled on the joystick and climbed, turned, came over the top of the arch he was creating in the sky and now he was racing back down again, feeling the pressure of the dive force him back into his seat before he flattened out and came in again. He positioned the nose of the plane absolutely in line with the bow guns and fired the cannon and the machine guns in his wings, seeing the tracer bullets home in on the target. Gerhard saw the entire gun battery ahead of him rocking with the impact of his rounds. There was fire coming in at him from the upper deck of the ship to his right. He looked towards it and saw a figure behind one of the machine-gun nests. It should have been a man. But in a fraction of a second he saw black hair, dark glasses, a woman . . . a ghost.

And then the plane was hit.

Gerhard felt the punch of heavy machine-gun bullets smashing into his wings.

All his other thoughts vanished as his entire concentration was focused on the here and now. First question: was he all right? He looked down and saw no blood. His limbs were all working. He was unhurt.

He was past the ship now, climbing again and his controls seemed to be functioning and then he heard Schrumpp's voice in his ear: 'You're on fire, Meerbach! Your right drop tank!'

He looked down at the wing and saw the flames blazing from the tank. He didn't think twice. The tank had to go before the fire spread to the wing itself. Gerhard pressed the release button. Nothing happened. He pressed again. Still the tank remained fixed to its position, the flames now growing. If it got any worse there was a danger the whole tank could blow.

Gerhard suddenly felt a clawing fear in his guts. He wasn't at a high enough altitude to bail out, but if the plane hit the sea he was a dead man. And all of a sudden his indifference to death, his loss of interest in life had disappeared. His natural survival instincts would not be suppressed. He desperately wanted to live.

But the damn tank still wouldn't release.

In a final desperate act he started working his flaps at random, shaking one wing and then the other up and down. He could see flames now licking along the edge of the wing. He threw his plane into every contortion he could think of, veering from left to right and then climbing into a vertical ascent, praying that the force of gravity would rip the tank from its moorings, still waggling his wings as he rose.

The rate of ascent slowed as the propeller steadily lost its battle with gravity. He was almost at stall speed. But Gerhard did not pull out of the ascent. He forced the plane to claw its way higher. Any second now the tank would blow, or the plane would stall. Either option would kill him.

I mustn't die. I refuse to die!

And yet he was going to die.

But then he felt a jolt, and the plane lightened as the tank finally broke free, and it was the drop tank that fell into the Aegean and Gerhard who pulled out of the ascent into a controlled dive, letting the wind over his wings blow out the last lingering flames before he flattened out.

But now there was a problem. About twenty per cent of his remaining fuel had just disappeared into the depths.

'Everything all right?' That was Rolf.

'I think so,' Gerhard replied. 'There doesn't appear to be any damage to the controls, engine's running fine. Fuel is my only issue.'

'Then don't waste another drop. Head for home. Take it nice and easy. And good luck.'

'No, it's all right, I want to see this through,' said Gerhard and banked his 109 to circle over the stricken vessel. By his rough calculation he had enough fuel to carry him three hundred kilometres.

His base, however, was almost four hundred kilometres away.

His only hope was to begin his return journey immediately and yet something inside him, that same instinct that had so recently demanded that he should live, was now telling him to stay. It was madness. He had to go. And yet he stayed, and even as the Messerschmitts finished their attack runs and then peeled away towards the Greek mainland, and the last of the Stukas dropped their bombs, Gerhard remained over the smoking, sinking *Star of Khartoum*.

* * *

Got him!' Saffron grinned exultantly as she saw the flame burst from the German fighter as it flashed past her. She watched the pilot's desperate attempts to get rid of the burning tank that could at any second destroy him and followed his ascent, still frantically shaking his wings. When the tank finally plummeted to the sea she felt cheated, deprived of the kill she deserved, and when she saw the pilot start circling over the ship, like a spectator wanting to see the end of the game, she was seized by a bitter, helpless anger.

But there was no time to think about that any more. The other 109s were coming in from all sides now, aiming for the deck on which she and her father stood, trying to take them out of the battle, just as they'd dealt with the guns fore and aft. Two more of the machine-gun batteries went down: one more man killed, three too injured to fight on. Saffron heard the angry mosquito sound of bullets fizzing through the air around her and the clamour as they hit the wood and metal around her but she and her father remained miraculously untouched.

Then the fighters had gone, disappeared up into the sky again, and for a second there was nothing but the noise of the ship's engines, the sea against the hulls, the cries of the wounded and the shouts of the men still fighting the fire in the after deck house.

She dared to ask herself: *Is that it?*

And then she heard the answer in the wail of the first Stuka. She looked up and saw it falling through the air, at one and the same time utterly modern and horribly primitive: a shrieking steel pterodactyl coming to kill them, screaming its glee at the prospect of her death.

Leon wheeled the guns round to face the monster. Saffron brought them up to full elevation and they fired a long burst but saw no evidence that they'd hit the target. And now a second Stuka was peeling off the formation and then a third,

455

and it was clear that they were all going to attack now and it suddenly became very plain to Saffron that some of them might miss, and one or two might even be hit, but one would get through. But there was nothing to be done but to keep firing, fighting back as the first bomb went wide, and then the second.

The third bomb hit. Saffron watched its bulbous black form drop from the Stuka and head straight for the after deck. It landed. It buried itself in the planking.

But it did not explode.

The relief was so intense, the release of tension so absolute that it was almost exhausting. But then another Stuka was coming in and the fear and adrenalin energized Saffron again and she fired and thought she saw her tracer bullets ripping into the Stuka and sure enough the cockpit was smashed to pieces and the engine had burst into flame. But the siren was still wailing and the Stuka was still diving.

And it was heading straight for the top deck.

Saffron hurled herself towards the ladder, but did not bother climbing down it. She just jumped for the small patch of deck at the bottom of the ladder, next to the bridge and as her feet hit the planking and she stumbled and fell to the ground the Stuka hit the *Star of Khartoum* and the whole world seemed to explode around her.

The blast blew out the windows of the bridge and if Saffron had not fallen when she hit the deck she would have been killed by a thousand flying shards of razor-sharp glass. She blacked out for a moment and when she came to the ship was on fire. It took her a few seconds to get her bearings and work out what had happened. The Stuka had hit the upper deck on the far side of the ship from where she had ended up, so she had been sheltered from the worst of the blast. And as soon as she understood that, the next thought hit her. *Daddy!*

She clambered back up the twisted, buckled frame of the ladder and when she got to the top was met with a scene of total devastation. The funnel that had stood in the middle of the deck had been almost totally destroyed. Only a jagged stump remained, belching oily black smoke. The remnants of the Stuka were embedded in the side of the main deck house, with the tail, which was somehow still intact, sticking up at an angle. Three of the gun mountings were lying scattered around the deck. The fourth had disappeared completely.

But where was her father?

Saffron looked around, trying to make anything out through the choking smoke. Then she saw him. He was face down on the deck, pulling himself forwards, one leg struggling for purchase while the other dragged along, motionless beside it. Beyond him, just visible through the smoke, there was a slick red train of blood smeared across the deck.

Leon looked up. His face was ashen as he struggled to prop himself up on one elbow. He reached an arm towards her and mouthed, 'Saffy!'

She put a hand over her nose to give her some feeble protection against the smoke and ran to her father. He had collapsed back down onto the deck and rolled onto his back, barely conscious, his grey cheeks and forehead wet with sweat, gritting his teeth, his features contorted into rictus of pain. And now Saffron saw the source of his torture, for his right trouser-leg had been torn open, the flesh beneath it shredded as though some wild animal had been tearing at it with crimson teeth and claws, and right at the heart of the terrible wound, standing proud of the rest, were the broken, splintered, jagged-edged remains of Leon's thigh-bone.

Saffron felt the sickness rising in her gorge and the tears springing to her eyes. *No! You can't be weak! Not now!* she told herself. So she bent down over him and said, 'Don't worry, Daddy, I'm here.'

Then she grabbed him under the armpits and, with her back to the ladder, started heaving back towards it. The two ends of her father's broken bone rubbed together and he could not help himself: he screamed in pain. Saffron forced herself to be deaf to his agony. She just pulled all the harder.

The *Star of Khartoum* was mortally wounded, that much was obvious, but the Stukas' orders had been to destroy it, so two more of the planes dived down and one missed, for the smoke was so thick that the target was hard to see. But the other hit, at virtually the same spot as the unexploded bomb. But this one went off and that finished the job.

The ship was sinking fast. Its fate was sealed and meanwhile the Stukas were past the safe limits of their fuel consumption. Their commander gave the order to return to base and they headed back, accompanied by their faithful fighter escorts. The second bomb had killed everyone by the stern of the boat and caused terrible damage in the engine room too. Barely anyone on the ship was still left alive. But the lad by the bow gun had come unscathed through the whole inferno, just as Saffron had done. He saw her up on the top deck trying to drag her father to safety and helped her get him down the ladder and then another to the lifeboat deck. A couple more survivors, including the ship's doctor, had gathered there and were struggling to get at least one lifeboat into the water before the *Star of Khartoum* went down.

They made it, just, and were able to row about fifty yards from the ship before it finally gave up the ghost, split in two and sank.

The doctor did his best to tend to Leon. He had grabbed his medical bag before running for the lifeboat, reasoning that he might have wounded survivors to deal with, and was at least able to pour some disinfectant on the open wound and give him enough morphine to ease his suffering a little.

Then Saffron heard the drone of an aero-engine. In all the chaos and the noise she had not realized that there was still one solitary German fighter up there, the one she had hit, still circling above them.

'What's he doing?' she asked, to no one in particular.

The doctor looked up, saw the 109 and muttered, 'Bloody vulture.' Then he shook his fist and shouted a string of foul-mouthed curses at the sky. 'I do apologize,' he said to Saffron, reverting to his normal, civilized self. 'Doesn't make a blind bit of difference, but at least one feels a bit better.'

Then one of the other survivors, Bowyer, the ship's rating whom Saffron could remember bantering with Captain McAloon before the battle said, 'Uh-oh, doc, I think the bugger heard you. Look out, he's coming our way.'

W*hat am I doing here? Why am I wasting fuel for no good reason?*

Now that the adrenalin of combat had dissipated, Gerhard felt that bleak, depressive emptiness return. His mind went back to the vision he had seen, the delusion of a woman where no woman could be. His mind was playing tricks on him. Fate was taunting him. Slowly the emptiness inside him filled with acrid, vengeful bile. He wanted to lash out at any target he could find, just so someone else could feel as bad as he did.

Gerhard banked his plane into a turn that took it around the pathetic little lifeboat that contained the last few survivors from the sunken ship. As he dived out of the sun, flattening out just a few feet above the sea, he knew that he was betraying every principle he had, wilfully casting aside any shreds of decency and honour that he still possessed and joining his brother and all the black-hearted bastards like him in the legion of the damned. And he didn't care.

The lifeboat was rushing ever closer. He could see the people in it pathetically waving their fists. One quick blast from the 109's guns would obliterate that tiny boat and every man inside it. Gerhard's finger tightened around the trigger.

And then he saw the ghost again. Black hair. Black dark glasses.

His first instinct was to fire, and keep firing until the ghost was blown out of his mind's eye for good.

But a millisecond later something told him, 'No, don't,' and then he flashed over the lifeboat without firing, soared up into the sky, looped around and swooped down into another dive, back the way he had just come.

'Go on then, you Nazi bastard! If you want to kill us, here we are! Just get on with it!'

Bowyer's voice was near hysterical with desperation. The pilot was toying with them, taunting them. He could kill them whenever he wanted. So why didn't he?

'Here he comes again,' said Saffron. Faced with certain death, she found that she was blessed by an unexpected sense of calmness. Everything was going to be all right. She was going to be with Gerhard again, where there was no war to keep them apart, and everything would be all right.

She kept her eyes fixed on the plane and stood to greet it, standing quite still, offering herself as a sacrifice.

The ghost was her! Gerhard knew it was impossible, and yet that figure standing so tall in the hull off the lifeboat, shaking out her hair, looking straight at him . . . that was Saffron. He knew it as sure as he knew his own self. *She's alive! My God, it's true, she's alive.*

He slowed the plane down until it was as close to stalling speed as he dared go, then he slid back the canopy of his cockpit, feeling the wind rushing at his face like the breath of life itself. As he flew over the lifeboat, Gerhard waved. He could have sworn he saw her smile.

Then he was past the lifeboat and now he really couldn't make another fly-past. His fuel status had been critical before he had decided to remain over the ship. Now it was disastrous.

Gerhard didn't care. Saffron Courtney was still alive. Love

and hope came surging back into his heart. So what if his 109 had no fuel? He didn't even need a plane. He could fly back to Greece all by himself, on the wings of joy itself.

'Good Lord,' the doctor said, 'what an extraordinary thing to do. Do you suppose he was saying, "Well played?" You know, for putting up such a good fight?'

'Jerry don't say things like that, doc,' Bowyer said. 'Not 'is style at all. Nah, I reckon it was more like taunting us. Unless . . .' A sly, cheeky grin crossed his face. 'Well, if you don't mind me saying, Miss . . .'

Saffron didn't even hear him. She was still trying to come to terms with what she had seen, or thought she had seen in the cockpit of the passing plane. She didn't know whether to whoop with joy, or cry bitter tears at the endless cruelties of fate.

'Miss . . . ?' Bowyer repeated.

Saffron forced herself to pay attention to the people around her. 'What is it?' she asked.

'I was saying you looked such a picture, standing there, like a proper film star or summink . . . I reckon our Kraut chum took one look at you and thought even he couldn't go shooting a girl like that. I mean, what a waste, eh?'

'It certainly would take a very bad man indeed to shoot an unarmed young woman in cold blood,' the doctor agreed.

Saffron had not said a word. But then the thought struck her that she had not been unarmed, not when it mattered. *I hit that plane with my guns. And if it was Gerhard's plane . . . No, it was, I'm sure it was, why else would he have waved at me? . . . Oh God I almost killed him. And I'd never have known what I'd done, or how close he had been. And if I had killed him . . .*

And then she broke down in tears, and the doctor put his arm around her shoulder and said, 'There-there, my dear. It's all right. We have all had the most terrible experience and you

461

have behaved quite remarkably. But it's over now. We shall soon be rescued, I'm quite sure of that. Everything is going to be all right. Just you wait and see . . .'

It was early evening before a Royal Navy motor torpedo boat, sent from Crete in response to Captain McAloon's signals, finally found them. As Leon was being hauled aboard, the doctor took Saffron to one side and said, 'Your father is very badly wounded. Provided the wound does not get infected he should live, but whether he'll ever walk again is another matter.'

Saffron did not reply. She was too physically and emotionally drained by the battle and its aftermath to formulate any words. A sailor helped her aboard the torpedo boat and she was given a cup of tea, that standard British cure-all for any disaster, great or small. As the brew worked its magic, Saffron opened up her bag and gave a rueful shake of the head. After all the precautions she had taken and all the hell she had been through, those carefully wrapped and greased possessions had never even had a single drop of water on them. She took out one of her precious photos of Gerhard and hunched over it, so that she could look at him without anyone else knowing. It was wonderful to think that he was still alive.

But then Saffron shook her head again and put her petty treasures away as she reminded herself of all that had been lost.

The pride of the Courtney Trading fleet had been sunk. Many good men had lost their lives, and it had all been for nothing. Greece's gold was lying on the sea floor hundreds of feet beneath them and no one was ever going to find it again.

Gerhard ran out of fuel about ten kilometres north of Athens, still a hundred shy of his base. By then, though, he had risen slowly and steadily to an altitude of seven thousand metres. When the engine cut out he just let the plane glide, remembering his first glider flights over Bavaria, savouring the absolute peace and quiet after all the clamour of battle, letting his mind relish the image of Saffron, standing so proudly, so bravely and so, so beautifully in that boat, staring death in the eye, and not realizing she was actually looking at love.

Mein Gott! If I had pressed that trigger . . . But I didn't, and that's all that matters now.

He felt quite calm as his inexorable descent continued. All he needed was a reasonably straight stretch of road, even a flat field would do, though there weren't many of those in the rocky, mountainous Greek countryside. For weeks now they had been looking at maps of Greece as they were briefed for one mission or another and he knew that there was a highway that ran parallel to the coast. He looked down from his cockpit and sure enough there it was, with exactly the kind of straight he needed about ten kilometres up ahead.

The Messerschmitt came down over an advancing formation of tanks and men, skimmed the last couple of trucks with millimetres to spare and landed on an empty patch of tarmac. It came to a halt another couple of hundred metres down the road, slewed diagonally across the tarmac.

Gerhard got out of the cockpit, undid his lifejacket and the silk scarf round his neck, then took a packet of cigarettes out of his jacket. Smoking cigarettes, he had discovered, was as inevitable a part of going to war as bad food and bullets. Up ahead he saw another mass of men and armour coming towards him. An open staff car detached itself from the column and raced towards him and an officer got out. Gerhard saw the shoulder tabs of an *Oberst*, a full colonel, on his uniform. He slid down from the plane, threw his cigarette away and snapped to attention.

'What the hell do you think you are doing here?' the colonel asked.

'I was on a mission, *Herr Oberst*. My aircraft was hit and I lost a lot of fuel. I could not return to my base and so I landed on this road, instead.'

'Well you're blocking the way. I've got to get an entire division to the outskirts of Athens by nightfall. So I order you to move your machine.'

'I'm very sorry, sir, but I am unable to do that. As I say, I have no fuel. If some can be found and your men back up a little bit, I should be able to take off without too much trouble.'

'Back up? We haven't backed up for the Tommies. Why the hell should we retreat for you?'

'Alternatively, sir, the land on either side of the road is quite flat. It should be no trouble for your armoured vehicles and trucks to go around the aircraft.'

'I hope this mission of yours was worth it,' the colonel said, grumpily.

'Oh yes sir,' said Gerhard, as a triumphant smile crossed his face. 'We sank a British vessel that was carrying a cargo of great strategic importance. The mission was ordered by *Reichsmarschall* Göring himself. He will be very pleased by its success.'

The colonel took the point. This cocky fly-boy, with his kills painted on the side of his aircraft and his Iron Cross around his neck, was protected by Göring himself.

'I will have my radio operator order some aviation fuel to be brought here as soon as possible. I expect you to leave here as soon as you have been refuelled.'

'Of course, *Herr Oberst*, that will be my pleasure.'

But until that time, Gerhard thought. *I will sit on my plane, smoke my cigarettes, and think about the girl I love.*

All in all, this had been one of the better days on which to be at war.

* * *

Visiting time at the hospital was restricted to set hours in the morning and afternoon. In the fortnight since he had been brought back from Crete to Egypt, Harriet had tried to spend every minute that she was allowed by Leon's bedside, but she was also conscious of the need to prepare their house for his eventual homecoming. The surgeon who had operated on Leon's leg was confident now that it would be saved. But it would be several months before he could even think of walking and even then there was still a possibility that he might be confined to a wheelchair. In either case Harriet would have to make the house easier for him to navigate, and do it before he left the hospital, for she feared he would be too proud to admit he needed help when he finally did come home. So it was that one morning she was at home, rather than the hospital, talking to an architect about replacing steps with ramps and adding handrails to help Leon guide himself, at least in the early days, before he acclimatized. Saffron, however, had taken her place and was sitting at her father's bedside when there was a knock on the door.

'Shall I see who that is?' she said.

Leon nodded.

She went to the door and opened it to find a fresh-faced, bespectacled man in an army captain's uniform. He didn't seem to Saffron's eyes to be more than three or four years older than she was.

'Oh,' he said, when confronted by a beautiful young woman in a summery cotton frock, looking at him with limpid, dark blue eyes.

'Can I help?' she asked, since the captain seemed incapable of making any further conversation.

'Ah, yes, absolutely, of course . . . My name's Carstairs, Military Intelligence. Just wondered if I could have a word with Mr Courtney. I have some information that I have been asked to pass on to him.'

'Then by all means come in, Captain Carstairs.'

He advanced a few paces into the room and stood at the end of the bed while Saffron closed the door behind him.

'Excuse me, Mr Courtney,' Carstairs said, 'but what I have to say is rather hush-hush. It concerns the sinking of the *Star of Khartoum*. For your ears only, as it were.'

'May I ask you a question, Carstairs?' Leon asked.

'By all means, sir.'

'Have you ever been in action? I don't just mean: have you served in a campaign, back at headquarters? I'm talking about the rough stuff, the sharp end, where people get killed.'

'Ah, no sir, I can't say that I have. I'm more of a desk-wallah. Analysis of intelligence is my game.'

'Have you analysed a newspaper lately?'

'I'm sorry, sir, I'm not quite with you.'

'Well, there have been a few stories in the Cairo press about my daughter's actions on the *Star of Khartoum*, fighting off the Luftwaffe. People are saying she deserves a medal. So if you have anything to say about that voyage, then you can say it to her as well, or not at all. Do I make myself clear?'

'Yes sir, absolutely. Might I ask you, Miss Courtney, may I count on your absolute discretion?'

'Of course.'

'Very well then. My message is this . . . You may have become aware that the cargo loaded aboard the *Star of Khartoum* was . . . how can I put this? Of unusual value, let us say.'

'I am,' Leon agreed.

'And I dare say that the knowledge that this cargo has been lost added considerably to the, ah, distress that you might have felt at the sinking of your ship and so many members of its crew . . . and, of course, your own personal injury, sir.'

'You might say that, yes.'

'It may even made you wonder whether it was all worthwhile,' Carstairs said, and the silence that followed confirmed his

466

supposition. He cleared his throat and spoke again. 'What I have to say may, I hope, reassure you that you have, in fact, made a much greater contribution to the war effort than you know. You see, the thing is, the cargo you believe was on the *Star of Khartoum* was, in fact, ah . . . elsewhere.'

'What do you mean?' Saffron exclaimed.

'I mean that your ship was a decoy. The real cargo was on another vessel and has now reached its destination safely, every ounce of it.'

'But that makes it worse, not better. All those men were sacrificed for nothing!'

'No,' Leon corrected her. 'It means that the *Star* was risked, and eventually sunk so that the real cargo could get through. That was an entirely worthwhile mission. My only question to you, Carstairs, is, how did you know that the Germans would take the bait?'

'Well, we left a few clues for them: for example, all those trucks lining up outside the Bank of Greece where prying eyes could see them. In reality, the transfer was made several nights earlier, much more discreetly. And even more importantly, perhaps, we had reason to believe there could be a leak from our end, either here in Cairo, or at the harbour in Alexandria, or even from the vessel itself.'

'You mean a spy in our midst?' Leon asked.

'Something like that, yes.'

'One of our own people?'

'Possibly, or someone else with a reason to support the Nazi cause. There are plenty of nationalists, Jewish as well as Muslim, who want to see the back of us and their enemy's enemy is their friend.'

'Jews supporting Hitler?' said Saffron. 'That hardly seems likely. I've been to Germany, Captain. I know what life is like for Jews there.'

'But not for Jews here, Miss Courtney. Most of them are

467

perfectly friendly to us, but there are some Zionists who want us out of the whole region, Palestine in particular, but Egypt too. Of course, they hate the Muslim radicals even more than they hate us and the feeling is entirely mutual. So if or when we ever leave, they will merrily start slaughtering one another. But for now, we are their common enemy.'

'Well, I wish you luck in finding your man, Carstairs,' Leon said. 'If there is anything I can do, just let me know. You can count on my cooperation.'

'Thank you, sir. That's very good to know. Good day, Mr Courtney, I wish you a speedy recovery.'

'Let me show you out, Captain,' said Saffron and she followed Carstairs to the door and watched him make his way back out into the corridor.

An Egyptian cleaner was busy mopping the linoleum floor. Saffron paid him no attention as she went back into Leon's room.

Leon was tired. He had no energy to spare so he got straight to the point. 'I think your uncle Francis is the spy. He knew about the shipment, and even though I didn't tell him, in so many words, what we were putting on board that ship, he knew enough to be able to give someone else the means to find out the details.'

'Do you really think he'd do that?'

'I wish I could say, "No." But the truth is, I think he's bitter enough and angry enough to betray his family and his country. And we all know what he thinks about fascism, he's never made any secret about that.'

'But what does he have to be angry about? You saved the company and made him a lot of money.'

'That almost makes it worse, I think. When someone gets into that frame of mind, they stop looking at things fairly. And if you do something decent that just makes them better off, they almost resent you all the more. Frank needs me to be the villain in the warped fantasy that goes on in his head. If I don't play that role then he has to go to even greater lengths to invent reasons why I am, despite all appearances, doing him down.'

'What a terrible way to live one's life.'

'Absolutely. But once a person gets stuck in that rut it's almost impossible to drag them out of it unless they really want to change their attitude themselves. In the meantime, we have a second problem. Not only do I suspect that Frank is the spy, I also wonder whether Carstairs wasn't tipping me off that his mob know that it's him.'

'What would be the good of that? What can we do about it?'

'I wish I knew. If I was still in one piece I'd go round and confront him, knock the truth out of him if needs be.'

'And then what? It wouldn't look very good for us – as a family or a firm – if one of the Courtney brothers turned out to be a Nazi spy.'

'It wouldn't look very good for anyone. I suppose that I could give him a choice: go into exile somewhere like Morocco or Spain – a neutral country where he can't cause any trouble – or I could hand him over to the authorities and let him be tried for treason. It's a hanging offence, after all. I'd imagine even Frank would be prepared to toe the line to save his neck.'

'But you can't do that. Not for the time being, anyway.'

'Don't remind me.'

'Maybe I could, though, or Harriet. Or, I know, how about Uncle Dorian or Grandma? Would he listen to them?'

'We can't involve them without telling them exactly what we were doing in Athens, and that's not on. I wish I had my strength back. I swear I'd find the nearest bus and push my darling brother under it.'

'I think it's probably just as well that you can't do that,' Saffron said. 'Now, get some rest. The important thing is for you to get well again. And if the worst comes to the worst, and

Uncle Francis is exposed as a spy, and the scandal ruins Courtney Trading, you will still have Lusima and Harriet and me, and we will all be perfectly fine.'

'Yes, that's true. But what about Dorian and Grandma and my sisters?'

'They can all come and live at Lusima too. We're hardly short of space!'

'Darling Saffron,' Leon said, squeezing her hand, 'what a lovely, kind, splendid daughter you are.'

'You're very sweet, but this daughter is going to be strict with you. Harriet will be here to see you later, but in the meantime, you must get some rest.'

She kissed her father's forehead, said goodbye and left the room.

Outside in the corridor she noticed that the cleaner had disappeared even though she could see very clearly from the marked, bone-dry state of much of the linoleum that he had only done a small portion of his work. *If Harriet ran this place they'd never dare behave like that*, Saffron thought, and was smiling to herself as she followed the signs to the exit.

The moment Saffron had gone back into her father's room, having said farewell to Captain Carstairs, the cleaner who had been wiping down the corridor floor picked up his mop and pail and scuttled away down the corridor towards the stairs. Two minutes later he was coming out of the hospital's staff exit and heading for the Old City. He had news for Hassan al-Banna and the sooner he heard it the better.

Two hours later, a message was on its way, via a forward listening post of the Afrika Korps to Berlin.

When Saffron arrived home, Harriet asked her how her father was.

'He was on rather good form, I thought, but he became a little tired so I told him to get some rest before you come to see him.'

470

'Did he do as he was told?'

'He did, actually. I think he was feeling co-operative towards me. He said I was a lovely, kind, splendid daughter, which was very sweet of him.'

'Well that's just what you are,' said Harriet.

'Do you mind if I pour myself a drink?' Saffron asked. 'I rather fancy a nice, cold G'n'T.'

'My dear girl, you don't have to ask me permission. You're grown woman. Just be a darling and make me one too. And don't be stingy with the gin!'

Saffron took her glass out onto the terrace, which looked across the garden towards the Nile. She thought about everything that she had heard at the hospital, and what her father said about Uncle Francis. It appalled her to think of all the death and destruction his betrayal had caused, and it shamed her, too. For he was a Courtney, just as she was, and his actions shamed the whole family.

Perhaps it's right that he should be exposed. Perhaps we deserve to have our names dragged through the mud along with his.

But then Saffron told herself that she had not done anything to be ashamed of, and nor had her father. Why should they be tarred by Francis's brush? And what good would come of having the story of his treachery made public? No one would benefit except for those who wanted Britain and its Empire to fall. So the fewer people who knew what he had done, the better.

But he can't just get away with it, he just can't!

Saffron sipped her drink. She ran the problem through in her mind. Then the solution suddenly presented itself, like the answer to a complex equation. She ran back over her reasoning to see if she could find a flaw, but there was none. The answer was correct.

And now Saffron knew exactly what had to be done.

* * *

Is the mint tea to your taste?' asked Hassan al-Banna.

'It'll do,' replied Francis Courtney gracelessly.

'Perhaps a little more sugar would improve it.'

'Possibly.' Francis gave an impatient sigh. 'Look, I'm not hear to prattle about mint tea and spoons of sugar. You wanted to see me. I'd like to know why.'

Al-Banna shook his head, regretfully. Allah was all-knowing and all-wise. There had to be a reason why He had sent this oafish, ill-mannered, ungrateful infidel into his life. But there were times when it was hard to know what that reason might be. *Perhaps He just wants to try my patience.* Yes, that might be it.

'Our mutual friends are not happy. You misled them about the *Star of Khartoum.*'

'What do you mean I misled them? I told them where it was going, what cargo it was picking up and where it was then going to sail. Then they sank it, which was the aim of the exercise. I'm the one who should be unhappy. They were meant to get rid of my brother and that little brat of his. But the two of them are still alive. What have they got to say about that, then . . . eh? Eh?!'

'They have more important things to concern them than the life or death of two insignificant individuals.'

'So what does concern them, then?'

'The gold was not on the ship.'

'So where was it then?'

'Our friends do not know. But if I were you, Mr Courtney, I would make it my business to find out. If you could tell them where it really is, they may be less inclined to suspect that you deliberately misled them.'

'I did no such thing! I told them what I knew, what my own damn brother had told me. He's the one who misled you, if anyone did. Not me.'

'I do not believe so. There is no evidence to suggest that

472

your brother is connected to British Intelligence. I think he was the first dupe. I think they used him to be their decoy. He told you because he wanted to persuade you that it was vital to send the *Star of Khartoum* to Greece. The question is: did British Intelligence know that you would pass the information on to us? If they did, then you have been compromised and your position is, hmm . . .' Hassan searched for the right word. 'Vulnerable . . . yes. You are very vulnerable.'

'You mean they're going to do me in?' asked Francis, his face suddenly ashen. A dribble of sweat ran down his temple. 'But I have done nothing wrong. It's not fair!'

'Only the English are foolish enough to believe that life should be fair. The situation is perfectly reasonable, however. You have caused our friends a great deal of trouble, all of which was wasted. Now you owe them. If you can find out where the British have taken the Greek gold reserves, and prove that your information is correct, then there will not be a problem. If you cannot . . .' he shrugged. 'Allah is just. You will receive precisely what you deserve.'

Francis was almost weeping from fear, and anger and a furious sense of self-pity. He had done everything he could to help the cause. He had passed on information that he believed to be both true and of vital significance. How was he to know that Leon was lying to him? And Leon had been lying, knowingly and deliberately misleading him, he was sure of that.

He stopped off at the Sporting Club for a couple of whiskies on the way home and then walked, only somewhat the worse for wear, the short distance to his flat, in a smart new block between the club and the river. He opened the door, threw his jacket and hat onto the end of the sofa and went to pour himself another drink.

The doorbell rang. Frank frowned. 'Who in Hades wants to see me at this time of night?' he muttered to himself and then felt a stab of fear as the thought struck him: *Have the bloody Germans sent someone to do me in?*

No, that wasn't possible. He had been warned of what would happen, but given a chance to make amends. And as long as they thought he could find the gold's real location, he was more use alive than dead.

He took a deep breath, as much to sober himself up as anything else, and opened the door.

Then he saw who it was and barked, 'What the bloody hell are you doing here?'

'Hello Uncle Francis,' said Saffron, 'aren't you going to let me in?'

'Oh, yes, I suppose I must. Come on then.'

Saffron stepped through the door, noticing the bitter twist to her uncle's mouth as she walked by him. The front door of the apartment opened onto a wide hall that had been expensively decorated, with marble tiles on the floor, walls papered in a deep, rich, oriental red and a modern, black lacquer console table with a matching mirror above it, against the wall to one side. Francis led her through to the drawing room at the end of the hall. The far wall was almost entirely comprised of glass doors that opened onto a balcony, with a spectacular view across the Nile towards the Old City.

'I adore your flat, Uncle Francis,' Saffron said. 'I've often wondered what it was like. When was it you moved in?'

'Summer of '39, just before the balloon went up. Typical bad luck, I could have got it for half the price, more like a quarter actually, if I'd waited another three months.'

'Isn't it nice, the way the company's success has made life so much nicer for everyone? Dorian's studio in Alex is divine.'

'I played my part, you know. It wasn't just your blessed father.'

'Oh I know. You brought in all that German business. It's so sad that all had to end. I say, you couldn't get me a drink, could you?'

'Oh, yes, of course. Forgot my manners,' Francis blustered. 'I don't have many people over, if truth be told. Hardly anyone in fact. A chap forgets how to be a decent host after a while, if he doesn't keep his hand in. Do you drink? Alcohol, I mean?'

'Yes, of course I do,' Saffron giggled. 'I'm quite grown-up, you know, almost twenty-two.'

'Are you really? Good Lord, how time flies. So, what's your poison?'

For a second, Saffron caught a flash of the man Francis Courtney used to be and might have still been had he not chosen to live in bitterness, rather than hope; accentuating all the ills done to him, rather than the kindnesses; suspecting the motives of others, rather than trusting in the common decency.

'Could you make me a martini?'

'Don't see why not. I'm a whisky man myself.'

Saffron found herself a chair and placed her shoulder bag open on the cushion next to her, while Francis made her cocktail. It was cold and strong with just the faintest suggestion of vermouth. 'Mmm,' she said, 'that's perfect. You should open your own bar, Uncle Francis, call it Courtney's Bar and Grill.'

Francis had sat down. His glass, which he had refilled after making Saffron's martini, was already empty.

'I say, Uncle, you need a refill. Don't get up, I'll get it for you.'

She took his glass, walked across to the drinks cabinet, refilled it and put it down on the side table next to Francis's chair, just next to a marble table-lamp shaped like a classical column. Then she walked over to the windows, opened one up and stood there, leaning against the frame. 'Your view is quite breathtaking,' she said. 'Makes me think of that song . . .' She hummed the first bars of 'You Belong to Me': 'See the pyramids along the Nile . . .'

Come on! Saffron thought as she tried to remember the second line. *Get out of that chair. You have to be standing up!*

'Do come and look, Uncle Francis, one of the restaurant boats is going by. There are people dancing on the deck. Listen! Can you hear the music?'

Francis downed his glass and got unsteadily to his feet. 'I see 'em go by all the time, but if you insist . . .'

Saffron waited till he was standing by her, almost as close as a lover might be, and then she said, 'So, Uncle Francis, why did you betray us to the Germans?'

I did no such thing!' Francis protested. He suddenly became aware that he was drunk. He couldn't think straight, couldn't work out how to get out of a hole that seemed to be getting deeper and deeper, the longer the night went on.

'Yes you did!' the girl snapped. She'd dropped the sweet-little-niece act now and there was a tough, aggressive pitch to her voice as she went on, 'You told them your brother was sailing to Piraeus . . . Your own brother! The man who saved you from going bust. The man whose money enabled you to buy this ridiculous gin-palace where you can live, all alone, no one coming round, boo-hoo-hoo.'

'I earned the money that bought this place! I did! Not him!'

'If you did, it was only because you sold yourself to the Nazis. Admit it, you work for them. You told them where the *Star of Khartoum* was bound, didn't you?'

She stabbed a red-painted fingernail at his chest to emphasize the point.

'You told them it was picking up the Greek gold, didn't you?'

She poked him again, harder this time.

'Stop doing that!'

'Oh, don't you like it when a girl shows you up? Well I can't say that I care what you do or don't like. My father, your brother,

476

is lying in a hospital with his leg smashed to bits. He may never walk again . . . because of you.'

Damn it, she jabbed me again! Francis thought. 'I said, stop it!' he barked, getting properly angry. He took a step towards her, making it threatening, expecting her to back away.

Saffron stood her ground.

'I'm not scared of you. I've been to war, actual fighting, the kind you've never seen. I've been put up for the George Medal, you know, for extreme gallantry in the face of enemy fire. They came at us time and time again, you know, the Germans . . . the ones who somehow seemed to know exactly where we were . . . who picked the *Star of Khartoum* out from all the other ships desperately steaming away from Greece, trying to get back to Alex . . . And it was all . . .'

Stab!

'Because . . .'

Stab!

'Of you!'

She poked her hand at him again, but this time he batted it away.

Saffron slapped him hard across the face, jerking his head and making him feel dizzy as he stumbled back from the force of the blow.

Christ! Have I hit him too hard? Saffron thought. Her uncle seemed dazed, lost. *No, come on, you can't give up now! You mustn't!*

And then the anger in him cut through his incapacity and adrenalin sharpened his wits and gave him a little new strength.

'I'll get you for that, you little bitch!' he snarled. And he came at her, punching at her, aiming for her pretty face, wanting to smash it, driving her back into the room.

Saffron put her arms up to defend her head and winced as his blows bruised her flesh and thudded against her bones.

477

'Yes!' Francis shouted, punctuating his words with his fists. 'I told the Germans everything! I wanted you dead! Both of you!'

Then, without warning, Francis changed his point of attack and aimed a short, hard punch beneath Saffron's raised elbows so that it thudded into her solar plexus. She gasped as the air was driven from her body and as she struggled desperately for breath, she dropped her guard.

'I want you dead!' Francis screamed again and he hit her right in the mouth, splitting her lip and catching her nose as well.

Saffron cried out in pain as the blood streamed from her nostrils and mouth. She stumbled backwards, caught the backs of her legs on the side of the sofa and fell backwards onto it, landing beside her bag.

She looked up and saw Francis coming towards her. The drinks he had consumed had made his step unsteady, but that was small consolation to Saffron. For now she saw him grab hold of the table-lamp that had stood beside his chair. As she scrabbled backwards on the sofa, dragging the bag with her, he ripped the plug from its socket, pulled the shade off its mount and grabbed the lamp just below the light bulb. Now he was brandishing it like a marble club, with its thick, square base acting like the head of a mace.

Francis was completely in the grip of his rage, ranting incoherently as he came towards the sofa. Saffron shoved her right hand into her open bag.

He raised the lamp up above his head. He half twisted his body as he prepared to put all the strength behind the swing that would send the stone column smashing into her skull.

And that was when Saffron pulled her right hand from the bag, grabbed it with her left, raised both hands and, as his eyes widened in horror at the sight of the pistol she was holding, shot Francis Courtney right between the eyes.

* * *

Saffron took a deep breath and looked around. She had been expecting to have to manufacture a scene to fit the story she wanted to tell. But Uncle Francis had unknowingly played his part to such perfection that no trickery was required. The impact of the bullet at point-blank range had knocked him backwards and he had dropped the lamp. But it was lying right next to his body, which would back up her account of what happened. Meanwhile, the blood was still flowing from the punch to her face. She ran her tongue along the backs of her teeth, gingerly testing them to see if any were loose. None were, and when she put a hankie to her face to mop up some of the blood her nose felt bruised and bleeding but not actually broken. That was a relief. A battered nose gave a man a certain roguish charm but it was not something any young woman would wish to emulate.

Satisfied that all was as it should be, she called the police. Saffron wondered whether to make herself sound like a panicking, hysterical female but decided against it. She was known for keeping her head under fire. She should certainly sound upset at what had happened, but no one would be surprised that she still had her wits about her.

'I wish to report a violent death,' she said, when she was put through to the duty officer, who was English, for the police operated in Egypt as they did throughout the Empire, with native junior ranks under British command.

'It's my uncle. We had an argument,' Saffron explained. 'He was very drunk and he lost his temper. It was awful . . . he attacked me and he . . . he punched me in the face. Then he tried to kill me, with a marble lampstand and I, I . . . well, I shot him. And I think he's dead.'

'Stay there, Miss, we'll be round in a jiffy. Don't touch or move anything. Where is the body?'

'In the drawing room.'

'Then I suggest you go into the kitchen and wait there.

I strongly advise you not to try to leave the premises, Miss. Otherwise I'll have to put out a warrant for your arrest and we wouldn't want that, would we now?'

Saffron did as she was told. She half-expected to hear one of the neighbours hammering on the door, wondering what was going on. But the block had been built with its occupants' privacy in mind, so the walls were thick. And there had only been a single shot. Anyone who had heard it, Saffron concluded, might well not have known what the sound was and would probably wait to see if there were any other noises before doing anything. So when there finally was a knocking on the door, it was the police. Saffron, who had checked her appearance in the hall mirror before answering the door, had been startled but also gratified to discover that her throbbing, hurting face looked even worse than it felt.

There were four of them: a plainclothes detective, two uniformed constables and a photographer. 'My name is Detective Sergeant Ralph Riley,' the plainclothes man said. 'Could you give me your name and address, please, Miss?'

Saffron did as Riley asked and showed him her identity card by way of confirmation. He ordered the two constables to stand guard outside and take the names of any inquisitive neighbours who might come by to have a look. He told Saffron to sit down at the kitchen table and wait for a few minutes. Then he and the photographer went into the drawing room to examine the crime scene. Ten minutes or so later, Riley reappeared, sat down opposite her and asked her to give her account.

'I came round to see if I could persuade Uncle Francis to come and visit my father, who's in hospital,' she said. 'Daddy and I were on a ship that was sunk in the Aegean and he was badly wounded and it's just awful that his own brother hasn't been to see him. Well, my uncle became very cross. I think he resented my father because of a business deal between them, even though he had done very well out of it. And I think he was quite drunk, too. He had two full tumblers of whisky, very quickly, one after the other while I was here, and I got the impression he'd already had quite a bit to drink by the time I arrived.'

Riley looked up from his notebook. 'Hang on, I've just realized . . . I thought your name sounded familiar . . . Saffron Courtney, of course, you're the young woman that's been in the paper. You're up for a medal.'

He sounded as though he was just about to ask her to sign her name in his notebook and inscribe it to his wife.

'That's right,' Saffron replied.

'Well, I never, you really have been out of the frying pan and into the fire, haven't you?'

'I suppose I have, yes.'

'Now, the crime scene all looks quite straightforward. You have clearly suffered a blow to the face. When we've finished our chat I'll have the photographer take some pictures of you to confirm that fact. And unless there was a third person here that you haven't been telling us about . . .'

He looked at Saffron.

'No, we were alone in the flat,' she said. 'My uncle doesn't have any live-in staff and he made a point of saying that he saw very few people here.'

'I'm sure the neighbours can confirm the truth or otherwise of those statements. But it certainly seems as though your uncle hit you. There are blood spatters on his right hand and the cuff of his jacket. And I dare say we will find your uncle's fingerprints all over that lamp that you say he was intending to use as a weapon against you. There is only one thing, however, that puzzles me, Miss Courtney.' The detective looked at Saffron and now there was nothing remotely starry-eyed about him as he said, 'Why would a young woman paying a social visit to her uncle just happen to have a Beretta 418 pistol about her person?'

'Because I always carry it, Sergeant.'

'Why would that be, then?'

'Force of habit I suppose. I used to be Major General Wilson's driver. I had to take him right up to the battlefield. We MTC girls are civilians, of course, so we aren't armed. But my father felt I should have some means of defending myself, just in case of trouble and General Wilson . . . well, I shouldn't really say this, because I don't want to get him in hot water . . .'

'I wouldn't worry, Miss. He is a general, after all.'

'Well, he said he would turn a blind eye, provided that I could prove to him that I knew how to handle a gun, which I could. I grew up in Kenya, you see, so I was used to shooting, so that wasn't a problem. He also insisted that I had to keep my gun out of sight. So my father got me the Beretta, because it could just be popped in my shoulder bag, and it's been with me ever since.'

'Have you had reason to use it before? In anger, I mean . . .'

'Yes. During Operation Compass, at the beginning of this year, we ran into an Italian patrol and had to shoot our way out.'

'Have you shot a man before, Miss?'

Saffron suddenly found her composure beginning to break, and this time there was nothing feigned about it at all. She bit her bottom lip and then said, 'Yes, I have . . . That's how I knew what to do . . . but . . . but it's a horrible thing to have to shoot another human being . . . and he was my uncle, my own family . . .'

She started crying and pulled her bloodstained handkerchief out of her bag.

'I'm very sorry, Miss Courtney, but I will need that hand-kerchief. Evidence,' Riley said. He got up from his seat and fetched a tea-towel that had been hanging on a rail in front of the cooker. 'There you go.'

'Thank you. It just hit me . . . what had happened. My uncle wasn't a nice man, Sergeant. But I wouldn't want . . . I wouldn't want all this.'

'I'm sure you wouldn't. I'll just ask the photographer to take your picture and then one of my men will drive you home. I must ask you to stay in Cairo. Are you expecting any orders to go anywhere, by any chance?'

'No, I'm on extended leave.'

'Then spend it here, if you don't mind, until I say otherwise.'

The following day, Leon told Harriet to hire the finest criminal lawyer in Cairo, Joseph Azerad, to handle Saffron's case.

'Have no fear, Mr Courtney, I will make sure that there is no case to handle,' Azerad said.

Leon had already informed him of Frank's admiration for Oswald Mosley. Azerad immediately called the head of the Cairo police and stated in no uncertain terms that it would be an outrage if a brave young woman who had served her nation with distinction and whose face was battered by the fists of an evil brute should be blamed for what was clearly an act of self-defence.

He also got in touch with contacts who worked on the newsdesks of the *Gazette* and the *Mail* and informed them that the famously beautiful and heroic Saffron Courtney had been forced to defend herself from an assault from her uncle, a known fascist sympathizer. He told the man from the *Gazette* that if he went to the Sporting Club he would soon find plenty of people willing to confirm Francis Courtney's status as a long-time Mosley supporter, and he gave the man from the *Mail* the address of the doctor who was examining Saffron's wounds and the time of her appointment.

Saffron, who had been forewarned, looked right into the camera, while raising a hand as if to protect herself from its intrusion. Her face had swollen considerably since the point at which the police had photographed her and was now covered with vivid bruises. No one who saw the pictures could possibly doubt that she had been assaulted, and another set of bruises on her forearms proved that she had tried to defend herself against her uncle's attacks before his fists eventually broke through.

By the end of the day it was clear that Francis had been holding the lampstand, close to the light fixture, supporting Saffron's testimony that he had been trying to hit her with the base, while the angle at which the .418 calibre bullet had entered his skull supported her claim that she had been helpless on the sofa, firing up at him as he advanced upon her.

By the end of the week the case had been dropped. Saffron received a telegram from Jumbo.

HEARD ABOUT EVENTS IN CAIRO STOP THINK YOU NEED A CHANGE OF SCENERY STOP COME TO JERUSALEM STOP BY ORDER WILSON

As Saffron packed her bags, Mr Brown was reading a detailed account of the shooting. And by the time he reached the last sentence he knew that he should fly to Cairo.

It took several weeks to arrange the journey, but he was eventually able to obtain a berth on an RAF Liberator bomber carrying a pair of senior officers who'd been transferred to the North African front. The pilot headed across the Bay of Biscay and then on a course over neutral Portugal before coming into land at Gibraltar. The following day he flew south over Morocco before turning east across the Sahara, to the south of the warzone in the Western Desert, before hitting the Nile, which he used as the guide to take him back up to Cairo.

When Mr Brown disembarked, he allowed himself a day's rest, for it had been a long, hazardous and tiring journey. Then he went to the High Commission and made some discreet enquiries. Having discovered what he needed to know, he boarded a train that would take him to El Kantara in northeast

Egypt, from which a sleeper service ran to Haifa, on the Mediterranean coast of Palestine. Once there, he changed trains for a final time en route to Jerusalem.

He really had gone to a very great deal of trouble. Now he was about to discover whether it had all been worthwhile.

It's very simple, Courtney,' Jumbo said, soon after she had arrived at the British army headquarters that occupied one wing of the magnificent King David Hotel in Jerusalem.

He led her up to the map of the Eastern Mediterranean and Middle East. 'Here's Cairo,' he said, pointing to its location towards the bottom-right of the map. 'Don't need to tell you that, what? And just to the east of Cairo, here's the Suez Canal, the gateway to India, the Far East and Australasia. If we were ever to lose control of the Canal, that would be curtains for the Empire. So, Rommel's charging along the coast road towards Cairo from the west, and getting rather too close for comfort. The Jerries have occupied Greece and Crete, meaning that they're now just a short hop across the Eastern Med from Crete to Alex.'

'But they could never get an invasion force past the Royal Navy, surely sir?'

'You're quite right, my girl. But look up here.'

He pointed his swagger stick at the territories of Lebanon and Syria, directly north of where they now were in Palestine. 'After the last war, we took control of Palestine and Transjordan and the French got their sticky mitts on Syria and Lebanon. Now those mandates are under Vichy control.'

'And the Vichy government is extremely sympathetic to the Germans.'

'And so . . . ?' Jumbo asked, exactly like one of Saffron's Oxford tutors leading her through an academic argument.

'May I ask a question, sir?'

'Fire away.'

'What forces do the Vichy French have in the region?'

'About forty-five thousand French, Lebanese and Syrian troops, the best part of a hundred tanks, three hundred aircraft and a modest naval force: couple of destroyers and three submarines. What does that tell you?'

Saffron stepped up to the map, looked at it for a few seconds and then said, 'If they were feeling daring the Germans could put men ashore at, say, Sidon, here, south of Beirut. Or they could go further north, up by the Turkish border, if they wanted to stay away from our fleet. In either case, they would land on friendly soil and link up with the Vichy forces. Then they could either go eastwards, towards the oilfields of Iraq and Iran. Or they could strike south and if they broke through our forces here in Palestine, they would then advance on Cairo and the Canal and catch us in a pincer movement: them from the north and Rommel from the west.'

'Oxford girl, aren't you?'

'Yes, sir.'

'Ever considered going to Staff College instead? By God, I wish the young men under my command had half your grasp of military strategy. Might I ask what you would do in my shoes?'

'Yes sir. I would attack, as fast and as hard as possible before the Germans have a chance to do anything.'

'And that is precisely what I have been ordered to do. They're calling it Operation Exporter. We're hitting the French hard with a mixed bunch of our own chaps, as well as Indians, Australians, and even Free French.'

'Will they fight their own countrymen?'

'Apparently they can't wait to get at 'em. Hate them all the more for being turncoats. Anyway we're hitting them from all sides, marching on Beirut and Damascus as well as securing all the major oil pipelines and ports. I'll be running the show from here, of course, but you know me, I like to see what's going on at the sharp end, so there'll be a fair amount of dashing about. Think you're up to it?'

'Absolutely, sir. Can't wait.'

'That's the spirit! And I can assure you of one thing, Courtney. This time we are going to win.'

Wilson was as good as his word. The disasters of Greece were followed by a series of triumphs in the Levant. It took just over a month to rout the Vichy French, destroying most of their aircraft and ships in the process. By 12 July, Saffron was in the old Crusader port of Acre where Jumbo was sitting down to talks with his French counterpart General Henri Dentz and a gaggle of pompous, but utterly ineffectual Vichy bureaucrats in the officers' mess of the Sidney Smith barracks. By ten that night they had agreed a ceasefire. Another day and a half of talks led to the signing of a treaty that handed over absolute control of all the French territory in Syria and Lebanon to the British. The armistice treaty was dated 14 July. It was Bastille Day, the French national day, an occasion for patriotism and pride. But on this occasion the dateline to an abject surrender.

A similar Allied campaign had defeated nationalist rebels in Iraq, securing the country's oilfields, and plans were afoot to do the same in Iran. A great swathe of the Middle East was now secure in Allied hands. In the desert a sort of stalemate had been reached. General Wavell had failed in an attempt to push Rommel back across the desert and relieve the siege of Tobruk, and been sacked as a result. But Rommel's lines of communication were stretched so tight, and his supplies of fuel, food and water had to make such a long and perilous journey across the desert to reach his army that he was finding it hard to make any more progress.

But all of this was now just a sideshow. A new conflict had begun, one that made every other campaign in the war so far seem like a mere skirmish. Hitler had reneged on his peace treaty with Stalin and flung the full might of his war machine at the Soviet Union in Operation Barbarossa, the most massive military operation in the entire history of warfare.

The carnage on the Eastern Front had begun.

You know, Meerbach, I think you might be right after all,' said Schrumpp one still, sunlit summer evening, as they stood outside the tent, pitched beside an airfield in the midst of the endless wheat fields of the Ukraine that served as an officers' mess. 'Even I'm getting bored with killing the Ivans in their decrepit old planes. It almost makes me nostalgic for the days of Spitfires and Hurricanes. If you shot one of them down it felt like a real achievement.'

Gerhard grinned, 'We'll make a proper gentleman of you yet!'

The squadron had ceased operations for the day, but now the drone of aero-engines could be heard, coming from the southwest.

'Can't be one of ours,' said Schrumpp. 'Sounds like a Tante Ju.'

'Must be someone important, then,' said Gerhard, for only the most senior officers and Party officials were transported around the front on one of Junkers Ju 52 airliners that had been requisitioned by the Wehrmacht for wartime service.

'Do you think we should make ourselves look a bit more like proper German officers?' asked Schrumpp, rubbing a hand over his unshaved chin.

'I wouldn't bother, they're probably not here for us.'

The tri-engined plane landed, came rolling to a halt and an open Mercedes staff car suddenly appeared from behind the control tower – or what still remained of the tower after the retreating Russians had tried to destroy it – and sped across the parched brown grass to meet the new arrivals.

'Here we go,' said Schrumpp as the fuselage door was opened

and a crewman placed a short step-ladder beneath it. Two men emerged from the plane: one in uniform and the other in a smart suit and tie, carrying a briefcase.

'What's an *SS-brigadeführer* doing here?' Gerhard wondered aloud.

Schrumpp shrugged. 'It's very strange. You hardly ever saw them in France or Greece, but now the whole place is crawling with them. I was talking about it to Rolf the other day. He says there's a new kind of SS unit. They're calling them Task Forces – and wherever we go they're right behind.'

'So what's their task?'

'Search me. But if it's the SS then it's probably to do with the Jews. Maybe they've come to plan those new homelands they're always going on about. I mean, that's the plan, isn't it? Ship the Yids out of the Reich and dump them all out here. You'd think we had enough on our hands conquering Russia without worrying about them too. *Ach*, the hell with it! Come on, old man, let's go and find another beer . . .'

Gerhard walked back into the tent, no longer paying attention as Schrumpp got the drinks, handed Gerhard his glass and then became caught up in another conversation with some other pilots. Gerhard winced every time Schrumpp or one of the other men in the squadron referred to 'Yids' or 'Hebrews', but at the ripe old age of thirty, he was a grizzled veteran compared to most of them. They'd been stuffed full of Nazi propaganda since they were schoolboys. They didn't know any better. But still, Schrumpp was right, this campaign was different.

When they invaded France, no one suggested that the French were an inferior race. That would have been absurd. But from the moment that they had first been told what Barbarossa was really about, the campaign had been presented as a war between races: noble German Aryans against sub-human Slavs and Jews. The propaganda films were filled with images of ugly, hook-nosed, shifty-looking men who embodied every stereotype of the evil, untrustworthy, endlessly conspiring Jew. And though the words were never said out loud, the tone of all the Party language was unmistakably destructive. These were people who did not just need to be beaten, or even enslaved. They were to be destroyed.

Gerhard could not begin to imagine what that actually meant. How could one wipe an entire race from the earth? It was inconceivable. But he did know that he could not bear to live in any world in which such thoughts could even be expressed as a nation's governing principles. Nor could he see how he and Saffron could ever be united, or be able to live in peace together in such a world. Of course one could not consort with one's enemies in wartime, that was normal. But it seemed to Gerhard that in the event of Nazi victory, the defeated peoples would always be enemies, to be degraded, exploited and enslaved. They were certainly not to be loved, let alone married.

So what am I to do?

Gerhard had always considered that he was not fighting for Hitler, but for Germany. There was no dishonour in serving one's country – his country. But was there a difference any more between Nazism and Germany? And if there wasn't, what in God's name was a decent man to do?

Saffron was lying by the pool at the King David Hotel, wearing a white two-piece swimsuit, reading *Rebecca* and sipping from a glass of beer, which she had sat in an ice-bucket to keep it suitably cold. The beer was making her drowsy, so she put the book down on the tiles beside her lounger and lay back. This was her first day of leave after weeks of frantic activity. An afternoon snooze seemed like the absolute height of self-indulgent luxury.

She was just on the verge of dropping off when she heard a familiar voice say, 'Hello Saffron. Not quite Oxford in November, is it?'

Saffron pulled herself up to a sitting position, gave a sharp little shake of the head to wake herself up, then lifted her hand to shade her eyes so that she could see as she said, 'Good afternoon, Mr Brown. I hope you haven't come all this way on my account.'

He gave one of his enigmatic smiles and said, 'May I?' as he lowered himself to perch on the end of the lounger next to hers. He looked at her in that disconcertingly direct way of his. There was nothing sexual or threatening in his gaze, but it made her feel uneasy nonetheless.

'Please do,' she said, steeling herself to keep her wits about her.

Mr Brown was as dapper as always. He had exchanged the dark, woollen suit he habitually wore in England for a pale beige linen one, but he still wore a stiff collar and tie in defiance of the heat. He replaced the Panama hat that he had politely removed to address her and sat, quite contentedly, saying nothing.

Saffron looked around. Her light cotton kaftan was lying bundled up behind her bag. 'Do you mind if I put some more clothes on?'

'By all means do,' Mr Brown said, still looking at her.

'Would you please avert your gaze?'

'Of course, how rude of me.'

Saffron picked up the kaftan, which she had bought on a trip to Grandma's favourite market stall in Cairo, and pulled it over her head. Then she reached into her bag, found her powder compact and checked her face in its mirror. She pushed a few stray strands of hair back under the headband she was wearing and then applied her lipstick. There was nothing quite like that essential splash of warpaint to make her ready for a verbal battle.

Mr Brown meanwhile had spotted a waiter. He waved him over. 'Some tea, please, lapsang souchong if you have it, Earl

Grey if you don't. No milk, no sugar, but I would like a few slices of lemon. Thank you.'

He turned back to Saffron. 'I heard about that business with your uncle,' he said, without the slightest preamble. 'Very impressive.'

'Really . . . why?'

'Well, I knew that you had a certain mental toughness that could, when properly trained, be used for this sort of work. And you've twice shown admirable courage and composure in battle. But I hadn't thought you capable of planning, executing and then extracting yourself from a cold-blooded murder quite so effectively, entirely off your own bat.'

'It wasn't murder, it was self-defence. I was attacked,' Saffron said, as calmly as she could manage, though her pulse had started racing at the very mention of the word 'murder'.

'You see, that proves my point. I have just accused you of a capital crime and you look me right in the eye, calm as you like and deny it.'

'I didn't enjoy killing him, you know.'

'I should hope not. That would make you a psychopath and I wouldn't want that. Psychopaths are unreliable. They always put their own compulsions ahead of their duty. But enough amateur psychology . . . You did us a great favour. We've known for a very long time that your uncle was cultivating a number of extremely undesirable friends. It was all just about tolerable before the war, but not once the balloon went up. Your uncle was a full-blown traitor. We rather think that he had your uncle David assassinated.'

'I thought he was killed by thieves.'

'Or his death was just made to look like a robbery. Anyway, as I'm sure you have already worked out for yourself, we couldn't have allowed dear Uncle Frank to be exposed. There was thus only one way of dealing with the situation and you took it.'

'My father doesn't know,' Saffron said, feeling surprised at how easy it was to talk to Mr Brown about this terrible thing that

492

she'd done. 'He believed my story. I'd like it to stay that way.'

'Of course . . . But speaking of your father, did he tell you about me?'

'Yes. He said that you'd turned my mother into a spy. And then he told me what she'd had to do.'

'Hmm . . .' Mr Brown considered that information. And then his face lit up and he exclaimed, 'Ah! The tea has arrived, excellent!'

The waiter pulled up a side table, placed the teapot upon it and was about to pour it into a cup when Mr Brown held up a hand. 'No, please, I prefer to do it myself.'

The man frowned. Saffron spoke a few words of Arabic, accompanied by gestures that evidently got the point across. 'Ah,' said the waiter, 'very good.' He went on his way and Mr Brown fussed for a while, getting his tea exactly as he wanted it. 'What languages do you have?' he asked as he was busying himself, not looking at Saffron this time.

'Of the African languages I'm fluent in Swahili, competent in Masai, and have a smattering of Afrikaans and Arabic, though I can't read or write Arabic script. In German I could read a newspaper and conduct a conversation but I certainly wouldn't pass as a native.'

'Not yet,' Mr Brown said. 'But your mother managed it.'

'Do you want me to do the same thing she did? Is that why you're here? Because I won't do it, you know.'

'I've never for a moment thought that you would. I'm here about a rather different line of work.' He sipped some tea thoughtfully, clearly concentrating all his attention on his tastebuds, gave a contented little grunt of approval and went on. 'About a year ago Mr Dalton, the Minister of Economic Warfare, authorized the formation of an outfit that was officially labelled the Joint Technical Board. It was a name one could put in funding proposals or stick on office doors without anyone knowing or caring what on earth it was.'

493

'Because it's so boring.'

'Quite so, but some of its small but growing number of members have a more accurate name for it. They call it the Ministry of Ungentlemanly Warfare.'

Saffron laughed. 'That sounds like more fun.'

'I'm glad you think so. Now let me tell you the truth about Mr Dalton's private army. Its actual name is the Special Operations Executive. Its purpose is to insert agents into Occupied Europe, to liaise with local resistance groups, establish spy networks, conduct reconnaissance on enemy positions and operations, carry out acts of sabotage and, in a few, particular cases, kill evil men whose deaths will save a great many innocent lives.'

'And you think I would be suited to that task.'

'I know you would. The missions that S.O.E. operatives undertake will be hazardous in the extreme. The chances of being caught, tortured by the Gestapo and then sent to a concentration camp, or simply shot, will be so high as to approach certainty. My job, therefore, is to recruit some of the most intellectually and physically gifted young men and women our nation possesses so that they can be trained to give their lives for their country. I do this because I know that the missions they undertake will be of supreme importance and that their lives will not be wasted, their sacrifice will not be in vain.'

'Are you trying to appeal to my idealism?' Saffron asked. 'I am not sure I have a tremendous amount of that.'

'No, I'm appealing to your decency. I think you are a fundamentally decent person, Miss Courtney.'

'I can think of at least one person who'd disagree.' Saffron said the words with a bitter flippancy, not expecting them to be understood. She had underestimated Mr Brown.

'You mean Fräulein von Schöndorf?'

Saffron saw at once what he meant by that. 'How did you

494

know?' she asked. 'How could you possibly know?'

'You might not believe this, but I was at a wedding when I caught wind of what you really got up to in St Moritz. Two silly young women were gossiping about you and the man I later discovered was Gerhard von Meerbach.'

'And now you wish to use it against me?'

'That's a rather harsh way of putting it. But the fact remains, you have had, and I believe are almost certainly still managing to conduct in some form, a liaison with the scion of one of the great German industrial dynasties, whose brother is a senior officer in the Nazi Schutzstaffel, or SS.'

'I'm quite aware of Konrad von Meerbach's rank and his politics. And I'm sure you know that you could make life very difficult indeed for me. So I suspect, Mr Brown, that you came here thinking that if you couldn't sweet-talk me into joining this Ungentlemanly Warfare show of yours, then a bit of blackmail might have to do the job. But you're too late. You can't use Gerhard von Meerbach as a weapon against me. He's dead.'

H*a! That took you unawares, didn't it?* Saffron had to admit it had surprised her as well. She hadn't planned to use the false report of Gerhard's death as any kind of tactical gambit, but then it had struck her: *If Gerhard is dead, then Brown can't use him against me.*

She picked up her bag. 'We had a way of communicating with one another. It was long and tortuous and took forever, but it worked. That's how I found out about this . . .'

She held out the telegram for Mr Brown to read. 'You see, he's gone. We saw each other for a few days in Switzerland at the start of '39, and a few more in Paris at Easter. We were doing nothing wrong, we loved each other very much and if this vile, beastly war had not come along, we would have married one another. But now he's dead, so it's over. *Kaput.*'

'Miss Courtney, I really am most awfully sorry,' said Mr Brown.

'Don't be. You didn't actually blackmail me and you certainly didn't kill Gerhard. Now, about the job offer that you were about to make . . . I accept. I want to be useful, just as my mother was in the last war. I'm very grateful to General Wilson for letting me be his driver, but I know I can do more than that. I believe I've proved that to your satisfaction, too.'

'Indeed you have, Miss Courtney.'

'Then you can count me in. I just have one request.'

'Go ahead.'

'Before I sign on the dotted line, I'd like to go home, to Kenya. If I'm going to risk my neck, there's someone I absolutely have to talk to first.'

G erhard was over Kiev on the way back from a mission, crossing the Dnieper River at a height of no more than three hundred metres, descending all the time as they approached the abandoned Russian air base that had become their new home.

Something caught Gerhard's eye as he passed over an area of open land on the edge of the city itself. He could have sworn he saw a long line of women, all stark naked, with armed, uniformed men on either side of them, and then a long trench with something in the bottom of it. *Was that a pile of bodies? Can't have been. Surely . . . can it?*

When he landed, Gerhard asked a couple of the other pilots if they'd seen it.

'Not me, skipper,' said Willi Kempen. 'Maybe it had something to do with that SS Task Force that arrived a few days ago. I heard there were posters up telling all the Yids to assemble by the cemetery at eight this morning. They're supposed to bring money, paper, warm clothing – sounds like they're being sent away somewhere.'

'I heard an army major arguing with one of those SS bastards a couple of days ago,' said Schrumpp.

'Whoa, Berti, watch your tongue! Don't you know our noble squadron captain's brother is in the SS?'

'True,' said Gerhard. 'But he's also a total bastard.'

When the laughter died down, Schrumpp got back to his story. 'So, this major was saying, "Who's going to do all the work if you kill all my Jews? I need carpenters to mend carts, mechanics for my trucks. How am I going to supply the boys up at the front if I can't fix my damn trucks?"'

'What did the SS man say to that?' asked Gerhard.

'He said he didn't give a shit about carts or trucks. His unit had orders to kill every last Yid in Kiev and that was the end of it. "If you don't like it, send a letter of complaint to *Reichsführer* Himmler." Those were his exact words.'

Later that afternoon, Gerhard took a long hard look at the maps of the locality. The area he had flown over was marked as Babi Yar. He fixed its exact position relative to the airfield in his mind, then went to Rolf and asked permission to make a quick test flight. 'I just want to check the flaps on my starboard wing. The controls felt a little stiff this morning. If there is a problem, I can have the ground crew fix it in time for tomorrow's mission.'

'Why bother? You could fly without any flaps at all and the Ivans still couldn't shoot you down!'

Gerhard said nothing.

'Oh, all right, go ahead,' said Rolf. 'But make it quick. We can't just go burning fuel for no reason.'

Gerhard went up in the plane. He put on a little aerobatics display for the benefit of anyone watching from the ground: not to show off his skills, but simply because that's what he would do if he were testing the handling of his plane. Gerhard pulled out of his final dive and levelled out at less than a hundred metres, then he eased back the throttle until his airspeed was barely one hundred and eighty kilometres per hour: as low as he could go without stalling. So he was able to get a very clear view of what was happening down below. He realized that the trench he had seen was actually part of a natural ravine. It was filled with dead bodies, presumably of Jews, piled so high now that they were almost spilling over the top. Gerhard saw naked men and women being led up to the edge of the pit where they stood in a long line. Then he saw SS men – one for every Jew – put pistols to their heads, fire and blow them into the ravine with the force of the bullet smashing into their skulls.

Gerhard made three passes over the area. On the third he gave a little waggle of his wings, just to make it seem as though he were congratulating the killers below on the fine job they were doing of exterminating Ukrainian Jewry. Then he headed back to base.

'Flaps all right then, sir?' the mechanic asked when he clambered out of the cockpit.

Gerhard nodded, just about managed to say, 'Fine,' and forced a tight, bitter smile.

Then he returned to the barrack-house where he was billeted, went straight to the bathroom and vomited his guts out into the basin. When his stomach was entirely empty, he rinsed out his mouth and proceeded to the officers' mess where he became joylessly, but determinedly blind drunk, sitting alone, waving the other pilots away.

They let him be. Plenty of men had reason to numb themselves with alcohol these days. It was just one of those things and no one thought any the worse of them. So Gerhard emptied the bottle and as he did he realized that what he had seen at Babi Yar, though it was happening far from the Reich, out of sight of its people, was the true face of the Nazi empire, the true faith that would one day be worshipped in that vast, impossible hall he had laboured over for so long. This was the

498

darkness in Hitler's soul brought out into the light, let loose upon the world.

Izzy was wrong. There was no distinction between Nazism and Germany any more. There was no possible way that any man with a conscience could say that he was fighting for German honour and pride, because that belonged to Hitler now. The Führer had been proved triumphantly correct. They were all his slaves, his soldiers, his people to dispose of as he pleased.

The following morning, Gerhard sat on the runway, waiting to take off on their latest mission, praying that the pills they all took to keep themselves alert would kick in before he fell asleep at the controls of his plane. He had lain awake all night without the slightest hint of sleep, and in the darkness he had made a resolution: *I would rather be dead than live in Adolf Hitler's world. And there cannot be any hope for me or for Saffron or for our love as long as he is alive. So therefore I must dedicate myself to destroying him and all his cohorts. From now on, that will be my greatest purpose in life.*

Now dawn was breaking and nothing had changed. Gerhard von Meerbach had dedicated his life to freeing Germany, and the world, from the death-grip of Nazism. He had no idea how to do it, or who would be his allies. He just knew it had to be done. And with that grim thought in his mind, he lined up on the runway, pointed the Messerschmitt's nose to the east, and flew up and away into the first golden rays of the rising sun.

Saffron had been walking since before dawn, watching the mountain as it emerged from the darkness, separating itself from the great escarpment of the Rift Valley behind it, glowing in the golden light of the sunrise on its flanks and then revealing itself in all its majesty as the mist on its upper reaches cleared. Fuel was so strictly rationed that she could not have driven all the way from the Courtney residence, and flying was out of the question. But Saffron was glad of the full day's walk that had taken her to within five miles of the mountain, and the night she had spent under the stars. With every step she took and every breath of Kenyan air that entered her lungs she felt more at home. For the first few hours she had passed through farmland and plantations, stopping occasionally to talk to the workers. Saffron discovered that her command of the Swahili and Masai languages came back to her in an instant, as did her memory of the names and faces of people that she met. Many were men and women she had known since her earliest girlhood and they greeted her like a long-lost daughter while Manyoro stood to one side, beaming as proudly as any father at the good impression she made.

Saffron loved the huge smiles, the ready laughter and the unrestrained emotions that she encountered along her way. That wonderful African warmth was such a stark contrast to the insipid, buttoned-up, joyless personalities of so many of the people she'd met in England. She didn't even mind when all the older women insisted on asking whether she had a husband yet and, if, so how many sons she had given him. Invariably they were shocked to discover that she was still single and childless. Saffron explained, again and again, that she would love to have babies, but there was a war on and she was too busy serving her country to have time for marriage and motherhood.

At this, Manyoro would shake his head in a great display of bafflement and sorrow and agree with all the wise Masai woman that there was, indeed, no limit to the foolishness of headstrong girls. But he would, he promised them, have a good, strong word with his niece and remind her where her true duties lay.

He had insisted on accompanying Saffron. 'You are my brother's daughter, little princess. You are going to see my mother. Of course I must come with you to keep you safe. No man or beast will dare to trouble you when I walk at your side.'

For her part, Saffron was only too happy to have Manyoro's company. She was proud of her independence and knew that she was as capable as any man of fighting her way out of trouble, or taking the hardest of all possible decisions and living with the consequences. Still, it was wonderful to feel protected and secure in the company of a father figure she loved, and whose love for her was as warm and reassuring as a cosy fire on a cold winter's day.

She knew, too, that while the deeds to the Lusima estate might declare it to be the property of Leon Courtney, and the revenues from its farms might end up in his bank account, Manyoro was indeed the king of all he surveyed. He was greeted by all the estate staff and their families with the profound respect due to a monarch and he responded with a suitably regal air of a man who loved all his people but was still, none-theless, their master.

He was not, however, an entirely contented king. 'Can you believe that I offered my services to the King's African rifles and was rejected on the grounds that I was too old. Ha! Look at me, am I not still a mighty warrior?'

'You are, indeed, the very mightiest of warriors, Uncle Manyoro,' Saffron agreed, with a suitably serious look on her face, for he was indeed a fine figure of a man, for all that he must now be the best part of seventy, at the very least. 'It is a scandal and an outrage that these fools turned their back on you. But then, my father never made any secret of his contempt for his regiment's senior officers, as you well know.'

Manyoro nodded. 'That is very true. And he had reason to feel aggrieved for they were lying jackals who betrayed him with lies and injustice.'

'Then you should not take this personally. These men are not worthy of you. In any case, your people would suffer if you went away to war. They need you. And we need the food that they grow here and the meat of the cattle that they raise

501

and herd. Believe me, Uncle, my people are hungry. They are attacked on all sides. They need all that you can give them. So you, and all the people of the Lusima estate, are doing the King and the Empire a very great service.'

'I can see that you tell the truth, princess,' Manyoro said, 'and I thank you for it. I know that your mother looks down on you now and her heart swells with pride to see her daughter grown to such a fine, brave woman. And I know that my mother will be filled with joy to see you again, for you are as a grand-daughter to her, too.'

As the sun rose towards its zenith, Saffron walked with Manyoro up the mountain path, passing through the cloud-line that marked the point at which the dry, savannah vegetation of the lower slopes, the grass and umbrella acacia trees gave way to the lush montane forests that were constantly watered by mists and rain. As they came closer to the summit, Saffron could feel the delight bubbling up through Manyoro like clear spring water through black basalt rock as he approached his birthplace, his truest home.

Then they surmounted the very last, steepest portion of the climb and stepped onto the tabletop plateau and the moun-tain's summit. Now the cries of delight were all for Manyoro. Little children scampered around his feet and he greeted them all by name for these were his great-grandchildren and he took huge pride that there were so many of them, and all so healthy and well-fed. Saffron had been here before, to be introduced to Lusima Mama, but it had been before she went away to Roedean, so she could only have been eleven or twelve, at the most: too young to fully comprehend the significance of the occasion, or appreciate the true stature of the elderly lady she was meeting.

Now, though, she was a grown woman. And so, as Manyoro led her through the trees to the shady spot where his mother now liked to spend her days, enthroned in the chair cut from the stump of a once-mighty hardwood tree, she felt awestruck by the vision that greeted her.

Lusima Mama was now so ancient that she seemed to have gone beyond any mundane embodiment of old age. She did not rise to greet Saffron, but lifted her hand so that her visitor might take it, and tilted her head so that her cheek could be kissed. Saffron placed the most delicate of touches of her lips against Lusima Mama's skin and it felt warm and dry and as fine as the most delicate, gossamer silk. The bones of her fingers seemed so light and fragile in Saffron's strong hands that she feared she might snap them with the slightest pressure. And though her limbs were still long and straight and the bone structure of her face retained its exquisite elegance, Lusima Mama's presence seemed less physical than ethereal, more like an elven queen from an African fairy tale than a mere mortal human.

As Manyoro discreetly slipped away, leaving the women to their business, his mother smiled and shifted her body to make room on the seat. 'Come, sit beside me, my child.'

Saffron did as she was told. She said nothing. Every ounce of intuition that she possessed told her that it would be best to allow Lusima Mama to lead the conversation. She let herself be examined by dark eyes that had lost none of their insight until Lusima Mama smiled and said, 'You are a daughter worthy of your parents. You have the beauty and courage of your mother, and the strength and fighting spirit of your father. I should like to meet the one you love so much. He must truly be a man among men.'

Saffron knew from her father's stories about the first time he met Lusima Mama that she had an unsettling habit of already knowing everything before one had said a word, but still she could not stop herself from gasping. 'How . . . how did you know?'

Lusima Mama laughed. 'I have the power to see things that

503

others can't. But I had no need of them to tell that you were in love. And no man could win the love of a young lioness like you unless he was truly worthy of possessing it.'

'Thank you, Mama,' said Saffron, speaking with a formality she felt that so venerable a woman deserved. 'You are as kind as you are wise. I'm sure I do not deserve such generous compliments. And of course you are right. I am in love and he is a good, and strong, and handsome man.'

'And he pleases you, too, does he not?'

Saffron found herself blushing like a schoolgirl. 'Yes,' she said, trying hard not to giggle. 'Like a lion.'

'But now you and he have been parted by the war, and find yourself on different sides of the battle as your tribe fights his.'

'Yes, and I don't know what to do. I feel I should serve my country. But I don't want to die . . . Not because I'm frightened. I just have to be alive for his sake. So I'm torn.'

Lusima Mama shook her head. 'No, you are not torn. Your head may be filled with different ideas, but your soul knows what it must do. And, once again, I need no trance, or powers of divination to see this. It is obvious. You must be fit for your man, just as he is fit for you. But how could you be worthy of him if you took the coward's path? Remember, child, that the lion is the hunter of the pride. You are a hunter too. That is your nature and you must not deny it. Now, give me your hand again.'

This time it was Lusima Mama who took Saffron's hand in hers. She stroked the skin between Saffron's knuckles and her wrist. 'I have not done this for many years,' she murmured. 'I have known that I only had the strength for one last journey and that I would know when it was time . . .'

'But Mama . . .' Saffron protested.

'Hush, child, you are the light in my son M'Bogo's life. I do this for both your sakes . . .'

Lusima Mama's eyes close and she fell quiet. The silence

504

stretched out for what seemed like an eternity and then her eyes were wide open, rolled back so far that only their whites were visible. As her divination began she rocked back and forth as if moving to the rhythm of another world and when she spoke her voice was not that of an elderly lady, but was a low, gravelly monotone that sounded more male than female.

'You will walk alongside death, but you will live . . . I can see you, but I cannot see the lion. He is there, but he cannot be recognized. You will look for him, but if he is ever found, it will only be when you have ceased your search, and if you see him you will not know him, for he will be nameless and unknown, and if your eyes fall upon his face they will not see it for they will not know it to be his. And if he is alive, it will be as if he were dead. And yet . . . and yet . . . you must keep searching, for if he is to be saved, only you can save him.'

The voice that was not Lusima Mama's voice fell silent, her body became inert once again and then, as if waking from a dream, she shook herself, blinked several times, fixed her eyes upon Saffron and smiled.

'Now you know all that can be known, my child,' Lusima Mama said.

I will not see her again, or not in this life at least,' said Manyoro, as he and Saffron walked back down the mountain path.

'No, that can't be right,' said Saffron, who could not bear the idea that she might have hastened Lusima Mama's passing.

'It is not a matter of right or wrong. It is just life, which ends when it must end. Mama wanted you to know that what came to pass today was always going to happen. It is not so much that she will go because you came, but that she lived until you arrived.'

Saffron nodded, knowing that Manyoro's words seemed true to her, even inevitable, in a way she could not quite explain.

'I hope you learned what you needed to know,' he said.

'Yes,' Saffron replied. 'I learned that my love and I were made for one another. I know that our destiny is to be together. I know that this destiny can only be fulfilled if I make it so. And I will make it so, Manyoro. I swear to you . . . I will.'

Praise for *Travelling to Infinity*

"Stephen Hawking may think in 11 dimensions, but his
first wife has learnt to love in several."
The Times

"Jane Hawking has written a book about what it was like
to be pivotal to her husband's celebrated existence...
but it is much more a shout from the outer darkness."
The Daily Telegraph

"What becomes of time when a marriage unravels? And
what becomes of the woman who has located her whole self
within its sphere? For Jane Hawking, the physics of love and
loss are set in a private universe."
The Guardian

"Jane describes the final, painful years of her
marriage in candid detail."
The Independent

"Jane Hawking's harrowing and compelling
account... rings very true."
Irish Times

"This is not a vindictive book, although the agony she went
through is palpable; if Stephen's struggle to keep his mind clear
is heroic, so is her determination to balance his escalating needs
and those of their three children."
Independent on Sunday

"Jane writes about her former husband with tenderness,
respect and protectiveness."
Sunday Express

TRAVELLING TO INFINITY

MY LIFE WITH STEPHEN

TRAVELLING TO INFINITY

MY LIFE WITH STEPHEN

JANE HAWKING

ALMA BOOKS

ALMA BOOKS LTD
Hogarth House
32–34 Paradise Road
Richmond
Surrey TW9 1SE
United Kingdom
www.almabooks.com

Travelling to Infinity: My Life with Stephen is an extensively revised
version (with new material) of *Music to Move the Stars*, first published by
Macmillan in 1999
Travelling to Infinity: My Life with Stephen first published by Alma
Books Limited in 2007
First paperback edition first published in 2008, reprinted 2010
This new edition first published by Alma Books in 2014. Repr. 2014
Repr. 2015 (five times)
Copyright © Jane Hawking, 1999–2014
All rights reserved

Jane Hawking asserts her moral right to be identified as the author of this
work in accordance with the Copyright, Designs and Patents Act 1988

ISBN: 978-1-84688-366-8
EBOOK: 978-1-84688-373-6

Printed in Britain by CPI Group (UK) Ltd, Croydon CR0 4YY

Contents

For my family

La parole humaine est comme un chaudron fêlé où nous battons des mélodies à faire danser les ours quand on voudrait attendrir les étoiles.

– Gustave Flaubert

Human expression is like a cracked kettle on which we beat out music for bears to dance to, when really we long to move the stars to pity.

Part One

1

Wings to Fly

The story of my life with Stephen Hawking began in the summer of 1962, though possibly it began ten or so years earlier than that without my being aware of it. When I entered St Albans High School for Girls as a seven-year-old first-former in the early Fifties, there was for a short spell a boy with floppy, golden-brown hair who used to sit by the wall in the next-door classroom. The school took boys, including my brother Christopher in the junior department, but I only saw the boy with the floppy hair on the occasions when, in the absence of our own teacher, we first-formers were squeezed into the same classroom as the older children. We never spoke to each other, but I am sure this early memory is to be trusted, because Stephen was a pupil at the school for a term at that time before going to a preparatory school a few miles away.

Stephen's sisters were more recognizable, because they were at the school for longer. Only eighteen months younger than Stephen, Mary, the elder of the two girls, was a distinctively eccentric figure – plump, always dishevelled, absent-minded, given to solitary pursuits. Her great asset, a translucent complexion, was masked by thick, unflattering spectacles. Philippa, five years younger than Stephen, was bright-eyed, nervous and excitable, with short fair plaits and a round, pink face. The school demanded rigid conformity both academically and in discipline, and the pupils, like schoolchildren everywhere, could be cruelly intolerant of individuality. It was fine to have a Rolls Royce and a house in the country, but if, like me, your means of transport was a pre-war Standard 10 – or even worse, like the Hawkings, an ancient London taxi – you were a figure of fun or the object of pitying contempt. The Hawking children used to lie on the floor of their taxi to avoid being seen by their peers. Unfortunately there was not room on the floor of the Standard 10 for such evasive action. Both the Hawking girls left before reaching the upper school.

Their mother had long been a familiar figure. A small, wiry person dressed in a fur coat, she used to stand on the corner by the zebra crossing near my school, waiting for her youngest son, Edward, to arrive by bus from his preparatory school in the country. My brother also went to that school after his kindergarten year at St Albans High School: it was called Aylesford House and there the boys wore pink – pink blazers and pink caps. In all other respects it was a paradise for small boys, especially for those who were not of an academic inclination. Games, cubs, camping and gang shows, for which my father often played the piano, appeared to be the major activities. Charming and very good-looking, Edward, at the age of eight, was having some difficulty relating to his adoptive family when I first knew the Hawkings – possibly because of their habit of bringing their reading matter to the dinner table and ignoring any non-bookworms present.

A school friend of mine, Diana King, had experienced this particular Hawking habit – which may have been why, on hearing some time later of my engagement to Stephen, she exclaimed, "Oh, Jane! You are marrying into a mad, mad family!" It was Diana who first pointed Stephen out to me in that summer of 1962 when, after the exams, she, my best friend Gillian and I were enjoying the blissful period of semi-idleness before the end of term. Thanks to my father's position as a senior civil servant, I had already made a couple of sorties into the adult world beyond school, homework and exams – to a dinner in the House of Commons and on a hot sunny day to a garden party at Buckingham Palace. Diana and Gillian were leaving school that summer, while I was to stay on as Head Girl for the autumn term, when I would be applying for university entrance. That Friday afternoon we collected our bags and, adjusting our straw boaters, we decided to drift into town for tea. We had scarcely gone a hundred yards when a strange sight met our eyes on the other side of the road: there, lolloping along in the opposite direction, was a young man with an awkward gait, his head down, his face shielded from the world under an unruly mass of straight brown hair. Immersed in his own thoughts, he looked neither to right nor left, unaware of the group of schoolgirls across the road. He was an eccentric phenomenon for strait-laced, sleepy St Albans. Gillian and I stared rather rudely in amazement but Diana remained impassive.

"That's Stephen Hawking. I've been out with him actually," she announced to her speechless companions.

14

"No! You haven't!" we laughed incredulously.

"Yes I have. He's strange but very clever, he's a friend of Basil's [her brother]. He took me to the theatre once, and I've been to his house. He goes on 'Ban the Bomb' marches."

Raising our eyebrows, we continued into town, but I did not enjoy the outing because, without being able to explain why, I felt uneasy about the young man we had just seen. Perhaps there was something about his very eccentricity that fascinated me in my rather conventional existence. Perhaps I had some strange premonition that I would be seeing him again. Whatever it was, that scene etched itself deeply on my mind.

The holidays of that summer were a dream for a teenager on the verge of independence, though they may well have been a nightmare for her parents, since my destination, a summer school in Spain, was in 1962 quite as remote, mysterious and fraught with hazards as, say, Nepal is for teenagers today. With all the confidence of my eighteen years, I was quite sure that I could look after myself, and I was right. The course was well organized, and we students were lodged in groups in private homes. At weekends we were taken on conducted tours of all the sights – to Pamplona where the bulls run the streets, to the only bullfight I have seen, brutal and savage, but spectacular and enthralling as well, and to Loyola, the home of St Ignatius, the author of a prayer I and every other pupil at St Albans High School had had instilled into us from constant repetition:

Teach us, O Lord,
to serve Thee as Thou deservest,
to give and not to count the cost...

Otherwise we spent our afternoons on the beach and the evenings out down by the port in restaurants and bars, participating in the fiestas and the dancing, listening to the raucous bands and gasping at the fireworks. I quickly made new friends outside the limited St Albans scene, primarily among the other teenagers on the course, and with them, in the glorious, exotic atmosphere of Spain, experimented with a taste of adult independence away from home, family and the stultifying discipline of school.

On my return to England, I was whisked away almost immediately by my parents who, relieved at my safe return, had arranged a family holiday in the Low Countries and Luxembourg. This was yet another broadening experience, one of those holidays in which my father specialized and which he had been arranging for us for many years – ever since my first trip to Brittany at the age of ten. Thanks to his enthusiasms we found ourselves in the vanguard of the tourist movement, travelling hundreds of miles along meandering country roads across a Europe in the process of emerging from its wartime trauma, visiting cities, cathedrals and art museums, which my parents were also discovering for the first time. It was a typically inspired combination of education, through art and history, and enjoyment of the good things of life – wine, food and summer sun – all intermingled with the war memorials and cemeteries of Flanders' fields.

Back in school that autumn, the summer's experiences lent me an unprecedented feeling of self-assurance. As I emerged from my chrysalis, school provided only the palest reflection of the awareness and self-reliance I had acquired through travelling. Taking my cue from the new forms of satire appearing on television, I, the Head Girl, devised a fashion show for the sixth-form entertainment, with the difference that all the fashions were constructed from bizarrely adapted items of school uniform. Discipline collapsed as the whole school clamoured for entry on the staircase outside the hall, and Miss Meiklejohn (otherwise know as Mick), the stocky, weather-beaten games mistress on whose terrifyingly masculine bark the smooth running of the school depended, was for once reduced to apoplexy, unable to make herself heard in the din. In desperation, she resorted to the megaphone – which usually only came out for a blasting on Sports Day, at the pet show, and for the purpose of controlling those interminable crocodiles we had to form when marching down through every possible back street of St Albans for the once-termly services in the Abbey.

That term long ago in the autumn of 1962 was not supposed to be about putting on shows. It was supposed to be about university entrance. Sadly it was not a success for me in academic terms. However great our adulation for President Kennedy, the Cuban missile crisis that October had well and truly shaken the sense of security of my generation and dashed our hopes for the future. With the superpowers playing such dangerous games with our lives, it was not at all certain that we had any future to look forward to. As we prayed for peace in school assembly under the direction of the Dean, I remembered a prediction made by

Field Marshall Montgomery in the late Fifties that there would be a nuclear war within a decade. Everyone, young and old alike, knew that we would have just four minutes' warning of a nuclear attack, which would spell the abrupt end of all civilization. My mother's comment, calmly philosophical and sensible as ever, at the prospect of a third world war in her lifetime, was that she would much rather be obliterated with everything and everyone else than endure the agony of seeing her husband and son conscripted for warfare from which they would never return.

Quite apart from the almighty threat of the international scene, I felt that I had burnt myself out with the A-level exams and lacked enthusiasm for school work after my taste of freedom in the summer. The serious business of university entrance held only humiliation when neither Oxford nor Cambridge expressed any interest in me. It was all the more painful because my father had been cherishing the hope that I would gain a place at Cambridge since I was about six years old. Aware of my sense of failure, Miss Gent, the Headmistress, sympathetically went to some lengths to point out that there was no disgrace in not getting a place at Cambridge, because many of the men at that university were far inferior intellectually to the women who had been turned away for want of places. In those days the ratio was roughly ten men to one woman at Oxford and Cambridge. She recommended taking up the offer of an interview at Westfield College, London, a women's college on the Girtonian model, situated in Hampstead at some distance from the rest of the University. Thus one cold, wet December day, I set off from St Albans by bus for the fifteen-mile journey to Hampstead.

The day was such a disaster that it was a relief at the end of it to be on the bus home again, travelling through the same bleak, grey sleet and snow of the outward journey. After the uncomfortable exercise in the Spanish Department of bluffing my way through an interview which seemed to hinge entirely on T.S. Eliot, about whom I knew next to nothing, I was sent to join the queue outside the Principal's study. When my turn came, she brought the style of a former civil servant to the interview, scarcely looking up from her papers over her horn-rimmed spectacles. Feeling exceedingly ruffled from the fiasco of the earlier interview, I decided it was better to make her notice me even if in the process I ruined my chances. So when in a bored, dry voice, she asked, "And why have you put down Spanish rather than French as your main language?", I answered in an equally bored, dry voice, "Because Spain is hotter than France." Her papers fell from her hands and she did indeed look up.

To my astonishment, I was offered a place at Westfield, but by that Christmas much of the optimism and enthusiasm that I had discovered in Spain had worn thin. When Diana invited me to a New Year's party which she was giving with her brother on 1st January 1963, I went along, neatly dressed in a dark-green silky outfit – synthetic, of course – with my hair back-brushed in an extravagant bouffant roll, inwardly shy and very unsure of myself. There, slight of frame, leaning against the wall in a corner with his back to the light, gesticulating with long thin fingers as he spoke – his hair falling across his face over his glasses – and wearing a dusty black-velvet jacket and red-velvet bow tie, stood Stephen Hawking, the young man I had seen lolloping along the street in the summer.

Standing apart from the other groups, he was talking to an Oxford friend, explaining that he had begun research in cosmology in Cambridge – not, as he had hoped, under the auspices of Fred Hoyle, the popular television scientist, but with the unusually named Dennis Sciama. At first, Stephen had thought his unknown supervisor's name was *Skeearma*, but on his arrival in Cambridge he had discovered that the correct pronunciation was *Sharma*. He admitted that he had learnt with some relief, the previous summer – when I was doing A levels – that he had gained a First Class degree at Oxford. This was the happy result of a viva, an oral exam, conducted by the perplexed examiners to decide whether the singularly inept candidate whose papers also revealed flashes of brilliance should be given a First, an Upper Second or a Pass degree, the latter being tantamount to failure. He nonchalantly informed the examiners that if they gave him a First he would go to Cambridge to do a PhD, thus giving them the opportunity of introducing a Trojan horse into the rival camp, whereas if they gave him an Upper Second (which would also allow him to do research), he would stay in Oxford. The examiners played for safety and gave him a First.

Stephen went on to explain to his audience of two, his Oxford friend and me, how he had also taken steps to play for safety, realizing that it was extremely unlikely that he would get a First at Oxford on the little work he had done. He had never been to a lecture – it was not the done thing to be seen working when friends called – and the legendary tale of his tearing up a piece of work and flinging it into his tutor's wastepaper basket on leaving a tutorial is quite true. Fearing for his chances in academia, Stephen had applied to join the Civil Service and had passed the preliminary stages of selection at a country-house weekend, so he was all set to take the Civil Service exams just after Finals. One morning he woke late as usual, with the niggling feeling that there was something he ought to be doing that day, apart from his normal pursuit of listening to his taped recording of the entire *Ring Cycle*. As he did not keep a diary but trusted everything to memory, he had no way of finding out what it was until some hours later, when it dawned on him that that day was the day of the Civil Service exams.

I listened in amused fascination, drawn to this unusual character by his sense of humour and his independent personality. His tales made very appealing listening, particularly because of his way of hiccoughing with laughter, almost suffocating himself, at the jokes he told, many of them against himself. Clearly here was someone, like me, who tended to stumble through life and managed to see the funny side of situations. Someone who, like me, was fairly shy, yet not averse to expressing his opinions; someone who unlike me had a developed sense of his own worth and had the effrontery to convey it. As the party drew to a close, we exchanged names and addresses, but I did not expect to see him again, except perhaps casually in passing. The floppy hair and the bow tie were a façade, a statement of independence of mind, and in future I could afford to overlook them, as Diana had, rather than gape in astonishment, if I came across him again in the street.

2

On Stage

Only a couple of days later, a card came from Stephen, inviting me to a party on 8th January. It was written in a beautiful copperplate hand which I envied but, despite laborious efforts, had never mastered. I consulted Diana, who had also received an invitation. She said that the party was for Stephen's twenty-first birthday – information not conveyed on the invitation – and she promised to come and pick me up. It was difficult to choose a present for someone I had only just met, so I took a record token.

The house in Hillside Road, St Albans, was a monument to thrift and economy. Not that that was unusual in those days, because in the postwar era we were all brought up to treat money with respect, to search out bargains and to avoid waste. Built in the early years of the twentieth century, 14 Hillside Road, a vast red-brick three-storey house, had a certain charm about it, since it was preserved entirely in its original state, with no interference from modernizing trends, such as central heating or wall-to-wall carpeting. Nature, the elements and a family of four children had all left their marks on the shabby façade which hid behind an unruly hedge. Wisteria overhung the decrepit glass porch, and much of the coloured glass in the leaded diamond panes of the upper panels of the front door was missing. Although no immediate response came from pressing the bell, the door was eventually opened by the same person who used to wait wrapped in a fur coat by the zebra crossing. She was introduced to me as Isobel Hawking, Stephen's mother. She was accompanied by an enchanting small boy with dark curly hair and bright blue eyes. Behind them a single light bulb illuminated a long yellow-tiled hallway, heavy furniture – including a grandfather clock – and the original, now darkened, William-Morris wallpaper.

As different members of the family began to appear round the living-room door to greet the new arrivals, I discovered that I knew them all: Stephen's mother was well known from her vigils by the crossing; his young brother, Edward, was evidently the small boy in the pink cap; the sisters, Mary and Philippa, were recognizable from school, and the tall, white-haired, distinguished father of the family, Frank Hawking, had once come to collect a swarm of bees from our own back garden. My brother Chris and I had wanted to watch, but to our disappointment he had shooed us away with a gruff taciturnity. In addition to being the city's only beekeeper, Frank Hawking must also have been one of the few people in St Albans to own a pair of skis. In winter he would ski down the hill past our house on his way to the golf course, where we used to picnic and gather bluebells in spring and summer and toboggan on tin trays in winter. It was like fitting a jigsaw together: all these people were individually quite familiar to me, but I had never realized that they were related. Indeed there was yet another member of that household whom I recognized: she lodged in her own self-contained room in the attic, but came down to join in family occasions such as this. Agnes Walker, Stephen's Scottish grandmother, was a well-known figure in St Albans in her own right on account of her prowess at the piano, publicly displayed once a month when she joined forces in the Town Hall with Molly Du Cane, our splendidly jolly-hockey-sticks folk-dance leader.

Dancing and tennis had been just about my only social activities throughout my teenage years. Through them, I had acquired a group of friends of both sexes from various schools and differing backgrounds. Out of school we went everywhere in a crowd – coffee on Saturday mornings, tennis in the evenings and socials at the tennis club in summer, ballroom-dancing classes and folk dancing in the winter. The fact that our mothers also attended the folk-dance evenings along with many of St Albans' elderly and infirm population did not embarrass us at all. We sat apart and danced in our own sets, well out of the way of the older generation. Romances blossomed occasionally in our corner, giving rise to plenty of gossip and a few squabbles, then usually faded as quickly as they had bloomed. We were an easygoing, friendly bunch of teenagers, leading simpler lives than our modern counterparts, and the atmosphere at the dances was carefree and wholesome, inspired by Molly Du Cane's infectious enthusiasm for her energetic art. Fiddle on her shoulder, she called the dances with authority, while Stephen's grandmother, her corpulent frame upright at the grand piano, applied her fingers with nimble artistry to the ivories, not once allowing the sausage bang of tight curls on her forehead to become ruffled. An august figure, she would turn to survey the dancers with a curiously impassive stare. She, of course, came downstairs to greet the guests at Stephen's twenty-first birthday party.

The party consisted of a mixture of friends and relations. A few hailed from Stephen's Oxford days, but most had been his contemporaries or near contemporaries at St Albans School and had contributed to that school's success in the Oxbridge entrance exams of 1959. At seventeen, Stephen had been younger than his peer group at school, and consequently was rather young for university entrance that autumn, especially as many of his fellow undergraduates were not just one year older than him, but older by several years because they had all come up to Oxford after doing National Service, which had since been abolished. Later Stephen admitted that he failed to get the best out of Oxford because of the difference in age between him and his fellow undergraduates.

Certainly he maintained closer ties with his school friends than with any acquaintances from Oxford. Apart from Basil King, Diana's brother, I knew them only by repute as the new elite of St Albans' society. They were said to be the intellectual adventurers of our generation, passionately dedicated to a critical rejection of every truism, to the ridicule of every trite or clichéd remark, to the assertion of their own independence of thought and to the exploration of the outer reaches of the mind. Our local paper, *The Herts Advertiser*, had trumpeted the success of the school four years earlier, splashing their names and faces across its pages. Whereas I was just about to embark on my undergraduate career, their student years were now already behind them. They were, of course, very different from my friends, and I, a bright but ordinary eighteen-year-old, felt intimidated. None of this crowd would ever spend their evenings folk-dancing. Painfully aware of my own lack of sophistication, I settled in a corner as close to the fire as possible with Edward on my knee and listened to the conversation, not attempting to participate. Some people were seated, others leant against the wall of the large chilly dining room, where the only source of heat was from a glass-fronted stove. The conversation was halting and consisted mostly of jokes, none of which were even remotely as highbrow as I was expecting. The only part of it I can remember was not a joke, but a riddle, about a man in New York who wanted to get to the fiftieth floor of a building but only took the lift to the forty-sixth. Why? Because he was not tall enough to reach the button for the fiftieth floor…

It was some time before I saw or heard of Stephen again. I was busily engaged in London following a secretarial course in a revolutionary type of shorthand, which used the alphabet instead of hieroglyphs and omitted all vowels. Initially I accompanied my father to the station at a sprint to catch the 8 a.m. train every morning, until I discovered that I was not required to be at the school in Oxford Street quite so early. I could travel at a more leisurely pace than my dedicated, hard-working father, so I ambled to the station for the nine o'clock train and met a completely different commuting public from the jam-packed, harassed-looking, middle-aged breadwinners in dark suits. Rarely did a day go by when I did not meet someone I knew – unhurried and casually dressed, either going back to college after a weekend at home or going up to London for an interview. This was a welcome start to the day, because for the rest of it, apart from a short break for lunch, I was confined to the classroom, surrounded by the clatter of massed old-fashioned typewriters and the chatter of ex-debs whose main claim to distinction seemed to be the number of times they had been invited to Buckingham Palace, Kensington Palace or Clarence House.

The revolutionary form of shorthand was easy enough to pick up, but the touch-typing was a nightmare. I could see the sense of the shorthand, for that was going to be useful for note-taking at university, but the typing was tiresome in the extreme and I was hopeless at it, still struggling to reach forty words a minute when the rest of the class had finished the course and mastered all the additional skills of the secretarial art. Actually the shorthand would be of short-term value while the typing skills would prove themselves over and over again.

At weekends I could forget the horrors of typing and keep up with old friends. One Saturday morning in February, I met Diana, who was now a student nurse at St Thomas's Hospital, and Elizabeth Chant, another school friend, who was training to become a primary-school teacher, in our favourite haunt, the coffee bar in Greens', St Albans' only department store. We compared notes on our courses and then started talking about our friends and acquaintances. Suddenly Diana asked, "Have you heard about Stephen?" "Oh, yes," said Elizabeth, "it's awful, isn't it?" I realized that they were talking about Stephen Hawking. "What do you mean?" I asked. "I haven't heard anything." "Well, apparently he's been in hospital for two weeks – Bart's I think, because that's where his father trained and that's where Mary is training." Diana explained, "He kept stumbling and couldn't tie his shoelaces." She paused. "They did lots of horrible tests and have found that he's suffering from some terrible, paralysing incurable disease. It's a bit like multiple sclerosis, but it's not multiple sclerosis and they reckon he's probably only got a couple of years to live."

I was stunned. I had only just met Stephen and for all his eccentricity I liked him. We both seemed shy in the presence of others, but were confident within ourselves. It was unthinkable that someone only a couple of years older than me should be facing the prospect of his own death. Mortality was not a concept that played any part in our existence. We were still young enough to be immortal. "How is he?" I enquired, shaken by the news. "Basil's been to see him," she continued, "and says he's pretty depressed: the tests are really unpleasant, and a boy from St Albans in the bed opposite died the other day." She sighed, "Stephen insisted on being on the ward, because of his socialist principles, and would not have a private room as his parents wanted." "Do they know the cause of this illness?" I asked blankly. "Not really," Diana replied. "They think he may have been given a non-sterile smallpox vaccination when he went to Persia a couple of years ago, and that introduced a virus to his spine – but they don't really know, that's only speculation."

I went home in silence, thinking about Stephen. My mother noticed my preoccupation. She had not met him, but knew of him and also knew that I liked him. I had taken the precaution of warning her that he was very eccentric, in case she should come across him unannounced. With the sensible assurance of the deep-seated faith which had sustained her through the war, through the terminal illness of her beloved father and through my own father's bouts of depression, she quietly said, "Why don't you pray for him? It might help."

I was astonished therefore when, a week or so later, as I was waiting for a 9 a.m. train, Stephen came sauntering down the platform carrying a brown canvas suitcase. He looked perfect-ly cheerful and pleased to see me. His appearance was more conventional and actually rather more attractive than on past occasions: the features of the old image which he had doubtless cultivated at Oxford – the bow tie, the black-velvet jacket, even the long hair – had given way to a red necktie, a beige raincoat and a tidier, shorter hairstyle. Our two previous meetings had been in the evening in subdued lighting: daylight revealed his broad, winning smile and his limpid grey eyes to advantage. Behind the owlish spectacles there was something about the set of his features which attracted me, reminding me, perhaps even subconsciously, of my Norfolk hero, Lord Nelson. We sat together on the train to London talking quite happily, though we scarcely touched on the question of his illness. I mentioned how sorry I had been to hear of his stay in hospital, whereupon he wrinkled his nose and said nothing. He behaved so convincingly as if everything were fine, and I felt it would have been cruel to have pursued the subject further. He was on his way back to Cambridge, he said, and as we neared St Pancras, he announced that he came home quite often at weekends. Would I like to go to the theatre with him sometime? Of course I said I would.

We met one Friday evening at an Italian restaurant in Soho, which in itself would have been a sufficiently lavish evening out. However Stephen had tickets for the theatre as well, and the meal had to be brought to a hasty and rather embarrassingly expensive conclusion to enable us to make our way south of the river to the Old Vic, in time for a performance of *Volpone*. Arriving at the theatre in a rush, we just managed to throw our belongings under our seats at the back of the stalls when the play began. My parents were fairly keen theatre-goers, so I had already seen Jonson's other great play *The Alchemist* and had enjoyed it thoroughly; *Volpone* was just as entertaining, and soon enough I was totally absorbed in the intrigues of the old fox who wanted to test the sincerity of his heirs but whose plans went badly wrong.

Elated by the performance, we stood discussing it afterwards at the bus stop. A tramp came by and politely asked Stephen if he had any loose change. Stephen felt in his pocket and exclaimed in embarrassment, "I'm sorry, I don't think I have anything left!" The tramp grinned and looked at me. "That's all right, guv'," he said, winking in my direction, "I understand." At that moment the bus drew up and we clambered on. As we sat down, Stephen turned to me apologetically, "I'm terribly sorry," he said, "but

I don't even have the money for the fare. Have you got any?" Guiltily aware of how much he must have spent on our evening, I was only too happy to oblige. The conductor approached and hovered over us as I searched for my purse in the depths of my handbag. My embarrassment equalled Stephen's as I discovered that it was missing. We jumped off the bus at the next set of traffic lights and fairly ran all the way back to the Old Vic. The main entrance to the theatre was closed, but Stephen pressed on – to the stage door at the side. It was open and the passage inside was lit. Cautiously we ventured in, but there was no one to be seen. Directly at the end of the passage we found ourselves on the deserted but still brightly lit stage. Awestruck, we tiptoed across it and down the steps into the darkened auditorium. In no time at all, to our joint relief, we found the green leather purse under the seat where I had been sitting. Just as we were heading back towards the stage, the lights went out, and there we were in total darkness. "Take my hand," said Stephen authoritatively. I held his hand and my breath in silent admiration as he led me back to the steps, up across the stage and out into the passage. Fortunately the stage door was still open, and as we tumbled out into the street we burst into laughter. We had been on the stage at the Old Vic!

3

A Glass Coach

Some weeks after the Old Vic episode, as the speed-writing course was officially coming to an end, my mother met me on my return home one evening excitedly waving a message from Stephen, who had telephoned to invite me to a May Ball in Cambridge. The prospect was tantalizing. In the Lower Sixth at school, a girl had been invited to a May Ball, and the rest of us were green with envy lapping up every detail of a gala occasion which seemed to be the stuff of fairy tales. Now, unbelievably, my turn had come. When Stephen rang to confirm the invitation, I accepted with pleasure. The problem of what to wear was soon solved when I found a dress in white-and-navy silk in a shop near the speed-writing school in Oxford Street, which was just within my means.

The May Balls, which with typical Cambridge contrariness take place in June, were still some months away. In the meantime I had to start replenishing my funds, depleted by the purchase of the ball gown, for my travels around Spain later in the summer, so I signed on with a temporary-employment agency in St Albans. My first assignment was a one-and-a-half-day stint – Thursday afternoon and the whole of Friday – in the Westminster Bank in Hatfield, where the manager of the branch, Mr Abercrombie, a patient, kindly man, was a friend of my father's. I was first directed to the telephone switchboard, but with no inkling of what to do, I panicked at the flashing lights and frantically pulled out some leads on the board while desperately trying to push others into the vacant holes. I succeeded only in cutting off all outside callers and in connecting up the telephones of people who were sitting opposite each other. After that, I gradually settled into a variety of temporary jobs as the spring advanced into early summer and the night of the May Ball approached.

When Stephen arrived one hot afternoon in early June to take me to Cambridge, I was shocked by the deterioration in his condition since that evening of the Old Vic escapade, and

I doubted that he was really strong enough to drive his father's car, a huge old Ford Zephyr. Built like a tank, it had apparently forded rivers in Kashmir when the family – minus Stephen who had stayed at school in England – had lived in India some years earlier. I feared that the snorting vehicle might well go much too fast for the present driver, a slight, frail, limping figure who appeared to use the steering wheel to hoist himself up to see over the dashboard. I introduced Stephen to my mother. She showed no signs of surprise or of alarm, but waved us away as if she were the fairy godmother, sending me off to the ball – with Prince Charming – in a runaway glass coach.

The journey was terrifying. It transpired that Stephen's role model for driving was his father, who drove fast and furiously, overtaking on hills and at corners – he had even been known to drive down a dual carriageway in the wrong direction. Drowning out all attempts at conversation, the wind roared through the open windows as we sped at take-off speed past the fields and trees of Hertfordshire into the exposed landscape of Cambridgeshire. I scarcely dared look at the road in front while Stephen, on the other hand, seemed to be looking at everything except the road. He probably felt that he could afford to live dangerously since fate had already dealt him such a cruel blow. This however was of scant reassurance to me, so I secretly vowed that I would travel home by train. I was definitely beginning to have my doubts about this supposedly fairy-tale experience of a May Ball.

Defying all road-accident statistics, we actually arrived in one piece at Stephen's lodgings, in a fine Thirties-style graduate house set in a shady garden, where the other revellers were busy with last-minute preparations. When I had changed in the upstairs room allotted to me by the housekeeper, I was introduced to Stephen's fellow lodgers and research students, whose seemingly contradictory attitudes towards him baffled me. They talked to him in his own intellectual terms, sometimes caustically sarcastic, sometimes crushingly critical, always humorous. In personal terms, however, they treated him with a gentle consideration which was almost loving. I found it hard to reconcile these two extremes of behaviour. I was used to consistency of attitude and approach, and was perplexed by these people who confidently played devil's advocate, arguing ferociously with someone – that is Stephen – one minute, and the next not only treating him as if nothing were amiss, but attending caringly to his personal needs, as if his word were their command. I had not learnt to distinguish reason from emotion, the intellect from the heart. In my innocence I had some hard lessons to learn. Such innocence, by Cambridge standards, was boring and predictable.

We all went off to a late dinner in a first-floor restaurant on the corner of King's Parade. From where I sat, I gazed out at the pinnacles and spires of King's College, the Chapel and the gatehouse, darkly silhouetted against the vast, luminous panorama of an East Anglian sunset. That in itself was magical enough. We returned to the house for last-minute adjustments before setting out on the ten-minute walk across the watery green spaces of the Backs to the old courts of Trinity Hall, Stephen's College. He insisted on taking his tape recorder and collection of tapes across to the College to install in a friend's room, put at our disposal when we needed a break from the jollifications, but he could not carry them himself. "Oh, come on," one of his friends grumbled benevolently, "I suppose I shall have to carry them for you." And he did.

Relatively small, unpretentious and tucked away from public view, Trinity Hall consists of a motley collection of buildings – very old, old, Victorian and, most recently, modern – enclosing lawns, flower beds and a terrace which overlooks the river. We approached the College from the other side of the Cam, standing briefly on the high arch of a new bridge which, Stephen seriously impressed upon me, had recently been built in memory of a student, Timothy Morgan, who had died tragically in 1960 having just completed his design for it. From that bridge we were regaled with a fairy-tale spectacle: it reminded me of the mysterious country house in one of my favourite French novels, *Le Grand Meaulnes* by Alain-Fournier, where the hero, Augustin Meaulnes, chances across a brightly lit château in the dark depths of the countryside and, from being a bemused observer, finds himself drawn into the revelries, the music and the dancing, never quite knowing what to expect. Here in Trinity Hall, bands were sending their strains out on the night air, the lawn leading down to the river was decorated with twinkling lights, as was the magnificent copper beech in the centre, and couples were already dancing on a raised platform under the tree. In the marquee at the top of the lawn I was introduced to more friends of Stephen's, and together we made a beeline for our ration of champagne, which was being served from a bath, then on to the buffet and to the various entertainments: to the tightly packed Hall where on a distant stage an inaudible cabaret was taking place, to an elegantly panelled room where a string quartet was attempting to compete with the Jamaican-steel band out on the lawn outside, and to a corner by the Old Library where chestnuts were being served from a glowing brazier. Our companions had drifted away, leaving us sitting up on the terrace by the river, watching the dancers writhe to the hypnotic rhythms of the steel band. "I'm sorry I don't dance." Stephen apologized. "That's quite all right – it doesn't matter," I lied.

Dancing was not totally out of the question however, because later, after yet another buffet and more champagne, we discovered a jazz band secreted away in a cellar. The room was dark, apart from some weird blueish lights. The men were invisible except for their cuffs and shirt-fronts, which shone with a bright-purple luminosity, while the girls could hardly be seen at all. I was fascinated. Stephen explained that the lights were picking up the fluorescent element contained in washing powder, which was why the men's shirts were so visible, but that, as the girls' new dresses would not have been contaminated with *Tide* or *Daz* or any other detergent, they did not show up with the same ghostly light. In the darkness of the underground room, I persuaded Stephen to take to the floor. We swayed gently to and fro, laughing at the dancing patterns of purple light until, to our disappointment, the band packed up and went.

In the early hours of the morning, the other colleges which had been hosting May Balls traditionally opened their doors to all-comers. As day dawned, we staggered down Trinity Street to Trinity College where, in a spacious set of rooms, somebody's extremely well-organized and mature girlfriend was preparing breakfast, but I just sank into an armchair and fell asleep. Some kind person must have led me back sleepwalking to the lodging house in Adams Road, where I slept comfortably until mid-morning.

The day's programme for the May Ball partners had been planned with the efficiency of a modern tour operator, except that it was much more stimulating. As well as researching their PhDs in Chemistry, Stephen's friends, Nick Hughes and Tom Wesley, were much involved, as editors, in the production of a guide to the post-war buildings of Cambridge, *Cambridge New Architecture*, which was to be published in 1964. Stephen shared their interest and acted as a part-time consultant in the project. They were all anxious therefore to show the objects of their deliberations to any interested parties. However sceptically these buildings are viewed today, in the Sixties they were the cause of great excitement, the assertive excitement of post-war development and expansion, unconcerned for old properties, meadows or trees which might inhibit the new wave of roads, buildings and university development. Conservation was not yet a popular concern.

With a zealous, pioneering fervour, our guides pointed out to us – their impressionably ignorant female guests – the features of a selection of new sites, either recently finished or still under construction. These included the Hugh Casson development of the Sidgwick Site, and Churchill College – the memorial to Sir Winston, whose concern at the lack of provision for scientists and technologists in this country led to the foundation of the College in 1958. We were also taken to Harvey Court, the Gonville and Caius development, which left even the contributors to *Cambridge New Architecture* lost for words. They described it hopefully as "an experiment which may eventually bully its occupants into enjoying the pattern of life it imposes", and added in its defence: "and it is Cambridge's most courageous attempt at finding some new ideal solution to the problems of college residence". Little did I know that some twelve years later I would be living next door to this particular experiment in modern living. Finally, as a sop to tradition, we visitors from less richly endowed universities were allowed to take a quick peep inside King's College Chapel.

After lunch we all went out for a ride in a punt, and then the question of the return journey loomed. "I think it would be better if I went by train," I hesitantly suggested to Stephen, but he would not hear of it. Anxious not to offend him, I took my place once again in the passenger seat of the dreaded Zephyr. The journey home was every bit as terrifying as the outward journey, and by the time we reached St Albans, I decided that, much as I appreciated the May Ball, I did not want to subject myself to that sort of dodgem ride ever again. My mother was in the front garden when we drew up at the gate. I tersely said "thank you and goodbye" to Stephen, and, with never a backwards glance, marched into the house. My mother followed me in and reprimanded me severely: "You're not going to send that poor young man away without even a cup of tea are you?" she said, shocked at my indifference. Her words pricked my conscience. I ran out of the house to try and catch Stephen. He was still there, parked at the gate, trying to start the car. Slowly the car began to roll back down the steep hill, because he had let the brake off before getting the engine started. He jammed the brake on and, with alacrity, came in for tea, sitting with me in the sun by the garden door. As we excitedly recounted the events of the ball to my mother, he was attentive and charming. I decided that I really rather liked him and could forgive his road madness providing I did not have to experience it too often.

4

Hidden Truths

A couple of weeks later we temporarily acquired an addition to our family as my parents had responded to a call for accommodation for visiting French teenagers and were taking care of a sixteen-year-old girl whose best friend, by an uncanny coincidence, was lodging with the Hawkings. One Saturday in June, not long after the May Ball, Isobel Hawking invited the two French girls and me to join her on a visit to Cambridge. To my relief, she drove sensibly, talked in a jovially concentrated intellectual fashion and brought a splendid picnic – "a cold collation" she called it – which we ate on the veranda of Stephen's ground-floor room in Adams Road. Thus my family and I were brought into closer and more regular contact with the Hawkings, and when Stephen came back to St Albans for a weekend, my parents invited him to dinner. They treated him with faultless hospitality, outwardly unperturbed by his appearance. He had reverted to his old Oxford ways. His lank, straight hair was longer than ever, and the black-velvet smoking jacket and the red bow tie had become a uniform, adopted to defy the very conformity which my parents represented. They, for their part, may have taken comfort from the fact that this was to be our last meeting for some time, as I was on the point of setting off yet again for Spain.

Early one morning in July 1963, my father drove me to Gatwick for a student flight which was due to leave at 9 a.m. and arrive in Madrid at one o'clock, but take-off was delayed while repairs were carried out to an engine. I was not at all concerned by the delay, nor by the need for repairs, nor by the fact that, after take-off, water – which eventually turned to icicles – dripped through the roof of the aircraft. Nor was I worried by the discovery that the captain and his co-pilot were happily enjoying a glass of beer when we students were invited to look into the cockpit. Bill Lewis, an acquaintance of our local GP, who was meeting me in Madrid, was much more anxious. "I thought you must be coming via the North Pole!" he joked when, at last, I emerged from customs at five in the afternoon. He took me home to meet his wife, who assured me of a warm welcome at their apartment every evening from six onwards, and then he delivered me to the lodgings he had found for me. Pilar, the landlady, was a small, vivacious, sharp-nosed, black-haired single lady who lived in a extraordinarily large, well-appointed flat just round the corner from the Lewises. Pilar's other lodger, Sylvia, was also English and worked at the British Embassy. Sylvia was not happy about some of Pilar's friends, who would turn up at all hours of the day and the night, and when she told me her concerns I hastened to lay my plans for leaving Madrid at the earliest opportunity, but not before taking advantage of every precious moment in the capital city and its environs to visit the Prado Museum and join many a tourist bus to the royal palaces at Aranjuez and the Escorial. Of course I also went to Toledo, the medieval city perched on a rock above the river Tajo, where in the thirteenth century Jews, Arabs and Christians had worked in perfect harmony in the pursuit of learning, and where in the seventeeth century El Greco executed some of his finest paintings. With a group of students I went on the pilgrimage to the Valley of the Fallen, el Valle de los Caídos, supposedly the monument to the dead of both sides in the Civil War but in fact a burial place only for the Fascists – and eventually Franco himself – constructed by Republican prisoners of war. I began to realize that the many mutilated beggars on the streets of Madrid were the tragic, living remnants of the Civil War, revealing an ugly, schizoid streak to Spain. In the mid-twentieth century, the country still bore out the disturbing contrasts depicted by Goya in the eighteenth- and early-nineteenth-century paintings and drawings I had seen in the Prado.

Back in Pilar's establishment, Sylvia and I had the uncomfortable sensation that things were coming to crisis point. We had persistently refused to go out with her in the evenings and, just as regularly, saucepans were now clattering through the air in the kitchen, while meals and mealtimes became a matter of chance. Feeling slightly guilty at leaving Sylvia in the lurch, I took evasive action and set off by air-conditioned train for the safety of Granada, where I settled in for a protracted stay at an international student hostel which housed a stimulating and unpredictable crowd, particularly the Spaniards among them, whose discussions could range from politics to poetry in the space of a single breath. To preserve my own sanity, I would sometimes have to escape from the intensity of their arguments to wander the streets of Granada in the heat of the day, watching the gypsy children at play in front of their caves, or to stroll through the Moorish palace, the Alhambra and the gardens of the Generalife, astounded at the sheer extravagant beauty of the place.

Lulled into a dreamy slumber by the perfume of the roses and the playing of the fountains, I would sit alone for hours under the arches in the courtyard of streams, in the Generalife, and from there would gaze across to the forbidding walls which concealed the intricate, creamy lacework of the inner courtyards of the Alhambra. Dazzling in the sun, the city lay at my feet, its glare broken only by the tall bottle-green spikes of the cypresses and the violent purple and pink patches of bougainvillea tumbling over reflecting white walls. A beautiful city but also a very cruel city. What other city could claim to have murdered its own most famous son? It was in Granada at the outbreak of the Spanish Civil War that the rebellious right-wing Francoist forces slaughtered the greatest Spanish poet of the twentieth century, Federico García Lorca, the poet who, through the colour, rhythm and vision of his verse, had introduced me to Andalucía long before I had set foot on its soil.

During these long periods of solitary contemplation in a setting of such dramatically haunting beauty, I found myself overcome by waves of loneliness. In the past I had known moments of extreme dejection without being able to identify a precise cause. The reason for them was now becoming apparent and it was natural enough: I longed to have someone with whom to share my experiences. Moreover, I realized that the person I most wanted to share them with was Stephen. The early rapport between us had held much promise of harmony and compatibility. Because of his illness, any relationship with him was bound to be precarious, short-lived and probably heartbreaking. Could I help him fulfil himself and find even a brief happiness? I doubted whether I was up to the task, but when I confided in my new-found friends of all nationalities they urged me to go ahead. "If he needs you, you must do it," they said.

Competing against this inner turmoil, the strong pull of adventure finally tore me away from the brooding magic of Granada and deposited me on a hot, smelly bus, crowded with market vendors and their wares – mostly still alive and flapping and squawking – on the slow crawl over the hills to Málaga. I was waiting in the bus station for the connection to La Línea, the last Spanish outpost before Gibraltar, when a man came up to me and asked if I would like to train as a Spanish dancer. To my surprise he explained that I had the right looks and figure. Although I was by now an old hand at fending off the predatory Spanish male, I was flattered. Despite my misgivings, the man appeared genuine. He was neither oily nor ingratiating, but quite straightforward in his approach. He handed me a card bearing the address of his dance studio. I was weighing up his offer when the bus for La Línea lumbered into view and hauled me out of temptation's way. Sometimes I have a faint twinge of regret at how that bus broke all known records for timekeeping in Spain by arriving on schedule. Who knows what my story might have been, had it arrived just a few minutes later?

From La Línea I passed through the very physical border between Spain and Gibraltar, a barricade of green iron railings about twenty feet high with a gate at the customs post. Gibraltar, with all its incongruous trappings of British colonialism, was a convenient stepping stone for my one and only trip to Africa, to Tangiers for my first encounter with the descendants of the people who had invaded Spain in 711 and stayed there for more than seven hundred years – the Arabs. I liked them. They treated me, a young English girl travelling alone, with great courtesy and, unlike the Spaniards, who automatically harassed any passing foreign female, they showed no such disrespect. They were a dignified people, proud of their artistic skills, which were everywhere on display in the booths of the Kazbah. They were also gentle and hospitable, curious to learn about life in Europe, as I discovered over many glasses of the hot, sweet mint tea with which they plied me whenever I bought the smallest item in their shops.

Quite a few saucepans had been flung around in Madrid during my absence, according to Sylvia. Pilar was more and more dissatisfied with the return that she was getting from her paying guests, having doubtless anticipated sizeable bonuses of one sort or another, and had turned Sylvia out of her room, so she was now sharing with me. This we decided was a good thing, because there was safety in numbers, but it was no good for Sylvia as a long-term prospect, since I would shortly be leaving and she could not possibly stay in the house on her own. I had deliberately refrained from telling the Lewises the truth about the lodgings they had kindly found for me, as I did not want to appear ungrateful for their help or their hospitality, but the time had now come to apprise them of the goings-on at *la casa de Pilar*. Sylvia came with me to the Lewises' six o'clock cocktail hour, and together we told them about the succession of decidedly repulsive male visitors to the apartment – for, albeit on a small scale, Pilar was running a disorderly house and was intent on procuring nice English girls for some of the flabby, ageing men of her acquaintance. We recounted how they attempted to grab us when we returned home at night, usually sheltering behind the *sereno*, the nightwatchman, who kept the keys to the front doors of all the apartment houses in the street and who would appear at a clap of the hands to open the main door. We lightly glossed over the shenanigans which went on all night in the other rooms in the flat, and the ominous rattlings of the locked bedroom door handle.

As Sylvia and I recounted these tales to the captive audience of British expatriates on my final evening in Madrid, Mrs Lewis spluttered over her gin and tonic, while her other guests grinned in amusement. Immediately the tendrils of the local grapevine started reaching out to find new lodgings for Sylvia as a matter of urgency. Most of the Lewis regulars, like Sylvia, worked at the British Embassy, though she had not met any of them before. They were amusing but modest, a good advertisement for the Diplomatic Service, which began to beckon as an exciting career prospect. I returned to England the next day, by student flight, sad to have left behind so many experiences, sights, sounds, acquaintances and intrigues, but dazzled at the array of contrasting, maybe even conflicting, possibilities that were opening up before me.

5

Uncertain Principles

My attempts to get in touch with Stephen on my return home from Spain were unavailing. According to his mother, he had already gone back to Cambridge and was not at all well. I was busy preparing to leave home to embark on a new stage of my life in London and, for the next few weeks that autumn, my attention was totally absorbed as I was drawn into the academic and social whirl of the Westfield scene in particular, and London in general. Concerts, the theatre and the ballet were all within easy reach. This was how I came to be travelling on the London Underground with a group of friends when we glimpsed the headlines announcing President Kennedy's assassination. It was at about that time, November 1963, that I heard from Stephen again. He was coming to London for dental treatment and asked if I would like to go to the opera with him. This was a much more enticing prospect than any of the Freshers' hops, which despite Beatlemania were dire occasions where the boys stayed stuck to the walls until the last dance. Though I had loved music since early childhood, I had had little formal training and had been to the opera only once – with the school to a performance of *The Marriage of Figaro* at Sadler's Wells. My single attempt to learn an instrument, the flute, had been quickly aborted at the age of thirteen, when I broke both arms trying to ice-skate on the frozen lake in the park at Verulamium, the site of the Roman city on which St Albans was founded.

One Friday afternoon that November, I met Stephen in Harley Street, where Russell Cole, his Australian uncle by marriage, had his dental practice. He walked haltingly, lurching from side to side, making taxis an expensive necessity for journeys of any great distance. Curiously, as his gait became more unsteady, so his opinions became more forceful and defiant. On our way to visit the Wallace Collection, only a short distance from Harley Street, he announced quite adamantly that he did not share the general hero-worship of the assassinated President. In his opinion, the manner of Kennedy's handling of the Cuban Missile Crisis could only be described as foolhardy: he had brought the world to the brink of nuclear war and it was he, not the Russians, who had threatened a military confrontation. What's more, Stephen declared, it was preposterous for the United States to claim a victory, because Kennedy had agreed to remove US missiles from Turkey to appease Kruschev. Despite the force with which he expressed his ideas and his difficulty in walking, Stephen was indefatigable, so, from the Wallace Collection, we made our way down Regent Street in search of a restaurant. We were just crossing Lower Regent Street when, in the middle of the road, as the lights were turning green, he stumbled and fell. With the help of a passer-by, I dragged him to his feet and thereafter gave him my arm to lean on. Shaken, we hailed a taxi for Sadler's Wells.

The opera for which Stephen had tickets was *The Flying Dutchman*. It was magnificent, sweeping us away in the power of its music and the drama of its legendary tale. The Dutchman, cursed to roam the seas through storm and wind until he could find someone who would sacrifice herself for love of him, was a wild, hounded figure, loudly lamenting his fate from the rigging of his tossing ship. Senta, the girl who fell in love with him, was pure and innocent. Like most Wagnerian sopranos, however, her weight kept her pretty firmly moored to her spinning wheel. Sensing that Stephen identified closely with the hero, I began to understand his demonic driving tactics. His father's car was the vehicle for his fury at the trick that Fate had dealt him. He too was flying hither and thither in search of rescue – in a manner that could only be described as foolhardy.

After that evening, I felt that I needed to find out more for myself about Stephen's condition. I made several sorties into London, searching out old acquaintances who had become medical students, and investigating the poky offices of various charities dealing in neurological illnesses. Everywhere I drew a blank. Perhaps it was better not to know. Was Stephen's fate any worse, I wondered, than the fate which loomed over us all? We lived under the shadow of the nuclear cloud, and none of us could count on our full threescore years and ten.

In the lull of the bleak winter days between Christmas and the New Year, I called on Stephen at home in St Albans. He was on the point of leaving for London to go to the opera with his father and sisters. However he was so obviously delighted to see me that

I readily accepted his spontaneous invitation – to accompany him and his father in a week's time to yet another opera, Strauss's *Der Rosenkavalier*. The opera seemed to be an established family pastime in the Hawking household, whereas I, a newcomer, was still assessing this hybrid art form. Though undoubtedly it could exert tremendous emotional power through the combination of music and drama, it could also appear ludicrous if for the merest second one's concentration lapsed. During the next term Stephen seemed to have access to an inexhaustible supply of opera tickets and was forever coming to London to take me to Covent Garden or Sadler's Wells. I once ventured to suggest that I would rather like to go to the ballet, as the ballet had been my passion since the age of four, but that suggestion was quashed with withering scorn. Ballet was a waste of time, and the music was trivial, not worth the effort of listening, I was told. Chastened, I refrained from telling Stephen when I managed to get myself a ticket for Tchaikovsky's *Romeo and Juliet*, with Fonteyn and Nureyev, through the student union. We went in a party of girls and sat in the cheap seats, far back and high up in the amphitheatre at Covent Garden, way above the Grand Circle where the Hawkings usually sat. That performance was sublime, and it left me deeply moved.

Stephen was still coming to London frequently for seminars or for dental appointments and, increasingly, I found myself travelling to Cambridge to visit him on Saturdays or Sundays. Those visits, though urgently awaited, often proved disappointing to both of us. The fare – at ten shillings return – made quite a hole in my allowance of ten pounds a month, and the course of love did not run at all smoothly. It did not need much imagination to realize that Stephen could not contemplate embarking on a long-term, stable relationship because of the dismal prognosis of his illness. A quick fling was probably all he could envisage, and that was not what I – in my innocence and in the puritanical climate of the early Sixties, when the fear of an unwanted pregnancy was a potent constraint – dared imagine. These opposing perspectives led to such tension between us that I often returned to London in tears, and Stephen probably felt that my presence was rubbing salt into the wound of his trauma. He revealed little where emotional matters were concerned and he refused to talk about his illness. For fear of hurting him, I tried to intuit his feelings without forcing him to voice them, thus unwittingly establishing a tradition of non-communication, which eventually would become intolerable. I met him yet again in Harley Street later that winter, after an appointment with his consultant. "How did you get on?" I asked. He grimaced. "He told me not to bother to come back, because there's nothing he can do," he said.

At Westfield, Margaret Smithson, my room-mate, came with me to the meetings of the Christian Union, where I hoped to gain some supportive insights for a situation which was becoming very confusing as I became more and more involved in it. Like his parents, Stephen had no hesitation in declaring himself an atheist, despite the strong Methodist background of his Yorkshire grandparents. It was understandable that, as a cosmologist examining the laws that governed the universe, he could not allow his calculations to be muddled by a confessed belief in the existence of a creator God, quite apart from the confusion his illness might be creating in his mind. I was quite glad to get away from the tedium of regular Sunday church-going, but was not inclined to abandon my beliefs completely. Even then, possibly under my mother's influence, I was convinced that there had to be more to heaven and earth than was contained in Stephen's cold, impersonal philosophy. Although by this stage I was completely under his spell, bewitched by his clear blue-grey eyes and the broad dimpled smile, I resisted his atheism. Instinctively I knew that I could not allow myself to succumb to such a negative influence, which could offer no consolation, no comfort and no hope for the human condition. Atheism would destroy us both. I needed to cling to whatever rays of hope I could find and maintain sufficient faith for the two of us if any good were to come of our sad plight.

The meetings of the college Christian Union were not well attended, and soon they were to be even less so. The topic for the term's discussions was the nature of divine grace, but it quickly transpired that the leaders of the group, including the young chaplain, whose name we irreverently traduced to the Revd P. Souper, were firmly of the opinion that only baptized, confessed, practising Christians could receive divine grace, salvation or whatever else they liked to call it, and only they had the right qualifications to enter the Kingdom of Heaven. Margaret and I were so indignant that we walked out, furiously compiling lists of all those dearly loved – good people, friends and relations – who did not fulfil all the correct criteria, and held our own long discussions on these topics, which we continued into the vacations, when I went to stay with her and her family in Yorkshire.

Language students nowadays regularly spend a whole year abroad. In the Sixties it was a luxury to be able to spend even a term in the country of one's target language. We Westfield students set out by train and boat in late April to spend the summer on a pre-arranged course at the university of Valencia. We arrived to find that no such course existed and that all the university could offer us was a few classes in Spanish on Shakespeare. The only obligation on us was to collect our certificates of attendance at the end of the term, whether we attended the lectures or not. We went to just one class, which made a travesty of Macbeth, and decided that enough was enough. I had had a lifetime's education in Shakespeare at school and could not bear the thought of having a supplementary dose in Spanish. My companions agreed, so, thereafter, we went to the beach instead.

Only two weeks later, though the others still went to the beach, I was forced to stay at home, confined to my room in the seventh-floor apartment with a blinding headache which at first I thought was sunstroke but which developed into a severe case of chickenpox. I was already feeling wretchedly miserable. I missed Stephen badly: communication by telephone was out of the question in those days, and he did not write to me although I sent him many letters. The only comfort was afforded by my Westfield friends, whose visits kept me in touch with the outside world, and by my landlady, Doña Pilar de Ubeda, and her middle-aged daughter Maribel, who were kindness personified. As I slowly started to regain strength, I wandered into the kitchen, where Doña Pilar gave me lessons in Spanish cookery, a far more useful accomplishment than studying Shakespeare in Spanish. She taught me how to peel an orange tidily in quarters, how to make *gazpacho* and *paella* and she took me shopping with her. Luckily, with a spotty face and in the presence of such an august matron, I was spared the approaches of the men idly lounging around in the streets. Back in the flat, I sat in the living room listening ad nauseam to the two records I had bought myself – Beethoven's *Seventh Symphony* and excerpts from Wagner's *Tristan and Isolde*. The latter reduced me to an exquisitely painful state of woe. At last the longed-for moment came. Setting out by train for Barcelona on the first leg of the journey home, I was glad to leave Valencia behind: despite the succulence of its oranges and the all-pervasive perfume of its citrus groves, it left the nasty taste (of constant sexual harassment and the bitterness) of a repressive regime that thought nothing of flinging students into jail overnight and removing uncomplimentary pages from imported copies of the *Times*.

My parents brought Stephen to meet me, and the initial moment of reunion was happy but short-lived. I soon became aware that in my absence he had changed: his physical condition had not altered markedly, except that he now regularly walked with a stick, but his personality was overshadowed by a deep depression. This revealed itself in a harsh black cynicism, aided and abetted by long hours of Wagnerian opera played at full volume. He was even more terse and uncommunicative, apparently so absorbed in himself that when he offered to teach me to play croquet on the Trinity Hall lawn, for example, he seemed to forget that I was there. Throwing the stick, which had become his constant appendage, to one side, he gave out curt instructions as I aimed my ball towards the first hoop, missing it. He then took up his mallet and, croqueting my ball round the whole course, reached the finishing post before I had even had a second turn. I stood open-mouthed, amused and perturbed at one and the same time. This was indeed an impressive tour de force, in which he scarcely bothered to veil his hostility and frustration, as if he were deliberately trying to deter me from further association with him. It was too late. I was already so deeply involved with him that there was no easy or obvious way out.

It was painful but perhaps beneficial that we were soon to be parted again: Stephen was about to set out for Germany, with his sister Philippa, on a pilgrimage to the Wagnerian shrine, the Festspielhaus in Bayreuth, with tickets for the complete *Ring Cycle*. Thence they were to travel by rail behind the Iron Curtain to Prague. Meanwhile I was to accompany my father to an international governmental conference in Dijon, where I was to stay with a local family, an elderly couple with a highly sophisticated twenty-five-year-old daughter who had a job and a boyfriend. I was not at a loss for diversion however, because Dad's conference, after a day or two of lectures and study sessions, generated its own entertainment in which I was privileged to share. Since we were in Bourgogne, that naturally revolved around the vineyards, the famous *Clos* of the region.

Consequently there began yet another stage, arguably one of the most enjoyable of my education – the cultivation of a discerning palate in the course of which I was pleasurably introduced to the great names and the great bouquets of Bourgogne, Nuits-Saint-Georges, Côtes de Beaune, Clos de Vougeot. The advertising slogan for Nuits-Saint-Georges aroused my innocent curiosity: tantalizingly the deep velvety wine was said to resemble "*la nuit des noces, douce et caressante…*"

From Dijon we drove to Geneva airport to meet my mother and then spent a couple of days in our favourite retreat, high in the Bernese Oberland, at Hohfluh, a tiny village atop the Brenner Pass overlooking the valley of the Aare at Meiringen and enjoying the most spellbinding scenery. Before we left Switzerland for Italy, Dad took us to Lucerne, the medieval city on the edge of the lake, and showed us the sequence of paintings of the Dance of Death, in the roof beams of one of the wooden bridges which spanned the river. He pointed out the white-clad figure of Death, selecting its victim and capturing him in a deadly embrace and then whirling him faster and faster to his doom.

Italy was ravishing, a feast for the mind and the senses. Art, history, music, light and colour met us and pursued us everywhere we went – Como, Florence, San Gimignano, Pisa, Siena, Verona, Padua – in a vertiginous display of florid exuberance. One evening in Florence, after a day in the presence of Michelangelo, Botticelli, Bellini and Leonardo da Vinci, my mother and I were leaning out of the hotel window, looking across the Arno to the Pitti Palace, where we were to attend a concert. It was then, in an expansive moment, that she confided to me her reasons for marrying my father at the beginning of the War. If he were wounded, she said, she wanted to be able to care for him herself. That remark was prescient for, only a few days later, when we arrived at our hotel in Venice, the Hotel Della Salute on a secluded canal behind the church of the same name, the manager produced a postcard addressed to me. It was a view of the castle at Salzburg and it was from Stephen.

I was overjoyed. Could Stephen really have been thinking of me as I had been thinking of him? It gave me grounds for daring to hope that he was looking forward to seeing me at the end of the summer. The postcard was uncharacteristically full of news. He had arrived in Salzburg for the tail end of the Festival, which was quite a contrast to Bayreuth. Czechoslovakia had been wonderful and remarkably cheap, a good advertisement for communism. He did not mention that a bad fall on a train in Germany had deprived him of his front teeth and that many hours of painstaking dentistry by his uncle in Harley Street would be required to replace them. In the glow of romance, albeit conducted at a distance, Venice, its canals, lagoon, palaces, churches, galleries and islands – became even more gloriously scintillating – yet, impatient for the possible opening of a new chapter in my life, I was not sorry to leave it and return to Switzerland. From Basle we were to fly home with the car on board an aeroplane, in a well justified stroke of extravagance after the many thousands of miles my father had driven single-handedly across the Continent over the years.

Stephen was pleased to see me on my return. Intuitively I understood that he had begun to view our relationship in a more positive light and had perhaps decided that all was not lost, that the future did not have to be as black as his worst fears had painted it. Back in Cambridge, one dark wet Saturday evening in October, he hesitantly whispered a proposal of marriage to me. That moment transformed our lives and consigned all my thoughts of a career in the Diplomatic Service to oblivion.

6

Backgrounds

Once the momentous decision had been taken, everything else began to fall into place, if not automatically, then with some determination and effort. We sailed through the next year, carried high on a tide of euphoria. Whatever misgivings my friends and family may have had about Stephen's state of health, they kept them to themselves, and the only comments I received concerned the eccentricity of the Hawking family.

Such comments did not worry me too much, because I liked the Hawkings and regarded their eccentricities with a respectful fascination. They made me welcome, already treating me as one of the family. They may have economized on material goods, preferring the old and tried to the newfangled, and they certainly did compromise on heating to the extent that people who were cold were brusquely told to follow Frank Hawking's example and wear more clothes, a dressing gown for example, even during the day. Moreover, as I had already discovered, there were areas of the house which could be charitably described as distinctly shabby. However, none of this was particularly new to me. It simply indicated that this household had a set of priorities which were not so very different from those I was used to. My own parents had scraped and saved for years. We were not wealthy, and we often had to make do and mend because so much of Dad's income went on our education and on those wonderful summer holidays. We did not have central heating at home, and I was well used to sitting by the fire with my face and toes burning while a freezing draught whistled down the back of my neck. At night in bed I would rest my numbed feet on my hot-water bottle, in the full knowledge that blistering chilblains would be the price of such small comfort the next morning, when an exquisite ice garden of opaque fronds and ferns would cover the window panes. If our house was smarter than the Hawkings', it was both because it was smaller and because Dad had given up all pretensions to any prowess whatsoever as a handyman – and for

49

good reason, since his attempts at repairs usually made matters much worse, bringing ceilings down on his head for example, while his attempts at interior decorating usually sent the paint flying everywhere except on the target – and had long decided that it was cheaper in the long run to pay professionals to do his odd jobs for him.

Rarely when I was present did members of the Hawking family bear out the stories about their habit of bringing books to the table. Mealtimes were generally sociable occasions, calmly presided over by Stephen's mother, who kept remarkably cool in the face of her husband's frequent displays of temper. Although he could be sharp and demanding, Frank Hawking was not hard-hearted. His outbursts were usually directed at the crass inadequacies of some inanimate object, like a blunt carving knife or a spilt glass or a dropped fork, never at people within the family circle. In fact, in handling young Edward, who was given to tantrums particularly at bedtime, he was a model of patience and forbearance. As for Stephen, apparently no longer subject to the savage black moods of the past, his placid, more philosophical nature promised a quieter lifestyle.

The talk at mealtimes was predictably intellectual, ranging over political and international issues. As Philippa had gone up to Oxford to study Chinese, the Cultural Revolution was a frequent topic. I knew little about oriental history or politics and thought it expedient to keep quiet rather than betray my ignorance. Spain and France seemed very parochial and unglamorous by comparison with the Orient, and nobody expressed any interest in them or in their cultures at all. The Hawkings, in any case, knew all there was to know about France, since Isobel had French relatives. They also knew all there was to know about Spain, since she and the children had spent three months living in close proximity to Robert Graves's household in Deià, Majorca, in the winter of 1950, when Frank was away in Africa, engaged on research in tropical medicine. Beryl Graves was a friend of Isobel's from her Oxford days, and Robert Graves was regarded as an icon in the family.

When the supper table was cleared away, we, the younger generation, would settle down to play a board game. A fanatical games player since his early childhood, Stephen had, with his close friend John McClenahan, devised a long and complicated dynastic game, complete with family trees, landed gentry, vast acreages, bishoprics for younger sons and death duties. This game unfortunately had not been preserved, so we were reduced to playing games such as *Cluedo*, *Scrabble* and occasionally the notoriously difficult Chinese game, mah-jong, with its delicately carved ivory tiles. Not only had I already been exposed to Stephen's prowess at croquet but I had also received similar treatment when he offered to teach me to play chess. However, when it came to *Scrabble*, I did not need a mentor as I was confident of being reasonably competent at word games, an art learnt as a very small child from numerous games of *Lexicon* with my loquacious and inventive Great Aunt Effie when we lived in her house in north London.

If there were not a quorum for board games, Stephen and I would sit by the fire after supper while his mother regaled us with episodes of family history. I enjoyed listening to her and admired her as a role model. An Oxford graduate and, before her marriage, an income-tax inspector, she was intelligent and witty, yet totally devoted to her family, appearing to have no ambitions for herself at all. At the time she was teaching history in a private girls' boarding school in St Albans, where her very considerable intellectual qualities were definitely underrated. With a bemused detachment, she took upon herself the task of introducing me to her own past and that of the Hawking family. The second child of seven, she was born in Glasgow, where her father, the son of a wealthy boiler maker, was a doctor. Although her family moved by boat to Plymouth when she was still a young child, she had vivid memories of her grandfather's austere house in Glasgow, where family prayers in the parlour, attended by every member of the household staff, constituted the only form of diversion. On her mother's side, she claimed descent from John Law of Lauriston, who after bankrupting France in the seventeenth century took himself off to Louisiana. In the telling, multifarious and far-reaching family feuds came to light, most of them concerned money, for it appeared that cutting a miscreant out of one's will was considered an automatic and quite acceptable means of expressing profound and puritanical displeasure.

Stephen's father's family were of God-fearing Yorkshire-farming stock. Their claim to distinction had come through an ancestor in the early nine-teenth century who had been steward to the Duke of Devonshire. In recognition of this elevated position he had built himself a sizeable house in Boroughbridge in Yorkshire, and had called it Chatsworth. The family fortunes had fluctuated somewhat since those days, with the consequence that, in the twentieth century, Stephen's grandfather's farming ventures had led to financial ruin and it was left to his grandmother to rescue her family of five children – four boys and a girl – from penury. This she did by opening a school in her house. Its success was said to be a measure of her strength of character. Money, wealth and its creation and loss were prominent elements in Isobel's story-telling, as was her marked tendency to judge others by their intelligence rather than by their integrity or kindness. Charm was regarded as a severe flaw in character, and those unfortunate enough to possess it were to be deeply mistrusted.

As his mother was one of seven children and his father one of five, Stephen naturally had legions of first cousins and a whole army of second cousins. My parents, on the other hand, were both only children, so I had no first cousins: all I possessed were a few second cousins, one in Australia and the rest in rural Norfolk. It therefore came as quite a shock to meet so many people who not only were closely related, but who also bore remarkable facial similarities to each other. On Stephen's mother's side, they characteristically had high cheekbones, close-set blue eyes and wavy, chestnut hair, while the faces of his father's relations were all long and heavily jowled. Only my brother bore any slight resemblance to me, yet here were all of thirty-three cousins who looked like each other, depending on which side of the family they belonged to, and who were all closely connected to Stephen.

Although quite a number lived abroad and divorce had been rather fashionable among them, I met many of them, their friends, husbands, wives and even their former spouses, during the course of that winter's succession of family parties. They treated me in an open and friendly manner, and I began to realize what an advantage a large family network could be: the loss of individuality in appearance was more than compensated by the sense of security which such a network could create. The novelty of this sense of extended family was exhilarating. By comparison my own immediate family circle of parents, brother and one grandmother and two great-aunts seemed a bit limited.

There was however one Hawking who notably lacked the self-assurance of the rest of the family. On hearing of our engagement, Stephen's Aunt Muriel announced that, as she put it, she "just had to come down from Yorkshire to see what sort of girl Stephen was marrying". Muriel was Frank Hawking's only sister. The most timid member of the family, she had stayed at home to look after her ageing parents despite being a gifted musician. Now in her sixties, she wore the marks of frustration in her sad, drooping face and large, soft brown eyes. She was devoted to her brother, Frank, and to his eldest son, and dutifully admired the family's intellectual qualities, although she herself did not share them. Her homely way of speech was often ignored by the other members of the family, though Stephen, who was her Methodist equivalent of a godson, always treated her with a good-natured tolerance. Frequently I would sit and chat to Auntie Muriel, just as I would sometimes escape to Granny Walker's attic, to get away from the competitive intellectual atmosphere of the dining room.

Stephen could be highly critical of people other than his closest relatives. His self-confidence restored, he delighted in bringing his Oxford ways into any conversation, deliberately setting out to shock with his provocative statements. His comment that Norwich cathedral was a very ordinary building profoundly upset my mild-mannered Grandma when I took him to stay with her for a weekend. He considered my friends to be easy victims and had no compunction in monopolizing the conversation at parties with his controversial opinions, often dominating the social scene with vociferous and tenacious arguments.

With me he would argue that artificial flowers were in every way preferable to the real thing and that Brahms, my favourite composer, was second-rate because he was such a poor orchestrator. Rachmaninov was good only for the musical dustbin and Tchaikovsky was primarily a composer of ballet music. So far, my knowledge of composers was embryonic: all I knew about Rachmaninov and Tchaikovsky was that their music had the power to move me profoundly and I knew nothing about Brahms's orchestration. It was only later that I found out, to my silent amusement, that although Wagner had despised Brahms, the feeling was mutual.

While I applauded Stephen's refusal to be drawn into small talk, I was nervously aware that his arrogance was in poor taste and was putting me in danger of losing me my friends, if not my relations. There came a stage when I even feared that he was jeopardizing my chances of any future academic activity. I was content to abandon all my budding hopes of a career in the Foreign Office for his sake, but I was unhappy about letting him destroy whatever opportunity I might have had for pursuing some sort of research. When I took him to meet my supervisor, Alan Deyermond, who was at that time encouraging me to think about doing a PhD in medieval literature, Stephen really excelled himself. Waving his sherry glass around as if the point he was making was so obvious that only a fool could disagree with it, he revelled in the opportunity to tell Alan Deyermond and all my contemporaries that the study of medieval literature was as useful an occupation as studying pebbles on the beach. Fortunately, as Alan Deyermond was also an Oxford graduate, he willingly picked up the gauntlet thus offered and gave Stephen a good run for his money. The argument was inconclusive, and both sides parted on remarkably amiable terms. When I protested on the way home in the car, Stephen shrugged. "You shouldn't take it personally," he said.

Stephen's conviction that intellectual arguments were never to be considered a personal matter was tested during that same year. Professor Fred Hoyle, who had rejected Stephen's postgraduate research application, was at the time pioneering the use of television to popularize science to great effect. He had become a household name and his success was enabling him to put pressure on the government to grant him his own Institute of Astronomy in Cambridge. It was a foregone conclusion that if his demands were not met, he – like so many other British scientists – would join the brain drain to the United States. He had power and popularity, and his recent theories were eagerly followed in the press, especially those which he was developing with his Indian research student, Jayant Narlikar, whose office was near Stephen's on the old Cavendish site in Cambridge.

In advance of publication, Hoyle's latest paper, expounding further aspects of the theory of the steady-state universe which he had developed with Hermann Bondi and Thomas Gold, was presented to a distinguished gathering of scientists at the Royal Society. Then the forum was opened to questions, which on such occasions are usually fairly deferential. Stephen was present and bided his time. At last his raised hand was noticed by the chairman. He, a very junior research student who as yet had no academic research of any note to his credit, struggled to his feet and proceeded to tell Hoyle and his students as well as the rest of the audience that the calculations in the presentation were wrong. The audience was stunned, and Hoyle was ruffled by this piece of effrontery. "How do you know?" he asked, quite sure that Stephen's grounds for disputing his new research could easily be dismissed. He was not expecting Stephen's response. "I've worked it out," he replied, and then added, "in my head." As a result of that intervention, Stephen began to be noticed in scientific circles, and thus he found the subject for his PhD thesis: the properties of expanding universes. Relations between him and Fred Hoyle however never advanced after that incident.

Arguments notwithstanding – scientific, impersonal or otherwise – everything we did in the course of that academic year contributed to a common purpose, our forthcoming marriage, for which a date in July 1965 was set. As it was by no means certain that I should be allowed to stay in Westfield as a married undergraduate, my top priority was to win the consent of the college authorities. Without it, the wedding would probably have to be postponed for another year, because we both knew that the promise my father had demanded of us on our engagement – that I would complete my undergraduate course – was not to be taken lightly. Since a year was a long time in the course of an illness such as Stephen's, as his father persistently reminded me, his survival for that length of time could not be guaranteed. This unpalatable truth was a factor that I should have to bear in mind constantly whenever I looked to the future. In the first instance, it was now up to me to persuade Professor John Varey, the Head of the Spanish Department, and Mrs Matthews, the Principal, that the situation was urgent. Professor Varey's response, when I tentatively broached the matter, was that the situation was most irregular, but that if the Principal gave her blessing, he would not object.

As my previous – and only – encounter with Mrs Matthews had been at the interview in 1962, I was not hopeful of a propitious outcome. At the time appointed by her secretary, six o'clock one evening towards the end of the autumn term of 1964, I knocked with trembling hand at the green baize door which separated her flat in the Regency house from the administrative area of the College. Mrs Matthews evidently sensed my nervousness from the moment I walked through the door. She bade me sit down and thrust a cigarette into one hand and a sherry into the other. "What's the matter?" she began, frowning and looking me straight in the eye with an anxious concern, "don't worry, I'm not going to eat you." I took a deep breath and did my best to explain my relationship with Stephen, his illness, the prognosis and our plans to make the most of whatever time we had left to us. She never took her eyes off me and betrayed very little emotion. When she had heard my tale through without interruption, she came straight to the point. "Well, of course, if you marry, you will have to live out of College, you understand that don't you?" My heart lifted slightly, aware that she had not vetoed our plans outright, and I was able to nod confidently because I had already done my homework on that score. "Yes, I know that," I replied, "I have found out that there is a room available in a private house in Platt's Lane." "Well, then, that's fine," Mrs Matthews replied, staring fixedly at the embers in the grate. "Go ahead and make the most of the chance you have." She paused and then, changing her tone to one of uncharacteristic absent-mindedness, she confided that she herself had been in a similar situation. Her own husband had been severely disabled. She was only too well aware of how important it was to do whatever one knew to be right. Equally she agreed with my father that I must complete my education. She warned me that the future I faced would not be easy. She promised to help in whatever way she could – most significantly, by conveying her agreement to Professor Varey.

Having surmounted that major hurdle, all that remained was to arrange my accommodation in Platt's Lane, which was easily done. Mrs Dunham, the landlady, readily agreed to let the attic room on the third floor to me, and both she and her husband proved to be hospitable and patient landlords. "Patient" because never once did they complain about my monopoly of their telephone in the study downstairs. Stephen had devised a way of ringing me for fourpence, the cost of a local call, via all the intermediate exchanges between Cambridge and London: this meant that there was no time limit on our conversations every evening. Quite apart from the frenzied pleasure of daily communication and love-talk, we had plenty to discuss as we laid our plans for our future. The illness assumed the proportions of a minor background irritant as we talked about job prospects, housing, wedding arrangements and our first trip to the United States, to a summer school at Cornell University in upstate New York, due to start just ten days after the wedding.

7

In Good Faith

Now that my immediate problems had been solved at a stroke, I was confident that in my final year I could finish my degree in London by commuting weekly from Cambridge, especially since current social research suggested that married undergraduates consistently produced better results than frustrated, unmarried students. My father generously continued to pay my allowance to help cover the rail fares, but the responsibility of finding a job and an income to support us both lay with Stephen. For his part, he was now taking his research seriously, realizing that he would have to have a substantial piece of work documented, if not published, to enable him to apply for a Research Fellowship. To this end, he started to expand the ideas which had caused such a stir at Hoyle's Royal Society lecture. He also found by way of compensation for his efforts that his work was actually enjoyable.

Consequently it was with more than just the joyful expectation of a young fiancé awaiting the arrival of his beloved that he greeted me in his rooms, now for convenience in the main body of Trinity Hall, one chilly morning in the February of 1965: he was in fact expecting that I would put my secretarial skills to good use by typing out a job application for him. The look of horrified dismay that spread across his face as I walked into his room with my left arm bulging beneath my coat in a white plaster cast, dashed all my hopes of even the merest display of sympathy. I was not wanting anything more than that, because the circumstances in which the fracture had occurred had been too embarrassing to confess over the telephone.

The truth was that the Westfield hops had livened up considerably with the arrival, the previous year, of male students into the College and the election of a more dynamic entertainments committee on the Students' Union. We now had proper bands playing Sixties' music, the Beatles and the twist. I loved twisting, and at a midweek hop had indulged in an innocent bout of twisting with someone else's boyfriend. The floor was highly polished, my high heels skidded on the slippery surface and down I went, falling heavily onto my outstretched left hand. The searing pain all too obviously indicated another broken wrist, this time from twisting rather than ice skating.

Still rather battered by this ordeal, I did not at first appreciate the reasons for the horror on Stephen's face – not, that is, until he gestured to the borrowed typewriter and the pile of pristine white paper neatly arranged on the table. Dolefully he explained that he had been hoping that I would type out his application for a Research Fellowship at Gonville and Caius College, which had to be submitted by the beginning of the following week. Guilty on account of the twisting, I set to work with a will to write the application out in longhand, using my intact right hand. The exercise took the whole weekend.

To have stayed overnight in Stephen's rooms was unthinkable. On more than one occasion, according to Stephen, the eagle eye of Sam, the surly bedder and guardian of the College morals on Q staircase, must have noticed a scarf or a cardigan of mine carelessly left hanging over the back of a chair in Stephen's study. Scenting the whiff of scandal and a captive prey – for he was no friend to young lady visitors – Sam would put his head round the door of Stephen's bedroom in the early hours, hoping to catch me squeezed illicitly into Stephen's narrow single bed. But his expectations of a juicy scandal to report to the college authorities were constantly disappointed, because many of Stephen's better-established friends regularly offered me hospitality at weekends. Many of these friends already had houses and cars and were now in the process of producing offspring which, for our generation, was the expected progression of events. Ours was the last generation for whom the prime goals were quite straightforward: the ideals of romantic love, marriage, a home and a family. The difference for Stephen and me was that we knew that we had only a brief space of time in which to achieve those goals.

Against all odds, the Fellowship application was actually delivered on time, and Stephen then waited to be called to an interview. It was not however to be quite as simple as that. On the strength of the notoriety of his startling intervention in the Hoyle lecture, Stephen had approached Professor Hermann Bondi at the end of one of the regular fortnightly seminars at King's College, London, to ask him if he would be willing to act as a referee for the Fellowship application. As Hermann Bondi was a neighbour in Hampshire of Stephen's Aunt Loraine and her husband Rus, the Harley Street dentist, a formal letter did not seem necessary. Some weeks later, however, Stephen received an embarrassed message from Gonville and Caius College. In reply to the College's request for a reference for Stephen Hawking, Professor Bondi had disclaimed all knowledge of any candidate of that name. Given the circumstances and the casual nature of Stephen's approach to him, it was perhaps understandable that he should have forgotten. The situation was rectified by means of hasty phone calls, and Stephen was duly summoned for an interview, where he had plenty of scope for impressing the members of the committee with his powers of intellectual argument, the more so since none of them were cosmologists, however eminent their reputations in other disciplines.

The novel idea of admitting a cosmologist to their midst must have appealed to the Fellowship Committee, while for us the appearance of Stephen's name in the list of Fellowship awards was a cause for jubilant celebration. Everything was working out just as we had dared hope, and the date for our wedding could be fixed, as planned, for mid-July. Oblivious to the gloom of medical prognosis and ecstatic in the happiness of love and the promise of success, we glided into that summer through a series of further celebrations, with only a cluster of small bothersome clouds, such as my second-year exams, the question of accommodation and the hitherto unfamiliar evil of income tax, gathering on the horizon.

To our indignation, an unseasonably chill wind of hostile reality blew one of these small clouds all too quickly across our path, temporarily dampening our elation. Flushed with the success of his Fellowship application, Stephen went – within what we in our youthful impatience considered to be a reasonable lapse of time, a fortnight or so – to call on the Bursar of Gonville and Caius (generally pronounced in Cambridge as Keys, the name of the second founder of the College, but written Caius because of the Latinizing tendencies of the Renaissance). The Bursar coldly informed the newly appointed Research Fellow that, as he was not due to take up his post until the following October, it was highly presumptuous of him to seek a consultation six months in advance. As to Stephen's query, a matter which was uppermost in our minds, he certainly was not disposed to tell him how much salary he could expect to earn from the Fellowship. For good measure he decreed categorically that the College did not, furthermore, consider it a duty to provide accommodation for its Research Fellows. Smarting from such high-handed treatment, we were left to surmise roughly what Stephen's income would be and to find somewhere to live. Since there were plenty of married Research Fellows in Cambridge, we assumed that they managed somehow. As for accommodation, we rather liked the look of some new flats which were being built near the market square, and put our name down for one of those with the agent.

So confident were we in ourselves, and so impatient for our future to begin, that we did not allow such mundane problems to bother us for long. Indeed the attitude of the Bursar and those of his ilk simply confirmed Stephen's healthy disrespect for pompous middle-aged authority, a disrespect to which I was becoming a willing convert. We well knew that in our idealism we were deliberately defying common sense and all that was cautious, conventional and ordinary. We were certainly not going to allow our grand schemes to be thwarted or our convictions undermined by petty-minded officialdom. Tilting at such bureaucratic windmills quickly became our personal version of Sixties' rebellion. By contrast, our main battle was with the forces of destiny. In this lofty undertaking, we could afford to ridicule the minor stumbling blocks put in our way by officious college bursars.

When one battles with destiny only the major issues – life, survival and death – are of real significance. So far the forces of destiny seemed to be either dormant or on our side, for in spite of the obstacles our foreseeable future in the Cold War atmosphere of the mid-Sixties was beginning to look as secure as anybody else's. For Stephen, the prospect of marriage meant that he had to get down to work and prove his worth in physics. In my simplicity I believed that faith also had a hand in determining our way forwards. In a sense, we both shared a faith, an existential faith, in our chosen course, but I, encouraged by my mother and by my friends, reached out to a faith in a higher influence – God perhaps – who appeared to be responding to my need for help by strengthening my courage and determination. On the other hand, while I was well aware that the Hawkings, for all their traditional Methodist background, professed themselves to be agnostics if not atheists, I found their tendency to sneer at religious matters unpleasant. Stephen and I spent our first Christmas together just two months after our engagement. The fact that he came to Morning Service with my family produced raised eyebrows and snide comments on our return to 14 Hillside Road. "So do you feel holier now?" Philippa quietly enquired of Stephen in a tone laden with sarcasm, and I sensed a tinge of inexplicable hostility towards me. He laughed in reply while his mother remarked, "He should certainly be holier than thou, because he is now under the influence of a good woman." It was difficult to know how to take these remarks – it was not easy to make light of them, because they smacked of conspiracy and seemed targeted at an essential element, my faith, on which I would depend implicitly in the task before me. This cynicism was very different from the mirth in which I wholeheartedly shared when we analysed the various forms of the marriage service. I was appalled to find that, according to the marriage service of the 1662 Book of Common Prayer, I was expected to become a "follower of godly and sober matrons". I opted instead for the 1928 version, where that ugly phrase did not appear.

Success has a knack of breeding success, and soon we were celebrating again. Another Saturday had been spent in Stephen's rooms writing out another application, this time for a prize, the Gravity Prize, endowed by an American gentleman who in his wisdom believed that the discovery of anti-gravity would cure his gout. It is unlikely that any of the essays submitted ever provided any relief for the poor man's suffering, but his generous prizes provided great financial relief to many a struggling young physicist. Over the years Stephen won the whole range of Gravity Prizes, culminating in the first prize in 1971. Although, to our vexation, Stephen's first entry missed the post that Saturday in 1965, his efforts were nevertheless to be crowned with a very timely degree of success when some weeks later I was urgently called down from my attic in Hampstead to take a call from Stephen. He was ringing from Cambridge – as usual, for fourpence – to tell me that he had been awarded a Commendation Prize, worth £100, in the Gravity competition. I danced round Mrs Dunham's kitchen in raptures. Stephen's hundred pounds – added to the two hundred and fifty pounds which my father had been accumulating for me in National Savings and which he had promised to give me on my twenty-first birthday – would enable us to pay off Stephen's overdraft and buy a car. Later that summer, just before the wedding, Stephen's close friend in Trinity Hall, Rob Donovan, negotiated a very favourable deal for us with his father, a car dealer in Cheshire. We had the choice of two vehicles: one, a gleaming, red-painted, open-topped 1924 Rolls Royce, was tantalizing but quite impractical and rather beyond our means; at the other end of the scale, there was a red Mini on offer. Reluctantly Stephen had to concede that the Mini was better suited to our purse and to our requirements, especially since one of those small clouds looming on my horizon was ominously marked "driving test".

As all my previous attempts had ended in failure, I did not suppose that turning up for the next test in a 1924 Rolls would endear me to the crusty, humourless examiner who, when last I encountered him, had failed me yet again. Drily he had commented, as he clutched his heart, that my driving was not that of a beginner but of a hardened driver; it was alarmingly carefree and much too close to the speed limit. He should have been grateful that, given my recent experiences, I did not exceed the speed limit, overtake on bends or hills and attack dual carriageways from the wrong direction. Ironically, considering his known driving techniques, Stephen still held a valid driving licence, although he was no longer able to drive, so it was within the bounds of the law for me to drive on a provisional licence while he sat beside me. When finally in the autumn of 1965 I passed the dreaded test, it may have been because my bête noire, the chief examiner, was reported to be in hospital.

All those successes and celebrations in the early months of 1965 clearly marked our way forwards, with the result that my concerns became more intensely focused on Cambridge and the wedding. Inevitably a distance was developing between me and my friends and contemporaries, both my student friends in Westfield and my old dancing and tennis friends in St Albans. The last time that I saw many of those early friends was either when we worked together in the sorting office at the Post Office before the Christmas of 1964, or at my twenty-first birthday party: this Stephen's parents kindly agreed to host in their large, rambling house, which was much more spacious than my parents' semi-detached.

It was a glorious day, hot and sunny with bright, clear spring skies, and my happiness was complete. Stephen's present to me, recordings of the late Beethoven Quartets, could only be interpreted as the ultimate expression of our depth of feeling for each other. That birthday was happily very different from the previous year, when Stephen had given me a record of the complete works of Webern and later taken me to a drama about the use of the electric chair in the United States. That afternoon my whole family, including Grandma, had sat in a silent circle in our living room listening to Webern's entire opus. Stephen sat solemnly in an armchair while Dad buried his head in a book, Mum immersed herself in her knitting and Grandma dozed off. With great aplomb my family managed to appear totally unmoved by the assorted atonic clashes, lengthy inconsequential pauses and grating dissonances of the music, while I, sitting on the floor on the verge of hysterics, had to hide my face in a cushion.

In 1965, however, my twenty-first birthday party went with a swing in the warm spring air under the coloured lights on the terrace. It was as magical as a fairy tale, although as in all fairy tales it masked a perceptibly hostile element. Again I sensed an ill-disguised frisson of resentment in Philippa's attitude towards me which I was at a loss to understand. Was it because I had been allowed to take over her home for my party just for one evening? Or was it because she regarded me as intellectually inferior, and "feminine" – a term of abuse in the Hawking lexicon – as well? She clearly found my faith ridiculous. "Don't take it seriously," was Stephen's answer when I told him of my anxieties on that score, but this glib reaction was not sufficient reassurance.

From Mary, the elder of the two sisters, I received a more good-natured response. According to his mother, Stephen had found it hard to forgive his sibling for coming into the world barely seventeen months after his own birth. Mary, shy and gentle by nature, had found herself in an unenviable position in the family, poised between two exceptionally intelligent, determined personalities, Stephen and Philippa. In self-defence, she had forced herself into a fiercely competitive intellectual mould, when really her talents were much more creative and practical. With an intense loyalty to her father, she had taken up medicine, and it was with her father that she communicated most freely. Although my parents had heard first-hand accounts through various friends in St Albans of Frank Hawking's blunt, abrasive behaviour towards his staff in the Medical Research Laboratory at Mill Hill, towards me he was chivalrous and considerate. It was unfortunate that he did not present himself in a better light to the outside world, since he was a sensitive man who possessed generous and honourable qualities. Repeatedly, with endearing Yorkshire directness, he impressed upon me how genuinely delighted he and his family were at our engagement, sincerely promising to help in any way possible. Understandably he was devastated by the diagnosis of his son's illness and, notwithstanding his pleasure at our marriage, his medical background forced him to take a strictly orthodox and pessimistic view. My father had come across information about a Swiss doctor who claimed to be able to treat neurological conditions by means of a controlled diet, and he had offered to pay for Stephen to go to Switzerland for a course of treatment. With the doubtful advantage of superior medical knowledge, Frank Hawking dismissed the Swiss claims as unfounded. He, for his part, was only able to warn me that Stephen's life would be short, as would be his ability to fulfill a marital relationship. Moreover he advised me that if we wanted to have a family, we should not delay, assuring me that Stephen's illness was not genetically inherited.

Stephen's mother, who confided in me that she was convinced that the first symptoms of Stephen's condition had appeared in an unexplained illness when he was thirteen, also thought I should be fully informed of all the horrific developments that could be expected to occur as Stephen's condition degenerated. However, if the only treatments available were to be dismissed, rightly or wrongly, as crank quackery, I did not see much point in having whatever natural optimism I could muster destroyed by a litany of doom-laden prophecies without any palliative advice. I replied that I would prefer not to know the details of the prognosis, because I loved Stephen so much that nothing could deter me from wanting to marry him: I would make a home for him, dismissing all my own previous ambitions which now were insignificant by comparison with the challenge before me. In return, with all the innocence of my twenty-one years, I trusted that Stephen would cherish me and encourage me to fulfil my own interests. I trusted too in the promise that he had made my father when he had asked for my hand: that he would not demand more of me than I could reasonably accomplish, nor would he allow himself to become a millstone round my neck. We had both promised Dad that I would finish my degree course.

The plans for the wedding proceeded apace, attended by much to-ing and fro-ing between St Albans and Cambridge and by the sort of disagreements typical of weddings everywhere: Stephen, supported by his father, refused to wear morning dress, although my father and brother insisted on maintaining a proper sense of style. Similarly Stephen refused to wear a carnation in his buttonhole, since he thought them cheap and vulgar, although for me they were redolent in their colour and perfume of Spain. Roses provided a satisfactory compromise. My father thought that no wedding was complete without a few token speeches, at which Stephen baulked and refused to say anything. The question of bridesmaids came and went unresolved, leaving a gap which on the day was ably filled by nine-year-old Edward as an impromptu pageboy. Happily it was agreed, without audibly dissenting voices, that we should be married in the Chapel of Trinity Hall by the Chaplain, Paul Lucas. The religious service on Thursday 15th July would have to be preceded by a modest civil ceremony in the Shire Hall in Cambridge the day before, as colleges are not licensed for marriages, and the cost of a special licence from the Archbishop of Canterbury at £25 was deemed an unnecessary expense. Having deliberately chosen a small venue, we were then hard-pressed to accommodate all the guests. Some friends and relations had to be axed from the list altogether, while others were consigned to the organ loft.

In the midst of this confusion, I was tussling with Napoleon III, the Paris Commune of 1871 and my final French exams. Shortly before the wedding, Stephen attended his first General Relativity conference, which that year was conveniently held in London. I joined him for the official government reception in Carlton House Terrace, where I met many of the physicists who were subsequently to play significant roles in his career: Kip Thorne, John Wheeler, Charles Misner, George Ellis and two Russian scientists. Many of them were to become lasting friends to both of us. It was at that conference that the world's relativists, including Stephen, were first seized by the fever of excitement at the black-hole research (at that stage known much less graphically by the more pedestrian description of collapsing stars) that was to grip them for decades.

After the civil-marriage ceremony on 14th July, intoned by the Registrar among the filing cabinets and artificial flowers of the Shire Hall, my mother-in-law came up to me and with her wry smile said, "Welcome Mrs 'awkins, because that's how you'll be known from now on." The next day, St Swithin's Day, Stephen's best man Rob Donovan skilfully manoeuvred us and our near and dear through the marriage service and the festivities in the precincts of Trinity Hall without mishap. This was quite a remarkable feat, if only because of the number of elderly relatives present and the immense width of Philippa's hat, to which she had attached a superabundant display of foxgloves, delphiniums and poppies, rivalling the College gardens in their herbaceous exuberance. It was a happy day, despite the grey skies and intermittent drizzle. At last, in the early evening, at the end of the reception in the College hall where my father had publicly thanked Stephen for taking me off his hands, Rob Donovan dropped us off on the outskirts of Cambridge. There in a side street he had parked our recently acquired red Mini, complete with L-plates, well out of the way of my brother's mischievous designs. I settled myself into the driver's seat and, with Stephen beside me, cautiously pulled away from the kerb, heading in the direction of Long Melford in Suffolk and the Bull Inn.

8

An Introduction to Physics

All too soon that first idyllic week of marriage was but a halcyon memory – a memory of winding Suffolk lanes and lush gardens, musty country churches and half-timbered villages. At the end of it, as we sat waiting for take-off to New York, having boarded the plane long in advance of the other passengers, that blissful week with daytime outings to sleepy hamlets, country houses and the coast was quickly superseded by the inexorable advance of science, the synthesized traditions and the pace of the New World.

At Kennedy Airport, we were joining the queue of passengers at passport control when a tall, neatly dressed air hostess approached us, intently examining the file she was carrying. "What are your names?" she asked, looking down a list. "Jane and Stephen Hawking," we answered, not expecting any special messages. "Oh," she said in some surprise, "I don't have your names on my list. How old are you?" Now it was our turn to register some surprise. "I'm twenty-one and he's twenty-three," I replied for both of us. "Gee, I'm so sorry," she gushed, "I thought you were unaccompanied minors!"

Indignant at the insult to our maturity and our married status, we pulled ourselves up to our full height and passed through US customs to the helicopter which was to fly us over New York City to La Guardia airport for the connecting flight to Ithaca in upstate New York. Our first view of New York was depressing. As we flew just above the level of the skyscrapers through a dense smog, the buildings loomed out of the haze like giant javelins poised to spear us on their tips. It was hard to believe that human beings lived and worked down there in that inferno. My suspicions that we had landed in a modern Brobdingnag were confirmed when we were ushered to the limousine that had been sent to collect us from Ithaca airport and take us to Cornell University. Everything – the cars, the roads, the buildings – was ten times larger than anything I had ever seen; even the wide expanse of pleasant green countryside seemed to roll on for ever. Yet for me, a linguist used to the challenge of a foreign language only twenty-three miles away across the Channel, the most baffling aspect was that we had travelled thousands of miles only to find ourselves among people who spoke the same language as we did, even if, like the rest of their country, the language had suffered a bout of inflation on the way.

Our lodgings consisted of student accommodation in a twin-bedded room on the third floor of a new hall of residence on the Cornell campus. As we were both well used to the student way of life, that was not a problem. What really unnerved us was that the third floor had been designated as family accommodation for the duration of the summer school, and we were thrown in to survive as best we could among families with babies and small children who wailed all night or sat out in the corridor protesting while their parents held parties in the lounge area. This unforeseen circumstance spelt an abrupt end to the honeymoon which we had intended to resume on the American side of the Atlantic. Although some of the toddlers were undeniably appealing, a stay in a mammoth nursery was not what we had expected.

The problems were compounded by the logistics of the campus. For the able-bodied these would not have presented any difficulty, but since the hall of residence was the best part of a mile from the lecture theatre and we had no transport, it was a struggle for Stephen to get to the lectures on time. He could walk alone, but progress was slow; he moved much more quickly if he had a helpful arm to lean on, so gladly fulfilling my new role I went everywhere with him. Meals presented another problem. Living, as we still were, on student grants, we could not afford to eat all our meals in the canteen, but as there was not a single utensil in the kitchenette on our floor, we did not have the wherewithal even to make ourselves a cup of tea. Eventually one of the conference secretaries came to the rescue and offered to take me by car down into Ithaca to do some shopping at the nearest Woolworths. As we glided along in her enormous station wagon, I politely asked, by way of conversation, if she had ever been to Europe. She did not mince her words. "No", was her reply. "You see, I don't like going places where they don't have bathrooms."

Duly equipped with a saucepan, cutlery, mugs and plates, plus an electric fan to mitigate the heat – which, unlike Spanish heat, was sticky and humid – I set up an improvised home base, for the first but by no means the only time in my married life, on the third floor of the hall of residence. Brandon Carter, who was a fellow research student with Stephen in Cambridge and had been a guest at our wedding, was an invaluable help: drawing on his childhood experiences in the Australian bush, he taught me how to make tea by the billycan method – in a saucepan, the same saucepan that was used for scrambled eggs, pasta, baked beans and all the other bedsit-type fare on which we depended in those weeks. Versatility was of the essence in this unforeseen introduction to the joys of domesticity.

Much of my day was spent in walking with Stephen to and from the lecture hall and shopping in the nearby campus store. To fill the intervening hours, which were as short as the distances to any other place were long, I resorted to my studies in the library. Then, to vary the monothematic diet of Hispanic studies, I hit upon the idea of borrowing a typewriter and a desk in the secretarial office and began to type out the preliminary draft of the initial chapters of Stephen's doctoral thesis. The universes in question may have been expanding, but they were littered with so many incomprehensible hieroglyphic shapes and forms – as well as conventional numerals and all the normal mathematical signs – dancing above and below the line, that it soon became obvious that this particular enterprise was going to become a typographical nightmare.

Although such a sudden encounter with the nitty-gritty of marriage to a physicist might not have been exactly what I had anticipated from the second week of the honeymoon, I was relieved to have some useful occupation. I was also glad to be able to witness Stephen's intense excitement at moving in international scientific circles where he was already becoming recognized. He was particularly gratified at the increasing collaboration between himself and Roger Penrose, a slightly older British physicist, on a mathematical project known as the theory of singularities or gravitational collapse. The theory proposed that any body undergoing gravitational collapse must form a singularity, a region in space-time where the laws of relativity cease to hold, probably because the curvature of space-time becomes infinite. In the case of a star collapsing under its own gravity when its surface and its volume shrink to zero, Roger conjectured that the singularity would be hidden in what was later to be called a black hole. Inspired by Roger's theory and by the work of the Russians Lifshitz and Khalatnikov, Stephen was confident that these equations could be reversed in time to prove that any expanding model of the universe must have begun with a singularity, thus providing the theoretical basis for the Big Bang. The equations would also provide him with a momentous conclusion to his thesis.

The arrival like a ship in full sail from her family home in Detroit of Roger Penrose's wife, Joan, bearing one small child in a sling on her front and clutching another by the hand, while her elderly mother brought up the rear, afforded some relief from the tedium of life on the third floor. Joan had majored in public speaking, a useful attribute in controlling a family of boys – and an even more essential accomplishment, as I was beginning to realize, for making one's presence felt in the world of physicists where wives – although there were plenty of them with hordes of small children in tow – were scarcely noticed. Some were loud and loquacious, others were inhibited and reserved, others were positively sullen and morose; the handful of wives who themselves had a background in maths or physics tended to adopt a more competitive, masculine style of behaviour, while those whose dormant, half-forgotten talents lay in other areas tended to be prickly and mistrustful. Physics seemed to have taken its toll on all of them and, whether or not they liked each other or got on well with each other, they all had one thing in common: they were already, to all intents and purposes, widows – physics widows.

There were a few memorable diversions. Every day, as we strolled across the campus, I grasped the golden opportunity to chat in Spanish to a Mexican couple who seemed as disoriented in Cornell as I was. Then, one Saturday afternoon, some acquaintances of some friends of Stephen's parents kindly invited us to join them at their summer house by a lake not far from Ithaca. Otherwise, our evenings were spent humming 'Waltzing Matilda' over our single saucepan as it bubbled on the hotplate in the kitchenette on the third floor, while Brandon regaled us with lengthy accounts of his adventures. These often concerned life in the Australian bush, but also touched on his interest in the mathematician James Clerk Maxwell and on a dramatic sailing trip which was to have reached the Mediterranean through the Bay of Biscay but never got further than Cherbourg. When these topics were exhausted, the conversation normally lapsed into a sustained cosmological argument between him and Stephen, while I washed up the saucepan and the plastic plates, wondering whether we were doomed to spend the whole period of the summer school confined to the campus of Cornell University and the third floor of the hall of residence.

Just as I was beginning to resign myself to an unchanging routine, Brian and Susie Burns, an Australian couple who had previously spent some time in Cambridge, offered us a lift in their car to Niagara. Our sudden first sighting of the Falls after the tedious drive through the endless, sulphurous suburbs of the city of Buffalo took our breath away. The might of the immense volume of dark water constantly on the move, relentlessly tumbling over the edge of the precipice, transformed into a mass of white foam and rainbow filaments of cooling spray, was as mesmerizing as the thundering roar was deafening. Our senses numbed, we stumbled across the bridge to the Canadian side to get a better view and stood hypnotized until it was time for us to take the short flight back to Ithaca. Against a threatening sky, we boarded the small plane and took off amid thunder and lightning. For the first time in my life, I was afraid of flying.

The next weekend, Brandon and some friends arranged a sailing trip on Lake Ontario. We set out in a gentle breeze and, once out on the lake, the day slipped by. I swam in the green waters and Stephen sat back deep in thought, enjoying the clear blue skies and the sound of the water gently lapping against the hull. By late afternoon, our companions had long since ceased to share our pleasure at the peaceful conditions and talked anxiously of sending up flares and putting out distress signals – we were becalmed. Brandon helpfully remarked that this was not a situation he had had to deal with in the Bay of Biscay as there you could always rely on the wind. Somehow, much later that evening, we managed to limp back into harbour as in a magnificent blaze the setting sun, sinking from view on the blackened horizon, bathed our weary faces in its amber glow.

It was not until the last week of the summer school that someone – I think it was Ray Sachs, an extrovert Californian physicist, the father of four daughters – had the bright idea of organizing a social event, a picnic in a field, for families. There we were introduced to more wives and more children, but the person who made the greatest impression on us was a quiet American from Texas, Robert Boyer, with whom Stephen had already established a professional rapport. Robert included me in conversation in a natural, friendly manner, and talked about matters other than physics. Indeed, it has to be said that individually many physicists could be quite charming, friendly and down-to-earth. In a group, however, their natural tendency was to slip inexorably into interminable discussions and arguments, almost always about physics. But there was a rival topic of conversation which increasingly exercised the minds, not only of all academics but of all young people: that topic, Vietnam, was liberally aired at that picnic. The growing menace of the war was regarded with fear and loathing; it threatened to cut a swathe through the nation's youth for a cause supported only by the military and the bigoted.

On the last evening, at the end of the summer school, as we sat on the steps of the hall of residence gazing out at a full moon suspended in a translucent sky, I was introduced to Professor Abe Taub, the avuncular mastermind of the summer school, who with his wife Cice was also taking the air and admiring the night sky. We listened in fascination as they talked of their life in California, of the views their house commanded of the Golden Gate bridge, of San Francisco and of the campus and science department at Berkeley where Abe was the leader of the Relativity Group. I detected a tentative invitation from Abe to Stephen and a corresponding eagerness on Stephen's part, though no formal propositions were made.

We wandered back indoors and were about to resume our conversation when, without any warning, Stephen, perhaps affected by a chill in the night air, was seized with a devastating choking fit, the first I had witnessed. The illness, seemingly long-suppressed, suddenly revealed itself in its true terrifying fury. The lurking spectre stepped out of the shadows and grabbed him by the throat, tossed him about, shook him like a doll, trampled him underfoot and hurled his rasping cough round the room till the very air resonated with loud, panic-stricken wheezing. Helpless in the grip of the enemy, Stephen was beyond my reach. I stood by unprepared for this sudden encounter with the dreadful power of motor-neuron disease, the hitherto unseen partner in our marriage. Eventually Stephen managed to gesture to me to thump him on the back. I did so vigorously, determined to expel the invisible monster. At last it receded, as quickly as it had come, leaving us drained and exhausted and the onlookers politely dumbfounded. This onslaught came as a great shock to us both, an ill-omen warning of a hazardous future. Dreams of California disappeared into the mists of the fantasy from which they had begun to emerge.

By the time we returned to New York, the Cornell experience had rapidly turned me – at the age of twenty-one – into a rather confused follower of sober, if not of godly, matrons. The demonic nature of the illness had announced its presence much more dramatically than in lameness, difficulty of movement and lack of coordination. As if that were not enough, I sensed that there was yet another partner lurking in our already overcrowded marriage. The fourth partner first appeared in the form of a trusted and quiescent friend, signalling the way to success and fulfilment for those who followed her. In fact she proved to be a relentless rival, as exacting as any mistress, an inexorable Siren, luring her devotees into deep pools of obsession. She was none other than Physics, cited by Einstein's first wife as the correspondent in divorce proceedings.

New York City provided both a necessary respite from such sombre considerations and the opportunity to restore the balance of our relationship, away from the inveigling companionship of other physicists. A medical colleague of Frank Hawking generously offered us a room in his Manhattan apartment for the weekend. It was ideally situated for our sightseeing excursions to the Metropolitan Museum, the Empire State Building, Time Square and Broadway. Unfortunately Broadway had little to offer in August, so, bizarrely, we spent the Saturday evening in a cinema watching *My Fair Lady*. I had few regrets when we said goodbye to New York. As the bus drove into Kennedy Airport, I looked back over my shoulder to the solid line of clearly etched skyscrapers standing to attention in a grey mass on the horizon, and thought that I had never seen an apparition of such monstrous brutality. I was impatient to return to the manageable, if cramped, proportions and genuinely old-fashioned but less frenzied ways of the Lilliputian world where I belonged. My place was on a continent mellowed by history and a sense of poetic values, where I fondly thought there was greater stability and where people had more time for each other.

9

The Lane

My sentimental illusions about the stability of life on the European side of the Atlantic were quickly dispelled on our return to England, where I found that my parents were about to move to a house only thirty doors up the road from the home where I had lived since the age of six. The break with the past was now irreparably set in bricks and mortar. Although, when last heard of, the flat Stephen and I had reserved over the market place in Cambridge was not yet finished, we had to find a home of our own urgently if only to house all our wedding presents. Loading our luggage and presents into the red Mini, we set off for Cambridge and went straight to the estate agent's. The flats were indeed finished, we were told, but, as the agent had no record of our names or of our booking, they were all already let to other tenants. The Old World was beginning to look distinctly unreliable after all.

We discussed our next move over a despondent lunch. Stephen decided to brave the Bursar of Caius once again in the vain hope that he might be persuaded to help, even temporarily. Together we bearded the ogre in his den. To our surprise, he had changed identity in the previous six months, and the new Bursar was also the lecturer in Tibetan. However that post was a sinecure, since there were never any students in Tibetan, so he had time on his hands in which to oversee the financial affairs of the College. Unlike his predecessor, he did not snap Stephen's head off in indignation but listened gravely, even sympathetically, to his request, and then came up with a brilliant solution, which coaxed a glimmer of a smile from his dour face. "Yes," he mused, "I think we might be able to help – only in the very short term of course, because you know that the College has a policy of not providing housing for Research Fellows, don't you?" We nodded with bated breath. He consulted a list. "There's a room vacant in the Harvey Road hostel: it's twelve shillings and sixpence a night for one man so we will put another bed in and it will be twenty-five shillings a night for the two of you." We had to suppress our outrage at such sharp practice because we had nowhere else to go, hotels being beyond our means, but vowed that we would minimize the amount of time we spent at Harvey Road.

Although the College authorities were harsh and ungenerous, the staff, particularly the housekeeper of the hostel, could not have been kinder. This proved to be characteristic of the college servants, whether cleaning staff, workmen, gardeners, porters or waiters. Unfailingly they revealed qualities of warmth and friendliness often conspicuously absent in the rarified atmosphere of the higher echelons. The housekeeper warmed our room, aired our beds, brought us tea and biscuits that first evening and breakfast in the morning. She even offered to do our washing for us, although that was not necessary as our stay was to be mercifully brief.

In the intervening day, Stephen's supervisor, Dennis Sciama, had come speedily to the rescue by putting us in touch with a Fellow of Peterhouse, who wanted to sublet the house he had been renting from that College. The house was unfurnished, but it was available immediately and moreover it was ideally placed for us, in one of the oldest, most picturesque streets of Cambridge, Little St Mary's Lane, within a hundred yards of Stephen's department, which had recently moved to the building of the old Pitt Press printing works in Mill Lane.

Since number 11 Little St Mary's Lane contained not a stick of furniture, we had to grit our teeth, dip deep into our funds, savings and wedding-present money, and go on a rapid spending spree to buy basic furniture, a bed and an electric ring. While we were waiting for the bed to be delivered, I went out to buy provisions, leaving Stephen propped up against the bare wall of the living room for want of a seat. To my astonishment, when I returned he was comfortably seated on a blue kitchen chair. He explained that a lady from down the road had come to introduce herself and, finding him leaning against the wall, had kindly brought him the chair, which we could borrow until we had more furniture. The lady in question was Thelma Thatcher, the wife of the former Censor, or Master, of Fitzwilliam House, who lived at number 9. Thelma Thatcher was to become one of the most benevolent and most entertaining influences in our lives over the next ten years. That evening we cooked our supper in the Cornell saucepan on the single electric ring, drank sherry from our crystal glasses and, using a box for a table, ate from our bone china, using our gleaming stainless-steel cutlery set. Stephen sat on the Thatchers' kitchen chair while I kneeled on the bare white-tiled floor. No matter that it was somewhat improvised, we celebrated our good luck in having a roof over our heads for the next three months.

Guarded at its entrance by two churches standing sentinel – the Victorian United Reform Church on the right and the medieval Church of Little St Mary on the left – the lane is hidden from the public gaze. Tourists discover it only by chance. These days the lane is closed to through-traffic thanks to a campaign by the residents, including Stephen and me, so visitors to the two big complexes on the river front, the Garden House Hotel and the University Centre, have to gain access via Mill Lane, which is not residential. Number 11 is the last of the main terrace of three-storeyed cottages on the right-hand side of the street, some of which probably date back to the sixteenth century. When we took up residence in 1965, the house had been recently renovated by Peterhouse, a college which, unlike Caius, did provide its Research Fellows with accommodation.

Iron railings on the south side of the lane enclose Little St Mary's churchyard, a wild overgrown garden which, that September, was ablaze with reddening hips and haws and heavy with the scent of autumn roses. The few gravestones which were still standing were so weather-beaten that their inscriptions had become illegible, despite the spreading branches of the towering sycamore trees and the gnarled stems of the wisteria which sheltered them from the worst ravages of the elements. Here Nature had gently absorbed the dead of previous centuries back into her bosom, resurrecting them in a profusion of blossoms which trailed over the railings and reached out to caress the crooked old gas lamp which lit the street at night with its sulphurous glow.

Thelma Thatcher was the self-appointed warden of the lane. She had planted many of the rose bushes in the churchyard, where she exercised Matty, her King Charles spaniel, wrapping each of her paws in plastic bags in wet weather. As a matter of course, she took it upon herself to keep an eye on the well-being of all her neighbours, whatever their age or circumstances. Scarcely had a week gone by than she had lent us more chairs, tables, pots and pans, found us a gas cooker to borrow – from Sister Chalmers, the Peterhouse nurse who was moving into a fully equipped college flat – set about finding us somewhere else to live on the expiry of the present tenancy and served us innumerable glasses of sherry in the elegant, highly polished, antique-filled living room of her fine, whitewashed old house.

In 1965 she must already have been in her seventies, though with her straight back, dark hair and stately figure she could easily have passed for ten years younger. She combined the sparkle of a gifted raconteur with intense practicality: once, she told us, in a moment of inspiration at a Quaker wedding, she stood up and announced that the helpers had forgotten to light the gas under the tea urn. In a manner which would have done justice to Joyce Grenfell, she delighted in playfully deflating the pompous egos of many Cambridge academics. Her style was aristocratic and assertive, but always supported by deeply held and sincere Christian values. A self-professed pillar of the establishment, representing everything that Stephen despised, she found her natural target in woolly-minded liberals. In her, however, Stephen met his match, and he had to respect her for her goodness and generosity even if, politically, she and he were poles apart.

In the next few months, Thelma Thatcher took us under her wing like a mother hen. She kept a kindly eye on Stephen when I was away in London, as well as attending to the needs both of her elderly husband who – according to her, had snatched her out of her cradle – and of her lively, independent daughter Mary, who was assembling a film archive on the domestic lives of the British in India.

All too soon, I had to return to my final year at Westfield. Parting from Stephen each Monday was desperately painful, and the regime was hard for both of us. Stephen was just sufficiently capable of looking after himself to be able to live in the house, but every evening, unless invited out elsewhere, he had to make the long, hazardous trek down King's Parade on his own to eat in College. Our Australian friend, Anne Young, unfailingly kept an eye out for him as he passed her window on the other side of the road, and generally one or other of the younger Fellows would see him home after the meal, when he would ring me to report on the day.

My routine was exhausting. I would leave for London on Monday mornings, spend the week in Westfield and then on Friday afternoons join the commuters once again. In my anxiety to get home to Cambridge, to Stephen – and to Nikolaus Pevsner's

Friday evening course of lectures on Renaissance architecture, which we attended together – I would bite my nails as I watched the minutes tick by on the Underground, wondering how long the train would sit in the tunnel, fearing that I was going to miss the connection from Liverpool Street. For years afterwards, my worst nightmares were dreams of being stuck in a tunnel on the Underground.

During the week, the pressure was on: translations into and from Spanish, essays and seminar papers all had to be submitted within deadlines, and the only time I had for doing them was in the evening. Weekends were taken up with shopping, washing, housework and typing Stephen's thesis, parts of which he would have written out in a scrawly, all but illegible longhand during the week, and parts of which he dictated to me as I sat typing at our shiny new dining table in the otherwise bare living room. The trials of that pre-university secretarial course were now bearing fruit. The shorthand had been moderately useful for taking notes in lectures, but the dreaded typing was proving to be a godsend in tabling the laws of creation, since it saved us a mint of money in professional fees. The thesis first glimpsed at Cornell – with its equations and signs, symbols and coefficients, Greek letterings, numbers above and below the line, and infinite and non-infinite universes – drove me to distraction. However, since it was a scientific thesis, it was blessedly short. Furthermore I derived some small satisfaction from the knowledge that my fingers were consigning the beginnings of the universe to paper. The thought that all these mysteriously coded numbers, letters and signs were penetrating the secrets of that deep, black infinity was awe-inspiring. Dwelling on the poetic immensity of the topic for too long was counterproductive, though, as it distracted concentration from all the little dots and hieroglyphs above and below the line, any of which if misplaced could have thrown the beginnings of the universe into dire disarray and upset the whole order of creation.

I was not a little proud, too, to be able make a contribution of my own, other than the purely mechanical one of typing. Stephen's use of English left much to be desired. His speech was scattered with expressions such as "you know" and "I mean", and his written style showed little concern for the English language. As the daughter of a dedicated civil servant, I had been taught from an early age to use the language precisely, with appreciation for its clarity and its richness. Here was an area where in joining forces with Stephen I could assist him on an intellectual rather than just the physical plane, and also help bridge the gap between the arts and the sciences.

The weekends were also the time for buying more equipment and furnishings, for exploring Cambridgeshire and for seeing friends. We spent the whole of one Saturday afternoon in an electrical shop trying to decide whether we could afford the extra five pounds for a larger fridge than the one we had budgeted for. Considering that Stephen's salary, as we had at last found out, was eleven hundred pounds a year, while our weekly rent and housekeeping when we were both at home – not counting numerous other outgoings – was ten pounds, an extra five pounds on any purchase was a major expenditure. On Sunday afternoons, if the Mini could be extricated from the Caius communal garage, we would tour Cambridgeshire, visiting villages and churches, always looking out for a suitable house or plot of land to buy. Sometimes our expeditions had to be abandoned before they had begun because the Mini was so impossibly hemmed in by ageing Bentleys and Rovers in its corner of the garage that it would have taken a crane to get it out.

One Sunday afternoon, having manoeuvred the Mini out of the garage, we tried to visit the local National Trust property, Anglesey Abbey. As the car park was a good half mile from the house, I drove up along the leafy avenue to the main entrance, expecting a sympathetic welcome for my partially disabled passenger. In fact we were met with rude intolerance and sent away. We went straight home, and I penned my first letter in furious protest, not only at the lack of facilities for the disabled in Britain but also for the scant respect with which they were treated, thus initiating a role for myself as a campaigner for the disabled.

Often, on our Sunday afternoon jaunts, we would happen to be in the vicinity of some of our married friends at teatime and, clinging to the illusion of a spontaneous student lifestyle, we would drop in on them. Slightly older than us, many of these friends had already had their first babies. Consequently we found ourselves drawn more and more into their pattern of domesticity, especially when I became the fascinated and slightly bemused godmother to two of the said babies. Stephen was also being drawn into other circles: those of the Fellowship of

Gonville and Caius. One Saturday evening in early October, I accompanied him as far as the College Chapel for the service for the induction of new Fellows. At the suggestion of the Chaplain, I watched the service from the organ loft and then he invited me, a mere wife dressed in my housecleaning clothes, to dine at High Table. This was an unprecedented break with the past, as it was a long established rule in Cambridge colleges that wives – especially wives – were banned from High Table. High Table was the preserve of the Fellows who cultivated self-importance with the same exquisite care that lesser mortals might be expected to lavish on a prized stamp collection or a breed of racing pigeons. Their conversation revolved around the finer details of the most abstruse subjects – their own subjects naturally, about which they could expatiate at length while avoiding the embarrassment of having to discuss subjects about which they knew little or nothing. Mistresses were preferred to dull, silly wives. Indeed a Fellow might invite any woman to dine provided she was not his wife. It went without saying, of course, that, together with wives, undergraduates were also banned from High Table. Unbeknown to the College authorities, their renegade Chaplain had breached both hallowed rules.

Stephen's induction was soon followed by his first attendance at a meeting of the governing body of the College. Before he had time to understand what was happening that Friday afternoon, he found himself deeply embroiled in College politics. To his confusion, he seemed to have walked right into a re-enactment of the C.P. Snow novel, *The Masters*. The only minor difference was that in the novel the wrangling over the Mastership was deemed to have taken place in Snow's own college, Christ's, whereas the scenes that Stephen was witnessing were taking place in Caius. Here was life imitating art in the most extraordinary manner. As Stephen discovered after the event, the charge against the incumbent Master, Sir Nevill Mott, was that he was using his position to favour his own protégés. At the time it was impossible to tell what was happening. The governing body was in an uproar, tempers were flaring and immoderate accusations were being flung about. As a result of a quick calculation, Stephen had the uncomfortable sensation that the votes of the new Fellows might be decisive – indeed his own vote might be the casting vote – but as they had little idea of what they were voting for, their voting pattern was inevitably arbitrary. Stephen's introduction to college politics came to a dramatic end with the resignation of the Master that very afternoon.

During the course of the next year, the ructions over the Mastership crisis subsided as the new Master, Joseph Needham, tearing himself reluctantly away from his gargantuan task of compiling the history of science in China, guided the College back to stability. Although I found him terse, apart from one memorable occasion when over port in the Combination Room after dinner he expansively warned me never to drink sweet French wine – Barsac and suchlike – because of its high disulphide content, his distinguished wife Dorothy was to give me invaluable help in securing a foothold for myself in Cambridge academic circles. She, notwithstanding all her scientific brilliance, was one of the most modest, likeable academics I ever met.

10

A Winter Break

On the strength of his thesis, Stephen was gaining a reputation for himself as a prodigy in his field. In response to his share in the coveted Adams Prize with Roger Penrose that winter, for an essay in mathematics entitled *Singularities and the Geometry of Space-Time*, his supervisor Dennis Sciama assured me that he was sure Stephen had a career of Newtonian proportions ahead of him and that he would do all he could to encourage its progress. He was as good as his word. For all his ebullience, Dennis Sciama selflessly promoted his students' careers rather than his own. His desire to understand the workings of the universe was more passionate than any personal ambition. By sending his students off to conferences and meetings, whether in London or abroad, and by making them scrutinize and report back on every relevant publication, he dramatically increased his own fund of knowledge as well as theirs, and succeeded in nurturing a generation of exceptional cosmologists, relativists, astrophysicists, applied mathematicians and theoretical physicists. The distinction between these various terms was never quite clear to me, except that the identities changed according to the titles of the conferences: they would all become astrophysicists if the next conference was a conference of the Astrophysical Union or relativists if it was a General Relativity conference, and so on. That autumn the relativists of the July conference in London began, chameleon-like, to adopt the trappings of astrophysicists in preparation for the next conference, in Miami Beach in December.

It was fairly late in the term when Stephen learnt that funds were available for us both to go to Miami. I was doubtful about taking time off from Westfield, even though I would only be missing a couple of days at the end of term, but surprisingly Professor Varey raised no objections, so on a dull December afternoon, after a long wait for the fog to lift at London airport, we took off. It was already dark in Florida when we arrived, so it was not until the next morning that we discovered that our hotel room was right on the beach, looking out over the turquoise waters of the Caribbean. Having just stepped out of cold wet London after a hard term's work, I marvelled at the unreality, the improbability of the situation, as though I had walked into a different dimension, through the looking glass perhaps. This impression was to grow as the stay progressed. The blue skies and sunshine were certainly welcome, especially since Stephen's choking fits were becoming more frequent, and his sister Mary had earnestly advised me to take him away somewhere warm for the winter. At least by a happy chance we had the prospect of a week in the sun.

On the opening day, Stephen, together with his casually dressed colleagues, disappeared into the preliminary sessions of the conference, while I explored the venue. The hotel, built in a curve around the swimming pool, looked remarkably familiar. Was this a sense of déjà vu, I asked myself, for I was sure that I had seen it somewhere before. Suddenly it dawned on me that this was the hotel where the opening shots of *Goldfinger*, the James Bond thriller, were filmed. It was in a room in that hotel that the girl had died of asphyxiation after being covered from head to toe with gold paint! The Hotel Fontainbleau was a modern concrete structure with marble floors, plate glass and huge mirrors covering whole walls. In deference to its name, it was furnished in every nook and cranny with Louis XV-style furniture.

The furnishings were not the least of the incongruities, since the astrophysics conference was a major incongruity in itself. The smartly dressed hotel staff looked distinctly uncomfortable with the delegates, who were by no means models of sartorial elegance in their open-necked shirts, shorts and sandals. One day I ventured into the conference hall, intending to sit in for a while on one of the lectures. At first I was perplexed, not seeing any recognizable faces in the audience, then I noticed that the dress of the delegates bore no relation to the clothing the physicists had been wearing at breakfast, in that these people were all dressed in dark suits with ties, their hair neatly brushed and brilliantined, with not a trace of a beard anywhere. I listened to the speaker only for a moment before realizing that this was a conference of Jewish funeral directors promoting biodegradable plastic coffins.

From the exotic colours and summer sun of Miami we flew into autumn – to Austin, Texas, a small university town which in the mid-Sixties was trumpeted in the press as the home of the brightest and best in cosmology. George Ellis, who travelled with us from Miami, was spending a year in Austin with his wife, Sue, whom I had met briefly at our wedding. As we were to stay with the Ellises for a week, this was my opportunity to get to know them both better and forge the beginning of a lifelong friendship which would survive the vicissitudes of many turbulent episodes in all our lives. Pensive and reserved, George was the son of a much respected former editor of the *Rand Daily Mail*, a paper acclaimed for its resistance to apartheid in South Africa. It was at Cape Town University that Sue, the daughter of a traditional Rhodesian farming family, had met George. Both George and Sue were fierce opponents of apartheid and had become self-imposed political exiles from South Africa, insisting that they could never think of returning to live there. Where George was thoughtful and introverted, Sue was outgoing without being overpowering, vivacious yet sensitive to the needs of others. A talented artist and sculptor, she bubbled with warmth and creativity, qualities which she was putting at the disposal of a school for deprived children near Austin. Among her pupils were not merely the victims of broken homes and physical abuse, some were even tiny black child prostitutes who had been rescued from the Chicago slums and brought to Texas for rehabilitation. It was not hard to imagine what an asset Sue must have been to that particular school, for she had a way of making a fascinating artefact out of the smallest twist of paper, length of wire or handful of matchsticks, and her caring friendliness made her instantly popular among children who from an early age had learnt to mistrust adults.

In creating a structure to her life in Texas, Sue appeared to be the exception rather than the rule among science wives. For them there was little of any interest apart from the Max Beerbohm manuscripts and cartoons in the university library, and the gridlike streets of opulent houses in a landscape dominated by black-billed crane-like oil pumps, nodding up and down as they extracted the liquid gold from the yellow earth. The feeling of remoteness from the rest of civilization was overwhelming in an environment where even radio reception was a chancy thing. This sense of isolation was reinforced by the length of time, all of twenty hours, it took Stephen and me to get back to London via Houston and Chicago, where we were stranded for hours by snow on the runway.

Though Stephen may have harboured ambitions of joining the physics group in Austin, one salutary experience made me more than glad to put America, for all the advantages of its southern climate, behind us once more. We were visiting friends of the Ellises one Sunday afternoon when Stephen had a bad fall, which resulted in his coughing up a spot of blood. As his worst fear was brain damage, he insisted on our hosts calling a doctor. Their consternation was remarkable. They were embarrassed that their guest had had a fall, but it was truly unheard of for doctors to home-visit, especially on a Sunday afternoon, and they doubted very much whether they would be able to persuade any doctor to come. After a long succession of telephone calls, they were finally put in touch with a general practitioner who, as an exception, agreed to come and inspect Stephen. When he arrived he received right royal treatment. As he conducted his tests, which indicated nothing amiss, I concluded that America was a fine place for the healthy and successful, but for the strugglers and the infirm, for the people who, through no fault of their own but through accidents of birth, prejudice or illness were less able to help themselves, it was a harsh society where only the fittest survived.

11

Learning Curves

Our return to England from Texas on Christmas Eve heralded yet another change in our lives. After Christmas in St Albans, we went back to Cambridge to resume residence, not at number 11 Little St Mary's Lane but at number 6. Our tireless supporter, Thelma Thatcher, had rung the absentee owner of the empty house at number 6, a Mrs Teulon-Porter ("such a strange lady, my dears") impressing upon her that it was an absolute disgrace that her house should be vacant at a time of "desperate housing shortage for the young". Mrs Teulon-Porter responded to the urgent call by catching the first bus to Cambridge from her home in Shaftesbury. Despite the misgivings about her strange personality, she was offered generous hospitality at the Thatchers' while she attended to her empty property.

Mrs Teulon-Porter was a small, wispy, grey woman, already advanced in years. As Fräulein Teulon, she had come to England in the 1920s, had bought number 6 Little St Mary's Lane and then had married her next-door neighbour, the late Mr Porter. Both she and he were passionate historians of folklore and were closely connected with the Cambridge Folk Museum, which might have accounted for Mrs Thatcher's conviction that they dabbled in the occult. Various items in the house testified to their shared interest: an Anglo-Saxon rune-stone, probably from the churchyard, was incorporated into the fireplace; the door screen was a slice hewn from the trunk of an elm; the offcut wood from a cartwheel had been converted to form a heavy, curved stool; and an eighteenth-century postillion's box, made of oak, had been upended and attached to a wall to form a small cupboard.

Mrs Teulon-Porter seemed harmless enough to us – perhaps because she had been so well tutored by her hostess at number 9, but her house, despite all its quaint additions and its ideal location, struck us as very pokey and gloomy, musty-smelling and sticky with Dickensian grime. The façade in red brick and stuccoed pargeting suggested Edwardian renovations, while the front rooms on all three floors dated from the eighteenth century, charmingly so if one could overlook the dirt. The two flights of stairs were narrow and steep, but did not at that stage present any unsurmountable difficulties. The back of the house – looking out onto a dingy yard enclosed by other houses and a high back wall – appeared to be on the point of collapse, because the foundations had subsided so badly that the floor of the kitchen and, correspondingly, the kitchen ceiling and the floor of the bathroom above, sloped at an alarming angle. Mrs Teulon-Porter did not appear to consider this eccentricity at all hazardous. According to a plaque in the outside wall, John Clarke had masterminded this exemplary piece of engineering in 1770.

It required imagination and Mrs Thatcher's no-nonsense approach to convince us that this really was our dream house. Certainly its situation was perfect. The front rooms, right opposite the old gas lamp, enjoyed a full view of the churchyard, wistfully poetic even in winter, and although the proportions of the ground floor were rather spoilt by the staircase of the house at number 5 butting into the party wall, the two bedrooms were quite sufficient for our requirements. "My dears, all it needs is a coat of paint, you'll be surprised what a coat of paint can do," Thelma Thatcher declared authoritatively, determined not to let her masterly scheme be upset by trivialities.

Thus persuaded, we entered into negotiations with the owner. Stephen boldly made her an offer of £2,000 for her property. Not surprisingly she turned it down, timidly averring with one eye on Mrs Thatcher that she would expect it to fetch at least £4,000 on the open market. She would however agree to let it to us for £4 a week until such time as we could raise the £4,000 needed to buy it. In the meantime we were virtually free to treat the house as our own and redecorate it at will. The arrangement was to everyone's satisfaction. Mrs Thatcher shepherded her guest back to number 9 and there plied her with such liberal quantities of sherry, or possibly gin, that the next we heard was that Mrs Teulon-Porter, before departing for Shaftesbury, had agreed to have the dusty old coal shed and lean-to removed from the back yard and the outside of the house repainted.

Since the house was already vacant, Mrs Teulon-Porter was content to allow us to start redecorating inside before moving in. As Stephen's thesis was now at the bookbinder's, the time which I had previously spent typing it at weekends could now be devoted to my next occupation, that of house-painting. It was rewarding, but bore worryingly little relation to the Spanish studies which I was supposed to be revising for Finals. However, as the house was in a truly depressing state and as we could not afford to have it professionally redecorated, I had no choice but to do it myself. Armed with a collection of brushes and a plentiful supply of white emulsion, I attacked the grimy walls of the living room. My intention was to paint the two most important rooms, the living room and the main bedroom, before moving in, and then tackle the rest – the attic, the two flights of stairs, the kitchen and bathroom – more gradually over the ensuing months.

As I disliked the smell of paint, I usually worked with the front door wide open. The Thatchers were frequent and admiring visitors, plying me with cups of tea and encouraging comments. One day, Mr Thatcher paused as he was passing, bending his military frame slightly to peer in at the open door. "I say," he exclaimed, "you look such a fragile little thing, but, by Jove, you must be tough!" From the top of the stepladder I smiled, flattered by this commendation from a veteran of the First World War who still bore the disfiguring marks of that conflict on his gaunt face. A few days later we were told that the Thatchers had decided to pay their odd-job man to paint the living-room ceiling for us: "Dear Billy's housewarming present to our new neighbours," was Thelma Thatcher's way of describing her husband's extraordinary generosity. The Thatcher's odd-job man, a somewhat portly version of John Gielgud, was a retired artist who filled in his time with larger-scale painting while his wife ran a print shop on King's Parade. He was an amiable man who, I suspected, derived much quiet amusement from my initial attempts at wielding a paintbrush. Indeed, under his benevolent tuition, I soon acquired many of the tricks of his trade, like starting a wall from the top, or applying the brush in a circular motion over an uneven surface, or using a hard edge to paint a window frame.

Stephen's reputation in relativistic circles may have been rapidly ascending the ladder of fame on account of his pursuit of singularities, but my advance in learning was exhibiting an equally dizzying if more erratic series of highs and lows: propelled upwards by intensive doses of medieval and modern languages, philology and literature during the week, and brought to earth by a crash course in the skills of interior decorating on Saturdays. Finally, when I began to find the area of wall and ceiling still to be covered rather more daunting than I had anticipated, we calculated that we could just afford to ask the decorator to paint the kitchen for us, a particularly unpleasant task since the grime and grease were probably as old as the house.

Although my parents had only just moved to their new house, they and my brother Chris came to Cambridge one weekend early in 1966 to redecorate the top-floor bedroom and, in token of his willingness to help, Stephen's father spared a day from his globetrotting to paint the bathroom while I applied a coat of enamel to the old chipped bath. Then, magically, fully justifying Thelma Thatcher's convictions, our tumbledown eighteenth-century cottage acquired the air of a des res, and in the transformation the angles of its floors and ceilings had become simply eccentric curiosities. Our few pieces of furniture, which various colleagues of Stephen's carried the five doors along the lane, fitted in perfectly – although, of course, when we bought them we had not given a moment's thought to the possible proportions of their eventual resting place.

Proud of our restoration of the little house, Stephen and I decided that the new Bursar of Caius was due for another visit, especially as Stephen was by now beginning to feel more sure of his place in the College hierarchy. Early in the New Year, we had braved the annual Ladies' Night, Bishop Shaxton's Solace, when wives were officially welcomed to the College precincts and treated to a banquet, as if in compensation for the contempt in which they were held for the rest of the year. Bishop Shaxton had, in the sixteenth century, bequeathed the munificent sum of twelve shillings and sixpence for the solace of every Fellow who had to spend Christmas at home rather than in the College. The equivalent in modern terms of twelve shillings and sixpence per head was sufficient to provide a lavish five- or six-course dinner with unlimited quantities of the best wines for the Fellowship and their spouses. Typically the meal would consist of soup, a whole lobster, an undefined small game bird each – usually served complete with head and limbs – a substantial creamy pudding, a cheese savoury and then, of course, at dessert, the famous port – or claret – which tradition demanded should only ever be passed clockwise round the table. In theory it was a magnificent spread, but in practice college halls tend to be draughty places, and usually the food was cold before it reached the table. Our first experience of Bishop Shaxton's Solace was a chill one, not only on account of the temperature of the food, the wine and the hall. We were seated on the same table as the former Bursar – the one who had so scathingly dismissed Stephen's perfectly reasonable request for a job description before our marriage. That was bad enough, but our discomfort was compounded by finding ourselves placed out on a limb at the end of the table. After the meal, eaten in a frosty silence, an elderly band appeared from the shadows and struck up antediluvian foxtrots. I had never learnt the foxtrot, as the advent of the Beatles had cut short my brief flirtation with ballroom dancing, and now I could only watch in pensive, glum frustration as our tight-lipped dinner companions deserted us for the dance floor – looking like close-furled black umbrellas, they authoritatively steered their submissive, upholstery-clad wives round the hall, deftly exhibiting a precise, manicured display of ornamental footwork. I was twenty-one: all around me our dining companions were in their forties and fifties, if not their sixties and seventies. It was as if we had been propelled into a geriatric culture where our generation was deliberately snubbed as irrelevant.

The only consolation was that Caius, as one of the richest, most solidly based colleges, could probably afford to lend us a couple of thousand pounds without the loan creating a blip in the college accounts. We were well aware that no building society would even begin to consider the house for a mortgage, but Stephen, undeterred by his previous encounters in the Bursar's office, thought it perfectly reasonable to apply to the College for a loan so that we could improve our offer to Mrs Teulon-Porter. While he was with the Bursar, I sat waiting in the outer office and broached a matter of some delicacy to Mr Clarke, the white-haired bursarial assistant, much more amenable than the Bursar himself. My discussion began in the nature of a complaint. Why, I asked Mr Clarke, had he sent Stephen the application forms for a university pension a few weeks back when it was common knowledge that Stephen's life was going to be so drastically foreshortened that, in all probability, he would not qualify? Was it not a bit heartless of him to have sent the forms? Stephen had taken one look at them and with a weary gesture had pushed them aside, not wanting to contemplate arrangements for a future that others might look forward to, but that was to be denied him.

Mr Clarke did not apologize for any insensitivity; quite the contrary, he shook his head as if unable to comprehend my problem. "Well, young lady, I just follow my instructions," he said, turning his bright blue eyes on me from beneath busy white brows. "My instructions are to send out the forms to all new Fellows, as all new Fellows are by rights entitled to a university pension. Your husband is a new Fellow, so he is entitled to a university pension, just like the rest of them. All he has to do is sign the forms to establish his rights." His words were still ringing in my ears when he added casually as an afterthought, "No need for any medical tests or anything of that sort, if that's what you're thinking."

I could hardly believe what he was saying. This was an area which, in our ignorance, we had tacitly dismissed as inapplicable to us. Now I was being told that it could be resolved with a mere signature and, moreover, that it would assure us of a commodity which neither of us had ever thought about before – that is to say, security. For one afternoon's business we had both been remarkably successful, and through our success had discovered this new goal in life, security, which suddenly assumed a comforting importance. Stephen had persuaded the Bursar to send the College land agent to inspect the house with a view to securing a loan, and I had secured Stephen's rights to a pension. With a loan to buy the house and a pension, our well-being would gain two firm anchors in an otherwise uncertain world.

The College land agent came to survey the house one sunny spring morning, when the churchyard was bursting into a profusion of yellow blossom. Our optimism soon quailed before his dry, unsmiling exterior, and when he issued his verbal summary of his projected report, our hopes were dashed beyond recall. The agent gave us the strong impression that we were wasting his time, calling him out on such a nonsensical errand. Could we not see that the back of the house was falling down? And, as if that were not enough, the third-floor attic was a definite fire hazard. He would not risk sleeping up there, or even using it as a study himself, nor would he advise letting anyone else do so. A two-hundred-year-old house was not, in his opinion, a sensible purchase. In any case, there were so many road-building schemes in the offing that he would not be surprised if the whole lane were demolished to make way for a new access road to the city centre from the west. He could not possibly recommend the property as an investment to the College.

Stephen was infuriated at such a short-sighted verdict, but despite his vociferous protests the Bursar accepted the land agent's report. Some time later, as we were driving past the land agent's office on the other side of the city, Stephen spluttered indignantly as he pointed to the premises. Like our house, the building rose to three floors, but on a larger scale, a good ten feet higher than ours. The third floor was quite obviously, from the discernible lighting, being used as office or study space. Furthermore the whitewashed, gabled, timbered property bulged and leant picturesquely in the manner of a decrepit sixteenth-century building. It made our little eighteenth-century house appear positively modern and well-kept. There was no immediate solution to the problem, except perhaps to save as much money as we could to raise a deposit for a mortgage on a newer house. A system began to evolve whereby Stephen earned the money through salary, teaching and essay competitions, and I, running contrary to the national trend of reckless extravagance encouraged by the Macmillan government, attended to the family finances, paying the bills and saving as much as possible through careful housekeeping. Delicious scraps of streaky bacon came at one shilling and sixpence a pound from the old Sainsbury's, with its marble counters and endless queues; duck livers from Sennit's the poulterer's were nourishing and cheap; the market proved a veritable cornucopia of fresh fruit and vegetables; and the local butcher introduced me to inexpensive cuts of meat – hand of pork and shoulder of lamb never costing more than five shillings – which proved no disgrace on the dinner table when we entertained our new friends from the College and the Department.

The Labour government elected in 1964 inherited from the Conservatives the dubious legacy of a nation engaged in a gigantic spending spree. In the spring of 1966, having exercised my right to vote for the first time, I joined the late-night crowds in the Market Square to greet the success of the Labour candidate in the repeat election, which had been called to increase the government majority. Sadly, our new MP, Robert Davies, died while in office and the Labour government was shackled by its mounting economic problems, frequent strikes and a constant preoccupation with the "balance of payments" crisis, the economic buzz phrase of the Sixties. With a failing currency, Britain was having to relinquish its role as a world power. Home news broadcasts were dominated as never before by economics, while the international background of the war in Vietnam and heightening tensions in the Middle East threatened to give rise to the anticipated superpower confrontation which would unleash the forces of the nuclear arsenals of both sides.

Stephen meanwhile had discovered a way of earning more money and improving himself in the process. He had wanted to study mathematics at Oxford, but his father had been convinced, wrongly as it happened, that there would be no jobs in maths in the future. Aware that he had already disappointed his father by not showing any interest in medicine, Stephen had compromised by agreeing to study physics. When he came to Cambridge as a postgraduate student, therefore, he had only a basic grounding in mathematics. As he was now working with Roger Penrose, an exemplary mathematician, he felt himself at a disadvantage, but he hit upon the happy solution of getting paid for teaching himself the maths course by giving undergraduate supervisions in it for Gonville and Caius College. Thus he steadily worked his way through the syllabus of the Maths Tripos. Needless to say, his progress far outstripped that of his students, whose lack of application he found frustrating, as he pointed out in the end-of-term reports that I wrote down to his dictation. With Brandon Carter, he also attended some of the undergraduate lectures in mathematics, notably the course given by the genial Master of Pembroke College, Sir William Hodge. During the course of the term, the rest of the audience gradually drifted away, leaving Sir William lecturing only to three listeners, Stephen, Brandon and another colleague, Ray McLenaghan. They regretted that they had not taken the opportunity to slip away sooner, but since their absence would have been extremely conspicuous, they felt obliged to stay the course.

It must have been during my final year in London that an uncle of Stephen's by marriage, Herman Hardenberg, a Harley Street psychiatrist, spent a long period in hospital in St John's Wood, just down the road from Westfield, suffering from a heart condition. I used to call on him sometimes of an afternoon when the day's lectures and seminars were over. Herman, the husband of Stephen's aunt Janet, herself a doctor, was a charming, gentle, cultivated man who liked to talk about the subjects that interested me, particularly about the poetry of the Provençal troubadours, the topic of my special paper in Finals. He had been reading C.S. Lewis's *The Allegory of Love*, and naturally approached the tensions of the poetry – where the poet-lover languishes for his unattainable beloved – from the psychological angle. Then our conversation would turn to family topics: I told him about our life in Cambridge and our work on the house. "I hope the Hawkings are treating you well?" he once enquired cautiously, making little secret of his mistrust of that family. I confidently calmed his fears on my account. That the Hawkings were eccentric, even odd, was well known; that they were aloof, convinced of their own intellectual superiority over the rest of the human race, was also widely recognized in St Albans, where they were regarded with a mixture of suspicion and awe. There were upsets and outbursts and there had been tensions in the air at the time of our engagement and the wedding, but these I took as part of the general tenor of family life. I had no substantial reason to complain of the way they treated me. Indeed, as I told Herman, they always seemed delighted to see Stephen and me, and always welcomed us warmly to Hillside Road.

12

An Insignificant Ending

With the approach of summer, the trees and plants in the church-yard competed for the attention of residents and passers-by in a riotous display of colour and perfume. Successive groups of tourists, particularly Americans, would come sauntering down the lane. Many of them would press their noses to our windows in an attempt to peer through the net curtains into our quaint interiors. Not all were susceptible to the beauty of the surroundings: there was the small boy who announced in a loud voice to his parents as they strolled along: "Gee, Momma, I wouldn't like to live here: the Holy Ghost might come up and get yer!" I could not allow myself to dwell on the newly revealed beauties of our surroundings. Apart from a brief celebration for Stephen's PhD in March, my every precious spare moment was spent revising – in London in the College library during the week, in Cambridge with my books spread out around me in the attic at weekends or, that Easter, in St Albans, where we spent the holiday quietly with my parents.

The Hawking household, on the other hand, was in some distress. Stephen's younger sister, Philippa, had recently been taken into hospital in Oxford for reasons which were not disclosed to me. I shared Stephen's concern for her and wanted to visit her, naively hoping that perhaps at last she and I would be able to settle some of those shadowy disturbances which lay between us as sisters-in-law. Because I loved Stephen, I wanted to get on well with his family, to like them and to be liked by them, and I could not understand why this particular relationship should be so difficult. On the day appointed for our visit, however, Stephen's mother told me in no uncertain terms that Philippa wanted to see only Stephen, not me, explaining that no one, least of all Philippa, wanted to upset "this thing (presumably our marriage) between Stephen and you". As Stephen said nothing to mitigate the effect of his mother's bluntness, I was on the point of going home in tears to my parents, but then the old Ford Zephyr would not start and, in a sudden twist of events, I found myself driving Isobel and Stephen to Oxford in our Mini.

While the rest of the party went hospital-visiting, I spent the afternoon in the waiting room, revising the great medieval epic poem based on the exploits in exile of the hero, *el Cantar de Mío Cid*. The time passed quickly as I became absorbed in the sophisticated psychology of the late twelfth-century poem, which deftly interweaves two main thematic strands into its texture: the public image of the invincible warrior and the private face of the devoted husband and father. When the Cid goes into exile, the poet describes his distress at parting from his family as "tearing the nail from the flesh". Later the poet documents how the eponymous hero's many attempts to be generous and encouraging to his cowardly sons-in-law are misconstrued and turned against him. This epic tale, like a distant voice whispering down the centuries, told of the complexity and the unpredictability of the human mind. Even in the twelfth century, the poignant distinction between the hero's private life and his public image was seen as an authentic concept.

On our return from Oxford, no further reference was made to the morning's episode. In the family tradition, it was brushed under the carpet with many other dusty remnants of psychological and emotional detritus, regarded as being too insignificant to merit any consideration in that rarified atmosphere where emotional issues were never discussed because of the threat they might pose to the intellect. It was therefore a surprise, just before the onset of Finals, to receive a letter from Philippa, addressed to me in a minuscule hand. She regretted the differences that there may have been between us but looked forward to a better relationship in the future, assuring me that she respected my desire "to try to love Stephen". Although I responded wholeheartedly to this olive branch, I was as perplexed by that comment as my mother had been some months earlier when the rumour had reached her ears that the Hawkings were thinking of moving to Cambridge to set up a home there for Stephen. Did they not expect the marriage to last, she asked indignantly. I was confused by these undercurrents and wondered why Stephen's family, of all people, seemed so intent on undermining our relationship and our happiness, especially when he was dependent on me for so much of his everyday existence.

As if to confound the doubters, we were closer than ever in the week of Finals. Stephen came to London to give me moral support and stayed in my top-floor room working on the singularity theorems, and occasionally dipping into translations of the great works of Spanish literature – among them Fernando de Rojas's *La Celestina*, the downmarket prototype of Romeo and Juliet with its old procuress, Celestina, one of the most entertaining characters in medieval Spanish literature – while I went out each morning to the examination hall. After the afternoon session, Stephen and I would make off to Hampstead Heath or to the gardens and house of Kenwood in search of respite from writer's cramp and mental constipation. We also visited my much-loved Great Aunt Effie, as irrepressible as ever in her late seventies, still living alone in her large house in Tufnell Park. By the end of the week I was just beginning to get into my stride, but the exams were already nearly over. I felt a huge sense of anticlimax rather than relief. The topics I had revised had proved elusive in the extreme, and I knew that the First which was expected of anyone bearing the name of Hawking would prove just as elusive.

With the last flourish of the pen on the last page of the last Finals paper, I irrevocably signed away my student days. The Beatles record, *Revolver*, which Stephen had given me for my birthday, seemed sadly incongruous. There were no parties, no celebrations, just a few hasty goodbyes before I stepped definitively into my other existence and we set off in the car to meet Roger Penrose, who was to guide us out to his home at Stanmore for dinner with his family. We stopped in the car park of Stanmore station for Roger to collect his car, an elderly blue Volkswagen. Undeterred on finding every tyre flat, Roger drove to a garage round the corner where he pumped them all up. When we reached his single-storey house at the end of a cul-de-sac, tucked away from the stockbroker mansions, we were given an enthusiastic welcome by Joan and by their two small sons, Christopher and Toby, who had been a babe-in-arms at Cornell the previous summer. Now, at eighteen months, he was fully mobile and expressed his infectious *joie de vivre* by racing the length of the living room at full pelt, biscuit in hand, leaving a trail of crumbs across the navy blue carpet. Soon he was hurling his small person into an armchair, clambering onto the arm of the chair and then jumping off, the while declaring, "Don't do that, don't do that!" Blissfully unconcerned by such antics, Roger and Stephen lapsed into the inevitable discussion about the mathematics of physics.

The Finals results were more or less as expected, not brilliant but good enough to allow me to start working for a PhD. From my observations of the dynamics of life in Cambridge, I could see that the role of a wife – and possibly a mother – was a one-way ticket to outer darkness, and that it was essential to preserve my own identity. Even though there were moves afoot to admit women to certain of the more enlightened men's colleges, there were many well-qualified but unhappy wives in Cambridge whose individual talents had been totally disregarded, spurned by a system which refused to acknowledge that wives and mothers might be capable of an intellectual identity of their own.

My weekly commuting to London had come to an end none too soon, for Stephen needed my help more and more. As he had to lean on my arm wherever he went, I walked round to the Department with him every morning, took him home for lunch, which – like every other meal – had to consist of meat and two vegetables to satisfy his enormous appetite, and collected him again in the evening. All thoughts of a career in the Foreign Office had long been consigned to the past, but even a simple job or a teacher-training course was out of the question, as my presence was so obviously constantly required in the small circle of the Department of Applied Mathematics, Little St Mary's Lane and the kitchen. A doctorate seemed to be the ideal solution. I could easily adapt my hours of study in the University Library and my work at home to Stephen's schedule. Furthermore, I was eligible for a student grant, which was a welcome bonus.

The literature of the medieval period attracted me as an area of research, but as our circumstances would not permit me to travel to remote libraries in search of dusty manuscripts, I could not expect to edit a hitherto undiscovered text. My research would have to take the form of a critical study, using texts that were already published, which would not be difficult considering the facilities available in Cambridge. I continued to be registered, however, as a student of London University for various good reasons, the most cogent being that Cambridge PhDs were subject to a fairly strict time limit of three years, whereas there was no such restriction on the London degrees, and it seemed unlikely that I should be able to devote myself uninterruptedly to my thesis.

I did not embark upon my chosen field of research, the medieval lyric poetry of the Iberian Peninsula, straight away because, thanks largely to Stephen, another topic had presented itself as a subject for a preliminary research paper. As a result of reading *La Celestina* while I was doing my exams, Stephen had come up with a bright idea which he put to me as we were driving back to Cambridge at the end of Finals week. Had I not realized, he asked, that the ultimate tragedy of death, destruction and despair in the drama was precipitated by the old bawd Celestina's rejection of a minor character, Parmeno, a youth who has a mother complex about her? The idea was a fascinating one, which won my supervisor's amazed approval: he was even more amazed when I confessed that the idea was Stephen's. I too was astonished at his powers of perception and invention, which could focus on the essence of a problem in any field, my own included. My task was to explore and develop the idea and justify the Freudian concept when applied to a text dating from 1499. The most gratifying aspect of the project was that it was a tribute to the success of our relationship: we were living and working in harmony, supporting each other, participating in each other's interests, despite the disparity of our chosen subjects, despite attempts to divide us and despite the inevitable difficulties of Stephen's worsening disability. We were very happy. We both gained confidence and courage from the strength of our mutual resolve and from our trust in each other. Then in the early autumn we found that I was expecting a baby.

13

Life Cycles

Following close on the confirmation of the pregnancy came the sad fulfilment of one of the inevitable laws of nature: Stephen's paternal grandmother, Mrs Hawking senior, whose acquaintance I had made just a month before, died at the age of ninety-six while Stephen's parents were away in China on an official tour of the country at the height of the Cultural Revolution. That August, on a trip north with Stephen, his mother and Edward to visit ageing relatives, I had been introduced to Isobel's elderly maiden aunts in Edinburgh and, on our return journey, we had stayed overnight in the Hawking ancestral home in Boroughbridge in Yorkshire.

In the early nineteenth century, the ancestor who had been steward to the Duke of Devonshire and built himself the grand mansion had also amended the surname from the vulgar 'awkins to the more genteel Hawking. The Hawking Chatsworth, with its sweeping staircase, high ceilings and bay windows, had seen better days. Poor Aunt Muriel managed the vast house alone, while at the same time attending to her disabled but still imperious mother. Like the house, Mrs Hawking was certainly a shadow of her former self, but it was not hard to discern in her wrinkled features the determination and fortitude of the woman who had raised five children and saved her family from bankruptcy. She lived in the only room in the house which was still warm and habitable, the drawing room. The other rooms, including ours with its half-poster bed, were cold, dark, damp and not a little eerie, in spite of Aunt Muriel's efforts to make them comfortable.

While his parents were away, Stephen's younger brother Edward stayed with my parents. When he came to Cambridge to spend a weekend with us, he found himself, at the tender age of ten, obliged to cook his own Sunday lunch – under his brother's instruction, because I was suddenly laid low with an attack of morning sickness. It lasted all that day and into the next, and the next, and so on for week after week. An experienced friend suggested that the best cure for morning sickness was a cup of tea first thing in the morning before getting up. This was fine in theory, but in practice I could not have a cup of tea without getting up to make it myself. My parents came to the rescue with the gift of a tea-making machine. Thereafter I was troubled by few of the effects of pregnancy and was able to resume my usual routine of study and writing with renewed vigour.

There was no shortage of helpful friends, all of them recent mothers, to advise on the pros and cons of hospitals, nursing homes, health treatments, prophylactic breathing, relaxation classes and breast-feeding. In despair at my ignorance in such matters, they even left their babies with me for practice sessions in changing nappies, but it all seemed highly theoretical since, on the whole, the pregnancy was so straightforward and their babies were so well behaved. I was convinced that babies just ate and slept, whimpering a little from time to time.

My own health was unexceptional by comparison with Stephen's, which was beginning to require some management. Before leaving for China, Frank Hawking had read in a medical journal that a regular intake of vitamin B tablets might benefit the nervous system, which could also be reinforced by a weekly injection of a preparation called hydroxocobalamin. The vitamin tablets could be obtained on prescription from Dr Swan, a Bart's man like Stephen's father, with whom Stephen was registered in Cambridge – but the weekly injections were more of a problem, since the surgery was on the other side of Cambridge and, in Stephen's opinion, a morning spent there waiting for an injection was a morning wasted. We tried it a few times, to Stephen's growing irritation. One morning we arrived back home from the surgery at about midday to find Thelma Thatcher out in the lane, broom in hand, engaged in her daily exercise of sweeping the road and the pavement. Noticing our despondent faces, she called to us, "Dears, dears, what's the matter?" I explained, and she immediately came up with a solution. "Oh, but that's easy! We'll ask Sister Chalmers to call in on her way from Peterhouse!" She hugged us both and then went off to get in touch with Sister Chalmers, who had kindly lent us her gas cooker when we moved into Little St Mary's Lane. At Thelma Thatcher's instigation, she was now commandeered into giving Stephen his injection at home once a week when she had finished her college surgery. This in our household coincided more or less with breakfast time.

A similar problem arose when the medical authorities suggested regular physiotherapy to keep Stephen's joints extended and his muscles active. Already his fingers were beginning to curl, and he could no longer write, except to sign his name. We attended just one physiotherapy session at Addenbrooke's, the new hospital on the outskirts of Cambridge, but by the end of it Stephen was so angry that he declared that he would not squander any more of his precious time waiting around to be treated. It was Dennis Sciama who came to the rescue on this occasion. He persuaded the Institute of Physics to sponsor twice-weekly domiciliary visits by a private physiotherapist from its benevolent fund. This is when Constance Willis entered our lives.

Constance was one of those stalwart English spinster ladies, cast in the same mould as the jolly-hockey-stick Molly Du Cane, the leader of the St Albans Folk Dance and Song Society – open, jovial and straightforward of manner. Before coming to stretch Stephen's muscles at ten o'clock on Tuesday and Thursday mornings, Constance Willis would visit two octogenarian patients in Trinity College: Mr Gow, the eminent classicist, and the Reverend Simpson, formerly Dean of the College – principally to help them put their socks on.

Between them, Sister Chalmers and Miss Willis minimized the inconvenience to Stephen's routine, enabling him to work approximately the same hours as any of his colleagues. In reality, although he might arrive in his office later in the morning than they did, he usually worked later into the evening as well. He would spend long periods deep in thought, and often at weekends would sit silently wrangling with the equations governing the beginning of the universe, training his brain to memorize long, complicated theorems without the aid of pen or paper. "Celestial mechanics," Mr Thatcher called it jokingly. "I suppose your young man is busy with his celestial mechanics?" he would ask if Stephen had passed him in the street without acknowledging him, a common occurrence which, together with Stephen's reluctance to expend any effort on polite small talk, tended to offend some of our more sensitive neighbours, acquaintances and relations, and for which I frequently had to apologize, explaining that Stephen had to put all his concentration into remaining upright.

Bouts of morning sickness had prevented me from attending old Mrs Hawking's funeral in Yorkshire. In fact I had never yet been to a funeral. That omission was sadly soon to be rectified.

Mary Thatcher, the only daughter of our neighbours, was planning an extended study tour of the Middle East, where she would divide her stay of several months between Israel and Jordan. Just before her departure that autumn I saw her walking along the lane hand in hand with her father, whose pace had become slower and more halting. They disappeared from view into the churchyard. This poignant vision of father and daughter struck me forcibly, for it seemed that in those precious moments they were anticipating their final parting. Soon after Mary had left, her father fell ill and was taken into the nursing home, where he died some weeks later.

As dry leaves danced through the streets before the biting December wind, Stephen and I stood hand in hand at the back of the lofty, cold church of the Holy Trinity, the Low Church which William Thatcher had attended in preference to the High Anglicanism of Little St Mary's. The stirring words of the funeral service, intoned as the coffin was carried into the church, sent a chill shiver down my spine. Watching and listening, I was haunted by the paradox that, in one stroke, death had erased all the learning, the experiences, the heroism, the goodness, the achievements, the memories of that life from which we were taking our leave, while within me I was carrying the miraculous beginnings of a new life, a blank page on which the long process of learning, experience, achievements, memories, had still to be written. Beside me stood the child's father, young and vibrant despite the onset of disability. His general health was good, and his determination to enjoy life to the full – and to succeed in physics – was gaining strength by the day. Walking was difficult, buttons were a nuisance, mealtimes took longer and the brain had taken over from pen and paper, but these were mechanical problems which invention and perseverance could overcome. It was unthinkable that he could be a candidate for the sad ceremony we were attending that day. Death was the tragedy of old age, not of youth.

Youth is essential to the very existence of Cambridge, despite the medieval buildings and the fossilized Fellows who come home to roost in their dusty nooks and crannies. The magnetism of the place draws in wave upon wave of young people for three years, or if they are lucky six, and then ejects them into the real world, as if rousing them from an enchantment. Many of our early friends had already gone off to positions in universities all over the globe, and their places were soon filled by new arrivals, some semi-permanent, some transient. One such visitor that autumn was our quiet American friend whom we had met at Cornell, Robert Boyer. He paid only a brief visit to Cambridge, and after a session in the Department came to dinner with us. He talked about his English wife and little daughter, and Vietnam, the main preoccupation of Americans in those days, as well as about singularities and physics.

One day not long after Robert's visit, the radio was blaring out the *News* headlines, while I was preparing lunch and waiting for Stephen to come home. Since his return from Texas, George Ellis had kindly brought Stephen home at lunchtime on his way to eat at the newly opened University Centre on the riverfront at the end of the lane. I listened intently as the main item recounted a sniper attack in Austin, Texas. A madman had climbed to the top of the university tower, from where he had shot at the lecturers and students crossing the square below. One of the victims had been shot dead. The report was all the more horrific on account of the familiarity of the scene. I could picture it in my mind's eye and realized at once that the sniper's targets could well have included some of our acquaintances. Later that day we heard that it was Robert Boyer who was the victim of the sniper's bullet. This was not death from old age, or from natural catastrophe like the recent Aberfan disaster in Wales, or from premature illness, it was death at the brutal hand of man. There was a sober truth in those stark words of the funeral service: "...by man came death..." Shocked and bewildered at such a cruel trick of fate, we searched for a lasting way of expressing our sorrow and our admiration for Robert Boyer.

14

An Imperfect World

Robert George was born, weighing six pounds five ounces, at ten o'clock at night on Sunday 28th May 1967, just as Francis Chichester, the lone yachtsman, sailed into Plymouth harbour to be met by cheering crowds on his return from his round-the-world voyage. Robert's birth was received with private rejoicing of such intensity that when Stephen went the next morning to impart the good news to Peck and How Ghee Ang, our neighbours from Singapore who had taken over the house at number 11 from us, he was so overcome with emotion that Peck feared that I had died in childbirth.

Robert, in his eagerness to come into the world two weeks early, had taken me by surprise. In March, Stephen's sister Mary, his cousin Julian and I, together with thousands of other graduates, had all received our BA degrees at the mammoth London University degree ceremony in the Albert Hall, the occasion marred only by the absence of the Chancellor of the University, the Queen Mother, on account of illness. Afterwards our parents treated us to a memorable party in a splendid venue, the Royal Society of Tropical Medicine, obtained for our use by my father-in-law.

Earlier in the academic year, Dr Dorothy Needham, the distinguished wife of the Master of Caius, had taken me under her wing and introduced me to a fledgling academic society, Lucy Cavendish College, pioneered by two scientists, Dr Anna Bidder and Dr Kate Bertram; their aim was to promote academic opportunities for mature women students in Cambridge. Association with Lucy Cavendish College allowed me to acquire MA status in the University, and this in turn, most importantly, allowed me to borrow books from the University Library. By late spring, the Celestina paper inspired by Stephen, 'Madre Celestina', was at the printer's, and I saw no reason to suppose that I would not be able to combine motherhood with research. On the last Friday in May, true to my usual routine, I spent most of the day blithely working in the University Library, assembling material for the thesis. I did not suspect that this was to be my last visit to the Library for quite a long time.

That evening, disregarding the strange tightening sensations in my thighs, I went with Sue Ellis, who was also pregnant, to a party for wives given by Wilma Batchelor, the wife of the Head of the Department. On the Saturday morning, after an uncomfortable night, the tightening sensations became stronger and more frequent, so I dashed into town to do a copious amount of shopping for Stephen before I was out of action. Feeling rather ill as I heaved it all home, I called in at the butcher's for a few final purchases. Chris the butcher took one look at me and insisted on serving me ahead of the queue. "Jane," he said, "I think you had better go straight home!" I gladly followed his advice.

Later that day, at the height of a thunderstorm, How Ghee, who was the father of two little daughters, drove Stephen and me to the nursing home, but I soon wished that I had stayed at home or applied for a bed at the maternity hospital – which, in those days, admitted only women from deprived backgrounds or those with complications. The ageing midwives were every bit as crusty as the spinster school ma'ams of my teenage years. As I walked down the corridor with Stephen leaning on my arm, I felt the onset of a strong contraction, like the tentacles of an octopus embracing and squeezing my abdomen. Assiduously following the techniques acquired in the newly introduced antenatal classes, I leant against a door post and focused my attention on the much-practised breathing exercises.

"What on earth's the matter with you?" the steely-eyed Sister enquired harshly. She was much younger than the rest of her staff and should have known better. There, after the procedure came to a standstill for the next twenty-four hours, the baby was finally delivered, not by one of the midwives but by John Owens, a cheerful young doctor from the surgery where I was registered. Meanwhile Stephen was my faithful companion, sitting at my bedside for long hours and even sneaking in on his mother's arm by the garden entrance at six o'clock the next morning.

I lay in bed, bored and frustrated, transported only by the magnificent, overpowering themes of the Brahms double concerto for violin and cello which I had memorized as my mantra, the music on which I had learnt to concentrate to distract my mind from the pain. The music took me back to the week's holiday arranged for us by my parents that Easter, just two months before the birth. The cottage they had rented was down on the edge of the cove at Port St Isaac in Cornwall, a very long way from Cambridge. They probably thought, mistakenly as it happened, that this would be my last opportunity to travel for a long time. During that week Stephen, in concession to my tastes, had given me the recording of the Brahms concerto for a birthday present.

As Stephen's self-confidence had grown, so he had gained in fierce determination. During our stay in Port St Isaac, an afternoon's drive took us to Tintagel, one of the reputed homes of the Arthurian legend, perched remotely on the north coast of Cornwall. Disappointingly, the ruined castle was not visible from the village and, according to the postmistress, the only approach was down the steep rocky gully, the Vale of Avalon. Stephen insisted on seeing the castle and – unable to deny him anything, so conscious were we of his shortened life expectancy – my mother and I, one on each side, guided, lifted, bore him down the wild, uneven descent, stumbling over the stones in our path with the wind blowing off the sea into our faces. The sapphire band of sea at the end of the path seemed to recede, and the castle proved elusive. After we had struggled on for about three-quarters of an hour, my mother was getting short of breath and was worrying about me in my advanced state of pregnancy, but Stephen refused to give up. By a happy chance, a Land Rover appeared from nowhere, climbing the rough track back up to the village, so we hailed the driver. He was reluctant to stop, but paused to tell us that the castle was still a long way off, round a headland. The castle was evidently beyond our reach, but we pleaded with him to take us back to the village. Finally with brusque impatience he agreed to take just one passenger. There was no question but that that passenger had to be Stephen. With similar single-mindedness, Stephen was pursuing plans to attend a summer school at the Battelle Memorial Institute in Seattle that July. With never a moment's hesitation, I agreed to the plans, seeing no reason why the three of us, Stephen, myself and the baby, should not enjoy seven weeks on the Pacific coast. After all, babies just ate and slept.

The joy the baby brought was intoxicating. Within minutes of his birth he was lodged in the crook of my arm, looking slightly purple but observing his surroundings with consummate lack of concern as if he had seen it all before. "A future professor" was my mother-in-law's predictable verdict on her first grandchild.

When he was next brought to me, he had recovered from the birthing experience and had gained a healthy colour. His eyes were of the deepest, brightest blue, set in a neat elfin face with rosy cheeks and pointed ears. He had no hair, only an incipient blond down in a whorl on the crown of his head and on the tips of his ears. The minute fingers, each equipped with its own tiny nail, clasped my own outstretched finger.

This beautiful little creature, the miraculous embodiment of perfection, had come into a painfully imperfect world. In the week after his birth, the Six Day War erupted in the Middle East with violent consequences which were to last throughout the decades of the child's upbringing and long into his adulthood. In my simple, post-natal frame of mind, I was convinced that if the world were to be run by the mothers of newborn babies rather than hardened old men inciting brash youths to violence, wars would cease overnight.

Gradually in the days following Robert's birth we acclimatized to a new reality. Grandparents helped out for a couple of weeks, and then we were on our own, evolving a dramatically changed lifestyle. Henceforth expeditions – to the Department or into town – involved three people plus a pram and a walking stick. Luckily George Ellis came to the rescue. Not only did he bring Stephen home at lunchtime, he also collected him after lunch and brought him home in the evening. One afternoon, after a couple of weeks, when we had begun to achieve some faint semblance of normality, I considered that the time had come to return to my books and my growing card index of the language of the medieval love poetry of the Iberian Peninsula. The baby was fed and changed and placed in his pram out in the backyard under the blue sky. He looked comfortable and drowsy in the warm afternoon air. I expected him to sleep for at least an hour. Stifling my own tendency to yawn, I crept upstairs to my books and cards in the attic and spread them out on the table. No sooner had I found my place than a raucous cry came from below. I hurried down to Robert, picked him up, fed him and changed his nappy again. He did not really appear to be very hungry. I laid him down gently in his carrycot-pram and went back upstairs, only to be followed by the same cry. This little scene was re-enacted many times that afternoon until finally I realized that this tiny baby was neither hungry nor sleepy: he just wanted to be socia-ble. So at the age of one month he started work on a PhD thesis, helping me by wriggling on my knee and gurgling while I tried to write. That single afternoon completely destroyed whatever illusions I might have held about combining motherhood with some sort of intellectual occupation. Nor did I have any notion of the demands on the body of the birth process. I fully counted on being up and about my normal business within a week, little realizing that the nine-month gestation and the trauma of the long birth would take their toll of my strength. I had no idea that feeding the baby would be such an exhausting and time-consuming commitment which, combined with the topsy-turvy schedule of infant demands, day and night, would mean that I would often slip into a doze when eventually he went to sleep.

As July approached, I began to have severe qualms about the Seattle trip, especially as the arrangements were becoming more and more complicated. Charlie Misner, an American visitor to the Department who had become Robert's godfather at the christening in Caius Chapel in June, wanted Stephen to visit him at the University of Maryland after the Seattle summer school, to talk about singularities. Both he and his Danish wife, Susanne, assured us that we would be welcome to stay with them and their four young children in their large house in the suburbs of Washington DC. I could not allow myself to appear half-hearted, but I was not sure how we were going to get to Seattle in one piece, let alone further afield. The tiredness I felt as I tried to pack for Stephen, myself and our six-week-old baby was devastating. I had not expected anything like this, nor had I expected that my own body, previously so utterly reliable, would let me down so catastrophically.

Somehow, assisted by a posse of anxious parents, none more so than my mother, we managed to check in at London Airport on time on the morning of 17th July, 1967. Our goodbyes were hasty, because the airline promptly provided a wheelchair for Stephen, who found himself obliged to sit in it and be wheeled directly through customs and passport control to the departure lounge. Laden with Robert and with assorted bags of provisions for the flight, I hurried along behind. The ventilation system at Terminal Three had broken down that day, the hottest day of the summer, with the result that hot air was being sucked into the building but none was being let out, making a veritable inferno of the departure lounge. We had just reached the lounge when the loudspeaker announced that our flight was delayed.

While we sat waiting in the stifling heat, Robert eagerly gulped down the entire contents of the bottle of diluted rose-hip syrup which was supposed to last him all the way to Seattle. The first announcement was soon followed by another, inviting Pan American passengers to collect complimentary refreshments from the bar. I deposited Robert on Stephen's knee and went over to join the queue for our free sandwiches. When I returned, I froze in absolute horror at the sight that met my eyes. Robert was still safely sitting on his father's knee, smiling beatifically and leaning comfortably back against Stephen's chest, with Stephen's arm around him. Stephen's face wore an agonized expression. Down his new trousers there flowed a vast yellow river. He sat helplessly trapped as the yellow tide streamed into his shoes. For the only time in my life, I screamed – I dropped the sandwiches and screamed.

Screaming sounds a pretty irrational reaction, but surprisingly it was the most sensible in the circumstances. My screams summoned much-needed help with amazing alacrity. A portly, green-clad nurse appeared from nowhere and took charge. One severely critical glance at me was enough to convince her, quite rightly, that I was hopelessly unequal to the situation. She commandeered the wheelchair and pushed it and its occupants, father and son, back through passport and customs, disregarding the officials in our path, to a nursery where she cleaned up the baby, leaving me the task of rubbing Stephen down. While we were in the nursery, the last call for our flight was announced over the tannoy. Unmoved, the nurse rang through to central control and told them that the flight would have to wait for us. Thus at the age of seven weeks, Robert acquired the distinction of having delayed the departure of an international flight.

Stephen had to sit in those trousers for the whole nine-hour length of that spectacular flight. He sat in them over Iceland, which was etched in the sea like a jewel in a satin case, over the ice floes of the North Atlantic, over Greenland's snow-capped mountains and glistening glaciers, over the frozen waters of Hudson Bay and the arid wastes of northern Canada. Then at last, signalling the end of Stephen's ordeal, Mount Rainier loomed on the horizon as we came in to land at Tacoma airport. A day or two later, I took the trousers to the dry-cleaner's, but Stephen refused to wear them ever again.

Part Two

1

Sleepless in Seattle

The provisions made for us in Seattle in 1967 by the Battelle Memorial Institute were very generous. As well as a spacious single-storey house, lavishly equipped with all mod cons – including a dishwasher and a tumbler-dryer – and an enormous car with automatic controls, they provided a twice-weekly deposit of clean nappies and the corresponding collection of the dirty ones by that singularly American institution, the diaper service. If such arrangements did not altogether fill me with confidence, it was not because I was unappreciative, but that I was overwhelmed by being washed-up on an alien shore, albeit in luxurious isolation, deprived so soon after giving birth of the support and help of my mother, family and friends at home. Here I was solely responsible both for my ailing husband and for my new baby, and there was no George Ellis to give Stephen a helping hand round the corner to work.

The Battelle Institute, the secretary assured me, was very close at hand, only two miles or so away – but two miles or twenty, it did not make much difference: Stephen had to be taken there by car, and to take Stephen by car, I also had to take Robert. This meant helping Stephen dress and eat in the early morning, and then feeding and bathing Robert – in that order or in reverse – depending on whose needs were the most pressing. Then the monstrous car – a Ford Mercury Comet – had to be backed round to the front of the house, and my two charges, tiny but voracious Robert in his carrycot, and then Stephen on my arm, taken one by one down the steps of the long path and settled, the one on the backseat and the other in the front. Methodically carried out, this routine could have been tolerable. As it was, although we tried our hardest to minimize the number of morning sessions that Stephen missed, the system was reduced to breaking point – our darling baby, who had just learnt to sleep through the night in England, was now, in Seattle with an eight-hour time change, sleeping soundly all day and wide-awake and full of sociable intentions all night. In addition Seattle was enjoying – or suffering – its most intense heatwave ever.

For some time, in a spirit of nervous self-preservation, I restricted my excursions only to the Battelle Institute and the corner stores – notably, of course, the dry-cleaner's. I drove the massive car with such trepidation that eventually, despite the heat, I decided to do what no American mother would have dreamt of doing: I walked down to the stores pushing my carrycot-pram and loaded the shopping into it beside the baby.

With the jubilation of a shipwrecked sailor sighting a rescue boat, I greeted the arrival of the Penrose family. Eric, the latest addition to the family, was somewhat more mobile than Robert, but frequently recumbent. When the two prams stood side by side, or the two babies were placed down together on a rug, Joan would remark that they were continuing the Hawking-Penrose dialogue. Thanks to Joan, my social scene brightened considerably. She introduced me to some of the other wives of the delegates and took me on various excursions to downtown Seattle, where I browsed in the department stores and bought baby clothes. Under her influence, my confidence grew as I began to find my way up and down the north-south axis of the freeway through the centre of Seattle, even managing to locate an old childhood playmate from Norwich, who had married a Boeing engineer.

Then one Sunday, even more adventurously, Stephen's mapreading guided us to a ferry port, and we crossed Puget Sound to the Olympic Peninsula, where I took Robert down to the water's edge and dipped his toes in the shimmering but icy waters of the Pacific Ocean. Another weekend, with Robert propped up between us asleep on the bench-seat in the front of the car, we drove the hundred and fifty miles north, across the border to Vancouver, to visit our Australian friends from Cambridge, the Youngs, who had come to rest in the University of British Columbia. Vancouver was as cold and misty as Seattle was hot and dry, and had the Canadian charm of being more relaxed than its American neighbour.

Back in Seattle, we assembled with the rest of the group one hot Saturday morning down on the Waterfront for one of the few excursions organized by the Battelle Institute – a ferry ride to the Indian reservation on Blake Island. While waiting for the ferry, Jeannette Wheeler, the wife of a leading American physicist, came up to introduce herself. That very year, in a flash of inspiration worthy of Archimedes, John Wheeler had lighted upon the name *black hole* for the phenomenon that Stephen and many others were studying, while he was having a bath. Down on the Seattle Waterfront, Jeannette – a regal, grey-haired lady who, by all accounts, was a member of that select group, the Daughters of the American Revolution – took charge of Robert's pram while Stephen leant on my arm. Two little old ladies peered lovingly into the pram, and one of them reached out to tickle the toes of the sleeping infant, uncovered in the heat of the day. Horrified, Jeannette Wheeler barked at her not to disturb the sleeping baby. The poor little lady jumped out of her skin and, with her companion, edged away nervously into the crowd. Personally, I thought a bit of tickling of Robert's toes to wake him up during the day might be a very good idea. Then I might get some sleep at night. As it was, he slept for most of that day, waking only to gaze angelically into the weather-beaten face of the elderly Indian squaw who rocked him on her knee while I ate dinner at the long communal table in a big old-fashioned barn.

At least on this particular excursion, my only responsibility, apart from attending to the baby's needs, was to push the pram with one hand and support Stephen with the other. The other interesting excursions where I had to drive long distances left me so tired and so strained that I was on my knees with exhaustion by the time Gillian, my school friend, came over to Seattle from Vancouver Island, where her husband Geoffrey, an engineer, had a two-year appointment. Gillian – and Geoffrey, who was able only to spend a weekend with us – were my salvation. Geoffrey took over the driving, taking us on long journeys – not least a day trip to Mount Rainier – collected shopping and helped Stephen in and out of the car, while Gill willingly gave a hand in the running of the kitchen. For one week, I could relax a little.

While Gill was still with us, an incident occurred which we both still remember with distaste. The token monument which Seattle retained from the World Fair of 1962 was the Space Needle, a concrete pylon some three hundred feet high, topped by a viewing platform in the shape of a flying saucer. On Gill's last Saturday with us, we went up the Space Needle in the express lift and admired the views – over the sparkling green waters of Puget Sound and the white crests of the Olympic Peninsula to the west, the rugged Cascade range of mountains to the east, and to the south Mount Rainier, the massive dormant volcano. The views were majestic, but with Gill carrying Robert and Stephen leaning on my arm we soon wilted in the sweltering sun and returned to the lift to join the queue for the descent. Near us there stood a couple of girls, teenagers perhaps, but not so very much younger than Gill and me. They watched us, nudging each other; then, as we were all standing together in the lift, they started making spiteful, rude remarks about Stephen's appearance, as he leant languidly against the wall, in temperatures that were enough to make anyone look bedraggled. As they laughed and giggled, my anguish grew. I wanted to slap their faces and make them apologize. I wanted to shout at them that this was my courageous, dearly loved husband and the father of the beautiful baby, and a great scientist, but in my English reticence I neither did nor said any of these things: I simply looked away, busying myself with Robert, trying to pretend that they were not there. Never did an express lift, travelling at four feet per second, take so long to reach the ground. As we emerged from the lift, one of the girls glanced over Gill's shoulder at Robert. "Is that your baby?" she asked me in perplexed admiration. "Of course!" I snapped. She and her companion hurried away, I hoped in shame. Gill remarked, "What strange people!" understating what she and I both felt. Fortunately Gill and I had stationed ourselves between Stephen and those girls, so he was unaware of what had happened.

After this episode I was ready to go home forthwith. Nonetheless, one evening towards the end of the summer school, at the Battelle cocktail hour, Stephen was offered the tantalizing possibility of a two-week stay at the University of California in Berkeley, and immediately a Brazilian participant in the Battelle summer school offered us the empty flat of an absent friend. The offer was attractive in financial terms and, since we had already come so far, another two weeks on the West Coast, in California of all places, did not seem a great hardship. I had not entirely lost the spirit of adventure which had taken me round southern Spain in my student days, and this would be our opportunity to discover for ourselves that Utopia with which Abe and Cice Taub had tempted us in Cornell in 1965.

Encumbered by masses of paraphernalia – the pram and inordinate amounts of luggage – we flew down to San Francisco, where I was required to master yet another enormous car and negotiate yet another maze of freeways. Fortunately Stephen was a better navigator than he had been a driver – except on those occasions when he would spot an exit at the last minute and yell at me to cross four lanes immediately. After swerving a few times and bumping over a few kerbs in good Keystone-Cop style, we at last found the address of our absent landlords, a homely two-room flat in an old wooden house with a distant view, through the haze and the mist, of the Golden Gate bridge. The accommodation, though much more in keeping with our style and age than the sumptuous middle-class, middle-aged house in Seattle, posed a fearsome logistical problem as it was on the top floor of the house, on the second storey. The routine which we had hoped to leave behind in Seattle had to come into play again, except that every outing now required not two but three trips up and down – not one but two flights of stairs. Robert, at fourteen weeks, was too heavy to be carried in the carrycot, so that had to be taken down to the car first, then Stephen – leaving Robert on a rug on the floor – then Robert himself. In compensation for all this inconvenience, we maximized the use of the car and often, of an evening or exceptionally of a late afternoon, we would drive up into the parched hills behind Berkeley, or sometimes, more adventurously, north along the San Andreas Fault – a deserted, marshy area where the cracks in the road testified to the tremendous natural forces lying beneath the surface. Once we drove down to a desolate cove on a coastline not unlike Cornwall, where, defying the American way of life, hippies lived free of the constraints of a materialistic society in shacks on the beach.

Abe Taub, the Head of the Relativity Group in Berkeley, secured a temporary appointment for Stephen in his department, and one evening he and Cice invited us to dinner in their house high up in the hills overlooking the bay. It was further away than we expected, and by the time we arrived the evening was already drawing in. Unable to see where to park, I drove into a gully by the side of the road. The wheels locked and the car was stuck. After trying unsuccessfully to heave the car out of the ditch on my own, I went to seek help from the Taubs and their distinguished guests, among them a highly sophisticated and influential Parisian mathematician, Professor Lichnerowicz. The men took off their smart jackets, rolled up their sleeves and set to the task with chivalrous gusto. When at last we were extricated from the ditch and shown into the house – embarrassingly late and very dishevelled – Robert started to whimper. He had played this trick on us once before in Seattle. Sleeping soundly until the very moment when his carrycot was put gently down in a darkened side-room, he would suddenly start to protest, as though sensing that there was a party elsewhere from which he was being excluded. The only remedy was to allow him to spend the evening on my knee at the table, alongside all the other guests. Cice Taub remained unflustered by so many disruptions to her genteel gathering and, perhaps taking pity on my haggard appearance, invited me to accompany her and Mme Lichnerowicz to the Berkeley Rose Garden the next day.

The Rose Garden became my haven of peace and solitude in the frenzied environment of the Bay area, and a respite from the strenuous routine demanded by our living arrangements. It had a calming effect on Robert, who would lie in his pram under the pergolas watching the patterns of light on the roses and the leaves above his head. I sat by him in the shade, breathing in the perfume of the roses, immersed in my book, Stendhal's *The Charterhouse of Parma*, and gazing out over the Bay from time to time. My thoughts were drawn to Spain – to the gardens of the Generalife above Granada where, only a few short years before, I had tried to imagine a future for myself with Stephen. That future had become a reality, and had exceeded our wildest hopes. I was tired but resilient, and my happiness far outweighed my tiredness. Stephen was already recognized and sought after in scientific circles for his intuitive grasp of complicated concepts, his ability to visualize mathematical structures in many dimensions and for his phenomenal powers of memory. The future stretched ahead of us, now physically embodied in the small, thriving person of our baby son.

If the future had acquired a reassuring aura of certainty, the key to it lay in managing the present. Living each day as it came, rather than projecting some fanciful mirage on to the distant future, was becoming a way of life. From that perspective, the general outline of the future was fairly clear-cut: in the short term our star was in the ascendant. In the long term, the huge question mark that hung over the whole human race might well obliterate us all. The Vietnam war had escalated – to use the coinage then current – into the ugliest of conflicts in which the horrors of modern chemical science were being cynically unleashed on a simple peasant population, propelled by the uncontrolled military industrial complexes of both East and West. A mere spark somewhere else on our troubled planet could ignite a global conflagration.

We lived for the present, but even that had an annoying way of tripping us up with unforeseen obstacles. For example, the Brazilian couple who had, with the best of intentions, found us the flat, offered to take us on a tour of the sights of San Francisco. For once, I looked forward to sitting back and enjoying a day out. They arrived early one Saturday morning, bringing with them a Brazilian friend who spoke no English. I helped Stephen down the stairs, expecting to install him in the Brazilians' car first before going back up for Robert, who would travel on my knee. As we excitedly emerged into the street, we looked around for their car. Apart from our own Plymouth, there was only a decrepit grey Volkswagen parked in front of the house. "Where's your car?" I asked our Brazilian host for the day. He looked at me in surprise. "No, no, we are no going in our car, it too small for all of us. We take your car." With sinking heart I unlocked our car. Stephen sat in the back with the Brazilian ladies and our "host" settled himself in the passenger seat in the front, directing me, the chauffeur, while holding Robert on his knee. One look at him was enough to make Robert bawl as he never had before. He bawled all day – across the Oakland Bridge, all through the hours of torrid, nose-to-tail traffic jams in which we sat roasting, all through Haight-Ashbury, up and down all the steep streets of central San Francisco. I would gladly have bawled my head off too. Desperately wanting to comfort my frantic, hot, uncomfortable baby, there I was, trapped in the driving seat in a senseless situation, not of our own making.

There was a lull when at last we reached Golden Gate Park. Distancing ourselves from our passengers, we joined a large hippy peace gathering and sat on the grass with the flower-power people, swaying to the beat of the music. Around the lawns were people of my own age, yet somehow I was already much older than them. Stephen and I shared their idealism and hatred of violence. We, too, had asserted a comparable freedom against a rigid society in our fight against bureaucracy and narrow-mindedness – yet, to maintain our difficult course, we were constrained to follow a routine as organized and as rigid as any imposed by the society against which they were rebelling. The Vietnam war, though we shared their antagonism to it, was not our main target. Our efforts were directed against illness and ignorance.

After that day, I decided that never again would I depend on other people. However, putting that resolution into practice was easier said than done, for Stephen had already accepted a pressing invitation to spend time in Charlie Misner's department at the University of Maryland. Washington DC was on the way home, we reasoned, so another few weeks would not make much difference. Indeed breaking the journey halfway would help us all, including Robert, to cope with the jet lag. We also looked forward to seeing Stephen's sister Mary, now a qualified doctor, who was working on the East Coast, and to visiting Stephen's old friend John McClenahan and his lively Spanish-speaking American wife and her family in Philadelphia.

On the flight east, we sat in the same row as a middle-aged lady who sobbed for the whole journey. Since she occasionally cast longing glances at Robert, I passed him to her to cuddle for a while. A pale smile flickered across her face as he beguiled her with his tinkling laughter. Her companion leant across the aisle to tell me that she was returning home from Vietnam, where her only son had been killed. The hippies were right to protest at being used as cannon fodder when many of them had neither the right to vote, nor even the right to buy themselves a drink, since the age of majority was still twenty-one. Many of them were lucky in that, as students, their military call-up would be deferred and then their college professors would try to help the most able of them avoid the draft, while others would escape abroad, to Canada perhaps. The son of the mother on the plane had not been so fortunate.

Our visit to the Misners in Maryland was evidently not best timed, because Susanne was engaged in a stressful daily battle with the school authorities who were rejecting Francis, their eldest son, on account of his mild autism. We saw Stephen's sister, Mary, and spent a weekend with the McClenahans, but I was exhausted and depressed, especially because I had had to resort to feeding Robert with baby formula. I sat on the bed in the basement guest apartment of the Misners' luxury home in Silver Spring tearful at the breaking of that first bond with my baby.

If the recourse to bottles had unhappy psychological repercussions for me, it had even worse physical consequences for the Misners. One evening, Charlie and Susanne, who was beginning to relax a little from her daily struggle, put on a splendid dinner party to introduce us to some of their friends. All the children were asleep and we sat round the table eating and drinking, talking and laughing. Later we sank drowsily into comfortable armchairs while Charlie put on a slide show of charming family photos. In my semi-somnolent state of idle contentment, I suddenly became conscious of a very nasty smell coming from the kitchen. The horrible truth was soon revealed when other people began to frown and cough, as they too detected the poisonous odour, and I realized that I was responsible for it. Before dinner I had put Robert's plastic bottles and their rubber teats on the stove to boil, and in the convivial atmosphere I had forgotten all about them. The contents of the saucepan had evaporated completely, filling the kitchen with an evil black smoke which was quickly penetrating every corner of the spotlessly clean house. Utterly mortified, I would not have been surprised if we had been turned out into the street, baby and all, there and then. To Charlie and Susanne's lasting credit, they did no such thing and the next day, summoning a prodigious degree of charity, they even managed somehow to make light of the shameful episode. They must have been heartily glad to see the back of us some days later when they cheerily waved us and our four-month-old baby goodbye. Their relief at seeing us go could not have been greater than mine at the prospect of going home.

2

Terra Firma

That trip to Seattle – and beyond – changed our lives, in some ways for better, in others for worse. The money Stephen had earned in lecture fees during those long months across the Atlantic had a healthy effect on our bank balance. On the strength of it we were able to go out and buy a badly needed automatic washing machine and, in good American style, a tumbler-dryer as well. This would have been an extraordinary supply of consumer goods for any British household in the Sixties, but Stephen decided – after one searing exposure to domestic reality – that our lifestyle demanded even more electrical aids. That domestic reality arose one Friday evening later that winter of 1967, when we gave a large dinner party for an eminent Russian scientist, Vitaly Ginzburg, who had come to Cambridge from Moscow on a three-month visit. Not only was the length of his visit exceptional in the repressive climate of the Cold War, but he had also been allowed to bring his glamorous blonde wife with him. The amount of crockery and cutlery piled in the kitchen afterwards indicated the success of the dinner party. Leaning himself against the kitchen wall, Stephen picked up a tea towel, but so disgusted was he by the waste of time occasioned by so much washing-up that the following day he enlisted George Ellis's help and went off into town to buy a dishwasher.

There were other less tangible effects of the American trip. It was well established that the phenomenon that Stephen was researching had an inspired, easily identifiable name, the *black hole*, which was much less cumbersome than *gravitational collapse of a massive star*, the process predicted in the mathematics of the singularity theorems, and it lent unity to scientific research. It was, too, a name which caught the imagination of the media. As a result of the Seattle summer school Stephen had firmly consolidated his international position as a pioneer in this research, and we had widely enlarged our circle of friends. Stephen calculated that, by the time we returned to England in

October, Robert had flown such a vast distance in relation to his age that, even in his sleep, he was in theory still moving. Luckily Robert himself did not appear to be disturbed by this particular consequence of his first visit to America. I too had travelled far, but unlike Robert I suffered long-lasting and tormenting results from these travels. They had sown the seeds of a paralysing fear of flying, which grew like a giant weed in my mind in the months and years after our return home. By comparison with my carefree attitude to flying as a student only two years previously, this fear was both frustrating and incomprehensible. It was not until some time later that the reason for the phobia emerged. When I reviewed the events of those four months in America, I realized that the problem lay not with flying – since we had flown in many different aeroplanes over vast distances without incident – but with the attendant circumstances, the stresses and strains of being wholly responsible, a mere seven weeks after giving birth, for two other fragile but very demanding lives. That onerous and exhausting responsibility slowly crystallized into a fear of flying for want of any other outlet. The simple fact of being able to rationalize the fear did not make dealing with it any easier, because I was ashamed to admit to such a weakness, especially when our lives were strictly governed by Stephen's laudably brave maxim – that if there was physical illness in the home, there was no room for psychological problems as well.

Despite Stephen's excitement at the marked success of his research and his determination to avail himself of every conference, seminar or lecturing opportunity across the globe, the question of further travels luckily did not arise that winter, a winter which we spent in a comfortably stationary state, re-adjusting to the familiar routine of academic life. Stephen's Research Fellowship had been renewed for a further two years, and now that Rob Donovan, his former best man, was also a Research Fellow of Gonville and Caius College, Stephen could regularly count on his help for going into College to dine once a week. My routine was rather less predictable and consisted of a constant struggle to reconcile the needs of the baby with the demands of my thesis. When I played with Robert, my conscience told me that I ought to be working on the thesis. When I worked on the thesis, my natural instincts encouraged me to want to play with the baby. It was not a very satisfactory state of affairs – nevertheless it was the only way I could maintain my intellectual self-esteem in an environment where babies were disdained and regarded only as necessary facts of life. Theses, on the other hand, were respected. In the late Sixties, the university offered no crèche facilities – though, true to its male chauvinist instincts, it had for many years boasted a rifle range.

The fact that I was able to persevere with my research at all was largely thanks to my mother and to the succession of nannies employed to care for Inigo Shaffer, the baby son of neighbours in the lane. My mother would often come over to Cambridge by train early on a Friday, arriving just as I was taking Stephen to work, and would look after Robert so that I could spend the best part of the day in the University Library collecting books and other material to study at home during the next week. Sometimes Inigo's nanny would take Robert over for an hour or so, or – as the boys grew older – invite him to play with Inigo for an afternoon, leaving me free to return to the Library. This system also allowed me occasionally to attend and give seminars in London, confident that Robert was being well looked after and that Stephen, helped by George Ellis, was able to have lunch with the rest of the Relativity Group in the newly opened University Centre.

Thus I was able to pursue my project, an investigation of the linguistic and thematic similarities and discrepancies of the three main periods and areas of popular love poetry in medieval Spain. While Stephen mentally roamed the universe, I travelled in time – back to the *kharjas*, the earliest flowering of popular poetry in the Romance languages. I began my research by documenting the Mozarabic vocabulary – an early dialect of Spanish from Muslim Spain – used in the *kharjas*, which consisted of little more than poetic fragments incorporated as refrains in longer Hebrew and classical Arabic odes and elegies. I intended then to extend the exercise to the Galician-Portuguese *Cantigas de Amigo* of the thirteenth century, and finally to the fifteenth-century Castilian popular lyrics or *villancicos*. These three areas of lyric flowering, disparate in time as well as in place, shared many common features: the love songs were all sung by a girl, either looking forward to meeting her lover at dawn or lamenting his absence or illness. Often the girl would confide her joy or her grief spontaneously to her mother or her sisters, yet in many instances the imagery of these seemingly fresh and unsophisticated lyrics was derived from the language of the Christian religious background.

There were many conflicting theories, not to say contentions, attendant upon the provenance and interpretation of the poetry, especially of the *kharjas*, and it was through this maze that I had to find my way as a novice research student in the University Library. My time was spent scanning the huge green-jacketed catalogue volumes, pursuing arcane articles in unfamiliar journals, seeking out cryptic references in footnotes and searching the stacks and the shelves for the numerous works of literary criticism on which I would write notes at home during the course of the following week. Just occasionally I actually came into contact with original medieval manuscripts, an unforgettable experience, but not one which advanced my research very efficiently, because the temptation to marvel over the beauties of the illustrated initials and the precision of the script was far too distracting.

Though the prospect of having to plough my way through reams of critical material was daunting, I relished those hours in the Library. I loved the curiously deferential effect that that shrine of erudition produced on its worshippers as, like shadows, they flitted through its vast silent halls. Each student, whether young or old, was wrapped in his own small capsule of scholarship, assured of the freedom of being able to read and write without interruption. An even greater compensation for the tedium which some aspects of the research entailed was to be found in the poetry itself, particularly in the *kharjas*. The *kharjas* had first been interpreted, edited and published by Samuel Stern, an Oxford Scholar who in 1948, in Cairo, had discovered their bare bones, written in apparently nonsensical Arabic or Hebrew script. He found that by transcribing the fragments into Roman script and then adding vowels, the enigmatic Arabic and Hebrew texts could be made to spring into being as tiny snatches of Romance love poetry, breathing a pulsating life. For example, Stern had transcribed one group of Hebrew letters into Roman consonants thus: *gryd bs 'y yrmnl's km kntnyr 'mw m'ly sn 'lhbyb nn bbr' yw 'dbl'ry dmnd'ry.* With the addition of vowels, the text reads as follows: *Garid vos ay yermanellas com contenir a meu male Sin al-habib non vivireyu advolarey demandare.* Apart from one archaic form, and one Arabic expression, *al-habib*, the poem is now perfectly intelligible, even to a modern Spanish speaker:

Tell me little sisters,
How to contain my grief.

I shall not live without my lover
I shall fly away to look for him.

In another *kharja*, in a clear reference to her Christian background, she cries forlornly:

Venid la pasca ayun sin ellu…
…meu corajon por ellu

Easter comes still without him…
…my heart for him

When the lover does return, he comes like the sun with the glory of the dawn, for in these poems the lovers meet at dawn – and will meet at dawn down the ages of Spanish popular lyric poetry, unlike the sophisticated Provençal tradition, where aristocratic lovers part at dawn:

non dormiray mamma
a rayo de mañana
Bon Abu 'l-Qasim
la faj de matrana

I shall not sleep, mother,
in the morning light
Good Abu 'l-Qasim
the face of the morning

But for me, the most poignant fragments were those heart-rending lyrics in which the girl weeps in despair at her lover's illness:

Vaisse meu corajon de mib
ya rabbi si se me tornerad
Tan mal me doled li 'l-habib
enfermo yed cuand sanarad

My heart leaves my body
will it ever return?
My grief for my lover is so great
He is ill – when will he recover?

In one *kharja*, the only decipherable word is *enfermad* – ill – and in another the girl herself falls ill with the cares of loving:

> *Tan t'amaray tan t'amaray*
> *habib tan t'amaray*
> *Enfermaron welyos cuidas*
> *ya dolen tan male*

> I shall love you always,
> I shall love you always, my love,
> My eyes are ill with weeping,
> they hurt so much!

3

Heavenly Spheres

Although in tactical terms it was sensible for me to be registered as a London student, in reality it meant that I was very isolated in Cambridge. London seminars and supervisions under the auspices of my supervisor, Alan Deyermond, were always stimulating, but my opportunities for going down to London were infrequent. In Cambridge, where I read in the Library and wrote at home, I had no forum for discussion. Thanks to Dr Dorothy Needham, I had become an affiliated student of Lucy Cavendish College, a newly founded Collegiate Society for mature women students, and, by dint of careful organization – which involved having Robert fed, bathed and tucked up in his cot, and Stephen's meal ready for him on the table – I managed to go out a couple of times a term to the Lucy Cavendish dining nights which took place in Churchill College.

A solution to my problem of academic isolation came in a most unexpected form – through Robert's growing friendship with our neighbours' child, Inigo Shaffer. One of the guests at Inigo's first birthday party was a vivacious, auburn-haired six-year-old girl, Cressida Dronke, who, peering out from behind a hideous pair of multicoloured reflecting sunglasses, regaled the company of very small boys and their astounded mothers and nannies with a long and fascinating account of a production of *Romeo and Juliet* to which her parents had just taken her. There was apparently nothing unusual in this early introduction to Shakespeare, for Cressida had been a hardened theatre-goer since babyhood.

I already knew of Peter Dronke, who lectured in Medieval Latin, from his awesome reputation as one of the most gifted intellects in Cambridge, not confining himself simply to medieval Latin but ranging over the whole gamut of medieval literary studies, including my own. The happy chance meeting with the Dronkes led to my acquiring an unofficial, surrogate supervisor in Cambridge. Peter was always ready to share his vast fund of knowledge and to pass on helpful suggestions, constructive criticisms and useful references, while his wife Ursula, herself a scholar of old Norse and Icelandic sagas, was a constant source of kindly encouragement. Another important consequence of meeting Peter and Ursula was that they invited me to join the coveted, informal seminars which they hosted in their own home on Thursday evenings during term time. Only Peter could truly be said to be the master of all those sometimes abstruse topics expounded in the seminars, for their range was eclectic, covering most of late classical and medieval European thought and literature. We, the students, sat respectfully on the mustard-coloured carpet, literally at the feet of some of the greatest scholars of the day.

I was surprised and amused to find how close those seminars brought me in philosophical terms to the study of cosmology, albeit medieval cosmology. Inevitably many discussions dwelt on the twelfth-century intellectual expansion which emanated from Paris, particularly from the cathedral school of Chartres, where it was believed that God, the universe and mankind could be examined and comprehended by means of numbers, weights and geometrical symbols, effectively turning theology into mathematics. The new universities of both Paris and Oxford were at the heart of a continued, intense intellectual debate, in which primarily the nature of God, creation and the origins of the universe exercised the minds of scholars and theologians. The vigorous renaissance which took place in the twelfth century owed much to the innovative ideas coming from Spain, where in the year 1085 the Christian forces had recaptured Toledo from the Moors, with the result that that mixed, multilingual city had become one of the richest cultural centres in Europe, renowned as a thriving school of translation on account of its heritage of Arabic literature and supposedly lost works of classical antiquity.

In the thirteenth century, Alfonso the Wise of Castile expanded the role of Toledo as a major centre for translation and scholarship by participating in its activities himself, pioneering the use of Spanish rather than Latin for all documents and attempting various historical projects in that language. The translations produced at his court were even more significant than Alfonso's other projects and included a book on chess, the scientific theories on the nature of light of Alhazen, the foremost Arab scientist of the eleventh century – thus laying down the foundations of perspective on which Leonardo da Vinci would build in northern Italy in the fifteenth century – and, most importantly, the *Almagest*, the great work of Ptolemy, the Alexandrian mathematician and astronomer of the second century AD.

Originally written in Greek, the *Almagest* existed only in an Arabic version until Alfonso commissioned its translation in Toledo. Ptolemy's cosmological model of the universe was based on the Aristotelian concept of a stationary earth, orbited by the sun, the moon, the planets and the stars. In the Ptolemaic, or geocentric model, the earth is fixed at the centre of the universe while the heavenly bodies, the sun, the moon and the planets each move around the earth along the paths of their own fixed spheres. A system of smaller circular motions or epicycles is introduced to account for recognized inequalities in the motions of the bodies. Beyond the sphere of Saturn is the sphere on which the fixed stars are carried across the sky, and beyond that is the primum mobile, the mysterious divine force behind the cyclical movement of the spheres. This perfect, circular movement which propelled the planets on their course created a celestial music, the harmony of the spheres. The Ptolemaic model did not actually coincide with the scriptural view of the universe as being made up of the heavens, a flat earth and hell beneath, but since it could be made to match up with it without drastically upsetting previously held views of God's place in the heavens and of hell in the depths of the earth, it became a tenet of religious dogma in Christendom until it was questioned by the Polish astronomer Copernicus in the sixteenth century. For the Christian church the most important implication of this geocentric model was that Man, the inhabitant of the earth, was at the centre of the universe and that divine attention was focused solely on him and his behaviour.

Stephen came to one of these seminars about early cosmological models in the Dronkes' living room with a colleague from the Department, Nigel Weiss, whose wife, Judy, was a member of the seminar. The two scientists were forced to concede that the thinking of the twelfth-century philosophers, Thierry of Chartres, Alan of Lille and, in the thirteenth century, Robert Grosseteste and Roger Bacon among many others, was extraordinarily far-sighted, accurate and perceptive. Included in the ranks of the philosophers was a woman, the strong-minded

135

German abbess Hildegard of Bingen, who devised her own version of cosmology in which the universe took the shape of an egg. Hildegard of Bingen was far in advance of her times. Not only was she an early cosmonaut, she also proposed that women must make good the social and religious failings caused by the weaknesses of men and, to that end, should follow her example by undertaking missionary journeys along the Rhine, preaching, condemning heretics and righting social wrongs.

Several ironies struck me in the course of these seminars, particularly during the one that Stephen and Nigel Weiss attended. The most glaring one, of course, was that in the second half of the twentieth century the position of women in society, especially in science, had progressed at a snail's pace since the twelfth, despite Hildegard's brisk and frequent affirmations of the strength and glory of women. As far as the cosmologies were concerned, I was amused by the reflection that though advances in science may be revolutionary in the twentieth century, certain conceptual links with older theories die hard. The Ptolemaic system, which had gained ready acceptance in the thirteenth century but had later been supplanted by the Copernican solar system, still had a point of contact, however implausible, with an important cosmological principle of the twentieth century: the anthropic principle.

This was one of those subjects on which, during that period at the end of the Sixties and the early Seventies, Stephen spent long hours in concentrated argument with Brandon Carter, usually on Saturday afternoons when we drove out of Cambridge to the pastoral bliss of the country cottage which Brandon and his Belgian wife, Lucette, had been renovating since their recent marriage. Lucette and I would take Robert for long walks across the fields, conversing in French about our favourite authors, painters and composers, prepare tea and supper – and still Brandon and Stephen would be engaged in an intellectual contest over the fine detail of the principle, with neither prepared to concede.

The anthropic principle, as far as I understood it from Stephen's explanations in those rare moments when we discussed his work together, left me wondering at its close philosophical affinity to the medieval universe. As in the medieval, Ptolemaic universe, Man is once again placed at the centre of creation by the anthropic principle, or more precisely by what is known as its "strong" version. The proponents of the "strong" anthropic principle claim that the universe in which we exist is the only possible kind of universe in which we could exist, because from the time of the Big Bang some fifteen thousand million years ago, it has expanded according to the precise conditions, often involving chance chemical coincidences and very fine physical tuning, which are required for the development of intelligent life. Intelligent life is then able to ask why the universe is as it is observed to be, but this is a tautological question, the answer to which is: if our universe were any different, intelligent life would not exist to pose the question. In a real sense therefore, mankind could still be said to occupy a special place at the centre of the universe, just as he had in the Ptolemaic system. Whereas for medieval man, this special position was a strong statement of the unique relationship between human beings and their Creator, modern scientists appeared to be irritated or merely amused by any such inferences being drawn from the anthropic principle.

Although the modern universe is most certainly not bounded by the medieval concepts of heaven or hell, it is in many respects a more hostile environment than its neatly organized medieval counterpart, if only on account of its extremes of temperature and its vast expanses of space and time in which the human race appears to live in solitary isolation. In 1968 for a fleeting moment it seemed as if we might not be alone in the dark immensity of space after all. One afternoon in February of that year, when I called in at the Department, the tea room was buzzing with excitement. A research student in radio astronomy, Jocelyn Bell, and her supervisor Antony Hewish, had picked up regular, pulsating radio signals from outer space through the row of radio telescopes positioned on the disused Cambridge to Oxford railway line at Lord's Bridge, some three miles out of Cambridge. Could these signals be our first contact with extra-terrestrial life – little green men perhaps? Jokingly they named the first sources of these radio waves LGMs. The excitement died down when the sources of the radio pulses were identified as neutron stars, tiny remnants of stars, possibly only twenty miles across, with massive densities of hundreds of millions of tons per cubic inch. There was no chance that neutron stars could be supporting life.

While twentieth-century cosmologists might still retain some tenuous conceptual common ground with the Ptolemaic system through the anthropic principle, and might respect the intellects of the earlier twelfth-century philosophers of Chartres, Oxford and even Bingen on the Rhine, the Dronkes' medieval seminars served to bring into clear perspective the vastly divergent modern approach to the subject of creation. The main intent of the twelfth-century philosophers was directed towards reconciling the existence of God with the rigours of the laws of science, thus unifying the image of the Creator with the scientific complexity of his creation. To this end, Alan of Lille attempted to reconstruct theology as a mathematical science, and another student of Chartres, Nicholas of Amiens, tried to make it conform to Euclidean geometry, using geometrical symbols to explain the Trinity. However eccentric these notions may appear nowadays, they were undoubtedly genuine attempts to introduce a scientific objectivity to the teachings of theology and to explore and explain divine mystery through numbers and mathematical structures.

Conversely, their intellectual heirs, some eight hundred years later, seemed intent on distancing science as far as possible from religion and on excluding God from any role in Creation. The suggestion of the presence of a Creator-God was an awkward obstacle for an atheistic scientist whose aim was to reduce the origins of the universe to a unified package of scientific laws, expressed in equations and symbols. To the uninitiated, these equations and symbols were far more difficult to comprehend than the notion of God as the prime mover, the motivating force behind creation. Strangely, to the happy band of the initiated, the equations were said to reveal a miraculous, breathtaking mathematical beauty. This revelation, reflecting the hidden wonders of the universe, was almost a modern version of Plato's heavenly world of Forms. In the fifth century BC, Plato, Aristotle's teacher and a major influence on medieval thought, described a theory of Forms, or perfect heavenly Ideas, unrelated to the senses, discernible only to the mind. Each perfect Form or Idea had its counterpart in the tangible, corruptible, imperfect forms manifest on earth. The reverence with which modern scientists treated the mathematics of the universe suggested similar intimations of sublime perfection, but unfortunately these intimations of perfection were not easily accessible to those who were not fluent with mathematical jargon and for whom equations were impenetrable. Another difficulty, which apparently was a direct result of their obsession with mathematics, was the irrelevance for these scientists of the concept of a personal God. If through their calculations they were diminishing any possible scope for a Creator, it was logical that they could not envisage any other place or role for God in the physical universe.

In the face of dogmatic rational arguments, there was no point in raising questions of spirituality and religious faith, questions of the soul and of a God who was prepared to suffer for the sake of humanity – questions which ran completely counter to the selfish reality of genetic theory. Issues of morality, conscience, the appreciation of the arts, were best kept out of the arena lest they too became victims of the positivist approach. Still reacting against the organized religion of my childhood, I did not attend either of the two churches at the end of the lane regularly, but I sought sanctity in the garden of Little St Mary's, where Thelma Thatcher assigned a small patch of ground by the railings opposite our house for me to tend. There, under the rambling roses, I could weed, rake, hoe and plant bulbs for the spring and roses for the summer while pondering mysteries, theories and realities. Robert and Inigo played running along the winding paths and clambering over the mossy tombs while I worked. The ancient, sacred garden sprang to life with the music of their bright young voices, and our strip of ground blossomed with the pink-and-white striped rose that Stephen had given me for my birthday. It was the famous *Rosa gallica*, named Rosamundi after Henry II's mistress, Fair Rosamund.

4

Dangerous Dynamics

Since the churchyard garden was enclosed, Robert and Inigo could play there safe from harm, letting off their inordinate amounts of energy. From early infancy it was quite apparent that Robert was blessed with at least twice the normal fund of energy of a small boy. Quite apart from overturning all my notions regarding the sleep patterns of a newborn infant, he discovered, at about eight weeks, that his feet and legs were meant for standing on. Thereafter, he would not sit down, insisting on being held upright on my knee. Even when in Seattle we had been invited to take advantage of a free photographic session by courtesy of the diaper service, Robert resisted all attempts to make him lie gurgling on a rug or peep out coyly from under a blanket draped over his head, and reduced the photographer to a state of apoplexy when grudgingly he had to allow my arms to appear in the shot, in discreet support of the twelve-week-old baby who was firmly planted on his two small feet.

By the age of seven months, this inventive child had found out how to dismantle his cot so that all the joins, catches and hinges had to be tightly tied together with string to stop him falling out. Nevertheless, no sooner had Stephen and I turned our backs each evening and crept away downstairs, yawning and fondly trusting that repetitive readings of *Thomas the Tank Engine* had at last softly lulled our audience into the realms of sleep, than we would hear the tiny feet coming busily down the stairs to join us for our supper and whatever concert we might be listening to on the radio. Since he could no longer dismantle his cot, Robert learnt to vault over the bar and then drop onto the floor beneath. At about eleven o'clock we would all fall into bed together.

Even before he had perfected that degree of agility, Robert's dynamism had given us a quite a scare. In the spring of 1968, my parents took us to Cornwall once again with my brother Chris. Happily Robert was prepared to sit quite contentedly in the car, strapped in his seat, no matter how long the journey – but when at last in the early evening we adults sank drowsily into the comfortable armchairs in our rented cottage, Robert, already able at ten months old to walk nimbly round the furniture, set off on a tour of the ground floor. A sudden high-pitched scream from behind my back roused us precipitately. To steady himself, Robert had placed one small hand, his right, against an electric storage heater, which, unbeknown to us, was turned to its maximum setting, and the heat had seared off the skin of his palm. Thanks to my brother's medical training, Robert was pacified with a fraction of an aspirin – the only painkiller available – the hand gently treated and bandaged in a clean handkerchief, and we all, though shocked, managed to get a good night's sleep. Robert, Chris and I spent the best part of the next day searching out a doctor, because overnight the infant hand had swollen into one huge blister. The doctor, impressed at the quality of the first aid administered by a mere dental student, simply provided a pediatric painkilling prescription and more substantial dressings and thereafter commissioned Chris to continue to care for his small patient.

In the summer of that same year, the year of Robert's first birthday, How Ghee and Peck Ang with their small daughters left the house at number 11 to return home to Singapore. In true Little St Mary's Lane style, the Thatchers gave an informal farewell party for them, to which we and Inigo and his parents were invited, together with half a dozen or so other guests. Inigo and Robert were by this stage completely at home in the Thatcher household. They adored Thelma, and she reciprocated with a grandmotherly affection. They would call on her every morning, peering through her letter box, calling "Tatch, Tatch!" in the hope of being invited in to play with the collection of bright marbles on her solitaire table. They were frequent teatime visitors, sitting at her elegant Regency table on her elegant Regency chairs – though as a precautionary measure she did apologetically cover the yellow-striped damask seats with plastic sheeting. At the Angs' party no one took much notice of the small boys who were happily amusing themselves, until Thelma called for a toast to the Angs – How Ghee, Peck, Susan and demure little Ming – and their future happiness. We all turned to pick up our glasses of champagne from the occasional tables only to find that they were all drained dry. From upstairs, there came the sound of running water, of much flushing and splashing and peals of laughter. Two rather tipsy one-year-olds were having their own, much more entertaining party well out of sight in the Thatchers' bathroom.

Later that summer Stephen and I took Robert on his first bucket-and-spade holiday to the north Norfolk coast, where I encountered the unforeseen dilemma of needing to be in two places at once. As Stephen's speed of movement slowed down, so Robert's accelerated. Stephen found it difficult to walk across the soft, yielding sand, and so did I, as I supported him on one arm and carried bags, bucket and spade, towels and a folding chair on the other. Robert, in the meantime, would be racing away, heading for the open sea. Luckily, on that coast, the tide goes out as far as the eye can see, and that week was a week of low tides by day, so we managed to avoid undue mishap.

On the final morning I went upstairs to pack our bags, leaving Stephen and Robert downstairs in the main room at the front of the house. At the back, a sun room with an open mezzanine half-loft approached by a rickety ladder had been added to the cottage. For obvious reasons we did not use this room and kept the door to it firmly closed. After half an hour of packing I came downstairs to find Stephen sitting alone in the front room. "Where's Robert?" I asked in bewilderment. Stephen gestured towards the back room. "He opened that door," he said, "went through it and closed it behind him. There was nothing I could do, and you didn't hear when I tried to call you."

Momentarily I glanced at the door in horror, then burst into the room. There was no sign of Robert. My eyes travelled upwards, and there, to my astonishment, was my little son in his blue T-shirt and checked trousers, sitting at the top of the ladder on the open mezzanine floor, cross-legged like an infant Buddha, blissfully unconcerned by the drop beneath. I raced up the ladder and grabbed him before he had time to move.

If on that first visit to the coast, Robert did not succeed in hurling himself into the sea, it was only because his legs were too short for him to get to the water's edge before I caught up with him. After depositing his father on the folding chair on the firmer sand midway between the dunes and the shore, I would sprint over the beach at speeds which could well have won me an Olympic medal. Over the course of the next two or three years, Robert regularly threw himself headlong into any available stretch of water, be it sea, pond or swimming pool, as soon as my eye was distracted for a second. On a later visit to Norfolk with the Ellises and their little daughter – dark-haired, blue-eyed Maggie – Sue plunged into the sea like lightning to rescue Robert, who had run straight into the water and disappeared. When we visited the Cleghorns – the parents of Stephen's school friend Bill – out in the country, Robert made a beeline for their pond and fell in, amongst the weed, the mud and the frogs. And in the summer of 1969, when we spent the month of July at the University of Warwick at a summer school appropriately enough on Catastrophe Theory, Robert excelled himself by jumping into the deep end of the nearby swimming pool at every opportunity. Happily on those occasions, as his father was in lectures and not dependent on my supporting arm, Robert had the full benefit of my undivided attention.

That summer school coincided with that "great leap for mankind", the Moonwalk, which we watched on television in the student Common Room. Giant leaps, small steps and all-too-real catastrophes narrowly averted, these sonorous terms seemed to sum up the essence of our day-to-day lives. Giant leaps were needed to keep up with Robert's mercurial movements, while Stephen's steps were becoming smaller, slower and more unsteady. Each morning I would drive Stephen from the student hostel where we were lodging to the lecture hall on the other side of the new campus. At Stephen's pace, the lecture hall was some five minutes' walk away from the car park, across courtyards and through a maze of passages. Robert, just two years old, would shoot out of the car as soon as it came to a standstill, and hare away ahead of his father and me. The only consolation was that he had an unerring sense of direction which led him through the tortuous route to the lecture hall, where he would install himself in the front row. It became a standing joke among the other delegates that Robert's appearance in the early morning always heralded Stephen's arrival five minutes later. The lecturer would then adjust the order of his lecture notes, deferring any important results until Stephen arrived.

At home, we had to barricade the house to prevent Robert from escaping and throwing himself in the river. On our afternoon walks I was hard-pressed to find a means of expending all his energy without exhausting myself, especially as he would never turn round to go back home until he was on the point of collapse, and then he had to be carried or taken in the pushchair.

Generally I left the pushchair at home, because on our outward journeys, when speed of reflex was all-important, it tended to interfere with the swiftness of my reactions. "Put reins on him," my parents urged sensibly, worried by my haggard appearance. "You don't understand, he won't walk with reins on," I insisted, to their disbelief. "Nonsense," they said, thinking that this was just another example of my crackpot theories about personal freedoms. "All right, you try," I replied defiantly, handing them back the set of pale-blue, leather reins they had just given me. They picked up their cherubic, blond, blue-eyed grandson, and carried him and the reins down to the broad path along the river bank, away from the traffic. In no time at all, they were back at the house asking for the pushchair. "You were right," my mother sighed, "when we put the reins on him, he sat down and refused to move. When Dad tried tugging on the reins, he kept his legs firmly crossed and when Dad lifted the reins, he just left the ground, and there he was, dangling in mid-air on the end of the strap!"

Never in all the long years of my education and, unsurprisingly, nowhere in all those reams of medieval literature, had I encountered one jot of advice on bringing up children. Apparently through the ages, children had just happened, and it had never been thought necessary to teach their parents how to look after them. If this was an example of the workings of the geneticists' selfish gene, the selfish gene was intent on self-destruction. From six o'clock in the morning till eleven at night, Robert was full of golden smiles – cheerful, loving and utterly adorable – but his boundless energy brought me to my knees. I thumbed through my only guide, the already well-worn pages of Dr Spock's *Baby and Child Care*, searching for help and reassurance. Comfortingly, Dr Spock seemed to recognize the problem, but his solution – putting a netting over the cot – was not one that I could bring myself to adopt for fear that Robert might strangle himself. Then I turned to my doctor, Dr Wilson, who sympathetically recommended a glass of sherry – for me – in the evening "at about six o'clock, when Robert has gone to bed", and also prescribed a tonic.

Early one morning in the September of 1969, I was aroused from my slumbers not by a sound or by a light but by a smell – a sweet sticky smell which subconsciously I knew to be wrong. I opened my eyes to find Robert standing by my side of the bed with a broad grin all over his face and a viscous, pinkish liquid dribbling down the front of his blue sleeping suit. I jumped out of bed and stumbled down the stairs to the kitchen. A chair stood by the fridge and the floor was littered with empty bottles, all of them medicine bottles. One of the bottles had contained the sweet, syrupy antihistamine which the doctor had prescribed for Robert for a recent cold and earache, and which had a conveniently soporific effect; another had contained the stimulant which I had been taking to pep me up. At two years of age, Robert had pushed a chair into the kitchen, climbed up onto the fridge and reached up to the shelf where, for want of a medicine cupboard, the bottles were stored. He had swigged the lot.

Leaving Stephen to fend for himself as best he could, I dressed in haste and ran with Robert in his pushchair to the doctor's surgery. The surgery, only a couple of hundred yards away, was just opening, and we were given priority. As Robert was already starting to show signs of drowsiness, Dr Wilson sent us immediately to hospital, half a mile away in the other direction, by taxi. There the nightmare really began, as the seriousness of the situation became evident. Robert, his arms and legs jerking and flailing out in all directions, was taken from me and held down while his stomach was pumped out. At first, the nurses were terse, only asking what medicines he had taken, then, when they had tried all the interventionary methods at their disposal to rid the child's system of the poisonous cocktail, one of them turned to me and said: "He is extremely ill, you realize – there is nothing more we can do, we shall just have to wait and see what happens."

Only once before had Robert's health given cause for anxiety. The previous winter we had gone with the Ellises to Majorca for a week's holiday over the New Year. We had barely arrived when Robert fell seriously ill with a virulent strain of Spanish tummy which confined us to the hotel room for the whole duration of the stay. Unable to digest even plain water he wasted away before our eyes like the innocent child victims of the Biafran war in Nigeria, while the local doctor debated whether to take him into hospital or send us back home in advance of the rest of the party. As soon as the plane touched down at Gatwick, Robert began to make a miraculous recovery. By the time we reached my parents' house in St Albans, he was ready to play his favourite game of emptying all the tins from the cupboard and rolling them across the kitchen floor. That episode had been harrowing but this was far worse; the worst agony imaginable, the agony of watching one's child die.

They tied Robert down in a cot in a partitioned room on the children's ward and beckoned me to a chair in a corner. He tossed violently under the restraints placed across the cot to prevent him hurting himself. Mechanically I sat down, too numbed to speak or think or weep. Life drained away from my own body as our beautiful, darling child, our most precious possession, sank into a deep coma. This child had astounded everyone with his beauty, his happy nature and his liveliness. He was the living personification of all that was good and positive in our world and our relationship. I, and Stephen too, loved him more than anything else. We had created him out of love, I had given birth to him and we had nurtured him with passionate love and care. Now we seemed to be losing him through a combination of circumstances – my tiredness, his energy and the inadequacy of the precautions that we had taken for his safety. If he died, I should die too. My brain was capable of formulating only a single thought expressed in half a dozen words. They revolved round and round in my head, stuck in a single groove, to the exclusion of all else: "Please God, don't let him die. Please God, don't let him die. Please God…"

Every so often a nurse would come in to check Robert's breathing and his pulse. Pursing her lips, she would tiptoe away again while I, blankly staring into cold, empty space, stayed in my corner clinging to my formula, repeating it over and over again. Some hours later, the Ward Sister came in. She went through the customary procedures and then, instead of tiptoeing away, pronounced that Robert was in a relatively stable though still critical condition. His state was not hopeful, all that could be said was that it was not deteriorating further. Coming to my senses at this slightest of changes, I was shocked to remember that I had left Stephen alone in the house, scarcely able to look after himself. Where was I most needed – here in the hospital with my comatose infant son, or at home with my disabled husband who, without my help, might fall or hurt himself or choke? I must have mumbled a few intelligible words to the sister because she sent me out to check up on Stephen. I ran down the road through the fine grey drizzle to look for him.

Thankfully George had come in to help him get up and had taken him to work. By this stage he was having lunch in the University Centre, desperate for news but not knowing where to find us. I sat with him for a short while. There was nothing we could say to comfort each other, because there was no comfort to be had in our situation, except that we both shared the same sense of utter, bleak devastation, enveloped in an unremitting pall of greyness. I watched as Stephen ate his lunch. I could not even bring myself to drink a glass of water. It seemed pointless to try. There was no reason to stay alive. How could I live with such grief? We were crossing the threshold into that dark chasm where all hope is abandoned.

Scarcely daring to return to the hospital, I left Stephen in George's care. I entered the ward fearful of what I might find. All was silent. A young nurse followed me as I tiptoed into Robert's room. He was there in the cot, still alive. He was asleep, lying quietly on his back, as beatific as a Bellini cherub. To my surprise the nurse's face lit up with a smile as she pointed to the sleeping child. "Look, he's breathing normally now. He's sleeping it off, and soon he'll come out of the coma, he's past the worse," she said. Only tears, not words, could describe my feelings, tears of gratitude and relief. "You'll be able to take him home when he wakes up," the nurse continued – in a matter of fact fashion, as if this was just one more crisis in her busy routine, now thankfully resolved. I rang Stephen to tell him the good news, and at half-past three Robert began to wake up. "You can take him home now," they said. Within ten minutes he was discharged and we stepped out into the vivid reality of our everyday lives. Once back home, we sent word to our neighbours to come and join us for a celebration. They all came and we watched silently as if in a trance while Robert and Inigo pushed their toy cars round the floor, unconcerned and totally unaware of the day's drama.

That day Robert survived, but a little bit of me died. Some, though not all, of that extravagant youthful optimism which had fired me with so much enthusiasm now lay buried beneath a heavy burden of anxiety, that dull care in its ravelled sleave, which once it infects the mind is never banished. I had come so dangerously close to the worst catastrophe that a mother can bear – the loss of her child – that I became neurotically protective, often perhaps irritating Robert and his siblings by my concern for their safety.

Luckily the experience seemed to have left Robert unscathed. Nor did it reduce in any way his fund of energy, as our visit to a conference in Switzerland the following spring aptly demonstrated. While Stephen spent his days plunged into the murky past of the universe in the conference centre at Gwatt on the shores of Lake Thun, Robert and I went walking. This was where Robert discovered his passion for the mountains, the true outlet for his climbing instincts. When, later that week, we and the Ellises spent a few days in the family hotel at Hohfluh, high above the Aare valley where I used to stay with my parents, Robert was in his element. More than once, at less than three years old, he insisted on scrambling up as far as the snowline while I, several months pregnant again, plodded along behind.

5

Universal Expansion

A less dramatic crisis than Robert's calamitous encounter with the medicines loomed over us as the 1960s drew to a close: Stephen's Research Fellowship – which had already been renewed for a further term of two years in 1967 – was in 1969 about to expire. There was no mechanism for renewing it yet again, but because Stephen was unable to lecture, he could not follow the normal course of most other Research Fellows and apply for a university teaching post. Nor was there any point in expecting a full Fellowship, since College Fellowships, as opposed to Research Fellowships, are not salaried appointments but simply offer membership of an exclusive dining club, albeit a highly intellectual one, founded – it goes without saying – on the most estimable educational principles.

In 1968 Stephen had become a member of the newly opened Institute of Astronomy, a long single-storeyed building, luxuriously fitted out and set among trees in green fields in the grounds of the Observatory, on the Madingley Road outside Cambridge. This accorded him an office, which he shared with Brandon, and a desk – but it did not provide him with a salary, and it was unlikely to do so for as long as Fred Hoyle remained its director, since he had never forgiven Stephen for his notorious intervention at the Royal Society lecture some years before. Unlike in America, paid research posts in Britain were few and far between.

Such was the excitement generated by black-hole research over the past four years, however, that Stephen did not lack powerful advocates: Dennis Sciama willingly took up the challenge, as did Hermann Bondi, whose help my father enlisted on our behalf. It was rumoured that King's College had a salaried Senior Research Fellowship, which the governing body were prepared to offer Stephen. The authorities of Gonville and Caius bridled at these rumours and stepped in with a special category of Fellowship, a six-year Fellowship for Distinction in Science, before King's had a chance to make their offer.

With a secure job and a steady income, it was time for us to review our living arrangements. Although we drove out to the villages at weekends prospecting for suitable properties, we constantly came up against the intractable problem of transport: if we bought a new house in a village, even the closest village, I should have to drive Stephen to work every morning and collect him every evening, and such pressure could become irksome, especially with two small children in tow. It was impossible to better our situation in Little St Mary's Lane. With help, Stephen could still walk to work in the Department in the mornings, though occasionally he would get a lift out to the Institute in the afternoons for seminars and discussions with Brandon. For Robert there was a delightfully old-fashioned playgroup close at hand in the Quaker Meeting House, just across the fen, and the University Library – as and when I managed to find the time and the energy to work there – was within five minutes' cycling distance. We were within a stone's throw of the centre of the city, and the churchyard not only catered perfectly for Robert's outdoor needs but also fulfilled my gardening aspirations. The only drawback was that the house was so small and decrepit, despite my attempts to redecorate it.

Our enterprising friends, George and Sue Ellis, had bought and renovated a house at Cottenham, a fen village outside Cambridge, and Brandon and Lucette had done the same to their dream cottage out in the heart of the country soon after their marriage in 1969. Even in Little St Mary's Lane, various neighbours had cleverly enlarged and renovated their previously ramshackle dwellings, making sizeable, attractive townhouses of them, and at number 5 the author and biographer of Rose Macaulay, Constance Babington-Smith, had imaginatively adapted the limited space in her narrow house to meet her bookish requirements. Having seen, with a tinge of envy, how versatile the houses could be, we realized that ours was no exception. However, we were caught in the proverbial catch-22 situation. We had saved enough money for a deposit on a mortgage for a new property, and council grants were available for the renovation of old properties, but because of its age our house did not qualify for a mortgage and, of course, the College on the advice of its land agent had dismissed the property as a bad investment.

As we were mulling over this dilemma, a change of policy on the part of our building society removed the problem altogether, and mortgages – at a higher rate of interest – became available on older properties. An agreed mortgage from a building society had the added advantage that it would qualify us for an extra loan – at a low rate of interest – from the university. Quite suddenly, everything started to fall into place, though Stephen was sceptical. It seemed to me, as I pored with pencil and ruler over scraps of paper, that some of the ideas used by our neighbours along the lane could well be incorporated into our house to enlarge and renovate it. On the ground floor there could be an elegant through-room from front to back by making two rooms into one, with a new kitchen out at one side of the yard, while the first and second floors could be remodelled to provide a new bathroom, bedrooms and a roof garden. A retired surveyor, the aptly named Mr Thrift, who proved to be a true and also genial master of his profession, drew up detailed plans which enlarged the house seemingly beyond the bounds of probability, exploiting every inch of space.

He and I investigated grants – both improvement grants and grants for the disabled – and as soon as we had our draft plans ready laid, we were able to apply to a building society for a mortgage. Unlike the odious college land agent, the building society surveyor cheerfully inspected the house and, glancing at the proposed plans, nodded. "It'll be quite charming, won't it?" he said, indicating that he would readily approve the property for a mortgage. We were now able to approach our landlady again with a more realistic offer for the house, and this time she accepted. It really seemed that all things were possible. But we had scant opportunity to enjoy being householders: shortly after we had signed the completion, all the furniture had to be stored away in the front bedrooms, and we ourselves had to move out to allow the builders to invade our property. Further loans, including a generous one from Stephen's parents, and improvement grants were enabling us to embark on a major rebuilding programme.

George and Sue Ellis, with Maggie and one-year-old Andy, had gone to spend six months in Chicago, the home of the highly respected Indian theoretical physicist and Nobel Prize winner, Professor Subrahmanyan Chandrasekhar and his wife, Lola. Chandrasekhar, though a Fellow of Trinity College, had been forced to seek a post in America after being humiliated by his close friend Arthur Eddington at the Royal Astronomical Society in 1933. Chandrasekhar had anticipated black-hole research by predicting the ultimate collapse of massive stars under their own weight, only to have his theory scathingly ridiculed by Eddington and the astronomy establishment. In Chicago, the Chandrasekhars lived in the sort of style which only a childless couple can maintain. Everything in their quietly secluded flat was as white as snow: a thick-piled white carpet, a white sofa and chairs, white curtains – all in all, a white nightmare for a visiting mother, like Sue, with very small children whose fingers were permanently smeared in sticky chocolate.

Meanwhile, we gratefully took over the Ellises' eminently practical, child-oriented, converted country cottage in Cottenham for the duration of the renovations to 6 Little St Mary's Lane. It was only through living in the country that I fully understood the convenience of living in town. The house was delightful but the isolation was distressing, particularly because I felt sick all day throughout the pregnancy. Stephen had to be driven into Cambridge to the department each morning and collected in the evening, except on those occasions when he was ready in time to catch a lift with other Cottenham commuter neighbours. Robert was unsettled, missing both Inigo and his playgroup, while I sorely missed my friends in the lane, especially the Thatchers, and all attempts to work on my thesis were quite futile. My depression was not eased by the constant pounding of the news reports from the Middle East, which suggested that another confrontation between the Egyptians and the Israelis – and consequently between the superpowers – was imminent. Not only were the two countries regularly raiding each other's territory, but also a new aspect of war had reared its ugly head in the hijacking of civilian airliners. I became tense and irritable, and, I am ashamed to say, short-tempered with my nearest and dearest: with Stephen, with Robert and, to my lasting regret, with my dearly loved, but very slow-moving grandmother, who came from Norwich to stay with us for one very hot, enervating week.

At last, against all expectation, the house, which for months had looked like a bomb site, while what was left of it was held up by a solitary metal pole, was in a sufficiently habitable state for us to return to it in mid-October. It was not yet finished and each day brought a succession of different craftsmen, plumbers, plasterers, painters, electricians, all uncomfortably aware of the protruding deadline – or rather lifeline – to which they had to conform. Once back at home, Stephen and Robert could resume their normal routines and I could get on with scrubbing floors, rearranging furniture, hanging curtains and preparing the new back bedroom for the baby. This bedroom and a minuscule new bathroom alongside it occupied the space of the old sloping bathroom on the first floor. They overlooked a roof garden above the kitchen, which had been built out as planned into the yard at the side of the house. The area of the old kitchen was now the dining area of the through-room which extended from front to back, supported in the middle by a solid girder, mysteriously referred to as an RSJ. In the rear wall, constructed of mottled pink, black and yellow old Cambridge bricks, Mr Thrift had reinstated the John Clark's eighteenth-century plaque.

At the top of the house on the third floor behind Robert's attic, there was a new room which on the plans had to be labelled a storeroom, because the ceiling was a few inches below the statutory height for a habitable room, on account of a side window in the neighbouring property. However when the building inspector made his final survey, he cast his eyes round the room and impassively commented, "This could be quite a nice bedroom, couldn't it?" I hastened to point out to him, in no uncertain terms, that the room was full of boxes and suitcases in recognition of its expressed purpose. Soon afterwards, the so-called storeroom found its true function as a magnificent playroom – safe, out of sight, out of earshot and out of mind.

A fortnight later, on 31st October, when the workmen had left, we gave a party and invited forty of our friends to squeeze into our house – a happy combination of old at the front and brand new at the back. The excitement and the effort of putting on the party produced positive results, and the next day found me languishing in a state of some discomfort on the chaise longue which I had just finished upholstering. That night I went into hospital, having decided that I would never again put myself and a new baby at the mercy of the crabby old midwives in the nursing home, and insisting that this birth should take place attended by our serene, ever-smiling local midwife, in the maternity hospital.

In an unprecedented display of early-morning activity, I gave birth to a daughter, Lucy, at 8 a.m. on Monday 2nd November. Our midwife gave me all proper attention and then, naturally enough after being on duty all night, went home, leaving the baby and me in the care of the hospital nurses. But 8 a.m. on a Monday morning was an unfortunate time to be born. As soon as the nurses in attendance at the birth had washed and dressed the baby, they went off duty, leaving me stranded on the delivery table while the poor little creature – in the cot beside me but just out of my reach – screamed until her face turned bright red. I longed to comfort her, but I had been instructed not to move and, in any case, in my postnatal daze, I feared I might drop her. I lay cold and helpless on the hard table, distressed that the tiny red-faced infant in the cot was receiving such a rude introduction to life.

After two days in hospital I was ready and longing to go home – so ready that I had put my coat on and had wrapped my pretty little pink-faced doll, now much calmer, in warm lacy shawls – when a doctor appeared and ordered me back into bed, explaining that he was going to attach me to a drip containing iron rations to replenish my own failing supplies before letting me go home. Regretfully I obeyed and, instead of returning home to Stephen and Robert, I sadly took refuge in my book, *Buddenbrooks*, Thomas Mann's saga of a Prussian family at the end of the nineteenth century. My patience in the maternity hospital was rewarded the next day when Lucy and I went home, probably in much better shape thanks to the iron supplements that had been pumped into me. It was good to be back in the lane, where in early November the last roses, sweeter and more intense than any roses in summer, were coming into bloom in the garden. Robert arrived home from nursery school with Inigo, soon after midday. He flapped at the letter box, peering through it in excitement, and then rushed into the house, demanding, "Where's the baby, where's the baby?" As soon as he saw his tiny sister lying on a rug on the floor, he went straight over to her and gave her a kiss. Thereafter, although Lucy, once she had acquired the power of speech, hardly allowed him to get a word in edgeways, this fraternal relationship was one area where Dr Spock's good advice was never called for as Robert showed not the least sign of sibling rivalry.

Although Stephen's father and brother, Edward, had gone to Louisiana for the academic year in the cause of tropical medicine, his mother had stayed in England to be in Cambridge over the immediate period of Lucy's birth, because Stephen was beginning to need much more help with his daily needs. He could still pull himself up the stairs, but his walking was so slow and unsteady that he had recently, with the greatest distaste, at last taken to a wheelchair. In the four days of my absence in hospital, my substitute on the home front needed to be someone with patience, understanding and stamina, whom Stephen could trust implicitly. George was his stalwart helper in the Department, but he had his own young family to go home to in the evenings, so naturally Stephen preferred to have his mother look after him when I was out of action. She stayed on for a few days after my return home and was kind, good-humoured and energetic, if detached. The routine was exacting: the shopping and the washing had to be done, the house cleaned, meals prepared and Robert and Stephen looked after single-handedly. The days since that one occasion when Stephen had picked up a tea towel to help with the washing-up were long gone. His illness made it impossible for him to help with the running of the house, because there was nothing of a practical nature that he could do. The advantage for him of this practical inability was that it allowed him unlimited time to indulge his driving passion for physics, which I accepted, because I knew that he would never have willingly been distracted from it by the mundane considerations of cookery, housework and nappies, whatever his circumstances.

After my return home, my own mother took over from Isobel to enable her to join her family in America, where her restraining presence was urgently needed. In his detestation of reptiles, Stephen's father had disobeyed all local advice and had tackled a deadly cottonmouth snake with a broom handle in a fight to the death. Stephen was to visit his family in Louisiana in December on his way to a conference in Texas, six weeks after Lucy's birth, but it was agreed to my immense relief that he should go with George, and I should stay at home with the two children.

When all the grandparents had left, our routine changed again, revolving around the baby and Stephen, with a great deal of willing help from three-year-old Robert, Inigo's nanny and Thelma Thatcher. I felt myself very blessed in my two thriving children. Stephen, however, was worried about Lucy. She slept for long periods during the day and, at night, was positively angelic, so much so that he was convinced that there was something wrong with her. He expected all babies to be like Robert, active and energetic at all hours of the day and the night. I did not share this anxiety. I thoroughly revelled in the blissfully quiet period after her birth which was one of the most stable, contented periods in our lives, especially welcome after the activity of the rebuilding work.

The house was a delight in its brightly painted cleanliness and comparative spaciousness, and the baby a source of great joy; she was so tiny that I could hold her in the palm of one hand, and so quiet that when the health visitor came to call, she did not even notice her lying beside me on the bed. Little Lucy observed conventional bedtimes, allowing me to run a fairly well-ordered household, care for Stephen and Robert and sleep regular hours. At night I was also able to resume reading novels while Stephen was getting ready for bed. We agreed tacitly – since all reference to his illness was offensive to him – that it was important for him to continue to do as much for himself as he could, even if that took time. He could undress himself once I had loosened his shoelaces and undone his buttons, and then he would struggle out of his clothes and into his pyjamas while I lay reading, a precious luxury at the end of each long day. Stephen's night-time routine was a slow one, not only because of the physical constraints but also because his concentration was always directed elsewhere, usually onto a relativistic problem. One evening, he took even longer than usual to get into bed, but it was not until the next morning that I found out why. That night, while putting his pyjamas on and visualizing the geometry of black holes in his head, he had solved one of the major problems in black-hole research. The solution stated that if two black holes collide and form one, the surface area of the two combined cannot be smaller, and must nearly always be larger, than the sum of the two initial black holes – or more concisely, whatever happens to a black hole, its surface area can never decrease in size. This solution was to make Stephen, at the age of twenty-eight, the dominant figure in black-hole theory. As black holes had become a topic of general conversation, it was also to make him a recognized figure of some fascination to the population at large. In Seattle we had been orbiting the newly named phenomenon, the black hole; now we had definitely crossed its event horizon, that boundary from which there is no escape. The theory predicted that, once sucked across the event horizon, the unlucky traveller would be stretched and elongated like a piece of spaghetti, never to have any hope of emerging or of leaving any indications as to his fate.

6

On Campaign

1970, the year of Lucy's birth, saw the passing of the Chronically Sick and Disabled Persons' Act. Though it was hailed across the world as a historic breakthrough in asserting the rights of the disabled, the government refused to implement it fully for many years, leaving already hard-pressed individuals to conduct their own campaigns for its enforcement locally. However it did give substance to our many complaints against the various public bodies whose buildings did not allow easy access to disabled people.

Carrying a small baby in a sling on my front while pushing Stephen in his wheelchair, with three-year-old Robert trotting alongside, I was in the vanguard of protesters, campaigning on behalf of the disabled and their carers. A high kerb or a badly placed step, let alone a flight of steps, presented the sort of obstacle which could turn an otherwise manageable family outing into a disaster. Not robust enough – at only seven-and-a-half stones – to surmount the obstacle unaided, I would have to lie in wait, hopefully scanning the vicinity for a male passer-by from whom I could solicit help. Then I would have to hand my baby over to any kindly lady who happened to be around. Together, the accosted male, Robert and I would heave the chair and its occupant up or over the hurdle, always wary lest the helper should lift the wrong part of the chair – the armrest or the footrest – which might come away in his hand. Finally I would shower the helper with gushing thanks before we continued on our way. Often to my relief, the helpers would volunteer before I had to importune them. Often, as they lifted the chair with Stephen in it, they would ask in amazement, "What do you feed him on? He weighs a ton for such a slight chap." "It's all in his brain," I would reply.

Our letters of protest to the City Surveyor were met with a superior disdain, reminiscent of Stephen's early encounters with the bursars of Gonville and Caius. The City Surveyor had never before heard of disabled people wanting to cross the city as far as Marks & Spencer to buy their own underwear, so he failed to see the need for such an expedition – as if disabled people and their families had no right to venture that far. Injustice spurred us into action. Why should Stephen have to suffer restraints on his lifestyle other than those inflicted by an unkind Nature? Why should short-sighted bureaucrats be allowed to make life doubly difficult for him, when he, unlike those smug officials, the scourge of Seventies' Britain, was using his restricted allowance of life to abundant advantage every day?

After many battles we succeeded in persuading the Arts Theatre and the cinema to make seating areas available for wheelchairs. The University began slowly to revise its provisions for access, as did a few of the more liberal colleges. We took our campaign further afield – to the English National Opera at the Coliseum, where our needs were immediately acknowledged, and to the Royal Opera House at Covent Garden, where help consisted of offloading the responsibility for wheelchair access to two elderly front-of-house attendants who, poor things, while struggling with Stephen up the stairs to the stalls, dropped him. By a curious coincidence, the attitude of the City Council towards access for the disabled mellowed rapidly as Stephen's fame grew, but that was long after those strenuous years during which I pushed the wheelchair with two tiny children in tow.

Most of the colleges were slower to make adjustments, pleading poverty or the impracticality of adapting historic buildings without contravening conservation laws. Often, college dining halls would be accessible only via the kitchens, with their treacherous obstacle courses of steaming vats, sizzling grills and laden trolleys, and creaking, smelly service lifts already laden with stacks of crockery, trays of hors d'oeuvre and cases of wine. Then our late arrival at High Table would be greeted with pompous disdain, as if such disruptions were too frightfully embarrassing and boring. Our battle with one college, so advanced in its eagerness to admit women but distinctly tardy in its attention to the requirements of the disabled, continued late into the Eighties.

Quite apart from steps and kerbs, there were many unforeseen hazards in the course of everyday life. Once, when taking Stephen with Lucy on his knee out for a walk across the fen, the front castor of the wheelchair stuck in a rut, jolting the frightened occupants out of the chair on to the muddy path. On another occasion, when Lucy was slightly older, we avoided the ruts but came across a rather different obstacle in our path. To cut down on baggage, I had left the house with only my door key and no money in my pocket. As we turned through the wrought-iron gates into King's College, Lucy inevitably spotted an ice-cream van parked on the verge. She had begun to acquire language at ten months' old, when, lying on our bed, she had looked up at the light fitting and announced, "lat, lat," so demanding an ice cream at the age of one was well within her capabilities. Refusing to take my apologetic "no" for an answer, she slid off her father's knee to the ground at his feet, and staged a furious infant sit-down demonstration on the pathway. I could not carry her and push Stephen at the same time so Robert and I tried to cajole the agitated little ball of royal blue garments and auburn curls, but to no avail. The King's Choristers paused on their way from the choir school to evensong in the chapel and stood wonderingly round her in a circle, perturbed at the spectacle of so much anguish in such a tiny person. After an eternity an acquaintance of Stephen's from another group in the Department appeared on the scene and came to the rescue. While I pushed Stephen, he carried Lucy, still loudly proclaiming her indignation, home – without an ice cream.

As we had no time to read newspapers, we relied on my parents for useful snippets of information culled from theirs. Often they would send us bundles of cuttings, sometimes about discoveries in astrophysics, sometimes about benefits for the disabled. Since in one of the latter it was suggested that disabled people could reclaim the cost of the motor-vehicle licence, we approached Stephen's doctor for clarification. It transpired that the information in the article was ahead of its time: in 1971 there was no mechanism yet in place for reclaiming the licence fee – that was to follow some years later – but Dr Swan suggested that Stephen might like to apply for a disabled vehicle.

This amazing possibility began to open up exciting horizons. If he could manage the joystick controls of an electric car, Stephen would have a new, mechanical mobility in compensation for his diminishing personal movement. An application was accepted, the bureaucratic formalities completed, but just one hitch remained: the vehicle had to be parked under cover near an electric socket to charge its batteries overnight. As so often happened, a solution came from an entirely unexpected source when Hugh Corbett, the Warden of the University Centre at the river end of the lane, responded to our need and unhesitatingly offered Stephen a parking space under cover by a plug.

Although disabled vehicles were criticized for their instability, the electric car – which travelled at the speed of a fast bicycle – enabled Stephen once again to be master of his own routine, driving where he wanted and dividing his working day between the Department in the morning and the Institute of Astronomy in the afternoon. On his return home in the early evening, he would draw up outside the house, hooting the horn, and Robert would rush out excitedly and clamber onto a ledge beside him for the final fifty yards of the journey down to the University Centre, while I would follow on with the wheelchair to bring Stephen back home. As ever no system was completely trouble-free. The car was subject to frequent breakdowns, and often we found it hemmed in its parking place by other vehicles. Once it overturned, giving Stephen a nasty fright, though fortunately no injuries.

In summer the children and I would sometimes take a picnic out into the grounds of the Observatory and visit Stephen in his office in the Institute of Astronomy. The children's high-pitched voices would race ahead of them along the plush carpeted corridors, like gusts of fresh spring air, announcing their presence to their delighted father. The expressions on Stephen's face were always a much more powerful measure of his emotions than his spoken words, and on these occasions it was the smile on his face that conveyed his unmistakable joy in his children. The Observatory, purpose-built in 1823 with a dome in the centre and residential wings for the astronomers, had the appearance of an unusual but imposing country house, set in carefully tended orchards and gardens, where we acquired a small patch in which to grow our own produce. While the churchyard was ideal for growing roses and lilies, I baulked at the thought of growing vegetables in its soil. Out at the Observatory the children set to with a will, chatting incessantly while they dug, planted seeds and watched them grow. Then at the end of the day we would proudly take our armfuls of beans and carrots and lettuces into the Institute to show Stephen, before setting off for home ahead of him.

Those carefree afternoons spent on the verge of the country proved to be a respite from the increasing trials of life in Little St Mary's Lane. When we had chanced upon it in 1965, the lane was a haven of tranquillity. By the early Seventies, it was becoming a busy and dangerous thoroughfare to the University Centre, Peterhouse College and the Garden House Hotel on the river bank. Not infrequently a ten-ton lorry would misguidedly come down the lane intending to deliver its load to the Centre or the hotel, only to find itself stuck halfway where the road narrowed. The lorry would then have to back up to Trumpington Street, narrowly missing the façades of our houses and filling our front rooms with fumes.

If this was the main problem by day, by night our ears were assaulted by a barrage of thudding pop music from the Peterhouse so-called music room. The Fellows of Peterhouse had cleverly situated their music room – where regular pop sessions were held – as far away from the main body of the College as possible, in a room overlooking the churchyard. Perhaps they thought that it did not matter if the slumbers of the dead were disturbed. Unfortunately they gave little thought to the living of the neighbourhood – especially the very elderly and the very young – for whom the nocturnal wailings, poundings and crashings were intolerable. Advance warning of an imminent session could be detected in the afternoon with the whistling of speakers, the occasional chord on a guitar, the crash of a lone cymbal. On one such afternoon, Thatcher nodded in the direction of Peterhouse, "Isn't it lovely, dear," she said, "I think they're having a *thé dansant*."

More campaigning – this time not about disabled issues – was an urgent necessity. A succession of letters to the Governing Body of Peterhouse, anguished telephone calls in the middle of the night to the porters and even, on one occasion, to the Master himself, eventually produced a compromise, curtailing the hours for full-decibel power and reducing the volume after midnight.

The traffic, a real danger for the three small children, Robert, Lucy and Inigo, who liked to ride their tricycles up and down the road and pay social calls on the neighbours, was a more intractable problem and one which demanded a more organized campaign of meetings and many more letters, most of which did not meet with an encouraging response. However the complexion of the issue changed dramatically on account of a devastating fire which struck the Garden House Hotel in 1972, a couple of years after it had been targeted in a student protest for appearing to support the military regime in Greece.

By the end of the day of the fire, the scene of so many happy family gatherings was nothing more than a charred smoking shell, from which there soon arose ambitious plans for greatly enlarged premises. Architectural considerations apart, a horrendous volume of traffic would certainly ensue, so we, the residents of the lane, opposed the plans unanimously. Just as both sides were heading for a confrontation, we realized that the two apparently conflicting aims were not as incompatible as they had seemed. The managers wanted a new hotel, and we wanted the lane closed and its peace and safety restored; by joining forces instead of opposing each other, both objectives could be achieved, and this was in effect the final result of a tense meeting of residents and managers expertly chaired by the Thatchers at number 9.

If in Cambridge Stephen and I had begun to find ways of adapting and controlling our environment, elsewhere it was more difficult. On their return from Louisiana late in 1970, Stephen's parents decided to buy a country cottage. I hopefully suggested that a cottage on the east coast would be a wonderful asset for our family. In both Norfolk and Suffolk, though the sand was soft, the terrain was level and manageable, allowing Stephen to be pushed to the very edge of the beach from where he could watch the children at play. My idea was curtly dismissed. "The east coast is much too cold for Father; he would hate having a cottage there," Isobel remarked. This was puzzling, since Frank Hawking spent most of his time working in the garden in all seasons and all weathers – just like the hardy Mr McGregor in *Peter Rabbit* – and indoors he wrapped himself in a dressing gown for warmth rather than install more heating appliances, leaving everyone else to freeze in the sub-arctic conditions.

Isobel went prospecting for a cottage with Philippa, who had come back from a two-year period of study in Japan, and returned rapturously enthusing over their find – a stone-built cottage overlooking a bend in the river Wye above a village called Llandogo in Monmouthshire – a place of lovely walks and views, with streams and woods for the children to play in and explore. I had never been to Wales and was easily infected by their enthusiasm, the more so because in April 1971 we had acquired a large, shiny new car, a replacement for the ailing Mini, financed by Stephen's First Prize in the annual Gravity Competition for an essay which he had run off just after Christmas.

Despite its size – about three times larger than the Mini – even the new car was barely adequate for all our luggage, as I found when I experimented with various ways of loading it for the exploratory trip to Wales in the autumn of 1971. Once the wheelchair, the pushchair and the travel cot were stowed away in the capacious rear section, there was little room for the suitcases. The next expedient was a roof rack, but that created its own set of the problems: by the time I had packed for the four of us, closed the house, eased Stephen into the front seat of the car, folded the wheelchair and lifted it into the back, strapped the children into their seats, loaded their luggage, including the travel cot and the pushchair, and then heaved four heavy cases onto the roof rack, I was so exhausted that the 220-mile journey, three times as far as the distance to the Suffolk or the Norfolk coasts, became an ordeal rather than an adventure. Even when the M4 opened just shortly after our first trip, the distance still proved to be a major drawback.

Nevertheless, when we stopped across the Welsh border for a tea break and saw the road signs in a foreign language and smelt the tingling damp air, our sense of excitement returned. At last we could truthfully tell Robert, who had been asking how much further ever since we left Cambridge, that we were nearly there. Some miles of open hill roads and then winding, leafy lanes brought us at last to our destination. The description we had been given of the cottage was undeniably accurate. Its position above the river Wye was breathtakingly beautiful, commanding an uninterrupted view of the river, the valley and the tree-covered hills on the opposite bank, where in a glow of radiant colour, autumn reigned in all its glory. A stream ran down the hillside beside the house, and a path through the beech woods at the back climbed up over damp peaty undergrowth to the waterfalls at Cleddon. Not so very far away, on the Black Mountains and the Brecon Beacons, a chill wind raged incessantly, testing the stamina of even the toughest hillwalker. The house itself was certainly picturesque – whitewashed, slate-roofed, set into the green hillside, blue wood smoke curling gently upwards from its chimney – and its attractions were undeniable.

This faithful description had omitted several important details, however, such as the fact that the hillside was little short of vertical, so that the only possible movement was up or down, and the only stretch of horizontal surface suitable for a wheelchair was a track a mere hundred yards long to the blackberry thicket at the edge of the wood. Moreover the house itself was reached by a flight of a dozen steep stone steps, slippery with moss and lichen, while inside a long, steep staircase led up to the bedrooms and the only bathroom. It could not have been more inappropriate for Stephen. Although his father stood by, it took him ten minutes to get up or down the stairs to the bathroom and more than ten minutes to get up or down the treacherous steps to the road. All excursions had to be made by car because there was nowhere else for him to go.

The children loved the place and a part of me shared their enjoyment. The changing colours were mesmerizing and the clear air refreshing. I relished my mother-in-law's meals. She was an excellent cook, except on those occasions when she chose to economize by serving us fresh-ground elder or brackish nettles from the garden. Unlike Stephen, who would wrinkle his nose in disgust, I also enjoyed my father-in-law's home-made wine, especially the luscious, golden mead which he fermented from the honey produced by his own bees. After supper we would spend long, lazy evenings in front of the open fire, playing board games until the children's heads started to loll sleepily. But on those occasions when I went out walking or climbing with Robert, I felt very unhappy at leaving Stephen behind, sitting sadly indoors or out on the terrace. Nowhere could more effectively or more cruelly have emphasized the limitations of his disability. I was upset and baffled. It seemed that the Hawkings considered themselves free of all basic responsibility for Stephen. If we visited them, they would be prepared to help, but otherwise they appeared to disregard the inconveniences of motor-neuron disease.

7

Upward Mobility

Llandogo with all its obstacles in 1971 turned out to be a useful rehearsal for the next summer's excursion – to the annual summer school in physics at Les Houches in the French Alps on the lower slopes of Mont Blanc – which was the brainchild of Cecile de Witt and her American husband Bryce. The mother of four daughters and an outstanding physicist at a time when women physicists were rare, Cecile was one of those capable women – not unlike some of the Fellows of Lucy Cavendish – of whom I stood in awe. From her home in America she organized the conferences in her native France and invited her own hand-picked participants. At Les Houches she supervised all the arrangements, led the sessions and climbed the mountains. For Stephen, she commissioned a labour force, brought in bulldozers to construct a ramp up to the chalet where we were to stay for six weeks, and made every possible provision for our comfort. She could hardly be blamed for the weather in the Alps that summer.

Stephen flew out to Geneva with his colleagues while my parents and I drove the rest of the family to Paris for the over-night Motorail to Saint-Gervais, some twenty miles from Les Houches. We happened to arrive in Paris on the chaotic weekend of *le grand rush* in late July, when the whole of France goes on holiday, but somehow Dad managed to find the Motorail depot and somehow, with our small charges, we managed to fight our way through the massed hordes of travellers on to the train at the Gare de Lyon. The next morning, with the nightmarish journey behind us, the sun shone as we relaxed over breakfast of coffee and croissants outside the station at Saint-Gervais, and it still shone, bathing the white peaks in glistening magnificence, as we excitedly embarked on the winding journey up the Chamonix valley to the very heart of the mountains.

Scarcely had we climbed the steep track to the summer school, a cluster of chalets and lecture halls set among meadows and pine trees, than the sun disappeared, a mist descended and it began to rain. It rained and it rained and it was cold. Water dripped from every roof, every gutter, every branch and every blade of grass, and Cecile's carefully constructed ramp soon turned into a mud slide. In the middle of July, Dad and I had to resort to feeding the woodburning stove an endless supply of logs to keep the chalet warm and to dry the nappies with which every corner was festooned. Dear little Lucy did her best to help by spontaneously potty-training herself at the age of twenty months.

In these circumstances, despite the elevation and the vertical nature of all expeditions, Stephen was happy. From morning till night he was surrounded by colleagues from all over the world whose driving passion was the study of black holes. Occasionally some of them went off in groups for the day, weather permitting, to climb Mont Blanc, but that only added to the excitement and the tension and lent an additional aura of superiority to their overall image. Nothing was too difficult for this breed of superhumans who were capable of mastering the secrets of the Universe and also of conquering any physical challenge on earth. Stephen of course was included in this category, since obviously he was fighting his own physical challenges with the gritty courage of a hardened mountaineer. The rest of us – the hangers-on, the wives, mothers, grandparents and babies – were left to our own devices, to shop and cook and find our own entertainment. Raids on the local supermarket for its somewhat limited range of supplies provided eggs for a staple diet of omelettes cooked over a bottled-gas stove. Although there was a restaurant which catered for the delegates, it was too expensive for the whole family to eat there all the time, and in any case the conversation at table inevitably veered, in the friendliest possible way, towards the rarefied subjects of black holes or alpine mountaineering in which we – that is the family – were not able to participate constructively.

As and when the rain eased off we would set out for a walk, under the dripping branches, up the mountainside at the back of the chalet, past the lecture hall into the wood to search for wild raspberries and blueberries. Then we encountered another unexpected challenge. While Robert, true to form, would charge ahead, Lucy adamantly refused to walk more than a couple of yards at a time and would then put her arms up, wanting to be carried. Because Robert's limitless energy now seemed quite normal, Lucy's reluctance to move perplexed me, just as her sleepiness when new-born had perplexed Stephen. Our progress up the mountain track was slow, and rarely did we reach the clearing where the raspberries and blueberries grew before it started to rain again. On one of these expeditions, an extraordinary thing happened.

For once Lucy was actually walking on her own two feet with Robert, ten yards or so ahead of her grandparents and me. Bringing up the rear I was enjoying an unaccustomed freedom of movement, unencumbered by any other person, small or large, when suddenly I saw the children stop in their tracks. They stood stock-still, whispering to each other very quietly and, beckoning to us to lower our voices, pointed to the ground. There, wending its way across the path from one side to the other was the smallest, most perfectly formed adder, the white diamond markings on its body standing out clearly against the grey. It took no notice of us as it slithered into the undergrowth. It was beautiful to watch, but even more striking were the children's reactions, as if some primitive instinct had warned them to stand quiet and still.

However high-powered their physics and impressive their mountaineering feats, the American participants at Les Houches brought a carefree atmosphere to the centre which helped to mitigate the effects of the rain. There was nothing superficial about their relaxed friendliness. Kip Thorne and his botanist wife, Linda, had made the break from the constraints of their Mormon background to search for broader truths unshackled by religious dogma. Whatever their private thoughts, they never voiced any criticism of the rigours of their background, but brought the positive aspects of Mormonism, a deep caring and concern for their fellow beings, to a wider world.

Jim Bardeen, the quietest, most self-effacing physicist imaginable, was working closely with Stephen and Brandon Carter on the painstaking task of constructing the laws of black-hole mechanics from the basis of Einstein's equations of general relativity. The new set of laws detailing the physics of black holes had caused a hubbub of excitement when their similarity to the second law of thermodynamics had become apparent, and it was this similarity which was driving cosmologists to attempt to narrow the gap between thermodynamics and black holes by putting the theory of black holes into the language of thermodynamics. The laws of thermodynamics govern microcosmic operations; they dictate the behaviour of atoms and molecules, including their eventual decay into heat, which they exchange with the objects around them. However the conundrum that now faced physicists was that the laws of thermodynamics, although similar, could not work in the case of black holes, because the predictions were that nothing, not even heat, could escape from a black hole.

Stephen, Jim and Brandon were attempting to unravel this major enigma when, one afternoon, unable to endure another drop of rain, I bundled the children and their grandparents into the car and set off over the pass beyond Chamonix to Switzerland, convinced that the sun must be shining somewhere. Somewhere there must be a welcome transfer of heat from one celestial body to another, even if heat did signify decay, or "entropy" in scientific terminology. Jim's wife, Nancy, came with us and enthralled the children, singing to them, telling them stories, sharing jokes and reciting poems all the way to Martigny – where indeed the sun was shining – and back. Through the infectious gaiety which shone from her big brown eyes, Nancy concealed the deep pain of the recent loss of both her parents.

It was also in Les Houches that Bernard Carr, Stephen's new research student, came bounding into our lives one wet afternoon. Bernard was certainly different from the expected run of research students. He was talkative, sociable, unselfconscious, the result perhaps of being sent to boarding school at the age of six. His conversation ranged widely over many topics, often coming to rest on his other main interest, parapsychology, a subject which physicists, including Stephen, tended to regard with derision. For Bernard however, coincidences and telepathic communication were significant. Indeed he was astounded to find that his impromptu visit from Geneva – where he was staying – to Les Houches, was actually expected by Stephen, his new supervisor, who had already summoned him in an undelivered word-of-mouth invitation through a third party. Bernard's early ambition had been to become a spaceman. As a child, to his mother's consternation, he had once spent a whole day preparing for this objective by standing on his head in the cupboard under the stairs while his younger brother sat outside the door acting as mission control. His mother must have been grateful that his intellect destined him for the theory rather than the practice of space exploration.

When at last the sun consented to shine in France as well as Switzerland, and the mountains appeared from behind the clouds,

Kip and Linda offered to take Robert and me on a mountain walk, up towards one of the glaciers, the Glacier de Bionnassay on the west face of Mont Blanc. Leaving Lucy and Stephen with my parents, we took the cable car from Les Houches up to a ridge from where we could look down to the toy chalets and villages dotted about the valley. The summer school down to our left was just out of sight behind the dark trees, while to our right a steep path ascended the mountainside, following the track of the funicular railway which crawled laboriously up from Saint-Gervais to the top station at the Nid de l'Aigle, the Eagle's Nest. The dazzling whiteness of the mountain against the deep blue sky was intoxicating, leading us on, up and up, pausing now and then to share Linda's ecstatic delight at the wide range of alpine plants and flowers opening in the afternoon sun. We continued our climb, higher and higher, beyond the end of the railway line in the direction of the massive blue-grey expanse of the glacier, still searching for more specimens for Linda.

It was not until we reached the first of the climbers' refuges in the lee of the Dôme du Goûter that, as one, we realized that we were alone on the mountain. Far below, the trains had ceased to run and all the other walkers had melted away although the sun was still high. Eagles wheeled silently overhead, a distant stream trickled down the rocks; otherwise there was little movement: an eerie quietness prevailed. None of us had thought of checking the time of the last cable car down to the village. At a brisk pace, almost a run, we set off back down the track to the cable-car station, more than an hour's walk away. Against all expectation, there in the station was a cable car with an attendant standing beside it. We ran to him smiling with relief, but he turned a dour face towards us, barring our way. Implacably indifferent, he announced that the last cable car had gone at five-thirty and it was now nearly six o'clock. We pleaded with him breathlessly, pointing to our five-year-old, who was – for once – beginning to tire. The man was impervious, hard as flint. We turned away, anxious and angry. On the ridge above the station there was a hostel from where we tried to call the summer school, but there was no reply. We dared not wait any longer, as the sun was now lower in the sky, so we left money with the hostel keeper asking her to try to ring again and leave a message.

There was nothing for it but to head straight down the mountainside as fast as possible, taking the path when we could find it, scrambling through bracken and long grass when we could not. A patriarchal figure, like St Christopher in a medieval painting, Kip carried Robert, whose legs had borne him well for more than four hours, but were now aching with weariness. Fighting our way through the undergrowth, we watched in disbelief as the cable car, carrying the same disobliging attendant, sailed over our heads on its homeward run down to Les Houches. The air grew chill as the sun sank behind the mountains, and the sky darkened. We persevered, thankful at least that we were walking down the mountain not up it.

The village of Les Houches was by no means the end of the road. The summer-school enclave was another three quarters of an hour away, up the hillside further west. It must have been well after nine when we stumbled blindly into the brightly lit refectory where everyone was anxiously waiting for news of us. No message had come from the hostel and the worried group of family – my parents and Stephen – colleagues and students were fearing the worst. Tearful with tiredness and relief, we fell into each other's arms.

At the end of August, as we dodged the showers at the last social function of the summer school – a barbecue where a whole lamb was being roasted over a pit – Kip suggested that Stephen might like to visit Moscow for talks with those many Russian scientists whose freedom to travel was severely restricted. He promised to make all the arrangements for a private visit which could be timed to follow on from the Copernicus Conference in Poland in the summer of 1973. Kip's well-meaning suggestions made my blood run cold. While Lucy was a baby, Stephen had travelled abroad to conferences either with George Ellis or Gary Gibbons, his first research student, or with his mother. Now that Robert was five and Lucy one and a half, my period of respite from international travel seemed to be drawing to a close. Frequently Stephen would ask if I would go with him to conferences in far-flung places; just as frequently I would reply that I could not bear to leave the children.

Divided loyalties were beginning to tear me apart. Stephen was pursuing his career with an iron will, and conferences gave him the chance to assert his presence on the international scene. It had been my genuine aim to help him achieve all possible success, but since making that commitment, I had become the mother of his children, and to them I owed an equal responsibility. Although

Stephen obviously required my help for many of his personal needs, the children needed my help for all of theirs. They were small enough still to need a constant presence. If their future was insecure on account of the health of their father, then I, their mother, had to compensate for that by not abandoning them more than necessary. Although they would be in excellent hands with their grandparents, I found the prospect of being thousands of miles apart from them for any length of time excruciating.

The scenario was set for a grim, recurring competition. Stephen would ask if I would like to go with him to a conference in, say, New York and tensely I would decline. Tacitly ignoring my reluctance, he would repeat the same question week after week until I was reduced to a frenzy, overwhelmed with guilt at letting him down, yet saddened by his lack of understanding. This pressure exacerbated the fear of flying which had pursued me since the tour of America in 1967, hovering over me like a great black bird at the mere mention of air travel. I had flown only twice since then, once on the winter holiday to Majorca when Robert fell sick, and the second time to Switzerland in May 1970. There had been a trip planned to Tbilisi in Georgia in September 1968, but to my silent relief, many British scientists, including Stephen, refused to attend in protest against the Russian invasion of Czechoslovakia that August. My fear of air travel was not completely unjustified: in the late Sixties and Seventies, not only did aeroplanes fall out of the sky with chilling regularity, they were also the favourite targets for hijackings by the growing bands of international terrorists.

The sum total of all the conflicting pressures doomed me to years of misery and travel by the longest, most roundabout means. In 1971, when Stephen was invited to attend a conference in Trieste, he went by air while Robert and I took the train, leaving seven-month-old Lucy with my parents. After the long, hot journey across Europe, we stopped in Venice, where Robert, bewitched by the view from the top of the Campanile, refused to descend – until the sudden clang of the heavy bells at midday sent him running for the lift. He then insisted on sitting down at a table in St Mark's Square outside Florian's, which proved to be an expensive lesson – the equivalent of £6 for a tiny cup of coffee – so the next time we passed Florian's by and sat down on the steps around the porticoed square – only to become targets for the local pigeons.

Two years later, the proposed trip to Moscow via Warsaw was a very different undertaking: travel by air was indispensable and applications for visas had to be sent months in advance. There was no choice; I would be away from the children for nearly a month, as in those repressive days after the fall of Khrushchev, nobody other than me would be granted a visa to accompany Stephen. The prospect haunted me but the plans were laid, the tickets were booked – paid for, as always by some scientific organization or other – and, with some difficulty, the visas extracted from the Russian embassy. It was very dispiriting to think that in the space of a few short years, I had become a pale shadow of the student who had travelled alone round Spain, blithely disregarding all parental concerns, revelling in the spirit of adventure, and relishing air travel, even in clapped-out propeller aircraft. Bound for Warsaw and Moscow but wan with care, I slipped away from the children as they played happily in their grandparents' house in St Albans in August 1973.

8

Intellect and Ignorance

Astronomers were flocking to Poland in 1973 to celebrate the 500th anniversary of the birth of Nicolaus Copernicus, the Polish astronomer whose dissatisfaction with the complicated mathematics needed to account for the movement of the planets in the earth-centred universe of Ptolemy's theory compelled him to develop a new theory of the universe in 1514. Still considering myself as something of a medievalist, but a medievalist with more than a passing interest in cosmology, I was fascinated by the iconoclastic effect of the Copernican theory, which postulated that the earth and other planets revolved around the sun, and thus superseded the Ptolemaic theory which had become tantamount to an article of faith, both scientific and religious, though in fact it bore little relation to the biblical concept of a flat earth, above which was heaven and below which was hell. On my first visit behind the Iron Curtain – apart from a day trip to Yugoslavia from Trieste in 1971 – I also found in Poland a lesson in the nature of tragedy: the tragedy of history in a country which bore the scars of oppression and division, the philosophical tragedy for mankind of the schism between science and religion which resulted from Copernicus' theory, and the tragedy of genius.

Although Copernicus did not live to see how his theory was developed by Galileo in the seventeenth century, he must have been well aware of its dangerously controversial nature. He might be seen as the first scientist to open the Pandora's box of science, with its dual potential of advancing human knowledge and yet of posing uncomfortable dilemmas which would test man's moral integrity. The theory well deserved the term by which it came to be known: the "Copernican Revolution". Since, according to Copernicus, the earth was no longer at the centre of the universe, man was not at the centre of creation. Man, therefore, could no longer be said to have a special relationship with the Creator. This fundamental change in perspective was to liberate man from the oppressive medieval obsession with the divine image, enabling him to expand his intellectual capabilities and value his own physical attributes – and it was one of the powerful influences behind the philosophy of the European Renaissance, when architects built palaces rather than cathedrals, and artists and sculptors replaced the religious image with the human form, depicted for its own sake, for its beauty and strength. In scientific terms, the Copernican theory paved the way for the discoveries of Newton in seventeenth-century England, where a positive after-effect of an otherwise fanatical Puritanism had been the release of rational thought from the grip of religious superstition. Within Catholicism, however, the Copernican theory was to produce an ugly, anti-scientific reaction, the repercussions of which are still felt throughout society.

Perhaps wary of its implications, Copernicus did not permit his work *Concerning the Revolution of the Heavenly Spheres* to be published until just before he died; a copy of the printed work was reputedly brought to him on his deathbed on 24th May 1543. Nonetheless he had not sought to hide its contents, for the theory had been widely disseminated over a long period, and he himself had lectured to the Pope Clement VII on the subject in Rome in 1533. Perhaps the Pope did not fully understand the implications of the lecture because it was presented to him merely as a simplification of the cumbersome Ptolemaic mathematics, or perhaps he did not take it seriously, because it was not until some time later – in the seventeenth century – that it fell to Galileo Galilei to bear the full brunt of the Church's ire for his support and publicizing of the new system.

A charming popular account of the spyglass ascribes its invention to children who were playing around with bits of glass and lenses in the workshop of a Flemish spectacle-maker and found that by putting two lenses together they could see distant objects plainly. The spectacle-maker saw the potential of the gadget for the toy market, but when in 1609 Galileo heard of it, he worked out the underlying theory in one night and developed his own improved version, the telescope, which he demonstrated to that city's incredulous merchants from the Campanile in Venice. To their astonishment, they could see in detail the markings on a sailing ship on the horizon, two hours from port. Galileo then realized that his revolutionary navigational aid could be turned on the heavens. He built a telescope in Padua, discovered four new planets – in fact the satellites of Jupiter – and published his own watercolour maps of the moon. His observations, which showed that not all heavenly bodies necessarily orbited the earth, convinced him of the accuracy of the Copernican theory. In 1610 he somewhat naively publicized his proof of the theory obtained from his observations, and in the next few years found himself in conflict with the Church, for whom the earth was theologically fixed at the centre of the universe.

In 1600, Giordano Bruno had been burnt at the stake for daring to speculate about astronomical matters, yet Galileo was undeterred by Bruno's fate. Innocently supposing that no one would want to contradict visible evidence, he went on to become the main and most successful proponent of the Copernican theory, especially because he published his findings in the vernacular language, Italian, instead of Latin. The attack this represented on the traditional Judeo-Christian view of a conveniently earth-centred universe posed an unacceptable threat from within to a church already struggling to contain the forces of Protestantism from without, and in 1616 the Church authorities issued an admonition requiring Galileo not to hold or defend the Copernican doctrine.

The election in 1623 of Maffeo Barberini to the Papacy as Urban VIII alleviated Galileo's uncomfortable situation temporarily. Barberini was a highly cultured man and a lover of the arts, but he was also proud, extravagant and autocratic – he reputedly had all the birds in the Vatican garden killed because they disturbed him. He was however a friend of Galileo's and helped to bring about a limited relaxation of the 1616 injunction by commissioning Galileo to write a discourse – *Dialogo sopra i due massimi sistemi del mondo, tolemaico e copernicano* – giving the arguments for and against the two competing systems, on condition that the discourse should be completely neutral. Inevitably the book, when it appeared in 1632, was seen as a categorical statement of the force of the Copernican argument and led to Galileo's arrest and trial by the Inquisition. He was sentenced to house arrest in his villa at Arcetri where, old, blind and captive, the king of infinite space bounded in a nutshell, he eloquently lamented the disparity between the vastness of his area of research and the limitations of his physical condition, a situation with which it was all too easy for us to sympathize: "This universe is now shrivelled up for me into such a narrow compass as is filled by my own bodily sensations."

Despite the life sentence of house arrest, his creative powers were not dulled. A new manuscript, *Concerning Two New Sciences*, was smuggled out of Italy to Holland where it was published in 1638. With this manuscript, Galileo is said to have laid the foundations of modern experimental and theoretical physics, and with it the scientific tradition moved north, away from the repressions of southern Europe.

Although Galileo was a devout Catholic, it was his conflict with the Vatican, sadly mismanaged on both sides, that lay at the basis of the running battle between science and religion, a tragic and confusing schism which persists unresolved. More than ever today, religion finds its revelatory truths threatened by scientific theory, and retreats into a defensive corner, while scientists go into the attack insisting that rational argument is the only valid criterion for an understanding of the workings of the universe. Maybe both sides have misunderstood the nature of their respective roles. Scientists are equipped to answer the mechanical question of *how* the universe and everything in it, including life, came about. But since their modes of thought are dictated by purely rational, materialistic criteria, physicists cannot claim to answer the questions of *why* the universe exists, and *why* we human beings are here to observe it, any more than molecular biologists can satisfactorily explain *why* – if our actions are determined by the workings of a selfish genetic coding – we occasionally listen to the voice of conscience and behave with altruism, compassion and generosity. Even these human qualities have come under attack from evolutionary psychologists who have ascribed altruism to a crude genetic theory by which familial cooperation is said to favour the survival of the species. Likewise the spiritual sophistication of musical, artistic and poetic activity is regarded as just a highly advanced function of primitive origins.

Frequently over the decades of our marriage, stimulated by a scientific article or television programme, I found my mind exercised by questions of this nature and would try to discuss them with Stephen. In the early days our arguments on the topics rehearsed above were playful and fairly light-hearted. Increasingly in later years, they became more personal, divisive and hurtful. The damaging schism between religion and science seemed to have extended its reach into our very lives: Stephen would adamantly assert the blunt positivist stance which I found too depressing and too limiting to my view of the world, because I fervently needed to believe that there was more to life than the bald facts of the laws of physics and the day-to-day struggle for survival. Compromise was anathema to Stephen however, because it admitted an unacceptable degree of uncertainty, when he dealt only in the certainties of mathematics.

Galileo died on 8th January 1642, the year in which Newton was born and three hundred years to the day before Stephen was born. It was therefore not surprising that Stephen adopted Galileo as his hero. When in 1975 he received a medal from the Pope, he took the opportunity to launch a personal campaign for Galileo's rehabilitation. The campaign was eventually successful but was nevertheless seen as a victory for the rational advance of science over the hidebound antiquated forces of religion, a theological capitulation, rather than as a reconciliation of science with religion.

In the sixteenth century, Nicolaus Copernicus had led the life of a true Renaissance man, untroubled by the crises that Galileo was to suffer in the next century. Copernicus enjoyed all the advantages, breadth of education and experience of that period of intellectual expansion and travelled widely, as far as Bologna, Padua and Rome. He studied medicine as well as mathematics and astronomy. He made translations from Greek into Latin, fulfilled a number of diplomatic functions and presented proposals for the reform of various Polish currencies. Ironically, five hundred years later, such broad possibilities were denied to Copernicus' modern compatriots as they celebrated his quincentenary.

From the scientific point of view, the great advantage of the Polish setting for the commemorative conference was that it provided a meeting place for all the great minds from both West and East, since Russian physicists were able to travel to Poland, if not further field, with relative freedom. For Westerners, Poland was certainly more accessible than the Soviet Union: our Polish visas came through automatically, whereas the Russians were much less welcoming. The only inconvenience of entry into Poland, as a number of male delegates found, was that the bearer of a passport was expected to resemble his photograph down to the last detail. Since the year was 1973, many of the younger delegates and students were sporting long hair and fine bushy growths of beard, bearing little resemblance to their passport photos which could have been taken nearly ten years earlier when they were but whining schoolboys with satchel and shining faces. The only means of persuading the Polish authorities that they really were who they purported to be, and not decadent hippies intent on undermining the purity of communist culture, was to shave off their beards and cut their hair at the border post. They arrived in Warsaw looking like sheep from the shearer. Stephen was probably the only one among them whose hair was actually shorter than on his photo and did not have to subject himself to an urgent trim.

The Poland we witnessed in 1973 was a sad country, ravaged by Germany and dominated by Russia. It was hardly surprising that the Poles regarded all foreigners, ourselves included, with suspicion. We were all tarred with the same brush: if we were not German, we must be Russian. Protesting our Britishness was of no avail because we and the Americans came from the envied affluent societies to which the Poles would like to belong but from which they were barred. Plate-glass shopfronts bore ample evidence of western aspirations, but inside the shops the shelves were either bare or the goods they displayed were shoddy and prohibitively expensive.

Everywhere Poland showed signs of a country ill at ease with itself, caught on the horns of a dilemma between old and new, East and West. Torn apart throughout its history by both its neighbours, Russia and Germany, it had painstakingly reconstructed much that it had lost in the Second World War – especially, in fine detail, the old town of Warsaw. In contrast, Stalin's unwelcome post-war gift to the Polish people was a megalithic municipal building of which it was said that the best views of Warsaw could be seen from it – meaning that only by viewing Warsaw from the Stalin monument could one avoid seeing the monument itself. In that building the Copernicus conference took place. It was approached from without by means of a long flight of steps. Another long flight of steps led down inside the building from the foyer to the conference area. Each morning, Stephen's student Bernard Carr and I would carry Stephen to the top of the steps, sit him down on a chair and then bring up the wheelchair. Inside, for want of a lift, we would then take the wheelchair down the corresponding inner flight of stairs before carrying Stephen down to it. This process was repeated in reverse sequence at the end of the day, possibly also several times during the course of the day, subject to variations in the programme and the venue. Those steps did not impress us with Stalin's generosity to the Polish people: they impressed us only with his megalomania.

A repressive Communism, imposed by Russia, which condemned peasant farmers to appear as lean as the emaciated cows we saw them herding along the country roads or the teams of scrawny oxen they drove across the fields, had produced a defiant reaction in the people. Poland was the most devoutly Catholic country in Europe: the Polish Church had become a symbol of national independence and nobly fulfilled its role as the defender of liberty, producing martyrs from among its priesthood. Nonetheless, I was perplexed to find strong reminiscences in Polish churches of the Church in Spain, so unlike the refreshing simplicity of English Catholicism which had resulted from the reforms of John XXIII's inspired papacy. As in Spain, churches in Poland were ornate, darkly lit, incense-filled, full of extravagant plaster saints and virgins, imbued with that distasteful air of superstition. Clusters of little old crones, draped in black, crowded round the porches and genuflected at the altars just as they did in Francoist Spain. Polish independence as manifested through the Catholic church was a very conservative force, competing against a hostile political system with its own traditional opiate, whereas in Spain the attitude of the Catholic church was equally conservative but was generally one of political compliance with the repressive regime.

Cracow, to which the conference adjourned for the second session, was more assured of its identity than Warsaw, since its monuments – Wawel Castle and the church of St Mary – had survived the war intact, but the vicinity of Cracow was tainted with the chilling notoriety of Auschwitz. There was no official excursion to Auschwitz, but some Jewish participants organized their own outing and came back communicating to the rest of us their devastation at what they had witnessed.

The only place in that unhappy country where I detected any sense of peace and integrity was at Chopin's birthplace, a single-storeyed thatched house, set in a tangle of greenery at Żelazowa Wola in the country outside Warsaw. Although Chopin's family moved to Warsaw when he was a baby, he spent summer holidays at Żelazowa Wola, the country seat of his mother's aristocratic relations, the Skarbeks, and it was there that he put the finishing touches to his E-minor piano concerto. He also spent holidays with school friends in the country. On one such holiday, he and his friends went on an excursion to Torum and found the house where Copernicus was born. Shocked by the condition of the house, Chopin complained that the room where Copernicus was born was occupied by "some German who stuffs himself with potatoes and then probably passes foul winds".

The old house at Żelazowa Wola, with its sparse furnishings, polished floors, family portraits and collection of instruments, modestly conjured up the atmosphere of life in a cultured Polish family in the early nineteenth century. It was not just the aura of unworldliness that held me enthralled, but also the evocative silence. Mazurkas and waltzes hung on the air as though the main living room were still echoing with the strains of a family party. Nocturnes wafted in on a scented breeze from the shady garden. The setting lent a visual, tangible dimension to that powerfully emotive music. Above all, the house spoke of peace, the peace of a devoted family which had nurtured that most seductive of Romantic geniuses, the genius for whom, according to his good friend Delacroix, "heaven was jealous of the earth". Like Copernicus, Chopin lived abroad for much of his life. He left Poland in 1830 never to return to his beloved homeland. His requited love for the young Polish girl Maria Wodzi´nska, whom he met in Dresden, was thwarted by her parents, who disapproved of the match on the grounds of Chopin's ill health. Marriage to Maria might have taken him back to Poland. Instead he settled in his father's native country, France, where he formed a tempestuous liaison with the volatile female novelist of licentious repute, George Sand, and died of consumption in 1849 at the age of thirty-nine.

The tragic experience seemed to be the hallmark of that stay in Poland, where so many resonances seemed to touch familiar chords and reveal points of similarity with our own lives. The tragic experience pursued us to the very end, for it was in the scientific company of Claudio Teitelbaum, a young Chilean delegate to the conference, and his wife that strange fleeting poetic memories from my own past resurfaced. Although they were living in Princeton, the Teitelbaums had close connections with the government of President Allende – the newly elected socialist government of Chile – through Claudio's father, who was one of Allende's ambassadors. They were part of the circle of dedicated left-wing reformers which included Pablo

Neruda, the inspired poet at whose feet I had worshipped as an undergraduate. In 1964 Neruda had come to read his poetry at a gathering in King's College, London, and I still carried in my mind the sensual sonority – as rich and evocative as Chopin's music – that he brought to his love poems, caressing and emphasizing their lush strain of natural imagery. Neruda, a communist, was so deeply involved in Chilean politics that the presidency was within his grasp, but he relinquished his ambitions in favour of his friend, Salvador Allende. It was in Cracow, in the bare lounge of the hotel on the last day of the Copernicus meeting, that news reached us of the right-wing military coup against the legitimate Chilean government, allegedly with CIA support. Allende had died in the defence of the Presidential Palace. The Teitelbaums were stunned not only at the death of their much admired President but also at the death of their dreams of reforming the impoverished lives of the oppressed peasants of Chile. They with thousands of others were destined to spend many years in exile. Their destiny was fortunate by comparison with those who did not manage to flee the vicious reprisals exacted by the right-wing Pinochet regime. Two weeks later Pablo Neruda, a Spanish-speaking poet of genius like Lorca before him, died in the aftermath of right-wing revolution.

9

Chekhovian Footfalls

If the impressions I carried from Poland were confusing, Moscow was perversely reassuring in that there was no room for doubt among its citizens about their own political identity or about ours. We knew – and everyone else knew – that the Soviet Union was a totalitarian police state and that there was little to be gained by hankering after a liberal democracy. The Muscovites politely recognized that we came from a privileged society without holding that against us. On the flight between Warsaw and Moscow, Kip warned us to behave as though our hotel room were bugged, not just for our own safety, but for all the colleagues we would be meeting. Stephen had visited Moscow once before, as a student, with a group of Baptists – strange company for one of such forceful atheistic opinions. Even stranger was the fact that he had helped them to smuggle Bibles into Russia in his shoes.

Such reminiscences were hardly appropriate on the present occasion, which had acquired the importance of a high-level official exchange, with all the concomitant VIP treatment. On arrival at the Hotel Rossiya, a massive square block between Red Square and the Moskva River, we glanced round our suite, equipped with samovar and fridge, half-expecting to uncover a microphone strategically placed to record our private thoughts. We did not however resort to the lengths of the diplomat in a joke then circulating: he was said to have pulled up the carpet and snipped at the wires he found beneath it. A loud crash and a horrified shout came from the room below where the chandelier had fallen to the ground.

We had already noticed that the lift bypassed the first floor of the hotel; this was out of bounds and was said to be reserved on all four sides of the hotel, each a quarter of a mile long, for "administration", for which we read "listening devices". Moreover, many of the Russians who had come to meet us at the airport, bearing welcoming bouquets of roses and carnations, were reluctant to enter the hotel beyond the lobby. Significantly in the light of their reticence, Dr Ivanenko, an elderly scientist of modest reputation, was only too pleased to sit in Kip's room for hours at a time, precisely enunciating, as if to hidden ears, all that he had achieved for Soviet science. It was Ivanenko who always accompanied groups of younger Russian astrophysicists to conferences in the West. We generally supposed that he was their minder, especially because they were forever inventing schemes for evading him. His own behaviour could be mysteriously unpredictable. In 1970, while we were at the conference centre at Gwatt in Switzerland, he had disappeared during the course of a boat trip along the shores of Lake Thun, not to be seen again until he turned up sometime later in Moscow.

The purpose of Stephen's visit to Moscow was twofold. Primarily a theoretician, he had begun to dabble in the practical question of black-hole detection. In this he was following the example of an American physicist, Joseph Weber, who had been conducting a solitary struggle to build a machine for catching the minuscule vibrations of the gravitational waves which were predicted to come from stars as they collapsed into black holes. We had spent several afternoons scouring rubbish tips in Cambridge for disused vacuum chambers which might be fitted up, in somewhat Heath-Robinson fashion, with detector bars immersed in liquid nitrogen, to complement Weber's work in Europe. This aspect of black-hole research had also been taken up in Moscow, at the university, by Vladimir Braginsky, an experimental physicist who showed us his laboratory and cheerfully gave me the remnants of a stick of synthetic ruby which he had used in his experiment. He was blessed with an extrovert nature which concealed the extent of his scientific foresight and revealed itself in his penchant for risqué political jokes, even in a semi-public setting. It was Braginsky who at dinner one night kept the company captivated with a torrent of jokes, interspersed with a succession of toasts in vodka and Georgian champagne. Not all his jokes were hysterically funny. Most had a political edge, as for example the joke about transport: an American, an Englishman and a Russian were comparing methods of transport. The American said, "Well of course, we need three cars, one for me, one for my wife and a motorhome for holidays." The Englishman said modestly, "Well, we have a runabout for town-driving and a family car for holidays." The Russian said, "Well, the public transport is very good in Moscow so we don't need a car in town and, when we go on holiday, we go in tanks…"

Stephen had also come to Moscow for conversations with those Russians, many of them Jewish, whose freedom to travel had been severely curtailed. Yakov Borisovich Zel'dovich, a fiery, impetuous character, had been in the forefront of the development of the Soviet atom bomb in the Forties and Fifties. In the late Fifties and early Sixties, like his American counterpart, John Wheeler, he turned his attention to astrophysics, where the conditions inside an imploding star mirrored those of the hydrogen bomb. In consequence Zel'dovich became a foremost authority in black-hole research. However, because of the secrecy surrounding his earlier work, he never expected to be able to emerge from behind the Iron Curtain and come to the West to share fully the international excitement aroused by black holes. The seminal research in imploding stars which his group generated was broadcast to the outside world on his behalf by a rather shy and rather tense younger colleague, Igor Novikov, with whom Stephen developed a strong working relationship.

Like Zel'dovich, Evgeny Lifshitz, also a Jewish physicist in the group, suffered travel restrictions, as did the many gifted students who knew that they would have to wait years before receiving the coveted first travel permit, itself a passport to the rubber-stamping of further permits. Some were voci-ferous and intense, others reserved and pensive. However extrovert some of their personalities might appear to be, it was obvious that they lived under extreme tension in an undercurrent of fear. All were seriously concerned at the restrictions placed on their creativity by incompetent officialdom, and all were afraid of the power of the KGB if they tried to improve their situation.

Kip had many conversations on this theme with his Russian friends, while Stephen and I provided a useful front of social activity. One evening this previously successful ploy backfired. Throughout our stay, our hosts showered us with tickets for the Bolshoi: for the opera, *Boris Godunov, Prince Igor*, and for the ballet, *Sleeping Beauty* and *The Nutcracker*. Though Stephen was eager to attend the opera, he was very reluctant about the ballet. Indeed, on the only previous occasion when we had been to the ballet together, to a production of *Giselle* at the Arts Theatre in Cambridge, he complained of a headache in the first act and I had to take him home in the interval, only to find that he made an immediate and miraculous recovery. In Moscow we were consistently in our seats in good time for the opera, but when we arrived at the Bolshoi for *The Nutcracker* the doors were already closing. We were hurriedly ushered into a side aisle and the doors closed smartly behind us. Kip, who had been intending to use the cover of the ballet to escape with a colleague, Vladimir Belinsky, into the streets of Moscow for surreptitious discussions on matters political as well as scientific, found himself trapped. He had come into the theatre to help us settle in, and when the doors closed, he had no option but to sit patiently through the first act of *The Nutcracker* till the interval, while Belinsky waited for him outside in the foyer. At least Stephen had a companion in adversity.

Although we were well aware of these cloak-and-dagger operations lurking in the background, we began to realize that Stephen's scientific colleagues enjoyed in a limited fashion a freedom denied to the rest of the people, the freedom of thought. In its ignorance, Communist officialdom was unable to measure the significance of abstruse scientific research. Consequently it tended to leave scientists in peace as long as they behaved with caution and towed the party line – unless, that is, like Andrei Sakharov, they spoke out openly against the regime on overtly political grounds. Indeed, in his book *Black Holes and Time Warps*, Kip Thorne refers to the unnecessary fear he felt for the Russians, Lifshitz and Khalatnikov, when they courageously wanted to acknowledge the error of their claim that a star cannot create a singularity when it implodes to form a black hole:

> For a theoretical physicist it is more than embarrassing to admit a major error in a published result. It is ego-shattering… Though errors can be shattering for an American or European physicist, in the Soviet Union they were far worse. One's position in the pecking order of scientists was particularly important in the Soviet Union; it determined such things as possibilities for travel abroad and election to the Academy of Sciences, which in turn brought privileges such as near doubling of one's salary and a chauffeured limousine at one's beck and call…

Lifshitz's freedom to travel had already been long curtailed when, to his immense credit and with the greatest urgency, he had persuaded Kip on an earlier visit to Moscow in 1969 to smuggle out a paper retracting the claim and admitting the mistake. The paper was published in the West. As Kip thankfully remarks, "The Soviet authorities never noticed."

Stephen got on well with his Russian colleagues because they shared his intuitive approach to physics. Like him they were concerned only with the crux of any problem; the fine detail did not interest them, and for Stephen, who carried all his theories in his head, fine detail was a hindrance to clarity of thought. Effectively, like him, they discarded all dead wood for a clearer view of the trees. They adapted this approach to whatever subject was under discussion, whether physics or literature. They gave the impression of having stepped out of the past, from the pages of Turgenev, Tolstoy or Chekhov. They talked about art and literature – their own Russian masters and Shakespeare, Molière, Cervantes and Lorca as well. Like my student acquaintances in Franco's Spain, they recited poetry and composed verses for any occasion – including poems in Stephen's honour. To them, it seemed, one more repressive regime meant little, because their country had always been governed by totalitarian regimes and had no experience of democracy, so, like generations of Russians before them, they found their solace in art, music and literature. In a society dominated by *Soviet* materialism, culture was their spiritual resource. Through them, I felt I could touch the soul of the country, the mournful soul of Mother Russia, who always draws her exiled children back to her lonely rolling landscapes of rivers and birch forests. Their personalities shone out of the background of their bleak lives like the golden domes of the well-preserved though no longer functioning churches which would suddenly appear from behind the gaunt concrete blocks of modern Moscow, illuminating the grey dreariness with their gleaming brilliance.

These colleagues seemed just as happy to take us on cultural expeditions as to talk about science. Often our days were a combination of the two: scientific discussions would accompany our sightseeing. We wandered through the golden-domed cathedrals of the Kremlin, purged of their religious function by an officious Communism which nevertheless had not managed to eradicate their air of sanctity. We stood enraptured before the altar walls of icons, and we examined floors of semi-precious stone. We ambled through the art galleries, the Tretyakov and the Pushkin, and made the pilgrimage to Tolstoy's homely wooden house, with its stuffed bear standing on the creaky landing ready to receive visiting cards, and its little room at the back where the great man applied himself to his other passion, shoemaking. From Tolstoy's garden I picked up a handful of fallen maple leaves, rich brown, orange and yellow.

I asked to see a functioning church and was taken both to the extravagantly decorative, red, green and white church of St Nicholas in Moscow and to the Novodevichy Monastery on the outskirts. Despite the wailing chants and the mumbling icon-kissing of the elderly devotees, neither place could convey the essence of holiness with the power of the two decommissioned, empty little churches which stood abandoned outside our window, dwarfed by the bulk of the hotel. One was brick-built, topped by a gold cross; the other was little more than a golden dome. It seemed that in banning organized religion, the Communist regime had actually encouraged the growth of an inner spirituality, which was ever present for those who were receptive to it and alien to those who were not.

In the age of space travel, we were drawn back into the past through the lives of the dignified, poetic individuals with whom we were associating. There were few cars on their roads, their material possessions were scarce and their clothing was drab. Health care was available to them free of charge, but what we saw of it suggested that Soviet hospitals and doctors were to be avoided at all costs. During the second week Stephen needed a dose of hydroxocobalamin, the fortifying vitamin injection which, in Cambridge, Sister Chalmers came to give him every fortnight. With some difficulty, his colleagues persuaded a doctor to come to the hotel. At first glance, I thought that it was Miss Meiklejohn, the terrifying, doughty games mistress from St Albans High School, who had walked into our room. She produced her equipment from a black bag: a steel kidney-shaped bowl, a metal syringe and a selection of reusable needles. We both winced. Stoical as ever, Stephen sat quietly while she jabbed the bluntest of her needles into his thin flesh. Squeamish as ever, I turned away.

The endless, grey-raincoated queues in the shops where our friends bought their food brought back childhood memories of post-war London. Whether in GUM, the state department store on Red Square, or in neighbourhood shops, the system seemed expressly designed to discourage its customers from making any purchases whatsoever. First they had to queue to find out whether the desired items were available on the shelves, then they had to queue to pay for them in advance at the cash desk, and finally, clutching their receipts, they had to return to the original queue to claim their purchases. As privileged foreigners we could shop at the tourist shops, the Berioska shops, which were greedy for our pounds and dollars. There, wooden toys, brightly coloured shawls, amber beads and painted trays abounded. I assumed that all the goods were produced in the Soviet Union until I chanced upon a pair of black leather gloves which bore the label "made by the Co-op, Blackburn, Lancs".

In other Berioska shops, foreign visitors could buy fresh and imported foodstuffs such as grapes, oranges and tomatoes, which for the average Russian were luxuries. If the food produced in the hotel, supposedly a first-class hotel, was any yardstick, the average Russian lived on an erratic subsistence diet of yogurt, ice cream, hard-boiled eggs, black bread and cucumber. Such meat as the hotel managed to provide was usually concealed in minute quantities in floury rissoles, or was so tough and tasteless as to be good only for shoe leather. My smattering of Russian, learnt in an evening class some years previously, was not much help in choosing from the numerous pages of the menu, because once we had made our selection, we would be told that it was "off".

For the first few days, we despaired of getting an edible square meal until one evening we discovered a restaurant, secreted away on the top floor of the hotel, looking out over the red stars on the towers of the Kremlin. We found ourselves sitting near a Frenchman and watched in amazement as his meal was served. With the suave confidence of a Parisian dining in one of the best restaurants in his native city, he embarked on his first course, which consisted of a dish of caviar, smoked fish and cold meats, with a small glass of vodka. Then, while we pushed a flattened piece of chicken swimming in grease around our plates, his main course came to the table. Crisp brown slices of roast potato enveloped a steaming, succulent, baked sturgeon. Enviously we watched him eat, savouring the aromas which wafted in our direction. It was not until he leant back in his chair with a Gallic sigh and a gesture of deep satisfaction that it occured to me that here was somebody with whom I could actually communicate. All I had to do was ask him in French where to find sturgeon and caviar on the menu. Obligingly, he indicated items 32 and 54, thus holding out the delectable promise of an acceptable diet for the rest of our stay. It was our bad luck that the very next day, the top-floor restaurant closed down, and items 32 and 54 never featured on the menus of the other less classy restaurants.

Mistrust of the next meal became a constant preoccupation. However, with some anticipation we looked forward optimistically to one of the supposed highlights of our stay, dinner in the Seventh Heaven revolving restaurant of the Ostankino Tower, a radio tower on the outskirts of the city. The tower, a space-age status symbol, was closely guarded – supposedly because of its strategic importance – and only special guests were allowed to dine there. Even they were not permitted to approach the tower directly, but were frisked at the perimeter fence some fifty yards away, and then led along an underground tunnel to the lift. Cameras were forbidden, we were told, since during the course of its heavenly revolutions, the restaurant passed by a milk factory. For "milk", read "armaments", Kip said. The milk factory came round with disconcerting frequency as we tucked into our first good meal in weeks. Nor was the ride a smooth one – the tower lurched drunkenly halfway through each cycle – which may explain why Stephen and I spent the next twenty-four hours competing for occupation of the bathroom.

It was no surprise to us that our Russian hosts were not at liberty to invite us into their own homes, but there was one notable exception. On our last evening in Moscow we were invited to dinner at the home of Professor Isaac Khalatnikov. Khalatnikov was a beaming, expansive character whom we had first met at the General Relativity Conference in London just before our marriage in 1965. The taxi delivered us to an imposing block of flats, close to the river in the centre of Moscow. We had heard from contemporaries of the difficulties of family life in Moscow. Apartments were scarce. Entitlement to housing depended on one's standing in the Party. Newly-weds frequently had to live with their parents in two-bedroom flats. Later, families would often take in surviving members of the older generation, particularly the babushka, whose presence was well-nigh essential, even in such cramped conditions, because she would generally run the household and care for the children while her daughter or daughter-in-law was out at work. We were astonished therefore to find that the Khalatnikovs' apartment was exceptionally large, consisting of several spacious, well-furnished rooms complete with television and hi-fi. Furthermore the food on the table was a veritable banquet which would not have been out of place at a Western dinner party. The servings of caviar, meat, vegetables, salads and fruit were lavish and tastefully presented. Stephen and I were appreciative but mystified. Why, in a society which trumpeted its equality, did this family enjoy such an ostentatiously indulgent lifestyle? As usual Kip provided the answer: it had nothing whatsoever to do with Isaac Khalatnikov's distinguished scientific status. It was the consequence of his wife's connections. Valentina Nikolaevna, a rather sturdy blonde lady for whom my gift of delicate costume jewellery was singularly inappropriate, was none other than the daughter of a Hero of the Revolution. In a nation where all were said to be equal, some were more equal than others. By virtue of her birth, Valentina Nikolaevna was entitled to all the prerogatives of the new aristocracy, including preferential housing and the right to buy her food in the Berioska shops.

The maple leaves that I had collected from Tolstoy's garden proved to be an eloquent metaphor of the Moscow we saw in those weeks of our visit. It was with genuine relief that we joined in the cheers of the passengers when the London-bound plane took off in a swirling snowstorm in mid-September. Like the snow, the autumn leaves were harbingers of winter in a country where all those freedoms of speech, expression, thought, movement which we took for granted were permanently frozen. Yet their vivid colours sang of our irrepressible friends, those courageous people stranded in that political wasteland. As winter approached in Cambridge, we realized that together with the leaves and the souvenirs, the wooden dancing bears and hand-painted china, we had brought back with us an unwelcome legacy of Soviet oppression. For several weeks after our return, we were unable to communicate freely in our own home for fear that the walls might be listening to us. If this was a measure of the psychological pressure that our friends lived under all the time, our admiration for them could only increase. Thrilled as we were to be back with our children, such a realization was sobering. How, we asked, would we cope in those circumstances?

At Christmas time that year, my mother and I took the children to see the London version of *The Nutcracker* ballet at the Festival Hall. Lucy was entranced by the spectacle and thereafter insisted on being called Clara, like the child heroine of the ballet. She spent every spare minute dancing to a well-worn record and devised her own version of the Cossack dance by running the length of the living room and kicking one small leg in the air before turning and racing back to the other end. Like father, like son, Robert was less enchanted by the performance and would have preferred his father's favourite Christmas-time treat, the pantomime. He fidgeted his way through the first half of the ballet, and no sooner had the second half begun than he dragged his grandma out of the auditorium on the irrefutable pretext of having drunk too much orange squash in the interval. They were not allowed to return to their seats so my mother had to make do with a closed-circuit screening of the rest of the performance in the foyer, while Robert contentedly watched the barges plying up and down the Thames.

10

A Chill Wind

That winter in Cambridge we faced our own set of pressures, though not of a political nature. The conference in Poland and the visit to Moscow, combined with the previous year's discoveries at Les Houches, had opened up new possibilities and new problems for black-hole research. The secret aim of all physicists was to uncover the philosopher's stone, the as yet unformulated unified field theory, which would unite all the branches of physics. It would reconcile the large-scale structure of the universe – about which Stephen and George Ellis had written a book – with the small-scale structures of quantum mechanics or elementary particle physics, and the theory of electromagnetism. Black holes held out the tantalizing prospect that they might be the key to the first stage of this particular quest – in the enigmatic resemblance between general relativity and thermodynamics contained in their laws.

Such was the lure of this goal that not only was Stephen intent on following up his Moscow discussions with consultations worldwide at every available conference, he increasingly spent his every waking hour immersed in such deliberations. The question of travels abroad came up with disturbing regularity. I repeated the canon of my excuses, but it sounded feeble to claim that the strain of leaving the children was too great when the future of physics was at stake.

At the same time, I was confused by Stephen's tendency to spend quite so many hours in the evenings and at weekends, like Rodin's *Thinker* with his head bent low resting on his right hand, transported to another dimension, lost to me and to the children playing around him. However compelling the intellectual challenge of black-hole physics, I could not fathom such depths of self-absorption. I would at first suppose that he was engrossed in a mathematical problem, so I would cheerfully ask him what was on his mind, but often he would not reply, and I would quickly become anxious. Perhaps he was uncomfortable in his wheelchair or not feeling well, I would enquire. Had I upset him perhaps by refusing to go to the next conference? As he still would not reply, or merely gave an unconvincing shake of the head, my imagination would run riot as I began to suspect that all these factors and many more, not least dejection at his deteriorating condition, were oppressing him unbearably. The position he adopted was, after all, one traditionally used by artists to depict depression.

Undeniably his speech was becoming indistinct, necessitating boring sessions with a speech therapist to try and redress the slur. Some people, whom we preferred to think of as deaf or stupid, could not understand him at all. He required my help with the minutiae of every personal need, dressing and bathing, as well as with larger movements. He had to be lifted bodily in and out of the wheelchair, the car, the bath and the bed. Food had to be cut into small morsels so that he could eat with a spoon, and mealtimes were protracted. The stairs in our house were now a major obstacle. He could still pull himself up – that in itself was recommended exercise – but he needed to have someone standing behind him for reassurance. It was natural that when away from home, he wanted to have me with him all the time. Pent-up guilt at my own reluctance to take advantage of all those opportunities to travel the globe, and frustration at the lack of communication, would tie me in knots of anxiety and despair. I felt like that traveller who had fallen into a black hole: stretched, tugged and pulled like a piece of spaghetti by uncontrollable forces.

A couple of days later, Stephen would emerge from his isolation. With a triumphant smile, he would announce that he had solved yet another major problem in physics. It was only after the event that these episodes became a joke. As each new situation was marginally different from the previous one, I never learnt to recognize the symptoms. At the time I always worried that Stephen might really be feeling unwell. Each time I would compliment him on his success, but secretly I realized that the children and I had joined battle with that irresistible goddess, first encountered in America in 1965, the goddess of Physics, who deprived children of their fathers and wives of their husbands. After all, I remembered that Mrs Einstein had cited Physics as the third party in her divorce proceedings.

For Stephen those periods of intense concentration may have been useful exercises in cultivating that silent, inner strength which would enable him to think in eleven dimensions. Unable to tell whether it was oblivion or indifference to my need to talk that sealed him off so hermetically, I found those periods sheer torture, especially when, as sometimes happened, they were accompanied by long sessions of Wagnerian opera, particularly *The Ring Cycle*, played at full volume on the radio or the record player. It was then, as I felt my own voice stifled and my own spontaneity suppressed inside me, that I grew to hate Wagner. The music was powerful, so powerful that I was irresistibly drawn into the sensual luxury of those hypnotizing chords and thrilling modulations, but my daily round did not allow me a single moment's respite from the unending demands of shopping, cooking, housework, childcare and Stephencare. From the kitchen or the bathroom, or even the playroom on the top floor, I would be all too conscious of the inveigling power of the music, insinuating itself through enthralling harmonies and discords. I would try to disregard its beckoning, ambiguous strains, knowing it to be far too manipulative for my confused state of mind. The open clarity of Mediterranean culture was my touchstone, not the dark menace of northern myth, where all heroes were doomed to premature death and chaos and evil triumphed. Stephen might be as bewitched by this force as he was by physics – since both for him had become a religion – but I had to keep my feet on the ground. If I allowed myself to yield to the sombre tyranny of that music, the structure I had built around me would collapse and crumble to dust. Wagner came to represent an evil genius, the philosopher of the master race, the demon behind Auschwitz, and potentially an alienating force. I was simply too young to be able to cope with so much emotional pressure.

Thankfully our diet of entertainment was not limited to Wagner, but was vastly eclectic. It ranged from Wagner, inescapably, and Verdi and Mozart in the opera houses, through performances of the Elgar oratorios in King's College Chapel and Monteverdi Vespers in St Albans Abbey, to *Princess Ida* at the Arts Theatre – since, truly broad in his tastes, Stephen was a Gilbert and Sullivan fan as well as a Wagnerian. Apart from Wagner, his favourite entertainments however were the Footlights, the university review in summer, and the pantomime in winter. For both of these he suspended his usually acerbic critical judgement. I often found the Footlights tedious, since the standard of humour never quite matched up to the unrealistic expectations aroused by the *Beyond the Fringe* generation, and as for the pantomime, the smutty jokes wore thin through constant sniggering repetition.

To occupy those other solitary evenings at home when Stephen was immersed in thought but Wagner was mercifully suppressed, when the trappings of the day were cleared away and the children finally in bed, I bought a very compact piano on the pretext that Robert should start having lessons. In an environment where everyone was so naturally accomplished, it was embarrassing to admit that I really wanted to have lessons myself. I took some lessons with a retired schoolteacher who, sympathizing with my ambitions, sensitively refrained from telling me that I was too old to learn to play. Rising to the challenge, he trained me in the basics of theory and harmony and, to my satisfaction, allowed me to choose my own repertoire. Robert also had lessons – with a young teacher who drew pictures for him of fairies dancing in the treble clef and giants stomping about in the bass.

Since he had started school, Robert, previously so happy and lively, was becoming much quieter and more reserved. He was only four and a quarter when, in line with local education policy, he was obliged to start school. I was convinced that this was too early. Some time later I read that the psychological difference between a four-year-old and a five-year-old is the same as the difference between a seven-year-old and an eleven-year-old, and that starting school at such a young age is actually damaging to a child's development. Robert was a shy little boy and, when asked what he did in the lunch hour his reply, casually delivered, made me very sad. "Oh," he said with a shrug, "I just sit on the steps." His primary school had an excellent reputation for bringing out the best in fast-learning children from academic backgrounds, and was essentially a literary school where those children who could read quickly made rapid progress. Some years later Lucy, bubbling with creative and literary talent, flourished there. Robert however had great difficulty in reading. I feared that this might be a delayed effect of the medicine-swallowing episode, but my mother-in-law's comments were comforting. It was obvious that Robert was just a chip off the old block, she said, because Stephen had not learnt to read until he was seven or eight years old. I then fully understood why the winter spent by the Hawkings with the Graves family in Majorca had left such an unhappy impression on Stephen. If at the age of nine he had only just learnt to read, the daily sessions spent analysing the Book of Genesis under the eagle eye of Robert Graves must have been grim. Stephen wisely maintained that it did not matter what Robert read so long as he learnt to read, whereupon we plied Robert with the *Beano* and every imaginable joke book, so that each mealtime was accompanied with interminable jokes of the "Knock, knock", "Who's there?" variety and Robert's reading improved dramatically.

Dyslexia was not a condition that was recognized in educational circles in the early Seventies. Nowadays it is claimed that both Leonardo da Vinci and Einstein were probably dyslexic. We suspected that Stephen was dyslexic and were fairly sure that Robert was too, but, apart from a remedial reading class, there was no specific help for dyslexics in the state system. They were classed at best as lazy, at worst as backward, slow learners, already at the age of five, consigned to a second-rate future. I knew that Robert was not backward: this was the child who at the age of four, when we were gardening one afternoon, had asked quite seriously, "Mummy, who was God born inside?" This was the child who, at five, had sat down at the piano to explain the concept of minus numbers to me. "Look, Mummy," he said, "all these notes going up from middle C are plus numbers and all the ones going down from middle C are minus numbers."

I was sure that the emphasis that the school placed on literary rather than numerical skills was wrong for Robert. A new teacher who came to the school when he was just six announced that she was going to start an advanced maths group. I pleaded with her to let him join the group. She clearly found it hard to not to laugh. "But he can't read!" she remonstrated, "How can he possibly do maths?" I persevered, "Please just let him try." With the greatest scepticism, she agreed to let him join the class for three weeks. During those three weeks Robert did not appear to be having any trouble with the advanced maths and he seemed much less tense. At the end of the three weeks, he brought a message home from the new teacher, saying that she would like to talk to me after school. She came out to meet me at the school gate. "Mrs Hawking, I owe you an apology," she began fulsomely, "I really didn't think that Robert would be able to cope with the advanced maths when you asked me to let him come into the class, but I really must apologize because I was so wrong. He is extraordinarily good at maths, and is way ahead of all the others." But the maths class came to an untimely end after only two terms when the teacher left to have a baby, and then Robert was back at square one. As Stephen and I had blithely assumed that, in accordance with our socialist principles, our children would be educated in state schools, we were now presented with a resounding clash of loyalties because the needs of our child were not compatible with our political principles. The state system had not served Robert well so far. He needed to be praised for the subjects he could do well, particularly maths, and he needed encouragement, not castigation, in those he found difficult, particularly reading and writing. Only in the private sector could we be sure that the classes would be small enough for him to receive proper attention. The sonorously entitled Fellowship for Distinction in Science did not pay a large enough salary for us to be able to afford private education, nor did the Research Assistantships to which Stephen was subsequently appointed – at the Institute of Astronomy in 1972 after Fred Hoyle's departure, and also at the Department of Applied Mathematics in 1973. But by another of those ironic twists of fate, the finance became available – in a way that we regretted.

In 1970, shortly after Lucy's birth, Stephen's lonely Aunt Muriel had died. Instead of enjoying her new-found freedom after her mother's death, she had simply wasted away. The money she might have spent on herself, by going off on a round-the-world trip for instance, she saved cautiously to provide for the uncertainties of the future. The future never came and the money was left to some of her great-nephews and nieces, among them Robert on whom she particularly doted. Of itself, the inheritance was not sufficient to finance long years of education, but when set to work with an equal share from Stephen's father, it amounted to enough to buy a small house which could be let out quite profitably. Half the rent went to Stephen's parents while the other half contributed substantially to Robert's school fees. Cambridge was a good place for such a venture, because properties were still fairly cheap and the floating population of visiting scholars meant that there was a constant demand for rented properties. With my experience of renovating our own house, I was put in charge of the project. Buying and renovating another house and then letting it became an additional burden when my hands and my time were already full. The insight it gave me into the squalor of other people's lives was disheartening, but since I was all too conscious of the need to save money for the ever-mounting school fees, I had no option but to take up the paintbrush for an intensive week of solo decorating once or twice a year. Sometimes this exercise had to be carried out even more frequently to satisfy summer visitors.

Such taxing activity and wearing preoccupations left less and less time and energy for the thesis. I had succeeded in assembling material for the first chapter and had come up with a few original ideas of my own. I traced some close verbal reminiscences between the *kharjas* and the *Song of Solomon*, and I detected striking similarities between the *kharjas* and the Mozarabic hymns, the hymns of the native Christian populace under Moorish domination. With luck, all other things being equal, I might be able to snatch an hour for the thesis in the morning, while Lucy was at nursery school after I had taken Stephen to the Department. Keeping up with my own research stretched me to the limit. There was no longer any chance of broadening my grasp of other areas of medieval research, let alone investigating the other fields and topics which came up for discussion at the Lucy Cavendish dinners. I was out of touch with the political and international scene and had scant time for reading. I had little to offer and little to gain, other than a depressing awareness of my own inadequacy, from either Lucy Cavendish or the Dronkes' medieval seminars. When I did attend one or the other, I had to bluff my way through discussions and conversations or else maintain a dull silence. It was an uncomfortable situation in which I felt a fraud, and my attendance at both lapsed.

In Lucy Cavendish, I had just one friend, Hanna Scolnicov, with whom I felt at ease. Hanna, an Elizabethan scholar from Jerusalem, was enjoying the respite which she found in Cambridge from the tensions of her war-torn homeland. Hanna and I discovered that we had much in common. Although our circumstances were inevitably disparate, we were both trying to live normal lives and bring up our three-year-olds, Robert and Anat, against a background of tension and uncertainty. When we met, I had just given birth to Lucy and Hanna was expecting her second child. By the time Ariel was born the following summer, we had become friends for life. Moreover, in Hanna's husband, Shmuel, a classical philosopher, Stephen had found an intellectual sparring partner. Both Hanna and Shmuel were so much more intuitive and perceptive than many people who had known us longer and supposedly better. When Shmuel's sabbatical year came to an end and they nervously returned to Israel with their young family, there was even less incentive for me to attend Lucy Cavendish, and I became even more isolated and out of touch.

It did not matter much. Stephen's career was so obviously more important than mine. He was bound to make a big splash in the pond of physics, whereas I would be lucky to make the smallest ripple on the surface of language studies. And, as I reminded myself often, I did have the consolation of the children, both of them lively and funny, loving and adorable. Many people who might well have stared cruelly at Stephen, absorbed by the freakishness of disability – the same people who would have called him a cripple – were visibly nonplussed by the sight of a seriously handicapped father with such strikingly beautiful children, each one a miracle of lucid perfection. Stephen gained confidence through his pride in them. He could confound those doubting onlookers by announcing, "These are my children." The acute joy that we shared in their purity and innocence, their quaint sayings and their sense of wonder, gave us in turn moments of profound tenderness. In those moments, the bond between us strengthened till it embraced not just ourselves but our home and our family, reaching out to include all those people we valued most. The family, our family, had become my *raison d'être*.

I comforted myself that no amount of academic recognition could have equalled the creative fulfilment I derived from my family. If sometimes the long hours of childcare and baby talk seemed unremitting, I was well compensated by the privilege of rediscovering the world, its wonders and inconsistencies, through the eyes of small children. Happily my parents also delighted in this pleasure. Never were grandparents so keen to enjoy their grandchildren, and never were grandchildren so indulged by their grandparents. The children brought my parents some light relief from their own anxieties, which were focused on my grandmother, whose health and memory were failing fast. When eventually she moved to St Albans from her home in Norwich, it was too late for her to settle with confidence anywhere else, and all too soon, in her disorientation, she fell and broke an arm. I already knew when I waved goodbye to her one Sunday afternoon in early December 1973, that I should never see her again. I wept all week for that brave, gentle spirit whom I loved so much. It came as a great sorrow but no surprise when my mother rang the following Friday, 7th December, to tell me that she had died in her sleep.

11

Balancing Act

The gradual disappearance of close friends from our social scene did nothing to alleviate my flagging spirits. My school friends and college friends I saw rarely; either they had gone abroad or were raising families in other cities. The friends of the past few years were branching out, leaving Cambridge to climb the career ladder wherever the jobs happened to be. Rob Donovan, who had been Stephen's best man at our wedding, had with his wife Marian and their little daughter Jane left Cambridge for Edinburgh. Thereafter our contact with them was sporadic, though when we were able to meet, the strength of our friendship resumed in as lively and stimulating a manner as ever. We stayed with them outside Edinburgh in the summer of 1973, just before the planned trip to Moscow. As always in the company of old friends, our conversations ranged far and wide, recalling those Sunday afternoon visits soon after our marriage. We would gossip about the Cambridge scene, the latest convulsions in Gonville and Caius, developments in science, the complexity of grant applications and friends dispersed across the globe.

When we spoke of the Moscow trip, Rob insisted that we should not be lulled by lack of media coverage into supposing that in the post-Cuban Missile Crisis era the arms race had disappeared into the attic of history. Surreptitiously, both superpowers were developing a huge array of ever more sophisticated weaponry. Although the threat of nuclear warfare still hung over us all each time the superpowers, like snarling dragons, caught a whiff of each other's presence in some contested corner of the world, the fact that they were actually enlarging and refining their already enormous nuclear arsenals was not widely publicized. Rob's remarks worried and angered me. Now that we had children it was not enough to say that there would be consolation in all being blown up together. I was not prepared to stand back and let that monstrous apocalypse destroy the lives of my precious offspring. But what could I – or we – do? There was little use in appealing to the scientists who had developed these weapons in the Forties and Fifties – many of whom were known to us on both sides of the Iron Curtain – because the decisions were now in the hands of untrustworthy politicians, the devious Nixon in the United States and the inscrutable Brezhnev in the Soviet Union. It was almost harder to digest these unpalatable truths against the pristine background of Scotland's purple-headed mountains, where the honey-laden air sang of biblical simplicity, than in any man-made urban setting.

The Carters, Brandon and Lucette, with whom we also used to spend so many weekend afternoons, had moved to France with their baby daughter, Catherine. Brandon had taken up a research post at the Observatoire de Paris at Meudon. The Observatoire was set in the grounds of a château, rather like its Cambridge counterpart, and commanded magnificent views over Paris. I missed Lucette greatly for many reasons, quite apart from the fact that she was the only person I knew in Cambridge with whom I could speak French. A respected mathematician, she was clever and articulate without ever being pretentious. Her sincere interest in people and her enthusiastic sense of family were not typical of the Cambridge academics with whom she had mixed. She was musical, imaginative and blessed with a delicate sense of poetry. It was Lucette who through her rhapsodic delight in the trees and flowers, colours and perfumes of the churchyard, introduced me to Proust.

The greatest shock came with the loss of the Ellises. Their departure was especially distressing because they were not leaving Cambridge simply to go to another job, but because their marriage had ended. We identified so closely with them that when George and Sue separated, our own family seemed to be under threat. Our two families, each with two small children, had shared so much that we had become part of each other's support system. Sue was Lucy's godmother. We had bought and renovated our houses, had our babies, gone on holiday and attended conferences, almost in tandem. On the one hand, George and Stephen had written a book together, *The Large-Scale Structure of Space-Time*, and on the other, Sue and I had conferred and confided in each other over many of the crises of motherhood and the struggle to compete with the goddess Physics. George and Stephen were alike in that they could cut themselves off from the basic realities of the outside world, plunging out of the reach of their families deep into the realms of the theoretical universe. The many shared and parallel experiences had built an interdependence into our marriages, and when theirs failed, the solidity of ours was shaken.

All those friendships with couples who had now left Cambridge had been formed in special circumstances. They were the product of Stephen's contacts in the Department or in one or other of the colleges. He had shared interests, usually scientific, with the husbands while I discovered common interests with their wives. On the departure of the Ellises, our very close, foursome friendships petered out. Although we were on good terms with many of the younger Fellows of Caius and their wives and had made new friends among the more recent postgraduates in the Department, a subtle change occurred. I made many female friends through the children, but the husbands and fathers of those families did not necessarily have much in common with Stephen, and they were understandably deterred by the difficulties of communication. Moreover I tended to make friends among people with whom there was a perceptible bond of sympathy. They either had cause for sorrow in their own lives or they had some special knowledge of the needs of the disabled. Of all those several valuable friendships, two in particular, the most loyal and the most lasting, had very relevant points of contact with Stephen.

Among Constance Willis's team of assistants – "Daddy's exercisers" as Robert called them – there was a slim, fair-haired girl of about my own age, Caroline Chamberlain. In the summer of 1970 Caroline ceased to practise as a physiotherapist because she was expecting a baby at the same time as I was expecting Lucy. As she lived nearby in the Leys School – the local boys' public school where her husband taught geography – we kept in touch and were brought into closer friendship after our daughters were born. My mind was focused ever more intensely on the problems of disability, for it sometimes seemed that a trap was closing over all of us, over the children and me as well as over Stephen. Information was pretty well non-existent and I began to depend on Caroline's fund of professional knowledge for guidance. At once practical and cheerful yet very sensitive, she was well aware of the array of difficulties we faced at every turn and, despite all the pressures of being a housemaster's wife, would do her best to come up with an answer, be it a more comfortable posture, an item of equipment – such as a wheelchair cushion or a caliper – or the address of some useful pioneering organization.

At the school gate, that traditional meeting place for mothers, I found another stalwart friend in Joy Cadbury, whose children, Thomas and Lucy, were the same age as Robert and our Lucy. Joy's retiring gentleness confounded my perceived image of an Oxford graduate. Far from vaunting her intellectual prowess at the expense of others, she played it down as if it were of absolutely no relevance to her present lifestyle. The daughter of a Devon doctor, she had fulfilled her real ambition – to become a pediatric nurse – after graduating from Oxford. Joy took our situation deeply to heart, always ready to take the children off my hands in times of crisis, always ready to give an unobtrusive hand when the strain was overwhelming. She was not unfamiliar with motor-neuron disease, the incurable degenerative illness about which so little was known, because two hundred and fifty miles away her own elderly father was suffering its terminal stages.

In Devon, not far from Joy's family home, I had other allies in my brother and his wife Penelope. After Chris's first temporary job in Brighton, they had moved to Devon when Chris joined a dental practice in Tiverton. Artistic by nature and interested in character and relationships, Penelope understood my need to talk about personalities, influences and emotions and the ways people communicated with each other – subjects which in the Hawking family were virtually proscribed. In Chris and his wife I found a deep well of understanding and support; the drawback was that they lived so far away.

Not all new acquaintances could afford to bring me the encouragement which I found in Caroline, Joy and my relations. Some of my new friends were as marginalized as I was, though in different ways. Often they themselves needed support and turned to me for help. From the vantage point of the physical illness which dominated our lives and which was so immediately obvious and clearly defined, I had only occasionally in the past glimpsed other tragedies. With greater maturity I began to awaken to the many causes and complications of suffering. Some people were struggling with their emotions and with poverty after a traumatic divorce, others were alienated from their families, others were simply a long way from home. These situations and many others I could regard with a certain objectivity, and I tried to give some sort of sensible encouragement to the people experiencing them. Ironically the situations which were closer to my own were much harder to deal with.

Some well-intentioned friends promised to introduce me to a nurse whose husband was suffering from multiple sclerosis. I looked forward to this meeting, hoping that we might be able to bring each other the consolation of shared experience. It was hard even to mention the problems – the crushing responsibility, the emotional strain, the aching fatigue of bringing up two small children unaided at the same time as caring for a seriously disabled person who was wasting away before one's very eyes – without pangs of disloyalty. Stephen never talked about the illness, but nor did he ever complain. His heroic stoicism increased my sense of guilt at even giving voice to the slightest misgivings. But it was the very lack of communication that was hardest to bear, sometimes harder than all the physical stresses and strains combined. Whereas I had originally hoped that there would be fulfilment in unity of purpose, in fighting together against the odds stacked so heavily against us, it seemed that now I was little more than a drudge, effectively reduced to that role which in Cambridge academic circles epitomized a woman's place. Fundamentally I knew that I needed help – physical help and emotional support – in keeping my beloved family going.

Just once I summoned the courage to broach my woes – with the utmost caution – to Thelma Thatcher. Her response, if not a rebuff, was decisive in its severity. "Jane," she said, "I say to you what I always say when things cannot be altered: count your blessings." Her answer was honest and she was right. I had much to be thankful for – not least, my family and Stephen's dedicated hard work and courage. I was not destitute and I had no alternative but to accept my chosen lot, keep faith, work hard and make the best of it – as, I found out, Thelma herself had to do on losing her two infant sons. After all I was not unhappy: I derived intense happiness from the two most beautiful and enchanting children anybody could wish for – Robert with his silvery blond hair, neat round face and wide enquiring eyes, and Lucy, auburn-haired with a pink and white skin as soft as swansdown. I was just tired, exhausted from broken nights, back-breaking physical strain and the constant nagging sense of worry and responsibility. I was ashamed at having even attempted to unburden myself, and slunk away to count my blessings.

Practical as ever, Thelma called by the next day. "I've been thinking, dear, you must have more help. I'm just going to call on Constance Babington-Smith, shall I ask her to send her cleaning woman along to you?" Constance Babington-Smith's cleaning lady, bustling Mrs Teversham, was a treasure of the first order, as was her successor a year or so later, tall, angular Winnie Brown. Once a week, cleanliness and order were restored to our household. However, the housework was but a part of the problem. I still needed a sympathetic listener, someone who would patiently listen to my intimate anxieties with understanding and without reprimand. I was not expecting the flourish of a magic wand suddenly to put everything to rights, but I did cherish the hope that perhaps the new contact, the woman with the disabled husband, would be the person who would listen and respond with more understanding than anyone else, and possibly might be able to suggest ways of dealing with some of the practical difficulties of caring more or less single-handedly with severe disability. It was not to be. By the time we met she was on the point of departure for the USA with a new partner, leaving her husband in a home for the disabled.

Thelma Thatcher's stark philosophy of counting one's blessings was the only valid course open to me. I had pledged myself to Stephen. In so doing I had committed myself to trying to provide him with a normal life. It was beginning to appear that that pledge meant keeping up a façade of normality, however abnormal life might become for the rest of us in the process. I had no intention of reneging on my pledge, but isolated glimpses into the lives of others – such as the one I had just experienced – served to emphasize rather than alleviate my consuming isolation. Long ago we had discovered that there was no organization, no medical authority to whom we could turn for enlightened advice and assistance. Now, since there was no one to whom I could turn for personal support in finding a path through the maze of problems, I resolved to trust my own counsel, steering well clear of unsettling people and situations, pretending more than ever that ours was just a normal family, beset with a difficulty which was best kept confined to the background.

12

Event Horizons

One dark, windy evening – 14th February 1974 – I drove Stephen over to Oxford to a conference at the Rutherford Laboratory on the site of the Atomic Energy Research Establishment at Harwell. We stayed in the Cozener's House at Abingdon, an old country house on the banks of the Thames, which that winter was in flood. The rain pouring from heavy skies did not dampen our spirits, for Stephen and I – and a handful of his students – were tense with excitement, anticipating a momentous occasion: Stephen was about to produce a new theory. At last he had reached a resolution of the black-hole mechanics versus thermodynamics paradox which had been troubling him since the summer school at Les Houches. He had been spurred into obsessive calculation by the vexatious doubts cast on his earlier conclusions by a Princeton student of John Wheeler's – who had been so struck by the similarity between the laws of thermodynamics and Stephen's 1971 black-hole result that he claimed that the laws of thermodynamics and the laws governing black holes were actually the same laws. In Stephen's opinion, this claim was absurd, since to obey the laws of thermodynamics, black holes would have to have a finite temperature and would have to radiate; that is to say, the two sets of laws would have to coincide in all aspects, not just one. In his resolution of the question, Stephen's elaboration was innovative beyond all expectation.

Those intense periods of total concentration, which the children and I had witnessed, had led him to the conclusion that, contrary to all previously held theories on black holes, a black hole could radiate energy. As the hole radiates, it evaporates, losing mass and energy. Proportionately its temperature and surface gravity increase as it shrinks to the size of a nucleus, still weighing between a thousand and 100 million tons. Finally, at an unimaginable temperature, it disappears in a massive explosion. Thus black holes were no longer to be considered impenetrably black and their activity could be seen to obey, rather than conflict with, the laws of thermodynamics. The long gestation of this particular infant had been cloaked in secrecy. For my part, I felt a certain vested interest in attending its birth since its rivalry for Stephen's attentions had already caused me much heartache. Bernard Carr was to act as assistant midwife, projecting a transcript of Stephen's lecture on slides to the audience.

On the morning of the lecture, I sat outside the lecture hall in the tea room, idly flicking through a newspaper while waiting for Stephen's session to begin at 11 a.m. My concentration was interrupted by the raucous chatter of a gaggle of charladies in the far corner. Their spoons clinked noisily against the side of their cups as they stirred their coffee, and their cigarettes filled the room with smoke. Irritatingly their gossip was as pervasive as the smoke from their cigarettes, and I found myself compelled to listen as they mulled over the conference and the delegates. To my bewilderment, one of them observed to her two companions, "And there's one of them there, that young chap, he's living on borrowed time, isn't he?" Momentarily I could not think whom they meant. "Oh, yes," one of her companions agreed, "a right state he's in, looks as if he's falling apart at the seams, can hardly hold his head up." She laughed a light callous laugh, amused at her own comic invention. It reminded me of a comment Frank Hawking, already white-haired and seventy years old, had once made in my hearing to the effect that Stephen was likely to die before he did. That had shaken my sense of security and then as now, the offhand condemnation of Stephen behind his back and the dismissal of our vision for the future had made me smart in silence.

When Stephen came rolling out of the lecture hall in his wheelchair, ready for a quick coffee before embarking on his lecture, I scrutinized him carefully from head to foot. He was alive certainly – alive with excitement and anticipation – but I had to ask myself if he really looked as if he were living on borrowed time, and if he were really falling apart at the seams. I had to concede that, to a casual observer, he probably did, and that concession to outside perceptions made me very sad. Fortunately such concerns could not have been further from his mind. Firmly rooted in the physical world and as unaware as Don Quixote of unkind scepticism at his appearance and purpose, he was ready to charge into battle accompanied by his faithful Sancho Panza, Bernard Carr. Still shaken, I followed them into the lecture hall. I comforted myself with the reflection that those cleaning women had only seen the pitiable state of the frail body and were ignorant of the power of the mind and the strength of the spirit, conveyed so eloquently in that imperious cranium and those fine, intelligent eyes. My conviction that Stephen was immortal was nonetheless reeling from yet another blow.

With exquisite irony, Stephen reaffirmed his immortality in that very lecture, although at the time the chairman and some of the audience gave the impression that they thought that he had taken leave of his senses. I sat on the edge of my seat as I listened to Stephen, hunched in his chair under the lights on the stage, and read the slides which Bernard brought up on the overhead projector, clarifying the substance of Stephen's faint whispering speech. In effect the lecture was given twice, once by Stephen himself and again by the slides, so there was not the slightest doubt about the message: black holes were not as black as they seemed.

Despite the clarity of the presentation, silence reigned as the lecture came to an end. The audience seemed to be having difficulty digesting that simple message. The chairman, Professor John G. Taylor, of King's College, London, did not remain silent for long however. Aghast at this heretical attack on the gospel of the black hole, he sprang to his feet, blustering, "Well, this is quite preposterous! I have never heard anything like it. I have no alternative but to bring this session to an immediate close!" His behaviour seemed to *me* to be quite preposterous, reminiscent in fact of Eddington's attack on Chandrasekhar in 1933, except that Eddington had used "absurd" rather than "preposterous" to describe Chandrasekhar's theory. Not only is it usual for a chairman to allow time for questions after a lecture, it is also a commonly accepted courtesy that he should thank the speaker for his "extremely stimulating talk". J.G. Taylor (not to be confused with Professor J.C. Taylor, the particle physicist who, with his wife Mary, was to become a close friend some years later) extended neither of these courtesies to Stephen; rather he gave the impression that he would willingly have had him burnt at the stake for heresy. This conscious insult to Stephen was as intolerable as the cleaning ladies' mindless remarks. It implied a deliberate attempt to belittle him, suggesting that he had now proven himself to be incapacitated mentally as well as physically.

Whereas in the lecture hall one could have heard a pin drop, in the refectory after the lecture there was uproar. It was as if particles from radiating black holes were spinning in all directions, knocking the delegates sideways like skittles. Bernard settled Stephen quietly at a corner table while I went to queue at the counter for food. Still blustering and indignantly muttering to his students, J.G. Taylor stood behind me in the queue, unaware of my identity. I was rehearsing a few cutting remarks in Stephen's defence when I heard him splutter, "We must get that paper out straight away!" I thought better of drawing attention to myself and went to report what I had heard to Stephen. Although he shrugged in a good-humoured way, he sent his own paper off to *Nature* immediately on our return to Cambridge. Since it was reviewed for the magazine by none other than J.G. Taylor, it was no surprise that it was rejected. Stephen then requested that it should be sent to an independent referee and, on the second time of asking, it was accepted. J.G. Taylor's paper was also accepted but died a natural death, while Stephen's marked the first step along the road towards the unification of physics, the reconciliation of the large-scale structure of the universe with the small-scale structure of the atom – through the medium of the black hole. Undoubtedly the Rutherford experience served also to reinforce Stephen's determination to fight against all odds, whether physical or in physics. The same experience left me proud but perturbed by the many hidden undercurrents it had revealed. The theory of the evaporation of black holes paved the way for Stephen's election to the Royal Society the following spring at the unprecedentedly early age of thirty-two. In the seventeenth century Fellows had been elected as young as twelve years old, but that was in the days when privilege rather than merit ensured election. In the more recent past a Fellowship was an honour to which scientists aspired towards the end rather than the beginning of their careers, usually after acquiring a handful of honorary doctorates and serving on a few advisory scientific committees along the way. It is the crowning glory of a scientific career, second only in prestige to a Nobel Prize.

We were informed of the election in mid-March, a couple of weeks in advance of the official announcement, giving me time to arrange a surprise celebration. I planned a champagne reception in the dignified setting of the Senior Parlour in Caius, to which Stephen's family, friends and colleagues were invited, and I prepared a buffet dinner for a smaller, more intimate group of family and friends at home afterwards. There was no more fitting occasion on which to open the two bottles of Château Lafitte 1945 which had appeared a couple of years back on the Caius Fellows' wine list at the remarkable – though erroneous – price of forty-five shillings a bottle. The number of guests for the dinner party was limited therefore not by the capacity of the house nor by the amount of crockery we possessed, but by the quantity of extremely rare old claret in the two bottles, just enough for everyone to have a taste.

On the evening of 22nd March 1974, Stephen's students diplomatically steered him in the direction of the College where he was cheered as a conquering hero by friends and family, students and colleagues. The children did their best to pass round plates of canapés, caviar toasts, vol-au-vents and the miniature smoked salmon and asparagus rolls in which the Caius catering department excelled. Dennis Sciama agreed to propose the toast to Stephen and this he did very generously, listing all Stephen's many scientific achievements which, he said, would have more than justified his faith in him without this culminating honour of the Fellowship of the Royal Society. The children and I stood together in a glow of pride.

It was Stephen's turn to reply. It was a measure of the change in him since our marriage that he was well accustomed to making speeches in public these days but, of course, on this occasion the party had come as a surprise and he had had no chance to prepare what he was going to say. He actually made quite a long speech, speaking slowly and clearly, though faintly. He talked about the course of his research and the unexpected way in which it had developed over the past ten years or so, since coming to Cambridge. He thanked Dennis Sciama for his support and inspiration, and he thanked his friends for coming to the party, talking as was his habit always in terms of "I" not "we". With my arms round each of the children, I waited at the side of the room for him to turn towards us with a smile, a nod, just a brief word of recognition for the domestic achievements of the nine years of our marriage. It may have been a mere oversight in the excitement of the moment that he did not mention us at all. He finished speaking to general applause, while I bit my lip to conceal my disappointment.

In the very week of the publication of the Royal Society Fellowship list, Stephen received an approach – no doubt instigated by Kip Thorne – from Caltech, the California Institute of Technology in Pasadena, inviting him to take up the offer of a visiting Fellowship for the following academic year. The offer was lavish in the extreme. Quite apart from a salary on an American scale, it included a large, fully furnished house rent-free, the use of a car and all possible aids and appurtenances, including an electrically powered wheelchair to allow Stephen maximum independence. Physiotherapy and medical care would be arranged for him, and schooling for the children. Stephen's students, Bernard Carr and Peter De'Ath, were also invited to accompany him. We needed a change, a change that would bring us a renewal of commitment, a new perspective and a fresh impetus. A change would be good for the children, too, and this was an appropriate time to make it. Lucy had not yet started school and Robert would be moving out of the state system the following year. The offer from the Americans, who espoused our cause with generosity and imagination, was even more opportune – and our situation in Cambridge much more precarious – than we realized. Years later a close friend reported to me a scene witnessed at a somewhat frosty dinner party in Cambridge in that period in the early Seventies. To the surprise of that dinner guest, Stephen's likely fate was indicated in a remark delivered with consummate indifference by a senior don. "As long as Stephen Hawking pulls his weight, he can stay in this university," the speaker announced, "but as soon as he ceases to do that, he will have to go…" Luckily for us we were able to go of our own volition, not quite sure of what the future would hold, but in the event, we were actually to be invited back a year later.

If an opportunity to exchange the icy chill of the fen winds for the warm deserts of southern California was to be welcomed, the obstacles associated with such an enterprise could not be lightly dismissed. Weighing up the advantages against the disadvantages preoccupied me most. Whereas Stephen might well have mastered the fifteen-thousand-million-year history of the universe, my vision of the future had become restricted only to the foreseeable perspective of the next few days. I had learnt not to speculate on a more distant future, or plan for two, five, ten or twenty years hence. However the next eighteen months demanded careful consideration, especially in the light of my past chaotic experiences on the west coast of America. I steeled myself to confront my personal problem, the fear of flying. At least this time I should not have to abandon my children because they, of course, would be coming with us – but that, in a changed perspective, was the least of my anxieties. Far more worrying was the question of how I was going to manage to travel a third of the way across the world, solely responsible for Stephen in his very debilitated state, as well as for the children. Secondly how should I cope for a whole year, entirely alone, with neither parents nor neighbours on hand to help in time of crisis? Frequently in the past couple of years when I had been laid low with flu, headaches, backache and even pleurisy, I had been able to rely on my mother or the Thatchers to come and help. No such help would be forthcoming in California.

In addition, one of the most perplexing stumbling blocks for some time had been Stephen's absolute rejection of any outside help with his care. He staunchly refused to accept any help, apart from snippets of advice from his father, which might suggest either an acknowledgement of his condition per se or of the fact that it was deteriorating. This attitude, together with his refusal to mention the illness, was one of the props which underpinned his courage and was part of his defence mechanism. I well understood that if once he admitted the gravity of his condition his courage might fail him. I well understood, too, that the mere struggle to get out of bed in the morning might defeat him if he gave any thought to his plight. How I wished that he, for his part, could understand that just a little help to relieve me of some of the severe grinding physical strain which was stifling my true optimistic self might contribute to an improvement in our relationship.

My doctor had listened to my troubles and had conferred with Stephen's doctor. Together they had tried to initiate a rota of domiciliary male nurses to lift Stephen in and out of the bath at least a couple of times a week. This embryonic plan was aborted soon after it was conceived, because the pleasant but elderly male nurse was able to come only at five o'clock in the afternoon, and such an abrupt interruption or conclusion to his working day was, understandably, anathema to Stephen. Only a miracle could resolve the problems we faced. However, that Easter a miracle of an idea floated into my mind like a thistledown seed gliding to earth. It lightened my step and removed my anxieties at the impracticability of well-meaning attempts from the other side of the world to offer us a welcome change of scene. The idea was quite simple: we should invite Stephen's students to live with us in our large Californian house. We could offer them free accommodation in return for help with the mechanics of lifting, dressing and bathing. This was all the more essential since Stephen was no longer able to feed himself at all and needed a constantly watchful eye. With assistance from Bernard, he would not be humiliated by the unmentionable indignity of having to receive help from nurses – which he considered a detrimental step, an acceptance of the deterioration in his condition – but would be assisted by people from his own circle, if not family then at least friends, part of the household. Stephen's first reaction to the idea was automatic rejection, but when he had had time to think about it and realized that the fate of the Californian venture might hang on his decision, he changed his mind. I broached the idea to Bernard Carr and then to Peter De'Ath who, after due consideration, agreed that it would suit all parties very nicely.

There remained one major function to be fulfilled that summer: Stephen's admission to the Fellowship of the Royal Society on Thursday 2nd May. We set off from Cambridge in good time for lunch at Carlton House Terrace, the fine eighteenth-century headquarters of the Royal Society overlooking the Mall. As we approached north London, the car began to lurch uncontrollably and the steering became heavier and heavier. We had no alternative but to press on with the journey, hoping against hope that we would be able to reach our destination. At last, tugging the resistant steering wheel round, I turned with relief into the forecourt of Carlton House Terrace, there to embark on the well-rehearsed sequence of searching out the usual bevy of elderly porters, heaving the various parts of the wheelchair out of the car, assembling them, stationing the chair by the passenger seat and then lifting Stephen under the arms and swinging him round from his car seat into the chair. Then the porters had to be instructed in the careful lifting of the chair up the inevitable flight of steps to the main entrance. This time the sequence was more complicated because the car as well as Stephen needed attention: the front nearside tyre was flat.

As on many occasions, help came from the least expected quarter. It was the secretary of the Royal Society himself – a man of few words, flustered with the demands of the important guests and the significance of the occasion, for all of which he was responsible – who got down on his hands and knees, dressed in his smart dark grey suit, and changed the wheel for us while, unawares, we were being regally entertained to a formal luncheon by another Cambridge scientist, the President of the Royal Society, Sir Alan Hodgkin. The admission took place in the early afternoon amid much ceremonial in the lecture theatre. Speeches were made introducing each new Fellow who then stepped onto the platform to sign the admissions book. When Stephen's turn came, a hush descended on the audience and the book was brought down from the podium for his signature. He inscribed his name slowly and carefully to a tense silence. His final flourish was greeted by a burst of rapturous applause, which brought a jubilant smile to his face and tears to my eyes.

Stephen was not the only Cambridge scientist to be honoured that year, nor yet the only physicist from the Department. John Polkinghorne, the Professor of Particle Physics, was also being admitted to the Fellowship of the Royal Society on the same occasion. Having reached the apogee of his career in science, he was on the point of giving up physics to take up theology; that is to say, from being Professor Polkinghorne FRS, he was about to become an undergraduate again, embarking on the long haul of study for ordination, curacy and parish, with the particular motivation of healing the schism between science and religion which had originated with Galileo. In his opinion, science and religion were not in opposition but were two complementary aspects of one reality. This thesis would become the theme of his writings as a priest-scientist. Although we did not know him well, I admired his conviction and was greatly encouraged to find that atheism was not an essential prerequisite of science, and not all scientists were as atheistic as they seemed.

Part Three

1

"Oh, hi! My name is Mary Lou and I live in Sierra Madre. And who are you? Where are you from?" The speaker, a slight, tanned figure, invited our reply with a broad smile. As we had only just arrived at the party, hosted by some English expatriates, a week or so after landing in Los Angeles, we were not yet accustomed to such directness. There was a long pause while we overcame our surprise and realized that an equally spontaneous reply was expected. After all, it had taken the best part of ten years for us to be recognized at parties in Cambridge, and even then the approach was always tinged with a certain diffidence. Of late some of the senior Fellows – and more especially their wives – had regularly shown a benevolent interest in us, but over the years we had become used to sitting trapped at the ends of tables, or in corners on our own, never really expecting anyone to speak to us, always pleasantly surprised if during the course of the evening we happened to encounter a friendly face. Indeed one of the kitchen managers had once confided in me that it was difficult to place us at table at College feasts because no one really wanted to sit with us. Small wonder, then, that we were unprepared for Mary Lou's initiative. Her exuberance was infectious and I attempted to convey our elation at all things Californian in my letters home to our families and friends, as for instance in my first letter to my parents, written in the days before regular phone contact was financially feasible:

535 South Wilson Avenue
Pasadena, CA 91106
USA

30th August, 1974

Dear Mum and Dad,
This is so exciting! The flight was very long, but very straight-
forward by comparison with the last time we flew over the Pole
when Robert was a small baby. Like a born traveller retracing
his steps, Robert was entranced by the scenery, black peaks

growing out of snowfields, mountains rising out of a frozen sea where occasional waterholes glowed deep emerald in the ice, white specks of icebergs in Hudson Bay, then the deserts of America, the Salt Lake and finally the coastal mountains. In contrast, when we were high over the Atlantic, Lucy, quite unimpressed by the adventure, asked if we were on the ground yet...

We all revived on landing, although it was about 2 a.m. (your time), and were wide-eyed at the sight of so much that was new and unfamiliar – palm trees, huge cars, our own gleaming station wagon in which Kip came to meet us, freeways weaving in and out of the city in all directions, skyscrapers and, ultimately, the house with its white weatherboarding, looking much prettier than in the photos. It was dusk when we arrived and there was a light in every window – a Disney fantasy come true! It is as elegant inside as it is pretty out. And so comfortable! Huge sofas that you just sink into and bathrooms everywhere, all colour-coordinated, of course! Everything is brand new, all the imitation-antique furniture, the towels, the china, even the saucepans! These people must think that we are used to an astronomical standard of living. If only they knew! From the kitchen sink I can look out onto mountains, while Stephen is actually closer to his office than in Cambridge because the house is right opposite the campus. Like a small boy with a new toy, he is excitedly learning to manoeuvre his electric wheelchair, the same as the one he has at the Institute only much faster. It's years since he has had such freedom of movement, though the chair has to be lifted over kerbs and steps, which is a bit of a problem since kerbs are very high here as no one ever walks out in the street and the frame is very heavy. The two solid gel batteries each weigh a ton, not to mention the occupant. We have had engineers here all day attending to the wheelchair and making adjustments to all the other appliances. Nothing it seems is too much trouble.

The garden is rather bare and is tended by a team of gardeners, who came with shears, brooms and a vacuum cleaner. They cut back, tidy up and hoover the lawn, but would never recognize a weed if it stared them in the face. The grass needs a great deal of water, which comes up from an underground irrigation system – no need for hosepipes or watering cans. It's all so exotic! The first morning we stepped out onto the patio *to find a hummingbird hovering by a weird-looking plant, with spiky orange and blue flowers. All around the house are camellia bushes the size of trees and by the patio there is a huge Californian dry oak, just waiting to be climbed. Round the edge of the garden we have an orange tree in bloom and in fruit at one and the same time, two avocados, a fir tree and a small palm. So far, as it is so hot, we have eaten all our meals on the patio – just as well since the dining room is so beautiful with its plush red carpet and its mahogany table, we hardly dare step inside the door, let alone eat there.*

The children and I went for a bathe in the Caltech pool this afternoon. Lucy fell in and did not like it at all. She is regarded as terribly backward since at three she cannot swim, but Robert will be swimming within the week; at present he swims underwater. We are all so dazed with healthy, happy tiredness that Lucy has gone to sleep in front of the television, (novelty though it is, we hardly ever watch it because of the interminable adverts) and even Robert shows signs of dozing off. I think I may be asleep before him even so.

Much love, Jane

My father was due to retire from the Ministry of Agriculture on his sixtieth birthday in December 1974 after a long and dedicated career, and he and my mother planned to celebrate his retirement by coming out to stay with us in California. In the meantime we had a constant stream of visitors, some of whom stayed for a weekend or so while others, like Peter De'Ath, Stephen's PhD student, took up residence and helped Bernard with Stephen's care, until he found his own accommodation. I grew more confident at driving and did not find shopping for so many visitors a strain, because all the purchases were neatly packed into brown paper (not plastic) sacks and carried out to the car for me by smiling assistants. Moreover Robert – aged seven – was a brilliant navigator: he seemed to carry the freeway map in his head and, unlike his father, told me where to turn off well in advance.

On the children's first morning at the Pasadena Town and Country School, I delivered them somewhat apprehensively to the school gate, then at noon I returned to pick up Lucy from the nursery department and joined the car queue of waiting mothers, sidling round the block in their automobiles. As I edged to the school gate, I gave her name to the teacher standing guard on the pavement and he hailed her over the loudspeaker: "Loossee Hokking, Loossee Hokking!" he bellowed. No one came forwards and there was no sign of Loossee Hokking among the crowd of small children waiting patiently inside. A great commotion ensued. Could Loossee Hokking have been kidnapped – the worst fear of the school – on her first day? The place was in chaos. I parked the car and went in. The Principal came running out of her office and a bevy of middle-aged ladies scattered in all directions in frantic search of the lost infant. Loossee Hokking was not hard to find. She had liked school so much that she had taken herself off to lunch and was intending to stay until two-thirty. Thereafter she came out of school, sometimes temperamentally, a bit the worse for wear, as it was a long day for a three-year-old.

The children found a new friend in Shu, the eight-year-old son of our Japanese neighbours, Ken and Hiroko Naka, who had lived for some time in Cambridge before moving to the United States. Ken was a biologist, specializing in catfish eyes, some sort of scientific oddity closely resembling the human eye. The Nakas not only took Robert and Lucy to school every morning after that first day, they also planned all sorts of expeditions to fun parks and beaches for the three children. As I found out when I collected the children from school in the afternoon, Shu's conversation was peppered with computer jargon. While Lucy babbled on irrepressibly, Shu conducted his own monologue at which Robert nodded knowingly; doubtless attracted by this, his first introduction to information technology, the science that would eventually become his career. Delighting in his new-found independence, Stephen also secretly rejoiced in being the star of the campus – where he sat in an air-conditioned office all day. Ramps appeared everywhere on campus as well as in the driveway to the house. He had his own secretary, Polly Grandmontagne, and a regular physiotherapist, Sylvie Teschke, whose husband, a Swiss watchmaker, was anxiously anticipating the end of his livelihood with the advent of quartz watches. Bernard Carr, Stephen's student, began to settle into the routine of our household, unfailingly cheerful despite his somewhat erratic regime, which consisted of helping me put Stephen to bed at night then going out to parties, after which he would sit up till the early hours watching horror movies on account, he said, of his insomnia – and then he would sleep till lunchtime. Once I went upstairs to rouse him in the middle of the morning and found him sleeping soundly with his body in the bed and his head on the floor!

That autumn Mary Thatcher came on a tour of the United States, to lecture on her newly released film archive of the lives of the British in India. Like all our visitors we took her to the local attraction, the Huntington Gardens and Gallery, founded by Mr Huntington who had made his money on the railways and married his aunt to keep it in the family. Her portrait suggests that he paid a rather heavy price for the privilege, but the accumulation of wealth enabled him to purchase Constable's *View on the Stour*, various Chaucerian manuscripts and the Gutenberg Bible among other notable works for his Gallery, as well as establishing a beautiful garden. The garden was divided into fascinating specialized geographical and botanical areas: a viciously prickly desert-cactus garden, an Australian area with eucalyptus trees but no kangaroos, a jungle area, row upon row of camellias, a Shakespearean knot garden, a classical Japanese garden complete with bridge, tea house, and gongs, and a mysteriously philosophical Zen garden – mostly raked gravel dotted about with a few significantly sited rocks. In fact some of the best of European art was to be found within easy reach. If it were not in the Huntington Gallery, it would be in the Pasadena Museum of California Art, the J. Paul Getty Museum at Malibu, or Hearst Castle on the way up to San Francisco. Sometimes I felt quite sentimental if not a little homesick on seeing European art, particular the Constable, in the brash brightness of California. There was little room for those subtleties of life that we knew so well, the grey skies, the respectable shabbiness, the crumbling buildings, the diffidence, the snobbery. The Californian skies, the colours, the landscape, the people, their behaviour and their use of language I found starkly well-defined, honest and devoid of nuance. As for the food, it was gargantuan, but so stuffed with additives that we were glad to be able to grow some of our own fruit. Fifty-two avocado pears fell off the tree one weekend in October when we were away in Santa Barbara. We hurriedly picked them all up on our return and stored them in the bottom of the fridge to save them from the weekly cleansing operation by the gardeners.

That November I wrote to warn Mum and Dad what to expect.

Dear Mum and Dad,

We are so much looking forward to seeing you in just a couple of weeks but I hope you will be able to stand the pace here. Don't come to California for a rest! We live in a constant social whirl. As our house is the largest and closest to the campus, it has become the venue for the Relativity Group's entertaining this year. Kip and Linda have a lovely old Spanish-style villa up in Altadena but that is some way out of town and the area around them is so thick with thieves that as soon as they buy anything new, it disappears. The same goes for any cars parked in the street. So we have some of the parties here instead, cocktail parties, dinner parties, evening drinks parties – not to mention Lucy's birthday party to which she insisted on inviting the whole class plus teachers... Soon we shall be cooking a turkey for Thanksgiving. I don't know how many people will be coming but I'm leaving the traditional trimmings like pumpkin pie to the Americans who know how to do those things. There's no accounting for some of their tastes anyhow. Some people came to dinner last week and I served them a beef casserole. To my amazement they added autumn strawberries from a bowl on the table to their plates of stew!

You will meet our new friends too, especially the other Fairchild Fellows in Stephen's field, the Dickes and the Israels. Bob and Annie Dicke from Princeton are very much like you. He is intellectual and an excellent pianist, and she is warm and grandmotherly. The children and I often go to tea with her and swim in the pool at their block of flats, grandly known here as "condominiums". Did you meet the Israels from Edmonton when they came to Cambridge with their ten-year-old son Mark in 1971? They are very cosmopolitan in outlook but gentle, humorous and immensely knowledgeable, without a trace of affectation.

A special message for Chris: Robert developed toothache last week, although I had taken him to the school dentist just before we came out here, so on Thursday we went to see a dentist. California style. Potted plants, plush carpets, soft sofas and piped music greeted us. The dentist came out to talk to me after he had inspected Robert's teeth. "Well, Mrs Hokking," he began, then paused for his words to take effect, "this will be quite an investment... those young molars need remedial dentistry, stainless-steel crowns... around one hundred and eighty dollars, I would estimate…" I can imagine Chris's reaction but what choice do I have except to pay up?!

The children and I have joined the local library. Robert took out a book on the British Empire, which struck me as rather excessively patriotic, but not bad for a child who only a year ago was accused of being backward. I also have an addictive new interest thanks to another Caltech wife, Tricia Holmes. Tricia, who is Irish, has introduced me to the evening choral class at Pasadena City College. Once a week we sight-sing our way through a major choral work. I'm not a good sight-singer but it is very exciting. Last week it was Brahms's German Requiem, this week the Mozart Requiem and so on. Later in the year we shall be doing the St Matthew Passion over two weeks. The approach reminds me of the way Americans travel in Europe, a day in Paris, a day in London, two days in Venice, perhaps.

Lucy also has a special activity thanks also to Tricia Holmes, whose little girl, Lizzie, is more or less Lucy's age. Lizzie and Lucy go to ballet together, so the ballet shoes are in use again, and this time it's the real thing, no messing around with nursery rhymes and free expression, but no tears either. The teacher is young and rather seriously American. Her reservation is that she might be teaching Lucy by the wrong method… Since I last wrote we have taken in another migrant to fill up some of the space in this house. Anna Zytkov, a young Polish astrophysicist, has moved in until she can find somewhere to rent. No sooner had she arrived than I suggested a game of tennis, although I have not played in years. We had just begun to play when Anna fell over, and broke her ankle. Since then, in her immobilized state, she has built the most beautiful, fully furnished doll's house out of a large cardboard box for Lucy for her birthday. It is a real work of art, so delicately and imaginatively crafted that it makes the garish plastic artefacts that one sees in the shops look monstrously vulgar and clumsy.

We shall have a full house at Christmas. I think Anna will have left by then, but in addition to the six of us plus Bernard, George Ellis will be coming to stay for a couple of days when he and Stephen return from a conference in Dallas on the 21st, and on the 23rd, Philippa Hawking will be coming over from New York where she is working at present. We will be at the airport at 5 a.m. on the 16th to meet you! Be prepared for *all the usual end-of-term activities at the school – Robert is reciting from the Battle of Bunker Hill – and for a huge party here on the 21st.*

Much love till 16th
December, Jane

In early December, Stephen went off with his entourage to the conference in Dallas. While the children and I were alone in the house, I awoke one night to find the bed and the floor shaking beneath me. Our instructions were that we should run to the porch in the event of an earthquake, but I was too terrified to move, literally petrified. When finally I recovered my senses, I ran upstairs to see if the children were all right and was astonished to find them both sound asleep. I went back to bed, turned out the light and then it happened again. Even the aftershock was tremendous, quite unlike the little tremors that rattled windows regularly each afternoon. However, had there been earthquakes at Christmas, we probably should not have noticed them (just as Stephen failed to notice a major earthquake in Persia in 1962 because he was travelling cross-country on a bus at the time and was suffering from dysentery). Mum and Dad, George Ellis and Stephen on their return from Dallas, and Stephen's sister Philippa arrived in the middle of consecutive nights, and then we gave a party for forty or so friends and colleagues, who enjoyed themselves so much that they stayed till after 2 a.m. To prove it, we have a photo of a very distinguished elderly physicist, Willy Fowler, practising yoga on the living-room floor at 2 a.m. precisely!

Sixteen people came to Christmas dinner, which meant that the children had a ready-made audience for their conjuring show. Robert was given a conjuring set and he, with his ebullient assistant, regaled us with a winningly innocent first attempt at sleight of hand – a change from the constant diet of riddles and jokes which bemused us and kept the children in ecstasies of laughter. The contrast between his quasi-professional opening gambit – "If you want to ask questions, please ask them after the show and not before it" – and the disarray in his box of tricks, his pleasure when a trick actually worked and his suppressed irritation at his show-stealing assistant, not to mention his gaping toothless smile, were very endearing.

After Christmas and the Pasadena Parade on New Year's Day, we summoned the energy to take the family to Disneyland for a day. The queues were long and the children managed to ride on only two attractions each. We did have a good vantage point for the lavishly produced Disneyland parade though, but even that was a bit of a disaster because it was Lucy's misfortune to be offered an apple by the Wicked Witch in the Snow White section. She was so terrified that she hid behind my skirts. Then early in the New Year we drove over to Death Valley, the desert park, 300 miles to the north-east. It was a great relief to have my parents with me to share the driving, to help with loading Stephen and the wheelchair – not to mention the batteries – into the car, and to keep the children entertained while I attended to Stephen. We were awed by the weird primeval landscape, a giants' playground where the Valley floor is littered with sand dunes here, volcanic craters there, and scree and sand-coloured rock protuberances everywhere. Vast salt flats below sea level are all that remain of a deep ice-age lake. On all sides the Valley is enclosed by rugged snowcapped mountains, which in their many-hued stratifications bear witness to enormous geological upheavals in the dawn of time. In summer Death Valley is said to be the hottest desert in the world and is almost barren of vegetation: only cacti, desert holly and the creosote plant survive among its hostile rocks and stones, and only the tiny, prehistoric pupfish can withstand the extreme saltiness of its few shallow creeks. Constantly changing colour with the movement of the sun, the landscape is magnificent but not beautiful. The sorry tales of the pioneers who tried to cross the Valley in 1849 and the ghost-town remnants of the gold prospectors' dreams, together with the sterility and silence of the place, invest it with a menacing and forbidding atmosphere. My mother remarked how dynamic, tough and persevering those pioneers must have been and added that we shouldn't be surprised to find those same qualities in modern Californians, especially the women, the descendants of those pioneers.

We came home to a nice surprise. We had already organized a small farewell party for my parents, so it was a happy coincidence that on the same occasion we could celebrate the award, to Stephen and Roger Penrose, of the Eddington Medal by the Royal Astronomical Society. It was all very prestigious but we were not really sure what it signified, as the announcement came as a complete surprise. Nevertheless, it did have the effect of reminding Stephen to pay his overdue subscription. Lucy was determined to go back to England with her grandparents and packed her suitcase specially. She was so indignant when the plane took off without her that we had to make a quick dash to the nearest Kentucky Fried Chicken outlet to calm her down.

Martin Rees – now President of the Royal Society and Master of Trinity College, Cambridge, but back in 1975 simply one of our best, most unpretentious and kindest friends – had agreed to cast our votes that spring in the referendum on British entry to the Common Market. It was probably a complete waste of his time as Stephen's vote most certainly cancelled out mine. (Stephen had a habit of doing this in elections.) To my way of thinking, from California Britain appeared as a small offshore European island, which would do well to settle down to its rightful place within the Common Market instead of dwelling on past glories and lost greatness. Fortunately this is just what happened, despite Stephen's attempt to sabotage my vote.

Stephen meanwhile was getting up to all sorts of mischief. As a sort of insurance policy, he bet Kip Thorne that the constellation Cygnus X-1 did *not* contain a black hole, because he felt he would need some consolation in the form of four years' subscription to *Private Eye* if that actually proved to be the case. Kip for his part was content with just one year's subscription to *Penthouse* magazine if, as seemed likely, Cygnus X-1 did contain a black hole. Otherwise, Stephen was making contacts with particle physicists, which meant that his interests were moving way beyond the event horizon into the heart of the black hole. He was attending lectures by two eminent particle physicists, Richard Feynman and Murray Gell-Mann, whose gentlemanly behaviour towards each other concealed an arch rivalry. Stephen was present when Feynman turned up at the first of a course of lectures by Gell-Mann. Noticing Feynman in the audience, Gell-Mann announced that he would be using his lecture series to conduct a survey of current research in particle physics and proceeded to read from his notes in a monotone. After ten minutes, Feynman got up and left. To Stephen's great amusement, Gell-Mann then heaved a sigh and declared, "Ah, good, now we can get on with the real stuff!" and proceeded to talk about his own recent research at the cutting edge of particle physics.

Winter was scarcely noticeable, though it rained hard, sometimes for two or three days at a time. Then the sun would shine again in an azure sky and the clouds would clear from the mountains, revealing the splendour of the peaks sparkling with fresh snow.

The rain suddenly brought spring to the canyons which, so brown when we first arrived, were now green and lush, while the roadsides and cliffs by the beach rippled with wild flowers: orange poppies, blue lupines, sunflowers and daisies. We did not let the rain interfere with our activities. On George Washington's birthday in February, we went out for a drive and came back several hours later having driven 350 miles, the longest distance I have ever driven in one day. We climbed up through the swirling icy mists of Palomar Mountain to the world's largest telescope, and then crossed the scorching dryness of the Anza-Borrego Desert, where masses of flowers were coming into bloom. When Stephen's mother and his Aunt Janet came to stay in March, we piled into the car and went off to the Joshua Tree National Park, a high desert area above 3000 feet, where the Joshua Tree produces its lily-like flowers. At a lower elevation, there is a forest of cacti appropriately called "jumping chollas". One of them jumped at me, implanting its barbs in my leg, a rather mean thing to do on my birthday I thought, especially as the children had already sat on my birthday cake in the back of the car. Aunt Janet's medical expertise came to the rescue – of my leg, not the cake.

In April, Stephen received the Pope Pius XI Gold Medal for science at a full session of the Pontifical Academy. It seemed that the notion of the Big Bang as the point of creation appealed to the Vatican, and at last Galileo had found a champion when Stephen in his address to the assembly made a special plea for the rehabilitation of Galileo's memory – three hundred and thirty three years after his death.

While Stephen was away in Europe, the children, Annie Dicke and I took the boat across a very choppy sea to Catalina Island. In those days the island was a gem, unspoilt and free of traffic, but what impressed us most was the trip we took in a glass-bottomed boat. The sight of the tranquil, gleaming world of the seabed, where seaweed grew to a height of twenty feet and fish, unaware of our presence, darted with a quicksilver grace between its branches, held us spellbound. I wondered how we could be so ignorant of the silent beauty and mystery of that other world which was literally at our feet and on our shores. When I revisited Catalina Island in 1996, the island had lost its pristine beauty and was as polluted under the surface of the ocean as it was on land. That change was to be a potent image of the way our lives had changed in the interim.

As that year in California drew to a close, I sensed that although it had been positive and exhilarating in so many ways, it had begun to define a widening fault line between our shining public image and our darkening private face. It also brought me sharply up against my own limitations. At three years old, Lucy might have been a backward swimmer, but apparently I was a really retarded mother. In America in the early days of women's lib, a woman who did not have a job by the time her child was two was regarded as a miserable failure, inevitably lacking in "personal fulfilment". So I threw myself headlong into a crazy round of activity. The endless stream of visitors, the frantic socializing, books from the library and, of course, the children, kept me more or less occupied, distracting my mind from the dispiriting effect that life on the edge of the Caltech vortex had on anyone who was not an international scientific genius. Caltech, the temple where devotees came to worship at the altar of science, particularly physics, excluded all else. The Wives' Club struggled valiantly to entertain spouses with trips to places like the J. Paul Getty Museum and the occasional concert or play in the theatre, but there were quite a lot of unhappy, disaffected wives, demoralized by their husbands' total obsession with science.

I managed to avoid being swallowed up by the Caltech abyss, but nevertheless it caused me to question my own situation. One weekend in Santa Barbara, while Stephen was engaged in endless discussions with his colleague Jim Hartle, I sat on the beach, wrapped up against the icy wind, gazing out to sea while the children played. As I ran the loose sand through my fingers, I asked myself where my life was going. What did I have to show for my thirty years? I had the children, "my blessings" as dear Thelma Thatcher would say, and Stephen. Certainly proud of his extraordinary achievements, I didn't really feel that I shared in his success – yet everything that happened to him was crucial to me, whether an honour, sparkling with fame and glory, or one of those life-threatening choking fits seizing him unawares. I loved him for his courage, his wit, his sense of the ridiculous and the absurd, and that wicked charisma which enabled him – and still enables him – to twist most people, including me, round his little finger. So I was achieving what I set out to do – to devote myself to Stephen, giving him the chance of fulfilling his genius. But in the process I was beginning to lose my own identity. I could no longer count myself a Hispanist or even a linguist, and I felt that I did not command respect anywhere, in California or in Cambridge. Perhaps all the frenzied socializing and entertaining was really just my Freudian way of saying, "Please notice me too!"

It was in California that for the first time ever we met a family in similar circumstances to our own. The Irelands, David, Joyce and John, lived over in Arcadia, only a few miles from Pasadena. Like Stephen, David was a scientist by training. He studied and taught maths. Confined to a wheelchair, he was also severely disabled with a neurological illness and could do little for himself. Very positive in attitude, Joyce was an organized, energetic person and had married David in the full knowledge of his illness. Stephen was very nervous about meeting the Irelands and I felt for him in his anxiety, wanting to protect him – but though he was clearly shaken by David's condition, he managed to put on a cheerful smile and together we kept up the bright façade of normality. I wondered what the Irelands thought of us. They may have admired our determination but the façade would not have fooled them. They knew too much about the battles and the struggles.

In many respects their battles mirrored ours, but there was a fundamental difference between us. The difference was that their approach to David's illness was quite open – open with themselves and open to the outside world, not concealing the difficulties and the pain behind a brave smile. David consigned that spirit of frankness to a book, written to introduce himself to his son, John, in case he died before John was born or before John was old enough to know him. *Letters to an Unborn Child* is a very honest self-portrait and a moving account of the battles that David and Joyce underwent. It also recounts a journey in self-awareness, as David's confronts his major failing, the concealment of his true self behind a popular, jovial exterior. Through his eventual work as a counsellor, David discovered an enhanced faith in the love of God, a personal, unconditional love, outside the realms of time and space, and through this he could face the future without fear or bitterness. David's book taught me that my tearful frustrations, even the bouts of anger I felt at thoughtlessness and lack of consideration, usually when I was tired beyond endurance, were all valid emotions since, in David's words, "they release the poisons which sicken or kill us". Conversely, according to David, imperturbable self-control, bottling up powerful emotions and suppressing the emotions of others, is unhealthy and dangerous. I was struck by the irony of discovering these truths through the words of someone who was, if anything, even more disabled than Stephen, someone who, through his own suffering, had learnt to reach out and help other people.

One person who also reached out to other people was Ruth Hughes, the voluntary organiser at Caltech of the visitors' pound of toys and children's bikes. A refugee from the Nazis, Ruth was remarkably perceptive and concerned for me as well as for the children. She astounded me when I was introduced to her by saying that she had first seen Stephen in the Athenaeum, the Caltech Faculty Club, and while everyone else was praising his courage and brilliance – in a land where success is adored and failure deplored – she had said to herself that there must be someone equally courageous behind him or he simply would not be there. Nobody had ever said anything like that to me before and it quite threw me off my stride. Later when Stephen was awarded the Papal medal, Ruth presented me with a pearl brooch because, she said, I should be given something too.

2

Establishments

Before we left Cambridge for California in the summer of 1974, I knew that we would not return to 6 Little St Mary's Lane because the house was too small for our growing family and the stairs too perilous for Stephen. But Cambridge has very few residential properties within easy reach of the town centre, so the question of where we might move to was not easily resolved. Although our house might fetch a very reasonable price on the open market, we would never be able to afford to buy a larger, more suitable house anywhere near the Department, certainly not in the Grange Road area, where, before our marriage, Stephen had lodgings. This time however I had no qualms about approaching Gonville and Caius College, which was lapping up the reflected glory of Stephen's repeated successes and would be unlikely to treat us with the same harsh indifference that it had shown in the Sixties when we were young, unknown and struggling to make ends meet.

It transpired that the Bursar no longer dealt with the letting of College property. Luckily it had been taken over by the Revd John Sturdy, who had been appointed Dean shortly before Stephen's induction as a Research Fellow in October 1965, and who with his wife had befriended us from that time onwards, always supportive, always concerned for the children, always deeply caring. John, a studious, other-worldly Hebrew scholar of saintly appearance, was well complemented by his bustling, intensely practical wife Jill. In those early years, the Sturdys already had two children and were expecting their third baby at the same time as I was expecting Robert. Over the next fifteen years they adopted nine more from all backgrounds, colours and creeds. Jill took a degree in English, did a teacher-training course and then founded her own school to support and educate her family. At Christmas the Sturdys instituted a party in the College for the children of all members and employees, whether Fellows, kitchen staff or cleaners. John Sturdy or their eldest son, John

Christian, would dress up as Father Christmas and the children had a fine time boisterously playing musical chairs round High Table.

I was sure that I could count on John's sympathy. Even so, his speed of response was surprising. "Have you thought about where you would like to live?" he asked – as if the range of choice was unlimited – when we met to discuss the prospects in June 1974. Thinking my request to be rather hopeless, I sighed, "Somewhere in the Grange Road area, I suppose." "Well," he replied calmly, "let's go and look at the properties in that area and see if there is anything suitable for you." We looked at half-a-dozen houses, formerly family homes that now belonged to the College, on the west side of Cambridge, on the fringes of the Victorian village of Newnham. Some were too distant from the Department for Stephen, some were too close to noisy main roads and others were not spacious enough on the ground floor for a wheelchair. There was one house however, in West Road just off the Backs, which immediately caught my attention. Solid and extensive, with a Victorian self-assurance, it stood in large gardens next door to Harvey Court, the monstrous development which had featured in *Cambridge New Architecture* way back in the Sixties. We were already well acquainted with those gardens since they had been the venue every summer for Robert's birthday parties. My mother would arrive bearing a lavishly decorated birthday cake – sometimes in the shape of a train, sometimes a car, sometimes a fort – and my father and I would organize enough games and entertainments to keep upwards of a dozen small children amused for two hours, the most taxing two hours of the entire social calendar, apart from those dedicated to Lucy's birthday party, which being in the winter was, if anything, even more challenging.

With a few modifications, the ground floor at 5 West Road could be made very suitable for us, especially because it consisted of a sufficient number of large, well-lit rooms to accommodate the whole family, plus all the other necessary facilities, still leaving space to spare for parties for all ages. It was further from the Department than Little St Mary's Lane, but not inconveniently far, and was about the same distance from the primary school that Lucy would be attending. The gardens offered scope for parties and games of all descriptions – particularly cricket, practised with the greatest reluctance at St Albans High School, but now vital to the proper upbringing of my son. The house had been vaguely threatened with demolition in the early Seventies, I remembered, when the land on which it stood had been earmarked as the possible location for a new college, Robinson College. However, the site was too small and the house was spared. And only five years or so previously 5 West Road had been a thriving family hotel, the West House Hotel, but when its lease ran out the College had taken it over for use as undergraduate accommodation. The students had been given free rein to choose their own colour schemes, and the once fine Victorian dining room now had a black ceiling and scarlet walls. This did not upset me unduly as paint was superficial and easily changed. I was much more impressed by the dimensions of the house, so at the end of our tour I opted for the West House without hesitation – and, incidentally, effectively silenced the faction in the College which wanted to demolish any building, including that house, which had been built before 1960. Negotiations proceeded without a hitch and it was agreed that, on our return from California in 1975, we would occupy the ground floor. In part exchange for the rent, the College would have the use of our own house in Little St Mary's Lane for Fellows, since the College had relaxed its rules to allow Fellows to rent accommodation.

During our absence, partition walls were erected on the staircase to screen the ground floor from the undergraduates upstairs; the newly created flat was redecorated throughout, and ramps were built at the front and at the garden doors. In directing these operations from California, I enlisted the support of a courageous young man, Toby Church, who as a student had been struck down by a paralysing illness which had deprived him of the power of speech and the use of his legs. Toby had employed his engineering expertise to adapt his environment to his needs so that he could look after himself – with a little help from nurses – and also to build his own invention, the Lightwriter, a small, laptop keyboard with a digital screen into which he could type his speech. Unfortunately, the invention was not of much help to Stephen since operating the keyboard required too much dexterity, and Toby was not particularly interested in electric wheelchairs since he was concerned to keep his arm muscles in good shape by propelling himself around under his own steam. But as my intermediary, Toby propelled himself round to West Road many times in the course of the summer of 1975. On our return from California, it was a pleasure to move into such lovely surroundings. For all the sixteen years of our occupancy, we were conscious of our good fortune in being able to live in that house. The rooms were vast and high-ceilinged, with decorative plaster cornices and delicately embossed central roses around the light fittings. The tall sash windows gave onto a true English lawn, framed with carefully chosen conifers and deciduous trees: dark, forbidding yew mingled with the light fronds of willow. A giant sequoia – a Californian redwood, evidently a sapling newly introduced to Europe when the house was built – towered above the tumbledown conservatory at one corner of the building, communing with its partner, a *Thuja plicata* or western red cedar of comparable height at the far end of the lawn. The gnarled old apple tree faithfully produced its blossoms and its crop with such abundance that every two years the ground beneath would be carpeted with an excess of cooking apples from October to December. "Not stewed apple again!" the children would chorus at the supper table while their father would grin in mischievous collusion. Eventually he decided that he was allergic to stewed fruit, but that was not an excuse that the children were allowed to get away with.

In summer we would hang a hammock, swings and climbing ropes from the branches of the apple tree and listen to the twittering of the fledgling blackbirds inside its hollow trunk. To the left of the apple tree, in full view of the living-room window, lay the gracefully curving herbaceous border with its backdrop of flowering trees and bushes, lilac, almond and hawthorn. Even in the depths of the harshest winter, the beauty of the garden was still magical. Late one night after a persistent snowfall, I peered out through the heavy curtains and shivered in wonder at the transformation of the dank, brown winter garden outside. The full moon in a cloudless sky illuminated a glistening blanket of snow, covering lawn and trees with an enchanted, dazzling purity.

In its prime, the garden must have been a splendid sight. Despite the rampant goosegrass and pervasive ground elder, it still conveyed hints of its former glory in its myriad collection of perennials. Like the trees, they must have been planted as part of an overall scheme, perhaps as much as a century ago when the house was built. I tried to supplement the efforts of the hard-pressed College gardeners with a little weeding and planting in an attempt to subdue the goosegrass. Jeremy Prynne, a colleague of Stephen's in the Fellowship and College librarian, applauded my efforts and proposed that I should be elected to the College gardening committee since, as he remarked, many of its members could not distinguish a dandelion from a daffodil. However his proposal was rejected out-of-hand because it was inconceivable that a non-Fellow, let alone a wife, should be elected to a College committee.

From the time of our arrival in the autumn of 1975, the house, like the garden, was to lend itself enthusiastically to countless parties. There were the family celebrations, the birthday parties and the Christmas dinners. There were also the duty occasions – fundraising events as I became drawn into charity work, coffee mornings and musical evenings, departmental parties, parties for the beginning and the end of the academic year, conference receptions and dinners. In summer, there were tea parties (again usually for conferences, mostly of visiting American and Russian scientists) on the lawn with cucumber sandwiches and croquet, and there were the folk-dance evenings, barbecue suppers and firework parties. Such occasions were fun and they were usually appreciated, but it was hard work since I did not receive any help with the catering until years later. It was scarcely surprising that sometimes the unofficial companions of the official guests, the hangers-on, mistook me in my working apron for a college servant, and condescendingly demanded another glass of wine or another sandwich with scant respect, not realizing that I was the hostess.

We appeared to live in privileged surroundings, but there were disadvantages. Despite our occupancy, the house remained under threat of demolition. After the completion of the renovations carried out for our benefit, only minimal maintenance work was authorized. In winter, the central heating system, based on the original Victorian radiators, was scarcely adequate when the north wind blew snow through the gaps in the ill-fitting doors and windows. At one stage the gas fires, used to supplement the radiators, were found to be emitting more fumes into the rooms than they were sending up the chimneys. The wiring consisted of an eccentric combination of modern sockets fitted onto old wires of which no one knew the provenance.

Much more alarmingly, ceilings tended to crash to the ground with disturbing regularity, even though my father, with his catastrophic history of provoking the gravitational collapse of many a ceiling, was nowhere in the vicinity. By the grace of God, the damage was never more than material. One July night in 1978 the living-room ceiling lost its key and descended with an almighty thud amid a cloud of grime and plaster dust, smashing the stereo system to smithereens in the room beneath and sending the chandelier into a spin. Fortunately we had just gone to bed and the children were sleeping safely in their rooms. Equally luckily, no one was in the bath when a little later the bathroom ceiling also came down.

Outside, the roof regularly shed its tiles. This latter hazard was rectified thanks to a timely visit by His Royal Highness the Duke of Edinburgh, Chancellor of the University of Cambridge, who came to pay Stephen a private visit in June 1982. So afraid were we that a tile might crash onto the royal pate as His Highness entered the front door that I asked for a protective screen of netting to be put round the guttering. The point was taken and, some months later, the building was reroofed. Thanks to the royal visit we also acquired new bathroom fittings.

We were not the sole residents of the house since we occupied only the ground floor. Students, who had a separate entrance, lived on the upper floors, and mice lived in the dark depths of the cellar among the equipment belonging to the University Caving Club. The mice kept their distance after Lucy acquired a predatory cat, but it was less easy to attain a satisfactory modus vivendi with the students. As individuals they were as delightfully a friendly bunch as one could hope to meet, as we discovered on those occasions when we invited them in for a drink, or met them on the lawn in the middle of the night when the intermittent fault in the fire alarm roused the whole house for no good reason. But inevitably, the students' lifestyle, their routine and their habits were often at odds with ours. At times their presence made itself felt in a more tangible form than just loud noises and bumps in the night. About once a year someone would leave the bathwater running in the student bathroom upstairs, just above our kitchen. The last time this happened, I arrived home at lunchtime with a quarter of an hour to spare before the expected arrival of some cousins of Stephen's from New Zealand. I could hear the rush of flowing water the moment I turned my key in the door and smelt a musty dankness as I crossed the hall to the kitchen. The floor was already under a layer of water and the best plates and bowls, put out ready on the worktop, were collecting dirty puddles. The cheese, tomatoes, lettuce and bread swam in warm, grey pools, as more water poured through the ceiling and trickled down the light fitting...

Such drawbacks had not yet come to our notice however when, in September 1975, my mother and I cleaned out 6 Little St Mary's Lane before handing it over to the College, and I arranged the removal of our possessions to 5 West Road. Post-California our circumstances changed dramatically. We had come back to England to living quarters which were more akin to a mini-stately home, or a Master's Lodge, and Stephen was assured of his first official post in the University, a Readership, since while we were away a rumour had circulated in Cambridge that we were considering staying in California for good. Immediately the old biblical adage about a prophet being without honour in his own country proved itself and the Readership, later to be superseded by a personal Chair, materialized. Far from wanting Stephen to go, as had been predicted once by a senior don, the University had actually been impatient for his return.

The Readership brought with it the much-needed services of a secretary – in the form of Judy Fella, who introduced a fresh vitality and an unaccustomed glamour to the drab realms of the Department of Applied Mathematics and Theoretical Physics. Judy worked for Stephen for many years with tireless loyalty and efficiency. At last there was someone to take over the administration of his official life in England, just as Polly Grandmontagne had done in California. She typed his papers, including the hieroglyphs, dealt with his correspondence, organized his conferences, arranged his travels and applied for his visas, all of which amounted to a full-time occupation since he was now much in demand with celebrity status.

America was not unique in its adulation of success. In a more discreet fashion, cloaked in a diffident respectability, the same attitude prevailed in Britain. Afraid of being outdone in the scramble to acknowledge the brilliant scientific star blazing across their horizons, successive scientific institutions took their lead from each other and awarded Stephen their most prestigious medals. On many an occasion over the course of the next few years, my parents would come over to Cambridge in time to meet the children from school while I picked Stephen up from the Department, loaded him and the wheelchair into the car, and then set off for some smart London hotel – the Savoy, the Dorchester or the Grosvenor – where the evening's presentation dinner was to take place. Sometimes we were given overnight accommodation and that eased the strain on me since I was chauffeur, nurse, valet, cup-bearer and interpreter, as well as companion-wife, all at once. When finally all the intervening hurdles between the customary tenor of life in Cambridge and the glitzy London social scene had been surmounted, we would appear, always late, decked out in evening dress – complete with the hand-tied bow tie on which Stephen insisted – in a sparkling ballroom or dining room to be greeted by the assembled ranks of the scientific intelligentsia, peers of the realm and assorted dignitaries. They were all very charming and their wives were often kindly, but to me they all seemed so old, older than my parents: they were not the sort of people I was likely to meet in the street or at the school gate where my real friends were. The same people, along with the most affected members of London's glitterati, also turned up at other notable social occasions in the scientific calendar, particularly the *Conversazioni,* the evening gatherings in summer at the Royal Society, where the rich and famous mercilessly elbowed each other out of the way in the scrum for drinks and canapés, while the exhibitors, guarding their carefully prepared displays, patiently waited for the chattering assembly to show some interest in their painstaking research.

The artificial glamour of these occasions was simultaneously entertaining and irritating. While I enjoyed myself, I was inevitably aware of the hours ahead. There would be no coachman to drive us home from London after midnight or to help get Stephen ready for bed, and the next morning we would be back in our routine. I would be dressing Stephen, feeding him his breakfast, his pills and his tea, then I would clean the house and put two or three loads of washing into the machine before peeling the onions and potatoes for the next meal. Across the road, the tower of the University Library would loom accusingly, a silent but eloquent reminder of my neglected thesis. There would be no glass slipper either, even though there might be a glistening gold medal, set on a bed of satin and velvet, to remind us that the previous evening had not been just a passing dream. Even the medals disappeared from view after a day or two. Since the house was subject to occasional, opportunistic petty theft – handbags stolen from the hall, bicycles stolen from the porch – the medals had to be consigned to the bank vault, rarely to be seen again.

3

Buried Treasure

The reality of everyday life always began the night before, when, after giving Stephen his medications and putting him to bed, I would lay out the breakfast things for the children. At long last, Robert's enthusiasm for early rising found its true purpose, since he could be trusted to get his own breakfast and supervise Lucy's as well. In the morning I would get Stephen out of bed, dress him and give him a cup of tea and his early-morning vitamins, before taking Lucy to school on the back of my bike. On my return, usually laden with shopping, I would give Stephen his breakfast and attend to his personal needs before he went to work. After the freedom he had enjoyed in California, Stephen was in no mind to put up with the frustrations of a push wheelchair and applied to the Department of Health for an electric model, the fast one, since, according to the propaganda, such appliances were available free of charge. However, the truth did not conform to the promise of the advertising. All the force of Stephen's considerable persistence and doggedness were not enough to shift the grey officials of that particular governmental department into granting his application, for fear of setting a precedent which would open the floodgates to similar applicants. They told him that he could submit another application for the three-wheeler battery-driven car, which he now lacked the strength to control, or, indeed, for an electric wheelchair – but only the slow model, designed for indoor use like the one, purchased by a philanthropic fund, he already had at the Institute. We wasted hours arguing our case for the faster chair unsuccessfully. So much for the Welfare State. It had contributed so very little to our welfare that one might suppose that its purpose was actually to prevent the disabled from working to their full capacity and, consequently, from contributing as taxpayers to the National Exchequer. A handful of vitamin pills on prescription seemed to be the best it could offer with only minimal physical, practical, moral or financial support.

We became even more dependent on family, students and friends in the daily battle to function as a family. Stephen did acquire the wheelchair he wanted – from philanthropic funds, not through the National Health Service – and, discreetly accompanied by a student, rode to work in it every morning. His route took him along the path through King's College, where aconites and snowdrops bloom in winter and daffodils in spring, across the river over the humpbacked bridge and out of the College by a side entrance, to his office in the Department on the opposite side of Silver Street. That Stephen was at last able to enjoy the basic human right to move about freely, as and when and where he chose, was not a result of any government provision or benefit, it was the result only of his own hard work and of his own success in physics.

Transport for the children was another problem. I took Lucy to school on the back of my bike every morning, but Robert's school was some distance away. Thanks to a relative newcomer to Cambridge, John Stark, Robert got to school on time. Jean and John Stark and their two children had come to Cambridge from London in the early Seventies when John took up the post of chest consultant at Addenbrooke's Hospital; they had moved into the house that Fred Hoyle had built for himself a decade earlier. John kindly picked Robert up on his way to work, and dropped him together with his own son Dan, off at the Perse Preparatory School. I returned the Starks' help by collecting the boys in the afternoon and taking Dan home. I would occasionally stay and talk to Jean while the children played. A graduate of the London School of Economics, she found the male-chauvinist attitudes prevalent in Cambridge, and the domination of all walks of life by the University, cramping and discouraging. We shared our frustration at a system which had educated us to compete with men until the age of twenty-one or twenty-two, and then had summarily consigned us to second-class status. Not for one moment did we regret our roles as wives and mothers, but we did resent the low esteem which society, particularly Cambridge society, accorded those essential roles.

It was Jean who insisted that I should take up the thesis again, though I thought it foolish even to contemplate such a hopeless enterprise. It had been a presence in my life, sometimes welcome, sometimes much resented, for nearly ten years. I had completed only one third of the whole project, although I had amassed a vast amount of material, and I could not envisage ever finishing it. The only free time at my disposal was the sparse intervening period between Stephen's departure at midday and a quick round of the shops in the early afternoon, before picking Lucy up from school at a quarter past three – two and a half hours at the most. Nevertheless, thanks to Jean's insistence – and to the extraordinary example of Henry Button, one of my father's old Civil Service colleagues who had begun his research on the German *Minnesänger* in 1934 and finished it on retirement forty years later – the prospect began to appear less ludicrous.

As the three areas and periods of my research were so clearly defined, the return to it was less challenging than I had feared. I had already documented my ideas on the earliest lyrics, the Mozarabic *kharjas*, and could now turn my attention to the second area of medieval lyrical flowering – Galicia, the north-western corner of the Iberian Peninsula. There the language was more akin to Portuguese than Castilian, and the city of Santiago de Compostela had attained international renown and commercial success on account of the shrine of St James, whose coffin, according to one local legend, was said to have been washed up on the Galician coastline in 824. By the thirteenth century the songs of the Galician troubadours had ousted the waning poetry of Provence as the favourite amusement at the Castilian court, and their composition developed into yet another of the full-scale industries of that remarkable king, Alfonso the Wise. Among many widely disparate compositions is a large group, the *cantigas de amigo,* which consist of love songs voiced by women and which contain many of the themes and features of the *kharjas* – the lovers often meet at dawn, the girl confides in a mother figure or her sisters, the lover is often absent. They also exhibit folkloric elements in their style and language, which appear to hark back to traditional antecedents. In those few hours at my disposal each day, it was my task to sift out the traditional elements from the five hundred and twelve *cantigas de amigo*, evaluate any salient stylistic and linguistic features which they shared with the *kharjas*, compare their language with that of learned classical or biblical precedents and situate them against a more general European background.

I found many similarities between the *kharjas* and the *cantigas de amigo*, which were possibly the result of Mozarabic migrations northwards, away from later waves of fanatical Arab oppression. I also found striking differences, in that the *cantigas* do not contain any of the clear-cut radiance of *kharja* imagery or any sense of urgent anticipation. The imagery derives from the natural background of the mountains and streams of the north-western corner of the Peninsula, exposed to the turbulence of the Atlantic winds, and is identified with the emotions of the protagonists. Cultured poets would have read classical and biblical allusions into this imagery of wind and waves, trees, mountains and streams, where stags come to trouble the waters. But much more persuasive in the search for the origins of this poetry is the influence of a distant pagan past, veiled in the mists of a much earlier time than the confident Christian certainties of the *kharjas*.

A girl, closely identified with the beauty and whiteness of the dawn, gets up early and goes to wash tunics in the stream, a stream dedicated perhaps to one of the ancient Celtic fertility gods or goddesses of Galicia whose stones and inscriptions still survive:

Levantou-s' a velida,
levantou-s' alva,
e vai lavar camisas
em o alto:
vai-las lavar alva.

The lovely girl arose,
the dawn arose,
and goes to wash tunics
in the stream:
the dawn goes to wash them.

In some of these dawn poems she is interrupted by the playful antics of the wind – in pagan terms, the vehicle of evil spirits – in others by the mountain stag. The stag stirring up the water is symbolic both of the lover's presence and of their passionate activity, yet conceals any explicit reference to sexuality:

Passa seu amigo
que a muit' ama;
o cervo do monte
volvia a augua

The Sixth Form at St Albans High School. I am standing second
from the right in the back row, next to Gillian Phillips on my left
and Diana King on my right.

Wedding in Trinity Hall, Cambridge, 15th July 1965. From left to right:
my grandmother, Stephen's father, my mother, my brother Chris, Stephen, me,
Rob Donovan, Stephen's mother, Stephen's grandmother, my father.

Little St Mary's Lane

Stephen with Robert,
29th May 1967.

Robert aged nine months sitting between
Stephen and my father.

Lucy's christening, December 1970.

Family excursion,
Little St Mary's Lane, 1971.

Stephen turning back the waves,
Brancaster, summer 1971.

Picnic on the Cam with my parents, Kip Thorne, Brandon, Lucette and Catherine Carter,
John and Suzanne McClenahan and unidentified scientist with back to camera.

Robert, Lucy and Inigo Schaffer at play
in Little St Mary's Churchyard 1972.

FRS, May 1974.

David Hockney drawing Stephen and Lucy
drawing Hockney, Cambridge, March 1978.

Visit of the Duke of Edinburgh,
June 10th 1981.

PhD, Albert Hall, March 1981.

Stephen, Tim and me in audience
with the Pope, Rome 1986
(courtesy of Fotografia Felici).

Companion of Honour, Buckingham Palace, July 1989.

In the new house with the children and my parents, November 1994.

At Wimpole Hall, 4th July 1997.

With Jonathan and Bill Loveless, 4th July 1997.

Tim, Lucy and me with Stephen after the presentation of the Copley Medal
at the Royal Society, 30th November 2006.

leda dos amores'
dos amores leda.

Her lover passes by
who loves her a lot;
the mountain stag
stirs the water
happy in love,
happy in love.

The appearance of the stag at the fountain as a biblical reminiscence recalls the Song of Songs and the Psalms, but, at the
popular level, it could well be a vestige of the persistent pagan
fertility rites condemned by several scandalized bishops in the
fourth and fifth centuries

Many of the poems conveyed a bleakness and a melancholy
which set them apart from the bright immediacy of the *kharjas*.
Here the obstacles to true love are fickleness, unfaithfulness and
rejection, as well as the practical realities of warfare or social
convention, and they find expression through the medium of
trees, birds and fountains. Surveying the emotional wasteland
that her life has become, the lovelorn girl calls to her negligent
lover, reminding him how the birds used to sing of their love. She
accuses him of destroying the landscape of their love through
his cruelty. The repeated refrain, *leda m' and' eu*, expresses her
longing for the happiness she has lost.

Vós lhi tolhestes os ramos en que siian
e lhi secastes as fontes en que bevian;
leda m' and' eu.

You took away the branches where they [the birds] perched
and dried up the springs where they drank;
Let me be happy.

Although the return to the thesis revived my intellectual morale,
it was lonely work, sitting at a desk in the library, surrounded
by yellowing tomes, trying to evaluate the relative importance
of each of the numerous influences which had contributed to
the composition of these poems. Stephen's attitude to medieval
studies had not mellowed with the years. In his opinion they

were still as worthless as gathering pebbles on a beach. The medieval seminar, formerly such a source of encouragement and enthusiasm, had been disbanded; my links with the Cambridge Spanish Department had never been more than tenuous, and although my mother still loyally came to look after the children on Friday afternoons, I felt out of touch with the London seminars.

The plangent voices of the *cantigas* filled my inner world and accompanied me in my solitary activities. They were with me as I went about my household chores, they occupied my mind while I sat feeding Stephen his interminable meals – diced to small morsels, spoonful by spoonful, mouthful by mouthful – and whenever an opportune moment, however brief, presented itself, I would dash to my table in the bay window of the living room and jot down a few notes, a few ideas, a few references. Yet, studying those songs, annotating them, analysing them was not enough. I passionately wanted to be able to express those emotions myself, through song, the song of any period. After my introduction to vocal music in California, I longed to be able to sing well. Vocal technique was portable, unlike the piano, and could be practised anywhere at any time, even at the kitchen sink.

Although Stephen's contempt for medieval studies was unrelenting and his devotion to grand opera, especially Wagner, continued unabated, he did, nevertheless, encourage my new interest. Just once a week he and a student would come home early to babysit, so that I could go out for an hour to an evening class in vocal technique, which was taken by a distinguished baritone, Nigel Wickens, who was both a singing teacher and a performer. His tall, erect figure was made all the more imposing by his domed cranium, and on initial acquaintance he was not a little intimidating, particularly on account of the exaggerated precision of his diction. This, however, was but one of the features of his expansive personality. Well-versed in the arts of performance, he could hold his class in awed subjection one minute – and the next send them into convulsive laughter. A veritable musical magician, Nigel would open his box of tricks every week and reveal a wealth of glittering gemstones, displaying all the shades and colours of the emotional spectrum and encapsulating the rich legacy of a succession of musical geniuses, Schubert, Schumann, Brahms, Fauré, Mozart… geniuses whose songs touched the inner self, reaching in to tap the core of the soul, expressing hopes and fears, sadness and a sense of tragedy for which words alone were inadequate. Sometimes the sadness of the songs and the ill-defined sense of longing that they evoked were so painful as to be unbearable. After a couple of classes, I knew that I wanted to learn to sing properly, to train my voice from scratch and create my own instrument.

4

A Board Game

Well-settled in the new surroundings and secure in his employment in the university, Stephen was changing direction in physics, turning his back on the macrocosmic laws of general relativity and immersing himself more and more in quantum mechanics – the laws which operate at the microcosmic level of the elementary particle, the physics of the quanta, the building blocks of matter. This change, which was a consequence both of his black-hole research and of his contacts with particle physicists in California, was beckoning him to a further quest, the search for a theory of quantum gravity which, he hoped, would reconcile Einstein's laws of general relativity with the physics of quantum mechanics. Einstein had been deeply suspicious of the theory of quantum mechanics, developed by Werner Heisenberg and Niels Bohr in the 1920s. He mistrusted the elements of uncertainty and randomness implied in that scientific breakthrough because they undermined his belief in the beautifully well-ordered nature of the universe. He voiced this dislike forcibly to Niels Bohr, telling him that "God does not play dice with the universe".

The origins of the universe had held my imagination for the whole extent of my married life and before. My mother used to point out the constellations, sparkling against the bright, unpolluted clarity of the Norfolk night sky when Chris and I were children. Still in the Seventies, terrestrial lighting was dim enough for Robert and Lucy and me to be able to look up at the night sky and marvel at the remote, spangled beauty of the glittering stars in the darkness. We could speculate about immeasurable distances and incomprehensible time spans and wonder at the genius, their father and my husband, who could transform that infinite space and time into mathematical equations and then carry those equations in his head – as if, according to Werner Israel, he was composing a whole Mozart symphony in his head. Those equations held the key to many questions about our origins and our position in the universe,

251

not least the all-important question of the nature of our role as the minuscule inhabitants of an insignificant planet revolving round an ordinary star on the outer reaches of an unremarkable galaxy. These questions appealed to my imagination, even if my knowledge of the physics and the maths was only rudimentary. In contrast, the collisions of invisible particles, especially when those particles were not only invisible but imaginary as well, did not fire my interest with the same passion as the extraordinary mental journey through billions of light years to the beginning of space and time. Nor, I have to confess, did the set of scientists with whom Stephen was now associating attract me in the least. On the whole, particle physicists were a dry, obsessive bunch of boffins, little concerned with personal contact but very concerned with their own scientific reputations. They were much more aggressively competitive than the relaxed, friendly relativists with whom we had associated in the past. They attended conferences and came to the social functions arranged on their behalf, but, apart from a handful of ebulliently jovial Russians, their personalities made very little lasting impression. In among that grey morass it was an occasional pleasure to see the faces of those cultured, articulate, charming old friends from the relativity days – the Israels, the Hartles, Kip Thorne, George Ellis, the Carters and the Bardeens.

At least the most famous quantum physicist of them all left a long lasting impression, though he was certainly taciturn. Paul Dirac, a Cambridge physicist who in the 1920s had reconciled quantum mechanics with Einstein's theory of special relativity and in 1933 had won the Nobel Prize, was regarded as a legendary figure in physics. Stephen and Brandon considered themselves as Dirac's scientific grandchildren, since their supervisor, Dennis Sciama, had himself been supervised by Dirac. I had been introduced to Dirac and his wife, Margit Wigner, the sister of a distinguished Hungarian physicist, in Trieste in 1971. It was said of Dirac that when he introduced Margit to a colleague soon after their marriage, he did not say "This is my wife" but "This is Wigner's sister". After Paul's retirement in 1968 from the Lucasian chair – Newton's chair – the Diracs had moved from Cambridge to Florida, where he became an emeritus professor. The story was told that Dirac had once watched his wife knitting a garment. When she reached the end of the "knit" row, her husband, having worked out the mathematical theory of the craft of knitting, immediately instructed her how to turn the needles and "purl" the next row.

The Diracs visited us one afternoon in Cambridge. Margit was not dissimilar to Thelma Thatcher in her aristocratic bearing. If anything, though, with her flowing auburn hair, hers was an even more irrepressible personality, unselfconscious and gifted with a natural ease of conversation which contrasted strikingly with her husband's silence. As we sat having tea on the lawn, she talked about their travels, their family and their home in Florida, and she admired the children, chatting with them freely and openly, while her husband listened and watched. Margit more than compensated for his periods of taciturnity, attributed to the pressure put upon him by his Swiss schoolteacher father, who would only allow him to speak in impeccable French as a child at home in Bristol. She often spoke for her husband, just as I often found myself acting as Stephen's mouthpiece, especially when the talk did not concern physics. Stephen and Paul Dirac were not unalike in that they were both men of few words and preferred to put their well-considered utterances either to the service of physics or to trumping an otherwise meandering discussion. But in one particular respect they differed drastically.

In the week of their stay in Cambridge, Margit Dirac rang with an invitation to the ballet at the Arts Theatre. I hesitated, knowing only too well that Stephen would not be best pleased to spend an evening watching *Coppélia* even in the company of one of the world's most famous scientists. "No, no, my dear, it's not him we are inviting!" Margit exclaimed emphatically in response to my excuses on Stephen's behalf. "Paul wants you to come with us!" Paul's wishes brooked no further hesitation. A couple of evenings later I joined them at the theatre, slightly surprised to find that Paul really was there too, for I suspected that he would share Stephen's contempt for the dance that I loved so much. I was wrong: he seemed to enjoy the performance as much as anyone else. Despite his taciturnity, he and Margit exuded a comforting reassurance, making me very welcome, and for one evening I was not obliged to do anything at all, least of all worry about whether my companions were enjoying themselves.

At home, the routine was eased when a new postgraduate student of Stephen's, Alan Lapedes from Princeton, agreed to come and live in our spare room and, like Bernard in California, help with the more onerous tasks, especially the lifting. Reserved and self-contained, Alan was an uncomplaining helper, but I was wary of exploiting his willingness, since with other colleagues he often contributed to Stephen's daily care in the Department too.

Indeed problems with Stephen's bodily comfort were now considerable, because, true to form, he refused to resort to any palliative measures and often kept us tied to the house at weekends. During the week it was a perpetual source of anxiety and frustration, despite the efforts of Constance Willis's latest assistant, Sue Smith; she tried to make him take more regular exercise, by straightening his body and helping him to walk the length of the hall, supported by one helper on each side. However much Sue, with her engaging northern sense of humour, amused Stephen by telling him all the latest gossip in her own entertaining fashion, she could never persuade him to devote any more than those two hours of her visits to his exercises each week. "Now, you will do them, won't you, just for me?" she would plead, but he would simply regale her with one of his most beguiling, sphinxlike smiles.

The fact was that since Stephen was sedentary for all his waking hours, his limbs were much wasted through illness and lack of exercise. To outsiders, the mechanical advantages of the electric wheelchair, and the independence it conferred, hid the true extent of the ravages of motor-neuron disease because he was able to get about quite freely, flitting back and forth across the river, to and from the department. Any obstacle in the way of this revolutionary vehicle, however, required the assistance, not just of one able-bodied man but two or three to lift its 120 kilograms over a steep step or up a flight of stairs. If, on the way to an evening out together, we encountered a single step, we were in trouble.

Unlike me, Stephen, surprisingly, was not usually prey to the numerous minor ailments which the children brought home from school. He maintained a healthy appetite and a robust constitution, priding himself on never missing a day's work. Outsiders could have no concept, though, of how painfully emaciated his body had become, nor did they generally witness those horrendous choking fits which would come on at supper time and last well into the night, when I would cradle him in my arms like a frightened child, till the wheezings subsided and his breathing slipped into the easy rhythm of sleep. We tried to avoid these fits by experimenting with different diets, at first eliminating sugar, and then dairy products and finally gluten, the sticky protein in flour which binds bread and cakes. They were all suspected of irritating the hypersensitive lining of the throat. Although the children and I continued to eat bread and cakes, and cooking without sugar was not difficult, the challenge of gluten-free cookery in the 1970s – long before the advent of "free from" products on supermarket shelves – required some major adjustments in the kitchen since gluten-free flour in those days was a culinary nightmare. Even so, that challenge was infinitely preferable to those terrible life-threatening attacks of choking.

Just as we thought that we had escaped the worst of the winter's ills, the spring of 1976 lay in wait with a series of cruel tricks which made of it an obstacle course akin to a snakes-and-ladders board, though with many more snakes than ladders and with the dice weighted to land on the snakes. On 20th March the first small snake on the board snapped us up when Lucy fell ill with chickenpox. This unremarkable though uncomfortable ailment was certainly better disposed of in early childhood than at the age of twenty, as I knew from my own experience as a student in Valencia. By the following Monday, 22nd March, poor little Lucy was miserably red with spots, crying for all the attention I could give her by day and by night. As far as the chickenpox was concerned, we were no different from any other family with young children, but there the similarity ended. It was fortunate that Lucy made a speedy recovery during the course of that week, since the next throw of the dice was to send us hurtling down a much more precipitous snake.

On the Saturday morning at the end of that week, we all awoke with sore throats, and the next day both Alan and Stephen were distinctly unwell. The inflamed throats were accompanied by a high fever. Inherently mistrustful of the medical profession, still resentful of their shabby treatment of him in 1963 at the time of diagnosis, and as phobic about hospitals as I was about flying, Stephen forbade me to call a doctor even though he was neither able to eat nor drink and was coughing on every breath. Later the next day, in desperation, I called the duty doctor, but Stephen shook his head in furious rejection of all her suggestions for palliative measures, such as cough syrup or any sort of cough suppressant, because he had formulated a theory that such measures, in suppressing his natural reflexes, could be more dangerous than the cough itself. Effectively he had become his own doctor and was convinced that he knew more about his condition than any member of the medical profession. Stephen's mother, who had come over for tea on the Sunday afternoon, stayed on, and between us we nursed Stephen through a very disturbed night. The next day – my birthday – though very ill, pale, gaunt and racked by the choking, Stephen still refused to allow me to fetch help until late in the day when – as a major concession to me on my birthday – he let me call the doctor. When finally Dr Swan was permitted to set foot in the house at 7.30 p.m., his reaction was pragmatically straightforward: he called an ambulance at once, reassuring Stephen that he would be home again in a couple of days.

It was surely providential that at that blackest of moments when we arrived at the admissions unit – with Stephen thinking that he was about to be confined to a condemned cell and I, in an anguish of uncertainty, helplessly stroking his arm – the sound of a familiar voice, confident and authoritative, emerged from the doctors' office. It belonged to John Stark, the chest consultant who drove Robert to school every day. Stephen could not fail to respect John as a friend, whatever his opinion of doctors in general, and I was overjoyed to encounter someone in authority who could take charge of the situation without demanding lengthy explanations, someone with the medical expertise to relieve me of the impossible responsibility of caring for a very sick patient unaided. Nevertheless, because Stephen was so helpless in his inability to communicate with more than a handful of people, and because of his terror of being fed either a medicine or a food which could have harmful effects, I stayed in the hospital at his bedside all night. The next day showed a slight improvement in his condition – which had been diagnosed as an acute chest infection – as he gradually began to climb the first rungs on the ladder towards recovery, and two days later he was so much more cheerful that he seemed well enough to come home.

In the meantime, life at home had resumed a semblance of its usual pace. My parents had come to look after the children, Lucy had gone back to school and Robert went on a school day trip to York. When Alan and I collected Stephen from the hospital on 1st April, we entertained the foolishly optimistic hope that we were going to be able to get back to normal straight away. No sooner had we arrived home, so full of eager anticipation, than Stephen began to choke violently and incessantly and almost immediately slipped back into a desperate state. There was nothing that could be done to help him in his suffering, despite all the advice of the medical experts. He choked whatever position he adopted, whether sitting up or lying down. He could neither eat nor drink and was too weak to endure physiotherapy. My mother, Bernard Carr, Alan and I operated a rota system. One or two of us sat with Stephen all day and all night while the others slept. There was little doubt that the situation was extremely critical. I hardly needed the doctors to tell me that I should prepare myself for the worst.

Where medical science had admitted defeat, the concern shown by friends brought an unexpected revival of strength, inspiring a spontaneous renewal of hope. John Sturdy, the Dean of Caius, and his wife Jill came one evening, quietly and unobtrusively, to offer support through their prayers. Stephen's students and colleagues were unwavering in their devotion, visiting regularly and helping with his care, often through the night. Gradually, though still very frail and prone to choking attacks, Stephen began to improve until on Sunday 4th April he spent the whole day without choking at all and managed to eat a little pureed food. But that night his condition deteriorated again, and the following day saw us sliding back to square one. Robert awoke that morning with a high temperature, covered from head to foot in chickenpox blisters, and during the day he became delirious.

As my father was himself on the point of going into hospital in St Albans for an operation, my parents had returned home when Stephen first began to show signs of recovery. In their absence I had to throw myself on my good friends for help with the children, especially on Joy Cadbury, who for several years had hovered in the background, always ready to help with the utmost sensitivity when the need arose. In 1973 Robert had stayed with the Cadburys while we were in Russia and both he and Lucy always felt very much at home with their children, Thomas and Lucy Grace. They had already spent a couple of nights with the Cadburys when Stephen was in intensive care and I was with him at the hospital. The magnanimity with which Joy offered to nurse Robert, bespeckled with red blisters as he was, was quite beyond any call of friendship, *since* it was a foregone conclusion that both her own children would develop chickenpox within the next three weeks. I had no option but to let Robert go as the demands on me were so great, and my own resources were so depleted, that I could scarcely register what was happening to us.

In Joy's tender care Robert bounced back to health, though, of course, her children succumbed. My father came through his operation, and when, a day later, I managed to snatch an afternoon for a flying visit to St Albans, I was glad to find him up and about, walking round the ward. Stephen's recovery was slower and less predictable, mostly because he refused to take the penicillin he had been prescribed. He sat silently in his chair, resting his head on his hand, in the same melancholy posture he had first adopted in the Sixties. He did not speak, he choked frequently, and ate and drank in small, careful sips. He was not strong enough to go out, so the Department came to him and held its seminars in our living room. At last over the Easter weekend, he began to show signs of gaining strength. Only then could we begin to sleep at nights and I could relax my guard a little. The children came home, and in the one remaining week of the school holidays we looked forward to catching up on some holiday activities.

Stephen had other ideas. That Easter Monday, still in the early stages of convalescence, he summoned his students, commandeered the car and set off for a five-day conference in Oxford. As I stood in the doorway watching them go, my disbelief at such recklessness condensed into a desperate urge to escape – as far away as possible. Dennis and Lydia Sciama, who were aghast at Stephen's foolhardiness, recommended a hotel in St Ives in Cornwall. In a daze of miserable incomprehension, scarcely knowing where we were going or why, driven by a manic desire to get away from Cambridge, the children and I fled to London and boarded a train at Paddington for the West Country. The train whisked us further and further south. After Exeter it slowed down, crawling along at a snail's pace, snaking along winding branch lines. Oblivious to the slow passing of time, to the children's games, to their laughter and chatter, I gazed blankly out of the window, staring at the primrose-spattered fields of Cornwall without really seeing them, plunged into a stupor of exhausted dejection.

5

Celtic Woodland

It was obvious: we were living on the edge of a precipice. Yet it is possible even on the edge of a precipice to put down roots that penetrate rock and stone, roots that insinuate themselves into even the most meagre soils to form a sufficiently secure foundation for the branches above, stunted though they be, to produce foliage, flowers and fruit. At the end of April, on our return from Cornwall and Stephen's from Oxford, the children went back to school as if the nightmare of the Easter holidays had never happened. Quietly philosophical and undemanding, Robert had always taken his father's illness and disability in his stride, and fortunately he now went to a school which provided plenty of scope for doing all those physical activities that he and his father could not do together. Since Lucy followed her brother's lead in everything, she showed few signs of disturbance at the unconventional nature of her background. Our lives appeared to have taken up their usual rhythms, though perhaps with an even greater determination to focus on each moment of each day. As Stephen and the children settled back into their routines, I grasped every spare second to jot down a few thoughts on the thesis; I redecorated, yet again, the rented house owned jointly by Robert and his grandparents, upon which we depended for paying part of his school fees; I attended the singing class whenever possible; and I cooked for dinner parties for the advancing hordes of summer visitors to the Department.

In midsummer, a BBC television crew came to make a film about Stephen, as part of a two-hour documentary on the origins of the universe. By chance, the producer, Vivienne King, had been a student at Westfield in the same year as me. Although she had studied maths, she did not adopt a hardline scientific approach to the filming but wanted to present Stephen sympathetically, as a rounded figure set against the background of his family life. This image appealed to me because I feared that a hardline scientific approach could well present him as a sinister character, like the malevolent wheelchair-bound Dr Strangelove in Stanley Kubrick's film. The finished product, the first and best of its kind, contained the elements of a poetic idyll – albeit in a scientific context. Stephen was, of course, seen at work in the Department, interacting with his students, conducting seminars, expounding his latest theories. He was also interviewed at home against the backdrop of the two children playing in the summer sun among the flowers in the garden. When the film was broadcast worldwide the following winter as part of a major BBC documentary – *The Key to the Universe* – a school friend of Lucy's, the daughter of a visiting scholar, watched it back home in Japan. The mother wrote to tell us that her daughter had stood transfixed in front of the television screen when she saw Lucy sitting on her swing under the apple tree. "Lucy, Lucy..." was all that she could say as the tears poured down her cheeks.

This was certainly the image of self-sufficiency to which we continued to aspire, though that image and the sweet illusion of success were becoming less easy to sustain. Alan Lapedes was so exhausted on his return from the Oxford conference after Easter, that he had to go away for a couple of weeks to recover. After all, he had been ill with a chest infection too, but no one had given a moment's thought to his state of health, because his help had been urgently required in caring for Stephen. He had unstintingly helped throughout the critical period – and beyond, because when Stephen decided to go to Oxford, he had had no choice but to go with him.

Stephen's valiant attempts to appear fit and well may have stood him in good stead in the Department, but at home his spirits were alarmingly low and his constitution was dangerously weakened. He spoke only to voice his demands, and no sooner had one need been met, one command fulfilled, than another would arise, stretching me to the limit of my endurance. We needed help more than ever but no help was forthcoming, in spite of our doctors' concerted appeals to the National Health Service. In any case, Stephen still absolutely refused to accept any outside nursing help. My doctor applied to the local authority for a home help to assist with the domestic chores, since all our spare income was spent on augmenting Robert's school fees and did not run to the luxury of a daily help. No help materialized, however, because when the social worker came to assess us, one glance at our surroundings was enough to disqualify us from any benefits. She was only one in a long line of people who failed to distinguish between the gilded illusion that we struggled to maintain and the brutal reality at the core of our situation.

Help, when it came, assumed a form which, in its innocence, was so precious that although it eased the physical strain, it increased a hundred times my guilt at being unable to cope on my own. Robert, at nearly nine years old, stepped out of his childhood and began to fetch and carry, lift and heave, feed and wash, and even take his father to the bathroom when I was overwhelmed with the weight of other chores, or just too exhausted to respond. In Stephen's pragmatic philosophy of survival, Robert's arms and legs were as good a substitute for his own as anyone else's, and certainly better than having a nurse in the house, even temporarily. It disturbed me greatly that Robert's childhood, that unrepeatable period of freedom, was being brought to such an abrupt conclusion.

For the week of half-term at the end of May, I arranged the family holiday that we had not had at Easter – five relaxing days in our favourite hotel, the Anchor at Walberswick, only two and a half hours' drive from Cambridge. Despite all the efforts of the hotel staff to cater for all our needs, including the diet, the holiday was a disaster. Stephen choked from beginning to end, but took umbrage at the suggestion that he might prefer to eat his meals in the privacy of our own chalet. Consequently every mealtime was an ordeal, as his convulsive wheezings ricocheted off the walls and distracted the other guests from their food. He subsided into a depressed lethargy and built a wall around himself, communicating only to express his needs in a morbid game of "Simon says…". Robert's help was called for again and again when I reached breaking point – as I did often since this situation demanded more stamina and courage than I possessed.

I was desperate for help and asked myself frequently where I could find it, almost always drawing a blank. Our friends were all keen enough to help in the short term, but they had their own families, their own lives to lead. There was no one who could spare the time or the energy to give us the undertaking, the dedication we needed so badly – above all to relieve Robert of the premature burdens and responsibilities that were being placed on his young shoulders. In my despair I approached Stephen's parents, since they were the only people I could turn to. My own parents had given us huge amounts of help throughout our marriage and were wonderful grandparents, but there was little that they could do in this extreme situation where medical intervention was often required, nor did I feel that it was fair to ask them. Stephen's father had promised to help in any way possible in that euphoric period before our wedding in 1965. Indeed Frank Hawking had painted the bathroom for us when we first moved into Little St Mary's Lane; he and Isobel had paid for my stay in the nursing home when Robert was born, and they had also paid for us to have a cleaner once a week when Robert was a small baby. They had given us quite a large sum of money to help us buy our house, and had generously handed on a couple of family antiques to grace our living room. Isobel had come to look after Stephen when the children were born, and she had also been prepared to fly off with him to conferences across the world when small children and flying phobia kept me grounded. On our annual trip to the cottage in Wales, she and Frank could be relied upon to help with Stephen's care; she, with controlled good nature, often calming her husband's impatience, for clearly it took a considerable emotional effort and self-discipline for him to reconcile himself to the time-consuming restraints of Stephen's severe disability. Although their own property was so dauntingly unsuitable for a disabled person in a wheelchair, they were curiously meticulous about reconnoitring castles and beauty spots for excursions, counting steps and registering any other hurdles in advance of our arrival.

Their visits to Cambridge however were always much more formal than my parents'. Mum and Dad were demonstrative and passionate grandparents, involving themselves in every aspect of the children's lives and our own, whereas Stephen's parents behaved like guests rather than close relations – and of late I had begun to sense a distancing in their attitude, as if the veneer of normality we struggled to maintain was so convincing that no more involvement was required on their part. On our return from Walberswick, I wrote a despairing letter to them, begging them to bring their minds and their medical knowledge to bear on the situation to help ease the overwhelming difficulties which were threatening us. My promise to Stephen had not altered, but, with the best will in the world, it was becoming much more difficult to sustain, particularly in the face of the unrelenting stress, all day and every day and much of the night as well. If anything the pace of life had accelerated since Stephen's recent chest infection, with a major conference in Cambridge, more dinners, more sherry parties and more receptions. I was at breaking point, but still Stephen rejected any proposals to relieve either the children – especially Robert – or me, of the strain. His constant rejection of our need for more help was an alienating force, wearing away the empathy with which I had shared every dispiriting stage in the development of his condition. In his reply to my letter, Frank Hawking promised to confer with Stephen's doctor about the medical aspects of the case and said that there would be ample opportunity to discuss other matters at greater length during our forthcoming summer holiday in Llandogo.

There was actually very little opportunity to discuss these matters in Wales because of the characteristic Hawking reluctance to discuss anything of a personal nature. Dutifully Frank helped with Stephen's care every morning and then, usually clad in boots, waterproofs and a sou'wester, he disappeared into the wilderness to attack the weeds which were making a mockery of his attempts to grow vegetables in the rainforest conditions of the steep east-facing hillside. Isobel valiantly did her best to organize interesting excursions for us, dodging the showers in the afternoons – a teddy bears' picnic, a visit to Goodrich Castle, a hunt for four-leaf clover – all pleasant, sociable family outings, conducted without any reference to the underlying problems and tensions. One morning she came to me and in a tone of flustered defiance said, "If you want to talk to Father, you had better see him now." She pointed outside to where Frank stood in the pouring rain. I donned my raincoat and joined him under the dripping trees. We walked along the road, not speaking, splashing across the rivulets that were rushing straight down the hill to swell the river in the valley below. My thoughts and emotions were churning in such a chaotic whirlpool that they would not be so easily channelled into a coherent flow. I was afraid of appearing disloyal to Stephen, yet I had to persuade his family that all was not well, that ways and means had to be sought, and if necessary imposed, to lighten the burdens. If nothing else, it was essential to relieve Robert of the tasks that were oppressing him.

I succeeded in none of my aims. The merest hint of dissatisfaction with our situation was quickly identified as disloyalty to Stephen, summarily dismissed with the implication that it was a symptom of my own inadequacy. Frank did at least offer to discuss the situation with Stephen, but doubted that his words would have any effect. In any case, he asserted, there could be no question of forcing Stephen to accept more help. His only other comments were that Stephen was very courageous, that he drew his courage from his determination, and that he, Frank, was sure that Stephen was doing his best for his family. He was providing well for us, we had two lovely children and we were very fortunate in the position we occupied. I did not dispute the truth of all this, and by comparison with many disabled families we were no doubt well off, but there was little comfort in the repetition of such truisms. These were the blessings that I had conditioned myself to count for so many years. I knew well enough that Stephen's determination was his defence against the illness, but I did not understand why he had to use it as a weapon against his family. As for Robert, Frank expressed his concern for him by turning my argument on its head: Robert was too introverted, he said; he should be brought out of his shell so that, in the future, social ineptitude would not damage his career as Frank believed it had damaged his own, depriving him of recognition for his important work in tropical medicine.

There was no use in arguing. Though robust and in sterling health, Frank was old, a good ten years older than my father. Perhaps he was too old to understand how I felt and too old to adjust to what was being asked of him. For all his genuine concern for Stephen, he evidently found it difficult to see what was before his very eyes. To try and explain the obvious, to repeat the contents of my letter – that Robert's introversion was mainly a result of the home situation – would have been hopeless; the more so, considering that my purely practical suggestion that perhaps Frank and Isobel might begin to participate in the running of the rented house in Cambridge, especially when so much redecoration and refurbishing were required between tenancies, had been quashed outright on account of the distance – some fifty miles – between St Albans and Cambridge. The conversation petered out and we returned to the house.

Later the sky cleared. I was sitting on the terrace shelling peas for lunch when Isobel came and sat beside me. "So I gather you have talked to Father?" she enquired, eyeing me intently. "Not really," I replied. She pursed her lips and with the same defiance that she had shown earlier, she announced fiercely. "You do know, don't you, that Father will never allow Stephen to be put into a residential home?" So saying she stood up, turned on her heel and marched into the house. Her remarks stung me to the quick. I had never so much as thought about a residential home for Stephen, let alone mentioned such a preposterous idea. I had simply asked for help to protect my own young son from the psychological ravages of the physical disease which was afflicting theirs. Humiliated and even more despondent, I stood up. Abandoning the half-filled saucepan of peas, I walked slowly away from the house into Cleddon wood and there, in utter desolation, sat down on a broad, flat stone, scarcely conscious of the noise of the falls resounding in my ears. Never had I been so alone – alone there in the forest, on the hillside by the fast flowing stream. There was sympathy in nature when human beings could offer none, but nature was powerless to influence intellectual beings whose sole criterion was rational thought, who refused to recognize reality when it stood, bared before them, pleading for help.

In the second week of the holiday, when the sun shone dependably out of a clear sky, it appeared that I might have misjudged Stephen's mother. She took us to a hotel at the seaside on the coast and shared in Stephen's care for much of the time, sometimes feeding him his meals, helping to dress him and sitting by him on the path above the beach so that I could play with the children on the sands below and bathe in the sea. My spirits rose as my energies began to revive. It seemed that Isobel was responding to my pleas, after all, and was genuinely making an effort to help. I was grateful, but I smiled in puzzlement at some of the remarks she made. "Looking after Stephen is not really that difficult, you know," she observed breezily. "Robert doesn't seem to mind helping his father at all; in fact, I think it's good for them both," was her next cheerful remark. I was prepared to view such remarks as kindly meant, since the holiday that she had generously provided had been such fun and so beneficial to us all. However the persistent harping on the ease with which all my responsibilities could be accomplished, and the implication that my cries for help were not to be taken seriously, dampened my reawakening confidence in her. She did not seem to understand that, whereas my childhood naivety had long since died and my inherent youthful optimism had vanished, the thought that that was already happening to Robert at less than ten years of age was intolerable. "Really the wheelchair is not as heavy as you might think," she announced airily at the end of the week. "Lucy helped me to put it and the batteries in the car and between us we managed perfectly well." Lucy was five years old; the weight of the chair and its solid gel batteries had already made many a strapping student blanch.

Sad news greeted us in Cambridge at the end of August. During our absence Thelma Thatcher had been taken into hospital for an operation from which she did not recover. The ten years that we had known her, though a large proportion of our lives, were only a small proportion of hers, yet she treated us as if we were part of her family. Her soul was large, all-embracing, caring and practical, always ready to come to the rescue in times of crisis, always ready to help those worse off than herself, always ready with her quick sense of humour to pinpoint the ridiculous or the absurd. The children adored her and she adored them as their adoptive granny. For me she was a true friend and a staunch ally, whose judgement, I knew, was always sound, even though sometimes it might have been hard to digest. I had seen her just before we went to Wales. She was philosophical, dismissing her own health problems as insignificant, although she already knew that they were serious. Typically she was more concerned to talk about us. "I wish old Thatcher were stronger and could help her brave girl more," she said as she hugged me for the last time.

6

A Backwards Glance

That autumn, many scientists joined us for family meals at the end of long days filled with all the usual bustle associated with children and schools, clubs and after-school activities, as well as Stephen's requirements. Not much had changed in our circumstances – and Robert's help was still often called upon at home – but that week by the sea, the second week of the holiday in Wales, had restored both my stamina and my resolve, and I was better able to cope. Stephen was also in better health and spirits, although his recovery from the spring's bout of pneumonia did not mean that motor-neuron disease, which continued to exact its implacable toll of muscle degeneration, eating difficulties, choking fits and respiratory problems, had retreated.

In the Department the latest academic exercise to gain popularity was the symposium, a sort of protracted conference which extended over a whole year. This exercise held great attractions for Stephen since, with the increased funding now at his disposal, he could bring scientists to Cambridge from all over the world and work with them at leisure on lengthy projects such as books and papers – something which would have been an impossible undertaking in the hurried atmosphere of the customary four- or five-day conference. Although he was still wavering in his interests between general relativity and quantum mechanics, most of the visitors to the Relativity Group in the early part of the academic year were the old familiar faces, and most of them came from North America.

From my standpoint, the most formidable of them were the modest, amiable Chandrasekhars – not because of any clashes of personality, but because, just before they arrived for a dinner party, I learnt that they were vegan. I had supposed that they were vegetarian after mistakenly serving them a fish sandwich at a tea party, but had not suspected further complications. A last-minute revision of the menu was called for. Out went my planned recipes, and the search was on for meat-free, fish-free and dairy-free dishes – that were also gluten-free and sugar-free. My old Spanish stand-by, gazpacho, lent a touch of distinction to a meal of mushroom and onion risotto. It was really more appropriate to the Sunday supper table than to a dinner party for such distinguished guests.

In the middle of the term, the Cambridge coterie decamped to Oxford, where Dennis Sciama had moved to take up a Fellowship at All Souls College. Roger Penrose had been appointed Professor of Mathematics there, and he and Dennis regularly organized one-, two- and three-day conferences. While Stephen and his colleagues gave their seminars, I took the opportunity to get to know the museums and monuments of Oxford better. Over the past few years we had made six-monthly visits to the meetings in Oxford, even when the children were very small, and I too had begun to appreciate the charm of the place, at once more cosmopolitan and animated than its fenland counterpart. Stephen loved being back in Oxford. He carried the layout of the city in his head and, with a hint of pride, could direct me infallibly to any location, negotiating lanes and back streets with an easy confidence. He would nostalgically point out the wall he had once climbed over, only to fall into the arms of a policeman, and the bridge he and some friends were daubing with a ban-the-bomb slogan in the middle of the night, when a policeman sauntered by and arrested the friends, who left Stephen dangling in a cage beneath the bridge. These and other similar yarns had a somewhat apocryphal ring to them, though there were plenty of photos to attest to Stephen's disastrous antics on the river. There was little doubt, too, that he had been an eager participant in the sconce – a sort of beer-drinking contest, imposed as a fine for a breach of behaviour. Stephen's delight in those memories was touching: they provided a tantalizing glimpse of the old carefree rebel with whom I had fallen in love. They related, of course, to the days of his hedonistic youth, before the diagnosis of motor-neuron disease, which was, in chronological terms, a Cambridge phenomenon.

For conferences and trips further afield there were now plenty of colleagues and students who were glad of the opportunity to travel and to meet the famous names in physics. This was a great relief to me as I was still terrified both of aeroplanes and of leaving my children. I tried to be both father and mother to each of them and did not want them to suffer from having a severely disabled father, though of course I encouraged them to love and respect him. Unbeknown to Stephen, I shared my concerns with their teachers in the vain hope of protecting them against teasing in the playground. Occasionally, as in December 1976, when Stephen flew off with his students to Boston for a pre-Christmas conference, I could devote myself to my maternal role, attend the nativity plays, ballet shows and school carol services and take the children to the College Christmas party.

That December, Alan Lapedes, who had given us so much quietly dedicated help throughout the period of crisis, returned to his home in Princeton. I then spring-cleaned the spare room, our one room in the upstairs part of the house, for the arrival of our new resident physicist, Don Page, whom we had met in California where he was a former graduate student of Kip Thorne's. He and his mother had come to Cambridge on a tour of inspection. Naturally, they wanted to see whether the arrangement we were offering was suitable – and, I suspected, to judge whether I was a sufficiently respectable landlady. Evidently we passed the test, for Don bounced energetically into our household, like A.A. Milne's Tigger. He arrived with Stephen on his return from Boston on 18th December, and eagerly joined in all our Christmas festivities.

I had moved among physicists for long enough to know that they mostly come from somewhat unusual backgrounds. Don Page's background was so unusual that it was exceptional even among physicists. Born of missionary-teacher parents, he was brought up in isolation in a remote part of Alaska, where his parents provided his early schooling. He later attended a Christian college in Missouri, his parents' home state, and from there graduated to Caltech where he joined Kip's group as a postgraduate student. His fundamentalist beliefs were so firmly ingrained that the apparent clash between them and his field of study, gravitational physics and the origins of the universe, while paradoxical to many onlookers, did not appear to disturb him unduly, because he was able to compartmentalize his activities. On the one hand, his Christianity was devout, principled according to absolute values which, as yet unchallenged in their rigidity, could seem to lack sensitivity; on the other, those very evangelical convictions required of him a tireless zeal in all his endeavours.

While I respected his fervour – he attended church twice on Sundays, with additional midweek bible-study classes – and welcomed the supportive religious influence he brought to our lives, I sided with Stephen in refusing to be evangelized, particularly at breakfast time. Doubtless well-meaning, Don cherished the hope of making a spectacular conversion – comparable to that of Saul on the road to Damascus – through his early-morning bible readings and prayers. I could have told him that he was doomed to failure, for his broad, floodlit highway of biblical certainties was even less likely to meet with success than my own path, a quiet, unpretentious amble along the meandering lanes of simple trust in faith and deeds. Stephen had no patience with anything other than the rational power of physics, so I very much doubted that Don's earnest readings and literal sermons – at 8.30 in the morning when I came back from taking Lucy to school – were going to illuminate the way forwards. In any case Stephen always hid behind the newspaper, which was propped up on a wooden frame for want of an electronic page-turner, at breakfast. The upright newspaper was a barrier that the laden spoon had to negotiate when delivering his substantial breakfast of pills, laxative, boiled eggs, pork chops, rice and tea, and it was also a barrier to conversation.

This was not a barrier that Don had anticipated when he came down to breakfast in the early days, armed with Bible and edifying tracts. I said nothing, leaving him to address his invisible congregation as best he could. Shielded by the *Times*, Stephen would not be distracted from his perusal of current affairs, essential for a Fellow who prided himself on having the last word in high-table discussions – whether about Britain's precarious financial position shorn up by loans from the United States, or about the test runs of the Space Shuttle. I usually managed little more than a quick glance at the headlines, whereas Stephen read slowly, mentally photographing and digesting every snippet of information, every fact and figure, for regurgitation on some later occasion, probably at High Table.

As Don was finding his task heavy-going, it occurred to me that a distraction was needed, so I invited him to help himself to cornflakes, muesli, boiled eggs and toast, and asked if he had ever tried Marmite. He picked up the round, brown jar with its yellow lid. "No, no, we don't have this in the US; I guess it's some kinda chocolate," he replied, avidly ladling thick spoonfuls of the dark, treacly substance onto his slice of toast. "Try it and see," I said, whereupon he took a large bite. His open, childlike expression creased into wrinkles of repulsion at the pungent, salty assault on his taste buds. Even Stephen looked up from the newspaper, his broad grin revealing those alluring dimples in his cheeks. Good-humouredly, after a moment's puzzlement, Don was able to take the joke in good part, and never again did he bring his proselytizing zeal to the breakfast table.

The great advantage of having an American from Caltech in residence was that whenever Stephen wanted to go to Los Angeles – or anywhere else in the United States for that matter – in the interests of science, the American would want to go too. So although the following summer Stephen pressed me to accompany him to America for three weeks, Don was all too ready to go instead. This unexpectedly easy solution to a previously intractable problem cleared the way for me to fulfil a longing which had lain dormant for many years. It was in fact thirteen years since I had set foot on the Spanish mainland, and I longed to renew my contact with that country and its civilization, which had played such a significant role in my education before all my modest pretensions and aspirations were swallowed up. Pleasantries exchanged on dining nights with the Spanish butler of Caius had scarcely sufficed to maintain my once fluent command of the spoken language, and over the years that skill had dwindled pitifully to a handful of insubstantial polite formulae. The thesis was suffering from a serious lack of inspiration and motivation, partly on account of its length which had become unwieldy, partly because of the huge quantities of scrappy notes which remained to be incorporated into some sort of order, and partly because the topics were so remote that I was losing touch with them.

As always, my parents jumped at any suggestion of a holiday with their grandchildren, and together Dad and I planned an extensive tour through northern Spain and Portugal, coinciding here and there with the *camino francés*, the old pilgrim route to Santiago de Compostela. The mere exercise of planning brought back memories of those wonderful European holidays of old – especially because my father, with his historian's nose, had lost none of his talent for scenting out singular historical treasures which the ordinary tourist would have passed by.

Once all the summer activities were out of the way – dinner parties for a mini-conference, barbecues, lunch parties, children's tea parties, school sports days, college functions, mundane but necessary considerations such as servicing the car and cleaning out the rented house for reletting, and, ultimately, a vicious attack of measles which put Lucy to bed just before the end of term – Stephen left for California and we finally set sail for Bilbao. Although that grimy, industrial city on Spain's northern coast gave us a damp, cloudy reception, my heart leapt when I set foot on Spanish soil again. It continued to leap throughout that holiday, not only at the rediscovery of Spain, a liberated country where fascism was dead and democracy was tentatively establishing itself, but also at perceptible glimpses of my former self, the once hopeful, adventurous teenager, long buried under a heap of exacting burdens and more urgent priorities. By degrees I regained my grasp of the Spanish language, its grammar, syntax and vocabulary, for that too was part of my rediscovery. With its vitality the language reawakened my linguistic voice, so long reduced to a timid silence by the oppressive weight of intellectual prejudice in Cambridge, where one soon learnt to keep quiet rather than make a fool of oneself.

Cities with sonorous names – Burgos, Salamanca, Santiago, León, Coimbra and Oporto – and extravagant cathedrals, medieval monasteries, Mozarabic chapels, pilgrimage processions, sun-baked plains and gnarled olive groves blazed a trail of dazzling light and torrid heat into the chill drabness of our northern lives. In the rocky inlets, streams, pine trees and mountains, I discovered the landscape and the living traditions of the *cantigas de amigo*. The sensation that the ponderous weight of scholarship that I was trying to mould into a thesis had some basis in reality, that medieval studies were after all a more relevant, productive activity than collecting pebbles on the beach, gave me a tremendous boost. I promised myself that I would finish the thesis, come what may, even though it might not lead anywhere, even though it might simply be an end in itself. I felt impatient to record all that I had seen and relate it to the texts, but not so much so that I wanted to rush back to Cambridge before we had all squeezed every ounce of benefit from those weeks in Spain and Portugal. The children after all needed some compensation, in the form of a few days by the sea, for all the hours they had spent uncomplainingly in the back of the car. Lucy, whose imagination was so fertile that she could keep herself and everyone else amused no matter how long the journeys or how searing the heat, was fascinated by the cockle-shell motif of the pilgrim route to the tomb of St James at Santiago. She kept her eyes open for the shell on buildings, statues and signs, letting out a yell of triumph whenever she spied one. Perhaps not surprisingly after so many religious monuments, she and Robert became pretty confused in their grasp of the lives of the saints, with the result that, when we came down to the sea at Ofir in Portugal, they devised a crazy game in which Lucy played the part of John the Baptist, drenching her brother with sea water – while he, wrapped in a towel, played the part of a stoical pilgrim en route to the tomb of St James. Any religious connotations to this game were, needless to say, entirely spurious. While the children were engaged in this heretical and obstreperous pursuit, the one near-disaster of the holiday occurred when Dad found himself unwittingly shut in his room by a faulty door lock. There was no telephone in the room and the only possible exit was via the balcony: the only way to get off his balcony was to leap across a seventy foot drop onto ours and escape through our room. He joined us on the beach, bursting with pride at this daredevil achievement – which we all had to agree, with astonished amusement, was no mean feat for a sixty-three-year-old.

7

Impasse

In that autumn of 1977, with my mind once more fired with the glowing impressions of the Iberian Peninsula, I was determined to attack the thesis with fresh insight and vigour, although the organization of the material remained daunting and time was still a crucial factor. Stephen returned from California to promotion – to a personal chair in gravitational physics. His elevation to a professorship had implications beyond that of a modest salary increase, since the title and position assured him of enhanced respect and recognition wherever he went – with a few exceptions, one of them within his own Department. His promotion coincided with the redecoration and refurbishment of the Department, and for some time he waited for the carpet – to which as a professor he was entitled – to be laid in his office. After some months of waiting in vain, he decided to broach the matter with the Head of the Department, who tut-tutted peevishly at his request. "Only professors are entitled to carpets," he said. "But I am a professor!" Stephen remonstrated. Eventually, in somewhat belated confirmation of his status, his professorial carpet arrived.

Carpets notwithstanding, Stephen was afraid that the appointment might put a distance between him and his students, but he took comfort in the fact that the physical help he required of them disarmed any diffidence created by his lofty reputation. Although an undisputed intellectual potentate, he shuddered at the thought of conforming to the image of an establishment professor, aloof from students and colleagues. He preferred the image of the eternal youth with the boyish grin, poking fun at the very authority of which he himself was now a part.

While Stephen's physical condition may have been an effective equalizer in the sphere of the Department, his promotion, although welcome, created subtle problems for me in our dealings with the world at large, not least because his growing reputation so totally exceeded our circumstances. Only our very closest friends realized that on the home scene the struggle for daily survival continued unabated as before. Despite the piti-less onslaughts of motor-neuron disease, Stephen had become a national figure, the youngest Fellow of the Royal Society, the recipient of umpteen awards and medals, Einstein's successor and a professor at the University of Cambridge. The very paradox of his situation had made him the darling of the media. Not only in the popular perception but also, I began to suspect, in the eyes of his own family, his success was proof that he had conquered motor-neuron disease and therefore the battle was won: we could not possibly be in need of help. It was the most cruel irony that we had become the innocent victims of our own success. There was not simply a schism between the public face and the private image, they were actually in conflict with each other. Certainly the public functions – like the memorable occasion in the summer of 1978 when Stephen received an honorary doctorate from the University of Oxford – were enjoyable and gratifying, but that sort of limelight made not the slightest contribution to the help, both physical and emotional, which we needed more than ever because motor-neuron disease had not been conquered; it was still advancing at a slow but relentless pace. To the immediate family circle, the effects were devastating and the demands punishing. I could no longer keep up the pretence that it was just a background inconvenience, a fact of life. The disease dominated our lives and those of the children, in spite of all our efforts to uphold a precious veneer of normality.

Initially bright then reserved, Robert was now becoming so withdrawn that I feared that he was suffering from depression, a condition which, according to my doctor, was not unknown in children. For amusement he engrossed himself in computer manuals to the exclusion of other diversions. Stephen tried hard to fulfil his paternal role by buying elaborate electric train sets and complicated lengths of track, which Robert was not skilful enough to operate. Even when his old friend Inigo brought his more advanced electrical knowledge to bear, the trains never ran smoothly and Robert quickly lost interest. Apart from Inigo, who went to a different school, he had few friends and did not seem keen to cultivate new ones. It was obvious that Robert needed a male role model, someone who would romp and tussle with him, someone who would ease him out of a childhood already lost into adolescence, someone who would not expect anything of him in return, least of all help with their own physical requirements.

Lucy, effervescent and sociable, developed an early sense of independence, which enabled her to cultivate a wide circle of friends in which she found some compensations for the short-comings of her home life. From an early age she threw all her bubbling energies into a giddy social cycle of Brownies, swimming galas, Guide camps, sponsored runs, school plays and concerts and music and drama at the Saturday Music for Fun Club, as well as innumerable parties. Doubtless her huge collection of soft toys, and the fantasy world which she and Lucy Grace Cadbury invented for their Snoopy puppets, also played a part in helping her evolve subconscious methods for coping with her unusual background, though certainly she remained very sensitive to her circumstances. Both her age and her sex enabled her to avoid the some of the pressures that were falling upon Robert's shoulders.

My parents filled many of the gaps in the children's lives with trips to London, tea at the Ritz and visits to the theatre. However, there was a deep hole in my own life, which I could not even begin to broach to them. Thelma Thatcher was astute and forthright enough to identify it in one of her very last remarks to me before she died in the summer of 1976. "My dear," she said, leaning across her highly polished table and looking me straight in the eye, "I simply can't imagine how you survive without a proper sex life." I was so astounded by such candour from an octogenarian that I could reply only with a shrug of the shoulders. I myself did not know the answer to her question, but my sense of loyalty to Stephen forbade any open discussion of that topic, which for him was as taboo a subject as his illness. I did not allow myself to confide in Thelma Thatcher on that occasion and there was never another opportunity. Nevertheless I badly needed a confidante in whose age and wisdom I could trust. Quite apart from the physical aspects, the marital relationship was acquiring profoundly irreconcilable undertones. Intellectually Stephen was a towering giant who always insisted on his own infallibility and to whose genius I would always defer; bodily he was as helpless and as dependent as either of the children had been when new-born. The functions I fulfilled for him were all those of a mother looking after a small child, responsible for every aspect of his being, including his appearance – only just short of a nurse in that I refused to give injections or intervene in medical matters where I had no training. The problems were exacerbated by the sheer impossibility of talking about them. This was an intrinsic part of his battle against disease, which, with better communication, we could have fought together, side by side, supporting each other and developing strategies for coping with the difficulties. Instead it became an alienating force, bringing down a barrier of anguish between us.

Not for the first time, I sharpened my eyes and my ears, on the lookout for similar situations, words of advice or crumbs of comfort. My hopes were raised on a rare visit to Lucy Cavendish not long after kind Kate Bertram's retirement, when the new President was to introduce herself at a feast, a singular event for that College, and one which, despite my reservations about my own academic failings, I was reluctant to miss. After dinner, the new President rose to her feet and recounted the events of her life and of her academic career. Tears came to my eyes as she spoke of her marriage: her husband, too, had suffered from an incurable, disabling disease. Again it seemed for a brief moment that I had met someone with whom I might be able to talk freely, someone who would intuitively understand the tiredness and the despair behind the smiling but now hesitant façade. To my confusion, I heard her inviting the audience's sympathy for a choice that had faced her – between her academic career and her husband – when she was offered a prestigious American Fellowship. She had taken up the Fellowship.

Finally, in embarrassed desperation, I spoke to Dr Swan in the clinical atmosphere of his morning surgery. If his tone was one of concerned detachment, his words were as candid as Thelma Thatcher's. "The problems you are facing, Jane, are much like the problems associated with old age," he said candidly, "the irony is that you are a young woman with normal needs and expectations." He paused. "All I can suggest," he said, glancing up at me over his gold-rimmed spectacles, "is that you should make a life of your own."

In an unparalleled moment of chumminess that same autumn, Philippa coolly advised me that the time had come for me to leave Stephen. "Really, no one would blame you." she added condescendingly, as if in such facile advice lay the solution to all the problems. Whatever her motives – and certainly I had little enough cause to trust them – her advice struck me as being singularly ill judged. Certainly such a solution would have expelled me from the Hawking family circle with alacrity. She failed to understand that I could no more have left Stephen than I could have abandoned a child. I could not break up my family, the family that I myself in my optimism had created. This would effectively destroy the one achievement of my life and with it myself.

To pretend that I had never found other men attractive would be dishonest; however, I had never had an affair and my only relationship had been with Stephen. Those passing attractions had never been more than the briefest of encounters that consisted of no more than a fleeting eye contact. Indeed, I had long since lost my sense of individuality and any sense of myself as an attractive or desirable young woman. I saw myself as part of a marriage, and that marriage had grown from the original bond between two people into an extensive network, like a garden full of diverse plants and flowers, not only comprising parents and children but grandparents, loyal friends, students and colleagues. The central tree in that garden was the home, which I had created over the years, whether in Little St Mary's Lane, Pasadena or West Road. The relationship from which it had all sprung was now but one aspect of that complex diversity and, although that relationship had changed dramatically, the marriage itself was of much wider import and transcended the personal needs of the two people who had initiated it. A brittle, empty shell, alone and vulnerable, restrained only by the thought of my children from throwing myself into the river, I prayed for help with the desperate insistency of a potential suicide. The situation was such that I doubted that even God himself, whoever he was or wherever he was, could find a solution to it, if indeed he could hear my prayer – but some solution had to be found if our family were to survive, if Stephen were to be able to carry on with his work and live at home, and if I were to remain a sane and capable mother to the children.

It was an exceptional friend, Caroline Chamberlain – Stephen's former physiotherapist – at once sensitive and practical, who suggested that I might benefit from some diversion, such as singing in the local church choir. "Come and sing at St Mark's," she said, "we need extra sopranos for the carol service." Late one afternoon in mid-December we left the children with her husband Peter, while we went to the final rehearsals. This was the first time that I had sung in a real choir, as opposed to the choral class in Pasadena, and although my voice was developing nicely, sight-reading and counting were conspicuously absent from my skills, soberly reminding me of my teenage experiences as a hopelessly incompetent secretary. The other sopranos patiently measured the beat for me, a musical dyslexic, while the young conductor, pale and thin, politely internalized his dismay at the musical ugly duckling that Caroline had introduced into his organization. With practice my efforts improved, so that, come the carol service, my contribution was not as dire as he feared, and I was invited to join the choir for carol-singing round the parish later that week.

Lucy came carol-singing with me and trotted along from street to street, from house to house, calling at many homes, where the members of the choir and their choirmaster seemed to be not only well known but well received also. This was the area of Cambridge where Lucy went to school, yet apart from the school and the shops, I scarcely knew it at all. Here was a tightly knit community of friends and neighbours, elderly people and families, for whom the red-brick Edwardian church seemed to represent a nucleus, whether or not they attended it regularly.

In the dark winter night, as the choirmaster, Jonathan Hellyer Jones, walked beside Lucy and me, balancing on the edge of the pavement to protect us from the passing traffic, we struck up conversation. I talked as I had not in years and had the uncanny sensation that I had met a familiar friend of long acquaintance, a shadowy recollection brought sharply back into focus, given shape and form by this stranger. We talked about singing, music, mutual acquaintances – of whom there were several – and travels, particularly in Poland, where he had sung with the University Chamber Choir in the summer of 1976. He told me about St Mark's and its extraordinarily dedicated, warm-hearted vicar, Bill Loveless, who had given him great support and strengthened his faith through a very difficult period. He did not say what that period was, but I already knew from Caroline that eighteen months previously, Janet, Jonathan's wife of one year, had died of leukaemia.

We did not meet again for several weeks and our next encounter was quite by chance. In January 1978, while Stephen was away in America with his entourage for three weeks, I went with Nigel Wickens and a group from his singing class to an evening of Victorian entertainment given by the baritone soloist Benjamin Luxon at the Guildhall. In the crowded auditorium, I noticed Jonathan immediately, a strikingly distinctive figure, tall, bearded and curly-haired, on the other side of the hall. I was surprised when in the interval he recognized me and I introduced him to Nigel. "What a nice man!" Nigel remarked on the way back through King's College to West Road where he had parked his car. I agreed guardedly, preferring to concentrate on the other main topic of conversation, Nigel's forthcoming marriage to a talented American singer, Amy Klohr.

As a result of that chance meeting, Jonathan came to teach Lucy the piano on Saturday or Sunday afternoons, depending on his availability. She quickly warmed to him and his serious-minded hesitancy was soon dispelled by her liveliness. At first he came strictly for the length of the lesson, then he stayed a little longer to accompany me in the Schubert songs I was learning – while Stephen alternately directed the railway operations in Robert's bedroom and provided us with an audience of one for our own private *Schubertiades,* as we called them. After a few weeks of this routine, Jonathan began to stay for lunch before or supper afterwards, and to help with Stephen's needs, relieving Robert of all the chores which had oppressed him for so long. Then when we had got to know Jonathan a little better, Robert would lie in wait by the front door and pounce on him on his arrival, throwing him to the floor and wrestling with him. Jonathan took this unconventional form of greeting in good part and responded in kind to a growing boy's need for a good rough-and-tumble to release his excess energies.

Often during the course of each week we would come across each other quite by accident and wonder at the extraordinary coincidences which seemed to be bringing us together. We would stand by the roadside, talking, oblivious to what it was we were supposed to be doing or where we were going. We had so much to discuss, his bereavement, his loneliness, his musical ambitions on the one hand, and my fears for Stephen and the children and my despair at the difficulty of doing everything that was required of me with tolerance and patience on the other. Although younger than me, he had so much wisdom, so broad a perspective on life with which to enlarge my restricted view, so strong a faith and so luminous a spirituality with which to light my black horizon, that we truly trod the holy ground which, in Oscar Wilde's words, is present where there is sorrow. I had met someone who knew the tensions and the intensity of life in the face of death.

Other circumstances conspired to bring us together in the strangest of ways. I still attended dinners once a term or so in Lucy Cavendish – simply to maintain the contact rather than because I derived any pleasure from them. On one such occasion, having exhausted my own limited fund of conversation, I was listening to the talk across the table when I heard a distinguished elderly Fellow of the college, Alice Heim, singing the praises of a young man who visited her house regularly to play piano duets with her. The warmth with which she described him, his kindnesses to her and his musical talent startled me. He was unique, a veritable Apollo. Her ageing companions were more than a little perplexed by the effusions of their colleague. "What was his name?" they asked. When she replied, "Jonathan, Jonathan Hellyer Jones," my ears burned and I felt myself colouring with pleasure, as though I was the only person present who could share her appreciation of this champion who had entered our lives. Nor could anyone have been more surprised than I was, as much at my own blushing reactions as at Alice Heim's enthusiasm. I was uncomfortably aware that the warm glow resulted as much from embarrassment as from pleasure, as if I stood accused of a guilty secret. Yet there was no apparent reason for this friendship either to be a secret or to be tinged with guilt. It was based on our shared interests, on our concern for each other's situation, on the support we could bring to each other, and above all, on music. Nevertheless, though we had never touched and would not do so for a very long time, we were both aware that the guilty secret was an admission of the potentially physical nature of the relationship. The attraction between us was strong, but adultery is an ugly word, contrary to the ethical basis on which our lives were built. Was this the price I should have to pay to rekindle the flame of my passionate spirit? Was it a price that, in all honesty, I could allow Jonathan to pay? If I were to find myself in the company of the adulterous heroines of the nineteenth century, the price might be even higher. The end result might be only the jarring sound of Flaubert's cracked kettle rather than music to move the stars to pity.

8

A Helping Hand

During the following term Jonathan suggested that I might like to join the church choir, which was rehearsing excerpts from *Messiah* for an orchestral performance at Easter. As Robert and Lucy were old enough to be left for an hour in front of the television in the early evening, I joined the handful of choral parishioners for the Thursday rehearsals in the church. To me, a comparative beginner, the graphic complexity of Handel's choruses – in which sheep ran astray with alarming rapidity "turning everyone to his own way" – represented a challenge which I countered with an obsessive enthusiasm. In joining the choir, I also joined the church, where services fell loosely within the bounds of the Church of England formats that I had known since childhood. But this was Anglicanism devoid of sanctimonious dogma and stifling pedantry, thanks to the visionary dynamism of the vicar, Bill Loveless, whose surname could not have been more ill suited to his personality. Once a journalist on the *Picture Post*, actor, soldier and businessman, Bill had come to ordination in middle age. Happily still blessed with phenomenal vitality, he brought all his experience from other walks of life – and all his contacts too – to assist him in his pastoral work and in his unending search for relevant themes for his sermons, while for his monthly forum on topical matters he invited a succession of guest speakers – doctors, policemen, social workers, political activists and so on.

For Bill, true Christianity did not deal in absolutes, bargains with God or divine punishments. Its one guiding principle was a passionate love of humanity, affirming God's unequivocal love for all people, whoever they were, whatever their imperfections. The only command of this loving doctrine was to love one's neighbour. In this realm there was rest for all the weary and heavy-laden, and there I found solace. At last the crumpled rag of my spiritual being began to revive, but, although I derived comfort from my return to the Church, it also set me imponderable questions. What was being asked of me? How great a sacrifice was required of me? The circumstances in which I had met Jonathan, when I was at breaking point, were so extraordinary – and yet so ordinary – that I could not avoid the bizarre, perhaps naive impression that that meeting had been deliberately engineered by a benevolent power, acting through our good and caring mutual friends. We were both lonely, deeply unhappy people, in desperate need of help. Could that meeting really have been part of a highly unorthodox divine plan? Or was I just being absurd, even heretical and hypocritical? I knew my Moliere too well to want to find either myself or Jonathan being cast in the role of Tartuffe, the arch hypocrite.

Some people might regard the support that had appeared at my side, lifting the burden from my shoulders, as a happy chance, for others it might seem just a coincidence. For me, tense and overwrought to breaking point, it had the hallmark of divine intervention – although at that stage, in the spring of 1978, Jonathan and I had scarcely begun to confront our feelings, let alone give them any expression. The fundamental question was how to handle this heaven-sent gift. It could be used hurtfully, destructively, with the potential to break up the family in which I had invested so much of myself, if Jonathan and I even momentarily contemplated going off and setting up a home together. It would not be enough to claim that I had fulfilled my promise to Stephen in outrageously difficult circumstances over a very long period, because this was not a viable rationale in terms of the teachings of our church, which both I and Jonathan believed were the only true basis for human living. The alternative course was the only one we could follow. Then, that special gift could be used well, for the benefit of the family as a whole – for the children and for Stephen, if he were prepared to accept it as such. The latter course would not be easy since it would require a rigorous amount of self-discipline. In caring for Stephen we would have to try to maintain a distance from each other, living apart and not allowing ourselves to show any outward signs of affection for each other in public. In principle, our social lives would always focus on at least three, if not five people, never an exclusive twosome. The well-being of Stephen and the children would be the justification for our relationship with no thoughts for the future. In effect there was no obvious future for anyone who became involved with me. If it was selfish of me to monopolize the life of a young man who had already suffered so much tragedy, the answer was always the same: with his help we could survive as a family, without it we were doomed.

As, hesitantly, we began to admit to the attraction that was drawing us to each other, Jonathan would dispel these doubts by reassuring me that through us – all of us – he had found a purpose which was helping him to alleviate the hollow pain of his own loss. It was during the course of a rare visit to London, sitting in a quiet side chapel of Westminster Abbey, that he announced that he was prepared to commit himself to me and to my family, come what may. That most selfless and most moving of pledges lifted me out of the dark void that my life had become. The relationship was ennobling and liberating. It was still platonic and would long remain so. The mutual attraction, and the unruly emotions it threatened to provoke, were sublimated in the music we practised and performed together, usually in Stephen's presence at the weekends and sometimes on weekday evenings as well. It was enough that someone had come into my life on whom I could depend implicitly.

Stephen at first reacted to Jonathan with a certain male hostility, trying in true Hawking fashion to assert his intellectual superiority, just as he might when faced with a new research student. He was soon disarmed on discovering that this technique was unavailing, since Jonathan was not competitive by nature. Highly sensitive to the needs of others, he responded much more readily to Stephen's helplessness and to the charm of his smile than he did to the sonority of his reputation. Stephen became gentler, calmer, more appreciative, more relaxed. It even became possible, in the dead of night, for me to confide in him in an unprecedented manner. Generously and gently he acknowledged that we all needed help, no one more than himself, and if there was someone who was prepared to help me, he would not object as long as I continued to love him. I could not fail to love him when he willingly showed such understanding and, most importantly, communicated it to me. On the occasional days when Jonathan was attacked by the black dog of depression, it was Stephen who would reassure me that Jonathan would never let me down. Otherwise, once accepted, the situation was rarely mentioned. It was however greatly reassuring to me that I could trust Stephen with my confidence.

All pulling together, the three of us embarked upon an excep-tionally creative period. There were still those times when the combination of my tiredness and Stephen's innate cussedness would bring me to the verge of collapse, but generally we operated on a much more even keel. For Stephen, it seemed as if the respectability conferred on him by his Fellowship of the Royal Society and by the Papal medal constituted an automatic passport to a cornucopia of other honours. While he continued to advance his understanding of the universe, all sorts of august bodies continued to trip over each other in their eagerness to cover him with medals, prizes and honorary degrees. These had already included the honorary doctorate from his Alma Mater, the University of Oxford, and to his special gratification, an honorary fellowship at University College. The atmosphere at the six-monthly feasts in the College was warm and friendly, and Stephen's undergraduate excesses were a recurring topic of jovial reminiscence. As if to lend substance to the recollections, we were regularly accommodated in undergraduate rooms at some distance from the nearest bathroom across cold, damp flagstones.

In March 1978, Caius College, not to be outdone, commissioned a line-drawing portrait of Stephen from David Hockney. While Hockney sketched and drew, Lucy sat curled up, reading and drawing, in an armchair in a corner of the living room. Doubtless to the surprise of the Fellows of Caius, Hockney included her in the final version, a gentle acknowledgement of Stephen's family background to offset the official formality of the portrait. On the second day of the sitting, Lucy paid her own tribute to Hockney. We were sitting on the lawn, drinking coffee and taking advantage of a brief spell of spring sunshine, when she burst out of the house, bouncing across the lawn on her hopper, a big balloon made of tough rubber. Her dungarees were pulled up to the knee, deliberately revealing that like Hockney she was wearing odd socks, one white and one brown.

One cold wintry evening that February, Stephen and I had joined the distinguished gathering of Fellows on the coach going down to the Royal Society for the admission of Prince Charles as an honorary Fellow. (Before coaches were fitted with wheelchair lifts, Stephen had to be hauled aboard bodily – by the coach driver and me. This however was easier than driving and parking in London.) The occasion gave Stephen cause for much mirth, a welcome reminder of the old irreverent student, scarcely discernible under the present, weighty trappings of

Establishment recognition. At the ceremony, the new President of the Royal Society complimented the Prince on the dedicated royal patronage of the Society, founded as he said by Prince Charles's namesake, Charles II, and "continued by his son James II". Stephen guffawed and, in the loudest stage whisper of which he was capable, gleefully announced, "He's got it wrong! James II was Charles II's brother!" At the reception after the ceremony, Stephen enjoyed himself even more by demonstrating the turning circle of the wheelchair to Prince Charles and in so doing, ran close to – or over – the highly polished royal footwear, an exercise which he was to inflict at a later date on the Archbishop of Canterbury at a dinner in St John's College, Cambridge.

Jonathan's career was much less meteoric than Stephen's; in fact it had scarcely begun. Quite apart from the devastating tragedy he had suffered, the frustrations of being a struggling musician contributed to the gloom of the bleak, black days he sometimes endured. A former chorister and prize-winning scholar of St John's College, he was sufficiently ambitious to find the prospect of a life spent teaching the piano disheartening, yet his natural reticence and modesty tended to conceal his very real talent as an organist and harpsichordist. His intense love and knowledge of baroque music, particularly Bach, especially when performed on authentic instruments, found scant outlet in the humdrum routine of piano teaching in schools. Convinced that he had a mission to wean the ears of the public away from resonant modern instruments and Romantic interpretations to the subtleties of baroque performance technique, he hardly knew where to begin. Authenticity in performance became one of the subjects under discussion at mealtimes, when the children's chatter allowed the adults to get a word in edgeways. Stephen would tease Jonathan about the difficulties of managing a harpsichord, insisting that a steel frame would solve all the delicate time-consuming problems of tuning and retuning. Jonathan would point out that the instrument would then not only be unsuitable for authentic baroque performance, it would no longer be portable either. In fact it might as well be a piano.

Good-humoured banter notwithstanding, Stephen and I inevitably became more and more involved in music and encouraged Jonathan to take the plunge, to move away from teaching into performing. This proposition presented him with a dilemma of which he was already only too well aware. To become a performer he would have to give up most of his teaching and devote the time to practising and rehearsing, yet he depended on teaching for his income. It would be a long time before he could make enough money from performing alone. He did have one great advantage however: he possessed his own instrument. Not only did he have a fine upright piano in his tiny house – so reminiscent of 6 Little St Mary's Lane – on the other side of Cambridge, but most of the rest of the living space was taken up with a harpsichord which he himself had built. He was therefore well equipped to begin performing; he simply lacked the right opportunity.

The more the three of us discussed the dilemma, the more we realized that the only way for Jonathan to build up a repertoire and to become recognized as a performer, in a highly competitive environment, while still earning an income from teaching, was for him to create his own opportunities. This he could do gradually by self-promotion and by offering his services to charities. A symbiotic relationship developed between him and the various charities to which he subscribed, particularly the societies concerned with leukaemia and other cancers. He gave recitals free of charge and in so doing trained himself in the techniques of performance, not simply in playing the notes but in overcoming nerves and in planning and presenting the programmes, while the charities benefited from one hundred per cent of the takings, minus the costs of publicity.

Meanwhile I was at last catching tantalizing glimpses on the horizon of the end of my own intellectual pilgrimage. I scarcely liked to confess how long it had taken me to reach that point, for it was all of twelve years and two children. Alan Deyermond, my supervisor, had been right to insist on registering me as a student at London University, as any other university would have thrown me out long ago. The way had been hard and tortuous and just when I was despondently thinking that there was no end to it, Jonathan had appeared to cheer me along the final stretch. He showed a sufficient interest in the subject to spur me on; he would ask me at the end of each day what I had achieved, listen to just a few lines of the poetry and lend a hand in sorting out the card index and the masses of notes, scribbled on odd bits of paper. That interest and a little practical help was all I needed to bolster my resolve for the final hurdle, the last chapter of the thesis which was to be an analysis of the language of the popular poetry of Castile in the later Middle Ages.

The Castilian lyrics were lively and colourful, full of the medieval iconography of gardens, plants, fruits, birds and animals, symbolizing the multiplicity of the aspects of love. Many of them were also of religious significance and were common to the rest of Europe. The garden epitomizes the attractions of the beloved as well as the virtues of the Virgin Mary. The fountain at the centre is both the spring of life and the symbol of fertility. The apple is the fruit of the Fall and the pear the fruit of divine redemption, but, in the secular context, both are potent metaphors for sexuality. The rose is the emblem of the martyrs and of the Virgin, yet it is also the most appealing image of the sensual beauty of the beloved. Spain introduces its own set of vivid images, drawn from its flamboyant landscape. The fruit which the unhappy nun tastes is the bitter lemon, while happy lovers walk in the shade of the sweet orange grove. The olive grove, similarly, becomes the scene of lovers' meetings. The fact that many of these images have reappeared in the poetry of the Sephardic Jews who were expelled from Spain in 1492, and in the poetry of the New World, is indicative of their early folkloric composition. Thematically these poems present an unbroken tradition with their Galician and Mozarabic forebears, the *cantigas* and the *kharjas*. The songs are usually sung by girls, the motif of the lover's absence recurs, the lovers meet at dawn and the mother is a constant figure.

During sparse weekday minutes and half hours, the writing began to flow with an unaccustomed ease. At weekends, on Saturday and Sunday afternoons, the songs began to flow as well. I voraciously attacked whatever Nigel, my personal Svengali, put before me, whether Schubert, Schumann, Brahms, Mozart, Britten, Bach or Purcell. Thanks to Stephen, I rapidly acquired my own library of music as he showered me with volume upon volume of music for birthday and Christmas presents. Sometimes I would be called upon to sing a solo verse in church. Initially the stage fright was terrifying, but eventually, with practice, it subsided and then the voice, which Nigel had painstakingly crafted into an instrument, surprised even me. I was producing the sound but it bore little relation to my light, unsure speaking voice. It was strong and confident, the voice of someone else, poised and assured and affirmed.

One weekend that spring my brother Chris and his wife Penelope brought their baby daughter to stay and I introduced

Jonathan to them as a new friend. They did not demand accounts of a situation which I myself could not fully explain. They were also a receptive and appreciative audience for a few songs. Afterwards, Penelope remarked on the atmosphere in the living room that Sunday afternoon. She said that it was magical, as if a great sense of peace and calm had descended on our house. That comforting remark increased my confidence in my new friendship. Chris was much taken with Jonathan, and before he left he deliberately drew me aside to tell me what a wonderful person he thought Jonathan was, especially remarking on his magnificent Byzantine eyes. Later he rang from Devon. We talked for a long time, discussing my situation and the way that it was changing. I took Chris's advice very seriously to heart. "You have been steering your little boat single-handedly across a very stormy, uncharted sea for many years," he said, and then continued, "If there is someone at hand, willing to come on board and guide that boat into a safe harbour, you should accept whatever help he can offer."

Later that summer we received a visit from my old head-mistress, Miss M. Hilary Gent, who regularly included us in her annual progress round the country, taking in former colleagues and pupils from her long career in teaching. Miss Gent's memory for names, faces and circumstances was formidable. She relayed her own news network, linking old girls with old teachers and vice versa, and establishing acquaintanceship between people from different periods of her life who had never even met. Keenly observant, she had shown herself sensitive to my tiredness and low morale over the past few years and had done her quiet best to help by writing formal but encouraging letters, and by putting me in touch with old girls from St Albans who had come to live in Cambridge. I rarely followed up her introductions as my life had become too complicated and I preferred the company of the elderly – especially since I myself, at the age of thirty-three, was acknowledged to be living the life of an old person and I needed the philosophical reassurance of someone who had come to terms with the dilemmas of old age and mortality which beset me.

Once a fortnight or so I would visit the oldest person I knew, a diminutive, white-haired former artist, Dorothy Woollard. As I sat with her in her sheltered accommodation, listening to her tales of the past and commiserating with her malaise at her present restricted circumstances, her room represented a quiet oasis of solitude and reflection in my otherwise frenzied routine. DW, as we called her, had trained in the Bristol School of Art, and as a girl she had seen Queen Victoria, a tiny old woman in a black bonnet, on a royal visit to Bristol. She had painted the pictures for Queen Mary's doll's house in Windsor Castle, and during the First World War she had worked in the Admiralty, drawing charts. She had never married but had devoted many years of her life to caring for her adored teacher who was wheelchair-bound in old age. His portrait, her greatest treasure, hung in her room among a vast collection of her own masterly etchings and watercolours. At an age when most people would have retired from all activity, she kept herself occupied by translating books into Braille. She was still quick and nimble, even in her nineties, so much so that once she left the dinner table to demonstrate her ability to touch her toes to my astounded parents. She attributed her longevity – she lived to the age of a hundred – and her sprightliness in part to her afternoon tea, *yerba mate*, a South American brew which she served to me when I visited her. Amongst my elderly acquaintance only Miss Gent, who was probably at least ten years younger, could compete with her in alertness, clarity of thought and quick-wittedness. Both were blessed with the perceptive wisdom of old age and a sensitivity to the problems of illness – attributes which, in my experience, younger people often lacked.

Jonathan was with us when Miss Gent arrived one Saturday afternoon for tea. Immediately she and he began to talk. They talked for the rest of the afternoon while Stephen – the famous old boy of the preparatory department of St Albans High School for Girls – and I sat listening. It transpired that Jonathan, in his late twenties, and Miss Gent, in her late seventies, had many acquaintances in common, since music and the musical arena were but one of the many topics in which she was intimately knowledgeable. She interrupted their conversation to follow me into the kitchen when I went to fetch the tea. Unhesitatingly, with an openness which I found extraordinary for a wizened, elderly spinster, let alone my former headmistress, she declared, "I am so very glad that you have Jonathan." She looked at me searchingly, as though wondering whether to be more explicit. "You have struggled on for so long alone," she went on, "I don't know how you have managed; you really need someone to help and support you. He is a splendid young man." It was as if Thelma Thatcher with all her years of experience was talking to me, telling me that my relationship with Jonathan bore the mark of destiny, that the gift was really to be accepted.

My parents met Jonathan that summer. As usual they were reticent about expressing their opinions, traditionally indicated by their reactions rather than words. In this instance they behaved exactly as if Jonathan had been a presence in our lives for as long as they could remember; they did not stand on ceremony, nor did they pass any comments on his regular appearances in our household. For his part he tactfully ceded his place at the piano to my father, whose passion for Beethoven had fired my own love of music. So while my father pounded out the *Appassionata* and my mother plied her needle, replacing the buttons and repairing the cuffs and seams which had fallen off or apart since her last visit, Jonathan would discuss the merits of early instruments with her and tell her about his crusade for authentic performance. It was after we had met Jonathan's parents that I remarked to my mother what wonderfully kind people they were. My mother looked at me in some surprise. "Well, you ninny, what would you expect?" she said. "People who have a son like Jonathan are bound to be wonderful. How could they be otherwise?"

At the end of the summer we parted company, already anticipating our reunion in the autumn. Jonathan left England to attend and teach at a baroque summer school in Austria, and we set out, with Don in attendance, for Corsica. Now that the children were growing up and my self-confidence was re-emerging, the fear of flying was beginning to dissipate a little. Air travel no longer held the dreaded threat of separation from tiny dependent beings; instead it held out the enticing promise of a holiday by the Mediterranean on a French-speaking island. The fact that the holiday was also a conference in physics was not a hindrance to enjoyment. In fact it was the perfect compromise because Stephen and his colleagues would be doing what they liked best – physics – while the families would be enjoying the best sort of beach holiday, within a stone's throw of the conference centre. I was particularly looking forward to seeing the Carters again. I intended to confide in Lucette. With her intuitive understanding of people and relationships, she would be bound to offer good, sound advice.

9

The Unexpected

Cargese, the conference venue on the west coast of Corsica, was certainly the happiest compromise ever devised for single-minded physicists and their young families. While Stephen revelled in the physics, the children and I enjoyed the bright sun, the sand and the sparkling sea. The occasional bomb outrage and high prices preserved the island from mass tourism, keeping its beaches and coves clean and uncrowded, as Majorca used to be. Cargese was established as the home of a colony of Greeks seeking refuge from Turkish persecution in the eighteenth century. Their presence was still very much in evidence in street names, family names and in the name of our hotel, the Thalassa – the Sea. On promontories overlooking the town, Cargese proudly sported two churches, one Latin and the other Greek. The same priest officiated at both, alternating between the two on consecutive Sundays. Lucette and I attended the Greek rite, fascinated by such an exemplary display of harmony in what might otherwise be a divided community. Both churches contained images of John the Baptist; the Greek icon was compelling for its sharp Byzantine clarity, especially for the haunting depiction of the saint's long, slanting eyes, so reminiscent of Jonathan's. Even that image was not able to inspire me with the courage to tell Lucette about my friendship with him. Whenever I tried to summon the words, whether in English or in French, they stuck in my throat, trapped by my sense of self-reproach at the merest hint of disloyalty to Stephen. The glorious new relationship, which promised so much, was awakening doubts. Was it going to force me to live a lie, to lead a double life? That could turn out to be as difficult as the strain and distress of the preceding months and years. I took heart when I recalled Chris's advice and Miss Gent's encouragement, but in the company of physicists and their families – among whom Stephen was an awe-inspiring hero – my courage failed me.

In a quiet bay, away from the children's shouts, I wedged myself into a corner in the rock and wrote a long letter to Jonathan, trying to organize my thoughts and sort out my troubled conscience. I told him how much I missed him and how eternally grateful I was for the light he had brought to my life, like the light of the Corsican sun searching out the green depths of the ocean. I said how appreciative I was of all the unstinting help he had given us, of the transformation he had brought about in our home, easing the tensions and assuming much of the strain – but I also said that I could not risk damaging my family, that my first duty was to Stephen and the children, that since Stephen and I had lived through so much hardship together, I could not renege on my marriage when he, more helpless than a small child, needed me more than ever. Resting against a warm rock with the waves splashing at my feet, I was preparing myself for the worst. I knew in my heart of hearts that it would not be at all surprising if, after a period of reflection during his stay in Austria, Jonathan were to decide that association with the Hawking household presented too many physical challenges and too many emotional difficulties. Such a decision would be understandable. Why should he want to burden himself with all our problems and willingly walk into an emotional trap when he was young and free, with the well-deserved prospect of a full, happy life before him?

Memories of Corsica faded fast on our return home, but those weeks had bequeathed us a long-lasting memento. As I took up the reins of the Cambridge routine that autumn, it began to seem even less likely that Jonathan would want to involve himself with us again, and the prospect of a happy reunion faded into the mists with the waning light of the September sun. As the days grew shorter and a chill crept into the air, I anxiously studied the dates on the calendar, starting to suspect in bewildered amazement that I might be pregnant. For some time I had ceased to bother about contraception as it hardly seemed relevant and simply added to the difficulties. In every waking hour and many a sleepless hour at night, the realization grew that, in the carefree abandon of the Mediterranean climate, I had been wrong. Passionately though I had adored my babies, the thought of caring for another little person, who would be totally dependent on me in an intolerably demanding situation, without the benefit of Jonathan's help, was terrifying. That Jonathan should have considered shoring up the existing family, as he had done for nearly a year, had been remarkable. To expect him to take on another small Hawking, especially when he had no children of his own and no prospect of ever having any as long as he associated with us, was inconceivable. I was resigned to losing him and, with his loss, to losing all hope for the future. I would be alone again.

The pregnancy had only just been confirmed when Stephen left for a conference in Moscow. Since I was already suffering badly from morning sickness, his mother agreed to go with him in my place. Don was also away with his father on a well-earned break from all those duties, which he fulfilled most conscientiously. As winter approached in Cambridge, the icy claws of the dark, inner winter from which I had so nearly escaped began to reassert their grip. I wrote Jonathan a note telling him about the baby, wretched in the certainty that this note would amount to a signing-off, an abrupt end to those few months of recovery and blissful platonic happiness. I did not know whether he was back from the summer school in Austria and did not expect a reply. For some time I heard nothing, but he replied eventually, apologizing for having taken time to digest the news and to adjust to it. He declared that his commitment to us was unchanged. Although he knew nothing at all about babies, he was sure that I would need his help more than ever and he was ready to offer it.

I was deeply grateful and felt myself blessed with the support of someone whose own early tragedy had awakened a sympathy and a consideration for the misfortunes of others which were exceptional almost to the point of eccentricity. His hand reached out and rescued me from death by drowning, not just in deep water, but in deep water under a sheet of ice. His encouragement transformed the long months of pregnancy from a time of desperate anxiety and foreboding to a period of hopeful anticipation and even enjoyment. He gave me the fundamental emotional reassurance that restored me to my old optimistic self and enabled me to prepare for yet another challenge, safe in the knowledge that for the first time in many years, this was a challenge I should not have to meet alone.

There was no escaping the fact that a very definite time limit had been sprung on the thesis. It had to be finished by the time the baby arrived, otherwise it might as well be thrown in the bin. I recovered my incentive, setting to work with renewed purpose even though it was fated always to be done in fits and starts. As usual, the writing had to be fitted in among the accustomed round of domestic chores, Stephen's care, children's parties, children's illnesses, speech days, dinners, lunches, visitors and travels. The latter included a physics conference in Dublin. It was our first visit to Ireland and Lucy came with us. Her picture, not unlike the Hockney drawing of her, appeared on the front page of the *Dublin Times* when a reporter found her hiding behind a door reading a book at a formal government reception.

Because Jonathan gave so much help with Stephen's needs, with the children and with the chores, even with the shopping, it was actually possible to make good, if fragmentary progress with the thesis, although my writing was also competing for time with music and hospital appointments. It was at the first hospital appointment in November that I suddenly became aware of the reality of the fourteen-week-old embryo, a mysterious, ethereal creature, whispering the message of its existence through the clinical medium of a new scientific invention, the ultrasound scan. After putting me through the barrage of usual tests, the doctors wired me up, and when they were satisfied with their findings, they asked if I would like to listen too. The rhythmic swish-swish of the tiny heart – beating rapidly against the background of my own, slower and louder – was poignantly moving, awakening in me a deep bond with the new life I had heard but not seen. It was as if the child was appealing to me through the music of its heartbeat, and so, long before the birth, I began to cherish that unseen presence, already loving the child as much as I loved Robert and Lucy.

Music accompanied the baby's gestation throughout the winter. Jonathan, our self-appointed entertainments officer, frequently brought home tickets for concerts, many of which were in the newly opened university concert hall only five minutes away. We sat on the stage alongside the performers in full view of the audience, since there was no other provision for wheelchairs. Often the performers, a host of celebrated musicians, from Menuhin to Schwarzkopf, would delay their exits after their curtain calls to come over and greet Stephen. At home I sang whenever I could, practising my repertoire for its first public performance. The baby responded with animated appreciation, kicking hard in time to the music. We were rehearsing with two musical goals in view. One was my entry in the Cambridge Competitive Festival in March, the other in February was a concert we and some musical friends of Jonathan's were giving at home for charity. We invited as many people as would fit into the living room and, in the tradition of the numerous parties in our establishment, laid on food and drinks in the interval. Afterwards, in an advanced state of pregnancy and an even more advanced state of nerves, I stood up to give my first public performance – other than the occasional solo in church. It consisted of two folksongs by Benjamin Britten and a couple of songs by Fauré; which were also to be my entries in the competition. The audience were kindly appreciative and on their departure made generous donations to our two charitable causes, leukaemia research and the Motor Neuron Disease Association, which had been recently founded and for which Stephen had become the Patients' Patron. When, long ago, his condition was diagnosed, we were told that it was very rare, that little was known about it, and that since so few people suffered from it there was no basis for a support group. None of this was true. Through the Association we discovered that the illness – also known in America as Lou Gehrig's disease, after a sportsman who suffered from it in the Thirties – was in fact quite widespread. At any one time there could be as many diagnoses of motor-neuron disease as there were sufferers from multiple sclerosis, which until then had received much more publicity because there were more survivors. Motor-neuron disease ran its course much more quickly – usually within two or three years – distorting the statistics and leaving patients and their families crisis-ridden, with neither the time nor the opportunity to set up support organizations or self-help groups. On the founding of the Association, some information at last became available. It emerged that motor-neuron disease could erupt in one of two forms. The acute form paralyses the victim's throat muscles, precipitating an early death. The rarer form, the one which had attacked Stephen, resulted in a creeping paralysis of the voluntary muscles of the whole body – including eventually the throat – over a longer period, perhaps five years or, at the outside, ten. Stephen's survival for sixteen years since the time of diagnosis in January 1963 made him a medical phenomenon, as unexplained as the illness itself.

Over the course of the next few years, Jonathan and I gave many joint recitals of baroque repertoire for the fledgling Motor Neuron Disease Association in churches throughout East Anglia, managing to raise quite respectable amounts of money, and since Stephen usually featured prominently in the audience, the illness and the Association came to the notice of the public. As a local volunteer, I visited some of the afflicted families in the area, whose lives were being shattered by a diagnosis that had left all of them shocked and bewildered, as it had left us years before. I felt that I had a duty to try and give these families the benefit of our experience, passing on to them the practical techniques we had devised for managing the condition, and pointing to the fact that Stephen, the survivor, was the living proof that the diagnosis was not necessarily a death sentence if one had the will to fight. Perhaps it was because the people I met were all much older than ourselves that they did not seem prepared to fight with the same vehemence. They were hurt and troubled, certainly, but they revealed a much greater calm and acceptance than I expected. The frenzied lifestyle, which had become the mark of our rejection of the disease, was not for them. Instead, they lived quietly, appreciating whatever was done for them, thankful for all the love and care they received from their families, often awaiting their fate with resignation. I trod warily, fearing to trespass on their privacy by introducing bright, well-meaning proposals for exercises, diets, injections or vitamins. There was, it seemed, an element in their lives which ours lacked and which I found myself envying. It was not defeatism but inner peace.

Stephen's position as Patron of the Association, and my attempts to help as a fundraiser and volunteer, brought me face to face yet again with one of those ironies of our situation. Once more we were elevated to a pedestal and there we found ourselves aloof. We needed advice as much as anybody, but we could not seek it because the admission of our needs would have been a denial of the confident façade on which other people depended for boosting their own morale. The number of people blessed with the perspicacity to see behind that mask were not many. They included my family, Jonathan and his parents and a few exceptional friends.

Just before the baby was due, we were fortunate to get to know some new friends of comparable sensitivity in Stephen's Australian colleague Bernard Whiting and his wife Mary, when they came to one of our musical gatherings. Relaxed and easygoing, Bernard was to give Stephen a hand, in much the same way that George Ellis had in the past. Mary, a classical archeologist, was writing a PhD thesis and working in the Fitzwilliam Museum on a catalogue of the museum's extensive gem collection. She was no fossilized museum piece. Her flowing, prematurely grey hair framing finely etched youthful features lent her a graceful distinction, like a Raphael madonna. Her appearance was well matched by her personality, for she was both learned and spirited, her interests extending far beyond archeology into art, literature and music, especially baroque music, so that when she and Jonathan met they immediately had plenty to discuss.

Towards the end of March 1979, Robert, who was in the first year of the Upper School at the Perse, went away to scout camp. I was not at all happy about this camp for eleven-year-olds since it was to be in the corner of a field in north Norfolk, exposed to the biting winds of a reluctant spring. The field, by all accounts, was sodden under a couple of inches of water. There was a fall of snow during the camp and Robert came back exhausted, soaked to the skin and coughing persistently. Stoical as ever, he declared that the camp had been "all right". After a couple of days in bed, he recovered sufficiently to be able to go away with Lucy to the cottage in Wales, where they were to spend Easter with Stephen's parents. Meanwhile I made my debut on the concert platform at the Cambridge Competitive Festival, singing the Fauré and Britten songs to Jonathan's expert piano accompaniment while Stephen smiled his cheerful encouragement from the audience. The adjudicator politely commended the timbre of the voice, otherwise only allowing himself to remark that he realized that my breath control was somewhat inhibited. With the competition over, back at St Mark's we were rehearsing for the devotional service on Good Friday and for the Easter Festival, at which I was to sing a solo, 'Now the Green Blade Riseth', accompanied on the flute by Jonathan's old school friend, Alan Hardy. After rehearsing in the church in the early part of Holy Week, we were all set for the performance on Easter Sunday.

The thesis was very nearly finished; all that remained was the mind-bogglingly boring task of ordering the bibliography alphabetically and attending to all the minutiae therein, upon the insistence of my supervisor. Every comma, full stop and bracket had to be in its correct place, otherwise he would not pass the thesis for submission. On Maundy Thursday, with an almighty flourish, I put the final full stop to the final entry in the bibliography, thus bringing to a conclusion thirteen arduous years of seminars, research, annotation, card-indexing, organizing, compiling, writing, editing, footnoting and referencing.

The next day, Good Friday, during the devotional service, I felt dejected to the point of tears. Perhaps this was a reaction to the emotive force of that particular religious commemoration and the music that went with it, perhaps it was the anticlimactic effect of finishing the thesis, or perhaps I was missing my children, who were to stay with their grandparents until after the baby was born in a week or two's time. The following day the melancholy lifted. Very strong physical symptoms took its place, leaving little doubt that the baby was going to be born quite soon. I spent most of the afternoon in the garden with Stephen beside me, relaxing in the sun and picking bunches of violets. Don drove us to the maternity hospital early in the evening, but a routine inspection revealed little movement of any significance, so we were sent away again. We called at Jonathan's house on the way home and stayed for a takeaway curry, inserting ourselves as best we could in among the musical instruments in the restricted space of the living room. As Jonathan and Stephen were partial to curries, he often arranged a takeaway, especially on Sunday evenings when the kitchen, after seven days of churning out three-course meals for all-comers, only ran to scrambled eggs. Exceptionally, this was a Saturday-evening curry and it was an exceptionally hot dupiaza.

Back at home I spent a most uncomfortable night and, at dawn, woke Don to ask him to drive us back to the hospital. Because Stephen wanted to be present at the birth of his third child, special provision had been made to accommodate him in the delivery room. Joy Cadbury, who presided over the Friends of the Maternity Hospital, had kindly conferred with the matron to make suitable arrangements for the wheelchair. The only space large enough for Stephen and Sue Smith, his physiotherapist, who came in to look after him – plus the medical team, not to mention me – was the delivery room, so I had to spend the rest of the day lying on the hard surface of the delivery table waiting for the birth to happen. Don sat out in the corridor, occasionally peering round the door, while Jonathan wisely took himself off to spend that hot, sunny Easter Sunday at his parents' parsonage in the country. In such inclement conditions, the birthing processes slowed down to a standstill. I sent messages to Don that he could safely abandon his post in the corridor to attend morning service in one or other of his ecclesiastical locations, and while I lay awkwardly trying to ease my bulk into a comfortable position, I rued the urgency with which we had come to the hospital, especially when I realized that I could have been singing in church. There, Bill Loveless had to announce the cancellation of the musical interlude on account of the absence of the singer who was otherwise engaged.

The various attempts made to accelerate the birth had the sole effect of turning me into a human pin cushion as the morning slid into afternoon and the afternoon into evening. Don returned and went out again – this time to evensong. While he was away, a crisis developed: the foetal heart, that infant heartbeat that had introduced itself to me many months ago, showed worrying signs of fatigue. While the medical team had their backs turned, preparing their instruments of torture to bring the baby into the world without delay, I hastily summoned all my remaining energies into an almighty push and my Easter child was born. When they gave him to me to hold, my heart went out to him. Wrapped in an old green blanket, his face was blue from the battering he had received. Although he was larger than either Robert or Lucy at birth, he did not display the energy with which they had greeted the world but lay limply, whimpering in my arms. For a moment I was oblivious of the commotion of the cleaning-up operations around us, absorbed by the little creature whom I already knew so well. Then Don burst triumphantly into the delivery room. He was pleased to make the acquaintance of his godson and was even more pleased with himself on account of a little ditty that he had thought up on returning from church. To my embarrassment he would repeat it to everyone he met for several weeks after the event. It went like this:

On Easter Day,
the disciples went to the garden
and found the empty tomb;
I went to the hospital
and found the empty womb

10

Dissonance

During the week that Timothy Stephen (the baby's full name) and I stayed in hospital, Lucy was brought back to Cambridge to meet her younger brother – but Robert was stranded in St Albans for reasons which were not fully explained. Apparently the children had been playing barefoot in the stream in Wales and he had caught a cold. He was coughing again, so badly that when the children called on my parents for tea in St Albans, my mother put him to bed. There he stayed for the next week until Stephen's sister Mary, the doctor, decided that he was well enough to come back to Cambridge. His return coincided with our homecoming. He nursed his little brother on his knee, sitting in an armchair in the living room, but looked suspiciously flushed and unwell. The mother of one of Lucy's friends, Valerie Broadbent-Keeble, a respected pediatrician, came on a social call to visit Timothy and me. By coincidence, she arrived at the same time as Dr Wilson, my GP. The two doctors glanced only briefly at Timothy, who had adjusted to the business of living and was glowing with health; Robert, on the other hand, commanded their full attention. Both were visibly alarmed at his state of health and were fairly sure that he was suffering from viral pneumonia. Valerie went away to organize Robert's immediate admission to the children's ward at Addenbrooke's while Dr Wilson wrote out a prescription for penicillin.

It was a blessing that the new baby was still tired from the ordeal of his birth and consequently slept for long periods by day and, amazingly, by night as well, otherwise the weeks after his birth would have been an even worse nightmare than they actually were. I was needed by everyone all the time. Stephen's needs were obvious, the baby's needs were undeniable, Lucy needed reassurance now that there was a rival usurping her place as the youngest member of the family. Above all, Robert was seriously ill in hospital and needed me most. After one night on the children's ward, he awoke covered in weals from head to foot.

Either he had contracted an infectious disease or he was allergic to penicillin. As there was no way of telling which of the two was the cause, he was moved to an isolation ward at the top of the hospital for fear of infecting the other critically ill patients on the children's ward. In isolation, his meals were passed to him through a hatch, and the medical staff donned gowns, gloves and masks when they entered his room. He was allowed only restricted visiting and the visitors had to dress up in the same protective clothing as the nurses. Bored, lonely and ill, he lay in bed with the tears streaming down his hot cheeks.

My visits to the hospital had to be timed precisely in between the week-old baby's feeds. Once he was fed, changed and settled, I would dash off to spend the next few hours at Robert's bedside, reading books and playing games, before dashing home again for the next feed. This became my routine until Robert was discharged from hospital. Stephen's mother did her best to keep the home fires burning, shopping and cooking wholesome meals, but there was too much for her to do alone. Never was Jonathan's help more urgently required. He looked after Stephen, he did the heavy shopping, he took Lucy to school and he visited Robert, enabling me sometimes to take a break from a rigorously pressurized routine. It was unfortunate that he had only been introduced briefly to Stephen's mother before this crisis occurred. Since her visits to Cambridge had been much rarer than my parents', the opportunity had not arisen. I realized that I could not expect any of the Hawkings, unlike our close and tactful friends, to divine the significance of Jonathan's presence in our household. But I hoped however that I had earned their respect well enough over the many years in which I had cared for their son for them to trust me at least to try to do my best for him and for the children in the present demanding situation, and I trusted that they might muster some sympathy or discreet toleration. Above all I wanted to reassure them that I was not about to abandon Stephen or break up the home, nor was Jonathan encouraging me to do so.

There was no suitable opportunity to broach the matter to Isobel. When eventually she and I found ourselves alone in the house with the new baby one afternoon, she took the initiative, catching me unawares. She looked me straight in the eye. "Jane," she said, adopting a stentorian tone, "I have a right to know whose child Timothy is. Is he Stephen's or is he Jonathan's?" I met her steely gaze, dismayed that she had so readily jumped to conclusions – and the most uncharitable conclusions at that. All the discipline with which Jonathan and I had forced ourselves to try to sublimate our own desires and maintain a discreet relationship was being trampled underfoot. The simple truth was that there was no way that Timothy could have had any other father than Stephen. Isobel was not content with this statement of the truth; instead she carried on, as if riding the crest of a wave, "You see," she went on, "we have never really liked you, Jane, you do not fit into our family." Later she apologized for her outburst, but from my point of view it was too late.

The following day Frank Hawking responded to his wife's urgent summons and came over to Cambridge in the early morning. I watched from the house as, together, they went out onto the lawn and disappeared into the shrubbery, engaged in conspiratorial conversation. Soon afterwards they left, huffily defiant, scarcely bothering to acknowledge me at all. The combination of so many traumatic events in such a short space of time after the birth had the predictably disheartening effect of diminishing my ability to feed the two-week-old baby, who was emerging from his post-natal stupor, exercising his leonine lungs and his vocal chords with hearty enthusiasm. Stephen brooked no opposition in resolving the situation in his own fashion. He dragooned eight-year-old Lucy to accompany him into town and help him shop at Boots, where he bought an array of bottles, teats, sterilizing fluid and dried milk powder. Thus ended my pitiful attempts to nurse my third child and thus commenced a new chore for Jonathan. Every evening before leaving West Road for his own home, he would make up the next day's supply of baby milk and store it in the fridge, ready for use on demand.

Some weeks later, as I was making the preparations for Timothy's christening in early June, Stephen received a letter from his father. The letter announced that he had been in touch with an American team of doctors in Dallas, Texas, who were treating motor-neuron disease with a new drug. These doctors were issuing an invitation to Stephen to become one of the first patients to test the drug. It seemed that it was a fait accompli. We would all, Stephen, Robert, Lucy, Timothy and I, with the mere waving of a wand, move lock, stock and barrel to Texas, where Stephen would undergo an extended course of treatment lasting months if not years. The letter was passed to me without comment, without explanation, the tacit implication being that the decision rested on my shoulders.

My head swam and my heart sank at the complexity of the responsibility that I was being asked to assume. First and foremost, if there was a chance of a cure for Stephen, I could never deny him that chance. Yet I was only too aware that the demands on the family and on me would be monumental, far in excess of anything we had ever experienced before. The children would be summarily removed from the schools, the environment and the home where they were happy and secure, and would be dumped down in a huge, strange, American city. This would not be Pasadena. It was not clear where our income would come from, nor was it clear how our housing or transport would be organized. I, the mother of a six-week-old baby, was being asked to uproot the whole family, the three children and their paraplegic father, transport them a third of the way round the world and set up home for an indefinite time. There was no indication of how I was to achieve that objective, no promise nor any likelihood of help in this mammoth task other than young Robert's, nor any certainty that the treatment would be successful. Painful memories of Seattle in 1967 came crowding to the fore, multiplied a thousand times by the experiences of the past several years.

As the date of the baby's christening approached, I could not keep this most painful of dilemmas from my parents. The christening party divided squarely into two opposing camps. In a situation which required extreme tact on all sides, the Hawkings stood in one corner of the living-room, ostracizing the rest of the gathering – my parents, Tim's godparents and their families, and a few friends. The atmosphere was so unbearable that at one stage I left the room and took refuge in the bedroom. My father followed me, only too conscious of the intolerable pressure I was under. An intellectual match for the Hawkings but devoid of all affectation or snobbery, he pulled a piece of paper from his pocket. "Jane," he said, "just have a look at this, will you? If you approve, I am going to send it to Frank Hawking." As I read, gratitude for my father's intervention flooded through me: the letter was a masterly resolution of the dilemma, without in any way jeopardizing my loyalty to Stephen. Quite simply it stated that we all wanted Stephen's best interests, but that the Hawkings must be aware that the care of two young children and the new baby – their grandchildren – in addition to the burden of Stephen's care, made it impracticable for me to travel to Texas. He suggested that if they were convinced of the efficacy of the treatment, they should consider accompanying Stephen to Texas themselves. Yet again my father, sometimes exacting, always honourable, always unpretentious, had by quiet, intelligent application behind the scenes come to the rescue. The letter was sent. He did not receive a reply.

After so many years of thinly veiled tolerance, they had expressed their dislike of me with caustic bluntness when I was at my lowest ebb, soon after the birth of my third child, while my eldest child was critically ill. Their dislike had emerged and spread into unconcealed hostility. It was stupid of me not to have recognized their animosity and resigned myself to it sooner; it was stupid of me to have lived in innocent hope of better things. As they were Stephen's closest relatives, I had been bound to try to get on with them as best I could. In fact for this very reason, I was still obliged to maintain a veneer of civility. Whether I liked it or not, the close blood tie was the one invariable factor in this predicament.

The following winter news came that the Texan team were offering to send their treatment to Cambridge. However the consultant neurologist at Addenbrooke's stated quite firmly that the treatment was untested, unproven and inappropriate for motor-neuron disease. He suspected that Stephen would be used as a guinea pig, and that the researchers were looking for the scientific respectability and publicity associated with his name, possibly to attract funding. The treatment would have to be administered in hospital and the time involved would be considerable, with minimal chance of a positive outcome even in the short term. Motor-neuron disease had already done its worst to Stephen; there was little more that it could do and it was a well-known fact of medical science that the body was not able to repair damaged nerve tissue. The greatest risk to his survival these days came from pneumonia, not motor-neuron disease per se. The proposed treatment would be a waste of Stephen's precious time and scarcely more than one of those chimeras against which Frank Hawking had himself warned so decisively in the Sixties.

11

Turbulence

Perhaps I might have been less distressed at the behaviour of the Hawkings had I realized how implicitly I could rely on Jonathan's family. With unassuming goodness, they dedicated themselves tirelessly to other people, whoever they were, whatever their origins. They made no distinction between family, friends, parishioners or strangers. Anyone in trouble, rich or poor, could arrive on their doorstep by day or by night and be assured of help and a sympathetic ear, and probably a filling meal into the bargain. I could not believe that any parents, however well-intentioned, would welcome the sort of family that their eldest son had become involved in. I was wrong. On our first visit to their rectory, they treated us, Stephen, the children and me, as if we were the most welcome visitors, as if they were really pleased to see us. Never did they pass even the slightest hint of judgement on us or on our situation.

Like Bill Loveless, John Jones had been a late ordinand. He had come to Cambridge to train for the ministry, after his first career as a dentist in Warwickshire. In this mid-life change of direction, he was encouraged unequivocally by his wife Irene, so like my own mother in her quietly assured faith. From their hilltop vantage point, just outside Cambridge, they tended to their flock in the surrounding fenland and worshipped with a practical tenacity which would have been extraordinary in a young incumbent, let alone in one of advancing years. Not only did John, with Irene's assistance, look after the souls in his charge in Lolworth and its associated parishes, he also mended the fabric of the medieval building entrusted to him by an impecunious diocese. In the early Eighties the tower of Lolworth church was badly in need of repairs. As there were no funds available to repair it, John and Irene donned hard hats and overalls and set about removing several tons of bird droppings from the inside before relining and strengthening the structure themselves.

I found it unbelievable that these people, not related to us in any way, could find any good reason for wanting to welcome me and my family, nor could I understand why they should show such genuine interest in us and so much concern for us. They spread the light of kindness, sympathy and selflessness in darkness. It was not only Jonathan's parents who took us to their hearts but, inexplicably, his entire family as well, his aunts, uncles and cousins, his brother Tim and sister Sara. Formerly a physiotherapist, Sara was blessed with the same sort of intuitive good sense as Caroline Chamberlain in her approach to severe disability; she knew the toll that a paralysing disease could exact on the immediate family as well as on the patient. Sara and I quickly became the closest of friends. We were more or less the same age and we had our babies at more or less the same time. Sara's first baby, Miriam, was born in February 1979, two months before Timothy.

Thus I no longer had to look to the Hawkings for support. Instead, I began to foster the cool detachment that they had shown for years. Surprisingly, other more distant relatives of Stephen's stepped into the vacuum left by their absence. Michael Mair, a cousin of Stephen's who had been an undergraduate in Cambridge in the late Sixties when Robert was a new baby had returned to work in the eye department of Addenbrooke's Hospital. He and his South African fiancée, Solome, a radiographer, were enthusiastic cooks. Every so often they would bring a delicious, ready-prepared, calorie-rich meal for the whole family. In anticipation of their arrival, Robert and Lucy would stand in the porch, peering through the glass door and salivating long before they drew into the driveway. Never were those meals-on-wheels more welcome than in the months after Timothy's birth, as we struggled to get back onto an even keel, desperately weary from the gruelling effort of steering our little boat through turbulent seas.

The truth was that one adult minder was required to attend full-time to each one of the less able members of the family. Disabled to the point of not being able to do anything for himself – except handling the simple joystick controls of his wheelchair and of the computer which he had bought in celebration of Timothy's birth – Stephen had to have a well-known person, whether me, Don or Jonathan, in constant attendance. The baby, previously so docile, had begun to assert himself, responding to all the attention lavished on him with huge captivating smiles, so wide that they could have swallowed us up, but he protested loudly when our attention was deflected elsewhere. On these occasions my mother would laughingly point out his resemblance to his father. He had certainly inherited Stephen's cherubic dimples, but also like Stephen his mouth had the comical habit of drooping downwards at the corners to express affronted indignation, especially when he was hungry. In other respects, though a larger baby, he was the exact image of his older brother. I called them my twins – twins nearly twelve years apart. Indeed more than once, passing acquaintances would glance at Tim and cheerily call "Hello, Robert!" then in some bafflement would think they must have fallen into a time warp before they realized their mistake.

Luckily we were now able to afford the luxury of a nanny on a couple of mornings a week, so that I could see to all the administration involved in the production of the four bound copies of the thesis demanded by officialdom. My helper, Christine Ikin, later christened Kikki by infant Tim, was also the mother of three children. She came in from the country as regularly as the unpredictable bus service would allow, and cheerfully hoovered and cleaned and looked after the baby, while I contacted typists, proofread the results of their labours, collated hundreds of pages and sought out bookbinders. My association with medieval Spanish poetry had run its course and was coming to a grand finale. Since the thesis did not hold out the promise of any very obvious career, I had already reconciled myself to its being an end in itself rather than the means to greater advancement. In any case, a career was completely out of the question since ninety-nine per cent of my attention had to remain focused on the home and the family. Somehow I had to divide that attention fairly between the children and their father while still finding time to keep my brain alive.

Robert and Lucy were both finding it hard to adjust to new circumstances. Lucy now found herself in an uncertain situation in the middle of the family as neither the eldest nor the youngest child, and not until Robert went away to another scout camp later in the summer did she show any interest in the baby. Then she was suddenly called upon to fetch and carry bottles, nappies, pins and powder – chores that Robert had previously undertaken. At first she resisted defiantly, and then she burst into tears. At that moment I realized how badly she too had been affected by the trauma we had undergone since little Tim's arrival. Lucy had been left to fend for herself when in fact she needed as much reassurance as anyone else. I hugged her and told her that I had not stopped loving her just because there was another person in the family to care for. She warmed to her little brother straight away, as if in all those miserable weeks she had been longing to show her true feelings but had not known how. She fetched and carried just as willingly as Robert had done, and thereafter no one could have been more devoted to Tim or more susceptible to his winning ways.

Robert had been very ill, and although he had made a good recovery and was back at school, he often seemed subdued and forgetful. Dyslexia was still a severe handicap in his schooling. The school arranged a few sessions with an educational psychologist, who tried to instil into him techniques for coping with dyslexia, but she failed to identify the true extent of the problem. It was not until many years later that I discovered that at the root of it lay an overwhelming sense of inadequacy. From a very early age he had become aware that his father was a scientific genius and that people, in particular his teachers rather than his parents, had expectations of him that he knew he could not fulfil. His belief in himself swamped by self-doubt, his solution was not to bother with his studies at all since he felt himself doomed to failure in the eyes of the world, however hard he tried. The saddest part of it was that from as young as seven years old, when he first became aware that his father was a genius, he felt himself to be inferior. Robert had the doubtful advantage of a quick, scientific intelligence which destined him for a scientific career without achieving his father's fame. As for Lucy and Tim, they were later to suffer for not being scientific, and they were both acutely humiliated when told how disappointed their teachers were in them. Really all three children were in a no-win situation. But although their teachers' prejudices cast a passing shadow over their education, Lucy and Tim did not suffer as badly as Robert, for whom the expectations of society in general cast the long shadow of his father's reputation.

In the autumn of 1979 Stephen's reputation was enhanced very publicly in Cambridge by his appointment to the coveted Lucasian Chair in Mathematics. The chair, endowed in 1663 with one hundred pounds by Henry Lucas, was one of the most prestigious professorships in one of the most prestigious universities: it was Newton's chair. Stephen was now unequivocally ranked with Newton. He celebrated his elevation to the dizziest of academic heights by availing himself of the opportunity to give an inaugural lecture, a custom which had fallen into disuse, at least among scientists. A student stood beside him on the stage of the Babbage lecture theatre and interpreted his speech, which had become so faint and so indistinct that only a handful of students, colleagues and family could even begin to understand it. The rapt audience of scientists, many of them young hopefuls, strained to catch his utterances. The words were not designed to offer them the comfortable prospect of a secure future, for Stephen gleefully predicted that the end of physics was in sight. The advent of faster and more sophisticated computers meant that by the end of the century, in a mere twenty years' time, all the major problems in physics would have been wound up, including the unified field theory, and there would be nothing left for physicists to do. He, himself, would be all right, he declared jovially, as he would be retiring in the year 2009. The audience loved the joke, though I could not see that they really had much to laugh about...

Nor in fact did Stephen have much to laugh about. In summarily predicting the end of physics he had well and truly made himself a hostage to fortune, and his own Nemesis, the affronted goddess of Physics, caught up with him very quickly. Just a few weeks later, the new decade opened very inauspiciously for us all, especially for Stephen. After Christmas we all went down with bad colds, including the baby. By the New Year, the cold had settled on Stephen's chest, racking his body with harrowing choking fits at every sip of water or every spoonful of finely chopped food, even at every breath. These fits would come on at the end of the day and would last well into the night. Using the techniques I had learnt in yoga, I would try to encourage him to relax his throat muscles by quietly and monotonously repeating calming phrases. Sometimes I would succeed and would register the change from gasping panic to regular breathing, as sleep took over his sad, persecuted frame. Sometimes the sheer boredom of repetition would send me off into an interrupted doze while he continued to cough and wheeze beside me into the early hours. We would both be drained by the next morning, though he with true courage would never admit as much and would embark on his normal schedule undeterred by the events of the previous night.

While we all feared a repetition of the 1976 bout of pneumonia, Stephen himself predictably would not let me call the doctor, nor would he take any patent medicines, since he was still scared that the sweetener in cough linctus – even in sugar-free linctus – would irritate the lining of his throat and the cough-suppressant ingredients would either befuddle his brain or plummet him into a comatose state. So he coughed and choked, and choked and coughed, day and night, while the baby snuffled and wailed with a blocked nose and I panted for breath, since I was feeling none too well myself.

As ever my mother promptly came over from St Albans to run the household, while Jonathan, Don and I tried against the odds to care for its ailing occupants. Mum insisted on sending me to bed, at least in between the various tasks that I had to attend to. Bill Loveless paid me a visit on the following Saturday afternoon. I lay on the bed prostrate from tiredness and breathlessness while Stephen, the real patient, sat reading the newspaper in the kitchen, determined to sit out the crisis. I poured out my troubles to Bill. I still passionately wanted to care for Stephen, to give him a happy home life, to make all things possible for him within reason. Sometimes, as at present, his demands were totally in excess of all that was reasonable and the wall of his obduracy was making life unbearable. In consequence I was becoming more and more dependent on Jonathan to preserve my sanity, to share my burdens, and to make me feel loved. That dependency only increased my burden of guilt.

Bill took my hand in his. "Jane," he said, thoughtfully but firmly, "there is something I want you to know." If I was nervously expecting a stern rebuke, I was much mistaken. Gently he went on, "In the sight of God all souls are equal. You are just as important to God as Stephen is." So saying, he left me to ponder this surprising revelation, and went to talk to Stephen. Later that day Dr Swan called and recommended a short spell in the local nursing home for Stephen who, although ferociously indignant, reluctantly accepted his advice. I knew in a sense that Stephen was right because in the nursing home he was not known. The nurses there did not understand his speech nor were they versed in the very precise techniques required for looking after him. As soon as word spread that the Lucasian Professor had been removed to the nursing home, there was no shortage of offers of help. Once more the loyal students and colleagues, particularly

Gary Gibbons, Stephen's former research student, established an attendance rota so that Stephen should never find himself unable to communicate his needs to the nurses. Robert's headmaster, Antony Melville, remembering similarly tragic circumstances in his own family, spontaneously offered to take Robert into his own home, should the need arise. John Casey, a Fellow of Caius who concealed genuine sympathy behind a somewhat mannered façade, decided that the College should pay Stephen's nursing-home expenses and undertook to persuade the governing body and the Bursar. Perhaps that task was less insuperable than it sounds since, it should be noted, the Bursar, a retired Air Vice-Marshal, Reggie Bullen, was the most humane Bursar ever to hold that office in the College.

The following week, while Stephen was in the nursing home, I answered an invitation from Martin Rees, the Plumian Professor of Astronomy and Experimental Philosophy since 1973, to meet him out at the Institute of Astronomy. Endearingly unconvincing in his efforts to appear a hard-nosed scientist, Martin sat me down in his office and emphatically declared, "Whatever happens, Jane, you must not let the situation get you down." The unintentional irony of his words baffled me, but as I was too tired and distraught to comment on them to any effect, I said nothing, simply waiting for him to continue. He repeated what he had just said and went on to suggest that the time had come for Stephen to have nursing care at home. If I could find the nurses, he volunteered to find the funds – from various philanthropic sources – to pay for them. I was deeply grateful for his concern and his very practical offer, so carefully and considerately proposed. My gratitude was felt as much for the fact that he had noticed that we needed help as for the help itself.

There were three elements involved in bringing nurses into the home and certainly Martin's benevolent offer would take care of one of them, the financial side. I had no idea how to tackle the remaining two. Where was I to find suitable nurses and, more significantly, how was I to persuade Stephen to accept them? Whenever the baby and I went to visit him, he ground his teeth in anger at his temporary imprisonment, keeping his eyes firmly fixed on the television screen in front of him and refusing to look at us. There was little fundamental consolation that I could bring him, rather my presence seemed to madden him; yet if I did not visit him regularly I would quickly stand accused of neglect. Panting for breath under the weight of the hefty infant, I would struggle down the long corridor twice a day, rehearsing all the gobbits of information and titbits of gossip that I had been collecting for him. Our reception would always have a dampening effect, washing the colour and life out of those little yarns, diluting their impact until they were about as interesting as a firework display in a rainstorm. Stephen's parents paid him a visit one day without bothering to call on us at West Road.

We were expecting my father to arrive in Cambridge for lunch the next weekend when there was a ring at the doorbell. Mum and I were perplexed to find an unfamiliar car in the driveway and a middle-aged woman standing outside the door. Her husband was ushering my father towards the house. This couple had been travelling behind Dad six or seven miles outside Cambridge when they had seen his car slither across the road on a patch of black ice and crash into the opposite bank. They had come to his rescue. Although the car was a write-off, Dad, miraculously, seemed to be unhurt, though badly shaken. Nonetheless, we thought it best to call a doctor to check that all was indeed well. John Owens, the doctor who had delivered Robert twelve years before – and who, coincidentally had also attended Jonathan's wife Janet – came promptly and pronounced Dad to be in remarkably good shape considering the life-threatening ordeal he had undergone. Only a couple of days later we had reason to call the surgery again. Lucy, who had also had a bad cold, gave us and herself a fright when a capillary in her nose popped and started to bleed. No sooner had one copious nosebleed dried up than another began. This time the duty doctor was new to us. Rather surprisingly since he was middle-aged, he introduced himself as a trainee. Dr Chester White had taken up medicine as a second career in middle age, and he had only recently qualified. He gave Lucy a check-up, assuring us that there was no cause for alarm.

As he was about to leave, he turned his attention to me. "What about you? Are you feeling all right?" he asked to my surprise, "you look pretty exhausted." He sat down while I told him about Stephen and the crisis we were in. Little explanation was needed as he knew Stephen by repute and had seen him out and about in the street. He did not know, however, that we had battled on for years with minimal help from the National Health Service and was appalled to hear that we had the benefit of home nursing only on two mornings a week, when the district nurse came in to get Stephen out of bed and give him a bath and an injection of hydroxocobalamin. Stephen had been obliged to let the district nurses bath him when, in a cumbersome state of pregnancy, I found my room for manoeuvre in the bathroom severely restricted.

As I recounted the same old story of our wearisome struggle to keep going and to find a way through the obstacle course that our lives had become, I was under no illusions: Dr White would listen with the utmost sympathy but would be powerless to effect any improvement. Who could, even with the funds that Martin Rees had promised? I anticipated that he would say, as so many others had said before, "Well, I'm terribly sorry, but I don't know what to suggest." I was scarcely inclined to take him seriously, therefore, when with unusual perception he thoughtfully suggested two courses of action. First, he said, he would prescribe some medication for me and, secondly, he would get in touch with a male nurse on his list who did some private nursing and might be able to arrange a regular roster of care for Stephen.

The hope that these proposals held out was too beguiling not to be considered briefly, even if with a well-worn scepticism. There was just a chance that the hurdle of finding suitable nurses might be overcome as a result of this chance encounter, and the last hurdle – and undoubtedly the highest – Stephen's resistance, might also yield in the face of this initiative, since it was being imposed by an outside authority. The blame for this most detrimental of steps would not fall entirely on my shoulders. Within days Martin Rees had found a provisional source of funding to finance some nursing care for Stephen on his return home – but, as I feared, it took longer for Chester to get in touch with his nursing contact. That prospect, it seemed, was after all no more than another of those deceptive will-o'-the-wisps, a glimmer of hope extinguished before it had even been ignited. Perhaps it was just as well: in my heart, I disliked conspiring against what I knew to be Stephen's wishes, however intolerable the situation might be.

Then, one morning towards the end of January, Dr White's contact, Nikki Manatunga, the nurse, materialized out of the blue. A quietly spoken, hard-working Sri Lankan who had settled with his wife and two children in a village outside Cambridge, he showed no disquiet at my account of the difficulties and the requirements. On the contrary, he was confident of being able to put together a team of nurses from among his colleagues at Fulbourn Hospital, the local psychiatric hospital where he worked. A week later, when he came for his first shift, Stephen adamantly refused to look at him or to communicate with him in any way, except by running over his toes with the wheelchair. I apologized to Nikki who persevered with a smile, unperturbed. "It's all right," he said, "we're used to dealing with difficult patients." The next week he brought and introduced another nurse to the system and then another. An established nurse came with each new recruit and passed on the details of the routine so that there was always a smooth changeover with minimal intervention demanded of us, the resident carers. Slowly Stephen's irritation subsided as he grew to accept the presence of these dedicated, patient people, and eventually he realized that he could call upon them for help outside the strict hours of their terms of employment. He could take the nurses on trips abroad and be independent of his students and colleagues, even of his family. No longer would he have to rely on a small group of intimates for help with his personal needs. A new era was dawning for the master of the universe and, by extension, for the rest of us.

12

Ad Astra

In lifting the weight of Stephen's nursing care from our shoulders, Nikki's team allowed us as a family to start living life rather than just struggling through it. Caring for Stephen was relatively easy by comparison with the previous routine, especially since Jonathan was usually with us most evenings and all day at weekends, helping to feed Stephen, take him to the bathroom and lift him in and out of the car. He too was a helpless witness of the terrifying choking fits, which at every meal seemed to be squeezing the last lungfuls of breath out of their victim. We would wait hoping that the fit would pass, ready to call the emergency services, knowing that at these critical times the thread by which Stephen clung to life was at its most tenuous. The fit would pass eventually, and after a few sips of warm water he would resume his meal, discarding whatever item he suspected of irritating his throat. Then just as we were all beginning to relax, he would fall prey to another attack.

Jonathan was by nature susceptible to hardship and struggle, sensing where and how he was needed, helping with all those necessary domestic chores which formerly I had always done unaided: he brought in sacks of potatoes, emptied rubbish bins, changed light bulbs, checked air pressures in tyres and filled the cars with petrol. Now there was someone to help me drag home the mountains of weekly shopping from the market and from Sainsbury's. For years I had struggled across the Backs either pulling the heavy bags in a trolley behind me or carrying them on the pram, slung from the handle and squeezed into the tray underneath. Together we looked after the three children, but it was usually Jonathan who provided the taxi service to ferry Robert and Lucy to and from their various engagements, and it was Jonathan who indulged the baby's favourite activity: Timmie liked nothing so much as being thrown high in the air, up to the ceiling, abandoning himself, open-mouthed and wide-eyed, to that split second of suspense before coming back to earth and falling into the safety of Jonathan's arms.

Throughout the early Eighties, Stephen's ambitions and his successes continued to know no bounds. The catalogue of institutions, universities and scientific bodies vying with each other to shower sonorously named medals upon him – the Albert Einstein Award, the Einstein Medal, the Franklin Medal, the James Clerk Maxwell medal – and other honours, notably honorary degrees, read like Leporello's list of Don Giovanni's female conquests in Mozart's opera. Unlike Don Giovanni however, Stephen's conquests were not all restricted to Europe. There was no shortage of award-giving ceremonies in Britain, however, and when they were near to home, I took Stephen to them myself. On one memorable occasion we drove over to Leicester for a degree ceremony at the University, where the Chancellor was Sir Alan Hodgkin, the Master of Trinity College, Cambridge; he had formerly been the President of the Royal Society when Stephen was made a Fellow in 1974. Genial and unassuming, with a beaming smile, even when standing on the platform attired in full black and gold regalia, he welcomed Stephen into the ranks of the honorary doctors of the university by firmly pressing his hand – the hand which Stephen was using to control the wheelchair. That pressure sent Stephen, the wheelchair and Sir Alan Hodgkin – who was still, so to speak, attached to the apparatus – off into a whirling pas de deux, bringing the ensemble of ceremonial robes, mortar boards, bodies and wheelchair perilously close to the edge of the stage. I leapt to my feet and switched off the joystick control just in time to avert a horrible catastrophe.

Most of the ceremonies were in the United States, however, and it was fortunate that Nikki and his team were willing travelling companions. Thanks to them, Stephen was able to take advantage of every award-giving ceremony on the other side of the Atlantic – for which his fare and theirs would be paid. Then he would go on to the serious purpose of his trip – scientific discussions with his colleagues in other more interesting venues elsewhere. At this time he was particularly involved in the production – often as joint editor with Werner Israel – of several tomes of essays and conference proceedings concerning relativity and attempts to reconcile it with quantum physics. The conferences – or rather "workshops" – recorded in these tomes were Stephen's new passion, for he found that his international renown and his distinguished position as Lucasian Professor afforded him an advantage in attracting funding to the Department, though one of his pet complaints was *still* the lack of money for science. We had been used to receiving and entertaining regular seminar and conference delegates for years on a modest scale. These days Stephen could invite his colleagues – even his adversaries – to Cambridge on a grander scale and preside over all their deliberations as the ultimate authority. The workshops grew into much larger and much more prestigious affairs, with money not only to invite the most eminent speakers and delegates, but also to provide dinners and entertainments. Consequently my role as conference hostess was mercifully diminished. The days were over when I found myself putting on buffet dinners for forty or more people; under the new system, the workshop dinners were usually held in the college where the delegates were staying. My involvement was generally limited to hosting receptions, and the tea parties on the lawn, for which plates of cucumber sandwiches were, as usual, ordered from Caius kitchens. Otherwise, dinner parties at home were more intimate affairs for the band of our closest friends from abroad.

The lion's share of the complex administrative arrangements for these workshops – the delegates' travel, the accommodation, the venues, the methods of payment and all the printed material associated with the conference – as well as typing up the proceedings after the event, fell to Stephen's hard-working secretary, Judy Fella, although she was in theory only employed part-time. This was all in addition to her regular workload as the secretary to the Relativity Group. Her children were about the same age as Robert and Lucy, but she often worked long into the night, sometimes having to resort to the more advanced, experimental technology – installed by the fluid-dynamicists down in the basement of the Department – to produce camera-ready copy of the hieroglyphic signs and diagrams of the conference proceedings. Although Stephen appreciated her dedication, many of her secretarial colleagues failed to understand the unconventional pressures under which she laboured, and made life very uncomfortable for her.

It was in the Department rather than at home that a new wave of pressures, in the shape of the world's media, first made its appearance. For some time Stephen's discoveries had been well documented in the British and the American scientific press; the attitude was always one of deference in the strictly scientific context, with little or no reference to his physical condition. In the early Eighties the popular press began to take a more active interest in the phenomenon of the man himself. The contrast between the restrictions placed on him by his shrunken frame and his croaking speech on the one hand, and the power of his mind which allowed him to roam the outer reaches of the universe on the other, provided a fertile source for many imaginative flights of fanciful prose. Moreover the subject himself was far from averse to publicity; indeed was a willing interviewee, despite the incursions that interviews made into his already overloaded timetable. Judy took the extra demands posed on her schedule by the influx of journalists and television crews – not just from national networks but from all over the world – in her stride, though there were quite a few academics in the Department who understandably objected to finding that their tea room had been turned into a television studio yet again.

Stephen enjoyed bewildering the visiting journalists. He would apologize for not being able to bring a four-dimensional model of the universe into his office to demonstrate his theories, or, when asked about infinity, would reply that it was rather difficult to talk about it as it was such a long way off. Quite openly he would admit to disappointment that black holes had so far evaded detection, since proof of their existence would assure him of a Nobel Prize. The journalists made what they could of these witty, often cryptic responses to their questions and then went away to compile reverential articles from their baffling assortment of notes. Very few of them managed to achieve a balance in their reporting. Often their attempts to describe Stephen's physical presence lacked sensitivity, while their accounts of the science, perhaps understandably, relied on the interpretations of Stephen's students and colleagues.

The most insensitive journalist of all was a television producer from the BBC's *Horizon* team. The earlier snatch of film made some six years previously by my college friend, Vivienne King, had been a resounding success; she had shown Stephen in context and had avoided the pitfall – or the temptation – of depicting him as Dr Strangelove. It was still one of my worst fears that, in the hands of the wrong producer, Stephen might be portrayed as some sort of grotesque, wheelchair-bound boffin, twisted both in body and mind, destructively intent on the pursuit of science at all costs, and that is more or less what happened in the second *Horizon* film. When I asked if he would like briefly to include the family in the film, the producer disparagingly observed that the children and I were nothing more than wallpaper in Stephen's life, and when the film appeared six months later, the lunch scene in the University Centre at which little Tim and I were present was dubbed with a voice-over spoken by one of Stephen's students. He said, "Neither Mrs Hawking nor their son Timmie are particularly interested in mathematics, so when they come to lunch, we try not to talk about work." Afterwards, I learnt that, to his great embarrassment, the student in question had been commanded to read this by the producer. My former supervisor, Alan Deyermond, gallantly wrote to the BBC in protest at the injustice of such a deliberate insult. Irony of ironies, *Professor Hawking's Universe* opened with a shot of one of our wedding photos. The sole people to derive any tongue-in-cheek amusement from it were my parents, who featured in the wedding photo: overnight they became television celebrities in St Albans.

Even before the *Horizon* programme, Stephen had become a household name. In the summer of 1981, Prince Philip, the Chancellor of the University of Cambridge, expressed his wish to meet Stephen in the course of his rounds of the university departments. It seemed most appropriate to invite him to come for a private visit to the house, where he would be able to talk to Stephen without background disturbance. Robert, definitely a budding scientist at the age of fourteen, interpreted his father's replies to the Chancellor's questions about the age of the universe and the nature of black holes. As the visit on 10th June coincided with our guest's sixtieth birthday, I made and iced a fruit cake, decorating it with half a dozen candles which Timmie and Prince Philip blew out together before the royal visitor was precipitately whisked away to his next appointment.

When Stephen's name appeared as a Commander of the British Empire in the New Year's Honours List of 1982, we decided that, given the potential for calamity involved in controlling the wheelchair, Stephen should not go forwards to meet the Queen alone, but that Robert should accompany him. The investiture at Buckingham Palace was arranged for 23rd February. The occasion demanded new clothes for all of us, except for Timmie who was too young to qualify for an invitation and had to stay with my parents. Robert was kitted out with his first suit – which he never wore again since by the time another formal occasion arose he had outgrown it. Lucy, who was going through a tomboy phase, made it quite plain that she would only allow herself to be forced into a dress and a coat as a never-to-be repeated exception to her usual jeans and T-shirt.

As Robert and I were managing the exercise alone, we knew that we would be hard-pressed to arrive at the Palace from Cambridge at 10 a.m., so we drove down to London the evening before. There we stayed in the flat reserved for the use of Fellows on the top floor of the Royal Society, overlooking the tree tops of the Mall and the turrets and crenellations around Horseguards Parade. It was not until I was busily stowing all the new garments and their accessories away in the wardrobes late at night that I realized Lucy's new patent leather shoes were missing. She was innocently lounging in her scuffed, old-school clodhoppers and seemed quite content to go to the Palace looking as if she had just come in from climbing trees in the garden. The caretaker's wife thought there might be a shoe shop at the end of Regent Street, but doubted whether they sold children's shoes. We resigned ourselves to starting even earlier than planned the next morning. Leaving Robert to feed Stephen his breakfast, Lucy and I dashed up to Regent Street as the shops were opening – to buy the only pair of shoes available in Lucy's size. Sensible and unremarkable in brown leather, they were suitably smart but not as pretty as the shiny buckled pair that had been left at home. Ironically, they were to see plenty of wear, whereas the patent leather shoes lay untouched at the bottom of the wardrobe and were eventually given away.

Despite the last-minute crisis, we were still just on schedule when we set out for the Palace. We had not reckoned, though, on joining the mother of all traffic jams in the Mall: the whole population appeared to be converging on Buckingham Palace, giving the Mall the same air of frenzied urgency as the roads leading to Heathrow airport. Just as at the airport, most of the arrivals were being dropped at the gate, but it was our privilege to drive through those ornate, oft televised portals into a world apart. This was a world which seemed to operate on a different timescale from our own, a world where everything ran with a clockwork precision yet where no one showed the least signs of fluster or impatience, a bland courtesy and an easy charm being the hallmarks of all encounters.

Leaving the car, which suddenly looked embarrassingly old, battered and dirty, in the middle of the courtyard, we were shown to a different entrance from the other arrivals and were taken up several floors in an ancient lift. Lackeys ushered us with a genteel rapidity through a maze of corridors where we were able to pause only momentarily to glance at the furniture, the paintings, the Chinese vases and the exquisite, glass-cased ivories which lined the walls. When we came out into the main gallery, we were separated: Robert and Stephen were led away to join the waiting queues of national heroes and heroines, while Lucy and I were shown to our plush pink seats at the side of the magnificent ballroom.

There was plenty to absorb our attention while we waited for the proceedings to begin. Huge crystal chandeliers sparkled against the white and gold decorations. One end of the immense room consisted of a sort of red velvet temple, bathed in a soft gilded light, where elderly beefeaters from the Tower mounted guard over the dais where the Queen was to stand. On a balcony at the other end, a military band played a festive repertoire before launching into the National Anthem on the Queen's arrival. The morning's business was briskly introduced and the investiture assumed a remarkably familiar format, combining the time-honoured British traditions of school-prize-givings and degree ceremonies with the national penchant for pageantry on a grand scale, as each candidate stepped forwards from a seemingly endless line for his or her moment of glory face to face with Her Majesty the Queen. Lucy nudged me in alarm when she saw an elderly beefeater, who was standing behind the Queen, keel over – a victim of the heat, the weight of his costume and the hours spent on his feet. He was discreetly removed from the scene, feet first, without any disruption to the ceremony.

When Robert and Stephen appeared at the side entrance awaiting their turn, about halfway through the proceedings, my spine tingled with love and pride. As they crossed the floor to the centre and turned towards the Queen, they made a dramatically impressive pair – the indomitable but frail scientist slouched in his chair grinning broadly, accompanied by our tall, shy, fair-haired son. Stephen had every right to grin in pleasure at his own achievements. Perhaps he was also grinning at the irony. The formerly iconoclastic, angry young socialist had been nominated by a Tory government to receive one of the highest honours from the sovereign and was being taken into the bosom of the Establishment which he used to despise so vehemently.

Afterwards, over lunch in a posh hotel in central London, we inspected the insignia, a cross finely worked in red-and-blue enamel suspended from a red ribbon edged with a grey stripe. The inscription, "For God and Empire", like the Palace itself, belonged to the mysteries and the mythology of another age. When we studied the booklet of information that came with the "badge", as it was officially called, the only privilege we could discover that might be remotely relevant to us was that Lucy, as the daughter of a CBE, could be married in the Order's chapel in the crypt of St Paul's Cathedral. "Let's hope she remembers her shoes," Robert observed drily.

It was not only the British Establishment which was keen to number Stephen among its scions. He had already received the Papal medal in 1975, and in the autumn of 1981 he was invited to attend a conference organized by the Jesuits at the Pontifical Academy in the Vatican. The Pontifical Academy is the close-knit group of eminent scientists of unimpeachable character who advise the Pope on scientific matters. This conference was called by way of a papal updating on the state of the universe. At that early stage Stephen's nurses had not yet begun to accompany him on trips abroad, so Bernard Whiting, the Australian post-doctoral researcher who had been working with Stephen, agreed to accompany him to the conference, interpret his lecture to the audience and help me with his general care.

Since Timothy's birth, all my anxieties about leaving the children had returned and I could only reconcile myself to going to Rome by taking one or all of them with me – if not Robert, for whom school was now serious business, at least Lucy and Timmie. Happily, Mary Whiting, who knew Rome well, came too. Without the Whitings, the trip would have been an unmitigated disaster. The Hotel Michelangelo, supposedly the closest hotel to the Vatican though by our standards a good twenty minutes away from the conference venue, served no meals, not even breakfast. There was a lift but to get to it one had first to surmount a flight of steps. As if that were not enough, Rome was in the throes of cataclysmic rains. The mornings would dawn bright and sunny and we would cheerfully accompany Stephen into the Vatican, bowling along past the Swiss Guards at the gate, through the grounds to the Residence of Pius IV, a beautiful, rustic Renaissance building, constructed for the Pope in the sixteenth century. Later it accommodated female visitors to the Vatican and, since 1936, had housed the headquarters of the Pontifical Academy. There we would leave Stephen gleefully preparing to fight the Galilean corner and instruct the papal cosmologists in his revised view of the universe which had neither beginning nor end, nor any role for a Creator-God.

Until lunchtime at the Academy, the one reliably good meal of the day, I would stroll through the groves of bay trees and the children would play in the ornamental streams which trickled down the hillside. But the fine mornings would deteriorate into sultry, overcast afternoons when majestic clouds, worthy of Michelangelo, would billow over the dome of St Peter's. They would burst spectacularly amid dazzling lightning and crashing thunder, and would go on rending the heavens apart well into the night. Mary took us on guided tours to the places she loved and knew so well – to the Colosseum, the Forum, the Baths of Caracalla and out to the Catacombs of San Calixto – but our excursions were always tempered by the knowledge that we would be drenched to the skin if we were not back in the hotel by four o'clock in the afternoon. Thereafter we would have to hope for a break in the clouds around dinner time to allow us to dash out, wheelchair and pushchair in tow, for supper. Needless to say, the permanently gridlocked state of Roman traffic made it impossible to get anywhere near the hotel before the rains descended. Usually four o'clock and the first flash of lightning and roll of thunder found us in the vicinity of the railway station, searching for a bus to take us back across the Tiber.

Little Tim proved to be the unexpected hero of the hour: he loved the buses, grindingly slow, packed with bodies and suf-focatingly steamed up though they were, and the Italian pas-sengers adored him. "*Che bel bambino!*" they would exclaim, making space for me to sit down with him on my knee. "*Carissimo, carissimo!*" they would smile, stroking his blond hair and tickling his chin. He had just begun to discover the art of stringing sentences together in precise, grammatical English and was delighted to have a captive audience on whom to practise his new-found talent. "Do you have a house?" he would searchingly ask the adoring, though uncomprehending secretaries, students, businessmen and corpulent grandmothers. "Do you have a car?" He would continue with his own answers. "We have a house. We have a car. We have a garage. We have a garden." They would laugh, nodding sentimentally, while the rain streamed down the windows and the Roman traffic honked and hooted itself to a standstill in the darkening evening outside.

Mary took her role as guide so conscientiously that she would not rest until Lucy, Timmie and I had seen every church of note in Rome, including her favourite, the church of San Clemente. The medieval church, noted for its radiantly colourful eleventh-century mosaic of the Triumph of the Cross in the apse, is built above the ancient church, with its early frescoes dating from the sixth century, beside the remains of a Roman house. Having admired the brilliance of the mosaics, we followed Mary warily down into the dimly lit, red-brick lower church which, unaccountably, echoed with the sound of running water. "Oh," said Mary blithely, "that's the Cloaca Maxima, the main drain built by the Romans. It comes through here." The main drain sounded to me more like a rushing mighty river, but I supposed that Mary knew what she was talking about.

The bus ride back to the hotel in the pouring rain took even longer than usual that evening. The whole city had ground to a halt. From the conversation of the other passengers with the driver, Mary found out that the delay was caused by flooding – the Cloaca Maxima had burst the bounds of its Roman conduit and was pouring out into the streets of the city. In idle amusement to pass the time, we discussed whether this was a portent, a sign, an indication of divine wrath at Stephen's temerity in professing his heretical theories within the sanctified walls of the Vatican itself.

The Vatican – one of the most powerful, dogmatic and wealthy city states ever known – was presided over by a man whose personal attributes of holiness and courage were not in doubt, yet he sought to impose limitations on freedom of thought – just as rigidly as those atheistic scientists who would dispute our right to ask the question "why" the universe exists. The very man who should have been addressing the question "why" was busy telling the scientists that they had no right even to ask the question "how" about certain aspects of creation. At the end of the conference, the Pope told the assembly in his address that, although scientists could study the evolution of the universe, they should not ask what happened at the moment of creation at the Big Bang and certainly not before it, because that was God's preserve. Neither Stephen nor I was impressed by such injunctions; they were all too reminiscent of the attitudes behind

Galileo's arrest and confinement three hundred years earlier. Only now was the Church beginning to catch up with the history of Galileo's discoveries. There was detectable embarrassment that his theories had lain proscribed for so long. Though they were kept under lock and key, the papers relating to his fate were readily, almost apologetically, produced for Stephen's scrutiny – the implication being that it was simply an oversight that no one had thought of rehabilitating his reputation sooner. Nevertheless, the papal pronouncement indicated that the Church was still seeking to restrict thought, giving the undeniable impression that not much had been learnt from the lessons of those three hundred years.

13

Harmony Restored

Music, through which I had come back into the Church of England, had become the gateway to my spiritual rebirth and growth, and it was thanks to Mary Whiting that I was able to take up my singing lessons again soon after Timothy's birth. She positively begged to be allowed to take him out for a walk once a week in the hope that association with babies might help her have a baby of her own. On Wednesday afternoons therefore, though often tired, I resumed my lessons with Nigel Wickens, who was no stranger to the demands of parenthood after the birth of his daughter Laura. Under his guidance and to Jonathan's sensitive accompaniment – as and when his teaching commitments allowed – I returned to the joys of Schubert, Schumann, Brahms and Mozart. Variously they intensified then assuaged those emotions competing within my deepest self. Meanwhile Mary and Tim went to feed the ducks, walk in the park, sit on the swings and bury their faces in ice cream.

There were many opportunities to perform the solo repertoire in fundraising concerts for the causes which Stephen and I had espoused, and sometimes I was brought in to fill the gaps in other programmes, which was how my singing career reached its extraordinary apogee in the summer of 1982 with a short burst of song in King's College Chapel as an interlude in an organ recital that Jonathan was giving for a medical conference. My confidence both in my voice and in my ability to learn music quickly had grown sufficiently for me to feel that it was time to branch out by joining a choral society. It was just possible to contemplate such a step since I now enjoyed an unprecedented degree of freedom. While Stephen basked in the deserved glory of international acclaim, those early years of the Eighties witnessed my own transformation. On the one hand, the team of nurses brought desperately needed relief from the unrelenting physical demands that had previously consumed all my available energy. On the other, through Jonathan's unwavering support, and his devotion to the family as a whole, aspects of myself, which had long been suppressed, lying dormant in a dark corner in the daily struggle, emerged into the light. Partial living was no longer called for. I was beginning to experience the fullness of life myself, realizing that the sands which had run through my fingers on the beach in Santa Barbara years before had not, with the passing of time, spelt the end of my individual aspirations.

At a concert in the university church of Great St Mary, I encountered the sort of choir I was looking for – a mixed bunch of people of all ages and all walks of life – performing a wide repertoire and aspiring to a high standard. The dynamic young conductor, Stephen Armstrong, a recent graduate of the University, took me on and thereafter I found myself attending the once-weekly rehearsals, which demanded intense application for two solid hours at the end of a long day, and a great deal of learning in the intervening week. The day of the performance, usually a Saturday, was hectic. Concert or no, the family had to be fed and cared for, and the final rehearsal was always gruelling. Then the concert itself would be over in a flash and eight weeks' work would vanish in a single evening, sometimes creating a wild sense of euphoria at phrases that had gone exceptionally well, sometimes leaving tinges of frustration that others had not come up to expectation. Concert succeeded concert with quick changes of idiom and musical personality from baroque to modern via the classical and Romantic periods. From Bach to Benjamin Britten, the exhilaration from each performance well sung was heady. I did not mind what we sang; each successive work, each successive composer became my passionate favourite for the duration of the rehearsals and the concert, bringing about a timeless distillation of the fragile pathos of our lives, transforming painful intensity into consoling spirituality.

It was at this time, when my star was in the ascendant, that my mother fell seriously ill. Recently she and her only surviving cousin Jack had been overburdened with worry on account of Auntie Effie, who was now well into her nineties. Nor, I knew, did one need to look further than my own household to find one very obvious cause of chronic anxiety which could have exacerbated Mum's illness. At least the profound change in our own circumstances, occasioned by the advent of Nikki's nursing team, allowed me to give my parents some moral support at that most critical time and try to repay some of the care that they had shown us for so long. The revised regime also meant that, less harassed and less haggard, I could also give the children more attention. The baby had grown into the most irresistibly funny little child, observant, endlessly enquiring, dancing with an impish vitality. At about eighteen months, long before his encounter with doting Italian bus passengers, he had started to develop a precocious fascination for astronomy. In the early evening he would watch the moon from his high chair in the kitchen, following its course, distracted from the important business of his supper. As it moved across the sky – and across the window – he would grow impatient with his food, clamouring to be released from his harness. When it disappeared from view, he would dash excitedly into the living room to await the reappearance of its white shafts through the bay windows there. Each evening was for him a triumph of expectation – until the moon waned, abandoning him in the darkness of mystified disappointment. Then, at twenty-two months, he demonstrated a poetic though unscientific awareness of other natural phenomena. One cold afternoon in February 1980 as huge snowflakes came drifting down in a leisurely fashion, white and delicately geometrical against a leaden sky, he raced to the living-room window, shouting "I see tars! I see tars" – *tars* being his way of saying *stars*. He danced round the room, excitedly chanting his little refrain to the silent music of those softly falling starry constellations.

Tim's exuberance was enchanting but it could lead him to attempt potentially dangerous feats of independence in imitation of his brother and sister if left unguarded for the merest second. A couple of weeks before his second birthday, I was preparing the supper in the kitchen when suddenly the house seemed unnaturally quiet. There were no sounds of childish play – toy cars being pushed across the floor, the tin drum being thumped, chattering voices and laughter. The blood froze in my veins at the terrible silence. I rushed to the front door, only to find it wide open. Timmie had run away.

Robert, charging at full pelt ahead of Stephen and me, had frequently run away as a small boy but always to some purpose, and he had always put himself in the position of being easily found. Lucy had disappeared only once – on a fine day in the middle of summer when we were still living in Little St Mary's Lane. Thelma Thatcher and I had been anxiously searching the lane and the churchyard for her without success, when some passing Americans told us that there was a tiny girl standing with a doll's pram on the Mill Bridge. There she was – in her Bermuda shorts, one hand resting on the handle of the pram and the other holding up her transparent green umbrella. She was surrounded by an admiring band of undergraduates, who were clearly wondering what to do with this very self-possessed infant phenomenon.

Some ten years later in the isolation of 5 West Road, where there were no friendly adoptive grandparents to call upon for help and where the grounds ran for acres with neither a fence nor a gate, I stood at the open door in a frenzy of blank indecision, not knowing which way to turn. Had Timmie run out onto the road and down to the river, or round the house into the garden? The college staff, who were closing up their workshops for the day, heard me frantically calling his name, and came to help. Eventually Pat, one of the maintenance staff, soberly advised me to call the police. He stood by while, with my heartbeat resounding in my ears and my hands shaking, I dialled 999. I was upset that the officer who took the call did not react more dramatically. He did not seem to register the urgency of the situation. "Hold on a minute ma'am," he said jovially. He returned to the phone a moment later. "Can you describe your little boy and tell me what he is wearing?" he asked, still in the same irritatingly cheerful tone of voice. "Fair hair, blue eyes, blue top and green trousers," I replied distraught with worry. "That's all right then," the policeman said. "We've got a little boy in one of our police cars, but as he couldn't tell us where he lived, the officer is driving round in the hope of finding his mother." Timmie was brought home in a police car by a policewoman and the kind person who had picked him up just as he was about to set foot on the road – on his way, it seemed, to visit his godmother, Joy Cadbury. That same kind person had held him on her knee until the rather damp, blond, blue and green bundle was delivered back into my trembling arms.

Although they were less dependent on my physical presence, the two older children needed a great deal of understanding. Robert seemed destined to be a lonely child with few companions, while the transfer to secondary school parted Lucy from her band of cherished local friends whom she had known from birth. Because Robert had received a private education, thanks to his inheritance, we felt that we could do no less for Lucy, but she was the only one of her year to go from primary school to the girls' Perse. We gave her a kitten to comfort her and distract her, and in the hope that it might help pay her school fees, Stephen decided that the time had come to write a popular book, describing his science – the study of the origins of the universe – to the public in accessible language, avoiding the barriers of jargon and equations. I had often urged him to meet the challenge of explaining his research, reasoning that I, in particular, would benefit from reading it, and so would the taxpayers, in general, who were financing that research through government funding.

Both Robert and Lucy sometimes came with me to St Mark's where, ever inventive, Bill Loveless continued to cater for all ages and tastes. Not only did he keep the congregation of Newnham morally and intellectually awake with his monthly reviews of the state of the nation, he also put a prodigious effort into attracting families to the church by means of the family service. This service, always entertaining, sometimes unpredictable in the responses it could provoke, influenced a whole generation of children in an increasingly secular age. Lucy, who always had a part to play, whether lighting the altar candles or snuffing them out, reading the lesson, participating in the quizzes or performing in various dramatizations, loved it. One Sunday when I had left the children lazily dozing at home, Bill announced the inaugural session of a new youth club to be led by ordinands from the local theological college; it was to combine games, fun and serious discussion. Robert showed little interest when I told him about it, but reluctantly agreed to go that evening just to please me. At seven o'clock I drove him to the vicarage, promising to wait outside for ten minutes in case he did not like it. He liked it so well that I went home alone after the ten-minute wait, and thereafter he never missed a session. He met old acquaintances from primary school and made new friends, both girls and boys. They formed a cohesive and loyal group from that day onwards, encouraging Robert to develop the self-assurance and sociability which previously he had found so difficult. Only two weeks later, he met Bill Loveless as he was cycling home from school, and told him that he wanted to be confirmed. Bill became the trusted friend and mentor to both Robert and Lucy. He often reassured them and gently explained the complexities of adult life to them when the anomalies of their background – whether the scourge of Stephen's illness or the unconventional nature of Jonathan's presence in the family – disturbed their preconceived idealized notions of how family life and parents should be.

The atmosphere of those years was generally so much more relaxed that I was able to resume contact with my school friends again. They would come with their husbands and families for a Sunday visit once or twice a year. After a leisurely lunch during which many a topic – political, environmental, scientific, literary or musical – would be intensively discussed, the adults would amble round the garden and join the children for a game of hide-and-seek in among the glades and bushes of Harvey Court, the Caius property next door. This game became a tradition. With Stephen acting as lookout, the rest of us shed our adult reserve and recaptured for just an hour the intense excitement of childhood.

In the comparative harmony of that period, my relationship with Stephen entered a new phase where the tendency for us to slip into the roles of master and slave was arrested. We were companions and equals again – as we had been in our campaigning in the Sixties and early Seventies. The CND badge, which Stephen regularly wore on his lapel in television programmes, was but one indication of the several causes which we championed jointly. The inexorable increase in nuclear weapons, of which Rob Donovan had chillingly warned us in the early Seventies, had developed into a fully fledged arms race, a mad, uncontrolled competition between East and West to reach Armageddon as soon as possible and annihilate all living creatures on the planet. The Campaign for Nuclear Disarmament once again became a national force and local groups sprouted all over the country.

Our group, Newnham Against the Bomb, met once a month in the house of Alice Roughton, a retired doctor. A figure of immense and generous energies, trenchant convictions and fabled eccentricity, she was reputed to serve stewed squirrel and nettles at dinner parties. Her husband was known to prefer the garden shed to the house. We dozen or so members of Newnham Against the Bomb would sit round her smoking fire warming our hands on a glass of mulled wine, while we listened to presentations by knowledgeable but pessimistic speakers. Then we would plan strategies, discussing what we could do to stop the arms race. The prospects were not encouraging. We were after all pitting ourselves against the military industrial complexes of the two superpowers. There was some slight consolation to be derived from the fact that we were at least making an effort – and in any case, Stephen and I were used to playing David against many a monolithic Goliath.

Together he and I composed a letter and sent it off to all our friends around the world, particularly to those in the United States and in the Soviet Union. We urged them to protest at the escalation in nuclear weapons, which threatened to destroy the population of the northern hemisphere and produce so much radiation that the prospects for remaining life elsewhere would be negligible. We pointed out that there existed four tons of high explosive for every man, woman and child on the planet, and that the risk of a nuclear exchange being set off by miscalculation or computer failure was unacceptably high. Stephen used the same theme in his address to the Franklin Institute in Philadelphia when he was awarded the Franklin Medal in 1981. He remarked that it had taken about four billion years for mammals to evolve, about four million years for man to evolve and about four hundred years to develop our scientific and technological civilization. In the previous forty years, progress in understanding the four interactions of physics had advanced to the state where there was a very real chance of discovering a complete unified field theory, which would describe everything in the universe. Yet all that could be wiped out in less than forty minutes in the event of a nuclear catastrophe, and the probability of such a catastrophe occurring, either by accident or design, was frighteningly high. He concluded that this was the fundamental problem facing our society and was much more important than any ideological or territorial issues.

We made roughly the same points when we met General Bernard Rogers, a former Rhodes Scholar and Supreme Commander of Allied Forces in Europe, at a feast in University College, Oxford. After the meal, Stephen barred his way with the wheelchair as he was about to leave the dinner table. The General listened considerately while, in some embarrassment, I recited my speech on behalf of Newnham Against the Bomb. He then politely acknowledged that he himself was very concerned about the situation and had in fact been engaged in discussions with his Soviet opposite number. Within a few years, the rapidly changing economic and political situation behind the Iron Curtain overtook our local efforts. We shall never know whether our modest individual and group protests had even the slightest impact on the course of history, whether any of our letters ever reached their targets or whether our messages ever struck home to the heart of the political establishments of the East or the West.

Closer to home our campaigns concerned less apocalyptic matters, though they were equally impassioned, especially when they related to the rights of the disabled. The Cambridge colleges were so remarkably slow in implementing the Disabled Persons Act – which in its initial form had first reached the statute book in 1970 – that in the 1980s new buildings which made no provision for disabled access were still being commissioned. One of them, Clare College, not a hundred yards from our house, was sending out an appeal to attract funds for a building containing a library and recital room, which was advertised as a public place but had made no provision for disabled access. We campaigned vigorously in the media against this two-faced attitude and were met with comments such as: "If Stephen Hawking wants a disabled lift, he should pay for it himself." When finally Lord Snowdon – who had come to photograph Stephen for a glossy magazine – took up our cause on the radio, the College was forced to capitulate.

Stephen and I – and Jonathan – had supported the fundraising activities of the Motor Neuron Disease Association since its inception in 1979. For some time, Stephen as the Patients' Patron and I had attended meetings and conferences. In the early Eighties he was asked to become a Vice-President of the Leonard Cheshire Foundation as well and, in October 1982, I was invited to join the Appeal Committee to raise funds for converting a Victorian house at Brampton near Huntingdon into a Cheshire Home for the disabled. I attended monthly meetings in Huntingdon and soon discovered that my catchment area for fundraising was none other than the University of Cambridge – each college within the University and each individual Fellow within each college. Armed with a copy of the University register, my task was to sift through hundreds of likely donors and personally address pleading letters to each one, in preparation for the public launching of the appeal in the summer of 1984. The launch in Hinchingbrooke House augured well for the appeal, but unluckily for the charity it coincided with a six-week postal strike, while the national consciousness was distracted from giving to local charities by the horrendous pictures daily on television of starvation in Africa. Consequently it took many years of fundraising before the Home was opened. For Stephen and me, however, these campaigns were a wholly positive and unifying activity which gave us a joint role – outside physics.

14

Unfinished Business

In the early Eighties, there were two areas of unfinished business which I had to settle. First and foremost there was the thesis. I was summoned to Westfield for my oral examination in June 1980 in the presence of Stephen Harvey, the Professor of Spanish at King's College and of my supervisor, Alan Deyermond. The previous evening in Cambridge, Stephen and I had attended a performance of a Handel opera, *Rinaldo*, as part of the end-of-year celebrations in Caius. Much lauded though the performance was, it failed to make any impression on me because music, even the famous aria, '*Lascia ch'io pianga*', had temporarily lost its appeal. Like those occasions when Stephen had unwillingly found himself at the ballet, I squirmed in my seat in impatience, resenting the misuse of valuable time. I was fraught with worry that I would never be able to remember every point, every date, every reference in the 336 pages of the thesis the next day at 2 p.m.

The next day, tense and partially sighted, having lost a contact lens on the way to London, I groped my way through the exam until, with a mischievous smile, Stephen Harvey asked if I had read a book by the author David Lodge. Somewhat taken aback, I searched his face for clues to his meaning. Surely he wasn't referring to *Changing Places*, the hilariously authentic account of an academic exchange between Philip Swallow of Rummidge University (alias Birmingham) and Maurice Zapp of Euphoric State University (alias Berkeley)? I could not remotely discern any connection between *Changing Places* and medieval Spanish poetry; nonetheless I plucked up the courage to ask whether he was referring to any of David Lodge's novels. "No, no," he replied, "I mean *Modes of Modern Writing*" – which critical study, I had to admit, I had not read. After that, the exam proceeded in a more relaxed atmosphere. Later Alan Deyermond confessed that he had not read *Changing Places*.

The following spring Jonathan and Stephen – who bought me the flowing red robes of a Doctor of Philosophy – accompanied me to the Albert Hall and patiently sat through the mammoth degree ceremony. It was the end of a long and arduous journey. The fact that it ended in a blind alley was not significant. I had certainly not entertained any great hopes of a teaching post or even of hourly paid supervisions at the University of Cambridge, since my tentative enquiries as to whether there might be some teaching in the Spanish Department were politely ignored.

The chance to begin an occupation, if not a career, came unexpectedly and centred upon my other language, French, the language I had first encountered with some puzzlement on the side of HP Sauce bottles at the age of three or four. Fortunately the fascination for French engendered by the HP Sauce – together with sympathetic teaching in early childhood – had been strong enough to outweigh the powerful disincentive of Miss Leather, the gaunt, feline senior French mistress who regularly meted out "fifty French verbs" as her preferred form of punishment. It was said in her obituary that she could keep a classroom in absolute silence, even in her absence.

In the early Eighties, just as I had finished the thesis and Lucy and her contemporaries were looking forward to learning French in primary school, language teaching was summarily removed from the curriculum, a victim of the Tory government's economy measures. One of my much valued friends from the school gate, Christine Putnis, the Australian mother of a large family of clever children, prevailed upon me and Ros Mays, another of the mothers, to teach French to a group of children after school hours. With some trepidation, we began a project which was to last for ten years. Every Monday afternoon we would greet our pupils with drinks and biscuits, and then subject them to an hour's worth of intensive learning, artfully concealed in puzzles, games, songs, drawings and stories.

A year or two later I found myself obliged to revise French for GCE O level with Robert. It was his school report, just before the O-level term, which spurred me into action. "He is unlikely to pass the exam," it said of his French. The thought of a child of mine failing French was so terrible that drastic measures were called for. Robert's friend Thomas Cadbury was brought in to provide some competition and to ensure seriousness of purpose, and a minimum of fifty verbs were conjugated in all persons in all tenses. This linguistic onslaught struck its target so successfully that after the exam results it was actually suggested that the chip off the old scientific block might consider French for A level, a suggestion given only frivolous consideration as he had been earmarked from birth for physics, chemistry, maths, more maths and, of course, computing.

Just as I was beginning to feel confident enough to take on further teaching more formally, in either French or Spanish, another meeting at the school gate provided a golden opportunity. One of the mothers put me in touch with a recently established private sixth-form college where she worked, the Cambridge Centre for Sixth-Form Studies (otherwise known as CCSS). The startling conclusion of an informal interview with the Principal was that I found myself agreeing to teach candidates for Oxbridge entrance, a challenging proposition, and one which I suspected to be some sort of initiation test. If I could get students into Oxbridge, then I myself would probably be taken on. The advantages were that I could choose my hours and, as the organization had only limited premises, I could teach at home.

I spent hours looking up old entrance papers in the university library, devising teaching programmes and ruminating on the moral and philosophical questions set in the general paper, which revolved in some way or other around those philosophical and linguistic brain-teasers so beloved of Bertrand Russell such as: "There is a barber in Athens who shaves everyone who does not shave himself. Who shaves the barber?" or "Generalizations are false". Epigrammatic quotations were also a favourite of the examiners, who found an ample supply in the works of Oscar Wilde: "The truth is rarely pure and never simple", for example. Such formulations rubbed shoulders with essay titles inviting discussion about the ethics of nuclear deterrence or the positive and negative values of science, as for instance, "The genius of Einstein leads to Hiroshima". All these topics and many others like them were food to my starving brain.

My appetite whetted by university entrance papers, I next devoured the stuff of the A-level syllabus. Grammar, translations, comprehensions, literary texts – all required hours of thought, preparation and revision, but provided a sumptuous feast on which to feed my hungry intellect. What's more, I actually found that I enjoyed teaching and I liked the age group of sixteen- to eighteen-year-olds who were put into my charge. As my pupils were always about the same age as one or other of my own children at some stage of their education, I felt a natural affinity with that adolescent age group and quickly found that even the most difficult pupils would respond to a friendly approach. Many of them had been placed in boarding school at the age of six, and by the age of sixteen had demonstrated their frustration in some dramatic way or other and had accordingly been expelled. Now they had a second chance and had to be eased into taking it. There was also a clutch of overseas pupils, often multilingual, whose parents wanted their offspring to benefit from an English education within the security of supervised accommodation. These pupils were usually the most highly motivated and the most stimulating, though often, because of their multinational backgrounds, they were uncertain of their true national identity, and lacked written fluency in any of their languages. The strength of the A-level course was that it taught pupils to think analytically and critically for themselves and it introduced literature to people who might never have read a book in their lives. It was particular gratifying when, after two years of study, a pupil would come and thank me for opening his or her eyes to the delights of reading.

The pleasure was the more intense when one of those appreciative pupils was dyslexic. Through my own family I had such wide-ranging experience of the multitude of problems associated with the condition that I knew I could offer special encouragement. In an uncomprehending educational system, whether state or private, the dyslexics in a class, like my own sons, would typically be told that they were slow, stupid or lazy and would be sent to sit at the back of the class. Dyslexics are not stupid. Generally their intelligence quotient is higher than the rest of the population but their overdeveloped brain has squeezed out some other facility, usually associated with language or short-term memory. An intelligent child whose powers of communication are limited and who is sent to sit at the back of the class becomes a frustrated child who needs patient and considerate teaching to recover his self-esteem and express his latent intelligence.

Teaching at home for a few hours a day at my own convenience was the perfect arrangement. Kikki's successor, Lee Pearson, a gentle, reliable girl, took charge of Timmie in the mornings while I taught. My pupils would arrive as Stephen was leaving for work and when the bell rang, I had only to shed my apron before answering the door. I felt intensely happy: the skills that I had to offer were being mobilized. I won the respect of my pupils, and gradually discovered a professional identity for myself as I awoke from an intellectual coma.

15

Departures

Although through teaching, first at primary-school level and
then later for A level, I was beginning to find some sense of
my own worth, there remained the other area of unfinished
business, the one major barrier to the recovery of my true self:
the fear of flying. Flying phobia, the black consequence of that
fateful trip to Seattle so soon after Robert's birth when I nursed
my small bundle on aeroplanes the length and breadth of the
United States, had deprived me of many an exciting opportunity
to accompany Stephen – to California in midwinter, to Crete in
spring or to New York on Concorde. It had forced me to invent
patently feeble excuses, because every suggestion of travel by air
sent cold shivers down my spine, putting me immediately on the
defensive. It had caused tension in the home and it had made
me very unhappy. The anxiety had started to produce physical
symptoms so marked that, before the trip to Rome in the autumn
of 1981, I was actually sick. I was desperate to find a cure.

It was with great excitement that, while idly thumbing through
a magazine in the dentist's waiting room later that winter, I came
across a reference to a clinic where flying phobia was accepted
without embarrassment as a treatable condition. Enquiries and
a letter from my GP eventually put me in touch with the York
Clinic at Guy's Hospital where Mr Maurice Yaffe, a senior
psychologist, treated sufferers, either privately or in groups on
the National Health Service, with a variety of techniques. There
was nothing clinical about Maurice Yaffe: his personality and
manner were absent-mindedly donnish rather than medical; he
never mentioned the word "phobia", only "difficulty". As he
enthused over the delights of cheap air fares, we, his patients,
became adjusted to a perspective which encouraged us to concentrate on the pleasures of Paris, Rome or New York instead
of on the agonies of getting there. Then a very basic course in
aerodynamics left no doubt in the minds of the sceptical that
aeroplanes were meant to fly. Finally Maurice Yaffe unveiled his

own brainchild, a simulated aircraft cabin, housed in a small room in the basement of Guy's Hospital. Within minutes of taking our seats in the simulator, we found ourselves soaring away to Manchester – Manchester because the video film which appeared in the cabin window was of a flight to Manchester with all the appropriate sounds and sensations of take-off and flight: the announcements, the revving engines, the crying babies, the floor tilting, the undercarriage jolting and slight turbulence as the plane supposedly passed through cloud. After an initial feeling of panic followed by twelve or so flights to Manchester, the whole business became so boring that I forgot to be frightened and began to relax. The culmination of the course was a weekend in Paris, arranged in fine detail by Maurice Yaffe, though not of course paid for by the National Health Service.

If Paris was the first step on my road to liberation, California was but another short step away in psychological terms. There in the summer of 1982, we renewed old friendships the length and breadth of the state and revisited old haunts. Jonathan had arranged to attend a conference on early music in Vancouver that August and combined the conference with a visit to us in Santa Barbara, where he was often taken for one of Stephen's students. Indeed, he lived with the students in their accommodation and to all intents and purposes shared their rota of duties, although, unlike them, he was paying his own way.

Little Tim was amazed at the size of the country. "They did build a big country!" he would mutter to himself as he gazed out of the car window over deserts and mountains. As we watched the sun setting over the Santa Inés range from our apartment every evening, he would declare solemnly, "It's the end of the world, it's the end of the world." Some time later, I asked him what he liked best about California – the J. Paul Getty Museum, the deserts, the mountains, the sea or the Huntingdon Museum and gardens. It was a stupid question to ask a three-year-old. He answered me in what he considered to be my own terms, for, as quick as a flash he replied, "The Mickey Mouse Museum..."

I was now ready to fly east again as well as west. With a cautious eye on employment possibilities, Lucy had begun to study Russian for O level. In retrospect, this was not a good choice since, despite changing times, it did not lead to a brilliant career and produced only much frustration. However, the rigours of studying seventeenth-century church Russian at Oxford and a

346

winter spent in Moscow amid the privations of 1992 were still on the distant horizon when Lucy flew with her father, a bevy of nurses and me to a conference in that city in October of 1984. Lucy's attempts to speak Russian were met with ecstatic delight, especially when she stood up to propose a brief toast to "*mir i drujba*" – "peace and friendship" – at the closing banquet of the conference. It was one of those Russian banquets where the hors d'oeuvre are lavish – caviar, smoked fish and meats, nuts, pickles and, of course, the ubiquitous cucumber – and last for hours, interrupted by toasts, speeches and, in the case of one misguided Japanese delegate, an endless dirge delivered in a monotone which he himself had composed in unintelligible English. The main course, the usual lump of unidentifiable meat and mashed potato, arrived at the tables just as everyone was leaving.

Eleven years earlier, our acquaintances had demonstrated the utmost caution in their dealings with us. Now they seemed not to care a fig for officialdom. The young guide who was sent to "mind" Lucy and me was much more interested in accompanying us to buy clothes in the hard-currency shops to which we had access than in directing our movements. Two of Stephen's closest colleagues, Renata Galosh and her husband, Andrei Linde, openly invited us to dinner in their small flat on the outskirts of Moscow. They provided a delectable meal, in part down to an amicable relationship with the manager of some restaurant or other, and in part because of Renata's preserves from her dacha in the country, among them home-made strawberry juice strained from precious home-bottled fruit.

Although the flying phobia was more or less under control, it was simply not practicable for me to accompany Stephen on each one of his international expeditions: travel had become an obsession with him and he regularly seemed to spend more time in the air than he did on the ground. He found it hard to accept that, quite apart from Lucy and Tim, I was not prepared to abandon either Robert or my students as their A levels approached in the spring of 1985, a period which he had designated for an extensive tour of China. Bernard Carr and Iolanta, one of his nurses, manfully took charge, heaving Stephen on and off aeroplanes and trains, and valiantly manoeuvring the wheelchair up onto the Great Wall. They came back exhausted – nor was Stephen in the best of health, though he was triumphant at his achievement. He coughed frequently and appeared to be even more sensitive to irritants in foodstuffs. Many a night would be spent nursing him in my arms, trying to calm the panic which itself precipitated even worse choking fits.

However, the summer holidays promised a respite. We were to spend the whole of August in Geneva, where Stephen was planning to have discussions with the particle physicists at Cern, while the rest of us could enjoy the environs of Lake Geneva. At Cern Stephen would be working on the implications for the direction of the arrow of time of quantum theory and of the observations from the particle accelerator. This was a topic upon which he had expatiated at some length, with Robert's help, to the Astronomical Society at the Perse School. It was at this lecture that I resigned myself to the realization that physics had become so abstract that, even when explained in pictorial form, it was beyond my comprehension. No amount of film played backwards of broken cups and saucers jumping back onto tables and reassembling themselves could persuade me that the direction of time could be reversed. Such a supposition could potentially alter the course of human history if visitors from the future could interfere with the past. It seemed however that it was essential to prove mathematically that this was not a possibility, since the proof would ensure that nothing could travel faster than light.

Stephen's travels in time and space notwithstanding, it had been a good summer: it had begun when the cat had a large litter of kittens on the kitchen floor. The prettier specimens were farmed out to various friends and acquaintances, until eventually all that remained was one undistinguished black-and-white tom, which one of my more susceptible students, Gonzalo Vargas Llosa, a young Peruvian, insisted on taking to join his uncaged rabbit in his room. Lucy completed her first French exchange with a Breton girl whose boatman father had won the lottery, and there were parties. Robert set the style by celebrating his eighteenth birthday, just before the onset of his exams, with a ceilidh on the lawn on a warm clear night under a full moon. There were also concerts of every description, choral and instrumental, recitals and even a pop concert at the Albert Hall to celebrate Tim's sixth birthday, as he had become a great fan of Sky, devoting himself single-mindedly in his every waking moment to emulating their tremendous, sustained drum rolls. An unscheduled concert of a different nature took place on our back lawn when, one Sunday at the beginning of July, just as Stephen and I were returning home from an expedition into medieval Suffolk with the delegates to that summer's physics conference, the lights failed in the University Concert Hall up the road. Jonathan was to play the harpsichord in the concert that evening and brought news of the disaster. The weather was fine and dry, so the obvious solution was for the players to set up their instruments on the lawn while the audience grouped round, sitting alfresco on whatever rugs, cushions and mats we could muster.

Although Jonathan was regularly asked to play with modern and amateur orchestras such as the one which performed on our lawn, he had long lamented the lack of authentic baroque performance in Cambridge, where many young hopeful keyboard players vied for the few opportunities available. On the other hand, he was too remote from the London scene for involvement there to be a feasible prospect. Had it not been for his commitment to us, particularly to me, clearly he might well have moved to London, where he could have advanced his career much more easily. The only course was for him to start his own orchestra, but that was a daunting prospect in terms of the time, the commitment and the money required. He was becoming so frustrated by the musical isolation in which he found himself, and he hankered so desperately to perform as part of an ensemble that when, in the spring of 1984, he went into hospital for an operation, I decided to take charge of the situation. First I picked up the telephone and booked the University Concert Hall, and then I rang round various contacts and booked a small but complete orchestra of baroque players. Jonathan came round from the anaesthetic to the news that, in his temporary absence from consciousness, he had been appointed the director of the newly formed Cambridge Baroque Camerata which was due to give its inaugural concert on 24th June. Frenzied planning, programming and publicity filled the intervening weeks, which were also the weeks of his convalescence.

On the night, Robert ran the box office, Lucy sold programmes and various friends acted as ushers while I ran to and fro, liaising between front of house and backstage and attending to Stephen who sat at the side of the platform. To our amazement, the queue for tickets stretched out into the forecourt. We counted each and every member of the audience as they filed into the concert hall that June evening, since a full house was crucial to the financial success of the enterprise. "Financial success" did not mean making a profit; it merely signified breaking even. All seats were taken and the performance, entitled *The Trumpet Shall Sound*, received rapturous applause. Emboldened by the success of the 1984 concert, the Cambridge Baroque Camerata ventured onto the concert platform again in 1985 with another own-promotion, a programme to mark the tercentenary of the births of Bach, Handel and Scarlatti. Fortunately the gamble paid off a second time – although on some later occasions, unexpected rival attractions such as televised football finals would decrease the size of the audience dispiritingly. The London debut of the ensemble, planned for October 1985 in the Queen Elizabeth Hall, had to be regarded as an investment for the future, as it certainly would not break even, but it would bring the Cambridge Baroque Camerata to the attention of a wider public.

Our household seemed to have recovered a considerable degree of equilibrium. For no one were the results more satisfactory than for Stephen himself, who had finished writing the first draft of a popular book about cosmology and the origins of the universe. The book ranged wide, from a discussion of early cosmologies to modern theories of particle physics and the arrow of time – with particular reference, of course, to the significance of black holes. In conclusion the author looked forward to the time when mankind would able to "know the mind of God" through the formulation, at some not-too-distant date in the future, of a complete unified theory of the universe, the theory of everything. Stephen had been given the name of an agent in New York where the book was being offered to publishers, and meanwhile in England we discussed tax-efficient methods of receiving royalties, which we expected to bring in a modest supplementary income regularly over the years, like textbooks which were said to be far more reliable in the long run than bestsellers. It was unlikely to fulfil the original aim of paying Lucy's school fees, as she was already well into her secondary education.

At the end of July, a few days in advance of the rest of us, Stephen, his new secretary Laura Ward, some students and nurses, flew out to Geneva. I was anxious to stay to see Robert off on a scout expedition to Iceland before leaving Cambridge myself. The plan was that within the week we would meet Stephen and his entourage in Germany at Bayreuth, the Wagnerian Mecca, for a performance of the *Ring Cycle*, and then all travel back to

Geneva to a house rented for the duration of the holidays. At last I had begun to achieve a happy balance in my life and felt that with the help of Purcell, Bach and Handel, I could cope with the effects of Wagner's sinister modulations in a spirit of good-humoured tolerance.

It was quite casually, without a second thought, that I waved goodbye to Stephen as he left home on 29th July. Geneva after all was no distance compared with China and it was renowned for its standards of hygiene. We were all concerned for Stephen's father, who was in the throes of a chronic illness, and feared that he might die during our absence. He bore his illness with the same gruff pragmatic stoicism that he had brought to all situations and which he used to conceal pain or embarrassment. Despite the vicissitudes of my relationship with the Hawking family, I had not ceased to respect him, the more so because of late he had begun to write me truly appreciative letters, praising my care of Stephen and the children and my management of the letting house. However, my greatest anxiety at this time was for Robert, my eldest son, whom I saw off in the company of the Venture Scouts three days after Stephen's departure. Their plans – to trek across a glacier and to canoe round the north coast of Iceland – filled me with silent foreboding.

Part Four

1

Darkest Night

It was seldom that Jonathan and I were alone together for any length of time. We tried to observe a code of conduct in front of Stephen and the children whereby we behaved simply as good friends, suppressing, sometimes with difficulty, any display of closer affection in our attempts to avoid hurting anyone. Each evening I would stand behind Stephen at the front door as he saw Jonathan off, dispatching him to his own house on the other side of Cambridge. In our efforts to keep the home going by this unconventional method we had the support of many people, among them my elderly home help, Eve Suckling. These were people who had witnessed the situation from the inside and who were wise enough not to draw hasty conclusions. Even Don, whose absolute values had been shaken one evening in the spring of 1978, just before Tim's birth, when he found Jonathan and me comfortably lolling against each other on the sofa, had conceded that the situation often demanded of him much more than he had expected, and sometimes more than he could give – certainly more than he could give indefinitely. He admitted that he had lived with us long enough to find that the ceaseless rigours of our way of life often brought him into uncomfortable conflict with his own conscience. Always we knew too that we could count on the guidance of Bill Loveless to strengthen our resolve and help keep our perspective within the disciplined framework that we had tried to establish for it while viewing our weaknesses with compassion. More than once he was heard to say that our situation was unique and that he could not say how we should deal with it.

Occasionally, when Stephen went abroad or when we were to take the car to join him somewhere on the Continent, we tentatively allowed our relationship to blossom. But so sensitive was I to its unorthodox nature that the experience was often watered with tears of guilt, since an unthinking word from one of the children or an unexpected encounter on a beach or campsite could quickly destroy the brief, heady illusion of freedom and send my conscience plummeting into despair. Discretion and deceit were divided by only the finest line, and it was never easy to judge on which side of the line we stood. There were a couple of other celebrities in the public eye who were seriously disabled, and it was public knowledge that their spouses had found solace with other partners while still caring responsibly and lovingly for them. Perhaps it was because those spouses were husbands rather than wives that it was easier for them to bring their new relationships into the open than it was for me.

Nevertheless, those short periods of respite, even if spent under canvas in a raging wind or sometimes sharing a small foreign hotel room with two or three children, allowed us a freedom from nagging anxiety and constant care – they restored our flagging morale and, paradoxically, reinforced our loyalty to Stephen. Our travels would often take us through France, giving me the opportunity to introduce Jonathan to Brandon and Lucette, who were now living outside Paris, and to Mary and Bernard Whiting, who with their two small children were living in the heart of that magical city. They all wholeheartedly welcomed Jonathan as an essential element in our family life. In 1985 however, our route took us through Belgium and Germany rather than France. It had become an accepted part of the family routine that Stephen would attend a summer school in some desirable part of Europe, flying out with his students and nurses, and that Jonathan and the children and I would arrive by car in a more leisurely manner, taking a few days' holiday on the way. So on Friday 1st August 1985, after Robert's departure to Iceland with the Venture Scouts, Jonathan, Lucy, Tim and I set out for Felixstowe to board the ferry for the overnight crossing to Zeebrugge.

We had planned to spend the weekend by the sea on the Belgian coast before driving through Belgium and Germany to Bayreuth, where on 8th August we were to meet Stephen for the performance of the *Ring* – but just one night on the coast, where stinging sandstorms were blowing along the beach under leaden skies, was enough to turn us inland to look for campsites in the Ardennes, the hilly, forested area of Belgium near the German border. Not only did torrential rain begin to lash our windscreen before we had even reached Brussels, but a strange itchy feeling also began to creep around the nape of our necks, like prickly burrs caught in our pullovers and anoraks: the truth was that we were giving a free ride to the head lice that had infested Tim's school just before the end of term. We had all carefully washed our hair with the prescribed shampoo, while Stephen, for good measure, had insisted on also having his locks doused with a foul-smelling lotion, which he wore throughout a whole day in the Department. He remarked that evening that, apart from his faithful attendant-student, no one had come near him all day.

On that summer holiday in Belgium we were little better than tramps, soaked to the skin, and lice-ridden until I could find the appropriate shampoo. We ambled on still in the pouring rain from Belgium into Luxembourg, where we paused for a picnic lunch in Echternach, a leafy town on the German border. After being cooped up in the car all morning, Tim raced gleefully up and down a long alleyway of trees in a park. Inevitably he slipped and fell flat on his face in a muddy puddle. The apparition rising from the dirt was of an unrecognizable small boy, previously blond, caked in mud from head to foot, from the very tips of his eyelashes to his shoelaces – every item of clothing, including his anorak, oozed brown mud. Jonathan steered me onto the front seat of the car and then hastily brought out the washing-up bowl and set up the camping stove on the pavement. He warmed some water and then washed the offending creature and his clothes as best he could in full view of all the passers-by – to Lucy's intense mortification. The final leg of that journey took us via some friends of Jonathan's in Mannheim to Rothenburg, a medieval showplace within easy reach of the Wagnerian holy of holies. We pitched our tents in the early evening and lingered drowsily over food and wine in a pleasantly atmospheric restaurant. On the way back to the campsite, I stopped at a phone box to ring through to Geneva to check the arrangements for meeting Stephen in Bayreuth the next day. The phone was answered by Laura Ward, who had replaced Judy Fella when the latter had left to go on an extended trip to South Africa with her husband. Laura's voice was tense with unexpected urgency. "Oh, Jane, thank goodness you've called!" she almost shouted down the phone. "You must come quickly, Stephen is in a coma in hospital in Geneva, and we don't know how long he'll live!"

The news was shattering. It plunged me into a black pit of misery. Quite irrationally forgetting all those travels to distant places that he had survived perfectly well without me, I asked myself how I could ever have let Stephen go off alone with his entourage, deprived of the protection of my intimate knowledge of his condition, of his needs, his medicines, his likes, his dislikes, his allergies, his fears? How could I have seen him off without a qualm of anxiety and then have set out on holiday myself – with Jonathan?

While we were still in Cambridge, Stephen had rung, as he usually did on arrival, to say that all was well. He was living in a nice house in Ferney-Voltaire, well situated, if a little distant from the laboratory. He had wished us well for our journey and looked forward to seeing us in a week's time at Bayreuth. After that, in the mishmash of all my other concerns, especially my anxiety for Robert on his canoeing trip round the north coast of Iceland, I had scarcely given him another moment's thought, knowing him to be safe and in good hands. Apart from the troublesome cough, which he had brought back from China, he had been fine when he left home. It was incredible that he could have fallen into a coma in Geneva. We sat in the car numbly discussing the news. We decided to strike camp and set off for Geneva immediately, but on our return to the campsite we found everything closed for the night: the main gate was shut and the only entry or exit was by means of a wicket gate for pedestrians. There was no way we could leave until the early morning. I lay awake in my sleeping bag, listening to wolves howling and farm animals cackling somewhere in the distant black night. "Please God, let Stephen be alive!" I whispered, impatient for dawn.

As soon as the campsite opened, we loaded the car and set out on a mad dash across Europe to Geneva. Hundreds of miles of German pasture land sped by without our noticing as we raced to the Swiss border. The one advantage of being in Germany was that there were no speed restrictions. We paused at the frontier for some refreshments for the children, though I had no stomach for food, and then resumed our frenzied progress along the heartlessly tranquil shores of the blue lakes, Lake Neuchâtel and then Lake Geneva. We spoke little, each absorbed in an unhappy turmoil of confusing reflections. Even the children were quiet in the back of the car. Geneva glistened in the late afternoon sun as we approached it, but we had only one goal: the Hôpital Cantonal, where the fearsome truth of life or death awaited us. A combination of Jonathan's map-reading expertise and my ability to ask for directions in French brought us to it – a clean, clinical complex of buildings, white and glowing on the outside, highly polished and shining with stainless steel all over the inside. We were taken straight up to the intensive-care unit, and there Stephen lay, quiet and still, his eyes closed in a comatose sleep. A mask covered his mouth and nose, and tubes and wires, attached to various parts of his body, trailed in all directions; across monitors an endless dance of luminous green and white wavy lines traced the rhythmic patterns of his life forces battling to maintain their superiority over the old enemy, death. He was alive.

The medical staff on the ward gave me a curt reception. "How many years is it since you last saw your husband?" they asked coolly. It was obvious they thought that Stephen and I lived separate lives and that his illness had developed since we last met. They were baffled when I replied that I had seen him only last week. "Well, then, why is he travelling in his state of health?" they asked with the shocked incomprehension of inbred medical caution. I could no more answer that question than they could themselves, though I tried to recount the usual story of Stephen's indomitable courage combined with his scientific genius, etc. etc. – an oft-repeated tale that was too long and too complicated in the telling for my drained emotional state, and nobody believed it anyhow. Instead they gave me a garbled version of what had happened.

Apparently, Stephen's cough had worsened after his arrival in Geneva. Perhaps, as they did not live with him every day and every night, his companions had not realized that this was fairly normal. Much to his annoyance, they had insisted on calling a doctor. After hours of argument, the doctor in turn had insisted on consigning him to hospital. There pneumonia was diagnosed and, after more argument, Stephen was put on a life-support machine. He was not in fact in a coma, as his secretary had said, but had been drugged to permit a potent mixture of antibiotics and nourishment to be fed into his system through various drips, while the ventilator did his breathing for him. He was not at present in danger, since all his functions were governed by machines. I could all too easily imagine that this had been the realization of his worst, most terrifying nightmare. His fate, which lay in his own control of his medical care, had been taken out of his hands by strangers who knew nothing about him, not even who he was.

At the rented house in Ferney-Voltaire, our arrival was greeted with relief by the students, nurses and the secretary – all at a loss since, with the removal of the key player, their presence was superfluous. They also were all in a muted state of shock, silently questioning what else they could have done. While Stephen lay drugged in hospital, there was nothing for them to do. However, in the succeeding days, as I found myself sucked into a vortex of administrative, emotional and ethical problems, they invented new roles for themselves, which they fulfilled with quiet efficiency. The students did the shopping and the cooking, the nurses looked after the children and took them on outings – this, after all, was supposed to be their summer holiday – and Laura, the secretary, was in perpetual contact with Cambridge and Cern, trying to sort out our financial and insurance problems. The news was a bitter blow for Stephen's family, especially for his mother. Her husband was an invalid, and now her son's life was critically threatened too. We were in touch by phone daily, and she was consistently supportive and philosophical. In her unemotional way, she already seemed to have resigned herself to Stephen's death. It was cruel that three generations of Hawking menfolk were at risk at the same time, yet so far apart: Frank was old and ill in the small, manageable house in Bedfordshire to which he and Isobel had recently moved; Stephen was critically ill in Geneva; and goodness knows what had become of Robert. It was just as well that I did not know that his canoe had overturned in the North Sea off the coast of Iceland.

There was no anxiety about the well-being of the fourth and youngest Hawking, Tim. His immediate future was a problem however, since he had to be returned to England and my parents by some means or other; I was far too preoccupied in Geneva to be able to look after him, and the nurses would shortly be leaving. Although Lucy had her own passport, Tim was registered on mine, so I approached the British Consulate for help in getting him home. One could have been forgiven for thinking that the consular officials were being deliberately obstructive. The hard-faced, dark-haired woman at the consular desk summarily waved me away after I had spent ages waiting for an interview, even though I explained the extraordinary circumstances fully. There was no chance of Tim's returning to England without a passport, she said: for that, I would need to produce his birth certificate. I sighed. Tim's birth certificate was in the living room at home, in the William and Mary desk which had belonged to Stephen's grandmother.

On an off-chance, I telephoned our home number, not expecting it to be answered. To my surprise Eve's voice came on the line at the other end: providentially, she was in the house doing a spot of spring-cleaning. She went to the desk, found the birth certificate and sent it out to Geneva by express delivery. Triumphantly I waved the document at the same consular official a couple of days later, but she was not impressed. "That will not do," she said, as acerbic as ever, "that's only a short birth certificate, and we need the full one – from Somerset House." I stared at her in disbelief. "And in any case," she went on, "there are papers to fill in that your husband will have to sign." "I have already told you," I replied through gritted teeth, "that my husband is unconscious and paralysed on a ventilator in intensive care in the Hôpital Cantonal. He cannot possibly sign anything." "Well," she continued obtusely, "if your husband does not know that you are taking the child out of the country, you certainly cannot have a passport for him."

In one final attempt, near to tears in exasperation, I pleaded with her. "I am only trying to send the child home." She paused for a second, during which her mood mollified slightly, as if only at that moment had my words registered on her brain. "If you can get someone else, a British person with some qualifications, a teacher perhaps, to sign the papers and bring a photo, then we might consider it," she replied. To our private amusement, Jonathan filled in and signed the forms, since he fulfilled all the official requirements. We took Tim to a photo booth and made him practise his signature. At last, on 13th August, a full British passport was issued in the name of Mr T.S. Hawking; it bore the appealingly innocent photograph and the untried spidery signature of a six-year-old. Thus equipped, Mr T.S. Hawking travelled home – business class for want of a seat in economy – to England with Lucy and the nurses, and went to stay with my parents.

In his absence, Robert was the source of the sole piece of good news that summer. Bernard Carr, always a loyal ally in extremis, flew out to Geneva to take over from the students as the situation began to change. He brought Robert's A-level results, which were excellent, the only glimmer of light through the blackest of clouds. Those results assured Robert a place at Cambridge, at Corpus Christi College, my father's college, to read Natural Sciences.

2

A Slender Thread

If the comparative triviality of Tim's passport took an inordinate amount of time to resolve, it was in the topsy-turvy nature of things during that period that a far more serious matter was resolved in seconds. Two days after our arrival in Geneva, the doctor in charge of Stephen's case asked to see me as a matter of some urgency. He took me into a bare, grey side room. At first I thought that he simply wanted to verify the facts of Stephen's exceptional existence. The nursing staff had begun to accept that Stephen was no ordinary patient, nor was he the victim of neglect by his family. Having ascertained various details about his phenomenal longevity and his self-management, the doctor came abruptly to the point. The question was whether his staff should disconnect the ventilator while Stephen was in a drugged state, or should try to bring him round from the anaesthetic. I was shocked. Switching off the life supply was unthinkable. What an ignominious end to such a heroic fight for life, what a denial of everything that I, too, had fought for! My reply was quick and ready. I did not need either to think about it or discuss it with other people, as there was only one possible answer. "Stephen must live. You must bring him round from the anaesthetic," I replied. The doctor went on to explain the complications of the procedures that would ensue. Stephen would not be able to breathe unaided, and when he was stronger he would have to undergo a tracheotomy operation. This would be the only way of weaning him off the ventilator, as it would bypass the hypersensitive area in his throat, which had been giving him so much trouble. The technicalities of the tracheotomy, a hole in the windpipe below the vocal chords, would require permanent professional care. I did not pay much attention to this gloomy, if realistic, prognosis. I had made the decision that was required. The important truth was that Stephen was alive and would remain alive as long as I had any power to influence events.

I emerged from the interview room to a remarkable sight. There, standing in the corridor, was a Fellow of Gonville and Caius College, though not someone whom either of us knew at all well. James Fitzsimons and his French wife, Aude, had been on holiday with Aude's family in Geneva when word had reached them from the College that Stephen was ill in hospital there, and they had come to offer help. They could not have arrived at a more propitious moment. I was profoundly shaken by the events of the past week and was disturbed, though defiant, at the interview. I realized that the crises were by no means over, and indeed a worse crisis could be looming, for it was not at all certain that Stephen would even survive resuscitation from his drug-induced sleep.

James and Aude brought fresh energy and buoyant, though sensitive, resolve to bolster our resources. As Stephen was slowly restored to us, James joined our long vigils, taking a share in the rota, which consisted of Bernard, Jonathan, the remaining students and myself. We were not there to act as nurses – there were plenty of those in the hospital – but to strengthen Stephen's fragile hold on life and reawaken his interest and his curiosity from their unprecedented state of inertia. James was a fluent French speaker and was able to relieve me of some of the pressures of communicating Stephen's every indistinct request to the nursing staff. His attempts to mouth those requests were impeded by the tubes and masks covering his face. Those of us close to him had to try to anticipate his needs and ask the right questions; he would respond in the negative or the affirmative by means of his painfully expressive eyes, now open again, and by raising his eyebrows or frowning.

To alleviate the tedium, we read aloud from whatever holiday material we happened to have with us. With my student, Gonzalo Vargas Llosa, I had begun to explore the works of the blind Argentinian multilingual polymath Jorge Luis Borges, whose ideas excited me: I was particularly fascinated by his preoccupation with paradox and ambiguity, time and timelessness and the cyclical nature of historical events. His writing appeared to mirror in literary, even poetic, form much of the substance of scientific discovery in the twentieth century, and might be conceived as literary versions of Escher's spatially irreconcilable drawings, themselves artistic representations of a mathematical concept, the Möbius strip. I had intended to read Borges's *El*

Libro de Arena (*The Book of Sand*) over the summer holidays, so, hoping that its conundrums and enigmas might appeal to Stephen, I commissioned Bernard to bring an English translation to Geneva with him. Whether Stephen appreciated the rather complex, cerebral games of Borges's writing, I did not discover. I relished the stories for the intellectual escape they offered from the nerve-racking tension and clinical monotony of the intensive-care unit. But my fascination was even stronger when I found that I was being absorbed into the puzzle of the literature myself, especially through the first story, 'The Other', an apparently autobiographical story set in Geneva. Borges is seated on a bench in Cambridge, Massachusetts in 1969, looking out over the Charles river. A young man comes to sit beside him and the two converse. The young man, however, asserts that they are sitting on a bench overlooking the Rhône in Geneva in 1914. He is, of course, Borges's youthful self, and he recounts details of his home life at number 17 Route de Malagnou in Geneva. The ideas in the story – of identity, time travel, dreams, prediction, of history repeating itself and of knowing the future, were stimulating in themselves. But the coincidence that I had, unknowingly, chosen to read this story to Stephen in Geneva gave me the startling impression that I had entered it myself and become a part of it, adding yet another dimension. Bernard, still engaged on parapsychological research as an antidote to physics, enjoyed the coincidence. One afternoon, as Jonathan and I were leaving the hospital, I suggested driving out of the city to catch a brief glimpse of the Alps. Our route took us along the Route de Malagnou. On the way out of the city and on the way back, we scoured the street for number 17, the house in Borges's story. We could see 15 and 19, 14 and 16, but of number 17 there was no trace.

Once Stephen had regained consciousness, the pace quickened. As soon as possible an air ambulance, paid for by Caius, was commissioned to bring us back to Cambridge. Carrying an enormous amount of luggage, Jonathan set out for home by car on the same day that Stephen and I – accompanied by a doctor, paramedics, portable ventilators and other equipment – were loaded carefully into an ambulance, whisked to the airport, decanted into a small, red jet and sent hurtling into the sky the moment the hatch was closed. Had it not been for the circumstances of our flight, I might rather have enjoyed it – even Stephen roused himself sufficiently to peer out of the window as we soared above the clouds. This was the way to fly: our private plane was given priority over all the other airliners queuing up for space on the runway; there was no time for anxiety, none of the usual hassle and no delays. At Cambridge airport, John Farman, the head of the intensive-care unit at Addenbrooke's, was waiting to meet us with an ambulance on the tarmac.

Although Stephen had undeniably received excellent treatment in Geneva, there was an irrepressible sense of relief at being back home, where we and our situation were well known. Many a familiar figure appeared in the intensive-care unit that day, including Judy Fella, Stephen's former secretary. She had already been active on his behalf and was ready to give whatever help was needed. There were no gasps of surprise at Stephen's ambitious travelling schedule or incredulity at his domination of motor-neuron disease from the staff at Addenbrooke's. The minimum of general explanation was needed. Nevertheless, detailed explanation was required of the management of his case, of the routines that he himself had developed, of the precise quantities and frequencies of the medications he took, of the positions he liked to adopt when lying in bed, of his insistence on a gluten-free diet, even when being fed by tube. Each and every one of these matters, and many more like them, became the subject of lengthy discussions and investigations.

Three days after the flight, by which time Stephen's condition had stabilized in intensive care, John Farman thought it might be possible to ease him off his dependence on the ventilator; he was keen to encourage him to breathe unaided in the hope of avoiding the threatened tracheotomy operation. By Tuesday 20th August, Stephen seemed to be making good enough progress for the experiment to be tried. He was comfortable and gaining strength, and we – that is, as many friends and relations as could be mustered – had devised a rota, mounting guard over him by day and by night. Usually the long-suffering students, or our team of nurses or physiotherapists, including Sue Smith and Caroline Chamberlain, would sit with Stephen by night, and the family and other friends took turns by day. The nurses promised to ring if Stephen needed me that night, as they embarked on the delicate process of detaching him from the ventilator.

The telephone rang in my bedroom in the early hours of the morning. The ward sister said little, except that she thought

I should go to the hospital straight away. She offered no explanation. As my parents were looking after Tim, I had only to dress and leave a note before slipping out at first light. Stephen was very ill: a blotchy grey pallor had taken the place of his whitish complexion, and his bulging eyes were drained of all colour. His limbs were rigidly frozen in spasm, while a brutal cough had returned to torment his throat, like a cat toying with a mouse, letting it go, then pouncing with sharpened claws. In between each attack, he desperately tried to draw breath. Fear was written large all over his face.

The expression on the nurses' faces gave me to understand that they thought that very little could be done for him, and that the end was near. I thought differently. That the old demon was back and currently had the upper hand was obvious, but I detected a familiar element in the choking. That element was Stephen's own understandable tendency to panic. But it had been controlled before, and there was just a chance that it could be brought to heel, using the simple relaxation techniques that I had learnt in yoga classes and which I had practised successfully on him at home in past crises. I sat at the head of the bed and put one arm round the back of his neck. While I stroked his face, his shoulder and his arm with the other hand, I slowly whispered soothing words into his ear, as one might when calming a fretful baby. I chose my words carefully, and tried to create a gentle, rocking rhythm to ease away the panic. I conjured up scenes of calm, blue lakes and balmy, clear skies, rolling green hills and warm, golden sands. Gradually, over the next few hours, as the tension subsided and as his body relaxed, the paroxysms yielded to a quieter, more regular breathing pattern. Finally he dozed off. I was exhausted but jubilant: my homespun attempt at hypnosis had worked! There was no escaping the fact, however, that Stephen was still critically ill.

I went away for a rest, leaving the telephone number of our good friends, John and Mary Taylor, who lived close to the hospital. As well as being regular visitors to Stephen's bedside, the Taylors had offered me the use of their house. That morning I took up their offer at 7 a.m. Mary offered me a bed, but I preferred to sit for a while in the garden to breathe in the fresh morning air, so welcome after the sterile, dry atmosphere of the hospital, and to let the early sun caress my weary frame. Mary brought me some breakfast and we sat talking. I was incoherent with tiredness but I had one overwhelming desire, and that was to speak to Robert. It was so long since I had last seen him and so much had happened in the interim. I had to assume that he was well and that no news was good news. According to the schedule he was due to be back at base camp before setting off on the final expedition, and was therefore no longer incommunicado. I felt that the time had come to warn him that his father was critically ill, though I did not intend to ask him to come home. "Phone him from here," Mary suggested with her customary generosity. I had not the will to protest: I did as she said, and dialled through to Iceland with trepidation. When I heard Robert's voice, my resolve crumbled and I broke down. Whatever my intentions, they were overridden by a cry from the heart which escaped before I could suppress it. "Please come home!" I heard myself pleading into the phone. "Right!" he said, without the slightest hesitation. He came home the next day and was met by the Taylors at Heathrow. I did not realize that, had he completed the expedition, he would have qualified for a Queen's Scout Award. When later I heard about the canoe-capsizing episode, he laughed it off as a triviality.

My return to the hospital revealed the sort of variations on the theme of illness that had become familiar over the past two interminable weeks. Stephen's life still hung by a thread, new strains of bacteria had been found in his lungs and the medication had been changed. He was breathing through the ventilator again, but cheered up considerably at the news of Robert's return. I discussed with John Farman the possibility of bringing in a professional hypnotist to encourage him to alleviate the panic attacks and relax those muscles which went into spasm when he tried to breathe. John readily agreed and brought in a GP of his acquaintance who was also a trained hypnotist. She had moderate success, using the same techniques that I had been using, but not enough to warrant parting Stephen from the ventilator for any extended period. There was, it appeared, no alternative to the tracheotomy, the operation which would allow him to breathe through a hole in the windpipe, bypassing the troublesome membranes and muscles in his throat.

As August slid into September and the doctors started to talk seriously about performing the operation, the lung infection was at last responding to treatment and Stephen was getting stronger. Whatever they may have felt about the risks of such a step, I was beginning to feel confident that Stephen would survive.

How could he not survive with so many people contributing in every imaginable way to his recovery? Some offered invaluable practical help, at his bedside, nursing and communicating; some helped with the day-to-day administrative problems or with running our home; others, more distant, offered moral support; others prayed. Many, like Jonathan, who had arrived back from Geneva, and his parents and mine, did all of these.

The operation was a success, and Stephen made such a rapid recovery that after four weeks in intensive care it became possible to lift him out of bed into his wheelchair, though he was still too weak to operate it himself. The prognosis improved daily until it was considered safe to move him out of intensive care onto one of the neurological wards. There was a price to be paid for recovery however: the operation had deprived him entirely of the power of speech.

3

The Burden of Responsibility

In Geneva we had been protected from the bustle of the wider world. There we had been able to focus on Stephen and his illness, our movements restricted to the route between the hospital and Ferney-Voltaire. Of that small border town, I saw only the statue of Voltaire, its most famous resident, who had settled there in 1759, putting a comfortable distance between himself and the French government, ready to flee into exile in Switzerland at a moment's notice. Apart from the several arrivals and departures, the outside world which existed at the end of the telephone line was unreal, remote from the intensity of the tragedy of which we were part. In Geneva, too, we took each day as our measure of time. We neither looked forward to, nor planned for, anything weeks or months ahead.

Back in Cambridge that protection fell away. On the one hand, there were all the usual matters associated with our way of life at home that had to be dealt with; children had to be fed and cared for, bills paid, Tim taken to school every morning and collected in the afternoon, school functions attended and my teaching commitments fulfilled. On the other, the preoccupation with the fluctuations in Stephen's condition continued to be just as harrowing as in Geneva and the hospital visiting consumed just as much time. My teaching hours had to be squeezed into the middle of the day – after leaving the hospital in the morning and before returning in the afternoon. It was only because my parents and Jonathan operated a comprehensive back-up system, and because many friends, particularly Tim's godmothers, Joy and Caroline, generously offered help in some productive or reinforcing way or other, that as a family we survived this most exacting and exhausting period.

Keeping the home going while ministering to Stephen in hospital was by no means the full extent of my responsibilities. There were many pieces of business to be sorted out, not least the future of Stephen's book. It existed in a first manuscript draft which had been accepted by a publisher. As soon as the contract was signed, in the summer of 1985, a New York editor started working on the manuscript, and his letter outlining preliminary criticisms was waiting for Stephen on our return to England, though Stephen was in no fit state to read it. It was no surprise that the manuscript was not publishable in its draft form, as many of the concepts it contained were far too abstruse for popular consumption. I myself had read it and marked in red the passages where the science was incomprehensible, and the publishers pointed out that every equation would halve the sales. In his present circumstances, it was unlikely that Stephen would be able to effect the fundamental changes required. Unless the manuscript could be amended by a ghost writer, we might have to return the advance, paid just before the beginning of the summer holiday. I approached one of Stephen's former students, Brian Whitt, to enlist his help with the rewriting, but all other considerations on that score I put temporarily to the back of my mind, since there were others, much more pressing, in the forefront.

As Stephen began to make progress and was transferred to the neurological ward, his eventual return home was mooted as a distinct possibility. It was not at all clear how this was to be achieved since, plainly, Stephen would need specialist nursing twenty-four hours a day. Our previous, relaxed system of support by psychiatric nurses at specific times and for limited periods would no longer suffice, nor was their psychiatric training adequate to deal with what was essentially a critical medical situation. The tracheotomy operation which had saved Stephen's life also brought its own concomitant risks, because the tracheotomy tube, inserted in his throat, had to be cleaned regularly by a sort of mini-vacuum cleaner to bring up the secretions which perpetually accumulated in his lungs, and the device itself was potentially a source of damage and dangerous infection. He was frighteningly frail and vulnerable. It was impossible to imagine a more extreme disability of the body.

Twenty-four-hour nursing for three hundred and sixty-five days a year would cost a phenomenal sum; predictably only a tiny fraction of this expense would be borne by the National Health Service. Funding would have to be found privately and nurses engaged privately too. The philanthropic foundations that had funded nursing for a couple of hours a day would be unlikely to pay for twenty-four-hour nursing at a minimum of between thirty and forty thousand pounds a year on an indefinite basis. Then, at that most critical time, a message arrived from Kip Thorne in California. The news of Stephen's illness had travelled far and fast, thanks to Judy Fella's concerned intervention and, in response, Kip advised me, as a matter of urgency, to make a representation to the John D. and Catherine T. MacArthur Foundation, an American philanthropic organization based in Chicago. In Kip's opinion, there was a chance that the MacArthur Foundation might be prevailed upon to make a large grant, on the scale needed for permanent nursing for Stephen, if the case were well represented. Murray Gell-Mann, the particle physicist from Caltech, was on the board of the Foundation, and Kip was sure that he would encourage the other directors to give our case a fair hearing, though there was some uncertainty as to whether the Foundation would sanction a grant outside the United States. Speed was of the essence, since their next meeting was but a few weeks away.

I had no practice in writing begging letters, but whatever reluctance I might have otherwise felt about such an exercise evaporated in the face of the overwhelming need. I put down all the appropriate information which might influence the committee, not omitting to mention that Stephen had been a frequent visitor to the United States and had received many honorary degrees there. I also included photographs, taken in happier times, of smiling family groups. It was essential to assure the Foundation that any grant would be handled by a team of professional accountants, so my next task was to negotiate with the University authorities to persuade them to administer the fund on our behalf. The negotiations were both complex and time-consuming, though the goodwill demonstrated was encouraging.

The need to set up a private nursing scheme was the more pressing since certain aspects of the treatment Stephen was receiving in hospital were less than satisfactory. On the intensive-care ward he had received the full attention of the specialist nurses. The situation changed when he went onto the neurological ward. If the ward sister was generally cheerful and competent, some members of her staff appeared to be much less so. There were far fewer of them in proportion to the number of patients than in intensive care, but the lack of dedication, understanding and continuity was often alarming, particularly since many of the patients were in a vegetative state, unable to protest, think or even speak for themselves. One nurse, in particular, appeared to take advantage of that state to mete out treatment that was less than human. She was on duty when I arrived for an afternoon visit. Stephen, now sitting up in his wheelchair, was grimacing and squirming in discomfort while the young nurse, totally impassive in expression, busied herself about the room, deliberately – or so it seemed – ignoring his urgent need to pee. I helped Stephen myself and sent the nurse out of the room. That was her usual attitude, Stephen explained quivering with anger. She always ignored his needs when she was on duty. He did not trust her and was afraid of what she might do or omit to do. I could see what he meant. In her impervious expression and blank, pale blue eyes there was a chill hint of sadism which I, too, found very alarming. There was no alternative, I should have to move heaven and earth to get Stephen home, and that meant sorting out all the problems associated with twenty-four-hour nursing as quickly as possible.

That Stephen was able to protest about the nurse's behaviour was thanks to a miraculous piece of equipment which had arrived out of the blue for his use. We, the family, students and friends, had done as much as we could to make him comfortable: we had tried to keep the rota of attendance constant with no more than a gap of a few minutes here and there, and I had bought a television for his room. Nothing could compensate for the terrible loss of the power of speech, however, and just when that loss appeared depressingly irremediable, the new means of communication arrived unforeseen and unannounced. In fact it was the result of Judy's tireless efforts behind the scenes. She recalled having seen a feature about communication for the severely disabled on the BBC science programme, *Tomorrow's World*, and after a global search for information had managed to locate the British inventor of the equipment. She brought him and his invention – a set of electrodes which when attached to the head could measure rapid eye movement – to the hospital, and persuaded a Cambridge-based computer firm to contribute the necessary computer free of charge. Stephen balked at the intrusive discomfort of the electrodes attached to his temples, but when one of his students adapted the mechanism to a hand-held control box, he was more willing to experiment with the device.

The computer was loaded with a programme which combined dictionary and phrasebook. Using the control, the operator could scan the screen for the words he wanted to use: as he clicked on each one, it would take its place in the sentence which was forming in the lower part of the screen where the observer could read what the operator was wanting to communicate. Frequently used phrases could be incorporated complete, and verbal endings could be added to infinitives as required. Initially it was a slow, laborious and silent way to communicate, requiring patience and concentration both of the operator and the observer. I found that, given one or two words to point me in the right direction, I could often interpret Stephen's thoughts telepathically and save him the bother of tapping them all out, though often he insisted on writing out the whole sentence to give himself practice. Once his hand and finger muscles had recovered some movement, the new device absorbed much of the tedium of that final period in hospital. Albeit painstakingly, he began to master the novel technique which allowed him once more to reach beyond the drab surroundings of his hospital room and make contact with the outside world. He could begin to talk to his students about physics again and he could begin to experiment with writing, as well as directing his own medical care.

Having set the wheels in motion for raising money, Laura Ward and I embarked on the search for nurses. Neither of us had any experience in interviewing or employing staff, least of all nurses, but I hoped that the various social-service departments in the hospital and in the community would give us support and advice in this process. Many social workers and nursing officers called, and sat chatting and drinking coffee while they talked about their pet animals and suchlike. The amount of useful information I gleaned from them could have been consigned to the back of a postage stamp. Laura and I were left to advertise and engage nurses, and then set up a working rota of three eight-hour shifts, as best we could.

Laura repeatedly placed advertisements in the local newspaper and dealt with the responses initially, asking for references which she then followed up. As time was short, we decided to interview all the candidates who showed any suitability before receiving references. They all seemed plausible, likeable even, and I was in a hurry to set up the nursing system with as many nurses as possible, so that Stephen could come home. I assumed that nurses were by nature dedicated and idealistic, and that I could trust them. I explained the situation as best I could and made it clear that, although we wanted Stephen to be able to live at home, it was important that the home, also the home of three children, should not be turned into a hospital. I expected to treat nurses as guests in my house, and in return I assumed that they would respect our right to privacy. What a vain hope that was!

Even among the people we had interviewed and liked, my preconceptions of idealism and service were not always well based. When the references started trickling in, we had to discard many of the candidates we had thought to employ. Some were said to be slovenly, others unreliable, a few even criminal. How was it, we wondered, that there was no central regulation of the movements of this last group, when the jobs in home nursing for which they would be applying would almost all, by definition, take place in vulnerable and delicate circumstances? We were still left with a handful of good candidates, even after eliminating the undesirables but, alas, when Laura wrote to the promising applicants offering them work, a depressing number either declined to reply at all, or replied saying that they had found other jobs or that they did not think the situation suitable. To our own deep dismay, there were some eminently suitable people whom we had to turn away, on the advice of Stephen's doctors, because of their lack of training in tracheotomy technique.

The alternative was to employ agency nurses. The severe disadvantage of agency nurses was that the essential element of continuity would be lost: a different nurse at every shift could only add to the considerable frustrations which Stephen, and the rest of us, were bound to experience. Equally prohibitive was the financial aspect: agency fees, over and above the nurses' pay, would fritter away the MacArthur grant in no time at all. The money had been approved, despite some understandable suspicion on the part of the Trustees about the role of Britain's much vaunted National Health Service. Why, they had wanted to know, was Stephen's care not covered by the NHS? I had to choose my words carefully in explaining how the American-inspired monetarist policies of the Thatcher government – which had been in power for the whole of Tim's lifetime – were destroying our already overloaded, free NHS. The truth was that in encouraging a new self-seeking materialism, those policies were destroying not just the health service and our educational system, but the very fabric of society. Indeed Mrs Thatcher had denied the existence of society: for her it consisted of nothing more than a set of individuals with no sense of common purpose. It was an unfortunate time to be ill, unemployed, very young, elderly or otherwise socially disadvantaged.

A couple of months later, Laura Ward fell ill and had to leave. By great good fortune, Judy Fella, who had already given so much unstinting help, was willing to resume her old post as Stephen's secretary until a full-time replacement could be found. Judy was more circumspect than I was in selecting nurses, urging caution in the face of my impatience to bring Stephen home. She was wary even of some of the nurses whose written credentials appeared to be impeccable. Indeed, independently, reports had reached my ears about a particular nurse who had been engaged for a trial period; I was warned that although she had been given good references, she had a reputation as a troublemaker, and that there were nurses who refused to work with her because of her apparently unhealthy obsessions with some patients. In the circumstances, I refused to listen to gossip which, in any, case might be maliciously inspired. I knew the nurse in question by sight; she was a mother and I had seen her at the school gate. She struck me as reliable and efficient, and because she was a regular churchgoer, I felt that I could trust her.

During the month of October, I brought Stephen – with a hospital nurse in attendance – home from the hospital each Sunday afternoon. It was a delicate, worrying undertaking. Sometimes the change of atmosphere would frighten him and precipitate choking attacks. He was still very weak and coughed a great deal. The mini-vacuum cleaner was often in use, clearing the sputum from his chest. Sometimes we would have to return to the hospital before the afternoon was out, because the strain was too great for him; occasionally he would relax and enjoy being at home, though I sensed that he found the outside world intimidating after three months' incarceration. In those three months of crisis, his indomitable instinct for survival had stubbornly maintained its hold on life. Now everything looked strange and unfamiliar to him, as if he could not trust what he saw. Part of him wanted to re-enter the flurry of unpredictable normality, part of him wanted the predictable security of the hospital. Nevertheless a date, Monday 4th November, was set for his discharge.

In those three months since early August, I had escaped for just one evening's respite from the harrowing routine in order to attend the London debut of the Cambridge Baroque Camerata on 1st October. The evening was warm after a hot, sunny day, giving London a carnival atmosphere in the midst of which I felt alien and uncomfortable. The concert, played to an appreciable audience, went well, though the atmosphere lacked the buzz of excitement which attended the orchestra's full houses in Cambridge. It was a mystery how Jonathan had succeeded in putting it on at all, since his every spare moment had been spent either in the hospital looking after Stephen or at West Road looking after the family. Unruffled, he had calmly pursued his own activities – organization, administration, practice and rehearsals – late into the night, tucked away in his own house. As he performed and directed beneath the lights on the stage of the Queen Elizabeth Hall, always with an unassuming simplicity and understated elegance of style, no one could have guessed at the pressures of the preceding weeks. I was glad to be there to witness his success, yet I was smitten with guilt at having left Stephen forlornly behind in hospital, sitting out of doors in the autumn sun on a bare patch of ground which euphemistically called itself a garden.

By the end of October, the situation was different: Stephen was much stronger, but I was completely exhausted. I had developed chronic asthma and I slept badly, increasingly dependent on sleeping tablets and also subject to welts which came and went, producing sore tingling spots on the palms of my hands and in my mouth. All these were, of course, nothing more than the symptoms of severe stress. The doctors recommended a break, even if only a weekend, before Stephen's return home. In September, Robert had left Cambridge to spend his gap year in Scotland. He went to live temporarily with the Donovans outside Edinburgh and started working on the shop floor at Ferranti, where he learnt basic engineering techniques under the eye of an exacting foreman. Eventually he moved into digs in Edinburgh. It was not an easy life for an eighteen-year-old, and I feared that he was not looking after himself properly. The last weekend before Stephen's return home – which also happened to be the first weekend of half-term – was an opportune moment to get away. I could benefit from a change of air and routine, calm my stinging nerves and see Robert's circumstances for myself.

I was comforted to find him in good form – and Edinburgh was at its glorious, autumnal best. But three days, however sunny and bright, however clear and crisp, however stimulating with new sights and sounds, were scarcely enough to erase the incessant, intense, traumatic strain of the past three months.

Not three days nor three months nor even three years could have prepared me, or anyone else, for what was yet to come.

4

Mutiny

Stephen returned home in the early afternoon of 4th November. It was like bringing a new baby home from hospital. There reigned a sense of excitement tinged with nervousness, a protective fear lest the helpless, fragile being might suddenly cease to draw breath within moments of entering the house. Stephen, too, was tense and nervous, suspicious of the competence of the nurses engaged to care for him and anxious about every speck of dust in the atmosphere which might upset his breathing. He had little respect for the intelligence of other people at the best of times. Now, at the worst of times, he was inclined to regard them all as morons. His fears were warranted, but not altogether for the reasons one might have supposed.

The nurse who came that first afternoon was herself unwell; she was little more than an elderly waif and, although she fulfilled her duties admirably, she rang afterwards to say that she would not be able to come again as the strain was too great for her. This was a bitter blow, because that particular nurse had been booked for many of the twenty-one weekly shifts. There were others like her, pleasant, well-meaning people who could not cope with the stress. The agency was the only recourse, whatever the cost. For the next few weeks, as Judy and I tried to shore up the collapsing rota with a frenzied round of advertising, interviewing and instructing of prospective candidates, the agency provided nurses of varying degrees of competence. In fairness, these nurses probably had little advance notice of what would be expected of them. Never were Stephen's worst anxieties – and mine – more fully justified: the agency sent a different nurse on every occasion. Although generally they were well intentioned and well qualified, none of them easily understood what was required. Either Jonathan or I spent the whole shift repeating the same instructions over and over again.

Some nurses never mastered the angle of the cup to prevent tea from dribbling down Stephen's front into the tracheotomy tube or onto his clothes. Some did not chop his food into small enough morsels, others mashed it to an unacceptable purée. Some tried to give him his pills in the wrong order. Some jogged his hand on the joystick of the wheelchair, sending him off into a spin. Others made a complete shambles of the bathroom routine. Despite their medical experience, they were all terrified of the tracheotomy tube in his throat and were nervous of using the suction unit. Very rarely did the same nurse come back twice. When occasionally one of them was brave enough to cross the threshold for an encore, I greeted him or her as a long-lost friend in my relief at not having to repeat the whole procedure until I was sick of the sound of my own voice. I tried hard to be patient and reassuring, but my nerves were on edge, bristling with exhaustion, worry and dejection. Stephen's frustration was understandable, of course, and he made no attempt to conceal it.

If the daytime routine verged on the impossible, at night the problems were of a different order. Once in bed, Stephen no longer had the use of his computerized means of communication and was again deprived of speech. There were just two devices to help him. One, an alphabet frame, must have been the stock-in-trade of occupational therapists in the Dark Ages. The alphabet, in groups of large letters, was displayed around a transparent frame: Stephen was supposed to fix his eyes first on a group of letters, then on an individual letter within that group to spell out his needs letter by letter. The attendant was supposed to follow his eye movements and construct his meaning from them. The device demanded extraordinary patience and remarkable powers of deduction from all concerned. I tried to simplify the procedure by developing a shorthand code so that Stephen only had to focus on one letter for his meaning to become apparent. Either my code got lost in the muddle in his room, or the nurses thought they could do better; in any event, my invention did not last long.

The other device, which eventually superseded the alphabet frame and marked a considerable technological advance over it, was a buzzer. All night Stephen would hold the control in his hand, in much the same way as he held his computer control by day, and would exert pressure on it to illuminate a small box where any one of a limited number of commands would appear in sequence on a panel to indicate his needs. For a long time, even when he was in good health, it had been difficult to settle his rigid limbs comfortably in bed, and now that he was seriously ill the process took most of the night. In those early months I would stay with him until I was confident that he was well settled, since I knew that he was afraid of being left with an unfamiliar nurse. Then at two or three in the morning I myself would fall into bed, often to be woken soon after by the night nurse, who found that she could not cope alone.

Quite apart from the day-to-day and night-to-night problems, the months after Stephen's return were marked by many other life-threatening dramas. These usually occurred late at night, when the tracheotomy tube either blocked off or came unstuck. While the nurse tried to clear it or adjust it, I would dial through to the intensive-care unit in search of the doctors who were versed in the technique of changing it. A dash to hospital and endless hours waiting in the casualty department would follow, until a new tube was inserted and Stephen could breathe again. Since our last student helper, Nick Warner, a cheerful Australian, had left in the summer and had not been replaced, Jonathan slept in the upstairs room so that he could look after Tim and take him to school first thing in the morning when I was still recovering from the disturbances of the night.

As Robert had left home, his room, large and airy at the front of the house, was quickly converted into a room for Stephen. It was particularly suitable, because it had a washbasin and adequate cupboards for nursing and medical equipment – of which we received regular, massive deliveries. There was also plenty of space for an orthopaedic bed, bins, computers, desks, armchairs, all sorts of other paraphernalia and, of course, the wheelchair. This last item was becoming ever bulkier and heavier. The computer equipment which Judy had acquired for Stephen when he was in hospital had been superseded by a more sophisticated version, sent from California. The new computer had the added advantage of a voice synthesizer so that Stephen could be heard to speak the sentences that he typed up on the screen. No matter that the synthesized voice sounded unnervingly like a dalek: Stephen was once again endowed with the power of speech. The husband of one of the nurses, David Mason, a skilled computer engineer, set to work to adapt the computer and add its several parts to the wheelchair, so that Stephen would no longer be desk-bound but could carry his voice with him wherever he went. The weighty computer and voice box were strapped onto the back of the chair, and the screen was attached to the frame where Stephen could see it. Once, some time later, when we happened to come across an industrial weighing machine, we levered Stephen and all his contraptions onto it. The weight of the chair, batteries, computer, screen, various cushions and occupant amounted to one hundred and thirty kilograms.

There were recurring crises when the newly invented mechanism developed teething troubles, just as there were recurring crises with Stephen's own state of health. If David Mason were not called round as a matter of urgency at all hours of the day, then it was our faithful friend, John Stark, the chest consultant, or long-suffering Dr Swan or another duty doctor from the surgery, who would be summoned at all hours of the night. Physiotherapists were called out at weekends and our local chemist was roused after closing hours. In short, we floundered in an endless state of crisis throughout November into December, with its usual round of school carol services and other preparations for Christmas. We were again piloting our boat across troubled waters. These uncharted waters were shrouded in darkness, and we had on board a potentially mutinous crew.

The major share of my energies and my time were devoted to Stephen. I drank every sip of water with him, ate every spoonful of food and breathed every gasp of air. When my strength failed, Jonathan shared the burden, quietly and always reliably available in the background. What little time and energy I had left, I gave to my children and to my pupils. Teaching was my one opportunity to concentrate for a few hours a day on other matters – the time when language and literature could fill and enliven the vacuum created by despondency and crushing weariness. The pupils of that year became very special to me. Generally they showed an exceptionally mature understanding for teenagers, and from them I received the fulsome appreciation which strengthened my resolve to continue teaching, come what may, so long as I was capable of doing the job properly. It was essential to my own ragged mental health.

Stephen did not view my modest attempts to keep up my intellectual interests in the same light. He had suffered, and was still suffering, a horrendous ordeal, and was still very frightened; like Lear, he was child-changed – into a child possessed of a massive and fractious ego. On the one hand, his pathetic physical state expressed all too clearly his need for constant loving reassurance; on the other, he made himself inaccessible, barricading himself behind defiance and resentment. From being authoritative in the past, he became authoritarian, even – or perhaps especially – with those of us who had been through so much with him. He was indignant at some of the decisions I had been forced to take in family matters during his period in hospital, and would insist on his rights as a matter of principle. It was natural that he would want to reassert himself, but no one was disputing his right to be king of the universe and master of the house. It was difficult therefore to understand why he seemed to want to make the daily routine even more fraught than usual by means of various disobliging ploys, which usually involved deliberately stationing his wheelchair in the most obstructive position imaginable, or by disputing other people's right to privacy, particularly Lucy's. She and I were very close companions. Her open character, brimming with enthusiasm, and her independent spirit were endless sources of strength and encouragement even in the depths of despair. She and I talked at length, discussing all manner of subjects without constraint. It was obvious that in our extraordinary situation she needed space to herself. Her room had to be respected as her sanctuary, away from the constant commotion caused by nurses and wheelchairs. She was as intensely loyal to her father as she was to me, but she longed for privacy, away from the prying eyes, listening ears and gossiping tongues of the nursing staff. That privacy was constantly denied her.

I recounted my dismay at Stephen's apparently unreasonable attitudes to a doctor friend, who replied, "Just think, Jane, what he has been through! He nearly died, he was kept alive by machines and drugs. Can you tell me that all that would have no effect on his brain? There must have been times when his brain was starved of oxygen and it's more than likely that that shortage caused minute, undetectable lesions which are now affecting his behaviour and his emotional reactions, although, thankfully for him, his intellect is intact." Another friend, a senior nurse in a hospice for the victims of incurable degenerative diseases, was convinced that the families of those motor-neuron-disease patients struck down in the prime of life rather than in old age were the ones who suffered most anguish. In one sense these opinions and advice were comforting. They implied that Stephen was not completely responsible for his actions and that it was not just his excess of innate egoistic energy that was determining his lack of consideration, but the combined effects of motor-neuron disease and the recent trauma. These opinions, however, bore little weight elsewhere, even among medical circles, since it was apparent to all that, intellectually, Stephen had come through hell unscathed.

That, nevertheless, was not the full story. Judy, Lucy and I were well aware that Stephen's egoism was being fed and urged on by his nurses. I might as well have voiced my concerns – about keeping the home a happy place for all the family and not allowing it to become a hospital – to a concrete wall, for all the impact these concerns had on the nursing staff. They were indifferent to the fact that the house was also home to a shy, sensitive six-year-old and a spirited, intelligent teenager immersed in O-level studies. One of the very first nurses turned the whole house inside out as soon as she stepped through the front door. Fretting at the lack of sterility, she scrubbed everything in sight, trying to bring our home up to intensive-care standards, while Eve, who continued to give valiant service washing, cleaning and hoovering daily, watched incredulously. "She's daft!" was Eve's comment. Finally the new broom decided that it was too stressful to work in such an unhygienic atmosphere and left.

There were, it has to be said, nurses who were dedicated and perceptive, the most exemplary being Mr Jo, as we called him, who not only fulfilled all his nursing duties but occasionally brought us the most fragrant curries on Sunday evenings. Generally the dedicated people were older women – or men – trained in a more disciplined age, or people who had achieved a higher level of education than the norm, or people who were not strangers to problems themselves. There were others of similar ilk who promised to be as dependable but who, in the event, found the physical strain too much for them. For most, the words "professional discipline" and "understanding" were meaningless, and self-interest was paramount. Our tales of the harrowing months before their arrival meant nothing to them, nor did they give a moment's thought to the stress that we lived under all the time. A seven- or eight-hour shift might be stressful, but the nurse who performed that shift could go away to recover in his or her own home. That was not an option open to members of the family.

One common problem was that nurses, like social workers before them, were easily deceived by our surroundings. Because we lived in a large house, they supposed we must be super-rich. Discreet attempts to explain that we rented our flat from the College fell on deaf ears. None were deafer than those of the nurse who misread our outward circumstances and Stephen's professorship as evidence of wealth and power. Late one evening she came to me in the kitchen as I was putting out the breakfast things and brazenly demanded that I obtain a mortgage for her from the University. Not sure that I had heard correctly, I asked her to repeat her request in front of Stephen, who was already in bed. We went into Stephen's room where, standing beside the bed, she repeated what she had said. I explained that there must have been some misunderstanding as I had no influence with the University and was not in any position to obtain a mortgage on her behalf. Whereupon, at midnight, she started screaming and writhing, stamping and beating her chest, before whirling into a frenzied war dance round Stephen's bed. I ran to the phone and rang Judy, who came straight away. She smartly but tactfully removed the wailing banshee, who stood screeching her protests and threats of litigation out in the drive, while I rang the agency for a replacement.

Another nurse, a sad, lonely woman whom I befriended, soon turned out to be an alcoholic. She not only helped herself to judiciously measured thimblefuls of liqueur from our modest assortment of spirits stored at the bottom of the kitchen cupboard, she also picked up any loose change lying around. When she suddenly left, the taxi driver who drove her to Heathrow happened by chance to be an acquaintance of Judy's. He reported back that the nurse had not only paid his fee – some £45 – in two- and five-pence pieces, but had spent the whole journey regaling him with the intimate details of life in our household. That nurse might well have been party to everything that went on under our roof, because privacy was non-existent. It was virtually impossible to have a private, let alone intimate, conversation with Stephen – or anyone else for that matter – without first making an appointment and asking the nurse on duty to be so good as to leave the room for five minutes.

Because of the scarcity of time and the slowness of communication, I got into the habit of preparing what I wanted to say to Stephen in advance. I hoped that by presenting him with a succinct and logical argument, I could simplify the matter, be it financial or family, under discussion. Stephen objected to this, implying that yet again I was denying him his rights. He would insist on returning to first principles and would dispute my reasoning at every stage, sure of the superiority of his own arguments. Thus, minor matters became major issues, and the cheerfully optimistic frame of mind in which I had entered his room would quickly disintegrate into defeat and disillusionment. As Stephen recovered his power of speech, I became nervously withdrawn again, unsure of myself and so uncertain of my opinions that I ceased to voice them, as much the victim of psychological pressure as Stephen was the victim of illness. I observed this process as it happened, yet there was nothing I could do to stop it, because it was part and parcel of the situation. I was caught in a trap and began to have nightmares two or three times a week. The nightmare was always the same: I was buried alive, trapped underground with no means of escape.

In a last-ditch attempt to stem the tide of nursing insurrection, Judy and I decided to provide the nurses with uniforms in response to a request from some of them who complained that their clothes were getting spoilt by splashes and spills of fluid. One of the more senior of them had access to a supply of second-hand white overalls and brought us a dozen or so. A white overall worn with a belt and buckle would look smart and official; the agency nurses always wore uniform, so it seemed appropriate for ours to do so too. A uniform would also clearly draw a line between the nurses and the family and, we hoped, instill some sense of professional discipline. Stephen however refused to let his nurses wear uniform: he wanted to maintain the illusion that his attendants were just friends. Thereafter nurses had free rein to wear whatever they liked. Sometimes their dress and make-up would have been more appropriate to a street corner in Soho than to the home of a severely handicapped Cambridge professor and his family.

Lucy soon became used to having the newspaper whisked from under her nose by the duty nurse, as she sat eating her breakfast before school in her O-level year. It would then be ceremoniously set up in Stephen's place to await his arrival some ten minutes later. Quickly, the rest of the family became second-class citizens, as if we were the lowest of the low, crouching on the bottom rung of a ladder, at the top of which the Florence Nightingales administered to the master of the universe. In between there were the several echelons of students, scientists and computer engineers, all of whom were obviously more important than we were. When one of the nurses, Elaine Mason, asked why I did not give up teaching and take up nursing, learning to use the suction machine so that I could look after Stephen myself, it was the clearest indication yet that the rest of us, who had no medical qualifications, were being consigned to a despised obscurity. The facility with which Elaine Mason used her evangelical certainty to gloss over profound issues as being the will of God was disconcerting. When she airily announced in Stephen's hearing that looking after him was so much easier than bringing up her own two sons, I hardly liked to point out that she was nursing Stephen for only just a couple of sessions a week. Such remarks were all too reminiscent of the facile Hawking attitude that I had encountered in the past. As she was an efficient nurse, I tried to regard her insensitive pronouncements with the detachment they deserved.

In the face of such sanctimonious pseudo-philosophy, I found even greater solace in my attachment to St Mark's. I listened to Bill Loveless's sermons intently and also to those of his fellow preacher, a scientist and former missionary, Cecil Gibbons, who at an advanced age made it his duty to keep abreast of scientific developments and interpret them in a religious context. They both always had something pertinent and measured to say to me personally, whether about suffering, about man's place in creation or about good and evil, and under their guidance I began to formulate my own simple philosophy about some of the stumbling blocks to faith, principally by understanding that free will is a prerequisite of the human condition. If belief in God were automatically decreed by the creator, the human race would simply be a breed of automatons with neither evolution of thought nor motivation for discovery. Evil, I reasoned, was often reducible, even if distantly and hazily, to human greed and selfishness – predatory animal instincts, dictated by nature for survival in a distant evolutionary past, long before the development of finer intelligence and the dawn of conscience. Selfish, instinctive reaction, the root of evil, is outside the reach of God precisely because free will prevents His intervention. God could not prevent suffering, but He could alleviate its effects by restoring hope, peace and harmony. There was still the stumbling block of illness, degenerative, incurable, paralysing and devastating, which did not fit into this system – unless, that is, illness also sometimes happened to be the result, however remotely, of human fallibility, an error in research or treatment, in a chosen way of life or in the environment. If the cause of Stephen's illness was really a non-sterile smallpox vaccination given in the early Sixties, it might be accounted for thus. As for the present chaos, one could only hope that, by keeping faith, by still trying to give of one's best, a brighter, calmer day might one day dawn.

On the administrative front, Judy was beleaguered. She would prepare an agreed rota of nursing shifts a month in advance, only to find, in the event, that her careful organization had been mysteriously overturned and that the working rota bore little resemblance to the one she had prepared and distributed. Neither she nor I would have any idea whom to expect at any given time; the system would inexplicably break down, and agency nurses had to be called in. Shattered and demoralized by all the unforeseen – and often unnecessary – complications which had accompanied our best efforts to enable Stephen to return to the family and the community, Judy and I called a series of meetings to try and settle various differences once and for all. Word had reached her indirectly that, quite apart from the interference in the organization of the rota, trouble was being whipped up among the staff on issues which had no relevance to our private nursing scheme.

The grants from the MacArthur Foundation came in six monthly instalments. Every sixth months the University accountants would prepare a balance sheet to show the Trustees of the Foundation how their money had been spent, and I would submit a report on Stephen's health and care, together with another begging request for a further grant for the next half-year. In my second letter to the Foundation in March 1986, I explained how we had tried to engage our own team of nurses by placing regular advertisements in the local paper. I referred to the "indescribable problems" that this method had occasioned, with the result that we had often had to resort to the agency – hence the considerable bills for agency nursing. The grants, though generous, were only just enough to cover the bills. They certainly were not adequate to meet the demands which some mischief-maker among the nurses was now devising and which Judy thought to answer by calling the first meeting. Having thanked those present for all their help, I explained how the finances were obtained and organized in the hope that they might have a better idea of the difficulties we had experienced. I pointed out that the nursing bill came to at least £36,000 a year and was financed from the United States. I also emphasized that there was never any certainty that it would be renewed. It was therefore impossible to provide the nurses with anything more than casual employment on a part-time basis, which was strictly how the work was advertised. Consequently there was no scope for sickness pay, holiday pay, pensions or any of the other perks for which they had begun to agitate.

Thereafter a more subdued audience concentrated their attention on practical requests for laundry baskets, towel rails, adequate lighting, shelving and suchlike, and repairs to the potholes in the driveway. Judy and I took the opportunity to distribute the UK Council of Nursing's code of conduct, and asked the assembly to give its fourteen clauses their attention. Those recommendations had as much impact as the concerns I had already voiced about keeping the home, our home, a happy and well-balanced environment for Stephen and the children alike.

5

Out of the Ashes

Despite the mayhem wrought in the home by outside intervention, Stephen rose like a phoenix, and by early December 1985 he
was well enough to attempt short sorties to the Department. At
first I drove him there by car but, unless the weather was bad, he
was soon wheeling himself in his chair over his usual route across
the Backs, the only difference being that he was accompanied
by a nurse instead of a faithful student. All expeditions took
longer than before, involving much careful preparation of the
patient before setting out. Many essential accoutrements had
to be strung onto the back of the wheelchair, giving the whole
contrivance an extraordinarily cumbersome appearance. Lum-
bering and festooned with eccentric appliances, rather like
a tinker's cart, the chair dwarfed its occupant who, small and
wasted, drove it fearlessly into battle to reassert his sovereignty
over his intellectual domain.

It was unwise to dwell for too long on the Stephen's vulnerability,
though it was difficult not to fall into the snare of sentimental
overprotection: many had fallen into that trap. Some of us had
striven to achieve a balance between a deep concern for the minimal,
evanescent, physical presence and a somewhat mischievous ir-
reverence for the immense psychological and intellectual power.
This delicate balance, so essential to a healthy family life where no
one person should claim to be more important than anyone else,
had become impossible to maintain. At best, it entailed nerve-
racking attention to every detail of Stephen's care, yet a healthy
scepticism at some of his more outlandish and outrageous pronouncements. On a Sunday evening, for instance, Jonathan would
bring in the usual takeaway curry. Though neurotic and mistrustful
of the ingredients of my carefully prepared, guaranteed gluten-free
home cooking, Stephen would on Sundays consume a huge plateful
of curry with gusto, with never a thought as to the ingredients.
The children and I considered this glaring inconsistency fair game
for a little gentle teasing.

These were also occasions for wide-ranging discussions. Private conversation had become impossible, but in the relaxed atmosphere of those Sunday evenings – sometimes too at Sunday lunch when Robert, who came back to study in Cambridge in 1987, would bring his undergraduate friends home for a square meal – questions of science and faith would form the basis of sustained, good-natured argument. Cecil Gibbons had pointed out in one of his sermons that scientific research required just as broad a leap of faith in choosing a working hypothesis as did religious belief. Stephen usually grinned at the mention of religious faith and belief, though on one historic occasion he actually made the startling concession that, like religion, his own science of the universe required such a leap. In his branch of science the leap of faith – or inspired guesswork – centred on which model of the universe, which theory, which equation one chose as the most appropriate object of research. Then this, at the experimental stage, had to be tested against observation. With luck, the guess – or leap of faith – might, in Richard Feyman's words, prove "to be temporarily not wrong". The scientist had to rely on an intuitive sense that his choice was right, or he might be wasting years in pointless research with an end result that was definitively wrong. Any further attempts to discuss the profound matters of science and religion with Stephen were met with an enigmatic smile.

Insensitive to the subtleties of our relationship and unable to distinguish the mind from the body, the nurses, on the other hand, tended to smother Stephen in a blanket of sentimentality. This belied his strength of mind and undermined my attempts to keep the correct balance. For them he had become an idol, immune from criticism or even from the healthy scepticism which the psychiatric nurses had generated. They concentrated on the calamity of the illness rather than the victory over it, kowtowed to the patient's every whim and interpreted any innocent bantering as an insult to their idol.

The same sentimental mistake had been made earlier in 1985 by an artist commissioned jointly by the College and the National Portrait Gallery to paint Stephen's portrait. The paintings, unveiled that summer, showed the pathos of the body, slumped disjointedly in the chair all too clearly, but failed to show the willpower and the genius, conveyed with such persuasion in the set of the face and the light of the eyes. I regarded the portraits as a travesty and said so – to the exasperation of the bodies who had commissioned them. However, in the early months of 1986, the light of determination returned to those eyes as Stephen recovered his mobility and with it his unassailable position in the Department. The effect of his period of illness was not unlike the effect that exile from Cambridge had on Newton when the University was closed because of the plague in 1665. In the isolation of the manor house at Woolsthorpe near Grantham, Newton had found time for the contemplation and calculation needed to develop his theory of gravity. In those months when he was too weak to leave home, Stephen had learnt to use the new computer with the same single-minded motivation which he had shown in memorizing lengthy equations when, in the late Sixties, he lost the ability to write.

Through the loss of his voice, he discovered that he had gained a much improved method of communication. He could converse with anyone, not just the small band of family and students as in the past, and he was no longer dependent on having a student at hand to interpret his lectures for him. By turning up the volume on the speaker, he could address an audience as effectively, if not more so, as anyone else. His synthesized speech was slow, since it took time to select the vocabulary, but there was nothing unusual in that since his speech had always been measured. Stephen had always taken time to think before speaking to avoid cliché or inanity, and to ensure that the last word on any subject was his and his alone.

Not only was he empowered to express his own thoughts directly, deliver his own lectures and write his own letters, he was also able to work again on his book. His former student, Brian Whitt, had over the past months begun to help him with the methodical organization of the material and continued to help, particularly with diagrams and seeking out research material; but the project was now firmly back in Stephen's grasp. The book gave him the motivation to exploit the full potential of the computer, and the computer gave him the means of writing a revised version of the manuscript, incorporating the suggestions of the American editor. It began to look as if the book might become a reality: not only should we not have to repay the advance, we had, at long last, the prospect of financial security. The book might not make a fortune, but it might bring in a regular supplementary income, heralding the end of nearly a quarter of a century of economizing.

At home I endeavoured to juggle my own interests, teaching, music and the children, with the tiresome demands of wayward nurses. With Judy's stalwart help, I fended off impending chaos by conducting weekly interviews with new candidates and by attending to the requests for improvements from those already on the rota. We sensed that we had become the scapegoats for the frustrations which the nurses could not vent on Stephen himself. I discussed our predicament with an old school friend who lectured in nursing. She recognized the syndrome. "Nurses, like soldiers, are trained to act, not to think," she said. "If there is a patient needing treatment, their first duty is to that patient to the exclusion of all else. They act at an intensely physical level, which does not involve the intellect. Imagination is not a quality that is prized in nursing." This information certainly clarified the problem, but offered scant comfort, since it implied that nurses operated at the opposite end of the philosophical spectrum from the rest of us and, however much we might try to compromise, they, by definition, were unable to do so.

Meanwhile Stephen celebrated his return to normality. In the immediate short term, this took the form of a visit to the pantomime for his birthday and to the College Ladies' Night two days later. In the long term, he was already planning his travels for the forthcoming year, rashly undaunted by the Geneva experience. Paris and Rome were on his itinerary for the autumn, to be preceded by an experimental trip abroad in June – to an island off the Swedish coast for a conference in particle physics. How all this was to be achieved was another matter, especially since the dates for the Swedish conference coincided with Lucy's first O-level papers and I was reluctant to leave her at such a critical time.

In fact attention shifted dramatically from Stephen to Lucy in the spring of 1986. In March, she set off with a school party to Moscow, but not, as we had all expected, under the exuberant auspices of her Russian teacher. Each year it was Vera Petrovna's custom to dress up her charges like Michelin men, in layer upon layer of clothing acquired from second hand shops and jumble sales. In Moscow the girls would tour the city, visiting all her friends and relations, peeling off a layer of charitable clothing at each stop. However in 1986 she was refused a visa for the first time, so other non-Russian-speaking teachers had to accompany the party to Moscow and Leningrad. It was therefore a potential catastrophe when Lucy fell ill in Moscow with only her own knowledge of Russian to help her. Terrified of being abandoned in a Russian hospital, she told no one how ill she was feeling; she ate nothing and clutched her stomach for ten days. When she arrived home, she was too ill with a high fever and excruciating abdominal pain to go anywhere except straight to bed. The doctor came and diagnosed acute appendicitis. So there we were again – walking the all-too-familiar corridors of Addenbrooke's Hospital, sitting on the same plastic chairs, though for a dangerously inflamed appendix rather than a dangerously obstructed respiratory tract. We were told the next day, when Lucy was already recovering, that she was very lucky not to have had a burst appendix in Moscow.

Nevertheless, the arrival of warmer weather alleviated some of the tensions associated with winter susceptibilities, and life began to assume at least a thin veneer of its former hard-won normality. Defiantly determined that the home should still be worthy of that name, I tried to consign the complexities of full-time nursing attendance to the background, pretending, as we had so often in the past, that it was just another minor inconvenience. Once more we gave dinners and drinks parties for scientific visitors and participated in local activities at the schools and the church. Tim invited seventeen of his classmates to his birthday party, where a good, old-fashioned Punch and Judy show kept the guests enthralled for part of the time while, for the rest of the afternoon, my father, in time-honoured tradition at the piano, kept them amused with musical games.

As Stephen's health gradually improved, I ventured to take up some of my old activities, notably singing in the church choir and with the choral society which I had joined in the early Eighties. Since the latter's weekly rehearsals took place in Caius College Chapel by kind permission of the Dean, John Sturdy, this activity was quite compatible with Stephen's movements. He, accompanied by a nurse, would dine in the College while I sang – or tried to sing my way through an endless succession of colds – in the Chapel. Often he would call in at the Chapel after dinner to listen to the final stages of the rehearsal and we would then go home together. Lucy was adopting an increasingly independent lifestyle, which revolved more and more around the theatre and kept her out of the house.

Three nurses and a doctor were engaged for Stephen's trip to Sweden, stretching the MacArthur budget to its limit. It was however a profitable investment, since Murray Gell-Mann, one of the trustees of the MacArthur Foundation, was also a participant at the conference. He could see at first hand just how dire Stephen's circumstances were and just how much costly professional care was needed to sustain his life and his contribution to physics. In my next application to the Foundation in September of 1986, I was able to refer to our meeting with Murray Gell-Mann and to report that Stephen's health, though much more stable, continued to require the same degree of professional nursing: I predicted that it would be required indefinitely. Thereafter, the MacArthur Foundation agreed to support Stephen's nursing expenses on an indefinite basis and accepted my explanation that the National Health Service provided only a fleeting morning visit from the District Nurse to check the supplies, a weekly visit from the GP, one eight-hour shift out of the twenty-one, and additional help with bathing on a couple of mornings a week.

The small, traffic-free island of Marstrand off the west coast of Sweden proved to be the most delightful and suitable place for a convalescent physicist to flex his intellectual muscles. While Stephen and his comrades explored the universe by means of the trajectories of elementary particles, I relaxed, cherishing peace and solitude in the rocky coves and walking along the woodland tracks where daffodils still bloomed in June and the sun shone late into the night. The freedom of those few days in Sweden was a rare luxury, but one which just occasionally came my way thanks to the unexpectedly helpful intervention of Stephen's mother after the death of his father in March 1986. Stephen's father was not an easy patient in his final illness; the frustration of immobility was too burdensome for one who in earlier years had thought little of driving single-handed across Africa to enlist for service at the beginning of the Second World War, and who habitually in his late seventies would spend whole weeks camping and walking in the Welsh mountains. His funeral marked a sad end to a distinguished but inadequately recognized career in tropical medicine. I suspected that I was not the only person whose feelings towards him were decidedly ambivalent. I admired him and respected him, for he could be sensitive and considerate, even appreciative, but he could also be cold, harsh and distant.

After his death, Isobel's formerly stringent inflexibility appeared to mellow as she showed signs of greater compassion.

She seemed anxious to share the stresses of our family life in a new way and became popular with the children for her coolly sardonic sense of humour and for her apparently easygoing nature, which made few demands of them. She also showed a surprising and benevolent tolerance of my relationship with Jonathan, as if she had finally come to realize that he was not intent on destroying the family but was genuinely supportive of us all, including Stephen. I was grateful for her help and grateful for her understanding, especially when she offered to keep house so that we could resume our camping holidays on the Continent. If I could reliably look forward to a couple of weeks' summer holiday away from the strains of a half-life in a house where I was on duty in every capacity for seven days a week for a minimum of forty-nine weeks a year, juggling all my roles, trying to be all things to all the inhabitants, I felt that I could summon the strength to continue, however onerous those duties might be. At the end of the allotted time, I returned without question to Stephen.

Having spread his phoenix wings in Sweden without mishap, Stephen was eager to use them again and again. In September, the travelling circus – which now included a young physics graduate as Stephen's personal assistant – set off for Paris for a conference at the Observatoire de Paris at Meudon, where Brandon Carter worked. I was delighted to be able to spend time with Lucette, bringing her up-to-date on the events of the past year, and there I also discovered a new role for myself – as chauffeur and interpreter for the party. At least the nurses could hear, if not see, that I was good for something.

Only a month later we found ourselves again in Rome, where Stephen was to be admitted by the Pope to the Pontifical Academy of Sciences, despite the heresies he was still preaching about the universe having neither a beginning nor an end. Tim came too, as did the retinue of nurses and the young personal assistant whose responsibility it was to attend to the workings of the computer and the mechanics of Stephen's lectures. We tried to choose nurses whom we knew to be Catholic and who would appreciate the significance of the occasion. We were lucky in that two of the most reliable and pleasant nurses on the rota, Pam and Theresa, were both Catholic and were overjoyed to be invited. We needed three nurses however, and not all were as keen as Pam and Theresa. It was only at the last minute that Elaine Mason agreed to come with us: she did so only on the understanding that she would not have to shake hands with the Pope, as such a gesture would be against her principles.

The second visit to Rome was more formal than the first in 1981. The weather was better, and so were the provisions made for us: we stayed in a much more comfortable hotel, closer to the Vatican, and special tours of the art treasures of the Vatican were put on for wives and children while the scientists conferred in the Renaissance headquarters of the Academy. The climax of the visit was an audience with Pope John Paul II, to which all members of Stephen's party were admitted. With his hand gently resting on Tim's head, the Pope talked quietly to Stephen and me, pressing our hands and giving us his blessing. He then shook hands with the others, none of whom resisted. I was moved by the genuine warmth of his personality, the softness of his big hands and the holiness of the light in his bright blue eyes. I had no religious prejudices, and had come to Rome with an open heart and mind. The Pope touched my heart and my mind, for – politics and dogma apart – I sensed that he sincerely cared about the people he met and kept them in his prayers.

Encouraged by the success of these tentative trips abroad within Europe, Stephen's aspirations knew no bounds. That December he soared away to the usual pre-Christmas scientific conference in Chicago to reclaim his place on the international circuit. These days he travelled with all the ceremonial due to an Arab sheikh, surrounded by hordes of minions, nurses, students, the personal assistant and the occasional colleague. He was attended by so much luggage that the chassis of the limousines that came to whisk him away to the airport often had difficulty in clearing the ground as they left the driveway. The airlines had learnt to treat Stephen with respect, as a valued customer rather than as an inconvenience, and accorded him the sort of deference and assistance which, had it come twenty years earlier when I was struggling to look after Stephen and a tiny baby, might have spared me much stress. Nowadays, ironically, my presence was almost superfluous on the international travels. Alone among so many people, I often took Tim along for companionship, just as Robert had been my small companion in days gone by. Tim fulfilled this role admirably. He loved air travel and, as the plane was gathering speed for take-off – my worst moment – he would gasp, "Faster! faster!" dispelling my lingering fears with his contagious excitement. There was much that I could teach him and interest him in on these travels, not least a grounding in the Romance languages. In Spain, with patience and a total lack of competitiveness, he taught me to play chess, something his father had never succeeded in doing.

6

Maths and Music

Although eighteen months previously Stephen's chances of survival had been dismissed as negligible, he had confounded the pessimists yet again: he had survived and was back in the forefront of scientific research, theorizing on abstruse suppositions about imaginary particles travelling in imaginary time in a looking-glass universe which did not exist except in the minds of the theorists. His phenomenal resurrection and the consequent transformation of his prospects had galvanized him into even more intense industry. He was travelling again, terrestrially and universally, whenever and wherever he chose. Above all, just over a year since his first painstaking attempts to come to grips with the workings of the computer and his cautious return to the Department, he had completed the second draft of his book and was searching for a title. His state of health continued to be extremely precarious, the subject of perpetual anxiety, but with all the aids of modern medicine and twenty-four hour nursing care at his disposal, he virtually carried his own mini-hospital with him wherever he went. The nurses had learnt emergency techniques for changing the tracheotomy tube, and Stephen himself had taken charge of his medication as he reckoned, rightly, that he knew more about his case than any doctor.

Another nurse – tall, aristocratic Amarjit Chohan from the Punjab – had joined the rota. By night she worked in the operating theatres at Addenbrooke's, and by day (and in her free time) she came to look after Stephen. In lonely exile from her own home, the victim of thinly veiled racism, she adopted us with a passionate intensity which soon began to upset the other nurses. Stephen was flattered to find himself the contested prize in the battles which the more volatile, less stable of his attendants fought for his favours, and regarded their squabbles with bemused complicity. In Spain, Tim and I were astounded to watch while one of the nurses flirted unashamedly with a student and then actually resorted to fisticuffs with another nurse over some petty argument. Like distant thunder, rivalry between assertive personalities, each insisting on the superiority of her own method of care, rumbled menacingly. It was yet an additional wearisome problem at home and a source of embarrassment in public abroad.

The big event of 1987 which, among the imaginary trajectories and illusory universes, was exercising Stephen and all those caught up in his orbit was the celebration of the tercentenary of the publication of Newton's *Principia Mathematica* with an international conference to be held in Cambridge. Stephen was firmly established at the centre of this event, since the Newtonian tradition of leading cosmological research in Cambridge was consigned to his care as Lucasian Professor, and his work was the logical extension of Newtonian physics modified by the twentieth-century influence of Einstein's theory of relativity.

Isaac Newton was born in 1642, the year of Galileo's death and three hundred years before Stephen's birth. Although his education as a schoolboy in Grantham and as a "sizar" or servant-student in Trinity College was conservative, his major work *Principia Mathematica* was directly influenced by the mechanical and mathematical principles formulated by René Descartes, the great seventeenth-century French philosopher. In Cambridge in the 1660s Descartes' theories provoked "such a stir, some railing at him and forbidding the reading of him as if he had impugned the very Gospel. And yet there was a general inclination, especially of the brisk part of the University to use him". Newton took Descartes' principles home with him to Woolsthorpe Manor just after his graduation at the outbreak of the Plague. It was during that extraordinary period of creativity at Woolsthorpe Manor that Newton at the age of twenty-three developed his three major discoveries: the calculus, the universal theory of gravitation and the theory of the nature of light.

Newton may have been "brisk" in adopting Descartes' theories, but he was not at all brisk about publishing the results to which those theories had led him. *Principia Mathematica* was finally published in 1687 at the insistence of Samuel Pepys, the President of the Royal Society, and Edmond Halley, the young astronomer. In his *magnum opus,* Newton not only proposed the Law of Universal Gravitation, predicting the elliptical movement of the planets around the sun, but also developed the complicated mathematics of such motions. It is in *Principia Mathematica* that mathematics is harnessed to the service of physics and is rigorously applied to the visible universe. *Opticks*, Newton's other great work, also developed in the Plague years but not published until 1704, described light as a spectrum of colours which in combination formed white light, but which could be split into seven component bands. Newton set up a prism in the path of a sunbeam and watched as the white light entering the prism split into the colours of the rainbow, producing not the rounded image of the sun on the opposite wall, but an oblong image, where the seven colours from blue to red separated and fanned out "according to their degrees of refrangibility". If *Principia Mathematica* was inspired by the fall of an apple in the garden of Woolsthorpe Manor, the inspiration for *Opticks* was commercial – the improvement of the glass in the telescope, the instrument which Galileo had first turned on the heavens in the winter of 1609. Although Newton would have described himself as a natural philosopher, one might designate him the first great modern mathematician and physicist.

The product of an unhappy childhood, Newton could be dictatorial and not a little devious. He earned a reputation for vindictiveness in his treatment of the German philosopher Gottfried Leibniz, who claimed to have discovered the calculus first. Newton's discovery of the calculus, or fluxions as he called them, was prompted by his need in the mid-1660s for a general method of mathematical calculation, essential for dealing with the dynamics of planetary motion. It was put to immediate use in his theory of gravitation, but typically he failed to publish his results and was then incensed when Leibniz published his independent findings in 1676. There was nevertheless a humbler aspect of this embittered genius which appealed to me. When writing of his role in science, he speculated about his own importance, unsure of the significance of his discoveries: "I do not know what I may appear to the world; but to myself I seem to have been only like a boy playing on the seashore, and diverting myself in now and then finding a smoother pebble or a prettier shell than ordinary, while the great ocean of truth lay all undiscovered before me". "Collecting pebbles on the beach" was the very image Stephen had used in 1965 to pour scorn on medieval studies.

Newton left no stone unturned on his particular beach. Although in the opinion of contemporaries he was said to be tone-deaf, he had in 1667 produced a theory of music. *Of Musick* was a fairly unremarkable treatise containing nothing new; in it he considered questions of tuning the scale and compared in logarithmic terms the just and equal temperaments. He also used music to draw synaesthetic analogies between the seven notes of the diatonic scale and the seven bands of colour in the spectrum, basing those analogies on the breadth of the colour bands and the seven string lengths required to produce a scale.

The link between Newton's personal tastes and music was rather tenuous but, taken with all the other considerations, his theoretical interest was strong enough to justify putting on a concert of the music of his era to celebrate his tercentenary. Another of the considerations centred on the fact that Newton's genius was initially fired by the new approach to science coming from France, while with the Restoration of the monarchy in 1660 a wave of enthusiasm for the innovative French style in music came to England with Charles II – inspiring the other great English genius of the period, Henry Purcell. Since, together with the music of Bach and Handel, the music of Henry Purcell formed the basis of the Cambridge Baroque Camerata's repertoire, there could have been no more appropriate way of entertaining the delegates to the Newton tercentenary conference than with a concert of the music of that period. However much Stephen might have preferred it, a performance of the *Ring Cycle* was hardly feasible. The great advantage of such a prestigious occasion, to be held in Trinity College, was that it attracted commercial sponsorship for the orchestra at last, not only enabling Jonathan to put his musical enterprise on a secure footing, but also to make a recording of the programme, entitled *Principia Musica*.

Again, Stephen, Jonathan and I seemed to have struggled back to some sort of synthesis of our various talents and interests. Although the modern physics of quantum theory was completely beyond me, I could research Newtonian physics with some understanding of the concepts if not of the mathematics, and I could make myself useful liaising between the mathematical and the musical aspects of that summer's major endeavour. I enjoyed concert organization: it was hard work but, like teaching, it gave me a sense of self-worth. As well as the practical business of concert promotion, arranging the venue, the advertising, the ticketing and so on, there was the intellectual stimulus of researching the background to the music for the programme notes. In pursuit of information about the late seventeenth-century musical scene, I found myself drawn back into the precincts of the University Library, where the frenetic tempo of daily existence slowed to a reverent, unhurried pace. My researches yielded a welcome connection between Newton and Purcell in the writings of an eminent seventeenth-century musicologist and undergraduate contemporary of Newton's, Roger North, who concluded that the great "practical diversions" of his life had been "reducible to two heads: one, Mathematicks, and the other Musick". His delight in mathematics culminated in "Mr Newton's new and most exquisitely thought" hypothesis of light "as a blended mixture of all colours". As for music, there can be little doubt that "the devine Purcell" afforded him the greatest pleasure as he came "full saile into the superiority of the musicall faculty".

As in days past, the hours I could spend in the University Library were lamentably scarce. There was time only for dashing in to check a few references before rushing out with a pile of books under my arm. Before the Newton celebrations in July, there was a flurry of other activities to be fitted into the calendar. I was never at rest, propelled by an inner tension which pervaded every aspect of my being – physical, mental, intellectual, creative and spiritual. Yet again, I had to prove to myself that I was a worthy companion to Stephen's genius, and to the world at large I had to prove that we were still operating as a normal family. Apart from our academic activities, there were more parties and dinners, more work for charities, more concerts and conferences, more travel and more honorary degrees. Though other families led busy lives, by comparison with theirs ours was not normal: it was insane. I depended for my survival on all the support and reinforcement that my myriad activities and my family, friends and Jonathan could give me. Stephen's nursing companions, gifted in neither insight nor imagination, viewed these pit-props to be counter to Stephen's interests rather than supportive of them. Soon I, and the rest of the family, were made to feel that we should be apologizing for our presence, for our very existence, for breathing the same air as the man of genius. More often than not, it was Lucy who helped me keep a sense of perspective and Jonathan who encouraged me to retain some self-respect. Jonathan's frequent and comforting presence however had increasingly become the cause of much tight-lipped whispering and drawing-in of breath by those outsiders who, in their shallowness, sought to govern others by standards which, as events were to prove, they themselves were unable to sustain.

As Lucy was continuing with her Russian studies and was in her first year of A levels, she came to Moscow again in May 1987 with Stephen and me for yet another conference at the Academy of Sciences. The Academy, like so many other Russian institutions, was quietly dropping its former "Soviet" nomenclature in recognition of the dramatic change which was taking place in Russian society. "*Perestroika*" and "*glasnost*" were the words dancing on everybody's lips with an infectious excitement, bordering upon euphoria. "What do you think of the changing state of affairs in this country?" journalists asked Lucy and me after Stephen's public lecture. "The very fact that you can ask such a question is proof enough of the extraordinary change," we replied. Freedom of speech, freedom from oppression, freedom to travel – these were astoundingly precious liberties to people who had been restricted to the chilling, grey confines of a shadowy one-party state.

We too were much freer than on previous visits to Moscow. We could go where we liked without being accompanied or trailed, and the entertainment provided for us was not just the obligatory visit to the Bolshoi but a concert in a church outside Moscow as well. Religious fervour had gripped Moscow. In the church of the Novodevichy Monastery, for example, the air was thick with the smoke of hundreds of lit candles, around which the faithful were chanting and genuflecting as if to make up for lost time. By coincidence, I had spent the winter months rehearsing Rachmaninov's *Vespers* with the choir – in Russian – for performance in Jesus College Chapel in March. To my delighted surprise, the concert to which we were taken was performed by a similar group of amateur singers and consisted of unaccompanied Russian liturgical settings, sounding very much like the *Vespers* in an atmosphere that was tense with the novelty and promise of reawakening tradition. Against a richly gilded backdrop of icons, the majestic *basso profondo* voices summoned up dark Russian vowels, rolled them on the tongue and emitted them into the resonant spaces of the ancient church, where their deep-toned sonorities held the audience enraptured.

Through being in Moscow, I missed an occasion in Cambridge which was of profound significance not only to the children, Jonathan and me, but to the whole of the parish of St Mark's.

Our vicar, Bill Loveless, was retiring. So devastated was the congregation at losing its dearly loved incumbent that the parish went into a state resembling collective mourning for a long period after his departure. In the spring Lucy had taken the opportunity to attend Bill's final series of classes, leading to her confirmation. At about that time, in honour of his forthcoming retirement, the choir put on a concert at which I sang a couple of his favourite Schubert *lieder*, including *Die Forelle*, and afterwards we held a large farewell supper party at West Road. Even so, I was sad not to be present at his last Sunday service. He had a fund of wisdom of which I had only scratched the surface; indeed, one of his last sermons, on the theme of the search for a quiet mind, had impressed me deeply. In it he uncovered every aspect of my own lack of peace: my concerns, my fears – for Stephen, for my children and for myself – my inability to rest, the tensions and the cares, the frustrations and the uncertainties. He also broached that other group of emotional disturbances associated with an unquiet mind, those evoked by guilt, to which I was no stranger. Self-reproach trailed me like a menacing shadow. I listened for whatever scraps of comfort he could throw in my direction. Live in the present, he said, and trust in God through darkness, pain and fear. Then, as he quoted the biblical passage from Corinthians, "God will not suffer you to be tested more than you are able", I felt that his words were aimed at me alone. Guilt, he went on to say, is the risk that comes from striving always for the highest and the best; love is the only answer to guilt. Only in love can we sustain each other. His words offered a new resolution to the gnawing dilemma of guilt. Love was most certainly the force that sustained our household. According to that reckoning, I was being true to my promise: I had love for everyone, abundant maternal love for each of the children, love for Stephen as well as love for Jonathan. Love had many facets, Agape as well as Eros, and I wanted to continue to prove my love for Stephen by doing my best for him, but sometimes that love became so entangled with the legion of worries generated by the responsibility for his care that it was hard to know where anxiety ended and love began. Stephen himself was insulted by any mention of compassion: he equated it with pity and religious sentimentality. He refused to understand it and rejected it outright.

7

Extremes

With a little help from Shakespeare, Stephen had devised a title for his book; the manuscript had been moulded into a form acceptable to the publisher and a date in June 1988 was set for publication. The American edition was to be published in the spring, before the British edition. That first American edition had to be pulped at the last minute because of the fear of legal action on account of certain aspersions cast in the text on the integrity of a couple of American scientists. This misfortune allowed a minor omission to be rectified: Stephen had dedicated *A Brief History of Time* to me, a gesture which came as a much appreciated public acknowledgement, but the dedication had been left out of the American edition. The presses were put into overdrive to produce ten thousand copies of the amended edition within days, the potential libel was erased, my name featured in the dedication and the book was launched in the United States.

While Stephen was in America for the launch, Tim and I went to stay with his best friend Arthur and his parents, who were now living in Germany. The two little boys saw each other rarely these days, yet neither of them had made other close friends; when they met, they happily settled into their familiar routine, like long-lost brothers. As there had been a late fall of snow in the Black Forest, Arthur's father, Kevin, surprised us by asking if we would like to go skiing. I had never skied in my life and never expected to do so, although rumour had it that Stephen used to be a competent skier and Lucy regularly went skiing with her friends. Indeed, at that very moment she was in the Alps recovering from an arduous run of rehearsals for a play which she and her companions in the Cambridge Youth Theatre were to perform in Cambridge in April before appearing at the Edinburgh Festival in the summer. Tim and I jumped at the chance to learn to ski. He learnt quickly, hurling himself down the slopes at breakneck speed, threatening to overshoot the car park at the bottom. I watched helplessly while Arthur's mother, Belinda, desperately shouted instructions at him to snowplough – that is, to slow down by turning the skis inwards. The memory of broken arms when learning to ice-skate made me much more wary and nervous – until I realized that snow was a soft bed, if cold and wet, to fall into or onto. During that weekend in the Black Forest, I recovered some of my lost bravado. High up on the hillside, with the wind in my face and the sun shining on the glistening white snow, I rejoiced at the release from the treadmill of care and responsibility, and from the divisive, tedious squabbles of petulant nurses which had made our home life such an unendingly depressing struggle. Skiing demanded one-hundred per cent concentration, both physical and mental: the immediate objective was the bottom of the slope, and the only question the brain could accommodate was how to get there in one piece.

Stephen was in America for over three weeks. Soon after his return, we were to set off together to Jerusalem, where he was to collect the prestigious Wolf Prize, awarded jointly to him and Roger Penrose for distinction in physics.

My misgivings about the Israel trip were not solely caused by my reluctance to leave the family or to take time from teaching. Although I was looking forward to meeting Hanna Scolnicov, my friend from Lucy Cavendish days, I was not much looking forward to visiting the holiest, most ancient city in the world in the company of a party of physicists: I would have preferred a pilgrimage with more like-minded people, but I had no choice. There was a discernible tension in the air when Stephen said that, if I did not want to go, he was sure that Elaine Mason, the nurse who had accompanied him to America, would be happy to go in my place.

He had resented my refusal to go to America with him in March when Tim and I had gone skiing and, since his return, the communication lines between us had become brittle and taut. My suggestion that he should sack some of the troublemakers among the nurses met with the blank, incontestable reply, "I need good nurses". When I offered to collaborate with him on a proposed autobiography, a project which I hoped would bring us closer together, his reaction was dismissive: "I should be glad of your opinion." Only then did I start to perceive the truth of what other nurses had been trying to tell me for some time, namely that one of their number was exerting undue influence over Stephen, deliberately provoking and exploiting every disagreement be-tween us. Naturally my relationship with Jonathan featured large in the increasingly extravagant web of wile and deceit that was being woven and, as far as that was concerned, there was little I could say in my own defence, since clearly in the eyes of the world our relationship was a guilty one.

Before our departure for the Middle East, there was just time to see Lucy performing in the lively spectacle of *The Heart of a Dog*, a staged adaptation of the political satire written in the 1920s by the Russian writer Mikhail Bulgakov. The novella, in which Bulgakov voiced his concerns at the take-over of Russian society by the proletariat, was considered too abrasive for publication at the time and was not published in the Soviet Union until 1987, the year of our most recent visit. On the following Sunday, leaving my parents in charge of the home, we left for Israel.

Although there were delays at Heathrow, the main stretch of the flight passed without incident. Jonathan, who was away on tour with the Cam-bridge Baroque Camerata, had given me a Walkman and tapes of Bach's *Mass in B Minor* for my birthday, and with that I whiled away the time, occasionally peering out of the window down to the distant blue depths of the Mediterranean. As night fell and the sky and the sea darkened, a strip of neon lights appeared far below clearly marking the coastline, and we were told to fasten our seat belts for landing in Tel Aviv. The plane began its descent, and I watched as we skimmed lit buildings and roadways. I heard the rumble of the undercarriage being lowered and waited for the jolt of the landing on the runway. The bump never came. Instead the plane lumbered its way back up into the night sky. To my own surprise, I was fascinated, not frightened. There were no announcements. A hush descended on the cabin, and I sensed that the same questions were passing through the minds of all the passengers: had we been highjacked and were we heading for Lebanon?

Ten minutes later the captain's voice came over the address system. We had not been able to land in Tel Aviv because of sudden fog, he explained, and had been diverted to the only other available runway, a landing strip at a military airbase in the Negev desert, the neck of Israeli territory narrowing down to the Red Sea between Egypt and Jordan. The plane droned through the night to the desert, where it made an abrupt and bumpy landing on a short runway, not built to accommodate 747s – and there we stayed. By the time the fog had cleared in Tel Aviv, the period of duty for our crew had expired, so we – and they – had to wait for another crew to come out from Tel Aviv to collect us. I pulled down the blind, curled up and went to sleep. Stephen's assistant, Nick Phillips, nudged me the next morning just as the engines were beginning to turn. I drew up the blind and looked out on a perfect introduction to the Holy Land. Outside was a scene of timeless peace and beauty: golden sands, silken dunes and barren, purple hills, all tinged with the soft pinkish hue of dawn.

The focal point of the official visit was the presentation of the Wolf Prize in the Knesset against the backdrop of Chagall's immense tapestry of the history of the Israeli people. The ceremony took place in the presence both of the highly respected, liberal-minded President of Israel, Chaim Herzog, and the notoriously hard-line, right-wing Prime Minister, Yitzhak Shamir. They epitomized the two ends of the political spectrum in a country where good sense and fanaticism coexisted in equal measures. After the completion of the ceremonials, Stephen and Roger Penrose were so much occupied in scientific meetings, lectures and seminars with their Israeli colleagues that I was often left to wander and explore at will through Jerusalem. "Go into the Jewish quarter of the Old City, by all means," I was advised, "but don't go into the Arab quarter: it's too dangerous because of the *Intifada*." In my impatience to be independent of the official party, I shrugged off such caution with indifference, happy to find that the hotel, a modern block, was within easy walking distance of the Jaffa Gate of the Old City. Like a magnet, the grey walls on the opposite hill, as austere and forbidding as the walls of the Alhambra in Granada, drew me to them. Unprepared for the bustling, noisy mass of colourful humanity which ebbed and flowed in and out of the gate beneath David's Tower, I paused, looking about me and wondering which way to go, to the right or to the left. I was tempted to let myself be pulled along with the crowds and be sucked down the narrow street on my left, but mindful of the advice to keep out of the Arab quarter I set off to my right, past the grey-stone Anglican cathedral into a street which ran along the inside of the city walls. It was disappointingly dull and quiet. Hammering came from the occasional workshop, a few people going about their daily business hurried down the street, the sounds of a piano wafted from an upper window, otherwise there was little to claim my interest. It was pleasant but unremarkable. I carried on walking and came to a new housing development which was even more disappointing. However, an alleyway between the new houses on the left gave onto a steep flight of steps which descended to a leafy little square where I stopped for a drink, before carrying on down the next long flight. At the bottom was a broad open expanse, enclosed on the far side by a high wall of mellow, sunburnt stone. Black-coated men were praying and kissing the wall and bridal parties were being photographed against it. I had reached the Wailing Wall. I ambled across the open space, watching the crowds, some earnest and devout, others laughing and talking.

On one side of the space was a short tunnel, guarded by soldiers, under a mass of buildings. People were coming and going through it quite freely, so I joined them. In passing through that tunnel, I discovered – without the aid of complex mathematical equations – that time travel is a real possibility. In practical and political terms, that tunnel divided the Jewish and the Arab quarters of the Old City. In historical terms it divided secular modernity from an ancient past which vibrated with the sounds, the colours and the traditions of biblical times. Pilgrims and tourists mingled like visitors from another planet with the local inhabitants who, with their children and donkeys, got on with their daily lives as if the twentieth century had not happened. I walked on alone, pausing now and then on the edge of a group of pilgrims. I listened to the guide's explanation of each site and I joined in their prayers and hymns at a couple of the Stations of the Cross on the Via Dolorosa.

It was a strange experience suddenly to be alone, free to make my own discoveries and form my own judgements. I shuddered at the gloomy, repellent sense of intrigue which pervaded the Church of the Holy Sepulchre with its squabbling, rival sects and its queues of tourists waiting to pass through the inner sanctum. I could not wait to get out of its morbid atmosphere into the bright daylight. The view from the tower was its one redeeming feature. The panorama of flat, white rooftops was as striking as the view of the red roofs of Venice from the top of the Campanile. Far below, chickens cackled, cocks crowed and a donkey brayed.

It was with reluctance that I dragged myself away from the Church of St Anne, close by the excavations of the Pool of Bethesda, only a hundred yards from the Lion Gate with its views across to the Mount of Olives. The Church of St Anne, immense and domed, light and airy, was deserted when I went in. I clicked my fingers – a trick Jonathan had taught me to test the acoustics of a building – and was surprised to find that the church was even more resonant than King's Chapel. Emboldened by the silence of the empty church, I hummed a few bars of Purcell's *Evening Hymn* – "Now, now that the sun has veiled his light and bid the world goodnight…" – I listened in astonishment as the sound of my voice was caught by the pillars and flung up into the dome. There the song took on a life of its own and whirled in ecstasy before sliding back to earth in a whisper. The friendly Arab guardian of the Church appeared from a side door. He said that he liked to listen to the pilgrims who came to sing in his Church. Apparently I was lucky to have had it to myself, as usually choirs queued up for their turns. He invited me to return whenever I liked.

The Arab quarter of the city held no terrors for me; so, another day, I made for the Dome of the Rock, the spectacular holy place of Islam and the site of the stone where Abraham prepared to sacrifice Isaac. The entrance was closed and guarded by Israeli soldiers. It would be closed, except to worshippers, for the foreseeable future. In disappointment I made my way back up the street through the Arab bazaar with its motley assortment of tourist goods – Bethlehem blue glass, pottery and leather. I browsed among its antique stalls, which displayed bits of Roman glass, copper and coins, and its food stalls spilling over with all the delicacies of the eastern Mediterranean, nuts and olives, Turkish delight and halva as well as a cornucopia of fruits and vegetables. Like the stallholders I had met in Tangiers twenty-five years earlier, the Arabs here were polite and friendly. Having haggled over a pretty Roman glass bead at one of the antique stalls, a malachite and silver necklace at a ridiculously low price on another then caught my eye. The proprietor came out to talk to me without attempting to pressurize me into a purchase. He spoke good English and was just telling me about his cousin in Middlesex when he glanced down the street and hastily pushed me into his shop. He then took up a position, arms akimbo, in the doorway. His alarm was understandable. A troop of armed Israeli soldiers was forcing its way noisily up the alley. They did not seem concerned about respecting any property, barrows or stalls in their path and, from the stance adopted by my shopkeeper and others nearby, it appeared that they had a reputation for being light-fingered. When the noise of their passage, their boots on the cobbles and their shouts had died away, the shopkeeper came back inside sighing. He apologized for pushing me through the door and simply said, "You see, we have to be very careful." I bought the necklace and a richly decorated, hand-painted plate and said goodbye, promising to return. I did return on the last day only to find everywhere closed: the shops were boarded up and, apart from stray cats, the streets were deserted. The ancient pageant of light, life, noise and colour had vanished. Everywhere, every street, every corner, every square, was dark, eerie and intimidating – a ghost city which had closed its doors to time travellers.

As well as my sympathy for the Arabs, I felt a natural affinity with the Jewish people: many of our friends were Jews, highly intelligent, articulate and sensitive, whose families had been ravaged by the Holocaust. I could not, however, sympathize with the inhuman tactics of the Israeli army that I had witnessed in the Arab quarter of Jerusalem, even less could I sympathize with the loathsome driver who had been allotted to us. An American Jew of central-European origins, he voiced his opinions loudly and coarsely wherever we went. As he drove down the winding road to the Dead Sea, he gestured to a row of white houses up on the hills. "See there," he said proudly, "that's one of our settlements, we're building all those homes. The Arabs had this land for two thousand years and didn't do anything with it. They've had their chance, but now it's our turn and they want to push us into the sea." I had heard these wearying arguments before, delivered in the same Americanized monotone by other immigrant speakers. Further down the road, we came across a simple Bedouin encampment. "What can you do with people like that? Just look at them!" the driver expostulated, "they haven't advanced in two thousand years!" I could hardly contain my indignation. "Perhaps they like their traditional lifestyle," I retorted. I was saddened that peace was so elusive between two peoples of the same racial stock who had so much to offer each other. The best Jews and the best Arabs had a lot in common. They could both be intelligent, generous, friendly and amusing. Perhaps the Jews had the edge over the Arabs in rational argument, in science, technology and mathematics, but the Arabs had superior intuitive poetic and artistic skills. Between them, they held the key to the most successful and gifted culture the world has ever seen.

There were, inevitably, many official expeditions. Television cameras and reporters followed Stephen to all his meetings, eager for his reactions to a wide range of questions. Unfailingly one question recurred at every interview. I watched and listened from the sidelines and my heart sank as I heard it repeated again and again in some form or other. "Professor Hawking, what does your research tell you about the existence of God?" or "Is there room for God in the universe you describe?" or, more directly, "Do you believe in God?" Always the answer was the same. No, Stephen did not believe in God and there was no room for God in his universe. Roger Penrose was more tactful. When asked the same questions, he conceded that there were different ways to approach God: some people might find God in religious belief, others in music, others conceivably in the beauty of a mathematical equation. Roger's answers could not, however, dispel my sadness. My life with Stephen had been built on faith – faith in his courage and genius, faith in our joint efforts and ultimately religious faith – and yet here we were in the very cradle of the world's three great religions, preaching some sort of ill-defined atheism, founded on impersonal scientific values with little reference to human experience. The blank denial of all that I believed in was bitter indeed.

I sat in miserable silence in the back of the van as the driver conducted us round all the holy places of the Old and New Testaments – the dark little cave in Bethlehem, the bleached stones of Jericho, the parched mountains of the Wilderness, the rippling green flow of the River Jordan and the Sea of Galilee. Dumbly, in my corner of the careering van, I mused that this tragic land seemed to breed conflict. Against the impenetrable landscape, the sense of conflict was all pervasive and insidious. Even Stephen and I were in danger of succumbing to it, since we rarely seemed to be of one mind.

However, while Stephen finished his lunch in a lakeside restaurant at Tiberias, I swam alone in the turquoise waters of the sea of Galilee, and for a few precious minutes I felt myself to be at peace and in harmony with the landscape and its history. The threat of war over the Golan Heights had preserved Galilee from the ravages of the tourist industry, with the result that little could have changed in two thousand years. Tiberias was possibly even less of a resort in 1988 than it had been in Roman times, and the Lake was as calm and as unspoilt as a Scottish loch.

Had it not been for the heat, Galilee seen from the chapel of the Sermon on the Mount could well have been Loch Lomond. On the final day, we all bathed in the Dead Sea. Encouraged by me and supported by his entourage and the natural buoyancy of the salt, Stephen lay back, floating in the warm water, briefly re-establishing contact with the reality of nature, long denied him, rather than its theory with which he was in ceaseless communion. There was silence all around us. The only witnesses of Stephen's peaceful bathing were the hazy purple mountains of Jordan in the distance, the blue sky and a solitary bird of prey. It was impossible to drown or even to swim. My attempt to strike out in a breaststroke collapsed in splashing and floundering, and filled my nose with stinging salt. My swimming sessions would have to be reserved for the hotel pool, up on the roof where I swam a few lengths every evening after each day's hot, dusty excursion. The novelty of swimming with the whole of Jerusalem spread out below would have been entirely agreeable, had it not been for the presence of a suspiciously spotty child in the water. I recognized chickenpox, but trusted that I was well enough protected with antibodies against that virus as a result of my experience in Spain as a student.

8

The Red Queen

The trip to the Middle East was a prelude to the demands of that summer, which proved to be even more intense than usual. Although there was no escape anywhere from the endless bickerings of the nurses, the epicentre of the rumbling discontent had moved to the Department, as that was where Stephen spent most of his day. The young assistant, Nick Phillips, wrote to me to apologize for handing in his resignation, a move forced on him because he was so often the target of the ill-humour and criticism of one of the nurses. "Bad-mouthing" was the term he used in his note. I sympathized with him, but there was little that I could do to help. The nurses were a law unto themselves, and neither Judy Fella nor I had any influence. Whatever went on in the Department was completely beyond my reach: my concern had to be focused on maintaining a civilized atmosphere in the home.

With the start of the A-level exams and the end of those particular teaching commitments for the year, I turned my attention to the plans for Robert's twenty-first birthday party. We celebrated the actual day with a large family dinner at home, and planned another evening party a week later, on the lawn with a band, a repeat of his eighteenth birthday party – though this time it was to be a jazz band, and Robert sent out invitations to a "Mad Hatter's Fancy Dress Party". Just as preparations for the party were in full swing, three weeks after returning from Jerusalem, I awoke one morning with a splitting headache and itchy spots around my waist. The only comparable headache that I could remember was the one that had preceded the chickenpox in Spain when I was a student. Lucy took her younger brother to school and I fell back into bed. I saw no one until Eve came in, as usual, at ten o'clock. Her comforting Brummie accents were clearly audible outside my bedroom door. "Where's Jane?" she asked. Elaine Mason's languid tones rang out in prompt reply, "Oh, she's lying in bed... shamming." Eve took no notice, but came directly into my room. One look at me sufficed: "You need a doctor!" she pronounced firmly and loudly enough for all to hear.

The doctor diagnosed shingles, the reactivation of the chicken-pox virus, exacerbated by stress. He prescribed bed rest and a new drug to relieve the itching. Ruefully I remembered the spotty child in the rooftop swimming pool in Jerusalem and wondered how I was to fit bed rest into the long list of all those things to be done.

Thanks to Eve – who herself was suffering having broken her arm – and Lucy and Jonathan, I managed to rest a little. Jonathan shopped and ferried Tim to and from school and cub camp, in between organizing and rehearsing his next run of concerts, while Lucy interrupted her usual whirl of social activity to bring me cups of tea, cook and ward off unwelcome intrusions. Luckily Jonathan was no longer dependent on my administrative skills in the running of his baroque orchestra, since that enterprise was now established on a firm enough financial basis for him to be able to employ an administrator who attended to every minute detail of every concert. Since the Camerata was now a going concern and was giving concerts regularly, even in the remotest parts of the land, Jonathan was frequently away from Cambridge. He worked hard, rehearsing and performing, and often drove back from distant concerts in the small hours of the morning. His irregular schedule, typical of the life of an itinerant musician, was incomprehensible to the nurses. Not having witnessed or appreciated his talent in practice, the less imaginative of them supposed that his presence in the house during the day suggested that he was a ne'er-do-well, a lounger, sponging off Stephen's munificence. His presence gave rise to much whispering.

Lucy, meanwhile, was juggling her social life and rehearsals for the Edinburgh Festival with her summer exams. As my shingles improved only slowly, she found herself obliged to squeeze yet another unforeseen commitment into her already hectic routine. I had been intending to accompany Stephen to Leningrad for a conference in the third week in June, but it was obvious to everyone, except to Stephen and his subversive minions, that I would not be well enough to travel. As he made such a superhuman effort to overcome all obstacles, it was difficult for him to see why others, above all his wife, should not be capable of similar exertion and will power, especially since all other illnesses were insignificant by comparison with motor-neuron disease. It was clear that I could no longer live up to his expectations. I found myself having to open every sentence with awkward apologies, and each attempt to apologize for being me made me even more aware of my inadequacy. The more my sense of deficiency grew, the more intense the shingles became. The neuralgia and dizziness intensified to blinding proportions, while my nerves tingled like a thousand bee stings to the very tips of my fingers whenever I tried to communicate my feelings or my ideas over any family matter, however trivial.

There was one function which I could not miss, however ill I felt: that was the launch of *A Brief History of Time*, scheduled to take place at a lunch party for family and friends at the Royal Society on 16th June, a week after the shingles struck. *A Brief History of Time* was the tangible expression of Stephen's triumph over the forces of nature, the forces of illness, paralysis and death itself. It was a triumph and an achievement which involved us both in a way that was reminiscent of those passionate struggles and heady victories in the early years of our marriage. This triumph however was not a private affair but a very public event, attended by intense publicity. The figure I cut at that feast was little more than spectral: I lacked the stamina even to maintain a coherent conversation, let alone confront the onslaught of ensuing media interest with any display of confidence.

The day after the launch I rose from my sickbed again, donned my red dressing gown and a red paper crown, applied patches of violent rouge to my cheeks and appeared at Robert's party as the Red Queen: I made a rueful joke of the fact that, like the Red Queen, I was always running to stay in the same place. Perpetually tired and listless, I battled on to the end of term through a long string of engagements and the last classes of the academic year. I had neither the energy nor the inclination to intervene again in the feverishly explosive rivalries among the nurses, which grew ever more venomous with the meteoric rise of *A Brief History of Time* to the top of the bestseller list. So long as the nurses' squabbles did not further threaten the balance of life in the home, I tried to treat them with the contempt they deserved. The minimum amount of time I was – in theory – prepared to grant them, stretched to eternity as they aired their mounting grievances at length over the telephone, oblivious to the fact that I might have better things to do, but all too ready to be mortally offended if I replaced the receiver without hearing them out. Finally I found myself obliged to ask one of the nurses, Elaine Mason, whose behaviour seemed to be at the root of the troubles, to come for a discussion, in which I intended to tell her that I could not stand aside and see the nursing rota, my home and my family torn apart. I might as well have saved my breath. With a smug complacency, she condescendingly denied all such malicious intent, calling upon her husband to vouch for her immaculate character before sailing out of the house, head held high, while I sank into a hollow of all-enveloping despair.

By comparison the crank intruders who would ring – usually from America – in the middle of the night with no consideration for the time difference, seemed like light relief. At all hours, they would demand to speak instantly to "The Professor". Like a certain Mr Justin Case, they had all, to a man, solved the riddle of the universe, and were impatient to tell the Professor where his calculations had gone wrong. Mr Justin Case had to vie for the phone line at 3 a.m. with a Mr Isaac Newton, who was a regular caller from Japan. Lucy answered one call from a man who asked her to marry him. "Fair Lucy," he pleaded, "will you marry me? But read my thesis to your father first!" Another desperate caller from Florida insisted on speaking to Stephen because he was sure that the world was going to blow up in half an hour. "Sorry," we said, "he's away." "Well, then," came the forlorn reply, "It's the end of the world, and there's nothing I can do to save it!" Some actually turned up at the front door and lay in wait for Stephen there, not always to their own best advantage however. One, his upper half clad only in a string vest, was unprepared for the front door opening outwards. As the door was flung wide for Stephen to emerge at full pelt in his chariot, the poor man was thrown into a rose bush. His string vest caught on the thorns, and Stephen was well away by the time he extricated himself. There was also the Hollywood film star, who wanted to test out her own half-baked mystic theory of the universe; the fraudulent journalists, who promised to make donations to charity in payment for the interviews we granted them but never paid up; and the would-be unauthorized biographers, who were obviously out to make a quick buck at our expense. It was with impatience that I looked forward to the summer holiday, when we were to lay the ghost of the Geneva episode with a return to that city. Anywhere had to be better than Cambridge.

Hollywood stars and domestic difficulties notwithstanding, when we managed to communicate, Stephen and I gave some thought to the mundane matter of how to spend the Wolf Prize money. That and the anticipated proceeds from *A Brief History*, together with the modest savings that I had made over the years, amounted to enough to allow us to think of buying a second home. Stephen was interested in buying a flat in Cambridge as an investment, but I cherished the dream of a country cottage, somewhere away from all the razzmatazz, tensions and persistent invasions of our privacy. A cottage on the north Norfolk coast would have been my ideal, but that was beyond our means. A place in the country could give us longed-for peace and anonymity, the time and the quietude for Stephen to think and for the children to revise for exams, while I would be mistress of my own establishment, both house and garden.

It was not until we came across an eccentric Englishman – as Jonathan, Tim and I ambled through northern France on the way south to meet Stephen in Geneva that August – that the thought of buying a property in France began to cross my mind as a viable proposition. This gentleman, who had a minimal command of Franglais, was cheerfully setting himself up in business, buying and renovating French country properties and selling them to the British at prices which were extraordinarily cheap by comparison with those at home. As he unfolded his plans to a rapt audience of mystified French and fascinated English bystanders in a wayside restaurant, the exciting truth began to dawn that this was a possible outlet for our resources. We would enjoy all the advantages of a country cottage, abroad but less distant than Wales, and we and our children would be true Europeans, with a foothold in Europe, and hopefully bilingual into the bargain.

With all the hurly-burly of the start of the new academic year just after returning to England, I let the idea drop, and it passed into the category of a pipe dream. Our holiday with Stephen in Geneva had been a heartening success from the moment we met him at the airport, and after that harmoniously restorative spell, Jonathan, Tim and I had spent ten days camping in the south of France. We came back to Cambridge, refreshed and ready to take up the reins, altogether unaware of the new chaos that awaited us. First of all, Lucy's application to the University of Oxford – to her father's and paternal grandfather's old college, University College – had to be withdrawn and hastily resubmitted. The unexpected success of the Cambridge Youth Theatre's visit to the Edinburgh Festival had made it impossible for her to sit the entrance exams, so she would have to rely on an interview and her A-level results instead. Secondly, the tenant in the letting house belonging to Robert and his grandmother was threatening legal action, because in my absence in France Stephen had thought to resolve a problem that had arisen by ordering her to leave. Thirdly, the administrator of the Cambridge Baroque Camerata was finding the workload too great and wanted to resign. Fourthly, and most untypically for the discreetly private world of a scientific institution, the Department had turned into such a cauldron of intrigue that Judy, incapable of doing her job properly because of the indiscipline among the nurses, was brought to the point of tendering her resignation. This was a sad turn of events for those of us who had witnessed and appreciated her devotion to Stephen over a span of almost fifteen years.

I was afraid that the volcanic eruptions in the Department might overflow and engulf the house at the worst possible time – when Lucy was under greatest pressure. She was now studying for her A-levels and for Oxford entrance at the same time as rehearsing for yet another run of *The Heart of a Dog*, because the Youth Theatre's performance at the Edinburgh Fringe had been awarded one of the top prizes in the Festival, the Independent award for the best Fringe performance, which entitled them to a two-week run on a London stage. Unfortunately the London performances were scheduled to take place just before the crucial Oxford entrance interviews, so Lucy would have to go down to London to perform every day after school and then return to school as usual the next morning. As her resilience would be tested to the limits, it was essential for her to be able to count on a quiet, stable background at home. This simple piece of common sense did not impinge at all on the majority of the people who regularly came in and out of the house.

A rearguard action to keep the nurses' battles at bay was simply not enough to maintain calm at home. From being a well-known scientific figure in Britain and America, Stephen had suddenly achieved worldwide fame: he had become a cult figure with the success of the book. We had the first taste of this in October 1988, when Tim and I accompanied him to Barcelona for the publication of the Spanish edition of *A Brief History of Time*. He was recognized everywhere, attracting crowds who stopped to applaud him in the street. I was called upon to translate for journalists in press conferences and television interviews and, in my own right, was asked to give interviews for women's magazines. There was a satisfaction in working in tandem with Stephen again as his intellectual partner. However, the demand for interviews was reaching fever pitch, not only in Spain but everywhere, at home and abroad. It was easier to cope with the publicity abroad, because we were there expressly to sell the book, and that Mephistophelean pact required us to make ourselves available to the media. At home, where we had our daily routine to accomplish in quiet anonymity, the intrusions of the press became an irksome dislocation of family life. That television equipment had become a regular feature of Stephen's office, where nurses vied with each other to pose for the cameras, was not a problem. The problem arose when the journalists asked for an interview or pictures at home as well. This I was extremely loath to grant, and the children objected vociferously. It was bad enough having nurses in the house all the time: with television cameras and reporters as well there would be no privacy for anyone anywhere. My arguments cut no ice. They were represented as yet further evidence of my disloyalty to the man of genius. It was obvious that with my dependence on Jonathan and my refusal to train to be a nurse, I was already condemned. My reluctance to regale the press with stories of life with that genius within the walls of my home was just one more admission of my perfidy.

On 7th November, Lucy's two-week run in London began at the Half Moon Theatre on the Mile End road. She came out of school at 4 p.m., with just half an hour to spare before catching the coach. The play demanded huge reserves of energy and concentration of its young cast, who changed roles with every scene, sometimes appearing in individual parts, sometimes in the chorus. She would arrive home after midnight, and the next morning, by nine o'clock, would have to be back in school for a full day's work. Her schedule was punishing, but the general stress was eased somewhat by Stephen's decision to go off to California with his retinue for a whole month the day after the first night. Thereafter the quality of life improved dramatically at home, and we all heaved a long sigh of relief as we withdrew into comparative peace and seclusion.

With unaccustomed self-indulgence, I was sitting idly thumbing through the Sunday paper the next weekend when an article on the availability of property in France caught my eye. Beneath it there was a modest advertisement for an English agency, offering to search for suitable houses in the French countryside for its customers. I followed the telephone number up, and within a few days photocopies started arriving in the post from northern France. The photographs looked as if they had been taken in thick fog or a snowstorm, and the terminology used often sent me searching for the dictionary, but the prices were remarkably low. None of them were more than about half the price of a two-bedroom Victorian terraced house in southern England, and, although it was impossible to tell what state the properties were in, they were patently much more substantial in terms of ground area. Clearly further investigation was called for, which was how Tim, Jonathan and I came to be sailing to France one Saturday in mid-November.

9

Prospecting for Paradise

France in November was bleak and dreary indeed, and bitingly cold and dark. But at seven o'clock in the evening, Arras, our destination, was still brimming with life and activity as the shops disgorged their last customers out into the brightly lit streets. They were full of enticing displays of Christmas delicacies and toys, which promptly made a hole in our pockets. Moreover, much to our surprise, signs everywhere announced that *Beaujolais Nouveau* had arrived! The weekend began to assume a different perspective, especially after an excellent meal in the bar of our pension, where the ruby-red new arrival met with general critical acclaim. If all else failed, the weekend held the promise of dealing with most of the Christmas shopping and a certain amount of pleasure in liquid form as well.

The next day, the heavy sleet was hard and unrelenting, and although I could summon no interest whatsoever in quaint little houses dotted about the landscape, a pleasant, helpful agent and his assistant were waiting, prepared to give up the best part of their Sunday to escorting us round what they considered to be the most suitable properties on their books. What a Sunday that was, and what sights we saw as we huddled in the back of the agent's car! The rain beat down, now and then giving way to driving snow. When finally the sleet and snow had exhausted themselves, a dark, penetrating mist set in while we looked at tumbledown houses with leaking roofs, cardboard bungalows, and a house where the passage between the kitchen and the dining room was in fact the bathroom. We were looking for an old house with character, but basically in good condition, possibly with some opportunities for renovation, and with plenty of ground floor accommodation for the elderly and infirm members of the family, especially for Stephen. Nice views were desirable, and the distance from the main road was a prime consideration. Nothing we had seen that first day even approached our requirements.

As it happened, the next day dawned bright and clear and the countryside sparkled under a fine layer of crisp, fresh snow. On our way back to Boulogne we stopped at a small market town to call on just one more agent, Mme Maillet. She led the way out of town in the direction of the coast. The road climbed out of the hollow in which the town nestled, up onto the windswept reaches of an extensive plateau – in fact, a broad ridge between two river valleys. We passed a small race track on the right and sped through a tiny village. There was little sign of habitation, only the occasional church spire, water tower or ruined windmill. Then, suddenly, Mme Maillet turned right – we followed, and there it was, a kilometre or so away from the main road, long and low, whitewashed and red-tiled. "That's our house, Mum," said Tim, then aged nine. And so it was, unmistakably beckoning us across the fields, an old friend from a past existence, instantly recognizable, immediately appealing. "*Un vrai coup de foudre*", the French would say – love at first sight. Nor were we disappointed when we turned into the driveway of the Moulin – for that was what it was, an old mill house, its windmill long since destroyed. The low, smiling façade we had seen from the road proved to be but one of the three sides of the house, which embraced a courtyard, rather in the style of a Roman villa, the sort of house that Stephen and I had dreamt of in the golden days of our engagement. The aspect inside the courtyard was as delightful and welcoming as the exterior had been from the road. The living rooms, including the kitchen, all looked onto the yard or out to the garden and pasture at the back; they were wild and unkempt, at the mercy of a flock of hostile geese, except for a corner of traditional vegetable garden.

The sleeping quarters in the long side of the building which had first caught our eye and our imagination from the road were ideally suited to Stephen's needs, being on the ground floor, and the accommodation could be considerably expanded by completing the conversion of the vast, light, airy attic, which ran the whole length of that wing of the house. It was almost too good to be true. As far as we could tell, the house fulfilled every requirement; it was within an hour's drive of the coast, no further away from Cambridge than parts of the West country, and certainly closer than Wales. It enjoyed lovely views sweeping across fields to woods and it was well away from the main road although the access was easy. It was old and bursting with character but, apparently, in reasonably good condition. There was obvious potential for further improvements and, most significantly, the price left a sufficient margin for any renovations.

All the way home my mind was fixed on the Moulin, programming in the impressions, the excitement, the ideas. Once back in England, I hastened to write it all down and, with pen, paper and ruler, to make rough sketches of the property and plans for its adaptation to our needs, and fax them all to Stephen in southern California. Stephen replied positively. It was much less complicated to communicate with him by fax across the Atlantic than face to face, and I interpreted his terse comment "sounds good" as approval. Then the wheels for the purchase of the Moulin were set in motion at remarkable speed. Equally quickly I had to learn the language and the procedures for house purchase in France which, from the outset, proved to be very different at every stage from the English equivalents. I had to get to grips with French law and legal terminology, the French banking system, French building terms, insurance French-style, local taxation and the eccentricities of the public utilities. Sterling was buoyant against the franc at the time, so I had the consolation of benefiting from a favourable exchange rate. The comforting thought was that the same amount of money could not have bought us anything worth having in England. Deep down inside me I felt an assurance and a certainty that I had not known in years. This project, based on my input, my knowledge of French, would be my contribution to family life – although, of course, it would be jointly financed. So many of our excursions in the past had had a single objective, the pursuit of science. This project would combine all our interests and talents – languages, love of France and the French way of life, relaxation, gardening and music as well – with that scientific pursuit. The more I looked at my plans and drawings, the more I realized that the Moulin had an even greater potential than I had at first deemed possible. There was an old barn attached to the house which was ripe for conversion into accommodation upstairs, with potential for a conference room downstairs, permitting Stephen to have his own summer school, to which he could invite his scientific colleagues and their families. I had visions of establishing our own version of the Les Houches summer school in the undulating countryside of northern France, and it was my hope that there we would once again find the unity and the harmony which we had achieved before the events of 1985, and which since then had eluded us in England.

10

A Homecoming

My plans for the Moulin were put on hold at the beginning of 1989 because I was busy proofreading the French edition of *A Brief History of Time*. It proved not simply to be a question of checking the language, but of delving much deeper. The English edition opened with an introduction by the American scientist Carl Sagan; I was perplexed to find that this had not been translated into French and that, unknown to Stephen, Flammarion, the French publisher, had commissioned an introduction from a French physicist to replace it. I found the disparaging tone of certain remarks in the French introduction extraordinary, and I took it upon myself to delete them. The launch of *Une Brève Histoire du Temps* was scheduled for the beginning of March in Paris and would coincide neatly with the completion of the house purchase. The weeks before the launch brought a procession of French journalists and television cameras to Cambridge, while the completion of the conveyancing process focused my attention more and more on the other side of the Channel. My horizons were expanding, no longer constricted by the four walls of the home in England.

The intricacies of the French legal system, the mechanisms for setting up a bank account, the details of the insurance contract – all these I attacked with enthusiasm, helped by the delightfully idiosyncratic characters with whom I was coming into contact in the quietly rural Ternois region of northern France. The plans for renovation were already in the pipeline when, *en route* for Paris, I signed the house purchase agreement at a formal ceremony on 1st March, itself a considerable achievement, since all parties to the agreement had to be present and Stephen had decided that he could not spare the time to attend. He had after all only just returned from a trip to New York on Concorde. When news of the house in France began to percolate through to friends and relations in England, I was baffled by some of the reactions. "Stephen doesn't like the country," his mother announced adamantly in his hearing, as if intent on predisposing him against the Moulin. Had she forgotten Llandogo? Certainly Stephen's mistrust of the country might be justified after that experience. But to condemn the Moulin, which had been chosen so carefully and was being prepared so meticulously for his enjoyment, seemed very unfair. The image of Stephen that was being cultivated by his relations, and some of his nurses, was that of a playboy who lived for the bright lights of the city and who found the rural life boring. This image of him conflicted with my own perceptions of his character, and the aspersions cast on my venture were already undermining his interest in it.

The few days in Paris after the purchase of the house certainly intensified Stephen's love of the bright lights. He was fêted and pursued wherever he went, the darling of the media and the prized possession of the publisher. As I loved Paris too, it was no hardship for me to enjoy the bright lights as well. We dined at La Coupole; we ate in the restaurant on the Eiffel Tower, where Stephen was invited to add his name to the signatures of the rich and famous in the visitors' book; we visited the newly opened Musée d'Orsay and we entertained friends and Stephen's French relations, including his cousin Mimi, to a dinner in celebration of the launch. Photographers followed us everywhere, and journalists clamoured for interviews, for which either I or a French colleague of Stephen's did the interpreting. I was flattered to be asked for an interview by a leading radio journalist, Jean-Pierre Elkabbach, at the radio station Europe 1. When I arrived, my interviewer was involved in a long and heated discussion with Jean Le Pen, the nationalist leader. Jean-Pierre Elkabbach quickly recovered his composure and treated me with Gallic charm and deference. The interview was broadcast all over France, and as a result we and our circumstances were introduced to our new neighbours in our village in the north before we had taken up residence.

Within three weeks I was setting out for France again: this time with Tim and Lucy in a car laden to the roof with packaged cupboard and bookshelf kits, linen, crockery, cutlery, utensils and food. As if in our honour, we found that a new motorway had just been opened, cutting twenty minutes or so from the journey from Calais, so when we arrived, earlier than expected, at the Moulin, we found the house full of workmen, putting the finishing touches to the Herculean effort of making suitable arrangements for Stephen – and of converting the attic to bed-rooms, which they had completed in seventeen days. Their beaming pleasure in our delight was obvious as we toured the house that they had so swiftly transformed.

Stephen had recently bought a Volkswagen van which had been fitted with a ramp and fixtures to hold the wheelchair steadily in place. It also proved invaluable in transporting large items of furniture. Late that evening, Jonathan arrived at the wheel of the van, which was packed with yet more furniture and luggage. The next day he drove to the airport at Le Touquet – so fashionable with the British in its heyday – to meet Stephen, Robert and the entourage of two reliable and trusted nurses. The advances and royalties coming in from the several editions of *A Brief History of Time* permitted Stephen the rare luxury of chartering a small aeroplane from Cambridge airport to bring him to France by the simplest and most comfortable means possible. The genial Australian pilot had opened up spaces in the wing to store suitcases and bits of the wheelchair, and he invited one of the passengers, on this occasion Robert, to sit beside him in the cockpit of his tiny six-seater aircraft.

The weather was so kind during the Easter holiday that northern France acquired a deceptively Mediterranean aspect. The long white walls and low red roofs of the house and out-buildings glowed in the bright sun against an azure sky, while clouds of white blossom fluttered to earth like silken snowflakes in the meadow and the shrubbery. Even Stephen was impressed, though he complained that the countryside was as flat as Cambridgeshire. This was not actually true, as Robert was to discover when he set off on a bicycle ride. The house stood on top of a plateau, which was divided by many a meandering river valley with villages, water mills, ruined châteaux, abbayes, poplar trees and trout streams. Stephen appeared to like it – though, of course, he would never allow himself to admit it. Whatever his opinions about country life and quaint old houses, he certainly enjoyed the social scene. He and the children went out to buy pink champagne for the house-warming party, which we gave for all our neighbours and for all the people who had helped me with the purchase or worked on the house. Stephen was the willing centre of attraction: he demonstrated his computer and its ability to speak a garbled, Americanized version of the French language to everyone's amusement, and graciously acknowledged the abundant congratulations showered on him on the success of his book. The children had quickly made new friends, and even Tim was communicating effectively in French with a few well-chosen words and gestures, like *"football?"* or *"jouer?"*. He did however object to being kissed on both cheeks at every encounter, until Robert remarked to his mystification that in a few years' time he would be only too pleased to be kissed on both cheeks by the girls. As for me, in France I could be French, spontaneous and natural and true to myself, neither having to justify my actions nor apologize for my existence.

11

The Price of Fame

The shoots of my budding self-esteem, cultivated in the soil of French society, were to be quickly crushed back in England. Optimistic as ever, I did not anticipate that the arrival in late April of a Hollywood film producer would signal the opening shots in the next onslaught on our home life. He seemed friendly enough, inspiring my confidence with stories of his young family, and conveying a genuine sense of purpose in his plan to make a film of *A Brief History of Time*. His would be a serious, informative film of the book, and he liked my idea that it should take the form of a journey in time and the universe through the eyes of a child. The idea was appealing. So long as the film remained strictly scientific and could be imaginatively done, using the innovative technology of graphics, his plans augured well.

Hot on his heels came an American film crew, directed by a lively woman who also won my confidence with her sympathetic approach. It had become the accepted routine that film crews would first wreak havoc in the Department before turning their attention to our home for a reassuring touch of cosiness in the otherwise enigmatic portrait of the disabled genius. On initial acquaintance the directors would all appear to be pleasant, considerate, ordinary people, effusively promising that any disturbance would be kept to an absolute minimum. Their fly-on-the-wall approach would take no time at all and would require only a few shots, causing no disruption to our normal activities. Cameras, cables, arc lights and microphones would all remain at a discreet distance; the furniture would not be moved; we could dress informally and go about our daily business as usual.

The reality bore no relation to these promises. Without exception, in the short interim between pleasantries and filming, the procedures would – before our shocked eyes – become devastatingly intrusive. Disregarding the assurances they had given, all the producers and directors would plead shortage of time or scarcity of funds in mitigation of their sudden change of approach as soon as the cameras started rolling. Items of furniture would be shoved around, often damaged, never to be returned to their original positions; blinding arc lamps and glaring reflective screens on cold metal supports would supplant well-worn familiar clutter, obscuring the furniture and the books and newspapers; lengths of cable would snake hazardously across the floors in and out of every room; microphones would be hung from any available hook or shelf. We strangers in the harshly transformed landscape of our unrecognizable tubular steel home would be typecast in our parts: the principle (though untrained) actors in the drama, expected to react with natural grace and aplomb for the eye of the camera, that twentieth-century sacred object of worship. As I watched helplessly and participated reluctantly, a despairing voice inside me protested. Surely, it complained, there had to be a middle way between this insatiable nosiness and the starkly impersonal approach of the BBC Horizon film some years before. But an imaginative middle way would demand both more time and more money than any of the directors had at their disposal as they rushed frenziedly from one project to the next.

For want of any outlet, my silent rebellion at this extra burden rumbled beneath the surface. Despite the complaints of the children, especially of Lucy, for whom the glare of publicity and the intrusion of the cameras were most distracting as her exams approached, I was in no position to bar the cameras from the house for fear of further antagonizing Stephen, who positively relished the publicity. He had just returned from yet another trip to America, but the respite did not arm me with sufficient strength to combat the depredations of the film crew at what was always for me the worst season of the year, when tree pollens settled like pepper dust in my sinuses. The American director, who at first sight had appeared so friendly and likeable, rapidly became assertive, indeed embarrassingly so, when her cameras trailed us into town to film my usual routine of Saturday-morning shopping. It was unusual for me to be accompanied in this weekly chore by Stephen and his retinue, even more so that we should all have a fully fledged film crew trailing our steps. There was no possibility of taking evasive action. It might not have been so bad if they had actually lent a hand with the shopping instead of following us like shadows, poking their cameras and microphones into my face as I loaded the shopping trolley to the rim and dragged its heavy weight home behind me.

The primary function of this film was supposed to be a portrait of Stephen for an American television news channel; subsequently it was to serve the dual purpose of providing a snippet of biographical background for the other scientific documentary based on *A Brief History of Time*. Only the thought that this spate of filming would be serving both purposes made that horrible weekend bearable. By the time that an urbane interviewer-journalist and his wife arrived for drinks that Saturday evening, I was in no mood to welcome any more film or television personalities or technicians into the house. Scarcely had I introduced myself to them than the journalist's wife casually asked, just as I was handing her a drink, "Do you have a religion?" Her enquiry was delivered with an unabashed coolness which froze my frayed nerves. I turned on my vapid interrogator, more or less telling her to mind her own business, but then, instantly overcome with remorse, I heard myself foolishly inviting the entire team to dinner in compensation for my rudeness.

Alone, late at night, I lay in bed aware that a trap was closing over me. The stress of publicity was forcing me to behave in ways that were uncharacteristic and untrue to myself, yet there was no clear way out. It was obvious that, in the eyes of the media, I had become an appendage, a peep show – relevant to Stephen's survival and his success only because in the distant past I had married him, made a home for him and produced his three children. Nowadays I was there to appease the media's desire for comforting personal detail while inwardly my spirit rebelled both at the indignity and at my own helplessness.

Ten days after that bout of filming had come to an end, Stephen gave the Schrödinger lecture in a hot, stuffy lecture theatre, packed to capacity, at Imperial College, London. Schrödinger's equation, the fundamental equation for the science of quantum mechanics which he developed in 1926, bears the same relation to the mechanics of the atom as Newton's laws of motion bear to the movement of the planets. Stephen's lecture about imaginary time was as lucid as it could be, and afterwards he was fêted and pursued by representatives from IBM, the firm that had sponsored the lecture, who hankered for a photograph with him, presumably as one of the perks of their job. I stood diffidently to one side, thinking that I was the only non-scientist present, until I was introduced to Schrödinger's daughter, whom I had encountered once before at a similar occasion in Dublin in 1983.

She was quiet and unassuming, informing me for the second time that she was Schrödinger's daughter by someone other than his wife, but had later been adopted by Mrs Schrödinger. I was sorry for her; she was uncomfortably pursued by her father's legacy – as much embarrassed perhaps by his reputation as a womanizer as she was haunted by his scientific fame – and walked in his shadow. I feared for my children – hers was not a fate that I wanted for them.

The following Saturday, before setting off into town to sell flags for the National Schizophrenia Foundation, I opened Stephen's mail for him as usual. It contained a letter from the Prime Minister Mrs Thatcher in which she proposed recommending his name to the Queen as a Companion of Honour in the forthcoming Birthday Honours' List. The proposal sent us running for the encyclopedia. It revealed that this singular honour was one of the highest in the land, ranking above a knighthood and discreetly conveyed, without title, simply by the letters placed after the name. As Stephen was on the point of leaving for America, it fell to me to accept on his behalf.

Since Stephen had already been nominated for an Honorary Doctorate of Science at the University of Cambridge, the summer promised to mark the apogee of his career – though how that, with its inevitable flood of media interest, was to be reconciled with Lucy's A-levels and Robert's Finals, let alone stability and harmony, was not at all obvious. Our priorities were diverging drastically. Mine was the preservation of the sanctity of the home and the privacy of our family life – or such tatters of it as remained after the nurses had done their worst to tear it apart and after the media had plundered every corner of it. Stephen was, for all his fame, but one member of a family where no one person had the right to be more important than any other. Although his medical condition demanded more attention for him than for anyone else, the home had still to cater fairly for the needs of all its occupants, adults and children alike. The children must never have cause to resent the circumstances into which they had been born.

Stephen, for his part, delighted in the publicity. He revelled in his relationship with the media, who had made his name a household word all over the world. His fame, in the face of a sceptical and sometimes hostile society, represented the triumph not only of his mind over the secrets of the universe, but also of his body over death and disability. For him any publicity was good publicity and could always be justified by claiming that it would increase the sales of the book. A case of champagne arrived from Bantam Press later that summer in celebration of *A Brief History of Time*'s fifty-second week on the best-seller list. In the fifty-third week, it shot back to its commanding position at number one. It seemed that he had succeeded in reconciling two extremes in the task he had set himself: in his description of his branch of science, the most fundamental and the most elusive of all the sciences, he had managed to placate the scientific intelligentsia and attract the popular reader.

Although there was no denying that the book was a phenomenal success, I tried to keep the correspondence relating to the handsome royalties confidential. If our sudden flush of wealth were to become generally advertised, I knew that I risked losing many of my real friends with whom in the past I had scraped and saved to make ends meet, and I was also well aware that any publicity given to our enhanced financial status would attract exactly the sort of people with whom I did not want to associate. In the past, while Stephen's mind was focused on weightier matters, I had handled our financial affairs, always with an anxious eye on that uncertain future when Stephen might be too ill to work and the money might run out. I had run the family budget prudently and had accumulated sufficient savings to pay Lucy's school fees and to provide a buffer against the rainy day, which for us could run to months and years. Since the signing of the contract for *A Brief History* in 1985, I had also dealt with the correspondence on that subject with the agent in New York. Unaccountably, the arrangement whereby I handled the royalties was suddenly overturned behind my back. It was from the agent in New York that I learnt of this change: he told me that he had been instructed to send all correspondence relating to the book to Stephen in the Department and no longer to me at home. I had no idea what had provoked this change, and Stephen gave no explanation. It was as if, after many years of mutual trust, my ability to handle financial affairs efficiently and with discretion was being called into question. In the resulting confusion, even the most casual helpers were allowed to open and read private correspondence; it was spread out on desks and tables, left strewn around for all to see, as if in black-and-white confirmation of the undisputed supremacy of genius.

Stephen's second trip to America that spring allowed us all a breathing space from impossible tensions in which to return to those other elements of a more regular lifestyle, the teaching, the studying, the literature and the music, and to settle into simpler, more relaxed habits without the vain and wearisome distractions of fame, publicity and contentious nurses. Tim fulfilled one of his passions when we took off for a promised weekend to Legoland in Denmark, and later in May we returned to France for half-term.

The Moulin, welcoming us in its summer garb for the first time, opened its box of delights in a new guise. Further renovations had been completed, a bathroom had been added for Stephen's sole use, work on the barn had been started, and the garden was beginning to take shape. My dream of an English country garden was being realized in France so satisfactorily that even Claude, my valiant workman, confessed that he had begun to plant flowers in his own garden where previously he had grown only vegetables. Even more significantly, the Moulin opened the door to another world, the world of a past era, where the impossible whirlwind of our Cambridge lives slowed to a leisurely pace under the influence of the land and the sky, and where the only sound was the song of the lark, soaring high into the blue above the green cornfield in the morning sun. The place had already engraved itself on my heart. Its clean air and broad patchwork of fields fading to a distant grey horizon, its sleepy shutters and its aroma of newly chopped logs and old wood, its backdrop of tall conifers and shrubs shimmering in the sun, all sang of unaccustomed peace, solitude and salvation. There I could be alone, undisturbed by nurses, by the press, by cameras, by the clamour of incessant demands. I could dig my garden. I could immerse myself in books without fear of interruption and I could learn and listen to music without fear of criticism at such wasteful self-indulgence. There I could find my true centre, in close touch with nature, old-fashioned, perhaps, contemplative certainly, a daydreamer whose favourite occupation was gazing out at the wide expanse of the western sky each evening, standing spellbound at the everchanging magnificence of the setting sun as it dropped behind the silhouetted line of trees across the fields.

In those periods of reflection while I dug the garden, sowed seeds and planted rose bushes, I identified with the hero of one of the set texts that I had been teaching for the French syllabus in the past year. Candide, Voltaire's young hero, whose optimism in the "best of all worlds" – as taught by the philosopher Dr Pangloss – is sadly betrayed by experience, finally turns his back on the world and takes refuge in his garden. *"Il faut cultiver notre jardin..."* is his ultimate, pessimistic, personal solution to the malfunction of society. The clash of inexorable but often zany logic with searing, unresolved emotional problems lay like a corrosive material at the root of our existence in Cambridge, and that root was succumbing to the insidious effect of the invasive poison of fame and fortune. In France the soil was fresh and fertile, and there the garden was full of the promise of a future, a cyclical foreseeable future, decreed by the immutable laws of nature.

12

Honoris Causa

In the summer of 1989 all attention was concentrated on Stephen's multiple triumphs and the avalanche of media interest in them. The date for the conferral of the Honorary Doctorate by the Chancellor, the Duke of Edinburgh, was set for Thursday 15th June while, known only to ourselves, the royal honour from Buckingham Palace was to be confirmed the next day and published in the media on Saturday 17th. By a fortunate coincidence, this was also the date of a concert to be performed in Stephen's honour by Jonathan and the Camerata, two days after the honorary degree ceremony, also in the Senate House. Although in 1987 the Newton celebrations and concert had provided an attractive lure for commercial sponsors to support the Camerata, the sponsors themselves had become extremely vulnerable to the harsh vicissitudes of life in Thatcherite Britain. The ink was barely dry on the signatures to a generous sponsorship deal when the sponsoring business, a very gentlemanly British firm, was gobbled up by an American computer corporation that had no compunction in declaring that they were in business to make money, not to support the arts, music or any other charitable organization. They promptly pulled out of the sponsorship deal. This left Jonathan, whose schedule of contracted concerts for two years hence was based on the calculations of the sponsorship deal, potentially with a huge debt when he himself at the best of times earned little more than a subsistence income from music. At that most inauspicious moment for Jonathan and the Camerata, Stephen's fame and success offered the hope of salvation. A concert in Stephen's honour could be counted on to attract a large audience of people who would come to applaud Stephen as well as to listen to the music. It might also attract new sponsors for whom the high scientific profile would be attractive. Stephen would be fêted with his favourite pieces of baroque music and a retiring collection could be divided among the charities we all supported. This piece of planning augured well for everybody, and Stephen gave it his approval – along with his approval of the Prime Minister's letter, before he left for America in May.

The challenge of concert planning, forever flying in the face of sound economic sense, had previously added a certain spice and bravura to my other various dilettante occupations. That concert would have been no exception, had it not been for the perpetual incursions of the media. The journalists who came to interview me were a mixed bunch: some were reasonably pleasant, some were clinical, others were demanding. It was impossible to tell what sort of gloss they would put on an interview in advance. French journalists, Spanish journalists, representatives of all nations, came in an endless stream, all wanting a different slant on the science and on the background. They brought their superficial interviewing techniques to the situation; in turn, I developed my own techniques for dealing with them by deciding in advance how much information I was prepared to part with. I saw no reason why I should confide all the intimate complexities of my life to a journalist, a stranger whose interest in me was governed by the imperative to sell more newspapers. If I wanted to confess, I would turn to a priest, if I needed psychiatric treatment I would turn to a doctor, and if I had a story to tell I might one day write it myself, though regard for privacy – my own and other people's – might well outweigh the desire to tell that story. If, therefore, the questions posed by journalists overstepped my boundaries, I would turn the interview into a conversation, asking for their opinions and reactions rather than telling them my own. Inevitably I became the target of disparaging remarks. For example, one journalist reported that I had "cared for Stephen for just a couple of years after our marriage". My old Headmistress and stalwart supporter, Miss Gent, wrote to the editor of that newspaper, the *Times*, to rectify the mistake. She was shocked at his arrogant reply: far from offering any redress or apology, he asserted that he knew better than she did and he was confident that the facts in the article were correct. Our loyal friend George Hill, the husband of my school friend Caroline, ever anxious to protect us from the prying eyes of the gutter press, said that he knew about the misrepresentations in the *Times*, because he had peered over the journalist's shoulder when he was writing the piece. However, George had been so relieved to find no mention of Jonathan's part in our household that he had thought it better to let the article stand as it was rather than reveal Jonathan's close association with us.

If however, as once I did when being interviewed for the *Guardian*, I allowed myself to show any dissatisfaction with the trite old clichés about the rewards of living with a genius – those oft-repeated truisms which dwelt on fame and fortune as if illness and disability were not fundamental factors in our lives – I would be accused of disloyalty to Stephen. But as I saw it, if I continued to perpetuate the myth of cheerful self-sufficiency without even mentioning the hardships, I would be cheating the many disabled people and their families, who were probably suffering all the heartache, the anxieties, the privations, the stresses and strains that we ourselves had undergone in earlier years. It would be all too easy for an uncaring society to point accusingly at other disabled people and declare, "If Professor Hawking can do it, why can't you?" The hard-pressed carers might be pressurized into performing even more impossible tasks because of the unrealistic image of our way of life presented through the media. I could no longer truthfully offer the carefree, smiling façade, giving the erroneous impression that our lives were contented and easy, marred only by a little local inconvenience. For that *Guardian* interview my assessment was candid and truthful: I noted the triumphs but did not gloss over the difficulties. I voiced our criticisms of the National Health Service and emphasized the fact that Stephen's success, even in procuring funds to pay for his nursing, had been due entirely to our own efforts. I described how we fluctuated between the glittering peaks of brilliant success and the black sloughs of critical illness and despair, with very little level ground in between.

Such simple and fairly obvious truths proved most unpalatable to those people who had come to believe in Stephen's immortality and infallibility, and had conveniently detached themselves from the reality of his condition, namely his family and certain of his nurses. My comments were interpreted as treason where no hint of criticism could ever be countenanced. Such reactions only served to increase my sense of isolation. Were the people around me blind or mad, or was I losing my mind? Were those people living in a parallel universe where the roles were reversed and where, as they seemed to suggest, it was I who was infirm? Further accusations of disloyalty were flung thick and fast on the showing of a BBC film made that summer. In it I repeated the misgivings voiced in the two newspaper interviews, in a vain attempt to restore a sensible balance both to the depiction of our way of life and to the representation of Stephen's scientific theories as the basis for a new religion. My performance before the cameras, which rolled throughout the period of the honours and celebrations and afterwards, was not enhanced by a streaming cold and a raging sore throat – just a couple of the recurring infections and ailments which followed each other in quick succession from beginning to end of that decade. The heavy cold lent my interview and voice-overs a jaundiced tinge, deadening any humour and betraying an unintentional touch of bitterness.

Sadness there certainly was in my voice: it was the unfortunate outward manifestation of a profound inner sense of desolation and foreboding. Cassandra herself could not have forecast more accurately, or with greater dread, the catastrophe that I knew was looming over us all. Even Nikki Stockley, the young television producer, remarked how Elaine Mason had disrupted the filming process when she had tried to film in the Department. In public and at home, she was busily usurping my place at every opportunity, sometimes aping me, sometimes undermining me, always flaunting her influence over Stephen. She had engineered an unassailable stranglehold over the nursing rota, and had so successfully ingratiated herself that all remonstrance was useless: any comments would be reported back to Stephen, and I would be castigated for my interference. My appeals to the secretary of the Royal College of Nursing for help in enforcing the code of nursing conduct met with a flat refusal to become involved unless I could produce photographic evidence of malpractice. Such was the background of physical chaos and emotional torment against which the tapestry of the traditional honorary-degree ceremony unfolded, briefly transporting us into a fantasy realm of theatrical grandeur and champagne celebrations where all the froth of new clothes, archaic ritual, fixed smiles, polite chatter and endless handshakes spread like an insubstantial white layer over the smouldering reality beneath.

In a modest bid to ensure some privacy, Lucy had optimistically marked the calendar from 8th June as follows: *Lucy starts A levels and becomes a complete recluse(!)*. The day of Stephen's Honorary Doctorate, 15th June, she noted as, *L does 2 A levels*. Although she missed the accompanying festivities on account of the exams, there was little hope of fulfilling her reclusive intentions, so it was hardly surprising that on 22nd June an impassioned appeal appeared in brackets: *(Give me the sympathy I deserve!)*. In the circumstances, it was a credit to her that she managed to do her exams at all, let alone succeed in them.

15th June, the day of the two most intensive A-level papers was bright, hot and sunny – which was not of much help to Lucy. For Stephen's Honorary Degree ceremony, however, the weather was ideal. Never had the discrepancy between the best interests of different members of the family been more marked. Lucy left early for school in an advanced state of nerves, while the rest of us looked forward to a day of pomp and rejoicing, a true holiday from stress and dissenting voices. We left the house at 10 a.m. and strolled down the road to the Backs. The lawns and meadows by the river could not have looked more pastoral and peaceful: every blade of emerald grass and every leaf – green, gold or bronze – rippled in the bright morning sun, while the river gleamed like a silvery mirror, reflecting the infinite brilliance of the sky in mid-stream and the shady overhanging fronds of willow at the water's edge.

We arrived in Caius to find a buzz of unaccustomed excitement: the whole College had assembled to applaud Stephen in Caius Court, the Renaissance court near the Senate House. It took a few minutes to robe the honorary graduand in the ante-Chapel and a little while to get him comfortable in the chair in the heavy red gown, which would have been fine for midwinter, but was unbearably hot in midsummer. He refused to wear the gold-rimmed black-velvet bonnet, so Tim wore it instead. As we emerged from the Chapel, the Fellows, all begowned, preceded us taking up positions along the path to the Gate of Honour. From another gate, the Gate of Virtue, came a brass fanfare, and then the choir struck up the anthem 'Laudate Domino'. Another fanfare resounded round the court, chasing Stephen as he raced at full speed through the Gate of Honour, up Senate House Passage and into the Yard of the Senate House.

Robert had enlisted the help of muscular undergraduate friends to lift the wheelchair and its occupant up the long, winding staircase to the Combination Room in the Old Schools building, where the other honorary graduands, including Javier Pérez de Cuéllar, the Secretary-General of the United Nations, were assembling. Stephen just had time for a sip of apple juice before Prince Philip, the Chancellor, arrived. Good-humouredly he came over to talk to us and recalled coming to West Road in

1981. He teased Tim about his hat and stayed to watch Stephen's demonstration of the computer before being whisked away to meet the other dignitaries. We passed the royal personage as we made our way out to prepare ourselves for the procession in advance of the rest of the party. "Self-propelled, is it?" he asked. "Yes," I replied, "watch out for your toes!"

The procession, which had already formed by the time we joined it, began to move forthwith. The four of us – Stephen, Robert, Tim and I – walked slowly round the Senate House lawn at the tail end of the line-up, watched by the crowds outside the railings and the cameras within. The clouds of tension, friction and confusion evaporated in the fierce sunlight, and for a fleeting moment it was hard to believe that they had ever existed. In the Senate House all was cool, dark and solemn. The assembly of red-robed Masters of Colleges and Professors and the Chancellor in his gold-braided black robes took up their positions, and the audience of families and friends, dressed with the formality befitting an occasion of such pageantry, sat waiting in silent expectation. As the great oak doors closed on the midday brilliance and the thronging informal crowds of T-shirted tourists outside, the combined choirs of St John's and King's opened the proceedings with an anthem by Byrd, followed by a twentieth-century piece, and then the presentations began. A German theologian, the Lord Chancellor Lord Mackay, Pérez de Cuéllar and then Stephen, were all introduced by the Public Orator, and in a witty Latin delivered with such panache and such flourish that when he concluded his oration in honour of Stephen, Tim – not renowned for his Latin scholarship – burst into spontaneous applause. Pérez de Cuéllar was described as "having brought peace to the Persians and Mesopotamians" while the substance of Stephen's encomium was adapted from the first atomic theory as described by Lucretius in *De Rerum Natura*.

Amid much bowing, handshaking and doffing of hats, the Duke of Edinburgh conferred the degrees one by one, each presentation ending with a round of applause, which when Stephen's turn came attained rapturous proportions. Some of the graduands, such as the diminutive and frail figure of Sue Ryder, looked as nervous as young undergraduates; others, such as the opera singer Jessye Norman and Stephen himself, were old hands at the game and received their ovations with confidence and style.

The ceremony came to an end with more anthems and two verses of the National Anthem. Leaving Tim with his grandparents, Robert and I processed out with Stephen, sedately walking round the green again before heading down King's Parade in the blazing sun. Crowds cheered, smiling and waving, and cameras clicked.

When we reached Corpus Christi College – which by coincidence was Robert's college and the venue for the luncheon – we found ourselves surrounded by the nation's great and good, all wilting visibly in the heat inside the marquee, where champagne was being served, followed by lunch in another equally sweltering marquee. To add to Stephen's discomfort, the food was not suitable for him apart from the salmon. He was well entertained by his neighbour, but I had a fairly hard time with mine, a well-known authority on French history who seemed to have nothing to say for himself until I mentioned our house in France. Then he came to life. His wife had just bought a property in Normandy, he said, but he was a city man and did not much care for the country. Whereupon there was much mirth as he shared his views with Stephen and the latter grinned in agreement.

In the rising temperatures, the speeches were mercifully short. Starting with Stephen, "because everything begins with him", the Duke of Edinburgh expressed his admiration of the graduands, who "reflected the best of our civilization". Lord Mackay replied briefly, and then it was all over. The rest of the day was a disturbing mixture of frivolity and encroaching normality, as if the harsh reality of the gathering storm could not extend its reprieve for much longer.

At home a select group of relatives and friends had assembled, and the College had laid out a tea of smoked salmon sandwiches and strawberries and cream on the lawn, all to be consumed with champagne. Robert was not at that party, as he had another engagement: early that evening he was to row in the Corpus second boat, racing in the Bumps. I managed to dash away from the lingering guests just in time to see him row. The day, however long and eventful, was not yet over. Lucy came home in dire distress, as neither of her A-level papers had gone at all well, and then later in the evening, when all the guests had left and I was clearing up, the telephone rang. It was Robert. We chatted for a bit and then he blurted out that his Finals results were out and they were not as good as he had hoped. He was understandably very upset, and I too felt his humiliation and the irony of the situation keenly.

Robert, loyal and uncomplaining as ever, had dutifully assisted his father at the Senate House, had accompanied him in the formal procession, and had provided the team of helpers from among his friends to lift him up steps and over obstacles in Corpus Christi College. With thoughtful reticence, he had witnessed his father's good fortune without presuming on it, though always overshadowed by it. All through the ceremony in his father's honour, all through the excesses of media exposure, all through the compliments, the ovations and the accolades, Robert had kept to himself the galling news that his Finals results, published that very day, were disappointing. The underlying truth of the situation was that his profound sense of individuality had rebelled against the overpowering shadow of his father's genius by mutely refusing to compete with it. I could not help feeling a much deeper pain for my son in his dismay than joy for my husband in the full glory of his many-faceted success. I identified closely with Robert: I could only stand on the sidelines of Stephen's success.

If Robert had not achieved the academic success he had been hoping for, he made up for his disappointment on the river. Pursued by the BBC film crew, I took Stephen down to the races the next afternoon. Despite taking a wrong turning – the races take place on a stretch of the river at Fen Ditton five miles or so out of town – we arrived just in time to see the Corpus boat flailing past, hot on the stern of the Lady Margaret boat. News filtered back up the river in their wake that the Corpus boat had bumped its prey. My father, who in his day had also rowed for Corpus, was thrilled with Robert's prowess on the river. He always regretted that, under constant pressure to aim high, he had not been able to relax and enjoy his years at Cambridge in the 1930s – which is why, in his opinion, it was important that Robert had made the most of his time as an undergraduate.

13

Honourable Companionship

Late that evening of 16th June, we sat up to watch the announcement at midnight of the Birthday Honours. Inexplicably, Elaine Mason, the nurse in attendance, was disparaging and disapproving, but my father hopped up and down with excitement at his son-in-law's elevation to the higher echelons of the Establishment as a Companion of Honour. Like Stephen's father he derived a vicarious enjoyment from his proximity to the sort of public success that circumstance had denied him. The next morning I awoke to the more practical consideration of how to open the day in a suitably festive manner. I had not given any thought to the start of the day and Stephen's most important meal, his breakfast. Then I remembered that there was probably some caviar left over from a trip to Moscow and champagne from Thursday's celebrations in the fridge. The consequence of that extravagant breakfast was that none of us achieved very much that morning, only managing to stumble across the fen to the University Centre, where I had booked a table for lunch. In the early afternoon, however, I cycled into town to check on the organization of the evening's concert in the Senate House, and found Jonathan's family busy arranging the seating and the general layout while he rehearsed the orchestra. I left them to it and raced back home to collect my father for a lightning trip down to the river. We arrived just in time to see the Corpus second boat rowing down bearing a willow branch, the sign that it had made yet another triumphant bump.

That warm, cloudless June evening saw us back at the Senate House, astonished at the sight of the long line of friends and admirers who were patiently queuing to get in for the concert, aptly entitled *Honoris Causa*. I steered Stephen away from making a tactless beeline for the exam results, the Class lists, which were posted up outside the Senate House, and left him sitting on the same lawn around which we had processed only two days before. There he had his photo taken in company with various distinguished guests – from the firm sponsoring the concert, from his College and from the University – while I went to investigate why the queue was moving so slowly. Its length was partly explained by the fact that ten-year-old Tim was the only programme seller inside the building, though Lucy and my father were hard at work ushering the crowds to their seats. Having enlisted more help for Tim, I rejoined Stephen outside. The manager of the Senate House insisted to my embarrassment that Stephen and I should make a formal entry, and detained us outside until the rest of the audience was seated. We were greeted by a standing ovation. While Stephen beamed at the audience and pirouetted in his chair, I felt painfully shy and gauche and was glad to be able to sit down with my back to the audience.

A couple of minutes later, the sounds of the baroque trumpet in Purcell's sonata for that gloriously commanding instrument opened the concert, soaring above the heads of the audience to mingle with the ornate plasterwork of the eighteenth-century ceiling. Just as I hoped, the audience were so well satisfied at the end of their evening's entertainment that they contributed generously to the retiring collection, with the result that we were able to send handsome cheques to the three charities – the Motor Neuron Disease Association, Leukaemia Research and the Leonard Cheshire Foundation – as well as covering the costs of the concert from ticket sales. Ostensibly the evening had been a tremendous success: the charities had benefited; the Cambridge Baroque Camerata had secured a new sponsorship deal and had given a spectacular performance to a full Senate House; and, most importantly, Stephen had been lavishly fêted and applauded by hundreds of well-wishers. He, however, was edgy and disgruntled. His perceptions of the event were coloured by the grudging view that Jonathan and the orchestra had obscured his share of the limelight. This was as unjust as it was unlike Stephen's normal character. He had entered into the project with excitement and, when he had not been in America, had involved himself in its development with enthusiasm. Jonathan with his natural reserve had carefully stepped aside to allow Stephen to revel in the audience's adulation at the end of the performance, and indeed there could have been no doubt that it was Stephen's show. It was even less like Stephen that he should remind me that, since the honour bore no title, I had no part in it. The conclusion was as inescapable as it was unpalatable: he had fallen prey to flattery. The sycophantic sources of this flattery were not disinterested, and seemed to be feeding him ideas which were at odds with his formerly generous if stubborn nature.

The limelight was blindingly focused on Stephen for the rest of that summer, never more so than when we made our second visit to Buckingham Palace a few weeks later, though by comparison with the first visit, seven years earlier, this one was surprisingly intimate. We followed a similar routine – again staying at the Royal Society the night before – but with the difference that this time Tim and Amarjit Chohan, Stephen's Indian nurse, came with us, and Lucy had remembered to pack her smart shoes to go with the dark-brown dress which set off her blond hair beautifully. Again, just as before, the traffic in the Mall was at a standstill, though this time it was on account of the Changing of the Guard. To avoid the congestion around the main entrance, we were directed to the Queen's private entrance and were suddenly transported into a quiet, colourful country garden away from the hot stuffy turmoil of London and its traffic. An equerry, footmen and a lady-in-waiting greeted us with graciously imperturbable smiles and ushered us into the Palace, past the gleaming toy car that Prince Charles had had as a child and a couple of bikes, and up into the vast marble-pillared hall, which was lit along its entire length and furnished in red and pink damask. Huge displays of lilies stood like decorative sentinels, guarding the treasures.

We turned a corner and doubled back along the picture gallery, quickly retracing our steps over the marble hall, with scarcely a moment to glance at the portraits of Charles I and his family, gazing in mute detachment at each other across the floor. A couple of Canalettos, a Dutch genre painting and lots of portraits of Princess Augusta caught my eye. We turned into a passage so narrow that it might have led to servants' quarters, and were shown into a small side room full of paintings and furniture, the Empire Room. After a brisk briefing from the equerry, Stephen and I were hurried away from the family to meet the Queen, who was waiting in a room at the end of the passage. True to form, Stephen charged ahead towards the open door across the passage. There by the mantelpiece stood the Queen, wearing a royal blue dress streaked with white. She glanced in our direction with a friendly but apprehensive smile. This soon changed to a look of absolute horror when Stephen, bursting in haste into her reception room, rolled the carpet up in his wheels like a cowpusher on an American locomotive. The chair hoovered up the edge of the thick coffee-coloured carpet, tying it up in knots, bringing Stephen to an abrupt halt and blocking the way into the room. From behind the chair I could not easily see what was happening, and there was nothing I could do to release the royal pile. The Queen was the only person inside the room. She hesitated, and then for one moment made a gesture, as if she herself were about to step forwards and lift the heavy mechanism and its occupant out of the snare. Fortunately the equerry who had announced us squeezed past the chair, lifted the front wheels and sorted out the mess.

Naturally, Her Majesty was a little flustered – as was I – so we failed to shake hands and I forgot to curtsey as she uttered a short formal speech of welcome. After an awkward silence she must have decided that the best course of action was to go ahead with the presentation without delay, and so proceeded to announce that she was pleased to invest Stephen with the insignia of the Companion of Honour. I received the medal on Stephen's behalf and showed it to him, reading the inscription aloud as I held it out for him to see. "In Action Faithful, in Honour Clear" it read. The Queen remarked that she thought it was a particularly lovely wording, and Stephen typed up, "Thank you ma'am." We in turn presented her with a thumb-printed copy of *A Brief History of Time*, which rather nonplussed her – "Is it a popular account of his work such that a lawyer might give?" she enquired of me. It was my turn to be nonplussed, since I could not imagine anything remotely approaching a popular account of the law. I recovered my composure sufficiently to say that I thought *A Brief History* was more readable than that, especially the first chapters, which provided a fascinating account of the development of the study of the universe – before the physics became too complicated with elementary particles, string theory, imaginary time and that sort of thing. Thereafter the conversation continued haltingly for another ten minutes or so, ranging from a basic explanation of Stephen's science and interests to a demonstration of the workings of the computer and its American voice. The Queen directed her questions to me with a piercing, blue gaze, as bright as the large sapphire and diamond brooch on her shoulder. Although there was warmth and consideration as well as keenness in that gaze, it transfixed me. I was too terrified even to move my eyes, much as I should have liked to glance round the pretty turquoise reception room with its paintings and mementoes, and I stood awkwardly rooted to the spot, hardly daring to turn my head to left or right.

Over lunch on the top floor of the Hilton we recounted the details of the audience to the family, whose movements had been restricted to the Empire Room, not omitting the carpet episode, which appealed to their irreverent sense of humour. We described the subsequent conversation as somewhere between an oral exam and an interview with an intense but well-meaning headmistress, both equally terrifying. I had little doubt that the Queen had found it pretty difficult as well. Did we give the right answers, we wondered, as we looked out over the London skyline? There, directly beneath us, was the Palace, surrounded by the Elysian Fields where, after the audience, we had just walked. Stephen complained that he had not been able to converse as much as he would have liked because of a problem with the setting of the hand control of the computer, disturbed by the contretemps with the carpet. Be that as it may, the overall impression was that the occasion had gone well, and Stephen had yet another impressive medallion to add to his already extensive collection.

Just as we were leaving the restaurant, I was surprised to be presented with an enormous bouquet of orange and yellow lilies by the management. Although it came from a commercial institution, one of the chain of Hilton Hotels, the gesture was quite affecting. It reminded me of the pearl that Ruth Hughes had given me in California when Stephen was awarded the Papal medal in 1975, and it told me that somebody had noticed me.

14

Dies Irae

A week later Tim and I were in France again. The Moulin blinked sleepily in the evening sun as we drove towards it up the track and as I opened the gates. The crisp, fresh air penetrated deep into my asthmatic lungs, reviving my spirits, for I was physically tired after the long journey and emotionally taut after the recent peaks and troughs. The inner courtyard was quiet and still, enveloping us like a soft blanket and protecting us from the tyranny of the outside world. The silence was broken only by the chirruping of sparrows, echoing off the white walls. Then Tim added his piping voice to theirs, impatiently urging me to open the door so that he could get in and clamber up to his attic to check the state of his model aeroplanes, which swooped vertiginously over the stairwell, suspended from the banisters by an intricate web of thread and Sellotape. Inside we ran from room to room, inspecting every nook and cranny and renewing our acquaintance with every old beam. To our astonishment, the dusty black barn had undergone a Cinderella-like transformation and was ready to accommodate Stephen's entourage of nurses. The rubble, cobwebs and rotting rafters had disappeared, and in their place downstairs there was a large room with a tiled floor and a kitchenette, and upstairs two large bedrooms and a bathroom. A blend of solid new beams and usable old ones held up the structure, so confident in their age-old tradition that were it not for the sheen of newness on all the fittings, they could have been there from time immemorial. Then we ran out into the garden, anticipating more discoveries. Some strange enchantment had been exercised in our absence. Tim gasped, "It's just like Buckingham Palace!" – and indeed he was right. The plants and seeds in the herbaceous border had leapt to maturity, and where in May there had been small isolated clumps and diminutive seedlings, now a riot of densely nodding flower heads and dancing colour shouted ecstatic greetings. There were still things to be done, walls to be painted and floors to be covered, but the essential work was completed. The Moulin was ready to receive not only us, but the whole crowd of our summer visitors as well. My brother was to bring his family of four children at about the same time as Tim's friend Arthur, and his parents would be arriving for a weekend visit. Jonathan would be bringing my parents and Stephen would be coming out by air to Le Touquet, attended by Pam Benson, a most trusted nurse, and by Elaine and David Mason and their family.

Despite my mother's misgivings, I had in my optimism invited the Mason family, hoping that the experience of living with us in the same house but in more relaxed circumstances than in Cambridge would encourage a greater respect for the self-discipline which was basic to our routine. While I had no intention of interfering in any fond attachment that might have developed between Elaine and Stephen, I thought that, as a professional nurse, she might be persuaded to see that the success of our task depended on finely balanced teamwork. There was no room for troublemakers in this situation. Naively I trusted too that if she realized that Jonathan and I did not, as a matter of course, sleep together in the same room, she would learn to respect the modus vivendi which enabled us to go on caring for Stephen and the children indefinitely, come what may. Surely only the most bigoted fundamentalist could be blind to what we were trying to achieve and the effort and restraint that we put into that endeavour? It was ironic that in days gone by Stephen would have been scathing in his intolerance of fundamentalism and would have laughed to scorn anyone who tried to preach it.

We – that is me, Tim, my handyman Claude and a very helpful girl from the village – were still energetically applying white emulsion to the walls of the new part of the house downstairs when my absent-minded brother and his family of four children arrived a week early. Chris more than compensated for their unexpected arrival, however, by taking over the cooking. In his opinion, the best tourist attractions of France were the supermarkets, where he would happily spend his days browsing along the shelves in search of ever more extravagant ingredients to add to his cooking pot, the aroma of which, wafting from the new kitchen, made our mouths water every evening with the promise of gastronomic delights.

By the time Stephen and his motley crew flew in to Le Touquet in the middle of August, the new wing of the house had been well and truly tested by successive waves of visitors, including my parents, who had pronounced it entirely satisfactory both for its charm and its convenience. But a perceptible tension reigned among the new arrivals. My delight at seeing Stephen met with a cool response, arousing my suspicions that the underhand mutterings about his dislike of the French countryside had struck home, persuading him that he really did not want to spend any time on holiday in France, let alone in the country. All efforts to interest him in the glorious views from the house across sun-drenched fields to the distant blue line of hills and forests encountered the same bored, disdainful expression. Day after day, the truth forced itself remorselessly on me that his smiles and his interest were reserved for Elaine, and I had no doubt that he was being encouraged to despise me because I was flawed and did not conform to the image of perfection with which he was constantly being tantalized. He was being persuaded that I was no longer of any use to him, that I was good for nothing. Elaine was in a position of strength: her responsibilities were minimal and she could indulge Stephen by doing anything he asked; she could wheedle and coax, and her specialized training enabled her to attend to his every whim. Since his work and his physical condition were his two principal preoccupations, my role was logically much diminished, and hers was ostensibly greatly enhanced. The familial and intellectual bonds which I had valued and through which we maintained a semblance of normality had apparently become insignificant. Probably with her he had found someone tougher than me with whom he could again somehow have a physical relationship, whatever the other dimensions of their affair. I could not deny him this, and was prepared to accept it in our scheme of things – in the same way that he had generously accepted my relationship with Jonathan – provided that it was discreet and posed no threat to our family, to our children, to our home or to the running of the nursing rota achieved at such wearisome cost. It was also essential that it must not negate my relationship with Stephen, because I was convinced that without me he would be like a lost child, an unruly, assertive child but a helpless and naive one as well. My fate had been bound up with his so closely and for so long that I could never be indifferent to him, however difficult his peculiar set of circumstances – those of a disabled genius – had made him. Care for his well-being had become second nature to me. Whether it was the slightest sign of distress, discomfort or disapproval that his mobile features betrayed, I could not ignore him. The truth was that I still loved him with a deeply caring compassion. In that emaciated body, despite the power of the mind, his suffering was all too painfully apparent, and it was through that suffering that my feelings for him were constantly being aroused. These feelings were never intended to be patronizing; indeed often they could lead me onto an emotional tightrope, where despair and frustration at his stubbornness and unreasonable demands had always to be reconciled with deference for his dignity and respect for his rights as an extremely incapacitated person.

Our marriage, and the large and complex structure that it had become, was the definition of my adult life, summing up my most important achievements: Stephen's continued survival, the children, the family and the home. It was the long history of our joint battles against his illness and the story of his success against all the odds. I had dedicated most of myself to it – even if I had accepted help to allow me to persevere without becoming suicidal. True, I sometimes longed for more freedom of movement and resented the strict limitations it imposed, but I had never thought of running away from it except – when driven to utter despair – by drowning myself. The structure may have become dangerously top-heavy and unstable, but it was unbelievable that all that the marriage represented might now be swept away in a flush of passion. The fact that Elaine had an able-bodied husband and a family of her own was beyond the scope of my comprehension: that was a matter for her conscience in which I could not become involved.

The situation might have resolved itself peaceably had the personalities involved been different, had they been more considerate, less determined, less self-centred, less bent on the fulfilment of their own desires to the exclusion of all else. Perhaps, if I had been stronger and less confused, I could have handled the situation differently and with more assurance. As it was, the holiday was a disaster. Various mishaps combined to intensify Stephen's distaste for the country, even for the Moulin, which was so unlike his enthusiasm in the spring, and he became increasingly hostile to both the family and to Pam, the other nurse. When eventually I took it upon myself to point out to Stephen that his and Elaine's behaviour risked losing Pam from the rota, I inadvertently set fire to the conflagration which would consume us all. It engulfed the old house that day and the following night, shattering the cherished silence and shaking the aged beams, as it raged up around me. Flames of vituperation, hatred, desire for revenge leapt at me from all sides, scorching me to the quick with accusations – the unfaithful wife, the uncaring partner, the selfish career woman, work-shy and frivolous, more intent on singing than on looking after her frail, defenceless husband. I had had things my own way for too long, they said. I should "put Stephen first".

I faced the attacks alone. I would not demean Jonathan by bringing him into this uncivilized fray, but nor could I douse the flames. It was hopeless to try and point out that, throughout all the alienating distractions of physics and the grinding, ceaseless demands of illness, I had honestly tried to be a good wife to Stephen; that through the paraphernalia of medicines, medical equipment and nursing rotas, through the plethora of scientific papers, equations and meetings, I had honestly tried to do my best, however distorted my own life had become. That Jonathan's love and help had preserved us and saved me from ultimate despair would never be countenanced as a valid defence. My best was not good enough, and now I was being cast aside in favour of someone who beguiled the sick man with the flimsy straws of extravagant promises and unrealistic expectations. It was the beginning of the death of our marriage.

Alone in my room after the first wave of attack had finally subsided, helplessness reduced me to hot, angry tears. My spirit rebelled at the shallowness of so many of the people who had recently come into our lives. They had never come face to face with successions of multiple crises. They had never had to confront the overwhelming trauma of living in the face of death, day in day out for more than a quarter of a century. They had never plumbed the depths of emotion or been torn apart by moral dilemma. They had never been stretched to and beyond the utter limits of their physical and mental capacities. Their experience of these issues had been facile, skimming the surface of reality, motivated by self-gratification, dictating absolute values to others that they themselves could not observe. Indeed in their eyes I was a mere automaton with no justifiable claim to any human reactions at all. My need to be loved for myself alone was dismissed as preposterous.

After this fiasco Stephen and the Masons returned to England, and Tim and I stayed on at the Moulin. The lovely old house and garden gathered up my spent body and charred mind into the comfort of their embrace as the calm of rural France descended once more. If Stephen really did not want me, I reasoned, I could make a good life for myself in France. I could support myself by teaching English and Spanish, and Tim could become completely bilingual. At the beginning of September he started going to the village school, where he quickly made friends, unperturbed by the demands of the language. He would cycle off down the road to the village every morning while I stood waving and watching as he climbed the hill opposite and disappeared under the trees. At home we often spoke French. English and England had become alien to me, a country and a language which harboured and expressed extreme personal torment – not to mention the widespread political injustices of the Margaret Thatcher years – while France offered a new lifestyle, new friends and a sense of equality. Moreover France, a predominantly Catholic country, worshipped and prayed to the Mother of Jesus, the feminine intermediary to the masculine figures of the Trinity. There a woman had a recognized place in the divine order of things. Mary had a human presence which was tragic, loving and comforting. Often, in French country churches and cathedrals, I would be drawn to the figure of the Virgin Mary – a crudely painted plaster saint perhaps – who offered the solace of shared suffering.

Tim and I quickly settled into a routine which I was confident of being able to sustain. We could live in France permanently if need be, or eventually we could return to England when Stephen had resolved his problems. Jonathan, who had gone back to Cambridge to play a series of organ recitals, kept in touch regularly, urging us to stay in France if that was where we felt at ease.

Stephen also telephoned almost daily, but he urged us to return to England. He missed us, he said, and he needed us. He was so persuasive that I trusted that he really intended to restore some harmony to our lives and keep his nurses under control. Later that September, believing that my lost child really needed me, we set out for England across stormy seas, determined to avoid confrontation. The family, that is my parents and Robert, were delighted to see us when we arrived home late at night after long delays on the motorways. The reception I, but not Tim, received from Stephen was distinctly frosty. It was not the lost child who came to greet us, but the despot. At once I knew that I had made a grave mistake in coming back to England.

15

Too Much Reality

The following Monday, Tim returned to his primary school and I took up my teaching again, committing myself at least for the term if not for the whole academic year. Then, exactly a week after our return, Stephen gave me a letter announcing his intention of going to live with Elaine Mason. That evening, by a sorry coincidence, Robert was dealt a broken jaw by muggers who attacked him on his way home.

The execution of Stephen's decision was considerably delayed for the extraordinary and eminently practical reason that he and Elaine Mason had nowhere to go. In the meantime we lived in a maelstrom of chaos and confusion, while I clung like a limpet to the belief that the storm would eventually wear itself out and that, despite his present sad emotional disarray, Stephen would choose to stay with his family. As if blown along like a dry leaf in a gale, he came and went, often without any notice. Extreme pressure from outside was exerted on him, and each explosive episode would be succeeded by a period of calm as if nothing had happened. Those periods, though, were just the eye of the storm, only presaging further unforeseen elements which blew in at hurricane force. Reports reached me that the nurse was already announcing her forthcoming marriage to Stephen. I lived with the constant fear that there might well be a battle to gain custody of Tim, and Jonathan was banned from West Road under threat of a court injunction, so he had no choice but to keep to his own home. Open discussion was impossible, because an insurmountable barrier had arisen between Stephen and me and, the more he appeared to lose control of his own situation, the more I felt he sought to control me, as if I was simply a piece of property. The duty nurses posted unpleasant letters through my car window just as I left for work each day, and impossible demands were made of me each evening. Unpleasant remarks and false motives were attributed to me. I was told to give Jonathan up and "put Stephen first in everything". I even found myself reluctantly drawn into clashes about money, not just with Stephen but with Elaine Mason as well. Through the concentration required by teaching – especially by teaching the absorbing, intellectually teasing novels and short stories of Gabriel García Márquez – I managed to preserve some sanity, while among my colleagues in the staffroom I found a quiet sympathy and supportiveness which brought a sense of stability to the few hours each day that I spent away from home. At other times music soothed and solaced my battered emotions, though often its intensity caused my voice to falter and fade. Otherwise bedlam reigned and our home became the scene of unprecedented violence as other people's madness forced its way into our household and left Tim and me terrified, with not the least gesture of support from the two professional nursing bodies, the Royal College of Nursing and the UK Nursing Council, who refused to become involved.

Later that month, as I waved the two eldest children goodbye on consecutive days – Robert to Glasgow for a postgraduate-degree course in Information Technology and Lucy to Oxford – it seemed that my entire existence and the structure on which it rested were crumbling away. My personal identity, which I had desperately tried to construct over the years from all the disparate fragments – the jigsaw pieces of everyday life – had been shattered. I was alone and without shelter in the midst of a private war. Wherever I looked, I saw the rubble and ruins of the brave, bold but fragile edifice that Stephen and I had built. A dark chasm had opened up in the ground, swallowing up that edifice and with it more than twenty-five years of my life – all the years of my youth and young adulthood, all the hopes and all the optimism. In their place there was left little more than an insubstantial, vacant shroud, ghostly and withdrawn, the object of daily mental torture. The only certainty for the future was that my youngest and most vulnerable child, Tim, had to be protected and, however crushed and broken I might be, I had to muster the strength and the courage to fight for him.

Jonathan and I had never contemplated the possibility of a future together without Stephen. We had no fantasies, no dreams. The thought of change was alien to our thinking: I had closed my mind to it and did not seek it. In the past I thought that we had achieved a balance whereby everyone could flourish, even if that demanded considerable contortion, restraint and self-discipline at a personal level. This had evidently proved to be nothing more than complacent wishful thinking, for I was now forcibly given to understand that Stephen had been dissatisfied with our way of life for some time. I found this revelation quite surprising. If Stephen had been seething with resentment for so long, why had he not told me about it? How had he managed to be so successful, creative and dynamic if he was really unhappy? Apparently he had not liked being treated as but one member of the family when he considered his rightful place to be on a pedestal at the centre. Someone had come along who was prepared to worship at his feet and make him the focal point of her life. That someone was promising him that he would never have to employ nurses again, since she alone would care for him twenty-four hours a day, seven days a week and would travel everywhere that he wanted to go. Patently I could not match such single-minded devotion and, as a result, change of the cruellest kind was being forced upon me. I was threatened with being thrown out of the family home, and my role in Stephen's life was being systematically denied, as if all reference to me, all memory of me, had to be erased from all the records.

Once the term had started and Tim and I were entrenched in the Cambridge routine, there was no going back to France, yet I badly needed a bolt hole. Jonathan's house was out of the question, since a move there would signify that I was ending the marriage, which was not and never had been my intention. Any bolt hole had to be neutral territory, where Tim and I could escape the tensions, the battles, the venom and the recriminations which were creating bitter chaos at 5 West Road. There was just one option open. Although the College had been in possession of our house in Little St Mary's Lane for years – in part-exchange for the College flat – the property still technically belonged to us. As I knew that the house was unoccupied, I wrote to the Master pleading with him to allow Tim and me to use it temporarily until the battles had died away and the crisis had resolved itself for better or for worse. The Master was new to the College – I scarcely knew him nor he me. His reply was unequivocal: much as he regretted it, there existed a formal agreement between Stephen and the College for the exchange of the two properties, and until Stephen revoked that agreement, I could have no access to the house.

By day asthma stifled my breathing and befuddled my mind, while my hands tingled to the tips of my fingers with fright each time Stephen announced that he wanted to speak to me. Every night the terrible nightmares returned, waking me in a terrified panic: my heart pounded as buildings collapsed on top of me, burying me in a dark underground tomb. Tim too had nightmares in which he dreamt that he was being chased by baddies along corridors and down streets. By day he became excessively introverted and anxious. The doctor prescribed beta blockers for me and sent me to see a counsellor. The only remedy for Tim was to distance him from the troubles, but since Little St Mary's Lane was denied us, that was not easily done. I asked his headteacher to warn his staff of the intolerable strain that Tim was under at home. Too late I discovered that he had omitted to pass my anxieties on to his staff, and poor Tim often came home from his primary school in tears.

The battles continued to rage furiously for the rest of the term with only a short truce during the visit to Spain for the presentation of a prestigious award by the heir to the Spanish throne, the Prince of Asturias, in Oviedo. Being in Spain lifted my spirits and made that visit bearable. Although the truce brought its own minor superficial tensions in the form of repeated public appearances, press conferences and interviews, at least these gave me the opportunity to prove myself professionally again and reassert my own qualifications as a linguist and as Stephen's companion. The underlying tension which resulted from his lately announced resolve of buying a flat for his favourite nurse was much more severe. The mind which had mastered the mathematical secrets of the universe was no match for the emotional upheaval which now overwhelmed it. Like his Wagnerian hero, Siegfried, Stephen had wrapped himself in a protective cloak, the stiff cloak of determination – inspired by unrelenting reason, steeling him against sentimental frailty in the belief that he was invincible. But like Siegfried he was vulnerable, and helpless when his vulnerability was exposed to attack. Stephen's physical weak spot had been his throat, but he also had a second, psychological weak spot, which was an utter lack of resistance to manipulative, emotional pressure. He had never been subjected to it before and had no armour against it. This was the sort of pressure being exerted on Stephen: it built up a head of steam, hissing with relentless energy until it erupted in a series of emotional surges of volcanic force, which engulfed all obstacles with a red-hot flow of anger and passion. Then, quite miraculously, each new eruption would subside as quickly as it had exploded, and peace would descend once again on our home life. He would become gentler, more docile and regretful, genuinely concerned to put the turmoil behind him and resume the family life on which he had thrived in the past. Then he would admit that he was being tossed by conflicting emotions and needed support, understanding and the possibility of a reconciliation. This I was all too willing to give, for I shared the tragedy of his situation and wanted to help him get through it – but the lull would last only until the awful moment when another missive, another ultimatum, another summons, would seek out its target. I learnt to dread the outcome as Stephen dashed off, abandoning meals and social engagements to appease and become even further enthralled. And so it went on until Christmas. My parents' plans for celebrating their Golden Wedding were a catastrophe on the ebb and flow of that tidal force. With a randomness which had become perversely predictable, Stephen spent Christmas Day in the bosom of his family, but then late at night his van drew up outside and he vanished into the darkness, leaving home with Elaine to go and stay in a hotel before setting off for a conference in Israel the next day.

We did not see him or hear from him again until early January, when the children, Jonathan and I arrived home from a blissfully untroubled break in France to find him waiting for us as if he were expecting to resume business as usual. No explanations were proffered, and I knew better than to ask for any. That evening we gathered round the candlelit table, feasting on roast duck and orange sauce in celebration of Stephen's birthday. The cheerful letter I wrote to Stephen's mother the following morning, genuinely expressing my joy that the disruptions appeared to be over and that we could resume our attempts to lead a creative family life, received an entirely negative response. From that letter it became clear that Isobel discounted, even doubted, the effort that I had so long put into caring for Stephen and, on the contrary, saw me as the hedonistic beneficiary of his fame and success, intent now on denying him his chance of happiness with someone she really approved of and liked.

The stability was short-lived: all too soon the situation began to deteriorate again. After several more weeks in which the threats, the recriminations and the abuse once again gathered force, the children and I left to join Arthur and his parents for a few days' skiing in Austria at half-term. On our return to Cambridge, there was no sign of Stephen. He had gone. He had finally moved out, aided apparently by Elaine's husband, on the day we had left for Austria, 17th February 1990. The end had come. I felt neither sadness nor relief. I was numb.

It was not the end however. The very next day, Stephen telephoned from Elstree Studios, where the film version of *A Brief History of Time* was being shot, and asked me to join him there to participate in a family portrait, a biographical background for the film. It was an astonishing request. It was incredible that, having just left his family, he could expect us to go on performing like puppets for the cameras, still conveying the outdated happy and united façade. There was no longer any timid hesitancy in my voice. In taking his decision to leave us, Stephen had unwittingly relinquished his power over me, leaving me free to make up my own mind, no more in dread of his imperious reactions. I refused to go to Elstree. I had gained control of my life.

Thereafter, the high tragedy descended into farce. The phone rang incessantly as one after another the American producers and directors tried to cajole, flatter, persuade me to participate in their film. When they moved to Cambridge to set up an exact replica of Stephen's office in a disused church, they beat a path to the door, bringing with them their pathetic arguments. Millions of dollars were at stake, they lamented, wringing their hands; my absence would upset all their plans; without a substantial biographical element, the film would be unbalanced. I shrugged my shoulders and quoted back their original assurances, enshrined in the contract, about the nature of the film – a purely scientific documentary with only the briefest of biographical references. The more they revealed their lack of integrity by denying all such promises, the easier I found it to hold my ground – and the easier I found it to hold my ground, the stronger I became.

16

Null and Void

Whatever small comfort I may have derived from my new-found independence of spirit, the cataclysm had in truth left me a shattered wreck. In the darkness of defeat, I felt myself discredited and disowned, fumbling to find an identity, as if the preceding twenty-five years had been erased without trace. Indeed that impression was not simply subjective: it was given substance by the two charities for whom I had worked so hard. They could not risk their public credibility, they said, by continuing to have the two partners to a separation or divorce associated with their efforts, so they both dispensed with my services. Naturally Stephen's name was more useful than mine. This was a bitter blow. As I had suspected, outside the marriage and apart from Stephen, I was nothing.

It was nonetheless from this blind maze of disorientation that I began to sense the stirrings of an unprecedented, almost palpable strength in the air around me, a spiritual force, unrelated to my sapped physical state. It revealed itself in the spontaneous expressions of concern and love, reaching out telepathically to me from our many friends worldwide. These were the true friends, people who had known us for many years, friends who had witnessed the struggles and had often helped in times of crisis, friends who had generously delighted in the successes without being blinded to the harsh underlying reality. These were friends, too, from whom my attempts to come to terms with the situation had been no secret, friends who had known and admired Jonathan for his dedication to the family as much as for his musical talent. Many said that they wept when they heard the news. They brought me a sense of peace which enabled me to look to my own resources. Rather than wallow in resentment, I would put the energy which I had previously devoted to Stephen's well-being into a new project, a project of my own: it would be a book, but not the book of memoirs for which various publishers were already clamouring, since that was far too painful a subject and still lacked a clear perspective. My book would describe our experiences in setting up home in France, and would consist of amusing anecdotes and practical information, aimed at the considerable market of British buyers of homes in France. As not many of those Francophiles seemed to have any great command of the French language, I would compile a phonetic lexicon of useful terms relating to all areas of house purchase and residence in France: legalities, insurance, renovation, the utilities, the telephone system, local government and healthcare.

Most of the time which used to be spent running the home, attending to Stephen's needs, accommodating his nurses, organizing rotas, answering the phone to disaffected carers and putting on parties, I gave to that book. In writing it and compiling the lexicon, I learnt – like Stephen in the period after his critical illness – to use a computer. How I wished that one had been available in those years when I was working on my thesis! The computer and printer were a magnanimous parting gift from Stephen. Quite why he bought them I never discovered, but I suspected that the gesture was typical of the state of confusion in which he found himself, and which as ever he was too proud and self-contained to admit. I was, however, duly appreciative, since I could not have compiled the dictionary of useful terms without it. Although the French aspect of the project was endlessly entertaining and stimulating in the research and the writing, the publication was fraught with difficulty because, in my naivety, I fell into the wrong hands. A seemingly sympathetic literary agent took the book on board, but in fact, like so many others, he was interested only in the memoir.

Devious literary agents notwithstanding, the news of the separation fortunately remained concealed from the press for several months. Because it had not hit the tabloid headlines, we were allowed a beneficial period of respite. This limbo enabled Stephen and me to try to put our relationship on a new footing without the rub of media attention. We could meet as old friends without the stress of the day-to-day friction which had soured our relationship: he could come to West Road to see Tim at mealtimes, and we could discuss matters of family concern calmly and sensibly. The only difference was that he lived elsewhere with someone else.

The press finally learnt of our separation, literally as the result of an accident. One night, as Stephen was on his way back to his flat, he and the nurse in attendance (not Elaine) were knocked down by a speeding taxi. The wheelchair was overturned and he was left lying in the road in the dark. It was a miracle that he suffered nothing worse than a broken shoulder and spent only a couple of days in hospital. Inevitably the press got to hear of the accident, and naturally they wanted to know why his home was no longer at West Road. Reporters and cameramen, especially from the tabloids, came clustering round the gate like a pack of baying hounds, scenting scandal and terrifying Tim and me. We were being hunted. It was thanks to the good sense of the head porter at Harvey Court that they were put off the scent, and Jonathan, of whose existence they were unaware, managed to escape out of the back door.

Once the separation had entered the public domain, the College lost no time in sending the Bursar across to enquire when we were going to move. He was quite explicit: the College felt itself under no obligation to house the family if Stephen, with whom the College had signed the agreement, was no longer living there. He was in effect giving me notice to quit. I had neither the presence of mind to protest nor the will to fight. The previous day would have been – technically was – our twenty-fifth wedding anniversary. On that Monday morning in July it was made quite clear to me that everything that had occurred in those twenty-five years was of no importance to anyone else. The records had been wiped out. Those years might as well never have happened. Stephen was the only person who mattered. I was of no consequence, nor were the children. I had been given my marching orders and we were effectively being thrown out into the street. It was time to wake up to a new reality.

The only concession was that we were given one year's grace in which to readjust. This was particularly important, as Tim had been entered for King's College School, directly across the road, and it would have been the height of irony if we had been forced to move just as he was changing to a school less than five minutes from our front door. A further advantage of King's for Tim was that his friend Arthur was coming to school there as a boarder, so whatever the upheavals at home he could count on seeing his best friend every day in school. In fact Tim not only saw Arthur in school, but at home as well, because for the next two years Arthur came to live with us. It was a very happy arrangement for all concerned. Arthur became part of our family and gave Tim invaluable moral support in his changing circumstances.

It was my infinite good fortune that I was not alone. Jonathan had stood discreetly and steadfastly by my side despite being the target of considerable hostility. Equally discreetly and steadfastly, and with endless patience, he began to reassemble the broken shards of what used to be my personality, the while trying to come to terms himself with what had happened. From the outset he had been under no illusions: he knew that our relationship depended on a fine balance and on Stephen's acceptance that it was dedicated to the survival, not the destruction, of the family. Jonathan had feared the possibility of Freudian repercussions, but had underestimated the havoc that the intervention of an outside party could wreak by gossip and misrepresentation. There had not been any viable alternative, since he cared so deeply for me and for the family, including Stephen. For my part, not only could I not cope, I could not survive without him: he shouldered the physical burdens, and in his arms I found a longed-for emotional security. The new reality flung us together, though not with any joy or elation, only with sadness at the betrayal of our best intentions, coupled with muted relief that the long ordeal was over. Although Jonathan and I started to live together and began to look for a suitable house to buy, we were not intending to rush into marriage. We were committed to each other, but I was in no fit state, physically or emotionally, to marry anyone, let alone someone who deserved so much more than I could offer. In any case, since there had been no mention of divorce, I was technically still married to Stephen.

It was some consolation that, for all the chaos that *A Brief History of Time* had plunged us into, at least it had not left me destitute. We were able to buy and enlarge a detached house on a modern estate on the same side of Cambridge. At first sight I found the house and its garden dispiriting to the point of heartbreak. The house was cramped, featureless and uninspiring – a modern brick-and-concrete box, its inner walls covered in torn and faded hessian; the garden was pitifully bare and sombre, shaded from the neighbours by a row of overgrown leylandii. Yet again I would have to start from scratch and try to recreate a home in that characterless house and a flower garden from the unyielding grey clay which passed for soil. The attraction of the house was its position: it was still within cycling distance of the centre of town and of Tim's school. It also happened to be quite close to Stephen's luxury flat, which had to be regarded as an advantage, since Stephen insisted on seeing Tim twice a week. With uncomplaining loyalty, Arthur accompanied Tim on these regular visits, the outcome of which was never predictable and always disturbing. I was relieved that Stephen showed no urgency in pressing for divorce, because I dreaded that Tim might become a pawn in yet a further acrimonious battle. Occasionally a demanding letter would arrive, but as this clearly was Stephen's response to domestic pressure, these letters could be taken lightly, whatever their contents. Generally our discussions were civilized and even affectionate whenever we met.

As long as no divorce proceedings were filed, Tim was safe from legal wranglings over custody. Eventually that potential problem, because of his age, ceased to be an issue. For my part, I was leading a normal life, a tremendous luxury after more than twenty-five years of a life which had never really been normal. Jonathan and I cherished our normality and our privacy, though still living in fear of abuse by the gutter press which, we knew, would not hesitate to exploit our situation to please the salacious tastes of their readership. Occasionally those fears were justified, though never to lasting effect.

It was no secret that both the University and the College had designs on the land on which the house at 5 West Road stood. The two institutions were engaged in negotiations for the redevelopment of the end of the garden as a library for the Law Faculty, while for many years the College had been intending to build a hall of residence on the site of the house. In that last year of our occupation, we watched from the house in a silent state of siege as surveyors stalked the garden, armed with measuring rods, marking out distances with stakes and poles, while down by the holly hedge a pile driver forced its way deep into the light alluvial soil. With our removal the fate of the whole property – the old house, its lovely tranquil garden and its majestic backdrop of trees – would be sealed. In the name of progress, the University and the College were predictably intent on destroying yet another shady green space. In the mayhem of moving, there was little that I could do to save the house and garden except to ensure that the trees, especially the two magnificent sentinels, the wellingtonia by the house and the western red cedar, the *Thuja plicata* at the end of the lawn, were protected by tree-preservation orders. The self-styled arboreal officers conducted a survey and assured me that I had no need to worry: the trees were protected already because they were in a conservation area. I moved house satisfied that I had done my civic and environmental duty.

During the course of the next year, I visited the garden frequently on my way home from town to check that nothing untoward had happened. The threat appeared to have receded. All was quiet apart from the constant grinding action of the pile driver. The garden, the lawn, the trees were untouched, just as we had left them. I wandered in that sanctuary of nostalgia, sadly remembering the parties, the dancing, the games of croquet and cricket, and gazing at the blank, unseeing windows of the house, those windows that had contained so much joy and so much anguish. The house guarded its secrets closely, revealing its past in only a few scattered remnants, like the forgotten spoils of a battle – the rain-washed remains of Tim's sandpit, a battered toy bucket, a deflated football, a cracked flowerpot and the rusting rotary washing line which had given such good service. They told of lives and events of which the current student occupants of the house were scarcely aware.

Lulled by the unchanging tranquillity of the scene, my concerns for the garden were replaced by other more pressing matters. The literary agent was having scant success in finding a publisher for *At Home in France*, my handbook about buying French property. After various failures on his part, I thought I might try publishing the book myself, whereupon he sent me a copy of his contract pointing out that I was bound by its terms for four long years – unless, that is, I would sign a new contract giving him rights in perpetuity over any biography I might write about Stephen. I was angry, as much with myself for being so naive, as with this slippery customer of an agent who had taken such blatant advantage of my inexperience and my dejection. His deviousness fired my determination to publish my French book myself whatever the cost and to deprive him in perpetuity of any commission on any other book that I might write.

At about the same time the Inland Revenue turned their attention to the profits made from *A Brief History of Time*. As a result of the high rate of unemployment caused by the Tory government policies, the Treasury was short of funds and was instructing the Inland Revenue to increase its income from compliance investigations, particularly by looking into situations where a marriage break-up might have caused fiscal confusion. Although I was no longer involved in the handling of Stephen's book, the tax inspector brought the full force of his bullying professional belligerence down on my weary head. He harassed me with letters and phone calls, even ringing up at Christmas when my hands were deep in flour and my mind on carols, puddings and presents.

These and other preoccupations distracted me from the issue of the trees and the garden at 5 West Road. It was not until one Monday in July 1993 that I found myself thinking about them again; strangely these thoughts grew in strength until they became an irresistible urge to go to the garden. My rational self suppressed that puzzling feeling, since I was far too busy that Monday with preparations for the summer holidays as well as other activities. It was not until later in the week that I found the time to call in at West Road on my way home from a final pre-holiday shopping expedition. As I rounded the corner of the house, I encountered a horrific spectacle. Where I expected to find the well-known, much loved haven of flowers and greenery, all I saw was mass wanton destruction. The far end of the garden had been ransacked, obliterated. Where previously there had been trees and shrubs, roses and poppies, birds, hedgehogs and squirrels, now there was nothing more than a huge black hole in the ground, a muddy crater where Mother Earth was laid bare, ravaged and exposed. A quick mental count suggested that as many as forty trees had been felled, the most spectacular being the western red cedar, under whose shady branches Cottontail, Tim's little rabbit, had had her hutch. As I stood paralysed with shock and disbelief at the scale of the devastation, I remembered the strange call I had felt earlier in the week. Could those trees really have been calling me to their rescue? What had become of my attempts to protect them with preservation orders?

In response to my enquiries, the City Council could find no record of my earlier requests for preservation orders to be placed on the trees. The plans for the new building when presented to the planning committee had made only passing reference to a few insignificant shrubs and saplings, so the planning committee had given the go-ahead without further enquiry. The protection to the trees afforded by the conservation area was worthless. There was however a sense of poetic justice in the tragedy. The fate of the trees and the garden mirrored the fate that had befallen us. There could not have been a more potent or poignant metaphor for the end of our family life than that black hole in the ground.

Postlude

February 2007

I am beginning to write this new postlude while taking off for Seattle with a nine-and-a-half-hour flight ahead of me. Heathrow soon disappears below, yielding to an English patchwork of green fields as we bounce off the clouds. This is a journey I have flown many times since that first trip in 1967, and having a new grandchild on the other side of the planet is now a compelling cure for flying phobia. As we fly over the snow-dusted Scottish mountains, heading north-west to Iceland and Greenland, I travel back in time recalling that flight when Robert was a tiny baby and Stephen, his father, was showing the initial disabling effects of motor-neuron disease, and I marvel yet again at the coincidence that Robert should have settled in Seattle with his wife Katrina, a talented sculptor, and their baby son. I also marvel at the fact that Stephen, who was given approximately two years to live in 1963, is not only still alive forty-four years later, but has recently received the most prestigious medal of the Royal Society, the Copley medal.

In 1995, while visiting Robert, who had taken up a job with Microsoft six months earlier, I felt that there was a certain sense of poetry in the way that Seattle had described a circle around almost all the years of our marriage. Now I feel that poetry of coincidence even more strongly as we prepare to celebrate in that city the first birthday of our little grandson, named George, after my father. On this flight I am not alone: Robert is with me, returning to Seattle after my mother's funeral yesterday. Only a week ago she died very peacefully and quietly in her sleep after a sudden illness. I was at a rehearsal at the time and felt her passing as a slight frisson, a brushing of angel's wings. I scarcely needed to be told on my return home that there was a message for me from her care home, because I already knew what had happened.

It was in Seattle back in 1995, soon after the divorce had been finalized and a year after the eventual publication of *At*

479

Home in France, that I began to contemplate writing the long memoir of my life with Stephen. I was surprised therefore to find an invitation from a publisher to do just that awaiting me back in Cambridge. That September the words flowed quickly and passionately, as if urging me to free myself of a past that had often scaled the giddy peaks of impossible achievement and yet had plumbed the depths of heartbreak and despair. I had to exorcise that past and clearly define the end of a long era before embarking on a new future, and it was to their credit that the publication team allowed me to tell my story spontaneously. That first edition represented a great and cathartic outpouring of optimism, euphoria, despondency and grief.

My initial reluctance to tackle a biography – arising from diffidence about the loss of privacy that the exercise might entail – gave way before the gradual awareness that I had no choice in the matter. My privacy was compromised anyhow, because my life was already public property as a result of Stephen's fame, and it would be only a matter of time before biographers started to investigate the personal story behind his genius and his survival: that would inevitably include me. I had no reason to suppose that they would treat me with any more consideration than the press had in the past. It would therefore be far better for me to tell my own story in my own way. I would be revealing truths which were so deeply and painfully personal that I could not bear to think that their music might resound only with the ring of the *chaudron fêlé*, Flaubert's cracked kettle. Although my role in Stephen's life was drastically diminished – Stephen's remarriage had effectively slammed the door on our lines of communication – I could not close my mind to a quarter of a century of living on the edge of a black hole, especially when the undeniable living proof of the extraordinary successes in those twenty-five years was to be seen in our three handsome, well-adjusted, very loving children, as well as in the acclaim that Stephen enjoyed. As the words flowed, I discovered that the voice and the register were there within me, ready and waiting to surface and express that mass of memories accumulated over the years. They were memories which might simply be seen to relate the saga of an English family in the latter part of the twentieth century. Much of it would be quite ordinary, quite common to most people's lives, were it not for two factors: motor-neuron disease and genius.

Indeed motor-neuron disease provided a further equally powerful motive for putting pen to paper, in the desire to awaken politicians and government officials to the heart-rending reality faced daily in an uncaring society by disabled people and their carers – the battles with officialdom, the lonely struggles to maintain a sense of dignity, the tiredness, the frustration and the anguished scream of despair. The memoir would, I hoped, also reach the medical profession with the aim of improving the otherwise sketchy awareness within the NHS of the ravages of motor-neuron disease and its effects on the personality, as well as on the physical bodies of its victims.

As a result of the hardback publication in August 1999 of *Music to Move the Stars*, the original title derived from the Flaubert quotation, I received a sackful of supportive letters, mostly from women who empathized keenly with my situation, commended my decision to write and recounted the story of their own often troubled lives. Some had been carers themselves or had struggled to bring up families in adverse circumstances; others simply found resonances with which they could identify. Many admitted that the book had made them weep. From within Cambridge the expressions of support were quite overwhelming. All said they were gripped by the story, including a ninety-four-year-old who refused to go to bed until she had finished reading it! Many people, deceived by Stephen's television appearances into thinking that we enjoyed all possible help, were appalled to discover how little assistance we actually received, thus confirming my long-held suspicion that the public face and the private reality were far removed, if not at odds with each other.

The past had largely been consigned to computer, if not fully exorcised, when Jonathan and I were married in July 1997. Our wedding day proved to be an island of respite against the tumultuous background of illnesses, accidents and disasters which were affecting our families and some of our closest friends. We ourselves were not in great shape either: Jonathan had been taken ill with kidney stones while performing on the concert platform in Liverpool, and I had been hobbling about on crutches for some time with torn ligaments in both knees after a skiing accident. The multitude of problems that had befallen us and our near and dear had left scant time for the practicalities of planning, let alone for any mental, emotional or spiritual preparation.

In truth, nothing could have prepared us for the emotional and spiritual power of that day. Just a minute or two before leaving home, I suddenly became aware to my embarrassed amazement that a mile down the road there was a church full of people awaiting me. Then, on arrival at St Mark's in the company of my three children, even our new Vicar's calm, friendly greeting could not allay that mounting sense of awe and wonder. Perhaps her resplendent white-and-gold ceremonial vestments only added to the potent, dream-like quality of the occasion – a quality which became overwhelming as Robert, Lucy, Tim and I took up our positions in the porch from where we glimpsed my future husband, rising to his feet at the chancel steps. A wave of emotion engulfed us as the organist launched into the majestic opening chords of *The Arrival of the Queen of Sheba* and my children bore me, trembling and incapable of looking to right or left, up the aisle, depositing me at Jonathan's side. In a space to my left, looking wan and frail, sat my mother, in the wheelchair to which she had recently become confined.

There followed the hymns, the prayers, the readings and the anthems, their words carefully chosen, pored over, analysed, translated into French and Spanish, typed into and extracted from the computer many a time. All those words came alive in speech and song, lent breadth and depth, truth, urgency and clarity by the voices of the clergy, the readers, the congregation and the choir. The latter was composed of old friends, many of them professional musicians who gave a poignant rendering of 'How lovely are thy dwellings fair' from Brahms's *German Requiem*. As for the preacher, there was only one possible choice. Only Bill Loveless, who had known us both for so long and had sustained us through such times of trial, could have given the address. Despite ill health and old age, he climbed into the pulpit and launched into a passionate speech which bore all the hallmarks of his customary vigour and commitment. He spoke with heartfelt candour and honesty of the dilemmas and anguish of the past without glossing over the reality of our relationship. As he recalled former times, it occurred to me that so many of the friends from all over the world who had given us so much valuable support in days gone by, and for whom I regularly said a silent prayer from my pew on a Sunday morning, were all in the church, with us and around us – all that is except Stephen, my companion over such a long period and the father of my children.

The image of darling Lucy standing at the lectern to recite Shakespeare's sonnet about the marriage of true minds was quite unforgettable. She stood, radiant in cream silk, with her hands clasped under her six-month bulge as if to gain confidence from her tiny, fetal son while Alex, her fiancé, beamed with pride from the congregation. There were the odd distracting moments – such as the horrible scratchy pen which turned my signature on the registers into an untidy scrawl, bringing back humiliating memories of a failed art exam in calligraphy at St Albans High School. Then all too soon the service was over, and Jonathan and I were gliding down the aisle, borne aloft by the strains of Bach's 'St Anne Prelude' and by the joy on the faces of the congregation. We stepped out into the sun – it was the first fine day in weeks – there to kiss and hug all our guests and other well-wishers before setting off at the head of the long, slow-moving motorcade led by our friends from France, to Wimpole Hall for photographs, the reception, dinner and festivities which lasted into the night.

Jonathan and I were optimistically looking forward to a comparatively normal life together after our marriage. Since then I have learnt that there is no such thing as a normal life. Certainly we lead busy lives in which music plays a major role: I still revel in the choral repertoire and I also continue to give occasional solo recitals to Jonathan's accompaniment. I no longer teach – there are too many other demands on my attention, but I do manage to make time for dancing, which for so long in the past was not a feasible activity for me either as a practitioner or a spectator. Jonathan and I travel widely: as often as possible we step into that other dimension of rural France, where I work in the meadow garden I created to mark the millennium, while Jonathan plans new musical enterprises – either for The Cambridge Baroque Camerata or for the Choir of Magdalene College, which he has conducted and run for the past five years in his capacity as College Praecentor and Director of College Music.

Rarely however is there a time when we are not beset by troubles and anxieties. By the summer of our wedding my mother had become very disabled with arthritis, and was able to carry on living at home in St Albans thanks only to Dad's devotion to her care. Although I visited them regularly, there inevitably came the day when Dad, who was very hard of hearing, could no longer cope alone. Again we had to engage carers privately from an agency, again as no help was forthcoming either from the NHS or from Social Services. Our expectations that paid carers would be professional people were sorely disappointed. With a handful of shining exceptions, many proved to be of dubious character, doubtful honesty, uncertain qualification and inadequate training, and frequently Dad would have to call me to help out on a Bank Holiday when the replacement carer had failed to turn up. Often perplexed by the carers' idiosyncrasies, as for example when one of them served salad cream on a fruit pie, he never lost his sense of humour – but finally he took the decision to move with Mum into a care home just outside Cambridge.

Relieved to have them settled nearby and in good hands, I then found myself responsible for clearing and selling their house, a mammoth and exhausting task, but one that I was glad to be able to carry out while they were still alive. Still in full possession of his remarkable intellect, but sorely distressed by the perplexing contrast between his youthful inner self and his disintegrating outer frame, Dad succumbed to pneumonia, exacerbated by Parkinson's disease, in June 2004. He had refused to go into Addenbrooke's Hospital because he was so deterred by the terrible treatment Mum had received there only a few weeks previously, when she had had a chest infection. Against all expectations Mum outlived him, and not only celebrated her 90th birthday in March 2006 but also met little George, her fourth great-grandson and our second grandson.

Like so many of life's major experiences, there is no preparation for the stage when our parents become our elderly children and we are caught as the filling in a generation sandwich. Nor is there any warning of the trauma one feels at the death of one's parents, whatever their age. The two people who were always there unconditionally for me, and whom I have been able to depend upon unfailingly all my life, are no longer with me. It is as if a part of me is missing and now, just one week after Mum's death, I find myself flying halfway across the world in a miserably numbed state of shock. At home there are many encouraging messages of sympathy containing tributes to her selfless character, her genuine concern for and interest in other people, her dedication to good causes, her devotion to her family and her inspiring, deep-seated faith, but the sadness of the past week is very present. It travels with me wherever I go. Previously I could imagine how dreadful it must be to lose a child or a spouse, but I had no notion of how fundamentally shocking it is to lose a parent.

In the past ten years challenges other than attending to my elderly parents have arisen in the family. These I will not dwell on, but they have demanded special resources which I have found in the rock of faith that has sustained me from the early days of my marriage to Stephen. These days that faith is broader, more critical and more sceptical, but is nonetheless rooted in Christian ethics and finds its spiritual expression in music. The old optimism is gone and a determination to overcome adversity, probably learnt from Stephen, prevails in its place.

As far as the family are concerned, although Robert seems to be permanently based in the United States, we are lucky to have two of our children still living in Britain, and we see them often. Lucy is a full-time author as well as a single parent to her gorgeous son, William. A beautiful but difficult baby, he was diagnosed with autism in 2001.

Tim has rid himself of the self-doubt that characterized his childhood and has become sharp-witted and perceptive. Though he is proud of his father, he is particularly sensitive to the problems of living in the shadow of fame and would prefer to be considered for his own talents and hard work rather than because of his background. A linguist, like me, he read Modern Languages and then decided to do an MSc in marketing.

And Stephen... Remarkably since his second divorce Stephen has reasserted his control over his life, and despite bouts of illness, he has maintained his position on the world stage. We are able to associate freely again and enjoy many a family occasion together. It has been quite like old times, with plenty of banter and wit circulating round the dinner table while we wait for Stephen to have the last word. I was delighted to be invited to the Royal Society to witness the presentation to him of the Copley medal, the oldest medal of the Society. As on so many previous occasions I was touched with pride at his achievement, though quite what his science consists of these days I cannot tell, apart from his much publicized recantation of some of his former theories. I must admit I was less happy with his expressed intention, announced on radio on the day of the presentation, of going into space. Less ambitiously but perhaps more productively, he went off to Israel a couple of weeks later, a trip he undertook only on condition that he should be allowed to visit Ramallah and talk to the Palestinians. We gazed in awe at the double-page centre spread in the *Guardian* which showed Stephen driving his wheelchair through massed hordes of Palestinian onlookers. Before going into space he intends to bring his very special form of ambassadorship to Iran, though whether political circumstances will allow that to happen remains to be seen. On his return from Israel, he spent Christmas with us and we celebrated the New Year with him. Often he joins us for Sunday lunch and frequently we go to the theatre together. He and his mother came to my mother's funeral, and I was very pleased to see them there. Isobel looks frail but very fit, and is quite irrepressible, even if her memory is somewhat unreliable. In her jovial good humour and ready wit, she reminds me of the positive role model I once considered her to be. A couple of years ago she sent me a letter thanking me for all that I had done for Stephen. It was a noble gesture which helped alleviate some of the more painful memories, restoring our relationship to a civilized footing.

An enormous new hall of residence stands on the site at 5 West Road, where once we lived in that splendid house and relaxed in its beautiful garden. A few of the most significant trees however are still standing, a result of the campaign which I undertook in the 1990s when I discovered the havoc that had been wreaked in the garden after our departure. I watch as the plane en route to Seattle casts its shadow over northern Canada and releases its fumes over the receding frozen wastes of the Arctic, and I ask myself whether the bulldozing of our garden in the name of progress was not just another small symptom of the mad rush to exploit every available resource that is leading inexorably to the decline of the planet. Like that house and garden our lives were bulldozed, but the essential spirit of the family – truly the affirmation of all my young years – still exists and reasserts itself on those occasions when we can all meet and enjoy each other's company. Whether the spirit of the earth can eventually recover and reassert itself is the greatest question facing mankind, not unlike that menacing question way back in the Sixties, when Stephen and I first met, of whether the earth and all forms of life therein were destined to be obliterated by nuclear warfare.

Post Script – May 2007

Since I finished writing the Postlude, Stephen has completed his zero-gravity flight and returned to earth intact, giving rise to triumphant pictures in the media. The smile on his face as he floated in weightless liberation would have moved the stars. It certainly moved me profoundly and made me reflect what a privilege it was to travel even a short distance with him on the way to infinity.

Last Word – August 2014

Lucy's series of imaginative scientific adventures for children, beginning with *George's 'Secret Key to the Universe'*, has met with worldwide acclaim. She has battled tirelessly to obtain the proper provision for William, who has grown into a delightful, caring and very helpful young man.

Tim is now a successful marketing manager and travels widely in the course of his work.

Robert, still in Seattle, works somewhere on the Microsoft Cloud. He has a wonderful, very lively family who keep us interested, entertained and amused on their visits to Cambridge.

Stephen, the world's most famous scientist, remains at the centre of the family as well as at the centre of physics. In fact we are all just about to go on holiday together!

Acknowledgements

In *Music to Move the Stars*, the first edition of my memoir, I expressed my profound gratitude to all those people pictured within, friends, members of the family, colleagues and students, whose help and encouragement over the years had brought a positive influence to our family life. I also thanked my scientific friends, Kip Thorne, Jim Hartle, Jim Bardeen, Brandon Carter and Bernard Carr for their help in clarifying some of the more abstruse and intractable scientific issues which I had to address in the course of the writing, as well as gratefully acknowledging the advice of Peter Dronke in elucidating some of the finer points of medieval scholarship.

For *Travelling to Infinity*, the abridged version of the original memoir, I once again wish to express my thanks to all of the above and add the names of those who have made the new edition possible. Anthony McCarten has been a constant source of encouragement, and in his enthusiasm for *Music to Move the Stars*, introduced me to Alessandro Gallenzi and Elisabetta Minervini of Alma Books, who took the new project on with eagerness, alacrity and efficiency. I am extremely grateful to them for enabling my memoir to see the light of day again. I am indebted to Mike Stocks who took time from his own highly successful career as a writer to help tidy up the excesses of my prose. His tactful and supportive criticism has been invaluable and much appreciated.

Finally thanks are due to my family for once again allowing me to delve into their life stories and for showing forbearance and humour during the process.